PROTECT
AND DEFEND

ERIC L. HARRY

BERKLEY BOOKS, NEW YORK

PROTECT AND DEFEND

A Berkley Book / published by arrangement with
the author

PRINTING HISTORY
Berkley edition / April 1999

The Penguin Putnam Inc. World Wide Web site address is
http://www.penguinputnam.com

ISBN: 0-425-16814-X

BERKLEY®
Berkley Books are published by The Berkley Publishing Group,
a division of Penguin Putnam Inc.,
375 Hudson Street, New York, New York 10014.
BERKLEY and the "B" logo are trademarks
belonging to Penguin Putnam Inc.

PRINTED IN THE UNITED STATES OF AMERICA

10 9 8 7 6 5 4 3 2 1

To God's most beautiful wonders,
and the two greatest joys of my life:
Ethan and Jordan

Acknowledgment

No words of thanks would be appropriate unless they began with my wife, Marina, who nurtures both me and my children as we all go through the sometimes arduous process of writing a book.

I am also indebted once again to the U.S. Army Reserve's 147th IMA Detachment, who wargamed this book . . . twice. (The first time, the war didn't go so well for the United Nations's forces.) And finally, a special word of gratitude to a select group of men whom I have never met. They did in real life what I described in this work of fiction. In a cold so bitter the saliva froze on the roofs of their mouths, 25,000 U.S. Marines were suddenly and unexpectedly attacked by 120,000 Chinese soldiers. Under the most brutal conditions ever visited upon man they exhibited extremes in bravery and military prowess not soon to be repeated. What began for me as research for a novel now ends with these humble and inadequate thanks to the men of the 1st Marine Division—living and dead—who fought at the Chosen Reservoir in Korea from November 27th to December 10th, 1950.

PROLOGUE

"Our first work must be the annihilation of everything as it now exists."

Mikhail A. Bakunin
Dieu et l'État (1882)

The only signs of man were the huge black pipes running undefended from horizon to horizon. The man atop the shaggy native horse turned his collar up against the chill. Nightfall came slowly in that northern clime, but the wind began to bite long before dark. He eyed the featureless, dark blue sky. It seemed to weigh down on the earth, pressing the horizons below their accustomed positions. He had never seen true wilderness before. The sky there seemed to assume a greater prominence in the order of things.

With a gentle prod of his heels the horse started forward. Its rider had been awkward at first. He'd dug his heels into the horse's flanks then yanked back on the reins to slow the beast. Over the weeks of his trek to this remote spot, however, horse and rider had become one. He now sat comfortably in his saddle—his body attuned to the gentle sway of the animal's motions. A slight tug on the reins pulled the horse to a stop, and he climbed down.

He paused beside the horse to listen. The jet-black cluster of pipes and a few others like it supplied the homes and factories of Western Europe with almost half their energy needs. The massive volumes of natural gas rushing across the Eurasian plain made no sound. But as he moved nearer to the pipe, he could feel the heat.

Friction, he thought. *It's in there.* He untied the faded blue bedroll lying across his horse's rump and laid it on the ground with a faint clanking sound. When the coarse blanket was unrolled, the tools of his new trade lay spread before him as if on a surgeon's tray.

The emptiness swallowed the few sounds he made in the same way that it swallowed his thoughts. His mind wandered. The swiftly flowing stream he'd crossed a few kilometers back. The view of the night sky from a dozen camps in as many days. The perfect stillness of the deep woods on a windless evening.

The crisp, clean air of Siberia constantly bathed him with its ebb and flow. He breathed of it deeply, filling his lungs through his dry nose. The weather had cooperated. He'd never seen a more beautiful day than the one that was just ending.

The man forced himself to concentrate when he came to the delicate part of his long-practiced routine. Time passed—not quickly, but without notice of its passage. All the while memories made fleeting forays into the periphery of his consciousness. The bath he'd taken in a frigid stream. He had emerged to dry on the bank. The sun was hot on his bare skin. His horse had wandered out into the water, pausing to lap the cool liquid and then darting through the shallow stream every so often with surprising vigor, chasing and chased by the dragonflies. He would miss the horse, the summer nights.

As he had lain on the bank with the sun shining red through closed eyelids, other memories had come. Each roused him from his slumber with a start. That night they had come again. He had awoken in a full sweat—shivering from the cold. He had clutched his blanket to his chin—

staring out with pounding pulse at the blackness that surrounded the small bubble of light from his campfire.

He took a deep breath and paused to look up at the sky. He felt drawn to the reddish hues of the setting sun. Maybe here, in the great nothingness, he could change. He would remain in the wild, live off the land, suffer the immense hardships of a winter, maybe two. When he emerged, he would be a new man. Maybe the harshness—the sheer dominion of Siberia over all creatures great and small—would kill the old human and give birth to a new one. A new man cleansed of all that had passed.

It was at that moment he realized the truth. That no matter where he was or how far his travels took him, he would carry with him the baggage of all he had done. It was the punishment of God or of nature; it made no difference which.

He mounted the horse—the effort made greater by the burden of his memories—and rode a short distance alongside the pipeline. He pulled a crinkled piece of paper from his pocket and wearily climbed down. He opened a small can of thick white paint with his knife. He held the paper in one hand and a brush in the other, carefully copying the words from the paper onto the pipe.

Rising again to his saddle, he spurred the horse and slowly ascended a low hill. There he waited. He caught himself looking on instinct to all corners of the horizon. A habit born of life in the other world. The world of humankind. He saw nothing, of course; nobody.

A chill passed over him as the last sliver of bloodred sun sank into the west, and he wrapped his arms around himself, shivering. The cold would come early that night.

Four small charges popped within milliseconds of one another. Natural gas gushed from the torn pipes in phenomenal volumes. The tiny explosions had depleted the nearby atmosphere of oxygen. But when the heated and compressed gas jetting from the pipes found air, a mammoth fireball erupted. Like a giant can opener, the burning gases expanded and split the pipe for a hundred meters in each direction.

The jarring boom rolled over the barren landscape and startled the horse.

"Spokoyno," the man murmured. He patted the horse's hard neck that lay just beneath the short bristles of its coat. There were no echoes on the tabletop flat terrain. After the first concussive shock wave had passed, the only sound was from the burning gas. It filled the normally quiet world with a sonorous roar like that of a speeding train. A pall of black smoke rose high above the conflagration and blotted out the darkening blue sky.

The man scanned the now devastated length of black pipe. For a hundred meters in each direction, it was twisted and split and broken. But the large block letters he'd scrawled lay undisturbed just beyond the limit of the explosion's violence. The paint ran like white blood beneath the words. "Destruction is the mother of all creation!" he mumbled out loud as he read. A single ear of the agitated horse twitched to take in the sound of his voice.

He spurred the animal on. He was from nowhere, and it was to nowhere that he returned.

PART ONE

"The first two laws of thermodynamics can be summarized thusly: the natural course of the universe is to go from a state of order to a state of disorder. Those laws also describe systems built by man."

Valentin Kartsev (posthumously)
The Laws of Human History
Moscow, Russia

1

"Anarchy, anarchy, anarchy," Kate Dunn said into the brilliant lights of Woody's Minicam. Just behind her, the sustained roar of a hundred thousand voices echoed across Red Square. Her night vision was spoiled by the camera's lights, but she could see the demonstrators' fists pumping in air. The throng fell silent to await the speaker's next cue.

"Sound is good," Woody said with his eye glued to the Minicam's eyepiece. "But the light ain't worth shit. We won't pick up more than the first few people in the crowd down there." He plugged his headphones in. "Gimme some more sound," he directed.

"This is Kate Dunn, reporting to you for NBC News," Kate said. "How's that?"

"Fine." Woody's fingers tapped at the camera's controls. It was all automatic, but for some reason he always overrode the computer's settings with his own manual tweaks. Kate looked out over the crowd. She felt a flutter in her chest at the excitement of the moment. From her vantage atop the abandoned police van she could see the mob's leader in the distance bathed in harsh footlights from the speaker's platform. The angry man spat out another stream of invective. The sound truck's speakers were at maximum volume. It distorted the rabble-rouser's voice. Again the crowd roared. Their clenched fists shook at the Kremlin walls, where shadows danced from the flickering light of bonfires and thousands of torches.

Kate felt goose bumps ripple across her skin. "This is prime-time footage, Woody. I can feel it."

"Uh-huh," he replied. He worked the knobs on top of the tripod. His face was glued to the eyepiece. The scene around her was awe-inspiring, but she forced herself to close her eyes and go over her report. Not the words—she knew those cold—but the mood, the inflection, the calm of the veteran reporter's voice conveying in measured tones the excitement of dramatic events. She had watched foreign correspondents do it all her life. Her lips moved and she nodded her head in time with the crowd's chanted slogans.

"Show time!" Woody said. Kate opened her eyes, totally calm.

Woody's fingers counted down from five, but when he hit zero and pointed, she waited for the perfect moment. A thunderous shout rose from the hundred thousand angry Russians. They waved the black flags of the Anarchists in figure eights. In the quiet that followed the roar, she began.

"Anarchy," she said—thinking, *slowly, slowly*—"all current values are baseless. No political system known today works. Life as we have lived it is meaningless."

The roar rose up again, then the crowd fell silent. Kate was in rhythm with them. "These Russian Anarchists want to improve their 'spiritual condition' through destruction of all existing social order. 'From destruction, creation arises!' This is the slogan of a new generation."

A sustained cheer erupted, and Kate half turned to witness the spectacle. It was one of history's turning points, she could feel it. In the capital of a great power. Revolution sweeping the course of mankind down a hundred-year tributary. And she was there . . . reporting it all to a fascinated world.

"Among the ideologies considered to be of continuing significance," she said into the blinding lights of the camera, "anarchism alone has never been tried. That it still attracts fervent adherents such as those here tonight is testimony to its intellectual credibility. Single-minded obsession with individual liberty and skepticism of government, it seems, are as alive today as they were in the nineteenth century. Now, here, in this land of great social experimentation, we may soon learn whether anarchism is utopia, or leads down yet another detour through hell on earth."

A roar erupted just as she completed the sentence. *This is it!* she thought in the torrent of noise. *Don't screw it up now!*

"But what sort of idea *would* you expect to flourish in a Russia that has lost all hope?" Kate continued as fiery words were spat in Russian from distant loudspeakers. "In a Russia that has tried everything, and failed? What *sort* of ideology would take root in the minds of a hundred million lost souls?"

"Anarchi-i-i-a-a!" the crowd roared in stirring unison. Kate was almost overcome by a wave of emotion as her mind's eye viewed the scene from the camera's perspective. *Perfection, sheer perfection.*

"Anarchy. A rejection of everything, every ideology. When you can't create, *destroy*! 'To think is to say no!' A mean, uncompromising idea to vent the pent-up energy and frustration of a nation of the idle. An idea that captures the imagination and fires the empty bellies of a long-suffering people. The black flags, the feverish rhetoric"—she paused—"and the violence.

"With the world's attention focused on student protests in Beijing, the violence in Siberia earlier today came as a complete surprise. There, saboteurs launched concerted attacks on the system of natural gas pipelines that supply much of Western Europe's energy needs. Spokesmen for Western oil companies said late today that the reports, if accurate, would cripple the entire supply system due to the remote locations of the damage." Another roar went up, and Kate raised her voice and shouted into the microphone. "They further pointed out that no repair crews would be sent until the Russian government could guarantee their safety from terrorists." The crowd quieted in the repetitive pattern of exhortation and response. "As the gas pressure in the system steadily falls, prices on world energy markets are going through the roof. North Sea crude and other alternate sources of European energy rose more than forty percent by market close with no sign that—"

A stunning flash of light barely preceded a deafening boom that reverberated among the buildings enclosing Red Square. Kate ducked involuntarily at the stupendous sound. A hundred thousand people in Red Square flinched in unison. "Over there," Kate shouted. She pointed for Woody to turn the camera. Smoke billowed into the air from the end of the square in front of St. Basil's—from where army troops had gathered but stood idle. The chants quickly degenerated into random shouts from a multitude of shrill voices.

The crackle of machine-gun fire began the terror.

It was as if everyone panicked at once. "It appears that the army has opened fire!" Kate managed over the din. Woody moved to shoot the scene from close behind her shoulder. The heat of the bright lamp glowed warmly against her face. Objects hissed through the air all around, and Woody turned out the lights and lowered the camera.

"What are you *doing*?" Kate shouted over the noise of the crowd, which had turned as one and was streaming away from the guns. "Aren't you *getting* this?"

The *zzziiip* of what Kate suddenly realized were bullets and the rocking of the van under their feet sent the first jolt of fear through her system. Woody pulled Kate down to the flat metal roof as the steady, deeper rattle of heavy guns settled into a rhythm of machinelike killing. "We gotta split, Kate!" he yelled, pushing her toward the edge of the van's roof.

Kate tumbling through air into the dark sea of tightly packed bodies, barely managing to gain her feet at the last second. She looked up in horror to see the force of the horde topple the van onto its side. Woody leaped feet-first—camera in hand—into the human tide on the opposite side.

All around her was a crushing press of grunting, snorting panic. Growls and brief shouts burst forth. The men—much taller than her five feet three inches—elbowed and jostled their way toward the narrow exits a half step at a time.

Kate was terrified. The breath was pressed from her lungs in the crush. Her face was pinned between bodies and she couldn't even turn her head. There were arms clutching at her legs as screaming people were being trampled underfoot.

The bullets splitting the air all around and the booming explosions were now just background noise; a secondary concern. Her life depended upon footing. Upon tiny patches of cobblestone on which to place her next step. For to fall, she knew, was to die.

Kate began to claw and scratch for small openings in the mob. She grabbed onto lapels and sleeves and eventually hair as the crowd lurched this way and that. She maintained her balance as much by the grip of her hands as the placement of her feet. Suddenly the sea of humanity surged in an unexpected direction. Kate had guessed wrong. She fought for a toehold amid a tangle of legs. She was falling. She fought to grab onto something. An elbow smacked her squarely in the nose—blinding her with a white flash of pain.

Kate screamed as she slipped beyond the point of no return into the darkness of churning knees. The sea swallowed her up in slow motion, and the sounds of the explosions and the gunfire grew distant. There were different sounds down there, underneath the surface. The wails of the dying who lay on the stone pavement echoed amid the forest of stamping boots.

I'm going to die. The thought hit her with the physical effect of a body blow as her knees landed on cold paving stones and the flow of the bodies threatened to press her flat. All her senses abandoned her in that moment, the prickly grip of fear consuming her. She pounded her fists against the headless bodies that kicked her ever lower toward the oblivion of the earth. Pain shot unexpectedly through her ribs and she screamed long and loud—her eyes forced shut by the effort.

The pain in her ribs came from a tight grip. Fresh air bathed her face as she twisted and shouted and scratched her way up, up to the surface. To the air. Kate had been pulled from the depths. Someone had lifted her up from the grave. She couldn't see who it was. She didn't care. She fought viciously now. She would not fall again. Her jaw was clenched in a sneer. Everybody around her was an enemy to be pushed and slapped and scratched if advantage could be gained. Everybody but the man behind her. His two hands remained fixed on her ribs.

Slowly, the crushing force of bodies began to wane. As the pressure of the packed crowd fell, the pace of the crowd's flight picked up. The crackle of gunfire could still be heard in the distance as the demonstrators streamed toward the exits. Kate was swept along. The fighting and jostling of the crowd fell with the lessening crush. Still, however, the hands held her.

Kate stopped and turned. A tall man, in his late thirties or early forties, looked down at her in the semidarkness. He had tired eyes set in a handsome, pale face. His hair was pitch-black. He said nothing, turned, and disappeared into the masses before Kate could say a word. He wore the black garb of the Russian Anarchists.

Huge red flames boiled into the air over their heads as another stunning boom caused all to duck and turn. A second ball of fire shot skyward, and another boom rolled over the square.

The flames from the explosions rose into the air from behind the Kremlin walls—from *inside* the Kremlin! And then so did a helicopter. In the light from the blazing fires Kate could see the white, blue, and red tricolors of the Russian republic painted on its sides. It was the Russian president's helicopter. As it wheeled onto its side and hurtled away through the caverns of downtown Moscow, the night was lit by hundreds of burning tracer rounds fired past the fleeing aircraft at tremendous velocities.

BETHESDA, MARYLAND
August 16, 0000 GMT (1900 Local)

"It's anarchy, Elaine," Gordon Davis said to his wife. The local news reported the downtown killings as a "crime." But the appropriate words were anarchist atrocity. "They have no rules. They're incapable of feeling empathy for their victims. They're totally unsocialized. We'll *never* go back to the way we were. We're just going to have to live our lives in a country with wild animals running loose on the streets."

"I *know* you don't believe that," Elaine Davis said into her mirror. "I know what you really believe, Gordon. You're a totally hopeless idealist."

"We interrupt this program to bring you this ABC News bulletin."

They both turned to the small television in their large bathroom. "This just in to ABC News," the deep-voiced anchor said. "A major riot is reported to have taken place in Red Square in central Moscow."

Gordon saw his wife return to her makeup. *Another food riot*, he thought, knotting his tie.

"Western journalists on the scene report that anarchist demonstrators defied Russian Army orders to vacate the square by nightfall. Although it is unknown who fired the first shots, regular army troops had begun taking over barricades from Interior Ministry riot police earlier in the day, and by sunset were massed in the thousands. Estimates vary as to the number of demonstrators present, with some sources putting the turnout as high as two hundred thousand."

"Those poor people," Elaine said as she carefully drew a faint line under her eye with a pencil. Gordon had to look away. That process always made him nervous.

"At this hour the violence appears to be spreading outward from Red Square, and now seems to have consumed most of Moscow's center." Those words drew Gordon and Elaine's attention, not to the television but to each other. "Experts have kept a close eye on the situation in the Russian capital in recent days amid rumors of impending upheaval and worsening political instability. There are numerous *un*confirmed reports from Moscow tonight of widespread fighting between security troops and Russian anarchists, but ABC News must reiterate that those reports remain as yet unconfirmed. Please stay tuned to ABC for further word on this breaking story as it develops. We now return to your local programming, already in progress."

As the "Special Bulletin" screen replaced the picture of the ABC anchorman, Elaine said, "You think Greer will call the Armed Services Committee back into session?"

"No-o-o. Everything these days is China, China, China. Plus, everybody's down at the convention."

"Are you guys decent?" their older daughter, Celeste, interrupted from the bedroom door.

"Come on in," Elaine said as she powdered her nose at her vanity.

"Ta-da!" Celeste announced, smiling and holding her hands up to present her younger sister—Janet—who wore her new cheerleader uniform. Janet shook the pom-poms and kicked. "Doesn't she look like a complete dweeb?" Celeste asked. Janet shook a pom-pom in her sister's face.

"You were a cheerleader once *too,* Celeste," Elaine noted. "Just because you're 'way cool' now that you're going off to college doesn't mean you should spoil your sister's fun."

"That's right!" Janet shouted, again shaking the pom-pom in her older sister's face as she headed out. Celeste slapped it away and followed, an argument breaking out.

"The victim," the local news anchorwoman read, "age eleven, had a record of minor criminal activity and school suspensions. Eyewitnesses said that the boy pulled a knife in the stairwell of the school and was shot to death by the accused, also age eleven. School officials deny there is a security problem in the building's stairwells, although students claim assaults are common in the cramped and windowless space, where lights are repeatedly broken by gangs seeking to cloak their planned attacks in the darkness.''

"My *God*," Elaine said, stroking her eyelashes delicately with her mascara brush. "I don't know what I'd do if the girls had to go to public school. I'd never get a moment's rest I'd be so worried."

"It's horrible," Gordon agreed. The story of yet another murder played on their television, complete with a bloody sheet covering the corpse being loaded into an ambulance. The crowd gathering in the lights around the crime scene was entirely black, as was, Gordon felt sure, the victim. This crime was simply a garden-variety drug killing, not one of the more sensational reports.

"What are you going to talk about tonight?" Elaine asked.

Gordon straightened the top edge of his crisply starched collar. "Take a wild guess."

"Oh, Gordon!" Elaine said, turning to look at him. "Not at your daughter's *pep* rally, for goodness' sake!"

"Well, crime and violence is what's on everybody's mind!" he said, holding his hand out to the television. "Somebody's got to talk about it. We've got to get those people off the streets. I don't care how many cops, how many courts, how many prisons, how many electric chairs it takes, or whatever the cost. This country is in a major state of decline, and it's primarily due to crime and violence."

"Just who are 'those people,' Gordon?"

"Jesus Christ, Elaine!" he snapped, and she shushed him—looking at the door where the girls had been. "You and I both know who I'm talking about," he said in a lowered but still urgent voice. "People are leaving this country, Elaine! Native-born citizens just up and checking out of Hotel America. You saw that *Newsweek* article about

Vancouver and Toronto. If the trends continue, half the damn urban population of Canada will be former Americans by the middle of the next century.''

"I thought you said we'd all just have to get used to things. What can you possibly say? What can anybody do about the problem?'' Gordon slumped and frowned. "Plus, I don't think now's the time to launch any bold new initiatives,'' Elaine said, nodding at the news coverage of the Republican Convention. The Republican National Committee had asked that Gordon delay his arrival at the convention until the last day. The entire Davis family was scheduled to catch a flight for Atlanta at six o'clock in the morning. *"And,"* Elaine continued, "are you so sure that it's crime and violence that are the problem? Maybe they're just symptoms of something else that's wrong.''

"Oh, now you sound like Daryl! It's just 'the situation'?'' Gordon said sarcastically. They both let the subject drop, and Gordon checked his watch. "Let's not stay too late tonight, okay?''

"Did you give them the school's telephone number?'' Elaine asked, clearly trying to act nonchalant.

"Yeah,'' Gordon replied, not needing to ask who "they'' were. "And Daryl has it too. He promised to call if he heard anything—even rumors—from the convention hall.''

Elaine stood, and Gordon wrapped his arms around her. He could see her smile in the bathroom mirrors. "Just relax,'' he said. "We'll know soon enough.''

"You know, what if . . .'' she began, and Gordon's mind bolted ahead. He felt a rush of excitement at the wild speculation he had denied himself. "What if nobody calls?'' she finished. His mood crashed. "We've really built this up, and if—''

"They're going to call,'' Gordon said with more certainty than he felt and a note of irritation in his voice. The signs were all there. They'd done a full-blown background check. Gordon had had good talks with all the right people.

"You know what I think?'' Elaine said, pulling back and

smiling up at him. "I think there's a cabinet post with your name on it." She shook him playfully from side to side.

"Shhh! Don't jinx it," he shot back, kissing her to hide the grin that forced its way onto his face. "Besides, the president is still way up in the polls. Bristol has a lot of ground to make up by November before he can offer me anything."

"There's plenty of time for something to happen," Elaine said, sinking to Gordon's chest. "Life's a funny thing. I mean really, sweetie. Who ever thought you'd be a senator? You never know what's going to happen next. You just never know."

"We all think we're safe behind these walls," Senator Gordon Davis said, spreading his hands to encompass the ivy-covered gymnasium of his daughter's private school. The bleary-eyed parents sat impassively, waiting, Gordon imagined, for the blowhard politician to finish his spiel. "But we're not. We fool ourselves into thinking we can insulate. Isolate. Escape the violence out there that is eating away at the fabric of our country."

The silence was deafening. "It is a delusion. Like a cancer, anarchy is a disease attacking the cells of America— its citizens. Most of us here, the parents whose children attend this fine school, think ourselves immune from the disease. But let me remind you, ladies and gentlemen, that we live in a society. A collection of citizens. A nation. And if that host nation grows *sick,* then *all* the cells that make that nation up are at risk, the *healthy* as well as the diseased. Thank you."

Polite applause filled the gym. Gordon was an appointee who'd filled an unexpired term of a senator who had been driven to resign from office by a scandal. He'd never been an inspiring speaker. He left the podium to rejoin Elaine. It was the prep school's first gathering of the year—a pep rally to introduce the athletes and cheerleaders. Elaine cast her husband a forced and, he knew, disapproving smile. Worse yet was the scowl Janet aimed at him from the front rank of the cheerleading squad.

"Senator Davis, you have a telephone call," a school administrator whispered to him as the headmaster stepped up to the microphone to introduce the football team.

"Maybe this is it," Elaine said through her smile and gentle squeeze of his arm. The band struck up a march, the sounds of their blaring and discordant instruments painfully loud in the enclosed space, as Gordon followed the woman off the stage to a tunnel leading through the bleachers. Only Daryl Shavers, the chief of his senate staff, and the Republican National Committee staffers knew of his plans to be at the school that night. Only they had been given the phone number.

His heart began to pound. He tried for the hundredth time to deflate his expectations, not wanting to be disappointed. The Republicans were trailing President Marshall's Democratic ticket by eighteen points in the preconvention polls. The economy was humming along. Governor Bristol, the Republican nominee, was making no headway with his neo-conservative, social activist platform. *NBD,* Gordon thought to calm himself—using one of Janet's many acronyms. "No Big Deal."

The woman led Gordon into an office. He swallowed the lump in his throat. *But a cabinet post*, he thought. He was a born appointee.

"Hello?" he said.

"Senator Davis?" came the breaking voice of a kid.

"Who is this?" Gordon demanded, deeply disappointed.

"You gotta get out of that gym right now, sir. I'm sorry! I think I really screwed up. I've . . . I've already called the police."

"What are you talking about?" Gordon asked as another phone chirped and the woman picked it up.

"Just trust me, sir. Please! Go! Right now!" There was a click as the boy hung up.

The woman held up the other phone. "They said it's urgent."

Gordon raised the other receiver to his ear. "Gordon Davis."

"Sir, my name is Carl Jaffe. I'm deputy director of the Secret Service. We'd like you to get your family and head to the school's security office. We have some agents en route and they'll meet you—"

Long rips of automatic weapons fire erupted inside the gymnasium. The woman next to him jumped with a start then stared at the glass door, her mouth agape. The first screams rose but were drowned out by still more shooting. Gordon dropped the phone and rushed for the door. A torrent of booming gunfire assaulted his ears as he headed out of the office into a full-blown war.

Well-dressed parents, wild-eyed with panic, streamed out of the gymnasium with young children in their arms or being pushed along by firm grips on their shoulders. Some had lost all control and screamed wildly as Gordon waded into the flood of people fleeing the terror inside. The going was slow against the human tide. The rapid-fire bursts of the guns were brief and selective now. Shoulders and elbows pummeled Gordon in mindless flight from the terrible noise, some people bent over to run in a stoop. When Gordon reached the tunnel that led into the gym, he saw the first blood. It streamed down the face of a stunned middle-aged woman from beneath neatly groomed blond hair, coating her white silk blouse in remarkably brilliant crimson. Another long tear of fire—closer and much louder than before—caused people to throw themselves to the ground all around, clearing the tunnel momentarily.

Gordon slammed into a man in a calf-length black overcoat who dashed out of the gym looking over his shoulder. The man turned, and he and Gordon stared at each other for a moment—each stunned. The man stepped back and raised a smoking machine pistol. The muzzle of the ugly black gun traced a line up Gordon's body that he could almost feel as a prickly itch along his flesh. A shiver that began as a tingle in his groin rippled across his body as the man's blue eyes smiled and the gun steadied on Gordon's chest.

"No!" Gordon yelled just as a bullet smashed into the

metal stands right beside the gunman. The blond man
flinched and twisted, the muzzle of his gun spitting flame.
Gordon felt the weapon's hot breath, but the sting of bullets
did not follow. He darted under the sloping bleachers to his
right, the blazing gun swinging to follow him but the bullets
miraculously striking a thick concrete pillar in between.
Stooped over and hurling himself into the darkness beneath
the stands as fast as his feet would carry him, Gordon felt
jabs of pain in his ears from the sounds of the machine
pistol's fire. When the shooting stopped a second or two
later, he looked back through the maze of supports and
columns. A school security guard lay in the tunnel in a pool
of blood. In his hand he still clutched his pistol.

A stunning blow struck the side of Gordon's head. He
reached out into the semidarkness and felt his way around
the concrete support with which he'd collided. His head
was throbbing in pain, but his attention returned to the blue-
eyed gunman who peered after him from the well-lit tunnel.
He was slapping another long magazine into his weapon.

Flame erupted from the gun, and Gordon slid around the
thick pillar to the opposite side. Bullets cut through the air
all around and thumped into the concrete at his back. The
trusses and girders and concrete pillars under the stands
were lit in the strobe of the flaming muzzle.

The gun fell silent, but Gordon's ears still rang. "Come
out, come out, wherever you are," the man's lilting voice
came. It had a strangely resonant quality to it in the steel
hollows under the stands. He had trilled his *R*s deep in the
back of his throat. He was foreign. Another long rip of fire
clanged off the girders ahead of Gordon, sending great
showers of sparks through the air.

Gordon took off running, heading deeper and deeper under the stands. He dodged the increasingly thick forest of
obstacles visible in the blazing light from the killer's gun.
Sparks rained down on him from clanging ricochets, and
fierce spitting sounds tore open the air just inches from his
body. Sprays of splattered concrete stung his face and hands
as he ran dodging and weaving through the Erector set
maze.

The gun fell silent again, and Gordon slowed and stooped over low to the ground in a crouch. His breath came in shallow pants and his heart thumped against his chest so hard he added it to his list of worries. Darkness descended on the ever-lower stands around the curved end of the basketball arena. Gordon felt his way into the deepest, darkest regions—his face covered with a thin gauze of spiderwebs. The clacking sounds of another magazine being popped into the machine pistol presaged another storm of lead.

"You can run, but you cannot hide," the thickly accented voice tormented Gordon, who probed now through the near-total darkness. He held his hands in front like antennae, his fingers jamming into the hard obstacles just ahead of his body.

A burst lit the way ahead for just an instant, and Gordon dropped to his knees to crawl into the recesses of the stone-and-steel cavern.

Gordon dragged himself through the heavy coating of dust still covering the floor from the gym's construction. He squeezed his body as far as it would go into the wedge formed by the lowest row in the stands and pressed his back between two heavy girders that rose at an angle to the sides. Inside the gym above him, the shooting had stopped. But the shrieks and shouts and the vibrations of stamping feet against the steel at Gordon's back told a story of unspeakable horror. His wife. His two precious daughters. Tears welled up in his eyes, which he jammed closed to shut out the picture that flashed through his head. *Oh, God, no!*

"Sounds like some sort of *distu-u-urbance* up there, *ja*?" the man asked coolly—trilling his *R*s deep in his throat in a thickly Germanic accent. "Maybe you are worried about Mrs. Davis, eh?" He knew Gordon's name! "Maybe your delicious young daughters, *ja*?"

He was close. In the hard, enclosed space, every sound was sharp. It focused Gordon's mind, shutting out the background commotion from the bleachers above.

"Maybe you and I, ve could go find out, *ja*? Find out if

your family is safe?'' The man was cool, his manner almost serene. Gordon saw him now, creeping forward in the darkness—the dim profile of his pistol leading the way. He was moving slowly past Gordon, who lay totally still—curled in a fetal position and breathing slowly, quietly, through his parched mouth.

The gunman stopped, not ten feet in front of Gordon. He was fumbling with something. There was a sound like the tearing of paper. Then a snapping sound.

A brilliant flare seared the darkness with bright light, leaving an orange spot on Gordon's eyelids as his eyes shut involuntarily. When he opened them, the man was looking down at him—the flare in one hand, the machine pistol in the other. The light from below his chin cast long shadows up his face, forming dark crevices in the creases of flesh around his smiling mouth.

''Ah, there you are,'' he said, carefully placing the flare on the ground in front of him and rising to near full height just under the sloping ceiling of their world. ''Behold, Senator Davis, ze end of your vorld.''

He raised the gun with both hands. A swastika was carved sloppily onto his knuckles.

The stunning booms of automatic weapons in the cave-like environs threw Gordon into shock. His whole body clenched in a grip of fear so great that he could feel nothing. He opened his eyes to see the blond man lying on the ground next to the flare. Gordon stared at him, waiting for him to move. More shots rang out—these in a series of single but still-rapid booms. His pursuer jerked with each flash and boom of a gun. Gordon watched black blood fill a small depression beside his body.

Gordon's throat was pinched so tight with terror that he gagged, unable to draw a breath. Three men in dark suits appeared, stubby Uzis barely larger than a pistol held extended in two hands. They fanned out, combat style, ready. One crawled up to the coughing Gordon.

''Are you hit, sir?'' the tense man asked. Gordon managed to shake his head, but then turned and vomited into the dust beside him. He felt hands poke and press his body, lifting his jacket and patting him down as if for a weapon. "He's good," Gordon heard. He watched smoke from the man's gun barrel rise in the dying light from the flare. "Are there any more of them down here?" Gordon's savior asked. Gordon was transfixed by the darkening, reddish hue. The man shook his arm gently. "Sir? Can you answer me?"

"No," Gordon croaked, wiping his mouth and twisting his way through the dust toward open space. Toward the air that he suddenly craved. "I mean, no, there aren't any more. Just . . . that one." He coughed on the choking stench of gun smoke.

The three men each produced a small flashlight. The one next to Gordon pulled the lapel of his suit to his lips. "Big Top, Big Top, this is Red Leader," he said. "The package is secure. I say again. The package is secure." Gordon's head was still swimming as he looked up at the man. A wire ran into an earphone like a hearing aid. The man's pin-striped suit was immaculate. He wore a pin, an American flag, on his lapel—the universal badge of the Secret Service.

"Copy that," he said, then motioned toward one of the other two agents. "Skinner. You go." The agent took off for the tunnel without further instructions. He too had an earphone. The third agent turned the body of the terrorist onto his back.

It was then that Gordon's pounding heart and paralyzed mind calmed just enough to admit the "background" sounds from above. The flare burned itself out, leaving only the two agents' flashlights to light their world in narrow beams. They discussed the body. "That one got him," one said—the harsh white glow from his flashlight pointing under the dead man's overcoat.

"Jesus," the other said. "Look at that. Must be ten mags sewn in there."

Gordon's mind drifted off, away from the dark world filled with the acrid smell of smoke.

"Oh, God!" a woman wailed. "*Why?*" The words were barely audible over the ringing in Gordon's ears. But the woman's cries rose in anguish above the shouts of pain and despair of others in the gym above. Tearful, shattered sounds. There were families in the gym, nothing but families. Like Gordon's family.

"I've got to go," he said, rising to his knees.

The agents and their flashlights turned his way. "You'd better stay here, sir."

"I'm sorry, but I've got to—"

"Somebody is checking, sir. On your family."

They didn't know. They had to check. Alive or dead. Gordon sank back down into the dirt. Alive or dead. The weight that held him there was heavier than the steel and concrete above his head. Sounds of commotion. Sirens. The two agents both grew still, listening. Something was coming over their earphones. Gordon was focused so completely on the agent nearest him that the sensation was almost physical. "Red Leader copies." Gordon gasped for air. Which way was his life headed? "They're all right, sir," the man said, then lifted his lapel again in the dim light. "Copy that. We're coming out."

"You mean, my wife and daughters . . . I have two . . . they're all safe?"

"Yes, sir. They weren't harmed. We've got them under our protection." The two Secret Service agents stood. One helped Gordon to his feet, saying, "Watch your head," just as Gordon smashed it into the stands above. He was so drained, so exhausted, that he stumbled along in their grasp. The two agents swept cobwebs from his path with their Uzis.

Gordon stopped and turned to the head agent. "Were they after me?" he asked. He could see in the growing light from the tunnel the nodding head of the agent. "Why? Why me?"

"You don't know?" he asked quietly, almost whispering. Gordon shook his head. The agent explained. "Some kid—a computer whiz who hacked into a server and inter-

cepted E-mailed orders—phoned in a tip about an assassination attempt to the Bethesda police. They contacted the
Secret Service. The deputy director called the RNC and the
kid's story checked out. You were lucky, sir. We'd just
rotated off duty at Camp David and were heading back to
D.C. We were on the Beltway about six miles from here
when we got the call.''

"What . . . what story? What was the kid's story that you
checked out?''

There was a pause. The man considered not answering,
Gordon guessed. The two agents exchanged glances. ''He
hacked his way into the Republican National Committee's
computer and then blabbed what he found to whoever was
behind this. Senator Davis, sir . . . you're about to become
the Republican nominee for vice-president of the United
States.''

Gordon's head swam on hearing the words. *Vice-
president*, he thought. The two agents grabbed his elbows
and ushered him on like a prisoner. Through the dizziness,
the sirens, the shouting—the news somehow managed to
sink in. Gordon once again halted the men, this time on the
very edge of darkness which he knew would cloak the look
on his face. *Vice-president of the United States*, he thought,
holding onto a steel girder. *The first African-American nominee for vice-president in American history*.

CAMP DAVID, MARYLAND
August 16, 0423 GMT (2323 Local)

Thomas Marshall—president of the United States—awoke
in a sweat to thoughts of war. In the confused moment
before alertness came, he felt a sickening guilt over the
awful tragedy of it all. In his nightmare there had unfolded
a relentless march of errors.

There was a shout from outside his window. He opened
his eyes, fully conscious now in a room lit only by a digital
alarm clock. Not yet eleven-thirty. He and the first lady had
only just fallen asleep.

Marshall thought he heard another shout, and he propped himself up on his elbows. He'd had briefing after briefing on the student sit-ins at Beijing University. Several had come on the golf course as the Chinese government threatened the use of force. His muscles were sore from the thirty-six holes he'd gotten in that day. The Camp David relaxation was just part of the ritual. Disappear during the Republican Convention. Let them have their day in the sun before kicking their butts up and down the campaign trail.

His mind was leaden. The wine he'd drunk to relax himself for sleep had done the trick.

An engine—deep and heavy like that of a truck—groaned to life outside. There was another shout before the engine revved and tires squealed. Deep, male voices shouted urgently to one another. A string of firecrackers went off, then another, and another, punctuated by a sharp explosion. Marshall spun his feet to the floor and groped in the plush carpet for his slippers. His wife stirred and mumbled, ''What?''

Marshall padded over to the window and pulled the heavy curtain aside. There was a fire of some sort in the distance. From the direction of the main road. From the main guardhouse. The ''firecrackers'' were gunfire, he realized, and they came from there also.

A sharp boom rattled the windows and rocked him back a step in surprise. Flame boiled into the sky from along the road between the gate and the president's lodge.

''What was that?'' his wife muttered from the bed. The door to his bedroom burst open. He turned in time to see a dark figure rushing at him—profiled in the light from the sitting room. The large man tackled Marshall in a jarring collision. The curtains were still clutched in the president's hand, and the curtain rods fell onto the two men in a heap.

''*Tom?*'' the first lady shouted from bed.

''Stay out of the window, sir!'' the man on top of the president said. Marshall watched as the ceiling was bathed in the flash from yet another explosion. The popping guns of a firefight were slowly being drowned out by the whine of a helicopter's engines.

"Let's go!" another Secret Service agent shouted from the door. The president was amazed to see a man appear wearing a dark suit and carrying an M-16 rifle.

Marshall crawled beneath the window alongside the agent who had tackled him. He heard the first lady grunt. An agent had forcibly bent her over and draped a bullet-proof vest over her nightgown.

At the door, a third agent helped Marshall slip his pajama-clad arms through his own body armor. Strong hands pushed him down the darkened hallway toward the service stairs. "Let's go! Go! Go!" an agent shouted. At the end of the hall, two Marines with shaved heads wearing only T-shirts, boxer shorts, and combat boots were setting up a machine gun in the window amid the draperies the first lady had picked out. A long belt of bullets was being pulled from a metal box.

Down the stairway they ran. The president joined the first lady just inside the door to the rear lawn. A blacked-out Marine One helicopter sat on the pad forty yards from the house. Its engines drowned out all sounds of the fighting. The stairs behind them were crowded with Secret Service agents talking excitedly into their radios. An explosion lit the dozen or so Marines crowded around the door just outside.

"Hit it!" someone yelled, and out they rushed. The agents and Marines formed a human shield, around the president and first lady.

"What's going on?" the president shouted as they rushed across the lawn.

No one answered. In seconds they were aboard, and the aircraft took off with the door still open. The president was buckled into a seat by helping hands. Through the window he saw brilliant white flares dropped from the helicopter's belly illuminating the scattering group of escorts below. Fires rose into the air from the guardhouse and in a string along the main road. Marshall caught sight of tracer rounds flying in both directions in the dark woods by the gate. The thin treetops of the Maryland countryside scraped against the belly of the twisting, turning Marine One.

McLEAN, VIRGINIA
August 16, 0455 GMT (2355 Local)

"Hey, Dad!" Nate Clark's sixteen-year-old son appeared
at the door of his study. "Come take a look at this on TV."
Jeffrey Clark disappeared just as quickly as he'd appeared.

"What are you doing up, Jeff?" Nate barked. "It's almost midnight!" Nate rose from his desk and asked his
wife, "What about the American Express?"

"Paid it," Lydia answered. Her legs were slung over the
side of a padded leather sofa. She was gently kicking her
feet while reading a catalog. "What do you think about
this?" she asked, holding the catalog up to him just as
Jeffrey shouted "*Da*-ad!"

"Pretty," Nate mumbled mechanically before joining the
boys in the family room. "Look!" said fourteen-year-old
Paul—pointing at the announcer on television. It was CNN.
THIS JUST IN read a graphic in the background. "We have
no independent confirmation of any of this just yet," the
anchorwoman said. "If something like this were to be true,
it would be absolutely unprecedented." She hesitated, distracted, then said, "I'm being told we have Elizabeth Crane
on the line from the Maryland Highway Patrol. Ms. Crane,
can you hear me?"

"Yes."

"You're on the air."

The woman cleared her throat. "Well, about fifteen
minutes ago we received a call from the presidential compound at Camp David requesting backup units and stating
that there was a 'firefight'—that was the word he used—
under way. Two units responded and reported that there
were flames at the main guardhouse and at various places
inside the compound, and that gunfire could be heard from
the surrounding woods."

"Wait, let me get this straight," the anchorwoman interrupted. "Are you saying that there was some sort of
battle at Camp David? That there was gunfire and . . . and
a 'firefight,' as you said?"

"The units reported casualties at the gate, and the initial

call to dispatch was from a Marine guard on a cellular phone. The dispatcher also reported that the sounds of gunfire could be heard over the phone.''

"Do you know whether the president was still there at the time of the attack? My producer is telling me that President Marshall was reported there as late as this afternoon."

"We don't know anything more. We're advising all motorists who don't have to be out to avoid the area, and we're cordoning off all roads into and out of Camp David with roadblocks."

Nate headed for the telephone in the study. It began ringing before he got there.

"It's a Captain Fairs?" Lydia said, shrugging at the unfamiliar name.

"Hello," Nate said as he powered the television up.

"General Clark?"

"Speaking."

"Sir, this is Captain Fairs. I work for the chief of staff's office. We're sending men from the protective service by a few homes, and yours is on the list. And I've also got a message that General Dekker has requested you be in his office at zero six thirty."

"All right, I'll be there. What's the security for, Captain?"

Lydia shot him a look of concern.

"Just a precaution, sir. We're calling in extra security personnel here at the Pentagon. And there was some trouble at the SecDef's home—an alarm went off—but there was nobody there."

Lydia was already up and staring at the television. Nate couldn't hear the anchorwoman, but the pictures were from Chicago. Flashing police lights filled a city street slick with an evening rain. In the distance several cars burned. The street was strewn with sparkling debris.

Nate hung up.

"What is it?" Lydia asked.

"I don't know. Terrorists. Get the boys and let's go."

Lost in thought he heard, "*Nate?*"

He turned to her. "It's just a precaution," he said. "Someone may have broken into the secretary of defense's home. That's all."

Lydia headed for the family room in a daze. "Oh," Nate called out to her, "and send Jeff back."

Jeffrey appeared just as Nate pulled a nine-millimeter Beretta from the locked drawer. The sixteen-year-old's eyes widened. Nate slapped a magazine into the butt and pulled the slide, chambering a bullet. He carefully lowered the hammer and slipped the pistol into his waistband, but Jeffrey's eyes followed his father's hands. Nate put three full magazines into his blue jeans pockets.

"Come on, son," he said as he headed for the hall closet. He reached up and took the dark green canvas bag from the top shelf. He extracted the engraved silver shotgun in two pieces. In seconds he had it together and loaded two shells into the side-by-side double-barrel twelve-gauge. He handed it to his firstborn. "Be careful with this," he said. They joined Lydia and Paul at the garage door. "Lydia, you drive. Jeff, in the front seat." Nate grabbed a cordless phone and headed for the back door.

"What about me?" Paul asked, his voice breaking.

"Get in the back and keep your head down." He turned to Lydia. "I'm gonna go around the side of the house to check out the drive. I'll call if the coast is clear and climb in with you out on the driveway. Don't open the garage until I say so."

Nate slipped out the side door. It was dark and hot outside. The sound of the pistol's hammer locking back seemed overly loud. He felt an unpleasant surge of alertness. A flutter in his chest left him drawing shallow breaths. The pistol was at eye level, the butt of the gun and heel of his right hand supported by the palm of his left. He forced himself to blink. *Calm down*, he told himself. It had been a long time, but he remembered the physical sensations all too well. The sickening anxiety just when you most needed calm.

With his heart pounding, Nate headed up the walk—the

pistol leading the way. Pebbles crunched under his first
step, and he suddenly felt exposed. He stepped off the
gravel walk onto the grass and fought the urge to drop and
crawl. He swallowed and forced himself to stand more
erect. His shoulder muscles ached. There were too many
dark places. The bushes, the garbage cans, the tree line.
The tree line worried him most. He checked his rear, turning his entire body to keep his right eye in line with the
pistol's sights.

He shouldn't be doing this blind. He should be covered.
Riflemen on the bushes and behind trash cans. A machine
gun on the tree line. He inched his way down to the quiet
street and back to the side of the garage—checking for
wires across the narrow drive. He pulled the cordless phone
from his pocket and dialed the Range Rover.

When he heard the faint hiss of static, he felt a jab of
pain in his left side. The sensation was so sharp he probed
the spot. There was no wound . . . at least not a new wound.
In the decades since he'd been shot there in Vietnam he
had felt the pain return in random jolts as if the nerve end-
ings retained some memory of the agony they'd transmitted
that day. As he was lying in the dirt amid high weeds that
were his only cover, the pain had been so great that all he
felt after the tug of the suture was varying degrees of it
from icy cold to searing heat. And all he heard was the
steady hiss of white noise on the radio. Clark had clung to
the sound of the static on which his life had depended.

The car phone in the garage rang. Lydia picked it up
immediately. ''Come on out,'' Nate said, surprised at how
much effort it took. He sagged against the wall. The garage
door opened slowly, noisily.

On the flight back to the aid station, Nate had held his
hand out to the bare chest of Chuck Reed—his best friend
from the Point and fellow platoon leader. Sky-high on mor-
phine by then, Nate had felt him slowly grow cold as air
whipped through the open doors of the helicopter and life
bled from him more quickly than the IV could replenish it.
Chuck Reed had saved Nate's life, but lost his own in the
bargain soldiers made with each other.

The car appeared. Nate carefully lowered the hammer on the pistol and climbed in the back with Paul. Lydia wasted no time backing down the driveway. Jeffrey manually searched the radio for the fast-breaking news stories.

"You're sweating, Dad," Paul said in a quiet voice.

Lydia looked at Nate through the rearview mirror. "Leave your dad alone, Paul," she said softly.

"It's okay, Dad," Paul said. He laid his hand on Nate's back awkwardly.

Lieutenant General Nate Clark reached out and pulled the boy into his arms, hugging him. Hiding his face in the boy's hair. *Why me?* he thought for the thousandth time. *Why did I live when so many others died so young?*

2

Colonel Pyotr Andreev, commander of the Russian Presidential Guard, climbed the last metal rungs of the bomb shelter's air shaft. His dozen surviving security troops trailed just behind. Andreev's arms, shoulders, back, and lungs burned from the thirty minutes of strenuous ascent. But the broad, slatted vents that would close on the flash of a nuclear burst were now within reach. Andreev and two of his men began to pry open with bayonets the screen that prevented birds from entering the shaft. It was painstaking effort, for any noise would mean certain death.

Andreev squeezed out of the vent into the dim light of dawn and crouched amid the hedges that concealed the air shaft from view. He breathed heavily. Sweat soaked the dark trousers and white dress shirt that he wore under the ballistic vest and bandoliers full of ammunition. He peered through the bushes. Russian Army troops were forming into ranks in the headlights of armored fighting vehicles whose hatches were thrown wide open. The lick of flame from a doorway and from the wrecks of a couple of cars were the only evidence of the fierce fighting that had raged across the old fortress's grounds.

The sound of gunfire beyond the Kremlin walls, however, could be heard from all directions. The commander of the motorized rifle regiment sent to relieve the beleaguered Kremlin defenders had radioed that they had been ambushed by antitank missiles on Gorky Street. Andreev's men all looked at each other in silence—jaws agape as the ferocious, ripping sounds of firefights filled the fresh early-morning air. The Kremlin was roughly in the center of Moscow, and it seemed as if the entire city was engulfed in war. It was a sound that meant only one thing—the end of the Republic of Russia.

Andreev found their best route through the darkness to the ancient stone wall and the relative safety that lay beyond. The wall there appeared to be lightly defended. The dark forms of only two soldiers were profiled against the city lights. One was walking slowly along the wall away from them with his rifle slung over his shoulder. The other was peering intently through binoculars into the distance. Andreev led his men in a quiet dash across an open road just under the crest of a hill that shielded them from the busy main Kremlin square.

Andreev crept up the steps toward the soldier with the binoculars. His men were close behind with weapons raised. When he reached the top, he saw that the second soldier had rounded one of the towers that dotted the high walls and was now out of sight.

"Don't move," Andreev said in a low voice. The soldier's binoculars sagged, but otherwise he stood stock-still. He wore the blue-striped shirt of a "Desantnik"—a paratrooper—under his full combat gear. Andreev's men quickly disarmed the frightened soldier, then dropped a rope over the wall to the parklike grounds below. The soldier was forced to kneel and put his hands on his head. He stared down Andreev's rifle through wide eyes set in a face blackened with greasepaint.

"What unit are you with?" Andreev asked as his men rappelled one-by-one down the wall.

When he didn't answer, a grizzled sergeant in Andreev's

security force pulled a knife from its scabbard. Its menacing, serrated edge drew a darting look from the frightened paratrooper. "Hundred and fourth," he answered.

"From Omsk?" Andreev asked, and the man nodded. They had come all the way from Siberia. That meant air-force transport. *That* meant the rebellion was widespread and coordinated. "Why?" Andreev asked without thinking. The private's mouth hung open. He clearly didn't know how to reply. "What did your officers tell you your mission was?"

He closed his mouth and swallowed, taking one more look at the large blade before replying. "They . . . they said we would save Russia."

The rope shook—slapping at the stone. All of the men were now safely on the ground, and they were anxious for Andreev to join them.

"Get down to the men," he ordered the sergeant.

As the sergeant rappelled down the wall, bright lights lit the tops of trees. Andreev dropped to one knee behind the low stone wall. Across the open central square that had been their brief battleground, a five-car motorcade pulled up—their brilliant headlights lit. They were unconcerned with security now. They were in complete control. Emerging from the black limousine in the center was a lone figure.

Andreev instantly recognized the short, balding man in the blazing headlights. He wore a broad smile on his face and shook hands with a tall officer in full combat gear. They both then strode briskly toward the Palace of People's Deputies. The civilian's round glasses—like those worn by academics—gave him away. It was Valentin Kartsev, former general in the KGB and now the acknowledged "leader" of the Anarchists.

That son of a bitch, Andreev thought.

He raised his rifle. Resting the barrel on the stone in front of him, he brought the fixed iron sight onto Kartsev's midsection. At just over a hundred meters, Andreev knew he wouldn't miss, even in the poor light. *Die, you little piece of shit.*

The rope slapped at the wall again. Andreev's men would be holding the rope stiff at the bottom of the wall—standing there exposed while they dutifully waited for him.

His job was done. The president had fled God knows where. Andreev had other things to think about. His young wife, Olga. Their two little girls. Kartsev's back was to him now, and Andreev's aim had moved unconsciously to follow his target. Staring down the rifle at the man, he felt the tension in his finger hard against the trigger. The slightest pressure now would loose the sear, and the single bullet would shatter the bastard's back.

It was his chance. Andreev knew Kartsev. The man deserved to die.

The rope slapped the stone again.

Andreev closed his eyes and took a deep breath, carefully easing the tension on the trigger. He rose to a stoop, leaned over the young Desantnik, and raised his finger to his lips. The boy nodded. Andreev rappelled quickly down the rope to the grass at the base of the wall.

I had the shot. The thought nagged him. *I had the shot.*

HEATHROW AIRPORT, LONDON
August 16, 0500 GMT (0500 Local)

The flight computer flew the huge A-400 Airbus in for its automated landing. "I've got the lights," the copilot said. The pilot kept his hands lightly on the wheel as the computer trimmed the plane for its near-perfect descent onto the well-lit runway seven miles ahead. The night was clear. The flight from Hong Kong had been uneventful, but not so their departure. On board was Britain's foreign secretary, who was returning from a well-publicized protest. The tarmac had been lined with chanting anti-Western demonstrators.

The engines throttled up just slightly, and then up a little more—noticeably louder. "Airspeed two-twenty," the copilot reported.

"Must be some headwind," the pilot commented. The

sound of the engines rose. The pilot could feel the acceleration press his back to the seat. The airspeed continued to climb.

"Flight Niner-Two-Niner," the tower said, "you're above the glide path. Reduce speed to two-ten."

"Roger that," the pilot replied. "Disengaging autopilot." The fly-by-wire flight controls were responsive to even the lightest touch. The flight crew had to be extremely careful not to brush the wheel during normal autopiloted flight. The computer interpreted any movement of the yoke as a manual override.

The pilot pulled back on the wheel and the throttle in a smooth, coordinated motion.

Nothing happened.

"Speed two forty-*eight*," the copilot said.

The pilot jerked the wheel. Nothing. Even the lumbering Airbus should have lurched at that much control pressure. "Tower, this is British Airways Flight Niner-Two-Niner. I'm going around." He pulled the wheel back toward his chest. No response. He turned the wheel from side to side. The copilot stared at him in terror.

"State your problem, Niner-Two-Niner," the tower called.

"Heathrow Tower," he said, his voice flat despite the rising fear, "BA Niner-Two-Niner is declaring an emergency." The engines rose to a new plateau of sound, and the nose pitched down—still heading toward the lights at the end of the runway.

"Jesus!" the copilot said, pulling the throttles back all the way to reverse thrust and then jamming them forward. The whine of the engines didn't change. "Airspeed two-ninety! Altitude four hundred!"

"Reset the computer," the pilot ordered, firmly gripping the wheel.

The copilot flipped a protective cover up and pressed the button over and over. "It won't reset!"

The ground collision warning buzzer sounded. The pilot thrashed the wheel about wildly, cursing it, and kicking at the rudder pedals. The engines wound up to full power.

"Oh, Mother of God!" the copilot shouted.

"Flight Niner-Two-Niner," a supervisor's voice came over the radio from the tower. "Please advise situation, over."

From the first-class cabin in back the pilot could hear screams. The whining wind past the windshield made a sound like a dive-bomber in an old movie. "Shut everything down!" the pilot shouted, and the two men reached up to start throwing circuit breakers on the panels above their heads. The avionics of the advanced cockpit began to fall dark one instrument at a time.

The nose dipped down again. From the carnival-ride feeling the pilot got in his groin he knew it was too late. He and the copilot, strapped in their seats in the nose of the mammoth aircraft, hurtled toward the hard concrete runway.

Days later, in an office just off a hangar filled with debris, investigators listened over and over to a shout on the cockpit voice recorders. Finally, one thought to check the pilot's personnel records. The pilot had shouted his wife's name, but it was nearly instantly drowned out by the sound of the wrenching force that tore the life from all two hundred aboard.

OVAL OFFICE, THE WHITE HOUSE
August 16, 0700 GMT (0200 Local)

The sound of the ringing telephone filled the Oval Office. The principals of the National Security Council and the heads of the nation's law-enforcement agencies listened—waiting.

There was no answer.

"Try his dacha," Marshall finally said, and his aide called the Russian president's home outside Moscow. The phone rang and rang. Secretary of State Hugh Jensen looked at his watch and shook his head. "Tom," Jensen said in a low tone, "it's just after nine o'clock on a Friday morning in Moscow. We've tried all the telephone numbers we keep on file for President Krestyanov. One of them—their military command net number—is supposed to rove and guarantee contact twenty-four hours a day." He was hunched over his elbows. "There's nobody there."

After the meeting broke up, President Marshall read the *Chicago Tribune* at his desk in the Oval Office. THE TERROR CONTINUES a banner headline proclaimed. Marshall sighed as he skimmed. More lurid details of violence. CHINESE CRUSH STUDENT PROTEST, read a below-the-fold article. What would have been the top story—hundreds of democratic protesters feared killed—was relegated to second-class news. An article toward the bottom of the page caught his eye. BOLD VP NOMINATION CHANGES RACE. Marshall smiled at the presumably unintended pun. *"Changes race,"* he thought. He rocked back and put his stockinged feet on the desk to read the story about Gordon Davis.

The results of the first flash poll following the close of the Republican Convention were out already. Marshall's lead had fallen from eighteen to eleven points. The *Tribune*'s political analyst attributed it to a masterstroke by Governor Bristol. "Bullshit," Marshall whispered, snorting. "Just postconvention bounce," he mumbled.

The intercom buzzed. Marshall lowered the paper. "Yes?" he said.

"Sir, the Swedish prime minister is on line three for you from Stockholm."

Marshall made a face. *What the hell could he want?* He had his secretary summon his chief of staff, and then he pressed line three. *"Prime minister?"* he said in an energetic, vibrant tone—his public voice. "To what do I owe this pleasure?"

"Mr. President," came the deep and heavily accented voice, "I have news of some significance of which you should be made aware." The president's chief of staff walked in, carrying his coffee mug and nodding jovially at

Marshall's secretary. "Approximately one hour ago there was an unauthorized landing by a Russian aircraft on a runway outside Kiruna in the far north of our country."

"Who is that?" Marshall's chief of staff mouthed, pointing down at the phone. He placed his cup on a coaster and sat across the desk from Marshall.

"Swedish PM," Marshall whispered.

"In that aircraft," the slow voice came over the background hiss of the transatlantic connection, "was the president of Russia, the Russian prime minister, several members of the cabinet, and their families." The president rocked forward. The White House chief of staff leaned over the desk closer to the phone. "They are all seeking political asylum."

"Jesus Christ," Marshall whispered.

NATIONAL AIRPORT, WASHINGTON, D.C.
August 16, 1100 GMT (0600 Local)

A tanned and well-groomed man boarded the business jet. "Senator Davis," he said, "my name is Arthur Fein. I'm the head of Governor Bristol's vice-presidential team." He greeted Gordon's family. "You must be Celeste!" Fein said as the plush jet the Republican Party had leased fired up its engines. "And you're Janet. Look at you two!"

The girls smiled. Gordon marveled at how quickly they had recovered from the horror of the night before. It had to be the novelty of the limos and the press and the jet. *And they're young*, he thought. Elaine, on the other hand, had worn the same numb expression since their drive home from the gym.

Gordon turned to introduce Daryl—his chief of staff, right-hand man, and best friend. Fein instead greeted the two previously mute Secret Service agents. "You were on the Bush detail, right?" The man nodded. "Coffee, black, with two Equals, right?" Fein said, smiling and pointing at the man's face.

"That's right, Mr. Fein," the agent replied, smiling for the first time.

The noise of the engines on takeoff was too great to introduce Daryl. Fein was a study in comfort with his foot on the low coffee table and his hands—protruding from crisp white cuffs studded with gold cuff links—clasped in his lap. His suit was Savile Row—broad pinstripes down thick, heavy fabric despite the summer weather. His red tie matched the kerchief sticking jauntily out of his breast pocket. His blue shirt was topped with a starched white collar pinched together with a nearly hidden gold collar pin.

The moment the engine noise dropped, Fein shook Daryl's hand, laid a slim briefcase on the table, and said, "I hope you don't mind if we jump right in. We're going to be busy when we get to the convention, so this might be our best opportunity to get down to the nitty-gritty."

"I absolutely agree," Gordon said. Daryl extracted a legal pad filled with notes from an expandable folder that served as his briefcase. "There's a lot we need to discuss. What will our statement on the terrorism be? And on the Chinese crackdown in Beijing? You know I've got a strong record on crime. And the anarchy that's sweeping this country is really just a variant of . . ."

Gordon fell silent when Fein made a big production of laying a single sheet of paper on the table. "Okay," Fein said in a businesslike tone. "Day one. 'Hi, my name is Gordon Davis. I'm a young, handsome, conservative, well-groomed, well-spoken, well-educated African-American male with an equally attractive, perfectly functional, and loving wife and family. I'm a Norman Rockwell wet dream for the 1990s. I'm the great hope that we might all just possibly end up getting along together after all.' " He held his index finger up. "Day one." Daryl rolled his eyes. Elaine looked out the window.

Gordon picked the single sheet of paper up. On it were printed exactly what Fein had just said.

"Now," Fein continued, "for the next couple of hours I'd like to work with you on a few things . . . with your permission." Gordon leaned forward and rested his elbows on his knees. "First," Fein said, "you need to work on what I call 'white space.' You need pauses in your speech. They're very effective for placing emphasis. Slow it down. You have a tendency to try to jam as much content as you can into any given period of time. To get sound bites, you need emphasis. For emphasis, pauses are very important. So is voice modulation. No monotone. We *want* to capture some . . . of . . . that . . . *passion*!'' he said by way of example—his voice rising. His words stressed merely by the pacing of his speech.

Gordon was impressed. Daryl said, ''Jesus Christ'' disgustedly.

''Give it a try,'' Fein suggested. He sat back, folded his arms, and waited.

Gordon stared at him for a moment before asking, ''What do I say?''

Fein spoke slowly, his words spaced, the pauses intentionally filled with emphasis. ''That doesn't really matter.''

''*That* is something I feel very strongly about,'' Gordon said slowly—standing in the small lavatory.

''Even slower,'' Fein corrected from behind him.

Gordon repeated the words with an unnaturally slow pacing, watching himself in the mirror.

''There. See?'' Gordon saw Fein's reflection over his shoulder. ''Now lean forward a little.'' He pressed Gordon on his back. Gordon leaned forward. ''There. Leaning forward creates intensity. Next, empty one pocket and put your hand in it.''

''Which one?'' Gordon asked.

''It doesn't matter.'' Gordon laid his handkerchief and breath mints on the sink. He slid his left hand into the empty pocket. ''All right,'' Fein continued, ''chop the air with your right hand for even more emphasis.'' Fein made a motion like he was breaking a board with a karate chop. ''Pick any word and emphasize it with a chop.''

Gordon watched himself in the mirror. ''That is something I feel very *strongly* about,'' he said, chopping on the word ''strongly.'' It worked.

"Pick a different word," Fein said.

"What?"

"Pick a different word and chop."

Gordon looked back into the mirror. "*That* is something I feel very strongly about." The meaning changed with the gesture. "That is something *I*"—he stressed and chopped—"feel very strongly about." He smiled.

"See? The beauty of it is you can make people think you feel *passionately,*" Fein said, grabbing the air with both hands and yanking down, "about anything just by body language." He slapped Gordon on the back. "Let's go over it again."

"Move," Gordon repeated. "Forward and back, never side to side. Lavaliere mikes, not stick mikes. Never raise your hands above your head. Smile. Leaning forward emphasizes, leaning back deemphasizes. Eye contact. Modulate your voice. Speak slowly with lots of pauses."

"Then you can speed it up later in the speech to create excitement. Okay. Any questions?"

Gordon looked down at his handkerchief. "Why did I empty my pocket?"

"So all that stuff doesn't go flying when you take your hand out. As a matter of fact, you shouldn't carry anything in your pockets. Your wallet ruins the line of your suit." Fein pulled up on the shoulders of Gordon's jacket like a tailor.

"What do I do with it?"

"We'll have somebody carry it for you. Now, are you ready, Gordy? You're gonna knock 'em dead." Gordon smiled. "If you want to go through it one more time I could get the pilot to circle."

Gordon shook his head and stepped out into the narrow hallway. "I'm a policy wonk by nature. This just isn't my thing."

"But it *can* be!" Fein said, barring Gordon in the doorway with hands on both walls. "I've got a product the American people will buy, I can *feel* it. My job is to put that product in an attractive package. That's all. If you'll do what I say, Gordy''—he leaned forward and lowered his voice—''I'll put you one heartbeat away from policy-maker heaven.'' He arched his eyebrows, lowered his arms, and returned to the cabin.

Daryl spun into the short hallway and guided Gordon back into the lavatory. ''What the hell are you doing?'' Gordon asked.

''I was going to ask you the same question,'' Daryl replied.

''Look,'' Gordon whispered, ''he's a jerk. But he's . . .'' The words stuck in Gordon's throat.

''The first string? And I'm what?''

''You're my chief of staff. Listen, Daryl. These guys are pros at getting people into the White House! For Christ's sake, we're on our way to the convention to accept the nomination for vice-president of the United States!''

Daryl nodded. ''Okay, Gordon. But just don't forget who you are. What you believe in,'' When they returned to the cabin, Fein handed Daryl Gordon's handkerchief and breath mints.

THE PENTAGON, WASHINGTON, D.C.
August 16, 1115 GMT (0615 Local)

Lieutenant General Nate Clark passed the normally dark operations room. Junior officers from all four combat services were scurrying around, arranging piles of paper on the large map table in the center. The navy officers far outnumbered those of the army, air force, and marine corps.

''What's going on down there?'' Clark asked a young officer who loitered outside an office.

The man stiffened. ''They're PACOM, sir,'' he said. ''I don't know what's up, but they were in there this morning when I got in.''

''Does it have something to do with the protests outside our bases in Japan?'' Clark asked. The officer shrugged.

Men and women hurried in and out of the room in brisk fashion. Clark was destined for command of U.S. Forces

Korea, and PACOM—Pacific Command—would only indirectly affect Clark's theater. Still, his curiosity was piqued and he returned to the room.

When he stepped inside, several of the officers stood erect, but no command was typically given to come to attention inside the Pentagon.

"What's up, gentlemen . . . ladies?"

"Nothing much, sir," a navy captain said. "Purely precautionary." Two petty officers entered carrying boxes filled with files, which they placed in a row of similarly numbered cardboard boxes along the walls around the table. "There were some assassination attempts in Beijing last night. And there's rioting this morning in Harbin, but it's probably nothing."

At the end of the room two navy lieutenants were pulling a large, folded map out of one of the boxes. "Are you telling me PACOM convened a crisis action team on China?"

"Just a precaution, sir."

"But *everybody*'s got problems with terrorists today. Moscow, Berlin, Seoul, Tokyo—everywhere."

"Yes, sir, but not everybody put their armed forces on full alert. Call-up orders are going out every hour on the half hour over radio and television. And the PLA has been holding maneuvers just across the Taiwan Straits. The CNO's putting a carrier battle group in the East China Sea."

Clark nodded and wandered out of the room. *China?* he thought, leaning his back against the wall just outside the door. From inside the room he could hear the routine workings of the PACOM team. *That's not your show,* he kept telling himself.

"Who the hell was that?" he heard someone ask.

"Clark. Word is he's gonna get Korea."

Nate smiled. Korea was the prize of his career. It was the culmination of all his hard work. Few theater commands got the attention, or were expected to be as combat ready, as U.S. Forces Korea.

"He's a tall son of a bitch," the first man said. "What's he like to work for?"

"He's *infantry*," came a new voice. "Got passed over in Europe 'cause he wasn't a tank driver." Clark arched his eyebrows in amusement, having forgotten how gossipy these interservice teams could get. "He's a fuckin' case, though. Wife's Chinese." The smile left Clark's face. "Some sorta professor or something."

"You mean she's like, *Chinese* Chinese?"

"No-o! Chinese-American. Anyway, like I said, watch out 'cause he's infantry. Everybody thinks they're big teddy bears 'cause they never yell at the troops. But behind closed doors they'll chew you a new asshole if they think you didn't take good enough care of your men. 'Why didn't they get three squares yesterday?' " the talker said in imitation of a shout. " 'What the hell were they doin' standin' around in the sun? Didn't you see that shade a hundred meters away?' "

"All right, listen up!" Clark heard, the loud voice of the navy captain with whom he'd spoken. "We've got one hour to get this room in shipshape for our first briefing. Let's get that map going."

Someone asked, "What color should the Chinese Army be? Red?"

"Yeah, whatever," came the answer.

"Should I use blue for the Russians?" the same man then asked.

"Use green," someone replied. "Always save blue for the good guys."

On hearing the man's words, Clark's mood changed subtly. *Save the blue grease pencils for the good guys*, he thought. But there was no chance of that. There was no chance of any American units appearing on those maps.

"All right, first unit," the captain said loudly from inside. "Chicom—411th infantry Division, eighty-five percent strength, Jiamusi."

Clark headed down the corridor, repeating to himself over and over, "That's not your show. That's not your show."

•   •   •

From the moment Nate Clark walked into the large office, he knew something was wrong. He was ready for broad smiles, warm handshakes, and slaps on the back. Instead he was ushered into a semicircle of chairs facing the desk of General Dekker—chief of staff of the U.S. Army. "Have a seat, Nate," Dekker said. The two- and three-stars all sat on invitation of the four-star. The possibility of no command at all loomed. Retirement. *Why?* "Nate," Dekker began, "I know the scuttlebutt has been that you were in for U.S. Forces Korea. And quite frankly, that *was* going to be your command."

Clark's jaw was set, but he agonized over what error he might have committed.

"Nate, I'll come right to the point. The final decision is you're instead going to command U.S. Army Pacific."

Dekker paused, waiting for a response. Clark spoke slowly to control his temper. "That command is up for decommissioning."

"We've been fighting to keep it, Nate," Dekker said.

"It's a two-star billet."

"Not technically. Congress has completed the force levels review. It's a three-star command, and it *is* a command. You'll have Ninth Corps under you."

"Ninth Corps only has one division attached," he said, then began to wonder where he was headed. His choices were accept with a "yes, sir," or decline and resign here and now. "Who gets Korea?" Nate asked.

"Tim Stanton," the army's head of personnel said from Clark's left.

Tim was from Nate's class at West Point. *At least he's not from a class behind*, Nate thought. "He's a good man," he said.

"So are you, Nate," Dekker said. "Some would say— some of us here—that you're the very best. That's why you've been given USARPAC." He pronounced the acronym as if it were a word.

Clark heaved a deep sigh. On his green jacket were row

after row of ribbons. He had the perfect army résumé from platoon leader to corps commander. His career was to have been capped, quite possibly, by Dekker's job a few years hence. He'd even spent the better part of the last year since returning from Europe kissing the right butts all over the greater Washington area. Now he was getting a backwater command.

"Excuse me, sir," Nate said, "but I have to respectfully say that's all a load of shit."

Dekker wasn't pleased. He restacked some papers on his desk. The blue stone of his West Point ring glinted. He'd been a fourth-year and Clark's company commander when Clark was a lowly plebe. Dekker had always been one grade ahead of Clark.

"Nate, you are going to Fort Shafer to assume that command. You are going to kick their lazy asses off those Hawaiian golf courses, and kick 'em out of those warm winter barracks in Alaska, and turn USARPAC into a fighting command." He bore no trace of consolation now. "*That* is an order."

But Clark wasn't ready to play the good soldier. He took a deep breath and looked off.

"Goddamm it, Nate!" Dekker snapped. "USARPAC is responsible for the defense of U.S. interests and allies from the Urals to the California coast, and from the North to the South Pole—*ex*-clusive of Korea."

"What else *is* there but Korea?" Clark replied.

Dekker looked at each of the senior officers gathered around his desk. "This conversation didn't happen, is that understood? But we all know what the potential threat is."

"I'd like you to say it, sir."

Dekker took a deep breath. "China, Nate." There was dead silence. "They've been modernizing their military for over a decade. They're looking to bust out of their strait-jacket. If they go south, no problem. That's Vietnam's fight. West? That's India's. Fine. If they go north, let the Russians take care of it. But if they go east, Nate—toward Japan, Taiwan, the Philippines—they run into us. *You,* specifically.

What I'm saying, Nate, is that if this country goes to war with the People's Republic of China, it'll be *your* war. I want that command ready. I need you to make it happen.''

THE GEORGIA DOME, ATLANTA
August 17, 0230 GMT (2130 Local)

It was growing late. Gordon Davis and his family were exhausted.

The door opened. The roar of the crowd poured into the small but well-appointed waiting room. The noise extinguished the small talk between the Davises and the Bristols. A man with a clipboard and a headset entered. In the concrete corridor outside there lurked large, stony-faced Secret Service agents.

''All right,'' said the man with the headset. ''Governor Bristol, Senator Davis, we've got about five minutes before the chair sends it back to the Connecticut delegation. Your home state passed earlier, Senator Davis, so they can put you over the top. Right after they vote, the chair is going to suspend the roll call and request a nomination by acclamation. Then the standard stuff. Balloons, bands, yadda yadda. Now, let's run through real quickly what you're gonna do. First, we'll cue you to head out by yourself. It's twenty-two normal-length paces to your mark, which is number eighty-four. It's printed on some tape stuck onto the stage floor just to your left of the podium. The stage manager will have a diagram when you get up there. If it's covered in confetti, just remember twenty-two paces to the left of the podium. Okay?''

Gordon nodded.

''We've got about three minutes planned for the ovation,'' the man with the headset said. ''Three minutes and twelve seconds for the song 'Proud to Be an American.' Then we cut to your family. Mrs. Davis, you bring the girls out one on each side, the little one between you and the crowd.''

''I don't want them onstage,'' Gordon said. All eyes

turned to him, including his family's. "I'd just rather not, after last night."

The man with the headset said, "Senator Davis, let me assure you that security is extraordinarily tight. I've done dozens of stadium events in my life and I've never seen anything like this. The Secret Service even has sharpshooters up in the press boxes."

Arthur Fein stepped in and took Gordon's elbow. Off to the side of the room, Fein said, "Gordy, this is a prime-time, command performance. The networks tell us we might break records for the last day of a convention. Remember what I told you today's message was? Ten or fifteen minutes onstage tonight will put it out to a forty share."

"But I'm not even going to *say* anything," Gordon protested.

"All the better. We've got you and your lovely wife and daughters all standing amid an adoring throng. Balloons, confetti, rousing music on nationwide television!"

"Two minutes," the man with the headset said.

"Gordy," Fein said, squeezing Gordon's elbow. Gordon gently pulled it free. "We're gonna get all four anchormen talking about how, in a day when deep divisions fragment our society and—"

"Okay, okay," Gordon said. The words meant nothing to Fein. They were bullshit that scored points in the polls. Gordon turned to the coordinator. "If you can guarantee my family's safety . . ." The man nodded distractedly then led Gordon and his family from the room with one last slap on Gordon's back by Philip Bristol. The Davis kids passed awkwardly by their opposites from the Bristol family. They smiled but had nothing to say. They wandered through the concrete maze until they reached the stage. Gordon eyed the bare wood and exposed wires on the rear of the wall. On the public side, all was seamless blue. But the view from the inside revealed the flimsy facade.

Gordon walked into the bright lights of the raucous stadium. Tens of thousands cheered wildly. The chairman shook his hand as they passed. He kept up his count until he found some tape. Gordon smiled and waved, smiled and waved, smiled and waved. The whole time his skin crawled. With every flash of a camera, with every shout that rose above the others, with every rush of movement in the crowd, he tensed. When his family joined him, the feeling of dread redoubled. Twenty-eight agonizing minutes later—after "Proud to Be an American" and "We Shall Overcome" and the last of the balloons had fallen—it was over.

Walking off the stage now crowded with party luminaries, Gordon remembered he hadn't pointed or winked. He spotted a comical woman in the front ranks wearing a red hat and vest covered with campaign buttons. Gordon smiled, pointed, and winked as he made the shape of a gun with his hand and pulled the trigger. A hundred cameras flashed at once. The next morning, the picture was on the front page of every major newspaper in the country.

FINAL APPROACH, JFK AIRPORT
August 17, 0700 GMT (0200 Local)

"Papa, *smotri*!" the high-pitched voice chimed. Masha's finger pointed through the window at the New York City skyline.

"Only English, Mashenka," Pyotr Andreev whispered into his three-year-old's ear. "Remember what Mama and Papa said. Only English. It's a game, all right?"

"Okay," she said. Pyotr kissed her smiling face.

His wife Olga and five-year-old daughter Oksana sat quietly. Their escape from the collapsing Russia had, in fact, worked perfectly. One last hurdle remained. No one said another word as they landed, deplaned, and lined up at customs.

The security was extraordinary. There were uniformed officers with rifles along the walls. Every bag was opened and inspected carefully. Even the dog in the cage ahead of the Andreevs was removed. It yapped and kicked its short legs excitedly as another customs officer waved a long wand inside the cage, sniffing for explosives. The barking of the dog grated on Pyotr's nerves, but little Masha enjoyed it immensely. She looked back and forth between Pyotr and the noisy pet. Pyotr kept her hand in his, ready to administer a painful squeeze if she lapsed into Russian.

His throat was dry when their turn came. The officer looked at their Swiss passports, down at their pictures, up at their faces, back down again—repeating the process over and over. It reminded him of the old Soviet Union. Things had changed since the last time he'd visited America.

"You're Swiss?" the officer asked, unzipping a bag with a tearing sound.

"Yes," Pyotr replied. His heart pounded as he wondered whether they'd found all of the tags and cardboard inserts that came with their new luggage. On a quick trip to the bank in Zurich they'd gotten money and passports from the safe-deposit box. They'd bought Western clothes and toiletries.

"And you are here on vacation, Mr. Hoffman?"

"Yes. We are going to Disney World."

"Do you have tickets to California?" the customs officer asked casually as he probed through their clothing with hands covered by white latex gloves.

"Florida," Pyotr corrected. He pulled his ticket from his jacket pocket. "Orlando. We are going to Disney *World*, not Disneyland." The man looked at the Delta Airlines folder. He didn't reach for it, and Pyotr put it back into his jacket pocket. It really did have tickets to Orlando in it. The Andreevs, however, had no intention of using them.

Pyotr felt dampness under his armpits. The loud snarl of a zipper being run down the soft bag's side indicated they were through. Pyotr awkwardly wheeled a luggage cart down the concourse. The wheels turned this way and that. Just ahead of them, a man whose hands were thrust deep in his windbreaker stopped to get a drink of water. It was strange. An August day, the sun was hot. And the man wore a jacket. Not a sport coat or some other item of apparel more fashion than function, but a windbreaker.

Pyotr consciously had to avoid turning to look back over his shoulder as they passed the man. He stopped a couple of times to readjust the baggage on the cart. He saw nothing, but he felt it. That undefined sense of being followed.

OUTSIDE INTERIOR MINISTRY, MOSCOW
August 18, 1730 GMT (1930 Local)

The Russian crowd chanted in unison. "Authority is oppression!" one of the Anarchists on the street below had translated.

"How's the light?" Kate asked from in front of Woody's camera.

" 'Bout fifteen minutes left," he said as he carefully adjusted the focus.

Kate stood with her back to the railing of a second-floor balcony. Down below, the front ranks of a mob were taunting lines of riot police who encircled the Interior Ministry headquarters. "I don't really want to use the spots," she said. She was still spooked from the Red Square stampede on the first day of the fighting. Doubly spooked by the anonymous tip on her cellular phone that had led them to the Interior Ministry.

"No arguments from me," Woody said. "Batteries are low anyway."

Kate peered down over the railing of the sleazy hotel's dining room. They had bribed one of the kitchen workers with a one-million-ruble note, which at the day's closing exchange rate was worth ten cents. By tomorrow it would probably be worthless.

On the street, three lines of white helmeted riot police nervously stood their ground, holding clear Plexiglas shields and raised truncheons. They made occasional forays out to the ragged front ranks of the angry mob, raining blows onto someone's head or spraying long strings of pepper gas into faces before retreating. In return, the crowd was pulling up paving stones and lobbing them into police ranks.

"Okay, ready when you are," Woody said.

Kate tugged at her navy-blue jacket and then reached under it to pull down on her white silk blouse. It would only be a head shot, so she wore blue jeans and running shoes beneath. She took one last look in a small mirror and arranged her hair, then cleared her throat loudly for several seconds.

"Give me some sound," Woody said.

Kate fixed a serious expression on her face. "The Russian government collapses, but first a word from Purina cat chow."

"Your teeth are too damn white," Woody groused, fiddling with buttons. "Ever consider getting 'em capped?" She made a face. He held up his hand—five fingers spread out. Kate wiggled her shoulders and rolled her neck. Woody counted down with his fingers. When his last finger curled down, the red light came on and Kate began.

"The situation in Moscow hangs in the balance as darkness descends on the capital. Lines of troops loyal to the Russian president ring the Interior Ministry behind me, having retreated from one pitched battle with demonstrators after another in bloody street fighting during the afternoon. The whereabouts of the interior minister and his lieutenants is as yet unknown, although sources at the Duma—the lower house of the Russian parliament—indicate that he has fled all the way to the Ural Mountains."

"Okay," Woody said. He checked some readings. "Batteries are almost gone."

"And those are your last ones?"

"Yep." He looked up. "Okay, now's where we'll splice in the scenes of the shit we got caught in on the bridge and over by the embassy. Voice-over, voice-over, voice-over. Now." He lowered his eye to the camera, and he again repeated the countdown. Woody was milking every ounce of juice out of his precious batteries he could. Normally he'd just start taping and Kate would begin when she was ready. Kate tried to nail the next part of the report on her first try.

"In scenes reminiscent of 1917, angry mobs have taken to the streets while most ordinary Russians cower behind locked doors. We spoke of the fighting in Moscow with one family earlier today."

Woody rolled his index finger in the air. They would splice the interview in right there.

"Concerns such as those expressed by the Semyonovs," Kate continued without missing a beat, "must be on the minds of most Russians as night falls on a city of eleven million lit only by the fires of overturned vehicles and by the first torches, which I can see now, carried by the crowd on the street below." She squinted at the sight of the approaching group, who held torches high above their heads. They wore black, from head to toe.

"Woody," Kate said, pointing at the large group of black-clad men who pushed their way down the crowded street toward the Interior Ministry. Woody swung the camera toward the approaching phalanx and rolled his finger to keep her talking.

"There appears to be a group of Anarchist 'Black Shirts' approaching. That is how they have come to be known because of their distinctive black shirts and leather jackets. Each time a group of men such as this has arrived, the scene has erupted in violence. Each time the Black Shirts have attacked the police, the police have retreated. This time, however, there is no retreat for the beleaguered Russian security troops. This time their backs are literally to the wall of their headquarters building."

Kate backhanded Woody and he glanced at her without moving his head away from the camera. She pointed for him to get a shot at the lines of police toward which the Black Shirts pressed. He complied, but then returned to the shot now just below their balcony. In the long shadows cast by the buildings, the flickering torchlight would be dramatic. Kate let Woody get the shot he wanted. He had roamed the earth for twenty years to cover wars and famines and civil unrest, and she trusted that he knew what he was doing.

A dark orange light on the top of the camera began to blink. "The Black Shirts are headed straight for the ministry building now, and the crowd has begun to stir. Many of the demonstrators who have been here for some time are starting to take cover, and the general disturbance seems to have passed right into the lines of the police, who are looking around and craning their necks to see into the crowd they face. I don't think they've spotted the Black Shirts yet, but it's just a matter of seconds before . . ."

There was a beep and then a clicking sound as the tape mechanism shut down.

"Shit!" Woody said. He lowered the camera and slapped the Jamaican reefer decal on its side with his hand. "I can't fuckin' believe this, man!" Kate's eyes were trained on the now scurrying demonstrators, who had opened up a path for the Black Shirts. The *thonk* of tear-gas canisters lobbed into the Black Shirts presaged the choking gas to come.

Ripping bursts of machine-gun fire broke open the night. Woody and Kate lowered themselves onto the floor of the balcony. Popping sounds filled the air. Kate watched the growing confusion as police began to fall. Most of the rest threw their shields and truncheons down and ran. The flashing muzzles came not from the police, but from the Black Shirts who charged their lines.

Shots rang out from the upper windows of the ministry building. But the disciplined Black Shirts surged through the front entrance. Gunfire rose from floor to floor as Kate and Woody watched. By the time an explosion blew out the top floor windows, the glass landed in a tinkling rain on empty streets.

It was then that Kate realized what had just happened. There were no police, no security troops, no sign of the army. There was no more government to speak of left in Moscow. There was an end to all social order. There was anarchy.

3

THE WHITE HOUSE SITUATION ROOM
August 19, 0100 GMT (2000 Local)

President Marshall watched the television screens in the underground Situation Room. Around him sat his National Security Council—the vice-president, the secretaries of defense and state, the chairman of the Joint Chiefs of Staff General Dekker, and the directors of the CIA and National Security Agency.

"Is the mysterious Valentin Kartsev the man behind the Anarchist violence that's sweeping the world?" reported NBC correspondent Kate Dunn. "As Russia slides toward its third day of chaos, signs increasingly point to the growing power of one man—Valentin Kartsev, former professor of political science, former KGB general, Russian millionaire, mafioso kingpin, and chief Anarchist ideologean."

President Marshall and his senior national security advisors sat transfixed by the images. Solid masses of black-shirted men standing shoulder to shoulder in closed ranks and rushing toward their objective. Crowds of people ran in great swirls of motion this way and that as swaths of bodies fell before orange bursts of flame from automatic weapons. The smoke from explosions soon obscured the picture, and after the report concluded the screen cut to color test bars.

"That was the unedited, raw feed off the satellite from Moscow," the director of the NSA said. "We've got some other feeds from around Russia if you'd like, Mr. President, but this one is the first that purports to have some sort of inside information from the Anarchist movement."

"Where did that reporter get her info on this guy Kartsev?" Marshall asked.

"We talked to her producers in New York. They said she got an anonymous call on her cell phone—her second tip in as many days."

"So," Marshall said, "is this man Kartsev behind it all?"

The director of the CIA leaned forward. His shoulders hunched as he rested his elbows heavily on the conference table. "Things are such a mess over there right now, Mr. President, it's hard to say. The *real* player is the army, which our sources say could enter the fray full force anytime now. The problem, however, is that the same fissures that run through society run through the military as well. That raises some obvious risks."

"What would happen if the army split?" Marshall asked. "What are we looking at?"

Heads turned from one to another. There was a reluctance to take a position. Finally, Secretary of State Jensen ventured a response. "I think the consensus, Tom, is that things will get worse before they get better."

Marshall exploded. "Jesus Christ, I *know* they'll get worse if there's a goddamned civil *war* in *Russia*!"

"What I mean," Jensen said, "is that . . . that the situation won't improve much before *November*. There's real pressure building in the EC for some sort of action. The Europeans are scrambling for alternate sources of energy. With Siberian gas off the market, oil's up to fifty-five dollars a barrel."

"What the hell kind of 'action' are they talking about?" Marshall asked.

Jensen shrugged. "Intervention," he said simply.

The room stirred all at once. "Inter-*vention*?" Marshall exclaimed. "In a Russian civil *war*?"

Jensen held his hands up as if to fend off the president's verbal blows. "I'm totally opposed to it, Tom. *Totally* opposed. But there has been some talk about the feasibility of a peacekeeping mission *if* the UN can garner the support of the local Russian Army commanders in Siberia where the gas fields are. The violence out there has been limited, mainly directed against those pipelines. There's been very little civil or military disorder in the east."

"They're too worried about China," the secretary of defense suggested.

Marshall leaned back and rubbed his pounding temples. *"Who lost Russia?"* he could already hear the Republicans asking. "What do we know about this Kartsev?"

The CIA director pulled open a file.

"Kartsev, Valentin Konstantinovich. Born 1949 in Novgorod. Educated at the pedagogical institute in Moscow. Believed to be KGB informant on faculty of Moscow State University Marxism/Leninism department until assuming rank of lieutenant colonel in the KGB at their Dzerzhinsky Square headquarters in 1984."

"Lieutenant colonel at age, what, thirty-five?" the director of the FBI asked. "That's a pretty fast track, especially for someone who'd just been informing on a bunch of professors."

"He was one of Andropov's protégés," the CIA director replied. "Andropov was an intellectual. Widely read. Bookish sort. Before he died, he collected a coterie of similarly cerebral types with whom he'd spend hours spinning ideas. Kartsev, in his later years at the university, was among that inner circle."

"What about since 1984?" Marshall asked.

The CIA director again read from his file. "Liaison to the GRU—military intelligence. During the worst of the Afghanistan war—when intelligence about Russian atrocities, booby-trapped toys, torture, assassination, and the like were being picked up by the press—we got a 'walk-in.' A Russian Army officer assigned to their embassy in Karachi approached our station chief and fed us reports of 'excessive measures' by a renegade KGB unit that was responsible for all those operations. It was pretty clear to us at the time that he was simply feeding us straight from the Russian Army's high command, and so we took it all with a grain of salt.''

''What do you mean?''

The director shrugged. ''We figured it was just the army trying to keep its skirts clean by blaming the KGB. But some of the intelligence did check out. Kartsev's liaison unit—and their Afghan proxies—*were* operational in Afghanistan.''

''What happened to the officer who fed us the information?'' Marshall asked. ''Maybe we can talk to him.''

''He was recalled to Moscow for a briefing and was shot in a KGB prison three months later.''

Marshall arched his eyebrows. ''Nice people. What else does your file say about Kartsev?''

''He fled to Kirgizia when Gorbachev returned after the failed August coup of 1991. Severed his relations with the KGB . . . we think. He disappeared for a few years until his name started showing up on DEA and ATF intelligence reports for trafficking in drugs and weapons out of the former Soviet Union. The only other cross-references to Kartsev we've got in our database come from a variety of Western businessmen who have been offered partnerships—some of them lucrative—in deals with Kartsev or his affiliates. A couple did their deals, made a fair amount of money, and then were cut out by Kartsev. They just let it drop. One—a Dutch gentleman in the business of giving seminars on Western management techniques—apparently spurned Kartsev and tried to go it alone in Moscow. He was found dead in his Moscow apartment with thirteen bullet wounds to the back of the head. Small-caliber weapon. Neighbors heard nothing. No suspects.''

''Okay,'' Marshall said, glancing at his watch. He had a

campaign finance meeting. "So Kartsev's a bad guy. He's behind the Anarchists. The Anarchists are fanatical terrorists who're spreading violence around the world. The Europeans are inclined to go in there and root 'em out," Marshall rose. "I say more power to them. Good luck, and Godspeed."

"The Chinese aren't going to like it," Jensen said. "A UN force that doesn't include Asian troops being deployed on their border?"

"We're sitting this one out," Marshall said, ending the meeting. "Let the Europeans worry about the Chinese. I can't see how it concerns us."

SEOUL, SOUTH KOREA
August 19, 0444 GMT (1444 Local)

The mid-afternoon sun streamed through the windows. The South Korean president raised the large spoon to his lips. The soup was hot, and he blew on it as his mouth salivated at the faint aroma of garlic. He had stolen away to his private dining room from all-day meetings on the Chinese mobilization, and his stomach was growling noisily.

He touched the soup gently to his lips, testing its temperature. A 12.7-millimeter projectile traveling at the speed of sound punched cleanly through the window. Before the force it imparted could rip the entire pane of glass from its frame, the bullet cleaved the president's head off above the line of his ears. It was thirty minutes before the president's aides discovered the effects of the single shot.

WHITE HOUSE, WASHINGTON, D.C.
August 20, 1000 GMT (0500 Local)

"Mr. President? Mr. President?"

Thomas Marshall opened his eyes. He lay in bed in his darkened bedroom. "Hmm. What?"

"I'm very sorry, sir. But you have a phone call. It's Governor Bristol. He says it's urgent."

"Bristol?" Marshall croaked. He cleared his throat. "Phil Bristol?" The aide nodded. "What the hell would he . . . ?" Marshall rose, still pondering his unfinished question as he padded into the adjoining sitting room. *What would he want to talk to me about?*

A different aide handed Marshall the phone. He cleared his throat again. "Hello, Phil! What has you up so early?"

"Not early, Tom. It's late out here on the West Coast. I apologize for having to disturb you like this."

"If you're calling to throw in the towel and announce you're going to support the Democratic ticket during these troubled times, there's no need to apologize." Marshall was awake now. He winked at his grinning aides as Bristol politely chuckled.

"I'm afraid, Tom, this doesn't have to do with the campaign. I've got some official business to discuss with you. I've just called up a goodly portion of the California Army National Guard to deal with a situation we've got down in L.A. I wanted to tell you personally what I was doing with them."

Marshall's antennae were up. "What 'situation' is this you're talking about?"

"We've got a full-blown riot in progress. It looks like the Rodney King thing all over again."

"Good God, Phil. What the hell happened?"

Bristol told the president about the assassination of a civil rights leader in Los Angeles.

"The pot's been simmering down there ever since the mayor cracked down on crime," Bristol said. The president's political antennae tingled and twitched. It was Marshall who'd been hammering the "get tough on crime" theme ever since the first night of the terrorist attacks. "Apparently," his Republican challenger continued, "the LAPD community relations people had been warning the mayor about it. It seems the feeling on the streets was that your antiterrorism campaign had succeeded mainly in netting a large number of arrests from minority communities."

Marshall's jaw was set firmly now. Bristol thought he

already had his points up on the scoreboard. He was wrong. "So how bad is it?" Marshall asked.

"The looting and arson is spreading all through South Central. The fire department reports twenty-six structures ablaze—most they can't get to because of sniping. I'm worried particularly about the Koreans. Since the last riots there's been a mini–arms race among the store owners. The police have already stopped carloads of grocers and their families heading in to protect their property, all of 'em armed to the teeth. I'm determined not to let this get out of hand, so on my authority as governor of California I'm calling up the Guard to put a stop to it."

Marshall could already see the Republican media spin in his mind's eye. Bristol's private army crushing the chaos—the "anarchists"—on the streets of L.A. Lots of clean-cut citizen-soldiers responding to Bristol's strong, decisive leadership.

"Phil," Marshall said, "I agree with you one hundred percent. What's more, if things are *that* bad, I'm going to look into sending regular army troops in there to help you out."

"I appreciate that, Tom, but I don't think that'll be—"

"Nonsense! I'm not going to leave you out there all by yourself to deal with the situation. This damn business with the terrorists isn't a local problem, it's a national one. You're going to get every bit of help you need and more—no ifs, ands, or buts. I'll have my people get on this right now."

"Listen, Tom. I don't want to crowd your plate at a time like this. You've got enough to worry about with the international crisis. Why don't we just wait and see where we are this time tomorrow and—"

"I won't *hear* of that kind of talk, Phil. Unless you seceded while I was catching up on my beauty rest," Marshall said jovially, "California still *is* a part of the United States, and I'm still the president. I'll call after we've had time to check what assets we have available and do our own assessment of the situation. We'll talk soon. Good-bye, Phil."

There was a momentary pause. "Good-bye, Tom." Marshall hung up.

An aide took the phone, and Marshall grabbed the man's arm. "Get me the secretary of defense." He waited, chewing on the inside of his cheek. The aide handed the phone back to him. "Did you hear what Bristol is doing?"

"Yes, sir," the secretary of defense replied. "I just got word."

"I want you to federalize the California Army National Guard. Call them up."

There was a long silence as the political gears spun in the man's head. "Just the California Guard, sir? I mean . . . that would be a little . . ." He let the sentence trail off.

Marshall understood. A little too obvious. "I want a nationwide call-up to deal with domestic unrest."

"How large of a call-up do you want?"

"How the hell should *I* know? You tell me. But I want it big enough to put men on the streets nationwide," Marshall said as the idea grew on him.

"Well, say . . . about six brigades?"

"Sounds fine. And I want a full National Security Council meeting in three hours." Marshall hung up—pleased at having seized the opportunity presented him.

BETHESDA, MARYLAND
August 21, 1300 GMT (0800 Local)

Daryl Shavers entered the Davises' bedroom. Gordon nodded at his chief of staff, who joined him at the television. Fires still raged in the early-morning sky over Los Angeles. "Did you hear that Marshall federalized the California Guard?" Gordon asked. Governor Bristol's lawyers say Marshall can't even *use* the troops now. Once they're part of the U.S. Army, the Posse Comitatus Act prevents them from helping out the local police! It was a *blatantly* political act! We're just waiting on Fein so we can get started working up the right tone."

"Fein's already here," Daryl said. "His car's out front."

Gordon headed downstairs. Elaine and Daryl followed. Fein was in the dining room. The two girls were seated at the table. Laid out on a linen tablecloth was the Davises' silver service and their finest china and crystal. A woman Gordon had never seen before—wearing pearls at eight o'clock in the morning—hovered over Celeste, straightening the already orderly placement of the several forks on her right.

"Now," the woman said with a proper British accent, "the finger bowl arrives with dessert, but you don't use it until after you've finished. You should gingerly grasp the bowl with both hands and place it beside the upper left edge of the dish. Then take the doily from the plate and fold it carefully."

"*Excuse* me," Elaine said as she stormed past Gordon into the dining room.

"Good morning, Elaine," Fein said, smiling. "Gordon! Trust you slept well."

"Just *what* is going on here?" Elaine burst out.

"Mr. Fein's teaching us what to do at a state dinner," Celeste said, and smiled. When she realized Elaine was furious, she muttered "Mo-*ther*," in a lilting voice.

The dam of Elaine's outrage held. Fein jumped in. "Elaine, this is Mrs. Agnes Fillmore, formerly of the White House protocol office."

"How do you do, Mrs. Davis?" the woman said, smiling. "It's a pleasure to meet you. And I really *must* commend you. Your girls have truly impeccable manners."

Finally convinced that Elaine wouldn't break the peace, Gordon asked Fein to step out. They left Elaine and Mrs. Fillmore with the girls and closed the sliding pocket door into the dining room. "What are we going to do about the riots?" Gordon said. "Marshall's get-tough policies went too far. He stepped on his dick, and we should be all over him! What's Governor Bristol's position?"

Fein's expression didn't change as he answered. "This is a difficult time for the nation. Terrorists attacking government officials, new dangers abroad, and now lawlessness on the streets of our cities. It's as if anarchy is eating away at the fabric of society. At times like these, we must show *strength*''—he lightly tapped his clenched fist into an open palm—''a *resolve* in the face of our enemies, foreign *and* domestic.''

It was a sound bite. Gordon got the distinct impression that he was to memorize it verbatim. The dining-room door opened, and Elaine emerged as Mrs. Fillmore was saying, ''No, you push with your knife. You pile the food onto the fork. Never *spear* the meat like you're harpooning a whale.''

Gordon eyed his wife cautiously as she closed the door behind her. ''What's the plan?'' she asked. It was a good sign, Gordon thought. She was getting over the trauma of the attack.

''I've taken the liberty,'' Fein replied, ''of jotting down a few notes.'' He handed Elaine a single, typewritten sheet.

Elaine read it once in silence, then out loud in a wooden tone without looking up. '' 'One. Control emotion. No tears or anger unless we talk first. Two. Eye makeup is most important. Go light on the lipstick. But don't skimp on hairdressers or facials—twice per week. Three. Muted shades of clothing are better than sharp colors. Lots of soft blouses with long sleeves. Elegant scarves are good accessories. Four. In public, cross your ankles not your knees. No scratching, twitching, or squirming. Better to' ''—she swallowed and moistened her lips—'' ' . . . to listen than to speak. Always look interested in what the other person is telling you. Be prepared for stupid questions. Five. Keep smiling and smiling and smiling, and if all else fails' '' — she looked up—'' 'smile.' ''

TAMAN DIVISION BARRACKS, MOSCOW
August 22, 2000 GMT (2200 Local)

Kate Dunn lay in a ditch in the fetal position next to Woody. Her hands were clamped over her ringing ears as the fighting raged. She'd never been so terrified in her life.

Another anonymous tip had led them to the tense army base. Another scoop, Kate had thought as she and Woody had set up on the road just overhead. Woody had warned her that they were on the main road from the front gate. If the caller was right and there was going to be fighting . . . But Kate was energized by the prospect of the airtime they would get. She had shamed him into cooperating with joking comments about his manhood.

The night air around them was filled with all manner of speeding projectiles. They whipped close by their unprotected bodies with vicious cutting sounds or streaked through the dark sky overhead in burning trails. Cement chips flew off the concrete abutment against which they cowered. Kate realized in horror that the hulking armored vehicles that rumbled along the road above them were drawing and returning furious fire. Her world exploded as flame shot over her from the long, thick barrel of a tank. The shell burst against the wall of the barracks five hundred meters away. A brilliant flare of light erupted from the upper floor of the same building. From it emerged the wiggling and fiery tail of a rocket. The missile quickly locked onto its course—heading straight toward her. She jammed her eyes shut and clenched every muscle in her body, but nothing happened. When she opened her eyes, two shiny wires that had trailed the missile and carried the operator's guidance signals draped limply over the earthen ditch. The missile had missed the tank.

The dark forms of men dove into the ditch with loud grunts. Soon the slit was filled with over a dozen Russian soldiers. After shouted orders, they rose to charge barracks full of other Russian soldiers. They didn't get far before a brilliant explosion hurled several bodies into the air. Kate had felt the earth quake beneath her. She watched in horror as geysers of pyrotechnics gushed from vehicles and buildings. The men and the vehicles on both sides looked identical. The Russian Army was fighting itself.

The attack faltered. Men sprinted back across the tabletop flat lawn toward them in ones and twos. Their hands pumped furiously as they fled in panic. Most had discarded their weapons.

"How do you feel fighting other soldiers in your own army?" Kate shouted over the noise of battle.

The one Russian soldier who could speak broken English opened his mouth to reply. The low-light lens on Woody's camera recorded the faint green images of the soldier and of Kate's microphone to the soldier's mouth.

"Wery bad! When I shootit my gun, I . . . !" He raised his Kalashnikov into the air.

"You try to miss on purpose?" Kate asked.

"Yeah, yeah! I shootit the air!"

"Ask him which side he's on," Woody whispered, his eye pressed to the camera.

Kate was annoyed at him for feeding her a question, but asked it anyway. The soldier was confused. Kate rephrased the question. "Why are you fighting?" she tried.

"Ah!" the soldier said, nodding. "Because zey tell us to."

WHITE HOUSE SITUATION ROOM
August 24, 2200 GMT (1700 Local)

"Do you think it's a trick?" President Marshall asked as he leaned toward the speakerphone on the conference table.

After the momentary delay, the U.S. ambassador replied over the secure link from Moscow. "We can never know with any certainty, Mr. President. On its face, the general's offer appears entirely responsible. The Russians obviously have no interest in seeing the disorder spread to control of their nuclear arsenal. International supervision over the weapons is an eminently reasonable suggestion."

"May I get something straight, here?" General Dekker interrupted. All eyes turned to him. "Are we talking about deploying *U.S.* troops? To *Russia*?"

The ambassador answered. "To the eastern provinces *only*. To Siberia. The general assured me that the Defense

Ministry has absolute control over the nuclear forces in European Russia.''

Dekker sat with his forearms resting heavily on the polished wood table. ''And just what are they supposed to do if the fighting spreads out that way?''

''Their mission would be limited,'' the White House chief of staff chimed in. Marshall noted the heads of the Joint Chiefs turn to look at the civilian. The political animal who was the object of their loathing, however, was focused on his boss. ''This is a low-risk, high-return plan.''

''What returns are those, might I ask?'' came from Dekker.

The two men then locked eyes. ''Preservation of our national security, of course.'' Everyone there knew, however, that there were also political returns. That Marshall had been beaten up by Bristol for failing to counter Russian terrorism.

The president drew a deep breath. ''Would NATO go in there with us?'' he asked, turning to the secretary of defense.

''Great Britain, Germany, and France are all clearly behind the plan, which should bring in Belgium, the Netherlands, and Denmark. Bonn is only a day or two away from agreeing with Paris on a deployment into Ukraine, which they see as a strategic buffer between Russia and the West. They would view a Siberian deployment as a logical extension of their policy to the east. *And* it would allow them to secure Siberian gas supplies all the way back to the wellhead.''

''It's a mistake,'' Marshall heard, the words spoken softly. He turned to see Secretary of State Jensen sitting slumped in his chair with his arms folded over his chest.

''You care to elaborate?'' Marshall asked testily.

Without looking up, Jensen said, ''We're being sucked into a power vacuum. The collapse of the Soviet Union left an enormous geostrategic void over the entire Eurasian landmass. It's been pulling us eastward ever since the Bosnian deployment and the expansion of NATO into Poland, the Czech Republic, and Hungary. Now it's drawing NATO troops into the Ukraine and Siberia.''

Marshall huffed, then rubbed his eyes. "That's a fine subject for a *Foreign Affairs Quarterly* article." He slammed his hand down, startling several at the table. "But *god*dammit, this is the real world, and we've got real issues to deal with!" He turned to Dekker. "I'd like you to draw up some contingency plans. Figure out how many men it would take to secure those missile sites and nuclear weapons depots. Keep it simple. Use a minimalist approach. As long as we have the Russians' full cooperation, I wouldn't think we'd be talking about too large an operation. What about the Japanese?''

The secretary of defense nodded at Jensen, who remained silent. "We've worked out some arrangements—roughly the same payment terms as the Gulf War.''

"I'm not talking about *payment*," Marshall said. "I want them in there *with* us.''

Jensen looked up. The secretary of defense licked his lips. "On the ground?" he asked, clearly uncomfortable with the suggestion. "That might be highly unpopular in Japan.''

"We could offer them the Kuriles back," Marshall said. No one else spoke. "That should win over the nationalist vote.''

Marshall liked the idea, but everyone else squirmed.

"They'd have to amend their constitution to allow foreign deployment," the secretary of defense remarked.

"It's about damn time they *do*!" Marshall snapped, pushing his chair back from the table.

General Dekker spoke up even though it was clear Marshall wanted to leave. "Sir, if I might suggest, Japan is most useful for support. The POL—petroleum, oil, lubricant—either comes from Japan, or from a long way away. And if the army can't stage massively in Japan, its alternatives are Forts Richardson and Lewis in Alaska and Washington. That's a *helluva* long way away for a divisional supply train, sir. And we'd need more than logistical support too, sir. If it should ever come to it, we'd need them for medical support and for strategic air projection.''

"Well," Marshall said, "it doesn't seem that we're in disagreement, then. They can pay their share by meeting the petroleum needs of the deployment and by allowing full use of all bases and airfields.''

"What about the Chinese?" Jensen asked in a faraway tone.

"*Fuck* the Chinese!" Marshall said as he headed out the door.

McLEAN, VIRGINIA
August 25, 1200 GMT (0700 Local)

Nate and Lydia Clark sat cross-legged on the kitchen floor in their jeans. Nate held the front page of *The Washington Post* and stared at a photograph of charred bodies lying beside an infantry fighting vehicle on the streets of St. Petersburg. He crumpled it loudly and stuffed it into a water glass, which he laid in the cardboard box with all the other plates and glasses. One room per day, that was the way they had always done it. Panama, Frankfurt, Kansas, Brussels, Washington—wherever Nate's career had taken them.

"Did Jeff tell his girlfriend we're moving yet?" Nate asked.

Lydia rolled her eyes. "Not yet. He's in *lo-o-ove*! He just can't bring himself to tell her."

"Is he taking it hard . . . the move, I mean?"

Lydia looked at him with a knitted brow. "Nate, he's sixteen years old and has a girlfriend. He has to pull up stakes again and move thousands of miles away. Do you think he cares one *whit* that you didn't get the Korean command?"

"I didn't *mean* that."

"*Yes,* you did."

"No I *didn't*!" Nate lied. He avoided her face so as not to see the annoying grin that he knew she had fixed there. "Well," he said, "he'll be fine in two weeks. I mean, *Ha-*

waii, for Christ's sake! Once he gets a load of the girls on those beaches we're gonna have to chain him to the bumper of the car.''

Lydia leaned over the box and kissed him. She looped her hands around his neck and pressed her forehead to his. It was always like this. The disruptions to their domestic routine that each new assignment had brought were immense, but always they'd greeted the change with a sense of excitement. But before, Nate thought, they had always been on the way up. He gently pried her hands loose and resumed his packing.

Lydia left him to his thoughts for a while. He spent the time perfecting the arguments he'd failed to make in his meeting with Dekker. Finally, she casually said, "What do you think about the China thing?"

"What China thing?" he mumbled.

"You know. The possibility of going to war with China?"

Nate sat back on his heels. "What the hell are you talking about? Where'd that come from?"

"From *you,* dear, of course!" She was smiling, toying with him. "Darling," Lydia said in a tone reserved for the dim-witted, "you've been talking about China this and China that for a *week* now. You've had the 'C' volume from the encyclopedia on our nightstand since the day you came home from your big meeting. The television is droning on in the background and all of a sudden your newspaper flies out of your face so you can watch a story about riots in Beijing. Do you think I'm an *idiot*? Besides," she said, leaning over to cup his cheek with her cool, soft hand, "why else would the army take their very best general and put him in command of the whole Pacific?"

"I'm not 'in command of' the Pacific. I report to PA-COM—a *navy* billet for God's sake! I'll be reporting to an *admiral.*"

She sighed noisily. "Good thing you're not into all this political infighting crap. Just wanna do your duty for God and your country."

"Lydia, I spent the last year of my life brown-nosing my way through Washington cocktail parties because that was the only way I'd ever get another command. I've crawled up into and kissed the lower intestines of a dozen joint staff officers . . . !''

"Don't be crude," she said in a purely perfunctory manner. "Besides, you *got* a command! And a deployment to Siberia! As perverse as it may be, I'd think you'd be *excited* about that.''

He snorted. "You know what the manuals call deployments like these? 'Operations other than war,' " he said in disgust.

"You'd prefer *war*?" she asked.

"*No*. It's just . . . I didn't put this uniform on to command blue helmets. I'm trained for war, Lydia, not humanitarian relief missions, or peacekeeping, or counterterrorism.''

Her head hung, and her hair covered her face. "Be careful what you wish for," she mumbled, then looked up. "Nate, you may know facts and statistics about China from those files you keep locked in the safe upstairs, but *I* know what the Chinese think about their place in the world.'' From her tone, this wasn't Lydia-the-personal-therapist, but the Lydia whom he'd met while getting his master's in history at Berkeley—a degree being one of the better career tickets to get punched when there wasn't a war on.

"You remember, of course, that I wrote a Command and General Staff School *paper* on the rise of nationalism in—''

"But you're Eurocentric to the bone, Nate. You see China as an overpopulated country that a long time ago was a great power. Then the West hit its stride and developed steam engines and the riding lawn mower, and *boom* . . . China's a third-world country. Europeans think in nice straight lines. Linear progression. You start at A, then with hard work you advance and you get to B and then to C. But the Eastern way of thinking—the Chinese way—is the yin and the yang.''

"I *know* all that," Nate said.

"No, you don't! The Chinese view history as cyclical. It swings to one side, but always comes back 'round to the other. The yin and the yang. The Chinese have been down for five hundred years, but now they believe that they're going to be back on *top* for a few hundred years. When China was weak, the Russians occupied Asia to the north and called it 'Siberia.' But Russian power is on the wane, and China's is on the rise. China's GNP is already twice Russia's, and it's larger relative to the United States' than the Soviet Union's was during the Cold War. They're the third largest country in the world and have the largest population—one-point-two billion people. Can you imagine their power if they attain the per capita GNP of the Japanese, or even the Koreans or Taiwanese? Their economy has been the fastest growing on earth for the last quarter century, and what have they been doing with that economic might?"

Nate's gaze was unfocused. "Buying and making weapons."

"And so now they're mobilizing. Millions and millions of men—their biggest asset. How many physically fit men do they have of military age? Surely your files contain that fact."

They did. One hundred and eighty-nine million men, to be exact, with twelve million more eighteen-year-olds available for the draft each year. But Nate said, "They're just getting the glut of troublemaking teenagers off the streets. What was it Lin Hoa said in that speech he gave in Beijing? That Chinese youth are 'besotted by the drunkenness of prosperity.' The old Communist octogenarians are trying to dry out a population they think is too spoiled by Coca-Cola and blue jeans. That call-up is their way of giving this generation a little discipline."

Lydia was nodding through all of what Nate said. This time it was her eyes drifting off into space. She suddenly grabbed Nate's hands. "You're *right,* Nate. This is just like the Cultural Revolution in the sixties. A blooding of the young. A revival of the spirit of hard combat. The unity forged by fighting against the odds. They want *discipline*. Discipline to begin the new century. To assert themselves. To make the twenty-*first* century the Chinese century like the twentieth was the American. Don't you see? They want discipline, Nate—the discipline of war!''

Fort Shafer, Oahu, Hawaii
August 27, 0700 GMT (1700 Local)

Nate parked where he found LT. GEN. CLARK, CINCUSARPAC stenciled on the curb. The front steps of his new headquarters were bustling with soldiers in camouflage. The U.S. Army of the Pacific had quickly responded to his first official order—full-battle-dress uniforms would be worn till further notice. He got out and was saluted repeatedly by the crowd bottlenecked at the door. An armed detail was checking IDs, but the sea parted and Nate walked through. An MP captain led him to his office.

It was twenty by thirty feet. Carpeted wall-to-wall with a map of the Pacific theater. Lined in cherry bookshelves, glass display cases, and flag stands. His personal effects were neatly arranged. Pictures of his family. Books and bookends. Framed field maps with unit positions from Vietnam. Nate would use the office for barely more than a week. Another one was being prepared for him in Siberia.

A deeply tanned officer appeared at the door and stiffened. ''Major Reed, sir,'' he reported.

''Yes, of course,'' Nate said. ''I remember you from SHAFE.'' His return salute went straight to a handshake. ''You were on operations staff, right?''

The major laughed. ''If you can say a captain at Supreme Headquarters Europe was on operations staff, then yes, sir. But I *am* on operations staff now. I was *also* tasked to deliver your orientation briefing this morning. *And*,'' he continued, strangely self-conscious and not looking Nate in the eye, ''the thought was I'd deploy with you to Siberia. I've been in the Pacific for eight years—counting Korea. I know my way around the other services.''

Reed's distinct tan line betrayed that his hair had been longer before its recent trim. "I guess you and your counterparts in the other services play tennis and golf—or is it maybe surf, since this is Hawaii?"

Reed shrugged. "A good number of us run before second mess. Some classmates of mine."

Nate glanced down to see Reed's West Point ring and nodded. "As for you deploying with my staff, I could use someone who's familiar with the command and the theater."

"I consider it a privilege, General Clark," Reed replied. "A real honor! You know, sir, my father was a classmate of *yours*. I'm Chuck Reed . . . Junior."

Nate tried not to register the shock. After a moment he held out his hand, and Reed shook it again. Nate was surprised to find how dry his mouth was. "The last time I saw you," he said, "your picture, I mean, you were . . ." He held up his hands in the approximate size of a baby. They laughed.

Nate recalled the crumpled photo of the pretty wife and newborn child with clarity. Cadet Chuck Reed, Sr., had gotten married, as allowed, in their last week at the Point. It had been a big affair at the chapel with crossed sabers and hurled rice. He and Nate had left for Vietnam with Chuck's wife nine months pregnant. It was late in the war, and they could have gotten out of it, but that wasn't what new second lieutenants did. The picture of the baby had arrived in Vietnam with the first mail. The homesick twenty-two-year-old Reed carried it with him everywhere. When he got plowed on R&R, it was shoved in faces. Chuck and Nate had been fellow platoon leaders in the same infantry company. It was the first and only tour for both of them. Nate would recover from his wounds. Chuck would die from his.

"We got your letter," Chuck Reed's son said. "It was all we knew about how it happened. My mother still has it." Nate nodded, hanging his head. He'd always meant to visit. "We also got some letters from my father. He wrote us about the Vinh Phuoc River. That was your first action, right?'' Nate nodded. ''He said you saved his ass.''

Nate was dazed by the flood of memories. He spoke slowly. ''The NVA blew the bridge, so we had to ford the river. Your dad's platoon was all alone on the far side covering the crossing when they hit us.''

''And you crossed back over the river and pulled his nuts out of the fire,'' Reed filled in.

It had been a bad situation for two green platoon leaders. Nate looked up at the framed maps on the wall. The greens and browns of jungles. Swirling contour lines of broken terrain. Grids for artillery. His map of the Vinh Phuoc didn't survive its several immersions in the brisk, cold stream. ''We both lost men that day.'' Nate looked up at Reed. His father had died two months later trying to return the favor.

Reed escorted Nate to the briefing room. Two dozen colonels, one-stars and two-stars, stood in unison. Nate knew many of them. He rounded the long table shaking hands. ''Welcome to USARPAC,'' and ''It's a pleasure, sir,'' were the typical greetings. They were introduced by name, rank, and job. His heads of personnel, intelligence, and logistics—the J-1, J-2, and J-4—were all brigadier generals, as were the corps and divisional deputy commanders. The two-stars—major generals one rank beneath Nate's—were the J-3 in charge of USARPAC operations and the commander of the 25th Light Infantry Division. The various flag officers' assistants and commanders of miscellaneous subordinate commands were all colonels.

When Nate completed his circuit and sat, everyone settled in immediately. They were all aware of the news, he felt certain. ''A little over two hours ago,'' Nate began, ''the secretary of defense and the German defense minister were both killed in a terrorist bombing in California. All signs point to Russian Anarchists. We are headed into the base of operations of the Russian Anarchists—Siberia. They train there. They stage for their operations there. They return there—if they survive their missions. While Security Council Resolution 919 pursuant to which we will deploy establishes as our objectives humanitarian relief, peacekeeping, and securing Russian nuclear weaponry, our rules of engagement allow us to destroy any Anarchist facilities within our areas of operations.'' Nate looked into the faces of each of the men in slow succession. He wanted to make certain they understood the White House's unspoken objective communicated to him directly by General Dekker. ''Very well,'' he said, turning to Reed. ''I understand you've got a briefing for me.''

The young major strode to a large wall map depicting half the earth centered on the Pacific Ocean. When Reed spoke, he spoke to Clark. ''The U.S. Army of the Pacific has an area of responsibility extending from the east coast of Africa to the west coast of the Americas and from pole to pole. That hundred-million-square-mile AOR contains more than fifty nations and more than half the earth's population, which makes USARPAC the largest of the unified commands. Within that AOR also are the seven largest armed forces on earth, with over ten million ground troops under arms.'' Reed's pointer fell squarely on the People's Republic of China. Although his eyes remained on Clark, the pointer's placement clearly wasn't accidental.

''For deployment to Siberia,'' he continued, ''we will receive the 10th Mountain Division from Fort Drum, New York, which will go into Khabarovsk, and the 1st Marine Expeditionary Brigade, which will go into Vladivostok. In addition, we will get seven brigades and regiments of paratroops and infantry—two each from the UK, Germany, and France, and one from Belgium. Our theater reserve will be USARPAC's standing major combat formations: the 25th Light Infantry Division and 29th Infantry Brigade (Separate) here in Hawaii, and 1st Battalion, 501st Infantry (Airborne) at Camp Zama in Japan. The U.S. Army Readiness Group, Pacific, and IX Corps (Reinforcement) has also initiated USARPAC's force reconstitution plan by issuing orders to a variety of national guard and reserve units.

Among those are the 29th's round-out battalion based here
in Hawaii—the 100th Battalion, 442nd Infantry—and the
205th Infantry Brigade (Light) from the Minnesota National
Guard, which has good cold-weather skills. Action orders
to prepare for deployment have also gone out to the 73rd
Infantry Brigade of the Ohio National Guard, the 844th
Engineer Battalion of the Tennessee Army Reserve, and
medical personnel assigned to Tripler Army Medical Center
here in Hawaii, and Bassett Army Hospital in Alaska.''

Clark nodded once. Reed moved on to the next map.
Although as large as the map of the USARPAC area of
responsibility, it depicted only the Russian Pacific coast to
the east and Mongolia to the west. To the north was the
endless wilderness of the Siberian plains. To the south—
the People's Republic of China.

''Under the terms of the Russian Army's invitation, the
United Nations Forces Russia, or 'UNRUSFOR,' '' he said,
pronouncing the acronym as one word, ''may operate no
further west than Chita, Siberia, and no further north than
the Lena River. By similar invitations, German, French, and
British forces will secure the Trans-Siberian Railway to the
west of Chita all the way to the European rail grid. European forces will deploy by rail from Europe and will come
under UNRUSFOR command at Chita. U.S. forces will arrive by air or by sea and will come under UNRUSFOR
command upon debarkation.''

Reed's pointer slapped the map. It landed on the Chinese
border. ''The principal geographic features in UNRUS-
FOR's theater of operations are the Amur River and the
Trans-Siberian Railroad. The Amur—which the Chinese
call the 'River of the Black Dragon'—is the border between
Russia and China and the principal northeastern waterway
on the Asian continent. Sovereignty over the Amur River
basin has historically been contested . . . militarily. It broad-
ens in places into almost an inland sea, and in other areas
it snakes through steep gorges and spreads fingers out
through cuts in very rough terrain. It flows west to east
until it joins the Ussuri River at Khabarovsk and turns north

to empty into the Sea of Okhotsk. UNRUSFOR's headquarters will be at Khabarovsk in facilities provided by the Russian Far East Army Command. The Ussuri River runs south to north and forms the border between Russia's Maritime Provinces and China. At its southern tip is the only year-round port—Vladivostok. Further north, the port of Vanin will be available till it freezes over in November.

"The Trans-Siberian Railway is the other principal geographic feature in theater. The southern branch hugs the border. The northern branch runs from Vanin through the military industrial complex in Komsomolsk-na-Amur to points west. Both are double-tracked for simultaneous east-west traffic. They're Russian wide-gauge, so we'll have to use local rolling stock. But rail is virtually the only means of ground transportation other than military roads connecting the defense infrastructure. The importance of the Trans-Siberian Railway cannot be emphasized strongly enough. There are *no* roads connecting European Russia with the Far East. Whoever controls the Trans-Siberian Railway . . . controls Siberia. It's as simple as that."

Nate was quickly growing to appreciate Reed's abilities as a briefer. He now viewed the slender rail lines running east and west across the large map of Eurasia in the appropriate perspective, and the problems inherent in their defense assumed greater significance. "Tell me a little more about the terrain," he said.

Again, the pointer went to the map. "From Beijing to the Arctic Ocean, and from the Gobi Desert and Mongolian steppes in the west, to the Pacific Ocean, the terrain is 'taiga'—dense, virgin, evergreen forests covered in thick brush with spines as long as fingers. The topography is rugged and broken north of the Amur. To the south of the Amur in Manchuria and in the Russian Maritime Provinces, major mountain chains run north and south. The mountains' foothills are cut through with narrow, overgrown ravines formed by creeks that turn into muddy swamps in the short summers."

"How the hell does the local population get through all that with no roads?" Clark asked.

"There are roads all throughout Manchuria connecting villages to towns to cities—" Reed began.

"No," Clark interrupted. "I mean on the *Russian* side of the border."

"There are only a few small cities in Siberia," Reed replied, "and they're connected by rail. Out in the boonies, there is no local population to speak of, only a few huts used by trappers and hunters during the summer that are connected by narrow footpaths."

Clark studied the scale of the map, which was enormous. "Just what *is* the population in-theater?"

Reed turned back to the map, which was roughly evenly split by the Amur—China to the south, and Russia to the north. "There are less than two million Russians in UNRUSFOR's theater of operations, and that number is dropping rapidly as people are packing up and fleeing to the west."

"Straight into the civil war?" Clark asked. Reed nodded. *Fleeing what?* Clark thought. His eyes drifted south across the Amur River. "What's the population of northern China just across the border?"

Reed didn't take his eyes off his boss. "Approximately one hundred million, General Clark."

4

"And in conclusion," Gordon Davis read from the Tele-PrompTer, chopping his hand in the air for emphasis and counting to five silently, "let me say *this* to any Anarchists who think Americans are easily intimidated." The gathering of union workers listened quietly. "If you continue to sew your seeds of violence about this great and peace-loving nation, you will soon reap a *bitter* harvest from a just but mighty people!"

Yells and thunderous applause reverberated through the mammoth IBEW hall. A high-school marching band struck up a very loud rendition of "The Battle Hymn of the Republic." Gordon smiled, Elaine joined him, and they both smiled. Everyone was on their feet. Even though Gordon knew it was all staged for the cameras, whose lenses roamed the podium and euphoric crowd, he couldn't help but feel enthused.

His press had been good. He was cast as a compromise candidate—a healer of the nation's many divisions. Allegations of tokenism on the Republican ticket were not as forceful or as frequent as he had feared. But part of the reason, he felt certain, was the preoccupation of the media with the continuing wave of assassinations.

As he and Elaine left the stage, a cordon of over two dozen Secret Service agents held back the throng. Gordon raised his hand again to wave, feeling the downward tug of the body armor underneath his dress shirt. Backstage, Fein rushed right up to him, taking his elbow and shouting over the noise, "Perfect timing! You hit it just right!"

Gordon felt pleased to have the man's approval. Over and over Fein had proven his prowess. In the evening after their grueling days of campaigning, Fein, Gordon, and Daryl sat down to watch videotaped coverage of Gordon's various appearances. They were spun by the media just as Fein had predicted they would be. Fein's sound bites were served up as planned, and Gordon's campaign looked just like all the others. That was comforting to Gordon. It was an appearance of professionalism in which he took pride.

They headed out of the union hall through the kitchen. In the short distance from the exit to the limousine, a hundred reporters stood shouting questions from behind barricades. Gordon felt Fein's hand on his elbow guiding him toward the car. "Senator Davis! Is it true you smoked pot in college?" The lenses of half a dozen TV cameras focused on him.

"Yes, I did," Gordon replied calmly.

There was a pause before another reporter asked, "Did you inhale?"

Everyone broke out laughing at once. The hand gripping Gordon's elbow fell away. "Next question," he replied. Again there was laughter.

"Sir, the Republican platform is very conservative, but your voting record seems mixed. Would you call yourself a liberal, or a conservative?"

"Those are just labels," Gordon heard Fein mutter from behind. "I hold conservative views on national defense and the economy," Gordon said, "and liberal views on certain social issues."

"What about the article you published in the *Dartmouth*

Review criticizing affirmative action and minority set-asides? Do you today find them to be 'mere windfalls for the black middle and upper-middle class that tend to diminish the hard, honest work of black students and businessmen by casting doubt on the means by which their success is obtained'?''

Fein couldn't help him there. A voice from deep inside Gordon whispered that he didn't need help. That these were the questions that should be asked and answered. But a larger and growing part of the public animal he was becoming sensed danger. "I do not remember my exact words from that article.''

Fein stepped in and ushered Gordon to the open limousine door. "Are you against any other civil rights laws?'' was shouted from behind. When the door slammed closed, there was utter silence. Gordon, Fein, and Daryl sat in back by themselves as the car pulled past the mob of reporters.

"I thought you were some media guru,'' Daryl said to Fein. "Some *expert* who never lets things get out of control.'' Gordon frowned. He hadn't let Fein do his job. "Did you know, Gordon, that Arthur here used to be a marketing executive at Pepsico? Before he started selling people, he sold soda pop.''

"What kind of damage are we looking at?'' Gordon asked Fein, ignoring Daryl, who fell silent.

Fein shrugged. "You're a complicated package. Usually, with the veep, we just want one dimension. People get overloaded with too many messages, so we want one solid, consistent image coming out of the lower half of the ticket so as not to overburden the electorate with detail.''

"Jesus, Gordon!'' Daryl snapped. "Are you listening to this shit? 'Overburden the electorate with detail.' That means talking about the fucking issues! God forbid you do *that*!''

"You, however,'' Fein continued without so much as a glance at Daryl, "are obviously a ticket balancer. The party has a conservative platform. We've nailed down the right wing of the electoral spectrum. Now we can't let Governor Bristol creep too far toward the left—''

"You mean toward the fucking *center*!" Daryl interjected bitterly.

"—without risking alienation of our core. They won't vote for Marshall, but they could just stay home. And they represent not only votes, but probably a hundred million dollars in campaign contributions between now and the election. But *you* give us a very interesting opportunity. We've got computer models which project that for every right-wing voter we lose with you, we pick up two or three black or liberal voters. Now we can't move you too far to the left for risk of engendering internal dissension in our camp. But we're trying to poach some of the Democrats' traditional base by positioning you to the left of Bristol."

"So you're saying the pot thing could actually *help*?" Gordon asked. Fein nodded sagely, a twinkle in his eye. Daryl sank deeper into the plush leather seat. "But what about the affirmative action article?"

Fein shrugged. "It's impossible to predict. It's an art, not a science. But I do know that if we set you up as the anti—civil rights candidate, we'd be hounded straight to the gates of hell by the very people whose votes we're after. That article was written before your appointment to the Senate. You were a relatively young man. You've learned a lot of things since entering national politics." He shrugged again.

"Oh, for Christ's sake, Gordon!" Daryl burst out. "Just disavow the whole goddamn article." He leaned forward. "Oh! Oh! I've got it! We can tell them you were stoned when you wrote the article." He clapped his hands together and sat back, crossing his arms and smiling in a sarcastic pantomime. "Isn't this great? You're too goddamned *conservative* for the Republican Party! They want you not just to be their token *black,* but their token *liberal* too! A two-fer!"

Gordon stared at Daryl in silence. He wasn't angry, but sad. He realized now what had to be done. What *he* had to do. It would be the hardest thing he'd ever done in his life. Daryl was his best friend. They'd made every step together. Every step but this last one. Out of the corner of his eye, he could sense Fein looking at him. Fein knew what Gordon was thinking, and the party approved.

MOSCOW, RUSSIA
August 30, 1600 GMT (1800 Local)

There was a loud rapping at the door of Kate Dunn's apartment. She and Woody stared at the door, which flew open with a violent crash. A half-dozen men in dark suits rushed in and headed straight for Kate, who started screaming, *"Who are you?"* She tried to dodge outstretched arms but ran headlong into the clutches of a burly man with a meaty and close-shaven head who smelled of days-old sweat. Woody was shouting ineffectual challenges while being held against the wall.

"Let *go!*" Kate screeched as she was hustled to the door. "I'm an *American!* A *korespondentka!*" She jerked her body to try to free herself as she was dragged to the stairs. She kicked at the doors of her neighbors' apartments and screamed all three flights down to the street. A long black limousine waited at the curb. *"No-o-o!"* she shouted, digging her heels into the pavement. She was shoved roughly into the car. The door slammed shut behind her.

A small man sat impassively across from Kate.

The door wouldn't open. The car gunned its engine. Facing backward, Kate saw two cars following. They were jammed with the brutes who'd broken into her apartment. Another man and a driver sat in the front of their car behind a thick glass screen.

The lone man in back with Kate eyed her pleasantly without speaking. Her first impression of him was of a police inspector as he regarded her with a smile. But his pinstriped suit was too expensive, and he wore patent leather shoes at the ends of short legs crossed in feminine fashion. His most distinctive feature was the round, black-rimmed eyeglasses that stood perched on his bald head. On second thought, he looked less like a policeman and more like a professor. But the fear of him she felt tied her stomach in knots. "Who are you?" she croaked.

The man chuckled. There were gaps in his front teeth that gave him a faintly unpolished look. But his manner was altogether unthreatening. "You are a good reporter, Miss Dunn. Don't you know who I am?"

Kate fell into a state of semishock. "Valentin Kartsev?" she quietly asked.

"It's a pleasure to meet you." He spoke English well. His accent was mild and his manner cultured.

Kate dug her elbows into her sides to ward off the chill from the car's blasting air conditioner. "What do you want from me?"

"We each have our interests, and they happen to coincide. You want a story, and I'm going to give one to you. A very, very big story at that. You did well at the Interior Ministry and the Taman barracks. That is why we gave you those tips. That is why you were saved in Red Square. You are an appealing and resourceful messenger. You will get, what do you call it, *air*time. All I am proposing to you, Miss Dunn, is that you do your job. Report the news as you see it. If it is in my interest to assist you, then, well . . . it's a free country," Kartsev said with a wry grin.

The motorcade sped down the empty road heading out of town. Here and there they passed black clumps of charred vehicles that stood as monuments to the savage fighting now radiating outward from Moscow. "Where are you taking me?" she asked.

"On a tour of the most interesting country in the world," Kartsev said, then he turned to the window. The passing landscape reflected off the round lenses of his glasses as if projected onto a screen before his eyes. Kate was concerned mainly with drawing air into her lungs, but she looked out at the dreary Brezhnev-era apartment complexes that rose from the bare soil around Moscow like mushrooms. Dingy bed linens and drying laundry hung from open windows and crumbling balconies. Buildings rose high into the air despite being surrounded in haphazard manner by empty, unused land.

"This is the world's kitchen. Or, perhaps better put, its

laboratory. Unlike the Japanese, we Russians are not content merely to copy the West. We have always seen it as our destiny to improve upon your ways. Perhaps deep down we knew we could never surpass you by mere imitation, or perhaps it is a hopelessly quixotic vision of ourselves as pioneers. Regardless, Russians have always thought we were destined to be the world's incubator for grand strains of revolutionary social thought.''

Kate couldn't bear to look at him. They passed a village of faded little *izbas*—one-room shanties adorned with peeling blue and green paint. The main boulevard consisted of twin dirt ruts. An old babushka drove a horse with a switch alongside the highway. She wore a black dress and a shawl over her head, and her lips sank in around a toothless, wrinkled mouth. The horse pulled a flatbed cart that looked centuries old except for its big rubber tires. Kate said without turning, ''So you're going to enslave these poor people.''

Kartsev laughed in a kindly fashion. ''Miss Dunn, what a very 'archist' remark. Archism esteems control as its highest value. Monarchy, oligarchy, matriarchy, patriarchy— all are supported by their own ideologies, which justify the different systems of power. But *an*archism is not an ideology. It is not a prescribed set of values. We are to the state as atheists are to God. We are simply anti . . . archist.''

''But what is it that your movement stands for? What are you trying to accomplish?''

Another chuckle. ''We stand for nothing. We are not Republicans or Democrats. We have no programs or platforms. But what we are trying to accomplish is the building of an experimental, advanced, nonstatist society. We are really quite principled. We reject all the various claims to governmental legitimacy—mandates from heaven, the will of the majority, racial superiority. All arose from a voluntary communal exchange of autonomy for order. People traded their freedom for punctual railroads. But the government they get in return invariably perpetuates itself through coercion and force against its own people. If you don't believe me, just disobey the government. Quit paying your taxes. Build a walled compound and tell the sheriff to go away. They will not only take your property, they will attack you, lock you up, kill you—even in your country. We *reject,* Miss Dunn, the historic trade which gave rise to government in the first place. We reclaim our autonomy. At the expense of regrettable social disorder we obtain relief from the threat of official violence. And that, in my country, is very great relief indeed.''

Kate's mouth was dry. She coughed. ''So who is 'we'—exactly?''

''Everyone who rejects the social bargain. Everyone who opposes any institution which enforces order by infringing upon his or her liberty. Antitechnologists, laissez-fairists, syndicalists, individualists, pacifists, vanguardists, punk rockers, squatters, libertarians, atheists, radical ecologists, tax resisters, draft resisters, resisters of every sort. Anyone who has ever been falsely accused of a crime by the state, Miss Dunn, is a potential anarchist. So we are defined not by what we are for, you see, but by what we are against, which is any form of coerced social organization.''

''But it's those same 'social organizations' that get murderers off the streets so they don't kill again.''

''Which do you suppose would kill more people—murderers running rampant on anarchistic streets, or national armies fighting territorial wars across whole continents? Two states—usually autocratic—disputing the limits of their power through profligate waste of their young. War would not exist without the state, and the state would not exist without war. I intend to destroy the Russian state and every archist institution in this country. If structure exists even at the lowest levels of society they will sprout order, and hierarchy, and power mongering. Relations will organize around them like crystals form in liquid solution.''

''But doesn't everyone have the right to form a government?''

Kartsev smiled broadly. ''Rights are an archist concept. Rights have no meaning except when confronted with superior power. They are what is left to the people after the government has taken all it wants. Your country's Bill of Rights, for example, defines your most cherished freedoms how? By limiting the legal power of government to encroach upon them. But all those *rights* may still be overridden by the government, and guess who retains the power to interpret when? We Anarchists say there is no need for rights when there is no state to encroach upon them. But to answer your question, yes, people may form a government, and I will simply destroy it.''

The car slowed and turned into a gate. Two guards in long black overcoats stood at the gate with assault rifles strapped over their shoulders. The private drive inside wound through a parklike forest. ''Where are we?'' Kate asked, her voice quavering slightly.

''My dacha.''

Kate had been to a dacha to do a story—a tiny cottage on a poorly maintained dirt road. Kartsev's enormous manor came slowly into view. The motorcade pulled up to the front steps and one of Kartsev's men opened the door beside Kate. She got out. Instead of heading toward the mansion, Kartsev led her along a path of neatly brushed mulch. The path, Kate noted, led into the thin woods. It was an overcast day—slightly cool, slightly humid. Her hands grew cold and her heart thumped. Their footsteps crunched in unison. The footsteps of the two guards who followed were the only other sounds Kate heard. When the path ended, they continued out into the forest. The slender white birch trees were widely spaced and not very tall. The ground was nearly clear of brush.

Kartsev looked out of place in his expensive dark suit. He walked with his hands clasped behind him. ''So, what do you think of my country home?'' he asked.

Kate shrugged. ''Seems a bit remote. Lonely.''

Kartsev stopped. ''Oh, but we're not alone.'' He held his arms out to the empty woods. ''We are surrounded, you see, by the social scientists of Russia's past. Men and women who launched grand experiments into untried forms of self-government." He walked on. "I intend to keep accurate records—for posterity—unlike these less scientific predecessors." He swept his arm through air and looked out through the thin, young trees. Kate felt ripples of panic tingle her spine. A sudden sense of uncertainty on finding herself in the presence of total madness.

"Mr. Kartsev, there's nobody else here."

He smiled. "But you are wrong. You see, when I was seeking a site for my dacha, I came upon this great tract of unspoiled government land. They had been trying to privatize but had gotten no takers. There were rumors of environmental problems—chemical or radiological wastes—but I had an advantage. I had been with the KGB in my earlier days, and you never quite leave, you understand. So I knew the true story behind this parcel, and the more I thought about it, the more appropriate it seemed."

"What . . . what *was* here?" Kate asked. The serene woods betrayed no signs of the secrets they held.

"Beneath you is the main Moscow burial ground first of the NKVD, and then of its successor, my own KGB. You are standing right now atop the final resting place of a million of my fellow countrymen. They were brought here in ones and twos or by the truckload for decade upon decade. Here lie the great researchers of the past—my brethren in the quest for social knowledge." He beamed from ear to ear.

Kate halted and turned to face him. "What do you want from me?"

"I want you to spread the word."

"What word?"

"Anarchy." His lips curled, but his eyes—magnified by thick lenses—seemed devoid of humor. "Anarchy is not a new form of government, it is no government. No prisons, no camps, no armies. No employers. No parties. No religions. No clans, or cliques, or clubs, or any associations which involve the delegation of power over human beings. I want you to spread the word of our new kind of revolution like shock waves propagating outward. The bigger the bang, so to speak, the more powerful echos will be when they bounce back. I hope those echos will help destroy the failed structures that are holding my society back. Our social safety net hasn't allowed Russia to fall hard enough or far enough to eradicate those organizations so that new ways of life can sprout from the rubble. 'Destruction is the mother of creation,' Miss Dunn, and we are entering a highly creative period.''

Kate stared at him in disbelief. "Do you realize what's going to happen?"

The mild-mannered man's reply was delivered with academic detachment. ''Death. Ruin. Disruption. Homelessness. Disease. Packs of people roaming the streets for something to eat. Anything. Anybody. Funeral pyres will light the night, Miss Dunn.''

"The army will never let that happen."

"But the *army* is the first target. Have you not wondered where they are? Why they have not put down my Black Shirts? They are experiencing entropy. The first signs of their decay will be seen quite soon now. The army is an institution, after all. Its discipline threatens to maintain some semblance of order. A skeletal structure from which the sagging flesh of state will hang. We cannot allow that.''

"So you think if I show the world a violent and bloody revolution spread to America? That it'll incite the restive inner-city underclass in America and they'll storm into the streets and get slaughtered?''

"No. The audience I have in mind for your reports is that great middle class of your country. It's easy, you see, to get slaughtered. It's far more difficult to motivate people to actually *do* the slaughtering.''

THE BRONX, NEW YORK
September 1, 0130 GMT (2030 Local)

The shot was so easy he didn't even need the night-vision device. From the light of street lamps and two burning cars, the mounted policeman's chest filled the crosshairs of the optical sniper scope. The horse underneath the cop was the only problem.

The animal was spooked by the noisy crowd and the occasional stone hurled over the police barricades. It stepped this way and that—taking its rider in and out of the sights. *"Chyort!"* the sniper cursed under his breath from the rooftop four blocks away from the demonstration.

At that range, the angry shouts of the residents who protested the beating of three high-school students sounded more like the distant roar of a stadium crowd.

The next time the horse took a few nervous steps, the mounted cop steadied the animal with a firm tug on the reins. The sniper exhaled half a breath. The rider lay squarely behind the crosshairs. He squeezed the trigger almost involuntarily.

A single crack echoed among the buildings. The sniper quickly cycled the bolt, chambering a fresh round. But when he surveyed the scene, he saw what he had hoped for. The horse was out of control now—its rider barely hanging on and probably mortally wounded by the high-velocity round. He found another officer who'd turned his back to the mob to look at the commotion. His riot shield was out of place. Another squeeze, and another sharp recoil and crack.

The officer went down like a sack of potatoes. The bolt clacked again, but a third shot proved unnecessary. Someone in the police line opened fire. Then one of the rioters returned fire. Within seconds, blazing muzzles began to pop like flashbulbs from both sides. Before the man had packed his rifle, war had consumed the street.

Evelyn Faulk and her son André trudged their way to the south through the noise and commotion. The light was dim under the thick smoke rising from hundreds of fires all around the Bronx. It was two dozen blocks to the police lines. Neither the subway nor the buses were running. The few other people out that day headed furtively down sidewalks toward Manhattan like refugees from a war zone.

Evelyn's legs and back ached. It was slow going. Every few intersections they had to zig one block over or zag back the other way to avoid the unopposed looting of the city.

"Where we *goin'*?" André asked again.

"Just you *shush*!" she snapped back. She was doubly, triply angry. Angry at the thieves that ran loose like animals on the streets around her home. Angry at the police for running away and hiding behind barricades that did little more than protect rich whites from poor blacks. And angry at her own son. When the sun had risen after a sleepless night of shouts and gunfire, Evelyn had seen the look of anticipation in the seventeen-year-old's eyes. He was dressed and ready to hook up with his "crew"—children who'd grown up to be what others called a gang. She had seen all in André's eyes. To him, this was an exciting new world filled with adventure. To her, it was that trip to the morgue she lay awake imagining during the hours her son was on the street.

"Look at *that*," André said.

Evelyn followed his outstretched finger. There was trash strewn all about the entrance to Mr. Cantu's bodega. Empty soda cans, boxes of doughnuts only half-eaten . . . but no people. Evelyn and André crossed the street to peer inside.

Power was off all over the Bronx, and the store was dark. All they could see from the doorway was disarray. Flies buzzed about the spoiling food. The tiny bodega had been ransacked. Everything was overpriced, but the residents of Evelyn's neighborhood nevertheless cherished the store because its brave owners had not been chased away by crime. They had put bars on the windows and had guns behind the counter and—

"Come on, Mama!" André said suddenly, stepping outside. He tugged her back out onto the sidewalk.

"Let's go," he said. Evelyn pulled her arm from his grip and headed back inside. She nearly tripped over the man who lay on the floor in a white butcher's apron. It was stained with three black splotches. His eyes were wide. His

mouth gaped underneath his bushy mustache. Mr. Cantu
was covered in flies.

Evelyn felt like screaming, but she didn't panic. She
marched out of the store and grabbed André's arm. She
towed him straight down the block to the south. Her walk
was purposeful, and it forced André to break his long-
practiced saunter just to keep up with her pace. His
hundred-dollar high-tops flopped all about, their laces
untied, as was the fashion.

"Where we *goin'*, Mama?"

"Hush up, I said!"

By the time they got down to Ninety-sixth, people were out
in the streets like it was a holiday. There was no sense of
danger, just an air of excitement, an energy. Everyone was
talking and laughing and pointing at the smoke. There were
sirens of every sort near and far. But Evelyn hadn't yet
seen any police cars or fire trucks.

Except up ahead. They stopped at the sight of it. Lights
flashed through the gaps in the crowd. It looked like a riot,
but she couldn't see or hear any signs of a disturbance.
With tentative, wary steps, they waded into the mass of
people. "Excuse me. Excuse me," Evelyn repeated over
and over as the mostly indifferent crowd let her pass. They
seemed to have gathered only to gawk at whatever lurid
crime had been committed. After a minute or so Evelyn
and André reached the front ranks.

It was an amazing sight. New York City police cars were
parked bumper-to-bumper all along Ninety-fifth Street from
east to west for as far as the eye could see. The lights on
their roofs were all flashing. Evelyn grasped the brightly
colored wooden barricades erected a few feet short of the
cars. There was another barricade running along the opposite side of the street.

"What's going on?" she asked the woman next to her.

The woman looked her up and down and said, "They're
not lettin' anybody cross down from Harlem."

Evelyn looked at the barricades. It was like a wall had

descended across the city. But a few yards to her left, the wooden barriers opened into a corridor through the new border. A gauntlet of uniformed police officers with dogs lined the passage that led from the anarchy of the blighted northern borough.

"Excuse me!" Evelyn began again . . . but loudly. She pushed her way for the opening with André in tow. Police on horseback inside no-man's-land kept watch deep into the crowd. Tired men milled about in full riot gear, their helmets' visors raised. Clear plastic shields leaned against police cars, and long black truncheons lay on the pavement next to them.

A man wearing a black bulletproof vest and holding a large shotgun propped on his hip stood asking questions at the entrance to the crossing. Evelyn and André got in line and waited.

"This is America!" a man shouted up at the head of the line. An argument ensued. The man finally turned away in anger.

Next up was a woman wearing a white nurse's dress under a dark sweater. She got through with no hassles, but she had to lift her large purse high above her head as sniveling police dogs strained at their leashes on both sides.

"I'm a maintenance engineer at the Garden," the next man said.

"What does that mean?" asked the cop with the shotgun. "You clean up elephant shit when the circus is in town?" There was silence. "Go o-o-on," the cop barked.

Finally, it was Evelyn and André's turn. "Where you headed?" the tall white cop asked, addressing Evelyn but eyeing André. He ran a hand-held metal detector over their bodies, raising a latex-covered finger and spinning to indicate that they should turn around. Evelyn complied, but André just stared back at the man. Evelyn backhanded the boy. "What's the matter?" the cop asked. "Them looters steal your tongue?"

"Downtown," Evelyn said quietly.

"Oh, yeah? What ya doin' down there today?"

"I got me some business to take care of," Evelyn said softly. Her eyes were cast down toward the cop's black vest.

"Whoa-hoa! Some *business*, ya say? I suppose you gotta deal with your stocks and bonds and shit." Evelyn looked up. Through the open corridor ahead she saw taxis and people and activity. Life. "Go on!" the cop growled, a grin on his meaty face.

Evelyn and André headed through. A German shepherd reared up on its hind legs as it lunged. It was stopped by its leash, but not before its nose left saliva on Evelyn's good coat.

It was like crossing a border into a foreign country, André thought, although he had never seen a border before. Once they were across, they were free to roam the streets of the United States.

But the people on those streets shied away from André. Purses were clutched to sides or switched to the opposite shoulder. Conversations were halted until they were safely past. Eyes were kept warily fixed on him, André noticed, even by the well-dressed black businessmen. He smiled, thinking all he needed was to yell "boo" and they'd hand him their wallets.

They walked block after block. André finally said, "Where the hell are we *goin'*, Mama?" She said nothing. She just limped along with her head held high and her eyes fixed straight ahead.

"We're here," she said finally. She grabbed André by the jacket and pulled him toward a nondescript door. There were pictures like travel posters in the windows. U.S. ARMY RECRUITING CENTER, the sign said over the door.

"What the hell is this, Mama?"

"You can read!"

"Yeah, I know what it say, but—"

"Your daddy died on these streets." André hung his head. "It was Friday, and he'd been paid. He just couldn't give up that money. He'd worked *too* hard just to give it up. I will *not* lose you too, André. You *hear* me?"

André still avoided her eyes. "But the *army*?"

"Your daddy was in the army. I *married* him when he was in the army."

"I know all *about* that, *Mama!* And I know he got sent to a *war* too!"

"He was a boy just like you when he went off. He was a man when he came back from that desert." André frowned. "What you gonna do now that school's over, huh? I gave you all summer to think it over 'cause you done so good graduating, but what you gonna do now?"

André shrugged. "Get a job," he muttered.

"Doin' what? Loadin' trucks? Diggin' up streets on cold winter days? Honey, the *army* don't take no one without that degree. It *means* somethin' to them. And the army teaches you special things like computers. It'll teach you to get along with different people. You're a man, now, André. My oldest. Time to start actin' like one."

"Mama, if I'm a *man*, I can make my *own* decisions!"

She nodded, then nodded again. "Yes. Yes, you can." She sniffed. Her eyes moistened. It was killing André. He couldn't stand seeing her give up on him.

PHILADELPHIA, PENNSYLVANIA
September 4, 1500 GMT (1000 Local)

"They're everywhere," Olga Andreeva said. She held her hands over her mouth as they watched the buildings burn in Los Angeles.

"Nobody has said that Kartsev's people started this," Pyotr said, trying to calm his panic-stricken wife despite his own suspicions.

"Don't be naive! Of course they did this. Why else would it happen now? Just coincidence?"

"The police are being more aggressive. They just pushed the black people over the edge."

"Oh, you're so ignorant about such things. You think like a man. Everything must be straightforward or you miss it entirely."

The pictures on television now were of bodies strewn about one particularly devastated block. Andreev got his wallet from the kitchen counter and headed for the door.

"Where are you going?"

"Out," he said, standing in the door and looking both ways down the hall. "I'll be back soon."

Andreev stood before the glass-topped counter. "Can I ask what you're lookin' to use it for?" asked the sales clerk.

"Target practice," Andreev replied.

The salesman snickered then laid a huge, nickel-plated automatic on a rubber mat. "This here is an American gun—Smith & Wesson ten-millimeter." He pulled out two boxes of ammunition. "This is nine-millimeter Parabellum. *This* one," he said, placing the much thicker bullet down beside the first, "is ten-millimeter. The Smith & Wesson was developed for the FBI. It's got a thirteen-round combat capacity—twelve in a double-stack magazine and one in the chamber. It's heavy. It kicks like hell. It costs a thousand bucks. But it'll knock the holy shit out of your . . . *targets*." He and his grinning coworker laughed.

Andreev laid the beautiful weapon's butt in the palm of his hand. "I'll take it," he said instantly. It had a businesslike look about it, and the business of a pistol was killing human beings. He handed over a fistful of hundred-dollar bills. He had been paid well to protect the Russian president. Now that money bought protection for Andreev.

"You gotta fill these out," the salesman said, laying forms on the counter. "There's a seven-day waiting period, but if you're in a hurry . . ." He held a huge black plastic-and-metal shotgun by its pistol grip. The huge muzzle was gaping. "You might try this ten-gauge pump. Holds five rounds. I'd recommend a mix of shot and slugs. There ain't no waitin' period on this mother."

"I'll take that too," Andreev said, nodding.

The knock at the door made Pyotr and Olga jump. They knew no one in America. Pyotr got the shotgun and risked pressing his eye to the peephole. There was a small gathering of Americans in the corridor. He put the gun aside before he and Olga opened the door.

"Oh, hello," a kindly-looking old lady said. "We've never really introduced ourselves, but we're your neighbors." They all nodded, and the Andreevs nodded back. "We're forming a neighborhood watch. We were wondering if you'd like to join up."

"What is a neighborhood watch?" Pyotr asked.

He was met with stony stares. "That's," the old lady said, "a beautiful accent. Where are you from?"

"Switzerland," Pyotr said. The group eased. "A *neighborhood watch*!" an old man explained loudly as if Pyotr had a hearing problem. "You know, a patrol. We keep a lookout for signs of trouble."

Pyotr turned to Olga, she nodded, and he joined. After welcoming him, the old lady said, "Do you have a gun?"

Pyotr thought he didn't understand. "What?"

The woman stuck her hand in her purse. "A *gun*," she said, pulling a small revolver out with a frail, bony arm.

Pyotr was stunned, but he nodded. "Yes. Yes, I have one."

"Wonderful," the smiling woman said. "Then welcome to the watch. Oh, and welcome to America!"

UNITED NATIONS BUILDING, NEW YORK
September 6, 1500 GMT (1000 Local)

The Security Council meeting took a surprising turn. Angela Leighton—U.S. ambassador to the United Nations—leaned over to her aide as they waited for the Chinese handout to reach them. "What's this all about?" she whispered.

The man shuffled papers and shook his head. "It wasn't on the agenda."

The red folder was handed to Leighton. She opened it and saw a map of Asia. "Chinese Territories Taken by Imperialism in the Old Democratic Revolutionary Era (1840–1919)." She felt her jaw slacken, and she clenched her teeth. People were watching. On the map, the borders of China were clearly marked. But another set of lines bulged into neighboring countries. Huge tracts of China's neighbors were blotted out by shading. Most ominous were the shaded parts of Siberia.

"What the hell *is* this?" Leighton whispered. Other staffers gathered around the folder. The buzz of urgent conversations slowly filled the Security Council chamber. Legends written in Chinese, English, and French were cross-referenced to numbers on the map. An accompanying legend down the side margins gave the history of China's territorial losses. The next page gave greater detail. "1689—the Treaty of Nerchinsk. Russians cede Amur River basin to China. China rules area for 150 years. In 1858 and 1860, Russian Army forces regional Chinese authorities to sign treaties of Aigun and Peking, giving Russians north bank of Amur and east bank of Ussuri. Central Chinese authorities promptly repudiate both treaties."

"Oh, my God," Leighton whispered.

As the disturbance radiated outward from the chamber, the Chinese ambassador began his presentation. The British ambassador leaned over and said, "We need to talk." Leighton nodded as she donned her earpiece. Simultaneous English translation was being read by an edgy UN translator.

". . . at a time in our history when China was weak and Russia was strong," the Chinese ambassador read from his prepared text. "No Chinese government has ever acknowledged the legitimacy of those seizures. And now that balance of power has shifted." The sixty-year-old diplomat—young, by Chinese standards, and quite reasonable—looked up. He awaited the translation of his carefully spoken words into over a dozen languages. The room was astir with aides rushing out and staffers beginning to fill the gallery behind the circular table. "Asia is rightfully the territory of Asians. But as you can see from the map we have just handed out, rapacious Western powers seized the indicated regions by force or by proxy."

"It's not just Russian territory they're after," another of Leighton's aides whispered into her free ear. His finger traced the crosshatched areas spilling over China's borders to the west and south. "It looks like basically they're claiming every region that at one time or another paid some form of tribute to Beijing."

In addition to Tibet and Mongolia, Leighton observed, the Chinese were laying claim to Nepal, Bhutan, and Assam along the Indian frontier. And in Indochina to Myanmar, Malaya, Thailand, Vietnam, and Laos. In East Asia to Taiwan, Okinawa, and Korea. And, out of the territory of the old Soviet Union, the Pamirs, Sakhalin Island, Kazakhstan, Kirghizia, Tajikistan . . . and the Amur and Ussuri River basins in Siberia.

She turned the page. In Chinese, English, and French there was a resolution. She didn't need to read far. "Whereas, the former Republic of Russia unlawfully seized the territories of Greater China by military force, specifically 650,000 square kilometers of Siberia ceded by the Treaty of Aigun and 400,000 square kilometers ceded by the Treaty of Peking . . ."

"Get me the president," Leighton whispered to her aide.

Angela Leighton could tell from the president's tone that he wasn't taking the development seriously enough. She sat in a small conference room in the UN trying to decide how to brief him properly. "What could they possibly seek to gain out of perfecting some theoretical legal claim to all that territory?" Marshall asked.

She had to decide quickly how to begin. What to say in her five minutes in private. "Mr. President, may I take a step back for a moment and address the bigger picture. If you look at a map, China's present territory *seems* large enough, even given its enormous population. But only two-thirds of their land is under cultivation, and most of that not intensively. A lot of the territory they managed to hang on to during the imperial expansions is mountain or desert that can't even support modest populations. Manchuria, Inner Mongolia, and Tibet, for example—China's 'inner empire,' if you will—have both been heavily populated only in the last hundred years and contribute little to food production. The result is that the fertile central regions of China are all hugely *over*populated. But just across their borders to the north, Central Asia, Mongolia, and Siberia are one of the *least* populated regions on earth. Mongolia is half the size of the continent of Europe, but has a population of only one million people. Yakutia—which spreads across northern Siberia to the Bering Strait—is approximately the land area of the United States but has a population of 365,000! Sure, most of that land isn't arable, but the exception lies in the Maritime Provinces well inside the 'Greater Northeast Area' that was ceded to the Russians in the nineteenth century.''

"Wait a minute, Angela," Marshall said impatiently. "Are you suggesting that the Chinese are demanding a return of that territory to them? That they're looking to expand into some sort of 'outer empire'?"

"Yes, sir. And that would give them strategic control of all of Asia east of the Ural Mountains."

"But . . . that's *insane*! That sounds like some sort of . . . of 'Chinese *Lebens*raum!' " Marshall shouted. Leighton held the phone hard to her ear, but said nothing. "There's no *way* I'm going to be their Neville Chamberlain! Fuck that! This is a goddamn *election* year!" Leighton closed her eyes as the president ranted. It was the only way she could manage the incredible tension she felt building.

PART TWO

" 'For every action, there is an opposite and equal reaction'—Newton's Third Law of Motion. The behavioral sciences have laws as well. 'For every action, there is an opposite and unequal overreaction'—Kartsev's First Law of Man."

Valentin Kartsev (posthumously)
The Laws of Human History
Moscow, Russia

5

General Nate Clark and Major Reed walked down the sloping ramp of the transport. Nate stopped short of the waiting
entourage from his forward headquarters to watch troops
standing in loose formation at the rear of the giant C-17.
The morning was cold. The bright sunlight falling on his
arctic-white field jacket did nothing to warm him.

"Weapons in the *a-a-air*!" the platoon sergeant shouted.
The infantrymen with whom he had flown in raised the
muzzles of their rifles, squad automatic weapons, and machine guns toward the sky. Like Clark, they wore all white
except for their helmets, which were covered in the blue
cloth of UN forces. Heavy white packs lay to their sides.
Other platoons filed down the ramp and formed up in similar fashion.

"Safeties *o-on*!" the platoon sergeant yelled. Faint clicking sounds could be heard by the dozens. "Okay, ladies!"
the sergeant said to the all-male combat unit. "Lock and
load!"

There were clacks and tapping sounds of metal against
metal as magazines and belts of ammo were seated in weap-

ons. The most common sight was of soldiers pulling the charging handles of their M-16s to the rear, chambering a round.

"Grenadiers," the platoon sergeant shouted next, "load frags!"

The men with grenade launchers mounted under the barrels of their M-16s inserted stubby forty-millimeter, bullet-shaped grenades into the launchers' breeches.

"Check your safeties! Safeties on!" The men all looked at their weapons, which were still pointed away from their comrades. "All right, ladies! You now hold in your sweet little hands a *loaded* weapon! If it discharges a round, *someone* will die! It's up to *you* to make sure that someone is a very *bad* person and not the guy standin' in formation next to you!"

They headed off in two files. *Just like that?* Clark found himself thinking. Right off the airplane—with a hundred and ten pounds of equipment on their backs—they marched past huge piles of gray and muddy brown snow that had been bulldozed to the edge of the tarmac. They disappeared into the dense forests Clark had seen slide by beneath their plane on final approach. No questions asked. No idea what lay ahead.

It had been hot as shit when he had landed at Danang. They had ridden off in trucks beneath the smelly canvas. It had been two weeks before they first went into the field. Two days into their first battalion operation, Chuck Reed, Sr., had been left on the north bank of the Vinh Phuoc River. Three months later he'd been killed and Nate grievously wounded.

"Sir?" Clark heard—nearly jumping as Chuck Reed, Jr., tapped him on the shoulder. "Sorry, sir," the major said quietly. Clark realized that a Humvee had pulled up. He climbed into the heated armored car for the drive to his new command.

Nate walked into the crowded, windowless conference room. Senior officers from half a dozen allied armies rose.

"I'd like to introduce," Major Reed said in a loud voice, "Lieutenant General Nate Clark, United States Army, commanding general United Nations Russian Forces." Nate made his rounds, meeting his staff. Instead of the *J*- designations of USARPAC, the officers he met had been given jobs beginning with *G,* which were reserved for higher-level army groups.

"I am your G-3—operations—sir," the British general said before saluting. Nate returned the salute and shook hands.

The staff was entirely mixed European and American, but the senior officers under Nate were all European. The British got the real plum—operations. The G-1—personnel/administration—went to a Dutch officer that Clark knew well from his tour at NATO headquarters. The impressive man was fluent in all major European languages. The G-2—intelligence—was French. And the G-4—logistics—was German. It was the G-4 who provided Clark's amusement for the morning.

The German general pulled Clark aside. He spoke thickly accented English. "Excuse me, General Clark," he said, pronouncing the *G* in "General" as in the word "gun." "I wanted to discuss something, please." Clark nodded. "We might have a small misunderstanding. I was told that I would be responsible for theater logistics, but I overheard a member of your staff saying that *you* would run the railroad. I have substantial experience in the area of rail maintenance. Many of my reservists work on German rail lines in their civilian jobs. It seems to me that—"

Clark was already laughing. He explained to the confused officer what the expression "run the railroad" meant and sent him away with assurances that he was in charge of rail logistics.

Major Reed, who had heard the exchange, had a smile on his face that disappeared when Nate spoke to him in deadly earnest. "We're going to have to learn how to fight in coalition," Nate said. "Amusing ambiguities in language like that can turn into bags filled with dead men and women. Our allies are providing to us not only highly competent officers, but men who are almost totally fluent in *our* language. Almost. The official language of this coalition is English, but I want every American soldier from private to general to understand that *if* an order is garbled in communication, it's *their* fault. I want them sensitized to the nuances of idiomatic speech. I want them to be patient, but not patronizing. To define, to repeat, to speak slowly and use common words with precise meanings, not slang or jargon or colloquial expressions. It's a matter of life and death, Major Reed. You draft the memo. I'll sign it.''

DETROIT, MICHIGAN
September 9, 1500 GMT (0900 Local)

Daryl got into the limousine and looked around. ''Hey!'' he said to Gordon. ''Not only do I get to ride at the front of the bus, I get you alone for the first time in two days.''

Gordon felt awful. He'd been dreading this moment since Fein first cleared the time on his schedule with the advance men the night before last.

''I made some notes on the draft of your speech to the workers at the hospital emergency room,'' Daryl said as he rummaged through the shiny new leather briefcase his wife had just bought him. He handed a sheaf of papers over. ''I apologize that I didn't have time to type 'em up.'' He laughed. ''I guess you can read my handwriting after all these years, though.'' Daryl stared back at Gordon. His smile slowly grew stale.

''The speech was canceled,'' Gordon said.

Daryl's face betrayed momentary embarrassment before turning to the inevitable anger. ''Now, when the hell did they do that? That was going to be a major address on the health-care crisis! What was it? Too many sick people for the nightly news's taste?''

''It was security,'' Gordon said. ''The FBI arrested some terrorists in Chicago. They had hospital scrubs in their bags.''

Gordon looked out the window and ran his hand over his face. His skin felt different. He still wasn't used to the base makeup they applied in the hotel every morning.

"Something's the matter," Daryl said, almost whispering.

"We've gotta talk." From the change that passed over Daryl's face, he clearly understood just then what was happening. Gordon could tell from Daryl's eyes just before he looked away. Daryl was stunned—reeling. Gordon felt his eyes water. "I'm sorry." Daryl was looking out the window now at the passing landscape. It was a blur of empty roadside. The motorcade was traveling at high speed, and their route had been unannounced.

Gordon took a deep breath. "It isn't working out," he heard himself say.

Daryl looked at Gordon. He appeared so deeply, so profoundly hurt that he eyed Gordon not in anger, but warily. On guard. As if he didn't know what it was Gordon would do or say to him next to hurt him more. Or at least that was what Gordon thought.

"I need you back on the Hill to handle things for me there," Gordon said. "To take care of my office." Daryl's eyes sagged shut, a wince of pain at Gordon's words. "You will stay on, won't you?" Daryl was staring down at the three black television screens in the console opposite his seat. His eyes were unfocused. "Daryl, if we make it—if we get elected—I want you on my staff."

"Stop the car," Daryl said. He didn't bother to look at Gordon. "You can do that without asking Fein, can't you? You *can* stop the fucking car?"

"Daryl . . ."

"Stop the fucking car!"

"Daryl, you've got to be reasonable. We're out in the middle of nowhere." Gordon gestured out the window. The first low buildings, abandoned and boarded up, flew by on the way into the city. "I can't just stop this whole motorcade and let you out."

"Gordon, if you have a single shred of humanity left in

you—one last ounce of friendship for me—you won't make me get out of this car at a crowded campaign stop and see Fein and his people. Jesus Christ, Gordon, they all *knew,* didn't they? I realize what all those looks meant now. All those conversations that were stopped when I walked in. Why it was that I didn't seem to know what was going on anymore. Why I couldn't get anybody to . . . to help me . . .'' He was losing it. ''I stayed up till *two* A.M. last night making copies of the campaign budget figures. But when I put them in your chair before going to sleep on the sofa in my fucking *office,* I saw *another* folder there with a real pretty plastic cover! And when I looked inside, I find this new, *revised* budget that I hadn't ever *seen* before!''

Gordon felt so totally sympathetic toward Daryl's plight—so completely on Daryl's side—that it jarred him to remember that he himself was the enemy. That he had done this to his best friend—his longest political associate—just days after his nomination. But it had to be done, he reminded himself. Daryl just wouldn't drop the ''angry young man'' bullshit. There had even been some press rumblings that all wasn't well inside his team. Worse yet, the implication had been that the lines were drawn on the basis of race!

''Stop the car, Gordon,'' Daryl said, composed.

Gordon picked up the phone and said, ''Stop the car.'' The agent with the phone to his ear looked back through the soundproof glass. ''I said, stop the car, right now. Right here.''

The man hesitated, then said, ''Yes, sir,'' and hung up. He made several phone calls. All the while the motorcade hurtled toward the city. They were in the blighted slums now. The glittering buildings downtown toward which the vice-presidential party was headed loomed high over low-rent apartments. Every third building was boarded up. Some were burned out. Men congregated in empty trash- and rubble-strewn lots. Daryl didn't say a word. He just stared out the window.

Finally, the motorcade slowed to a stop. It had taken

quite a long time to arrange the unscheduled maneuver. It
was as if the inertia of the dozen cars, trucks, and vans had
resisted the effort. Agents poured out of their vehicles.
Shabbily attired pedestrians stopped and stared at the well-
armed, well-dressed security forces. Daryl opened his door.

"Daryl!" Gordon called out. When Gordon could think
of nothing to say, Daryl slammed the door. He looked totally out of place in his dark gray suit and starched white
shirt. He walked up to an unshaven man on the sidewalk.
The brim of the man's stained hat hung limply down
around the gray stubble of a scraggly beard. The man raised
a bony arm and pointed up the street. Daryl took off walking, his stride confident.

The limo's phone buzzed. Gordon picked it up. "Can we
get going, Senator Davis?" the agent in front asked.

The effort of speaking was almost too much. "Yes."

The motorcade took off again. Gordon kept his eyes
peeled along the sidewalk as they picked up speed. He
never saw Daryl, but he spotted Daryl's new briefcase. It
was sitting incongruously upright in an open, mesh trash
can.

ZAVITINSK MISSILE BASE, SIBERIA
September 11, 0000 GMT (1000 Local)

The crewman slid open the helicopter door. Nate Clark felt
subzero air fill the warm cabin. As raw as the weather in
Alaska had been during his brief acclimatization training,
Clark felt instantly that the cold of Siberia was of a different
order. And it was not yet technically autumn. The worry of
what was coming that winter was with him constantly.

After fleeing the downdraft of the rotor, Clark was met
by a civilian who introduced himself as an employee of the
International Atomic Energy Commission. He led Nate to
a nearby missile silo. Russian officers from the Strategic
Rocket Forces milled about the heavy blast door. It had
been swung open on its hinges. A crane slowly raised a jet-
black cone from the silo. In it, Nate knew, was a thermo-
nuclear warhead.

He couldn't help but look around at the nearby hills. They stood in the open. The exposed crane operator was now lowering his delicate cargo into a heavy, armored container mounted on a flatbed truck. His civilian host described their progress in removing Russian nuclear weapons for safekeeping. But Nate's eyes roamed the tree line. The skyline of the surrounding ridges. The swale that fell away from the flat, bulldozed missile pad.

On a nearby hill, Nate saw the regular string of dots for which he was looking. He thanked the civilian for the tour, then led Major Reed and the small security detail toward the firebase.

As they neared the base of the hill, men shouted in German from above. Clark and the others froze. German soldiers wove their way down the slope. The Germans saluted—wide-eyed on seeing the three black stars on Nate's collar—and led the entourage through their defenses. They kept repeating *"Minen"* as they pointed all around. The mines were all marked with thin sticks to which were tied colorful strips of cloth.

At the top of the first steep grade Nate was met by an officer. The man removed his glove to salute. He then shook Clark's hand and rammed his fingers back into his glove before introducing himself in English.

"Welcome to Firebase Zavitinsk, General Clark," the man said.

The German paratroopers were camped at the edge of the Zavitinsk Missile Base. At sunset, Clark knew, the IAEC technicians all returned to warm quarters. But in their outpost just north of the Amur River, the two hundred Germans hunkered down for the night. From his vantage on the hill, Nate's eyes followed the twin tracks of the Trans-Siberian Railroad into the haze to the east and west. After days spent organizing his staff, he had chosen these men for his first inspection tour.

They were the closest forces he had to the Chinese border.

"Sorry for the unannouced visit," Clark said. He zipped

his parka up to his chin and tugged the knit cap he wore under his helmet over his chilled earlobes. "How are your men adjusting to this weather?"

"This?" the handsome German colonel asked. His bright white teeth and eyes were set inside a red and weathered face. "The weather is not a problem today. There is sun."

"I meant the cold," Clark said as he followed the man down steps into an icy cut in the earth. His chin quivered with the first chatter of his teeth.

"Ah!" The colonel shook his head. "You must do what you must do, *ja*?"

They stood upright but still remained behind cover. The trench had been dug about three feet. An equally high mound of sandbags had been piled up around the lip. "These sandbags must give a pretty good fix on your lines," Clark commented. "Shouldn't you deepen your positions?"

The German shrugged, then kicked the toe of his boot into the dirt at the floor of the trench. "We dug until the first freeze. Now . . . ?" He shrugged again. "We could blast it out with explosives, but we don't have enough yet. Our supplies are . . . are not so gut." His smile was gone.

Clark looked around at the soldiers. One thing that would degrade a unit faster than cold would be empty bellies. "We'll fix that," he said.

"Besides," Clark's host continued, "when the snow comes, it will cover everything." The colonel held out his hand toward a dark bunker that opened off the trench. "Come, General Clark." Nate stooped and entered. His eyes stung immediately from the fumes of small chemical heaters. He was so uncomfortable bent over at the waist in the low room that he knelt on one knee. His escort knelt beside him.

"We keep living quarters separate from fighting positions by fifty meters," the German whispered. As Clark's eyes adjusted, he realized that the dark rolls covering the floor around him were men. Nothing but their faces protruded from black sleeping bags that fit around their heads like the hoods of parkas. "Separating the two areas makes less casualties from artillery."

Clark looked at him on mention of artillery. The only potentially hostile artillery in the area was Chinese.

"Artillery is a *problem,* yes," the colonel said, "when you do not control the surrounding area. If it got bad, we would reinforce and push the perimeter out. That would allow us to conceal and disperse our fighting positions. It would also give us some security against surprise attack. But we have good command and control in concentrated positions, and the soldiers fight better when they are together."

"I can imagine that your men wouldn't be too ecstatic about leaving these trenches," Nate said.

When the silence dragged on, Nate looked the German officer in the eye. "My men are not trench soldiers, General Clark. They would attack if I order it."

"I'm sorry. I didn't mean to suggest that they wouldn't."

Nate looked around the bunker. Interspersed with the bags full of sleeping men—who presumably had been on duty the night before—were machine guns, antitank missile launchers, and automatic grenade launchers.

"Why are all these crew-served weapons in here?"

"We store them in the living quarters during the day to keep them warm. At night, we keep all crew-served weapons and half the riflemen in their fighting positions."

Clark nodded again, and they rose to leave. Although it was relatively warm in the bunker—Clark guessed it was slightly above freezing—he still relished the crisp, clean air under the blue sky outside. The colonel led him down a narrow trench.

"The living quarters are connected to the fighting positions by slit trenches." When they passed men, they had to edge by sideways. Empty machine-gun revetments would be filled at nightfall. They stopped at a small, covered hole dug out of the side of the wall. "We have bombardment shelters every twenty meters. On top we put three sandbags," the colonel said, patting the three green sacks filled with dirt. "Half a meter overhead gives us protection from indirect fire, but we have trouble finding loose fill for the bags." He again kicked the toe of his boot into the frozen floor of the trench with a scraping sound.

They moved on. The narrow slit trench eventually opened into a much roomier main trench. There, a squad lounged around the floor—eating, cleaning weapons, writing letters. They all dropped what they were doing and rose to rigid attention.

"As you were," Clark said, but they remained ramrod straight. "At ease."

The colonel issued his own order in German, and the men relaxed but still remained standing. Clark shook the half-dozen men's hands. His nods were returned with a crisp bow of the soldiers' heads. Clark and the colonel then climbed up to fighting positions that had been carved into the forward walls of the trench.

The gently sloping hill had been cleared. The few stumps that remained wouldn't significantly restrict their fire. "I noticed your mines are still flagged," Clark said.

"Ah, yes, sir. We keep them out for the nighttime. When the snow falls, we will dig them up. The trouble with land mines is the pressure of the snow. Heavy snowfall will trigger them, *ja*?"

"What about trip wires?"

"We could lay trip wires. But you have to leave slack. When metal wire grows cold, it contracts. If you don't leave slack, it will set off the land mine. But if you leave too much, the wire just lies on the ground. Und all of it will be covered with snow soon. Plus the ground is frozen. We could just lay the mines on top, but the anarchists might take them in the night. Und even if we have the mines out there, the snow will smother the blast. So, mines are not that effective, *ja*?"

Clark nodded, having already concluded two things. First, the man knew what he was doing. Second, Clark did not. He had a lot to learn. From then on, it was less an inspection tour of a forward post than a field trip with an able teacher.

The young colonel led Clark through another maze to a round, heavily sandbagged junction. Men fell silent and shot to attention. Clark again shook hands. "These troops are for our *Gegenstösse*—our hasty counterattack. Our positions can be fought from every direction. We plan to let the enemy troops penetrate our weak points. Then, before they can consolidate their gains, we attack with these troops in a *Gegenstösse*. A hasty counterattack by a platoon is better than a *Gegenangriffe*—a deliberate counterattack— by an entire battalion the next day. But these men . . . they must attack over open terrain." The colonel peered out over the sandbags. Clark followed his gaze into the thick woods. The trees would protect the men as they dashed into the gaps in the lines. "Mobility is the key, *ja*? When the deep snow comes, we will pack it down in lanes with our snowshoes for them to go fast."

"You tramp down paths?"

"*Ja?* 'Tramping.' We tramp along axes of our counterattacks this way"—he chopped at the air with the blade of one hand—"*und* that way." He chopped again along a different bearing. "These men," the colonel said, turning to face the soldiers, "they are our very best, *ja*? Our most *daring*." Clark looked from face to face. They were all young. "They have to be for zis job?"

Clark nodded again. "Where are their weapons?" he asked.

"Ah, here!" The colonel stooped and picked up a small blanket at the feet of one of the men. He unwrapped the fabric and removed a small black machine pistol—a Heckler & Koch MP-5. "The teams are armed for close combat. Machine pistols und hand grenades only." He unzipped one of the men's white parkas. Hand grenades were affixed to bandoliers under the thick winter jacket.

They wound up the tour with a look at the artillery emplacements. Before Clark boarded the warm helicopter for the return to the warm command post in Khabarovsk, he mounted the sandbagged roof of a German bunker. From that vantage, he took in the panorama—the look, and feel, and smells, and sounds of a firebase. How many years had it been since his last? Since Vietnam?

Was it different, or the same? he wondered. Men worked all about the base. In Vietnam, they would have been stripped to their waists, soaked in sweat. Here, they were thick white shapes, moving about the altered landscape of the well-prepared defenses like men in spacesuits on the moon. But it was the same, Clark felt certain. It was all the same . . . all the same.

FORT BENNING, GEORGIA
September 15, 1300 GMT (0800 Local)

Gay and Roger Stempel sat in the front seat of their Mercedes as they drove Harold into the fort. "I still just can't believe he did this," Gay said for the hundredth time, the tissue wrapped around her finger and permanently pressed under her nose. "I *just* can't believe this." Harold's dad was silent. He'd given up replying. "You should've called a lawyer, Roger," she sniped, her anger turned on her husband.

"He's eighteen years old, Gay," Roger said. The car wound through the sunbaked Georgia base.

"Harold!" she burst out, turning and shaking her head. "What . . . what pos-*sessed* you to"—she looked out the window—"to join the *army*?" Harold looked at the sculpted green lawns, ignoring a question he'd tried vainly to answer. "I know you were upset being wait-listed at Harvard when all your classmates got early admission, but you *got* in! That's all that's important," she said insincerely.

"The Worths!" she suddenly blurted out, turning to Harold's dad. "We have reservations for dinner with the Worths in Boston!"

"I'll call Harry Worth and explain," he replied.

Gay Stempel rolled her eyes and groaned at the ceiling. She turned back to Harold. "Their son is an upperclassman. It's important for you to network from the very first day.

We set this dinner up to get you off on the right foot. It's the early days when friendships are formed, when everybody's new. Your father and I have told you over and over how much those friendships can mean to you later in life when you're trying to get ahead in your career and in society. And it's not as easy as it used to be. Everything is getting more and more competitive. Some of the better clubs require not just one, but two or *three* members to sponsor admission. Some even require four! *Four*, Harold!''

Harold ignored her as best he could. Just a few more minutes of this and he'd be free of her.

"Roger," she said, "maybe if he was on drugs, he couldn't have known what he was doing. Some sort of legal way out."

"That's probably the place," Harold said. He tapped his father on the shoulder and pointed to the gathering of green army buses whose former occupants filled the streets all around.

Gay growled in frustration and anger, flipping the sun visor down and lifting the small mirror. By the time they found a parking space, her face was freshly powdered. The large sunglasses took care of her puffy eyes.

The three doors all opened at once.

"Your *other* right, *maggot*!" shouted a disembodied voice from the other side of a bus. Harold tried not to look at his mother, but his father took her arm.

"I'm all right," she said, and shook off his attempt to help her. "It is so *hot*!" Gay said, fanning herself with the tissue as they rounded a bus.

There they encountered a sea of people in loose groupings. It was a motley crowd, wearing clothes of different colors and styles. They had long hair and short hair. They wore shorts and jeans. One poor soul had chosen to wear a suit. Black, white, Hispanic, Asian—everybody stood around waiting.

"Uh, son," Roger Stempel said, looking down at the ground and shuffling his feet, "this is a big step in your life. You know, your mother and I obviously had different plans for your next few years, but sometimes these things happen. You need some time to find yourself, so . . .'' He shrugged. Harold looked at him, but his father's gaze was toward the masses of recruits.

''It'll all work out,'' Harold said. ''It's only two years.''

''That's the attitude, son.'' His father put his hand on Harold's shoulder. A rare feeling of closeness seemed to bond them. ''All I wanted to say was, your mother and I understand how anxious you're going to be to get on with your education and the rest of your life when you come out. Despite all the words we might've had in the heat of the moment, we're still your parents, and I wanted''—he paused, reaching into his pocket—''*we* wanted you to have this.''

He brought Harold's hand up to his. ''It's a gold card. It has a twelve-thousand-dollar limit, not the two thousand like on the Visa card you had before. If you ever get into any trouble—*any* trouble at all—this card will get you out. We'll take care of it, no questions asked.'' His father sniffed and looked away, his eyes watery. He cleared his throat. ''Now let's go.''

Harold slipped the card into his pocket and waded into the amorphous clusters of men and women. As he watched people joke and chat casually among themselves, he again regretted not coming by himself and meeting people on the buses from Atlanta. Instead, he had acceded to his mother's wish that they drive down from New York. *It's gonna be just like Dalton*, he thought with growing anger. *I miss the first week of school because of Mother's fittings in Paris, and by the time I get to school everybody's already made all their friends.*

With a hug from his mother, Harold's parents were finally gone. Harold and his drill instructor—Sergeant Giles— stood side by side . . . waving. Harold heard the sergeant laugh, and he couldn't help but share the humor of his basket-case mom.

"You a fuckin' mama's boy, ain't you Stempel?" Giles said quietly.

Harold felt agitated suddenly. He looked up at the man. Giles smiled and waved once more as Harold's mother peeked out from around a bus before being pulled on by his father. The grin was still frozen on his face.

"You a pussy? Huh?" he asked. He didn't bother to even look down at Harold. "Do I got me a grade-A pussy for thirteen weeks, Stempel?" Harold pondered his response. But before he could think of one, the sergeant asked another question. "You know what happens to pussies, don't you, Harol' ol' chap?" It was a rhetorical question, Harold understood, demanding no response. As the intended meaning of the gibe sank in, Harold's lips curled in amusement at the wordplay. He nearly jumped out of his skin at the next sound—shot out of the DI's chest through his mouth like from a cannon.

"Answer me when I ask you a question, Private!"

Thus began Private Stempel's boot camp.

"What are you lookin' at?" was screamed straight into Stempel's right ear. Stempel concentrated on an imaginary dot straight in front of him. *"Answer me!"* came the tearing screech.

"Nothing, Sergeant!" Stempel yelled. His shout was lost amid the screaming NCOs who roamed up and down the line of recruits. Stempel kept in line behind the redheaded guy ahead of him. An electric razor came up the side of the recruit's head. Great masses of red hair fell to the floor in heaps.

"What are you lookin' at now?" a DI shouted. Stempel winced at the pain in his right ear.

"What is this piece of shit?" came a new voice from Stempel's left ear.

"It's the goddamn fuckup!" the sergeant at his right ear responded. Stereo drill instructors. "Every platoon has one!"

The last shock of the red hair fell to the cold concrete

floor. The air-conditioning had frozen Stempel into a block of ice. He stepped forward in his briefs, walking barefoot through thick mounds of hair.

The hot metal of the loudly buzzing razor dug roughly into the side of his head. The barber's free hand grabbed Stempel's chin, holding his head still. Stempel's hair was gone in seconds.

Stempel followed the barking shouts, all of which seemed to be directed at him. It was particularly bad when the line was delayed at a counter where soldiers handed out camouflaged uniforms. "Thumbs along your trousers!" someone shouted even though Stempel was wearing only Jockey shorts. "Stand up straight!" He stiffened, bowing his chest out and tucking his chin in. His hands were sweating profusely. "Close your mouth! You'll let *flies* in!" His mouth was dry. He was so thirsty.

A man with a tape measure wrapped it around his waist then down his legs. Folded uniform trousers and blouse were piled in his arms. He followed the bald redhead. Socks, boots, and underwear were laid on top of his other clothes. *"Get into your uniforms!"* thundered from somewhere. "You're *soldiers* now!"

It took Stempel the longest to get dressed. The room was empty, the shouts receding as he finished buttoning his blouse. One DI remained with him, leaning patiently against the wall. He clutched a clipboard to his crotch. His eyes were barely visible under the wide, sharp brim of his green hat. Harold tensed as the man walked over toward him.

"F-finished, Sergeant!" Harold shouted out, but the man blocked his way. Stempel came to attention. Their chests and faces were only inches apart. Stempel was prepared for the worst.

"Do you know what you're doin' here, recruit?" His words were so unexpectedly soft that Stempel didn't know how to answer. He couldn't tell what the man wanted him to say. "Do you understand what *we're* doin' here today— me and you?"

"Yes, Sergeant!" Harold said loudly, but without shouting.

"Look at me now, but I don't ever wanna see your eyes again." Harold looked up into the man's face. It was Sergeant Giles from the parking lot. "You gotta do this, son. You gotta do this, no matter how hard it gets. If I can break you here, I'll be takin' your manhood from you. I'm not sayin' we gonna make you a man. We cain't do that here. But if you quit, you'll be passin' up on maybe your one chance to be a man among men. To stand tall. To be a soldier. You catch my drift there, son?"

Harold swallowed but didn't trust his voice. He nodded, and Giles stepped out of his way. Harold broke into a run down the hall—batting his eyes to dry the moisture. A sign was posted over the door. VICTORY STARTS HERE, it read.

TOMSK, RUSSIA
September 19, 2230 GMT (0830 Local)

Clark waited in the French base's icy command bunker, the telephone receiver to his ear. The ever-pleasant White House operators had put him on hold. Even though he was at the most far-flung outpost in the most remote place on earth, the small satellite dish on the roof allowed direct dialing to any phone in the world. After Clark briefed General Dekker on the attack, the army chief of staff had transferred his call to the White House on express directions from the president.

There was a click, and then Clark heard, "Hello? General Clark?"

Although he'd never spoken to the man, his voice was instantly familiar. "Hello, Mr. President." The heads of the captains and lieutenants who filled the low-ceilinged room shot up in unison. "What happened out there?" President Marshall asked.

"A French legionnaire base was raided, sir. Fifteen dead, another forty wounded."

"Who did it?" the response finally came. The satellite delay was now quite familiar.

"Well, sir, they didn't leave any casualties, and we didn't take any prisoners, so we can't tell. But the guess is the Russian Army was behind it. The attack was coordinated. They used mortars. It was a professional job, not the sort you'd expect from irregulars."

"I think you might be underestimating the anarchists," the president replied. "They've been showing some pretty impressive organizational skills in their terrorist attacks." Clark began to object, but the president kept speaking. "What do you plan to do to prevent future attacks like the one last night?"

"There's not too much we can do, sir . . . with what we have here now. As you know, I'm sure, our European allies have siphoned off some of their troop commitments because of trouble along the Trans-Siberian Railroad further west. We've only got enough men to deploy to isolated positions at the missile bases and weapons depots. They're not mutually supporting, and they're not *self*-supporting. We can't do any patrolling in strength, which means ceding the countryside to whatever bands of renegade army or anarchist groups lurk out there."

"Is that a roundabout way of asking for more men? Because if it is, you're wasting your breath. More men only means more targets. We're going to keep this operation simple and quick. You're there only to secure those nuclear weapons, not to start policing the countryside. Once things are under control, you'll furl the colors and head home—you understand?"

Nate took a deep breath, then said, "Yes, sir. I understand. I understand completely."

WHITE HOUSE OVAL OFFICE
September 19, 2230 GMT (1530 Local)

President Marshall's chief of staff punched the button to disconnect the call.

"Well," Marshall said, "it doesn't sound like our man on the ground there is too happy."

"They always want more," his chief of staff replied. "More tanks, more troops, more jets. And you know what that leads to. Commitment. It's quicksand. We can't start throwing people in there like it's some sort of invasion. The Chinese would go ape shit! Besides, I thought we already acceded to Clark's requests when we gave him that extra brigade."

"But still," Marshall said. "What if the Russian Army really was behind the raid? What if there's more of it to come, and we've sent those men and women out there without enough support?"

"It was anarchist terrorists," his trusted advisor insisted, "and they got lucky. We should retaliate to let them know we won't be messed with, and to assure the electorate that we're not letting them push us around." Marshall winced on mention of the political ramifications. "You can't overlook the campaign! Those were French troops, and the French don't really give a damn about them. But if those body bags were filled with *our* people, there'd be hell to pay. We'd have to react strongly or take hits for coddling the Anarchists."

"React in what way?" Marshall asked.

With a shrug, the chief of staff suggested, "An Executive Order."

Marshall raised an eyebrow in surprise. "Are you suggesting that I authorize an assassination?" His question was met with another shrug. "And just whose death would you propose that I sanction in signing an Executive Order?"

The man was clearly waffling, but he replied nonetheless. "This guy Kartsev." Marshall frowned. "He's got *plenty* of blood on his hands if the reports we get are true!"

"That's hardly due process. Could we convict him in a court of law on what we know for a fact?"

"But we're not talking about trying him in *court*!" Marshall's chief of staff replied. "I'm talking about fighting fire with fire."

"You're talking about being *seen* fighting fire with fire. You're talking about the boost we'd get in the polls if one day Kartsev woke up dead. The media has demonized the guy—setting him up as the one man behind all the terrorism.''

''But he *is* behind the terrorism. I *know* you think that.''

''But *I'm* not a judge or a jury!''

''Oh, yes, sir. You *are*. That's why we've *got* Executive Orders. You sign it, and everything's legal.''

Marshall smiled and shook his head. ''Legal, sure. But is it moral?''

It was his advisor's turn to smile. ''What the hell does *that* have to do with anything? Kartsev is fucking *evil*! There's no *question* that what he's doing in those Siberian training camps is depraved and immoral. It's practically medieval! Young girls disappearing from local villages! Aerial photos of mass graves! The man tried to kill you and your wife. He's killed your secretary of defense and leaders all across the world. And he killed those fifteen French soldiers last night.''

''I'm not signing any Executive Orders.''

''Okay, okay. So you don't sign anything. So maybe you just pick up the phone and call the Pentagon. Every so often we get a Kartsev sighting out of the CIA. Maybe next time we do, he's somewhere out in the boonies. If it makes you feel any better, we don't 'assassinate' the guy with a bullet, we just have the air force drop bombs all around and maybe one lands on his head, okay? It's nice and neat and doesn't have any paper trail. If we miss, we just make sure what we *do* blow up has some military value.''

Marshall stared back in silence. Heaving a deep sigh, he finally picked up the phone and said, ''Get me General Dekker.''

6

Kate Dunn had simply left a note for Woody, gone to the Kremlin, and requested an interview with Kartsev. To her amazement, the black-clad guards at the gate led her straight in. Kartsev had sat in an ornate, high-ceilinged room sipping tea.

She had asked questions. He had answered. He had also checked his wristwatch repeatedly.

After ten minutes Kartsev had risen mid-sentence. The interview wasn't over, he'd assured her, but they had to leave. Just outside the room, they'd passed heavily armed Black Shirts. Her repeated calls of "Mr. Kartsev" had drawn no more than a smile over his shoulder. She had followed—blindly. The collapse of Russia was the biggest assignment she'd ever had, and he was her source, her guide . . . her protector.

Kate, Kartsev, and an entourage of armed escorts had descended several flights of stairs. The walls had grown bare and dingy. The halls had narrowed, and the Black Shirts had pressed in all around. Kartsev never gave an order. He never even looked up.

The Anarchist soldiers were all dressed the same. Nylon, zippers, boots, leggings, and gloves—all black. But the men who wore the gear were each distinct in some way. One had short hair to go under his black helmet, but a bushy beard hanging from his face. Another was shaved clean of all hair, his face deeply pockmarked and his unsmiling eyes black. There were compact men, tall men—Caucasian, Asian, black.

None had entered the large service elevator with Kartsev and Kate.

"Where the hell are we going?" she'd asked.

"To Siberia," he'd replied—smiling. "The last refuge of scoundrels."

She had peppered him with more questions, and he had always politely responded. He had not, however, answered. They'd left the Kremlin through a special subway car—the only people on the high-speed train. When they'd emerged, they were at an airbase somewhere outside of town. The only light on the runway had come from the open door of an unmarked business jet.

Thunder had rolled across the wooded hills. They'd paused on the tarmac to listen. Again Kartsev had looked at his watch. "Punctilious," was all he'd said.

The darkening sky above the tree line had flickered with man-made flashes.

"What's going on?" she'd asked.

"They're attacking the Kremlin," he'd informed her as the jet's door had been slammed closed behind Kate, "to kill me. The last scene of Act One," Kartsev had said, but never explained.

He had talked, however—nonstop, for hours. Never in direct reply to Kate's questions. Instead, he'd told her stories, mostly. Histories of ancient dynasties of which she'd never heard. He was brimming with obscure details about the darkest eras of man.

Kate had fallen into a fitful sleep.

•   •   •

The change in the engine's tone caused Kate to awaken with a start. "Where are we?" she asked as she looked out the small window.

"Tyumen Oblast, just east of the Urals," Kartsev replied.

The jet descended between two strips of parallel lights. The tires squealed. They slowed and stopped, not turning off the runway. The door was opened from the outside. Kartsev rose.

The engines wound down to a low whine. Kate stared out through the window at the runway lights. In the few moments before they fell dark she saw the outline of a limousine. It was replaced by the reflection of her face in the glass.

She followed Kartsev into chilly blackness. The sky overhead was clear and filled with stars. Wind whipped at her in the short walk to the car. They took the same seats as they'd had on the jet—facing each other. An aide climbed into the limousine's rear in a crouch. The man lowered small blinds over the windows by their strings. He then slammed the doors, and they were alone again.

Always alone. Kartsev never seemed to have people around.

The roads were deplorable. The car rocked back and forth as they periodically traversed major potholes or ruts. There would be no paving in this part of the world. They were hundreds of miles from anywhere. They might as well have been millions.

Kate's eyelids began to droop. The swaying motion, the warmth of the heater, the late hour—all conspired to leave her craving rest. Craving respite from her worries. Refuge from the sickening sense of danger that she felt.

She said nothing lest her voice quaver. Self-assured people, she'd always thought, were less likely to make stupid mistakes. *Like pretending to let Woody talk her out of going to the Kremlin*, she thought, *then going straight there when he was out scrounging up food. Stupid mistakes like following a madman into the middle of nowhere!* She tortured herself behind closed eyelids.

Her head fell back. She awoke with a start. Kartsev was watching her.

She was instantly alert.

"We're going to visit the training camps," he said, finally answering the question she'd repeatedly asked.

"Wha-*at*?" she blurted out. She sat upright. "To the *terrorist* training camps?" Kartsev nodded. *Calm*, she thought to herself. *Calm-calm-calm-calm.* "I *assume*," she began in an even but too-high tone, "you're going to show me the . . . the standard stuff." She had no idea what that was. "You know, rifle ranges, obstacle courses, that sort of thing?"

Kartsev shrugged. "If you'd like. But I thought you'd be more interested in the . . . *psychological* dimension."

She swallowed—twice—then asked, "Where are we—exactly?"

"For your own protection, Miss Dunn, it's really best if you don't know. Let's just call this . . . 'the end of the earth'." Kate felt her lower lip twitch—the beginning of a quiver. She tucked her cold hands under the seat of her blue jeans. "You won't be *harmed*," Kartsev said in what sounded almost like alarm. "I can assure you of that." She looked up. He stared at her openly, wearing a concerned expression. "You can go whenever you wish. You're . . . free."

Kate took a deep breath and broke eye contact. But he kept staring, she could feel it. Everything about his manner was unobjectionable. He kept a distance from the ugliness. It was a luxury, a perk of his high station.

"What . . . psychological dimension?" she asked, without looking up.

"Do you know who these terrorists are?" Kartsev asked. "These men who do unspeakable things?" She stared into her lap and shook her head. "They are Armenian Fedayeen from Nagorno-Karabakh, their Azeri enemies, Afghan Mujahedeen, Hamas, Hezbollah, and IRA. Tamil rebels from Sri Lanka, Khmer Rouge from Kampuchea, Philippine Communists, Angolan UNITA rebels, Bosnian Serbs and

Bosnian Muslims, Georgians, Kurds, Tajiks, Lebanese, even *gang* members from your own country. They're freedom fighters and bandits and criminals. They come from every mountain pass and urban alley which lies just beyond the edge of civilization. They're erratic primitives with shifting allegiances. They're habituated to violence. They have no stake in civil order.''

Kate heard the rustle of his jacket as he leaned forward. Her eyes remained fixed on her knees.

''The primary function of civilization, you know, is to restrain man from horrible excess. We're not the children of Rousseau, Miss Dunn. It isn't the evil government which keeps us from living in peace and harmony together like some Benetton advertisement. Homo sapiens are killing animals. We organize into the disciplinary structures of civilization out of fear of the alternative. With your Western social conditioning, you probably have little insight into the sullen world of our recruits. They live in very dark places. I'm going to give you a glimpse of the alternative to civilization, Miss Dunn. A peek into an anarchic world. I couldn't possibly make you believe with mere words what you're about to see with your own eyes. They're in the middle of their night now.''

She looked up at him then. She closed her dry mouth and swallowed. For the first time questions did not fill her head. There was nothing more that she wanted to know.

''The one thing, Miss Dunn, that all these men have in common is that they're impossible to reconcile to civilized order. For them, peace is not a desirable state of affairs. They were pathetic misfits before their wars. But when their societies collapsed, they led fantasy lives as action superheros as they killed women, children, and old men. So what do you think such men *do* when their war comes to an end? Their broken countries offer them no assistance. Would they get a laborer's job for minimum wage? These are men who rousted villagers from their beds to dig latrines, and then shot them because it was more convenient than returning them home. They murdered the men who'd slighted them before the war. They plundered from the weak what they could never have owned. They raped the women who'd spurned them. Unlike the soldiers in the great armies, Miss Dunn, who experience only war's sacrifices, these men developed a taste for the spoils.''

She steadied herself by thinking of a question. This was an interview. She should lead Kartsev. She was in control. "So, you provide a home for all the heros of ethnic cleansing?''

"Ethnic cleansing works very well, Miss Dunn. Roman legionnaires dispersed troublesome Jews. The U.S. Army virtually exterminated the Plains Indians. After World War One, ethnic Greeks were kicked out of Anatolia. After World War Two, ethnic Germans were brutally expelled from East Prussia, Pomerania, Silesia, and Czechoslovakia— killing millions. In each case, the violence was very effective in stabilizing an ethnically volatile region.''

"So," Kate said, snorting in disgust, "you search the world for the best ethnic cleansers, do you?''

He shook his head. "I don't have to. They come to us. We accept two types. The largest group is from the underclass. No education"—he bent his fingers back as he counted their characteristics—"no earning power, no abiding attractiveness to women, no future. For them, the half-understood rhetoric of a cause gives them some pretense of personal dignity. But—even more importantly—the end of the fighting for these men means the end of good times. It's really a 'catch-22' for them, because the longer the fighting continues, the more irredeemable they become.

"But men of the second type are the most dangerous of all," Kartsev said, again leaning forward. "Dispossessed military men. Cashiered officers. Soldiers with failed careers. They bring with them the military art. Their skills heighten the level of the killing to a different order of magnitude. Their only problem is that many have been inoculated with the moral and behavioral codes of Euro-American armies. They've learned a highly stylized, almost ritualistic form of warfare with rules and customs and traditions. Soldiers are trained to fight other soldiers. They learn to expect and deliver a symmetrical response. We teach them to respond a-symmetrically. To confound organized soldieries and police with unorthodox methods. It's like the British redcoats fighting American Indians. Or American Rangers in the streets of Mogadishu. They snipe, ambush, mislead and betray. It's quite amazing what just a few thousand of such men can do. The science of complexity offers a scientific demonstration of how seemingly inconsequential variables can spark immensely disproportionate reactions."

"Meaning what?"

"Meaning it doesn't take that much violence to change the course of history."

Kate's gaze rose to him now. "Are we still talking about terrorists' training? Or . . . or are you talking about something else?"

Kartsev smiled. "I believe we are entering a new age. An age of shattered belief systems like what last occurred in the sixteenth century. That sociopolitical earthquake led directly to the Thirty Years War—the greatest trauma of modern Europe. It annihilated an entire moral and social order. For a generation after, the remnants of disbanded imperial armies spread syphilis and banditry across continental Europe."

Kate swallowed again. "What is it you're taking me to see?" she asked in a quiet voice.

He grimaced, slightly. "We let these men live the way they want. We feed them . . . in whatever way they want to be fed. And what they need most is not bullets, or drugs, or food, but the raw material they value most—people. Women, mostly, but . . . whatever. In their world, they reign supreme. They do—"

"Stop it!" Kate said finally, clamping her hands over her ears. "You're evil," she said in a low voice.

The car pulled to a stop.

"Ah!" Kartsev said. "We're here."

He opened the door. Outside was a dimly lit building.

The cinderblock walls were painted white. They were unbroken by windows or doors.

"Are you coming, Miss Dunn?" Kartsev asked from the open door. Kate sat motionless and frozen by fear. "Well then," he said, holding out his hand, "I guess this is goodbye, then. The car will take you back to the airstrip, and the jet back to Moscow."

Kate looked down at his outstretched hand but didn't move. "Till we meet again, Miss Dunn." After two crunching steps in gravel, the door was closed in her face. Kartsev said something to the driver in Russian. Kate opened the door on the opposite side and vomited onto the ground.

When the limousine pulled off the road abruptly, Kate thought her worst fears were coming true. She could hear the front doors open. The horror ran wild through her imagination. But then she heard something more . . . thunder. Flashes of lightning pulsed through the blinds.

Despite the tension of the moment—or perhaps because of it—Kate sensed that something was amiss. The men from the front of the car were talking. *The night was totally clear!* Kate realized. There wasn't a cloud in the starry Siberian sky. And, there was something more. The lightning came in regular strings of popping lights, and the noise was less a rumble than a series of distant booms.

The doors closed again, and the car tore off at high speed.

FORT BENNING, GEORGIA
September 28, 2000 GMT (1500 Local)

Every muscle in André Faulk's body ached, but the white kid next to him looked half-dead.

"Listen up, gentlemen!" shouted the weapons instructor, a lieutenant wearing shatterproof black glasses. "This is your weapon." He raised a black assault rifle into the air, and despite André's misery he smiled. With rising excitement he looked over at the sagging white kid. Red in the face, eyes half-closed, mouth hanging open, he looked sick. "When this weapon's sear releases, whoever is standing downrange of the muzzle at that exact moment will take a 5.56-millimeter round going twenty-eight hundred feet per second. *This weapon,* gentlemen, will go off if you drop it!"

The white guy sagged against André's shoulder in a stupor. "Hey," André said. The DI lunged at him, spewing expletives at volumes that scraped at André's eardrums. After that interruption, the lecture resumed. Out of the corner of his eye, André saw the sick guy weirding out again, swaying this way and that with drooping eyelids. *He's fuckin' fallin' asleep*, André thought, *and they bust* my *ass!* It was practically the only time he'd spoken to another recruit, and it had gotten him in trouble.

"How about you, recruit?" the lieutenant said, pointing at the sleeping white guy. André smiled.

"Stempel!" rang out like a shot, and so did a burst of laughter from the group. "You stupid shit!" the DI shouted. He stepped high over men sitting cross-legged and stood over the poor dozing bastard. "Did we not give you enough sleep last night, Stempel? Is that what it is? So you just decided to nap your way through the most important fucking lecture *in your short and miserable life*?"

Everyone laughed again.

"What the hell are you laughing at?" the DI shouted, spinning on the forty seated men. The sergeant—fists balled and spine coiled—menaced the now unsmiling platoon. "You're a *unit,* and this son of a bitch is *in it*? Those friendly casualties the lieutenant is warning about is *you*! You think it's funny that Stempel here won't know jack about the fundamental safety procedures of a high-powered assault rifle?"

Everyone glared at the scrawny kid.

"Twenty push-ups!" the DI boomed. Stempel started to assume the push-up position, but the DI shouted, "Not *you,* Stempel! Everybody else! Gimme twenty! Count 'em!"

"One!" André yelled amid the other voices as he pressed his chest to the dirt. "Two!"

"*Now*, Stempel," the DI announced loudly, "I want *you* to laugh!" André kept counting. "*Laugh, goddammit!*" the DI screamed. Stempel started to laugh insincerely. "*Louder!*" With Stempel laughing, his fellow recruits did twenty push-ups. Many barely completed their last few, and others gathered around to shout encouragement. André finished and sat quietly, waiting. When done, Stempel was ordered to stand.

"Now, recruit," the lieutenant said, "why don't you give me the nomenclature of the M-16A1 rifle?"

The sickly Stempel belted out the words. "Sir, the M-16A1 assault rifle is a 5.56-millimeter, magazine-fed, shoulder-fired, gas-operated assault rifle capable of semiautomatic fire or three-round bursts through use of a selector switch . . . *sir*!" The instructor sat him down and resumed his lecture.

"I'm only gonna do this twice—once at regular speed, once more slowly!" He laid the rifle on a metal table. "To field-strip the M-16 rifle, you remove the magazine." The empty black box dropped into his hand. "Release the charging handle. Pull the charging handle to the rear." He slid a black metal piece toward the butt. "Remove the charging handle by pulling down and to the rear." It came off in his hand. "Push out the retaining pin"—which was tiny—"and drop out the firing pin." A single dart-shaped object came out. "Rotate the bolt to the right until the cam pin is clear of the bolt carrier key." The instructor lost André completely. "Rotate the cam pin one quarter turn and remove. Pull the bolt from the bolt carrier." The pieces were spread all over the table. "Hold the extractor down to control spring tension. Carefully push out the extractor pin and remove the extractor." A long spring that the lieutenant handled with care slid out with a piece of metal stuck in it. Each part had a name. The lieutenant went on and on.

André looked at the faces of the others for reassurance that no one else understood what the lieutenant was talking about when he saw Stempel's eyes. They were thick with tears and his nose was running.

LONDON, ENGLAND
October 2, 2100 GMT (2100 Local)

He pulled the van up to the manhole cover on the side street. He carefully lined the vehicle up with minute turns of the wheel and releases of the brake. When the spot was just right, he put the van in park and applied the hand brake. He twisted around and rapped on the wall with his knuckles. The narrow street was deserted. There had only been nine attacks in London proper since the "go" order had been given, including a Wembley Stadium job he himself had done. But people were still staying home at night.

A single thud vibrated through the floorboards of the old Volkswagen. After a few seconds a distant boom broke the peace of the evening. "Down ten, left twenty." The words came quickly over the radio in Russian. In back, his partners had to turn two knobs on the mortars' aiming mechanisms to adjust the fire—one click of the elevation knob, two of the azimuth. Another thud shook the vehicle. He heard the first wails of a siren in the distance.

Another boom jarred the night. "Fire for effect," came the radio call from the spotter. The back of the van came alive with thuds as the mortar men began firing through the open roof. These were not the light sixty- and eighty-millimeter hand-carried mortars. They were huge 120-millimeter tubes and projectiles. The rounds would be penetrating the roof of Number 10 Downing Street and exploding on the lower floors of the prime minister's residence.

Through the windshield he saw a bobby stop at the corner, then take off running. He cursed, threw open his door, and raced down the street with his machine pistol. When he rounded the corner, the policeman was nowhere to be seen. He slowed to a walk down the deserted city street. The front stoops of the row houses jutted out onto the sidewalk. He passed the first set of stairs with great care. The shadows on the opposite side were empty. He passed another. Nobody.

As he reached the third, he stopped. He had a feeling,

an internal estimate of the distance a fleeing man could have run. He raised the machine pistol, holding it one-handed into the air with his elbow bent.

He edged his way around the stoop. A dark figure squatted in the shadows. The bobby raised his head and then his useless billy club. He wasn't one of the new special squads. He had no gun.

Even as he leveled his weapon on the man, a wave of disgust washed over him. The bobby shied away, his back pressing against the painted bricks behind him.

I could let the man go.

The thought surprised him. It had come from nowhere. The two of them remained there—motionless, silent—as he turned the thought around and around in his head. He inspected it from all angles.

But why? came the response every time.

Fire blazed from the end of the machine pistol, lighting the darkness and sending the bobby sprawling.

JFK AIRPORT, NEW YORK
October 6, 1500 GMT (1000 Local)

"Hey, Kate," Woody said, gently shaking her. Kate Dunn opened her eyes. Bright sunshine streamed through the plane's window. They were parked on the airport tarmac. She was lying on her side and curled up in her window seat under a blanket. She felt a rush of excitement on arriving back in the States.

"We're home?" she said sleepily, turning to face Woody. The plane was empty save for two men in dark suits who stood over them. Woody sat there with his blanket pulled up under his chin.

"Looks like we've got some kind of official welcoming committee from Uncle Sam," Woody said. His eyes were puffy. He'd obviously slept through the landing too. He looked up at the two men. "I have nothing to declare."

"Would you two please come with us," one of the men said. He perfunctorily flashed a badge in a leather folder, which flopped open and closed in one motion.

"Hey, hey!" Woody said. "Not so fast. Lemme see that again."

The dour man's face showed a hint of a frown as he retrieved the wallet from his jacket. He flicked it open again and lowered it to Woody's face. Woody perused the FBI ID then turned to Kate. "Looks real to me."

They rose and collected their things. "Look, I've been through this before," Woody said as he pulled his camera bags from the overhead compartment. They were plastered with bright green decals in the shape of marijuana leaves. "I knew Jimmy Hoffa, *okay*? We had a little falling-out, that's all. But those garbage bags I dumped in the Gulf of Mexico were just some animal carcasses I'd picked up on the highway. I had nothing to do with any CIA contract killing, okay? Not that I'm saying the CIA killed him, mind you."

"Woody," Kate chided, but it did no good. Woody was having too much fun.

"Say," Woody continued, motioning the agent closer. "Is it true what I heard about J. Edgar Hoover?" he whispered. "That he was partial to dark, solid colors and the layered look because of his weight problem?" The two agents eyed each other, apparently vying to see who could appear more indifferent. "I mean sure, I understand that when he foofed up for parties and things that he'd make a statement with some florals or, like, a hot-pink one-piece thing. But, you know, for business I bet he was pretty conservative. Flats, no heels, right?" He grinned and nodded his head, pointing at the agent. "Am I right?"

"Let's go," was all the man said.

Woody kept up the running barbs on the private jet all the way to Washington. The agents had told them nothing other than their destination and that they just wanted to ask them some questions. "Man," Woody said, eyeing the small, well-appointed jet, "your tax dollars at work. Does this thing have a bidet?"

Kate tried her best just to tune him out, but grew more and more annoyed as the flight wore on. She knew it was his way of dealing with power. She had seen him try the same shit with Russian police, with varying degrees of success. When confronted with authority figures who robbed him of control, Woody just peppered them with comments, pinpricks in the elephant's hide. He was convinced that, sooner or later, he would gain the upper hand by so annoying them that they lost their cool.

"You know you really shouldn't wear navy with"—he nodded and made a face—"you know"—he nodded again and then leaned forward—"your dandruff problem," he whispered. The two agents sat stony-faced across a coffee table, facing Kate and Woody. The agent to whom Woody spoke smirked. But sure enough he shortly stole a quick glance at his shoulder. Woody tapped the side of Kate's leg with his knuckles. He thought he was getting somewhere now.

"Man, it's been a long time since I've been to D.C.," Woody said to Kate, then turned back to the agents—grinning. "It was back during the Iran-Contra hearings. I got some photos with a telephoto lens of Oliver North watering his lawn. He was wearing a T-shirt that had an American flag on it and the words 'These colors don't run.' " He grinned at the two men. "Get it? 'These *colors* don't *run*'?"

"I get it," the agent said. The flatness of his voice and his completely stern look signaled to Kate that he was ready to take offense.

"Pretty witty, don't ya think? Double entendre." Woody was grinning his stupid smile. "That's French."

"I know what it is."

"Do you speak foreign languages?" The man said nothing. Woody maintained a broad smile on a tanned face framed with long, graying hair tied in a ponytail. The government agent, many years younger, had short hair, pale skin, and no smile. "You don't, do you?" Woody asked. "That's really pretty provincial of you. I mean, it kind of makes you, like, the ugly American."

"Woody," Kate said.

"But, I mean," he objected, holding out his hand palm up to display the agent for Kate's inspection, "*look* at him. He went to some podunk community college. Took English lit courses he should've taken in high school and they give him a degree. Gets a gun courtesy of the U.S. government. Buys a three-hundred-dollar suit from some warehouse outlet. Thinks he's hit the big time. But he doesn't even speak any foreign languages."

"Leave him alone," Kate urged.

"You wouldn't even know what somebody said to you in a foreign language, would you? Could be 'Gee, Mr. Officer, you look swell today.' Or could be something else. Like . . . *'Yob tvoyu mat.'*"

The agent's leg uncrossed and he leaned forward. The other agent backhanded the man's chest to restrain him.

Woody was grinning ear to ear now. He leaned over to Kate, his eyes still on the angry agent. "They're not FBI. They're CIA. They're taking us to Langley, I'll bet you a hundred bucks."

"What the hell are you talking about?" Kate asked.

"It's an old trick. The CIA is prohibited by law from operating in the States, so they gin up these FBI badges and keep right on going."

"Jesus, Woody. You've got this paranoid conspiracy crap oozing out your ears."

"Or, they might be FBI—technically—but they're really CIA."

"Where in the world are you getting this shit?"

"They speak Russian, Kate," he said, finally turning to her. "The guy got pissed when I said 'Fuck your mother' in Russian. Now how many run-of-the-mill, gumshoe G-men do you think take all that time and effort to learn Russian, huh? You mark my words, we're headin' straight for Langley."

The nondescript government car pulled up to the main gate at the CIA headquarters in Langley, Virginia. Instead of heading for the front door, however, they pulled around to an underground parking garage.

Woody looked like the cat who ate the canary. He had turned toward Kate and arched his eyebrows at every turn the car had made on their trip out. He'd backhanded her repeatedly and pointed as the highway signs led ever closer. She had finally withdrawn her shoulder and said, "Cut it *out*!" Now he just sat there, loving every minute of what he viewed as a triumph over "The Man."

They were whisked inside the building and into a long, antiseptic corridor. There were no names on the doors. No signs directing people to different departments. "Where do you do all those LSD experiments?" Woody asked as they went through a set of double doors. They opened automatically, as in a hospital, and the small group entered another featureless hallway. "You know when I read about those experiments I sent an application to you guys volunteering for the program, but I never heard back."

They reached a T-shaped intersection. Sets of closed double doors led off in opposite directions.

"This way, please," one of the agents said. He took Kate by the elbow and headed to the right.

The other agent was taking Woody to the left.

"Don't tell them anything, comrade!" Woody called out to Kate as their respective doors opened. "Long live the party!" The doors closed behind them.

The "FBI agent" who escorted Kate did, she noticed, seem to know his way through the maze of corridors in the basement. He stopped at a door with the number "141" on it and knocked, waiting a moment before opening it.

She had expected a bare, concrete room with a single metal table, two chairs, and a harsh, bright light overhead. Instead, several men and two women rose from the sofas and chairs around the carpeted room. It looked more like the "Green Room" at a network television studio than an interrogation cell. There were even hors d'oeuvres on the coffee table and a small bar/kitchenette off to the side.

"Hello, Miss Dunn," a middle-aged woman in a business

suit said as she held out her hand. Most of the men and women wore plastic IDs pinned to their lapels. Some did not. "My name is Eve Fitzgerald," she said. "I'll be your liaison during your visit to Langley, which we really don't expect will take more than a few hours." She began the introductions. Somebody from "State." Somebody from the White House. The names went in one ear and out the other, but Kate saw their names were all conveniently printed in large letters on their shiny "Visitor" IDs.

The introductions did not include the several men who wore no IDs. And none of the people other than Eve were introduced as being from the CIA. Kate was having fun now. It was like a movie.

They poured Kate the tea she requested, and she settled onto a sofa. "You understand, Ms. Dunn," Eve said, "that our conversations will be recorded." Kate nodded. "And you consent to that recording?"

Kate chuckled. "This sounds like you're reading me my Miranda rights or something."

Eve smiled graciously. "Nothing you say here, I assure you, can legally be used by the U.S. government in any court. As a matter of fact," she said, smiling, "if you want to establish immunity from prosecution for failure to pay income taxes or something, you should go ahead and blurt it out now."

Several of the people in the room laughed, and it broke the ice somewhat. "I hope you don't give my cameraman Woody the same opportunity," Kate said with a smile. "We could be here several days while he confesses." There was more laughter. "But, in answer to your question, I consent to the taping or whatever."

"Wonderful. And let me take this opportunity to thank you for your cooperation. I know you must be tired, but we appreciate your agreeing to meet with us on such short notice."

Kate decided to let the comment pass. She could only imagine what kind of time Woody was giving them.

"Can I ask you, if you don't mind," Kate said, "just what it is I'm doing here?"

"Certainly, Ms. Dunn," a man seated directly across the coffee table from her replied. "There's really nothing all that secret about this, although we would like to get your agreement that everything that we ask you—the entire fact of your visit here—be held in confidence. That, I should say, *would* be a legally binding agreement."

He was so polite—they were all so friendly—that Kate almost reciprocated, but she hesitated. "Well, I'm not . . . I'm not sure I want to do that," she said. They stared at her in silence now. She felt their disappointment—their disapproval. They were being so nice, and she wasn't returning the courtesy.

The man with no name tag seated across from her nodded. "Very well. That is your right." He looked at another man—also anonymous—in the chair next to him.

The new mystery man said, "Ms. Dunn, we have all followed your reporting from Moscow with interest. The quality of it, let me say first off, is excellent. You seem to possess a rare blend, an ability to fact-find, together with a grasp of the broader perspective on the events unfolding around you. You are to be commended, and that comes from people who have spent a lifetime of judging the quality of information content."

Heads nodded all around, but no one else spoke. "Thank you," Kate said.

"Of particular interest, obviously, given what's going on in Russia today, have been your reports on the Anarchists. Especially your reports on a . . . Valentin Kartsev." Kate nodded. That would make sense. Still, on hearing Kartsev's name she felt a slight chill. "Can we get you something?" the obviously attentive interrogator asked.

"No," Kate said, embarrassed at being so transparent. "I'm fine."

The man cleared his throat. Kate looked for—but couldn't find—the camera. "We're going to ask you a series of questions. Most of them will be very innocuous—minor things about Mr. Kartsev that you may find amusing because of their seeming insignificance. And most will, quite honestly, be unimportant. But we ask them anyway because you never know when some little piece will fit and be useful. You understand?'' Kate nodded. ''But first, since most of the people present here are not going to stay long, I'm going to call your attention to the trip you took with Mr. Kartsev to the Siberian training camp.'' Kate nodded again, swallowing the lump in her throat. ''We are all familiar with your report on that trip. What we're interested in is this. When you left for your return to Moscow, was Mr. Kartsev still there at the camp?''

All eyes were on Kate now. She shrugged and nodded. ''I never got out of the car. Kartsev got out, said something to the driver, and then the car left him there to take me back to the airfield.''

''Excuse me,'' someone said from off to the side. ''Is this the car?'' he asked. He rounded the sofa and showed Kate a photo of the limousine. It had been taken from directly overhead and appeared to be in black-and-white. ''It could be, yes.''

The man returned to the wings, and Kate's questioner continued. ''What was Mr. Kartsev doing when you last saw him? Did you see where he headed after you parted?''

Kate shook her head, as much to rid herself of her recollection of that unpleasant night as in reply to the question.

Another glossy, eight-by-ten photograph was presented to her. The shot was also from directly overhead. It showed a complex of nondescript buildings visible through the canopy of trees. ''Can you tell where the car was when Kartsev got out?'' her interrogator asked.

She grasped the edge of the photograph, squinting as she searched for some landmark. There was a gravel road and a white windowless building. It seemed whiter where the spotlights were.

''That building,'' she said, pointing for the man holding the photo. ''That one right there.''

''C-nineteen,'' he said to her questioner. The man excused himself and joined a small group of people at the bar where they leaned over a sheaf of papers. The room was nearly empty within minutes. All politely bade her farewell. Only her "liaison" and two others remained. They asked her question after question for hours.

It was all very odd. The next few questions all centered on the flash and thunder of the attack. They were trying to gauge how far she had traveled when the bombs had fallen—how much time had elapsed since Kartsev had been let out.

"You think he's dead, don't you?" Kate finally asked. "Your bombs hit that building, and you think you killed him."

They didn't answer.

PHILADELPHIA, PENNSYLVANIA
October 10, 0000 GMT (1900 Local)

There was a knock at the door. Pyotr Andreev saw that it was one of the men from the neighborhood watch and unbolted the numerous locks.

"Pete! We got trouble, and the police ain't here yet. There's three guys in the parking garage wearing all that black getup. Anarchists!"

Pyotr handed their pistol to a frightened Olga and took the shotgun. "Jesus," the man said as he stared at the pump. The two men wound their way through the building. The ground floor of the three-level garage seemed quiet. "They were on the second floor," the man whispered. Pyotr led the way to the stairwell.

"Oh, there they are!" the old woman who organized the group called out. Pyotr cringed on hearing her loud voice. She approached, waving at Pyotr, who was crouched at the bottom of the steps. "Marge!" Pyotr's partner hissed. "Shhh! For God's sake!" Pyotr sighed.

Before the others arrived, Pyotr whispered, "You stay here. Make sure nobody goes down or comes up." He headed up the rusty metal stairs. His running shoes made no sound at all. A car alarm suddenly went off. He hurried up the last few steps, his progress masked by the strident alarm.

The three "Anarchists" were breaking into a sports car.

Two black youths were crammed into the front seat, the third was keeping watch. As Pyotr crept his way in a crouch toward the three men, the alarm fell silent. Bumper by bumper Pyotr closed on the car. He took one final check of the scene, then rose. The shotgun was on his shoulder and aimed at the lone sentry's chest. When the young man saw the ten-gauge's muzzle, his eyes widened in holy terror. "Hey! Hey!" he shouted, holding up his hands and revolver in plea.

"Freeze!" Pyotr shouted. "If you move, I will kill you!" The other two kids rose up from the car. "Freeze! Freeze! Freeze!" Pyotr shouted repeatedly trying to get control through intimidation. They slowly raised their hands into the air. They wore black, like Anarchists. Black overcoats. *But why were they breaking into a car?* Pyotr wondered.

"Hey, man, just be cool," one of the boys said. Their coats splayed out around them like capes.

"Move away from the car! Move! Move! Move!" Pyotr shouted.

"Yeah-yeah!" one kid said, his posture more relaxed after seeing that Pyotr was all alone. "Anything you say, man." His arms sagged, and he stood unmoving beside the car.

"Get out here!" Pyotr shouted again.

"Yeah, man, sure," the kid said, casually edging closer to Andreev. "Say, man—" he began.

"Stop! Don't move!"

"Listen, blood," the guy said, gradually lowering his arms, a friendly grin spread wide on his face. He drew closer and closer. Pyotr considered one last warning, but a quick check revealed the other two spreading out and slowly lowering their arms.

Pyotr squeezed the trigger. With a thunderous roar the shotgun hammered his shoulder. The shot caught the boy squarely in the thigh. He was blown backward onto the hood of the sports car. As Pyotr pumped the shotgun, the boom echoed through the concrete garage. When he spun the gun to the other two, he saw that they stood frozen with their arms stretched up to full extension.

The door to the police station's interrogation room opened. A graying officer in a well-pressed business suit interrupted the questioning.

"All right," he said, "you can go."

The detective who had been interviewing Pyotr said, "But I'm not through here yet."

"He's outta here. The investigation's closed."

"What the hell does that—"

"It's *closed*, Kozlowsky!" The detective sat silently for a moment, then slammed his notebook shut. His chair scraped noisily across the floor. The two men eyed each other before the detective headed out, leaving Pyotr alone with the older man. "You can go, cowboy," he said, not a trace of civility in his voice.

"Is that all?" Pyotr asked. "I am free?"

"You can *go*, so *go*!"

When Pyotr headed out the door, the cop grabbed his arm roughly. Through gritting teeth he muttered, "Don't shoot anybody else in this town, you hear?" The grip was painfully tight. The cop sent him on his way with a push.

As Pyotr walked through the open room filled with plain-clothesmen, eyes followed him surreptitiously. The buzz of activity quieted a bit as Andreev passed.

Olga and the girls wrapped themselves around him. Olga cried inside his hug, and the girls squealed in joy at the return of their father. Pyotr's eyes, however, scanned the uniformed officers behind the counter. Several looked away quickly. Something was up.

7

"Come on, Stempel!" Harold heard from a dozen voices. He tried desperately to recover as he dangled under the taught rope by his hands and locked heels. He had crawled halfway across the water obstacle, and now he was in dire trouble.

"You can do it, come on!" urged the fellow recruits in his training platoon.

Stempel struggled with all his might. But his arms, already aching from the exercise, were quivering. His heels slipped out of their clench. Now it was all he could do to keep the toes of his boots over the rope.

"Stem-p-e-e-l!" came the unmistakable voice of Staff Sergeant Giles. "Git over here! You're holdin' up the whole goddamn platoon!"

Stempel's toes both gave way. He swung down and barely hung on by his fingers. The rope was swinging and shaking. Another recruit behind him was holding on to the rope for dear life.

"Stempel! What the hell're you doin'?" Giles screamed. "Jesus H. Christ, son!"

Harold knew all was lost now. His arms squeezed his head. He couldn't draw enough air, and he began to grow faint. The yelling continued, but through his popping ears all he could hear was a droning noise of unintelligible shouts.

He tried one last time—not with the thought of succeeding, but to show he had made the effort. Bringing his knees up and dropping them, he began to rock and bicycle kick through midair. His grip on the rope was down to the last joints of his fingers, and they were frozen in icy pain.

"A-a-ah!" he grunted as he kicked one heel up toward the rope. He floated as he spun through air. A stunning crash of water engulfed him. It rushed in a burning flood up his nose. He fought to regain his equilibrium. He opened his eyes underwater and saw light between his knees. He spun and propelled himself for the surface.

Bursting out of the water, he spluttered and gasped for air. His back stung terribly from the flop. He thrashed at the water for balance.

"Stempel, git the hell over here!" the DI shouted.

Harold lowered his head and swam. In desperation his hands clawed at the mud. With his next breath he took in a watery gulp. He coughed and spit and coughed. A yank on his blouse tugged him onto dry land.

Sergeant Giles stood in the knee-deep water. "Stempel! *Git on yer fuckin' feet!*" Stempel rose in utter exhaustion. "Hands on yer head!"

Stempel complied, still fighting the dizziness. His platoon was urging the next man to shore. But some of the fire had gone out of their shouts. By falling, Stempel had lost the tight race with a rival platoon. They paid Harold no attention whatsoever.

Sergeant Giles stepped in front of Harold. With his face close and his voice low, he said, "You quit on me, boy."

"N-no, Sergeant! No!" Stempel spluttered, his hands still on his head.

"You quit on yer buddies, Stempel. That makes you a quitter. You know what quitters are when they're in the army, Recruit? Yella-bellies. They run out and leave their buddies to die so they can save their own hides. They're cowards, Private Stempel. Cowards.'' The tears welled up from Stempel's chest, and he tried desperately to stem the tide. His lips grew strained and his jaw quivered. He fought to maintain some semblance of composure, but his body betrayed him. ''You let yer buddies down,'' the DI continued. ''You're dead now. You're no good to yer country, you're no good to the army, but most importantly, Stempel, you ain't no good to yer buddies no more. You let 'em down. Go on back and change yer gear, Stempel. Hell, take the whole day off and think about it awhile.''

Stempel hesitated.

''Go *on*!'' Giles barked.

Stempel turned and trotted off with his hands locked over his head like a prisoner, glad to be free of the DI. Tears poured down his face. Looking back, he saw the rest of his platoon race on to the next obstacle, a tall wall over which hung a rope. They would all make it over the way they were trained—as a team, each helping the others. As much as Stempel hated every second of every day of training, he hated one thing more. He hated the thought of sitting on his bunk in the barracks all day waiting for the doors to burst open upon his platoon's return. He wasn't a part of them. They could cut it, but he couldn't.

''Faulk! Git over here!'' Sergeant Giles boomed.

The remainder of his platoon filed into the barracks. André hustled over to the drill instructor. The sun was setting, and this was the only fifteen minutes of the day they had to themselves. Every bone in his body ached, but he braced himself for another physically demanding waste of time.

''You and Stempel are both from New York, aren't you?'' the sergeant asked in a strangely civil tone.

''Uh—I dunno, Staff Sergeant!'' Faulk shouted.

''You don't know where you're from?''

''No, Staff Sergeant! I mean, I don't know where Private Stempel is from, Staff Sergeant!''

"Well, apparently you're both from New York City, so I'm gonna buddy you two up." He looked up at André, measuring his reaction. "You know what that means?"

"No, Staff Sergeant!"

"That means I'm makin' you responsible for gettin' Stempel through basic." He again paused, again studying André's face. André sensed that Giles was waiting, and searched his mind for some response. Giles wasn't asking him to take care of Stempel. He was ordering him to.

"Yes, Staff Sergeant!"

Giles nodded. "All right, then. Get on in there and get cleaned up. Dismissed."

André took a step back, did a crisp about-face, and ran toward the old wooden steps of the barracks. It was only after he got inside, passing the men standing naked or wrapped in a towel in line for the showers, that he began to get pissed about the order. By the time he passed Stempel's bunk, he was totally outraged. What the hell did the DI expect? What the hell could André do?

Stempel was filthy. He sat on the floor so as not to soil the tightly tucked white sheets of his bunk. He must have been there for hours. He picked lethargically at the knotted laces on his boots. He seemed resigned to being trapped forever inside the waterlogged footgear. He slowly looked up at André. On catching his eyes, he lowered his gaze and wrapped his arms around his knees, hugging them to his chest.

André knelt and patiently unraveled the knot.

CINCINNATI, OHIO
October 18, 1900 GMT (1400 Local)

"As this administration has shown," President Marshall shouted in a rousing climax, "we will *not* tolerate lawlessness in our streets! We will put a *stop* to that violence, no matter where the mission takes us, and no matter how hard that mission is! God bless the United States!" With a wave, he stepped down from the podium and into the open arms of an aide.

"I'm sorry to disturb you, sir!" the man yelled over the cheers and the marching band. Marshall held up a finger for the man to wait and stepped back up to give another wave. The roar of the crowd rose higher again. "Sir! I've got a message from the secretary of state." Marshall followed him through some cloth partitions. "Secretary Jensen just got a communication from Beijing! The Chinese ambassador paid a visit to the State Department on very short notice and delivered it verbally!"

The scene was a hubbub of noise and activity, and Marshall was totally distracted. He smiled and winked at the VIPs who still applauded as they watched him from the dais. "Sir!" the junior national security staffer called out. "The ambassador demanded that UNRUSFOR get out of Siberia in thirty days!"

Marshall turned back to him and cupped his ear. *"What?"* He was incensed. "Well, *fuck* them! I hope Jensen kicked their butts right out of the fucking building!" The staffer shrugged. "He *did* tell them to go to hell, didn't he?"

"I think, sir, the secretary wanted to speak to you before replying."

Marshall snorted, shaking his head as he felt the anger well up to new dimensions. His secretary of state was a gutless bastard. *I've got to fire his ass!* Marshall decided. He ached to do it right away. To pick up the phone, unload on the son of a bitch, and be done with it. But it wouldn't look good. He'd have to wait till after the election.

"Secretary Jensen *did* say that there was something stilted, formal in the ambassador's manner! He was communicating something with the utmost care and precision! The entire delegation appeared uncomfortable—like they were apologetic! Secretary Jensen thinks they may be signaling something about Taiwan!"

"What in the *hell* makes him think *that?*"

"The Chinese ambassador and his aides were wearing morning suits, sir, with tails, top hat, everything."

Marshall didn't need to be told the significance of that

news. Formal diplomatic communications come with certain trappings. On December 7, 1941, Japanese diplomats had arrived at the State Department wearing morning suits.

Marshall sat by the speakerphone in his hotel suite. He was surrounded by campaign staffers who were fascinated by the excitement of the conference call but had absolutely nothing to contribute.

"Our best analysis," Secretary of State Jensen said, "is that it's part of a power struggle in Beijing. Some faction is trying to garner support from the nationalists by talking tough on our Siberian deployment. And let's not forget how this plays among the Chinese populace. It's an authoritarian regime, but the faction that can claim popular support for their policies has an advantage in the political infighting."

"Okay," Marshall interrupted. "Just who is it we're dealing with over there?"

"It's really impossible to know," Jensen replied. Marshall rolled his eyes to the amusement of his campaign aides. "The preeminent power in China remains Lin Tsochang. In early August, several dailies across China reported that Mr. Lin's title would be elevated from its current 'Paramount Leader' to the exalted 'Chairman.' That, of course, is closely associated with Chairman *Mao,* who remains almost a deity in China. But, after the articles appeared, nothing more was heard. Since then, our official contacts we have still referred to Mr. Lin as '*Paramount Leader.*'"

Marshall waited. Finally, he said, "And . . . ?" to still more amusement in his hotel suite.

"Well, obviously it was a trial balloon that didn't fly. While Mr. Lin is hardly a liberal reformer, he was associated with a series of—quote, unquote—'liberal' decisions with respect to Hong Kong. The decision to allow opposition newspapers to reopen. An end to censorship of the local movie theaters. Withdrawal of those proposed restrictions on foreign travel by Hong Kong residents that sent such a scare through the population."

One of Marshall's senior staffers tapped his wristwatch. He had a photo op at a day-care center run by a consortium of local businesses with no federal government help. Then a swing by a local factory making digital video disks. Then a fund-raiser for a struggling Democratic congressman— one of the two dinners he had planned for the evening.

"Okay, Hugh, let's cut to the chase. In ten words or less, who are we dealing with, and what do they want?"

"Well, there's Lin Tsochang, who's head of state, commander-in-chief of the military, and general secretary of the Communist Party. He's clearly the most powerful man in government, but he's in his mid-eighties and in failing health. Arrayed against him is just about everyone else in the 'younger' generation—men in their late sixties. There's the chief of the 'State Council'—their prime minister—who runs the government day to day. He's gone on record calling for a new 'Cultural Revolution' to rid China of Western pornography and materialism. There's also the chairman of the National People's Congress—their speaker of the house—who's just to the right of Genghis Khan. Then there's the president—Mr. Lin's chosen successor. He personally ordered the riot police to Beijing University during the protests in August, killing sixty students. All those men are trying to outdo one another to establish their reactionary credentials to the seven-member Politburo and the much larger Central Committee and, through them, the fifty-million-member Communist Party. Every five years they hold party congresses. The sixteenth is only two years away, so it's the beginning of their campaign season. They have a very complex political system that we get little insight into. For instance, the party bosses in Beijing, Shanghai, and Hong Kong all have extensive power and—"

"Okay, Hugh," Marshall said, cutting him short. "Boil it all down for me. What's going on in Beijing?"

"It's probably a power play by nationalists, who want to be seen as righting the wrongs committed against a weak China by a stronger West. They view Mr. Lin and his supporters as vulnerable on the issue, and that's why this is dangerous, Mr. President. Mr. Lin will have to steal the wind from their sails by adopting even more nationalistic policies.'' The pollsters, briefers, speechwriters, and spin men in the room around Marshall were all nodding. ''He'll have to take a harder line, or we'll be staring across the table at dyed-in-the-wool hard-liners.''

''So you're saying I have to worry about an international political confrontation,'' Marshall recapped, ''solely as a result of *domestic* political developments in China?''

''All politics is local, Mr. President.''

KHABAROVSK, SIBERIA
October 22, 1430 GMT (0430 Local)

''General Clark.''

Nate Clark opened his eyes and rolled his boots to the floor. He slept in his fatigues even in his headquarters. It didn't feel right otherwise. He clicked on the lamp next to his bed. Major Reed stood beside his cot.

''What is it?'' Nate asked.

''It's the Chinese, sir. I think you'd better come down to the op center.''

''We've been monitoring these broadcasts for several hours,'' Clark's intelligence officer said. The British colonel and Clark stood over a shortwave radio. The bulky green device emitted the whiny and distant voice of a Chinese broadcaster speaking in a shrill and strident tone. ''They've been blitzing the airwaves with propaganda about the evils of capitalism—Taiwan- *and* Hong Kong–style. The addition of Hong Kong is new. We haven't made that one out yet. Then, a short while ago, all the television and radio stations broadcasting out of Hong Kong either switched to patriotic music or went off the air. The intelligence consensus appears to be that they are planning some sort of move. It may already have started.''

Clark locked his gaze on the man. ''Are they coming our way?''

A look of concern settled on his face. "They've certainly been building. Latest force strength estimates put the front-line units in Manchuria at eighty percent, up from sixty-five. But"—he shook his head—"my guess is no. They've only got thirty days' war stocks in the north, and their transport in-theater wouldn't allow for any large-scale operations without unacceptably lengthy halts for resupply."

"So what, then?" Clark asked.

The man shrugged. "Something else. I don't know what. But something is up."

Clark headed straight for his office, closed the door, and got on the secure phone. When General Dekker finally answered, Clark could tell that he'd been asleep. "I need one heavy division at Khabarovsk," Clark demanded, "and one marine division at Vladivostok. I need two air wings *on* the ground in Siberia—not four hours away in Japan. And I need your *personal* pledge to me that if the PLA begins to stage in north China, you'll back me to the hilt when I request either *three* times that many men, or that we pull out of Siberia altogether."

There was a long delay, much longer than necessary for the satellite relay. When Dekker replied, he didn't ask for an explanation. He had obviously been watching things in the Far East closely.

"You got it, Nate. I'll call in the staff tonight and take it to Himself in the morning. I'll get you the Big Red One—1st Infantry Division—and the 3rd Marine from Okinawa. We won't leave you out there by yourself. You've got my word on that."

When Clark hung up, he sat there in the quiet of the former Soviet military base ten thousand miles from home. His mind's eye roamed the frigid wastes of Asia. The tiny pockets of humanity that were his troops were scattered, isolated, vulnerable. They were no match even for random mortar attacks, much less for . . . what? For the Chinese?

Would two additional divisions do the trick? Six? Sixteen?

He hit the intercom button. "Get me Major Reed," he said to the man.

• • •

Nate Clark had led a mechanized infantry division into combat in the Persian Gulf. Of all the briefings, planning sessions, and operations and logistics reviews that led up to their attack into Iraq, none had been like this one. An oppressive weight hung over the large conference table around which were gathered senior officers of half a dozen nations.

Major Chuck Reed, Jr., rose. He was easily two pay grades the junior of any other officer in the room. He was also the best briefer Clark had ever run across. "The People's Liberation Army," Reed began, "is trained to hold fire and fight close in. That reduces the advantages of superior enemy weapons and brings to bear the Chinese advantage in numbers. But the Chinese tactics require extreme confidence and courage in their troops. They are an infantry army. Their spirit—their willingness to fight, to sacrifice, to die—is the key to their effectiveness. Lin Piao—Mao's defense minister—used to say that at ranges under two hundred meters, the PLA was the equal of any army in the world. To defeat the PLA, therefore, UNRUSFOR would have to win the war beyond two hundred meters. We would have to shatter the confidence, the courage, the morale of their troops before they get into range of small-arms fire, or risk being overwhelmed by an attack in the main."

The attention of the room was riveted on the junior officer. The normal order of a briefing—"METT"—had gone straight to "Enemy" and noticeably skipped the first subject "Mission." That was left to the defense ministries in Europe and North America, and defining UNRUSFOR's mission was looming as a monumental task.

"The PLA has three million men under arms," Reed continued. "They also have a militia variously estimated between seven- and twelve-million and fifteen special border divisions. Those have infantry capability but little integral heavy weapons or transport. The most recent battles fought in the theater began on March second, 1969, along the Ussuri River." Reed's silver-tipped pointer went to the

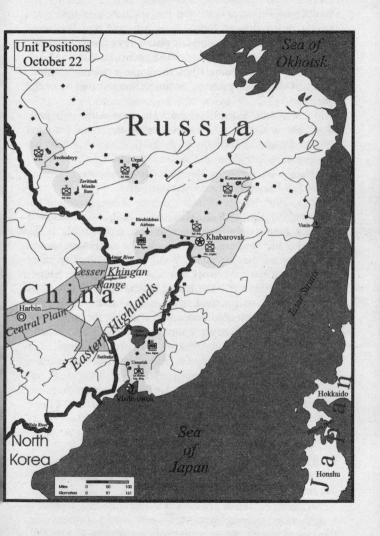

**Unit Positions
October 22**

Sea of
Okhotsk

Russia

Svobodnyy

Urgal

Zavitinsk
Missile
Base

Komsomolsk

Birobidzhan
Airbase

Khabarovsk

Amur River

Lesser Khingan
Range

Songhua River

China

Ussuri River

Harbin

Central Plain

Eastern Highlands

Tatar Straits

Suifenhe

Ussurisk

Vladivostok

North
Korea

Nalu River

Sea
of
Japan

Vanin

Hokkaido

Honshu

| Miles | 0 | 50 | 100 |
| Kilometers | 0 | 81 | 161 |

map. It ran north and south along the border between Vladivostok and Khabarovsk. On the Russian side there was strung tiny beads of blue—company- and battalion-sized units of German and Belgian paratroopers and American marines and support troops. ''The first two battles on March second and fourth were Chinese victories, killing almost a hundred Russian soldiers in small border outposts. On March fifteenth, however, the Russians moved heavy missile forces forward and fired across the border on a town deep inside China. The town was destroyed and several hundred Chinese civilians died. In total, the PLA lost approximately four thousand killed in combat.''

Heads were turned at the numbers of casualties incurred in such a low-intensity border skirmish.

''The PLA has two direct avenues of approach into the Russian Far East,'' Reed went on. ''Both would stage at Harbin. Both would have a single main supply route up the central plain. One turns east through the eastern highlands. It crosses the border in the Ussuri River valley north of Vladivostok but chokes off nicely at some mountain tunnels east of Suifenhe. It's the lesser threat. The other route is more difficult to interdict. It continues north through the Lesser Khingan Range and crosses the Amur to the west of Khabarovsk. There are enormous distances to defend.''

Reed waited as senior officers sketched their own maps. Clark watched. He knew what his subordinate commanders were experiencing emotionally. He'd lived it on nights, after duty hours . . . for months. He knew their study of Siberian maps. It was the study of distance. Of thinning lines. Of resources stretched due to nothing more than empty space. Their next question was universal, he was sure. *Are my people in harm's way?*

It was an attitude that would ensure defeat.

''Rates of advance?'' Nate asked Reed, although he'd already heard Reed's answer.

''A mechanized army with good engineering support— one hundred kilometers per day—except during severe winter conditions or the summer thaw and flooding. The *Chi-*

nese troops, however, are only motorized. They'd be slowed by their poor engineering support. They're transported by truck and dismount to fight, and those trucks are very soft targets. Attrition could reduce them to cross-country footslogging supplied only by strong backs and pack animals. At most they could make three kilometers per day. And keep in mind that without survivable tanks they'd have no way to rapidly reduce fortified positions.''

"Point one," Nate interrupted, "for you to take back up your chains of command. We need engineers. As many units as you can get out here. And I know that means call-ups. We'd probably call the entire army reserve and national guard. You know we won't lose Nine Corps to the Chinese. The U.S. Army does not lose an entire corps. So we need engineers to prepare positions. To map terrain obstacles. To build and maintain our road/rail network. And for engineering reconnaissance of the Chinese.''

"Without engineering," Reed said, "the *Chinese* would be canalized. Single echelons down a limited number of routes. With the exception of Lake Khanka—which is more trafficable—the infantry would have to chop those supply lines out of the forest. And vehicular traffic over makeshift roads would degrade them till they're impassable. Maintenance would tax engineering resources. When forward resupply grew infrequent, their momentum would be gone.''

"What about *our* engineering?" Clark asked.

"We need extensive surveying. But the most difficult engineering problems would be bridging the rivers between Vladivostok and Khabarovsk. So instead we'll use airmobile troops. We'll organize battalion or even brigade-strength raids. We'll choose the timing and stay till we win. Then we'll pull back and choose another mission. To maneuver, the *Chinese* would have to open trails twenty meters wide . . . with manpower. In the dead of winter. With total air supremacy by the enemy.''

Most kept their heads down. Their thoughts were probably of the mass death their operations would reap.

"The objective in the air is total victory," Reed said.

"Not a single Chinese plane flying in-theater, in fifteen days."

The talk went on. Commanders taking more control. Mixed accents but a common vocabulary. Easily understood talk of engineering maintenance. Elaborate directional aids for drivers sent through trackless forests on routes open day and night. Through blizzards that leave ten-foot snowdrifts. In the deep woods, the engineers proposed, they could build corduroy roads out of lumber. The armored people said no way. A battalion of tracks would destroy it completely. Better that their fighting vehicles knock down saplings. The engineers could improve from behind. But neither the Amur nor the Ussuri is fordable, the engineers reminded.

"But all those watercourses freeze in winter," Nate said. "The thickness supports vehicular traffic—even armored. That fact alone changes all our terrain analysis. In winter those water obstacles turn into supply routes paved in ice. It's in winter," he said slowly, "that we're vulnerable to Chinese attack."

WHITE HOUSE SITUATION ROOM
October 22, 1930 GMT (1430 Local)

Marshall had been awakened with the news. Thirteen Chinese missiles had struck Taiwan. Islands just offshore the mainland were being shelled. Plus Chinese soldiers were swarming all over Hong Kong. Beijing was silent as the troops went out of control. All the deals made with the city were being broken.

The president and junior staffers waited in the underground conference room.

"Why didn't we get some kind of intelligence warning?" Marshall asked. The captains and majors from the Military Office were mute. Several exchanged looks. "Or at least the British. The former prime minister assured me they still had good intelligence . . . before he was killed."

One of the army officers ventured an answer. "We

checked with the British, sir. The Chinese were in the middle of a troop rotation. Their handpicked special garrison was mainly kept in barracks. They were of the highest quality of soldiers. So the first warning the Brits got was when trucks came across from Shenzhen filled with ordinary infantry. They were armed and in combat gear.''

"First video is in, sir," a naval officer announced as he entered. He turned on the room's four screens. "We picked it up off Japanese TV."

Soldiers were smashing store windows with rifles. It didn't look organized to Marshall, but it did seem widespread. Boxes were being carted out of stores, presumably confiscated on authority of the army. Wheeled armored vehicles belched smoke on city streets. Civilians shook fists from doorways. Large helicopters swept in low over the sea. The video came to an end abruptly. It was replaced by color test bars.

Secretary of State Jensen arrived at the door.

"Can you believe this shit?" Marshall asked angrily.

"Could we clear the room?" Jensen asked.

The junior aides were all caught by surprise. Jensen and Marshall stared at each other in silence. When the door closed, Jensen took a deep breath. "We should get out of Siberia right now," he said. "Announce that we're going to step back from the confrontation with China. And if you don't agree, I'm going to have to tender my resignation."

Marshall was boiling. But he didn't so much as flinch. "Are you sure you mean that?" he asked.

"I've thought a lot about the direction of world events. I no longer feel I can lead your Department of State, sir."

I'm resigning, Marshall understood him to say. "Just where do you think we're headed, Hugh?"

"War!" Jensen blurted out. "We're headed for *war,* Tom. It's as plain as the nose on your face!"

"No, we're *not,* Hugh. I'll pull the plug before it gets that far. That was the plan all along. We're not there to fight for Russia's border. A few more months and we're out of there."

"This is our last warning from the Chinese," Hugh Jensen said calmly.

"The *Chinese*," Marshall replied loudly, "are kicking in *store* windows in Hong *Kong*! We'll *condemn* looting, Hugh, but by *God* we won't go to *war* over it. Hong Kong is *theirs*, for Christ's sake! What the hell can *I* do about it?"

Jensen looked up at the president. He wore a peculiar expression. "Tom, have you been briefed yet?"

"I've watched Japanese video from downtown Hong Kong with my own two *eyes*. What more do I need to—"

"No, I mean about Taiwan?"

Marshall stared back at him. "The missiles?"

Jensen rested his arms heavily on the table. It was as if he were physically exhausted.

"They've invaded, Tom. They've invaded Taiwan."

USS *LABOON*, STRAITS OF TAIWAN
October 23, 1730 GMT (0730 Local)

The scene was tense in the windowless Combat Information Center. But only a familiar eye could note the change to the darkened compartment. The sweat-soaked brow of the radarman. The sonarman whose hands pressed earphones to his head. The fire control coordinator hunched over his screen. The dark blue circle under the arm of the seaman first, who raised his fluorescent pen to draw targets on Lucite.

Lieutenant Commander Richards felt all the ship's systems. He was the captain, and they were his second skin. Situational awareness it was called. He sensed the direction in space of the F-14s that were swatting down MiGs by the dozen. The nearness of the noisy subs that were mere minutes from death. The distance of the Silkworm missiles that exploded harmlessly miles away.

But his mind was focused on a large round screen. The surface radar. The real danger, Richards knew, was in his ever-shortening range to the Chinese invasion fleet. The first landing the day before had drawn the Taiwanese Army to the west coast. This second and much larger force was circling the island to the northeast. It was aimed straight at the Taiwanese capital—Taipei.

"Any visual contact?" Richards asked his fire control coordinator.

"Negative, sir. We've got a whole screen full of radar targets, though."

At the center of the monitor was the *Laboon*. To the port and starboard a few miles away steamed its sister ships— the *John McCain* and *John Paul Jones*. Up ahead were hundreds of green blips. Chinese coastal patrol and fast attack boats. Minesweepers, training ships, and support and supply craft. Salvage ships and repair ships and even survey ships. There were barges being towed by oceangoing tugs. Only a fraction of the craft were true landing ships. But all were packed to the gunwales—a makeshift invasion fleet carrying seventy thousand men.

The *Laboon* had seen her first action in the darkness of early morning. She'd fired a dozen TASMs at targets leaving Xiamen. She'd then fired Tomahawk cruise missiles at the port itself. But now the orders were to go guns and torps. It was old-fashioned surface warfare. But it was co- ordinated with an all-out aerial assault. And six attack sub- marines would strike from the south simultaneously. They had to stop the fleet in the straits. They had to dump seventy thousand men into flaming water.

Richards shook the thought from his head. It was a scale of human tragedy beyond all comparison, but his job was to make it happen.

"Message from task force commander, sir," came from the communications officer.

"Put it on."

". . . to the *Laboon*, you are approaching the Chinese destroyer screen. Repeat. You are approaching Chinese de- stroyer screen."

The three American destroyers were vastly superior ships. But the Chinese combatants still carried lethal weapons. Over a dozen Taiwanese ships had already attacked. They'd smashed into the Chinese flotilla an hour before. The *Huei Yang* and *Lo Yang* had been sunk. They were old USN hull numbers DD-696 and-746—the former USS *English* and USS *Taussig*.

"We've got radar targets inside twelve nautical miles," the fire controller reported. They could engage at any time.

"Hold fire till we get a visual," Richards repeated. The CIC was cooled to seventy degrees. But the radarman in front of Richards was sweating profusely. "Listen up," Richards announced loudly. "There are Taiwanese warships out there mixing it up. Destroyers and frigates plus corvettes and fast attack boats. I don't want any friendly-fire casualties. Our rules of engagement require visual contact. We've got over ten miles of visibility. We're gonna do this slow and steady, you read me? I want positive ID before we fire."

"Aye, sir," replied the fire controller. He was a twenty-something lieutenant junior grade.

Rather than easing Richards's nerves, the man's reply had put him on edge. That his crew would follow his orders was a given. That the captain was responsible for his ship was an immutable law.

But the *Laboon* was not built to slug it out. Although the Arleigh Burke-class was made of steel, not aluminum, and reinforced with over seventy tons of Kevlar, even 3.9-inch shells from Chinese guns would make short work of her. And every hit by guns or missiles meant deaths.

"What's our speed?" Richards asked.

"Thirty-three knots, sir. Engines all ahead full. Course one eight six."

Richards could feel the vibrations of the deck. Four gas turbines turning two shafts. Two hundred thousand horsepower each. And the churning screws put the destroyer on a hundred screens. Every sonarman from the Philippines to the Ryukyu Islands could hear the noise.

"Range to nearest surface contact?" Richards asked.

"Eleven-point-two," the fire controller replied.

"Any visuals yet?"

"Negative, sir. There's a lot of smoke that's adding to the haze. But it should be any second."

Richards felt those seconds' passage. Visual contact wouldn't lessen the danger. It would raise it. If the *Laboon* could see the Chinese . . . the Chinese could see the *Laboon*.

"LAMPS is low on fuel, sir," the air controller reported. "Requests permission to land."

The destroyer carried an antisubmarine helicopter. It was returning from its sweep of the ship's rear. It was there the sonic wake of its propellers created a blind spot.

"Permission denied," Richards said. "Divert it to the *Eisenhower*."

"Radar contact bearing one nine five—range eleven-point-one—turning to port." Richards looked at his fire control officer. "She's maneuvering toward the *McCain*. Now tracking a new bearing. Bearing constant. Bearing constant. She's steadied up. Range ten-point-eight. Tracking bearing three-four—"

"Vampire! Vampire!" called the Air Defense Center. "I got *one* missile! Range *ten* miles. Bearing one *seven* nine! Bearing constant! Range decreasing! It's coming at us!"

"Begin evasive maneuvers!" Richards ordered. "Fire chaff and IR flares at four miles." The deck began to heave under their feet. "Unsafe the Phalanxes. Put 'em on auto." He steadied himself on the nearest console. "I'm going to the bridge."

Richards left the CIC. He was thrown from wall to wall along the short corridor. The ship was heaving wildly at top speed. The armored hatch was dogged tight. Richards opened it into bright daylight.

"Cap'n's on the bridge!" a seaman announced.

"Mr. Lawrence," Richards said. "I've got the bridge." Instead of climbing into his tall chair, Richards grabbed his binoculars. He walked to the angled glass overlooking the ship's single gun. The helmsman spun the wheel in the opposite direction. The deck heaved. "Put the CIC on the speaker,'' he ordered. He raised the binoculars.

Tinny reports of inbound missiles filled the bridge. ''Five miles. Speed six twenty.''

A new voice—his fire control coordinator—suddenly called out, ''*Visual* contact! It's a frigate. She's got empty missile rails.''

Richards raised the hand mike. ''Fire control, this is the captain. Do we have ID?''

The thudding booms of the chaff dispensers drowned out the first part of the man's reply. ''. . . Hull number five-oh-eight. It's the frigate *Xichang,* sir! Definitely Chinese hostile. Range nine-point-seven.''

''Fire two Harpoons,'' Richards ordered. ''Engage with guns.''

''Aye, sir! Engaging.''

''I got it!'' one of the lookouts shouted. ''Eleven o'clock. It's a sea skimmer!''

Richards saw the missile just off the port bow. White foam flew into the air with each swell. It obscured the missile. But in between he could see the small, round nose. And the smudge of heat blurring the sky in its wake.

''Constant bearing, decreasing range!'' the lookout reported. ''Missile inbound! Missile inbound!''

It was zeroed right in on the *Laboon.*

The ship shuddered. It fired a Harpoon. Then a second. Chaff dispensers boomed. All of a sudden the five-inch gun opened up. The bridge's window was filled with gun smoke. The sea breeze blew the windows clear and there was the missile.

''Hard astarboard!'' Richards ordered the helmsman. ''Bring her to two seven five! Continue evasive maneuvers!'' He was turning broadside. Presenting a fat target. But it was also bringing both of the six-barreled Vulcan cannons into action. If he'd maintained course, only the forward gun could fire. Now both would lock on radar image. When they got one, that is. The five-inch gun below the bridge fired again. Its automatic loader filled the breech every three seconds.

Richards opened the hatch and went out onto the port watch deck. Cold wind rushed by. The five-incher boomed again. He fixed his binoculars on the enemy ship. The seventy-pound shell struck the superstucture. The flash ripped through the radar mast. The frigate belched boiling white smoke.

Richards searched the sky for the inbound missile.

The missile popped up into the air a mile away from the *Laboon*. Richards looked not at the missile but at the nearest Phalanx anti-missile cannon. The six-barreled weapon sat top its white metal body. *Fire!* Richards silently urged. Both of the Vulcan cannons opened up. Computers unleashing two hundred shells a second.

The "Flying Dragon" missile arced skyward. It nosed over. It headed straight down for the *Laboon*'s aluminum funnels.

The two six-barreled cannon sounded like buzz saws. The air was filled with their explosive shells. The missile burst in a bright orange fireball. Cheers rose up from the lookouts. Richards watched the rain of debris just off the port beam. He started to breathe the air he'd denied himself.

"Incoming!" yelled the lookouts in unison. The shrill whistle of a naval artillery shell barely preceded hot tongues of fire. Richards felt the thunder of a near miss. A tower of water collapsed on itself.

"*Xichang*'s been hit again!" someone shouted from the bridge. Richards raised his binoculars. The frigate that had fired the almost deadly missile was listing and low. She was smoking from a direct hit amidships. Her guns had not yet fallen silent. But she was turning in fear of capsizing.

Two Harpoons in succession flew straight into its hull just above the waterline.

An orange explosion threw a geyser high into the air above Richards. The *Laboon* sailed straight through it. It was the *Xichang*'s and closest miss yet. Water rained down on the bow. Mist coated the lenses of his binoculars.

In the distance, the *Xichang* lit the hazy day with pyrotechnics. Her main magazine went off in a mini–mushroom cloud.

New visual targets were being called out, and Richards returned to the bridge and fired the remainder of his six ready Harpoons. The five-incher's twenty-round-a-minute rating was put to the test. The results were one more Chinese frigate set ablaze, and a destroyer turned turtle amid a pool of burning oil.

"We're through the screen!" came the report from the CIC. The calls of ship sightings now changed. "Hull number nine two eight! Landing ship tank. Range four-point-two!"

"Engage with ASROC," Richards ordered, calmer this time.

"Aye-aye, Captain," came the excited reply of the fire control coordinator.

A moment later an enormous burst of white smoke obscured the windows of the bridge. A huge torpedo lifted out of its armored canister mounted flush with the deck. It rode the belching white thrust of its booster. More sightings led to more anti-submarine rockets—regular torpedoes flown to the enemy vessels by powerful rockets. Richards followed the flight of the first ASROC.

It splashed almost anti climactically into the sea. It was three-quarters of a mile from the jam-packed landing ship. It was surreal. Richards counted off the seconds. A torpedo could make forty knots.

The Chinese LST broke in half. The ship's midsection literally rose into the air. The flat-bottomed ship slipped into the sea at the bow and stern. Crates and light vehicles splashed into the water all around.

The view through the windows of the still turning *Laboon* was constantly changing. Smoke rose into the air from horizon to horizon. Richards conserved his antiship missiles. A couple of five-inch shells or a single ASROC was all it took. They even turned broadsides to fire regular torps from the six tubes on the stern. In thirty minutes the Taiwan Straits were a flaming graveyard.

8

"In the battleground state of Texas," Kate read, her stop-watch running, "the election appears to be up for grabs. The latest NBC News/*Wall Street Journal* poll shows President Marshall and Governor Bristol running neck and neck both nationally and here in the Lone Star State. The results of that poll were borne out by a nonscientific survey we conducted of voters on their way to work." She hit the watch's stop button, confirming that the voice-over would roughly correspond in length with the taped footage. Kate swiveled her chair and hit "play" to watch the man-on-the-street interviews. She then switched to a second player to see her taped conclusion.

The unedited tape began with Kate wiggling her shoulders to loosen up. Her heavier-than-normal makeup wasn't obvious. She watched herself brush her bangs back. The navy-blue cloth overcoat was a good choice. She cleared her throat and looked into the camera.

"The voters seem to be asking two questions." Kate held the stick mike in her gloved hand. A small but distracting wisp of hair blew loose across her forehead. "First, how could the Marshall administration allow tensions with China to escalate into a shooting war? Although the invasion of Taiwan was devastating, Governor Bristol spent much of the day hammering the Democratic ticket with the bitter remarks to *Newsweek* magazine made by former Secretary of State Jensen." *Too long*, Kate thought. "Governor Bristol's finest moment came when he suggested the time for a show of U.S. strength was *before* our ally was attacked—not after." *Should have used the sound bite,* she thought. "But far more ominous for the president is the question many voters raise about the risks to American troops now stationed along the Chinese border in Siberia. Many analysts view the doomed PLA attack on Taiwan as having the purpose of galvanizing popular support in China, where the vast majority view Taiwan as a Chinese province and American defense of Taipei as meddling in purely internal Chinese affairs. But the question is galvanizing the Chinese citizenry for what? With the World Court having agreed to consider China's claim to much of eastern Siberia . . ."

She stopped the tape. Woody—if he would ever show up—would splice in video from the port of Vladivostok as Kate's report continued. She turned to another tape deck. Maybe she should cut instead to the Japanese story. "Shit," she whispered, then played the tape from where it was cued.

". . . J-j-a-apanese constitutional amendment would allow the military to deploy overseas. Parliamentary proponents argue for easing the World War Two–era restrictions due to skyrocketing tensions in the region. And the first act that the Diet should take—Japanese opinion polls suggest—should be to rename the 'Self-Defense Forces.' The leading candidate is simply the '*Armed* Forces,' but even those words are fraught with significance in an Asia still wary of Japanese militarism. Meanwhile war stocks pour into Japanese harbors from American ports. But they're all property of the United States military. And now that South Korea has gone on general alert, the East Asian rim of the Pacific Ocean is alive with instability. Urgent issues are debated nightly in Tokyo—both in posh clubs and along riot lines. Public officials here are quietly complaining of America treating Japan like another aircraft carrier—once a taboo topic, now considered sexy.''

"Damn!'' Kate said, stopping the tape. Did she want to take the time to edit the word "sexy'' out?

She instead turned back to the first tape player.

"The UN operation in eastern Russia is now entering its second month, and the Pentagon today announced the deployment of one additional army and one marine division to Siberia. Department of Defense spokesmen denied that the deployment was in any way connected to the Chinese attack on Taiwan and its ruthless suppression of Hong Kong. But the president's chief of staff made it clear that no such aggression would be tolerated in Siberia. In a *separate* story, President Marshall requested today that Congress approve a Pentagon call-up in excess of the president's 200,000-man limit. The current resolution would allow reserve activations to go as high as 500,000 men and women, although administration officials refused to rule out requests for more. The Pentagon also announced that the six brigades of national guardsmen previously deployed to the riot-torn areas would be formed into three new army divisions.''

Then cut back to me, Kate thought. She looked at her watch and leaned toward the open door. *"Woody-y-y!''* she shouted, then hit "play.''

"In responding to Republican attacks, administration officials point to their success in calming Anarchist violence worldwide. Confirming earlier rumors, a CIA spokeswoman today announced for the first time that they believe that Valentin Kartsev was killed in a bombing of Anarchist training camps shortly after my interview with him last month.''

Kate winced. She'd told Woody that the reference to her interview would ring hollow. They would now have to reshoot the entire piece.

"In a presidential race most thought would turn on the

domestic issues of the economy, terrorism, and civil unrest, it is foreign affairs that now looms as the deciding factor. In the photo finish for which President Marshall and Governor Bristol seem headed, the questions analysts are asking are: Will the boost that incumbents expect during periods of international crisis be offset by the perceived mishandling of Chinese aggression by the administration? And are there any more surprises in store for the candidates in the one week remaining before the election? This is Kate Dunn, NBC News, reporting from the campaign trail in Austin, Texas.''

Her toes were wiggling in her shoes. Her teeth were grinding despite warnings from her dentist. She willed herself to stop both.

''Woody-y, would you *please* . . . !'' she shouted.

He suddenly appeared in the doorway.

''Oh . . . hey,'' she said. ''Look, we've got a lot of editing to do before—''

''You've got a phone call,'' Woody interrupted. He held her cellular phone out to her. He'd borrowed it to order pizza. Woody couldn't quite suppress his excitement.

''Who is it?'' she asked.

He shrugged. ''Well, let's see. He's about five-foot-four and bald. He's a genocidal Russian nut who controls worldwide Anarchist terrorism.''

She grabbed the small phone and held it to her ear. There was the hiss of a long-distance connection.

''Miss Dunn, how wonderful to hear your *breathing*.''

Kate felt her skin crawl. ''Mr. . . . *Kartsev*?'' she asked, almost whispering.

''Yes, and I'm alive and well, contrary to all rumors.''

Kate was stunned. ''Where have you been?'' she asked, suddenly unsettled, insecure . . . as if he were there in the room with her.

''Staying out of harm's way, mostly. Doing a lot of writing as well. I have greatly enjoyed watching events on the world scene develop, as you can imagine.''

Kate finally came out of her trance when Woody handed

her a small rubber ring. A wire with a jack at the end was attached to the ring. It was a microphone. She plugged the jack into a tape recorder and placed the ring around the earpiece of the phone. The red light indicated the recorder was taping. "I've made substantial progress on my manuscript," he continued. "I hope it's going to be a work of some importance. It should spell out my thoughts and conclusions about what's happening currently."

"And so you've concluded what?" she asked.

"That it's difficult to control things as complex as world events. But it's surprisingly easy to 'get the ball rolling,' I believe the expression is. To be a catalyst. A bullet here, a bomb there, a computer virus or two and . . . voilà! It's analogous to plate tectonics theory. Only the forces are not geological, they're social. They lie pent-up. All they need is a triggering event to release them."

"May I ask why you called me, Mr. Kartsev?"

"Two reasons. I missed your company. It's the middle of the night, and I was having a bout of writer's block." Kate looked at her watch and wrote the time on a notepad. Quickly doing the calculations, she realized that he was somewhere in Siberia. "But secondly, I had thought you might want a story, and so I thought I would do you the courtesy of giving you one."

Her heart was pounding in anticipation. "What story?"

Kartsev cleared his throat. "Very well. Are you ready?"

CHICAGO, ILLINOIS
October 26, 2330 GMT (1730 Local)

A dozen people were clustered around the television in Gordon Davis's hotel suite.

". . . at precisely fourteen hundred hours Greenwich Mean Time tomorrow," came the voice of Valentin Kartsev, "all units of the Russian Army on both sides of the current civil war will lay down their arms. All soldiers and officers of the armed forces of Russia will immediately, as of that time, be discharged from further service and be free to return to their homes. No authority or other privileges will, after such time, be afforded any citizen of the Russian republic by virtue of his former service in or rank with the armed forces.''

''What will happen with the army's weapons?'' the female correspondent with NBC News asked.

''They will be left in place.''

''What about nuclear weapons?''

''They too will be left in place. We are relying upon the presence of UN forces to monitor the safekeeping of all weapons of mass destruction.''

''Why is this happening? Why is the army disbanding like this?''

''It was by agreement of the warring parties. Both sides were suffering terribly from battle losses, and even worse from desertions. Furthermore, as you are quite aware, I am sure, from your news reports, supply problems are so extreme in many parts of our country that military units have been reduced to marauding bands, terrorizing the populace in search of food. And military production has come to a complete standstill. It was in that state of exhaustion that the two sides met and agreed to desist from further hostilities.''

''Will there be an amnesty granted to soldiers loyal to the Russian High Command—the so-called White Army?''

There was a laugh. ''Miss Dunn. You seem to be missing the point. There will be no amnesty, because there is no one to grant that amnesty. Government in Russia in any form will, as of fourteen hundred hours GMT tomorrow, simply cease to exist.''

''Ho-o-oly *shit*!'' someone in the crowd gathered around Gordon Davis exclaimed.

The NBC News anchorman began his interview of the female reporter who had broken the Kartsev story.

''It was definitely Valentin Kartsev. There was one recorded interview with him by a Dutch independent film crew, and NBC had the voiceprints compared and found them to be an exact match. In addition, I asked the man several questions about details of our previous meetings which I believe could only have been known by Mr. Kartsev, and all were answered correctly.''

''Then the next question, Kate, is—was Kartsev telling the truth? Will the Russian Army just up and disband at nine o'clock Eastern Time tomorrow morning—election day in this country?''

''There is no way of knowing the answer until that time, but I found in my earlier dealings with Mr. Kartsev that he was totally candid and straightforward. He wasn't given to bluffing or grandstanding.''

''Thank you, Kate,'' the anchorman said. The camera zoomed in on him as he stacked a sheaf of papers. ''Well then, in a little over fourteen hours we'll learn whether the Anarchist revolution that has swept over Russia will achieve its final victory and leave that massive country completely ungoverned. To repeat this breaking news, what is known is that Valentin Kartsev—long claimed by un-named White Horse sources to have been killed in bombing raids ordered by President Marshall—has surfaced and dropped what can only be described as a bombshell of his own on President Marshall.''

There were cheers in Gordon's suite which he quickly hushed. The anchorman turned and the camera zoomed out to reveal a guest seated beside him. Behind them was a map of the United States. The studio was all set for election-night coverage. ''I have with me Bill Luck, our political commentator. Bill, it looks like the gang that couldn't shoot straight on Pennsylvania Avenue has managed to wing their collective feet once again. Will there be any fallout to this, or is the election pretty much decided by now one way or the other?''

''It definitely has *not* been decided yet. The latest polls are almost evenly split, and all of those polls are well within the margins of error inherent in the polling methods used. What the numbers *do* tell us, however, is that this election is going to be decided by which way a very small percentage of swing voters break between now and about twenty-eight hours from now when the last polls close in Hawaii.''

"Almost a year of campaigning and billions of dollars of campaign spending," the anchorman commented with a grin and a shake of his head, "after all the debates and speeches and position statements, this country's president is going to be chosen by a very tiny fraction of the electorate which hasn't yet made up its mind."

"Well, it *has* been a very newsworthy year, to say the least," the analyst added. "With all the fumbling and bumbling contributing to President Marshall's slide in the polls, we in my business couldn't have been any busier if Congress had enacted a Political Commentator Full Employment Act. So it's probably fitting, I suppose, that this election go right down to the wire just to keep people like me talking."

"If you had to call it, Bill, which way do you think it will go?"

The commentator shrugged. "If I had to take a wild guess, I'd say this last bit of news from Kartsev was the straw that broke the camel's back. I'd have to guess that the Republicans are going to be moving back into the White House come next January."

Raucous cheers erupted from the campaign staffers. Gordon was too stunned to react. For the first time he realized that it really might happen after all. That he might become vice-president of the United States of America.

FORT BENNING, GEORGIA
October 28, 0800 GMT (0300 Local)

André Faulk felt something hard probing at his side. He opened his eyes to see the barrel of a gun. Standing above him was a man wearing night-vision goggles under his helmet. His face was blackened with greasepaint. The man held his fingers to his lips to shush André, just as another man roused Stempel from his slumber. Stempel was supposed to have been on watch. But he was sound asleep in the fighting hole beside André.

"Huh?" Stempel said with a start, kicking André in the process. André kicked him back as Stempel stared up at the M-16's muzzle. The orange metal hood that would harmlessly deflect the blanks' wads was just inches from Stempel's chest.

The greasepainted man in front of André raised a rubber knife and swiped it slowly across André's neck. He pointed with it then toward Stempel. "You two are dead," he whispered, then again raised his finger to his lips.

From the bushes all around them there emerged over a dozen black-clad attackers. The dark forms advanced up the hillside toward their sleeping platoon. Stempel's head was darting this way and that. They both watched the "OP-FOR"—the Opposition Force composed of instructors—rush unopposed through their defenses. That was all he and Stempel could do. They were dead.

André punched Stempel hard on the arm. "Hey!" Stempel hissed. That drew a sharp "Shhh," from an "enemy" soldier carrying a machine gun right past them into the heart of their position. "What'd you do that for?" Stempel whispered, barely audible.

"You fuckin' fell *asleep,* that's why! God-*damn*, man!"

Stempel sank back into the hole, a desperate, sick look on his face.

They both jumped as the roar of gunfire shattered the quiet. Harold turned to see the dark hillside above light up. A dozen muzzles blazed. It sounded like ten strings of firecrackers lit off at once, only a hundred times louder. Harold clamped his hands over his ears, but lowered them when he saw Faulk staring at him in disgust.

Just as quickly as it had started, it was over.

From the darkness, André heard a skidding sound through the dirt. A man appeared out of nowhere. The hot muzzle of an M-16 was stuck in André's side.

"Get up!" the man yelled as André recoiled from the burning metal.

They were prodded roughly with the muzzle up the hill. At their camp they came upon a confusing scene. The rest

of their training platoon knelt under the swaying beams of
a half-dozen flashlights.

"Kneel down!" was shouted right in André's ear. He
and Stempel knelt beside each other, and their captors
roughly pulled their hands up onto their heads. "If you
miserable excuses for human beings learn *one* goddamn
thing from this training," Staff Sergeant Giles shouted,
"it's *fire your goddamn weapons*! If you don't do that,
you're not just useless, you're a dangerous goddamn *hole*
in the line!" There followed several long seconds of silence. "The Chinese don't take no pris'ners!"

With that as André's warning, there was a single boom
from a rifle. A hot strobe gave André the start of his life.
His profile lit the ground in front of him for an instant—
kneeling, hands on head, helpless.

"Mrs. Faulk!" Giles shouted. "The U.S. Army regrets
to inform you your son is *dead*!"

André was shoved roughly onto his face. His hands
barely came down in time to partially cushion his fall.

There was another shot, and Stempel landed roughly on
his chest with a thudding grunt.

"Mrs. Stempel! The U.S. Army regrets to inform you
your son is dead!"

"Good riddance," somebody mumbled from behind.

The process was repeated for each of the forty recruits.

Sergeant Giles kept at the recruits of the training platoon.
"Place the rifle butt on your shoulder, lay the front sight
on the enemy, and *pull the trigger*! If you do that, and that
alone, you'll be doin' what fewer than *half* the men who
preceded you in U.S. Army history did in any given firefight." He then took Faulk and Stempel apart from the others. The dim light of dawn turned everything gray. "All
right. What I want to know is, which one of you pieces of
shit was on watch? Which one of you assholes fell asleep
and let your entire unit get massacred?"

Stempel's head was hanging. His eyes were closed. He
was shaking, holding back tears, André realized.

"It was me, Staff Sergeant," André said.

Giles's eyes were already drilling holes in Stempel. He was slow to turn to André. When he did, he said in a calm voice, "You realize that even though this is training, you could be court-martialed for falling asleep on sentry duty?"

"Yes, Staff Sergeant!" André replied.

"And if it was during war, you could be shot?"

"Yes, Staff Sergeant!"

"But since I can't shoot you, I'm gonna have to do the next worst thing I can think of, whatever that is."

"Yes, Staff Sergeant!"

"He wasn't on watch, Staff Sergeant!" Stempel yelled all of a sudden, his voice thick with tears. "It was me, Staff Sergeant!"

Giles turned his attention back to Stempel. "Well, well, well," he said. " 'Pears to me that one of you is lyin'. Now, that's an *awful* serious offense." He looked back and forth between the two of them. "I cain't figure no way of tellin' which one is lyin', and which one is tellin' the truth. But it don't really matter much, since one of ya is lyin', and the other fell asleep on watch. So it looks like you're both fucked."

André caught a hint of a smile in his wrinkled eyes.

OFFICERS' BARRACKS, SHENYANG, CHINA
October 29, 1300 GMT (2300 Local)

Lieutenant Chin couldn't sleep. For three hours he had lain in his bunk tossing and turning, every muscle sore from the day's work. Snores filled the long, open barracks as the other junior officers slept soundly. Chin spent his time trying to trick his mind with soothing images of his family's farm. But it didn't work. They had given way to new images. Images of disgrace. The sight from earlier that day of the young lieutenant who, like Chin, was from a peasant family. During the morning's field exercise, he'd failed to follow water purification procedures before drinking from a river. He and his entire platoon had fallen ill. The regimental commander himself had stood the young officer up on the reviewing platform and shouted at him for over an hour. The entire regiment stood at attention below.

During the long tirade Chin could see the young man wince repeatedly. Not from the occasional blow on his legs or butt by the short swagger stick the regimental commander carried, but from the shouting—the words. "You can't *read,* can you? *Read this! Read it!*" All that Chin could hear from the young man were his sobs. Chin spun his legs to the floor in anger. Anxious. Wondering what it was in written manuals that he should know but didn't. He knew his job. He'd been taught everything important in classrooms and in the field. And he *could* read. He knew all two thousand characters. It was just sometimes he didn't understand.

He got up and walked the length of the darkened barracks to the lavatory. When he got there, he heard whispering from the mop closet. He groped along the wall for the switch, opened the closet door, and twisted the switch until it clicked, flooding the small area with light.

In the glare Chin saw four men squatting in a circle. Mops and brooms hung from the walls all around. One of the men rushed toward Chin and turned the lights off.

They were all officers in Chin's infantry battalion. To his great relief they appeared just to be talking.

"Come here," someone said in the darkness. He took Chin's arm and pulled him into the room. Chin squatted down to join the rest of them.

"Lieutenant Hung?" Chin asked, thinking he recognized the voice of a fellow platoon leader from his company.

"What are you doing?" a different voice whispered, ignoring his query.

"Getting a drink of water," Chin answered. His own voice was lowered to a whisper. "What's going on?"

There was silence from all sides.

"Who the hell is he?" someone else asked.

"Some ox driver from nowhere," replied Lieutenant Hung, Chin was certain.

"You go to school, ox driver?" Chin was asked.

"Yeah. Sure," Chin replied, immediately defensive. "Beijing Polytechnic."

There were laughs. "From ox driver to tractor driver," someone remarked.

"Your family buy your way into officer training, tractor boy?" Chin said nothing. The man poked right at his most sensitive core. "I bet you've never been more than twenty kilometers from your mama till school. Just out there with mud between your toes raking in all that farm money, selling to . . . ?"

He fell silent. Chin now understood what was going on. His anger was stored up after months of similar abuse from classmates during officer training. He and all the other boys from farming families always caught shit from these university snots. But they gave as good as they took, in Chin's estimation—taking rickshaws and eating at restaurants when on leave in the city. The farmers had money. The city kids were poor. That poverty bred jealousy.

"Selling to who?" Chin asked in the silence. *Go on— say it!* he thought hotly. *Selling to the Block Committees. Selling to the goddamn party officials. Say it!*

"Look, Chin, we didn't mean anything by it, okay?" Hung said. "Honestly. We were just giving you shit. No hard feelings?"

Chin knew he had them now. One mention of this little meeting and they'd all learn how heavy your legs get behind an ox team when mud gets caked up to your waist. Chin hadn't been farther than the market before the polytechnic, but it had been far enough to see the local reeducation camp along their route. It was filled with college pukes like them.

"Hey, come on, Chin. What about it?" another voice asked.

"Fuck you all," Chin said as he got up and left the closet. *Let them lose sleep tonight*, he thought. He waited by the door to the lavatory, straining his ears to hear their insults. One word—even an obnoxious inflection in their voice—and he was going straight to the company commander.

But they didn't mention him again. They spoke in low tones. The wobbling beam of a flashlight could be seen under the door. "All right," someone said. "Look this one up." The next word spoken was in a foreign language. "*Un-alien-able*."

After a few seconds someone read, " 'Not capable of being transferred.' "

"Ah," Chin heard several voices say at the same time. "That makes sense," someone whispered. "Read it again."

It was in English, Chin was almost positive. " 'We hold these truths to be self-evident, that all Men are created equal, that they are endowed by their Creator with certain unalienable rights, that among these are Life, Liberty, and the Pursuit of Happiness . . .' "

Chin listened, but he understood none of it. None of it but the word "unalienable"–"not capable of being transferred." He went to bed wondering what was it that was "unalienable"? What could not be transferred? Whatever it was, it was dangerous. Those college pukes were taking huge risks to read it.

His mind wandered as he lay there. What was it that couldn't be transferred? He thought and thought, finally drifting off to sleep.

FORT RICHARDSON, ALASKA
October 30, 0900 GMT (1700 Local)

Clark sat in the Humvee, the radio telephone to his ear. The *swish-swish* of the windshield wiper cleared the steadily falling snow. The heater kept the idling vehicle warm. Clark worried at the rate of fuel consumption by his mechanized army. During alerts, engines were run for several hours solely to ensure the vehicle would start when needed. It added up. There was a click over the phone. He'd failed all afternoon to get the president through ordinary channels, but there was always one line that remained open.

"National Military Command Center," the operator said from "The Tank" on the third floor of the Pentagon.

"This is General Clark, CINCUSARPAC. Get me the president." Moments later a communications officer with FEMA—the Federal Emergency Management Agency—who was in a van parked outside the Alamodome said the president was at a rally and couldn't come to the phone. Clark worked to control his anger. "Isn't it your job to keep the president in constant communication with the national military command system?" The FEMA officer acknowledged that it was. "And do you know who I am?" The man did. "Check your manuals if you have to, but there are only eight major commands, and USARPAC is one. Now, what's the significance of USARPAC being a major command and me being its commander?"

"You . . . you can get me in a lotta *trouble*?"

Clark ground his teeth. "I have direct access to the president, and I want it now."

There was a clicking sound, then ringing. *"Hello?"* was shouted over a blaring band.

Clark had to yell to be heard. *"This is General Nate Clark! Get me President Marshall!"*

"He can't come to the phone right now!" some kid said. "Can I take a message?"

Clark had left half a dozen urgent messages. *"You get me the president, or I'll have your ass!"*

"You're the Clark who's been faxing all those memos, right? The president got your requests for more troops, but I'm afraid it's not gonna happen tonight, General."

It suddenly seemed absurd. The fate of UNRUSFOR's 200,000 troops and perhaps the Asian continent for generations to come hung on the whim of a boy who would at most command a platoon in Clark's army. "Does the president realize the Shenyang Army Group—with 350,000 combat troops—is moving into staging areas near the Russian border. And the *Beijing* Army Group has been moving north since—"

"The president has taken care of it, General!" the staffer interrupted. "He sent a cable to Beijing. Now, tomorrow is Election Day, for Christ's sake! You've gotta understand!"

Clark understood. The connection clicked and the line fell silent. The hardware had worked perfectly, but the human link in the system had failed. Something always failed. War was never the result of a series of successes.

On seeing the native Alaskan scouts in the field, Clark immediately wanted them in Siberia. It was freezing out, but they went about their business as the unit's commander lectured Clark on his tour. "Artillery, mortars, land mines, and hand grenades either don't explode or are smothered in deep snow. Plus lateral fragmentation is zero. Command-detonated mines in the upper branches of trees is the only thing that works. Artillery rates of fire fall way off. Even with cold-resistant grease and oil, mechanisms get sticky and sluggish. Strikers and springs break like glass. Ammunition areas get covered in snow." They passed barrels of weapons protruding from well-concealed fighting positions. "Snow and ice gets in your sights and barrel. You can't take your gloves off to clean the weapon. But if you take it inside, you gotta strip it completely. It gets covered in condensation and will freeze up when you go back out."

"Your men handle this weather easily," Clark commented. "Is it because they're from the north?"

"No, sir. It's training, not acclimatization. There's a big difference between growing up where it's cold, and never bein' able to get out of bad weather when you're out in the field. Same goes for those northern Chinese. When it gets cold, they go to barracks. Unless they're trained to function in severe cold, they'll die after thirty minutes of exposure."

A Kiowa scout helicopter swooped low overhead and disappeared into the leaden, snow-filled sky. Clark had suspended peacetime operating minimums for army aircrews. He wanted pilots flying in dangerous shit to get ready.

"You gotta check your people constantly," the colonel continued. "Change socks. Wash your feet. Use foot powder. People get numbed by the cold. They'll take a nap out in the open and die. They'll get snow blindness 'cause they forgot their sunglasses. You gotta exercise 'em. Stamping your feet, clenching and unclenching, wiggling your toes, knee bends—they can keep you from losing an appendage. You gotta check the snow flower after they urinate. If it's dark yellow, they're dyin' of dehydration. And you can't let 'em drink liquor. We had a senior NCO up here on an exercise who took a swig from a bottle of Jack Black he'd left outside overnight. Alcohol doesn't freeze, so what poured down his throat was chilled to minus twenty degrees. Burned him so bad he almost couldn't breathe.''

Nate's two wars—Vietnam and the Gulf—had both been different. Hot. He asked about casualties.

''You evacuate on sleds—two men pulling on the flats, three in the mountains. Pile as many blankets on top as you've got. Luckily, casualties are low because the intensity of combat slows in winter. You spend your time in self-preservation. If temperatures go down to minus twenty, vehicles require five times as much maintenance. At minus forty, forget large-scale operations. Siberia gets even colder. Plus there's windchill. You can feel it just walking. Open vehicles and helicopter downdrafts are dangerous. Storms kill massively. Add a twenty-knot wind to minus twenty degrees and the windchill is minus sixty-five. It'd then take maximum effort to do even the simplest task out in the open. Exposed flesh freezes in thirty seconds. Your men go under canvas, your vehicles in laager, and you just survive. A ten-man arctic tent and a Yukon stove will get you by . . . but just barely.''

''Sounds like you just hunker down and ride the winter out.''

''Unfortunately, you can't do that, sir. You still gotta send people out. You patrol for the sake of morale. It's just you got two enemies—the opposing army, and the cold. And the cold is always there. It gets men down, and the only cure is activity. You can't just stand sentry. You get all bundled up cocoonlike in your hood and you look *out*

but don't see. You withdraw. It's dangerous—psychologi-
cally. You gotta patrol. Draw 'em out. Make 'em think
about livin'. *Care* about it.''

They proceeded into an ever-stiffening breeze. "How far
out do you patrol?" Clark asked.

"You can't go far or fast. Twenty inches of snow slows
foot marches to half a mile an hour. Any deeper and men
risk sweating and then freezing to death. Plan your routes
through thick woods or along high crests where the snow
doesn't accumulate. Frozen watercourses and lakes are also
easier and make good LZs—even airfields. But sound-
ranging teams with seismological gear can fix you on ice.
And ambushers can conceal themselves very well in snow.
You gotta look for shadows. Either that or hope they've
frozen to death during the wait.''

Nate's thighs were burning from walking in less than ten
inches of snow. "What about oversnow equipment?"

"Skis are good for long-range recon. You can tow up to
a squad behind a Humvee, or you can break a trail or tramp
a path for follow-on forces. But you gotta take skis off to
fight, and you lose 'em every time. Plus, ski troops can't
carry heavy loads or go through really deep snow. For the
deep stuff—bushland, draws, ditches—you either gotta use
snowshoes or hope it crusts over enough to hold your
weight. But hard-frozen snow is noisy as hell and sound
travels a *lo*-ong way on a cold night. Planning for patrols
boils down to how much you can leave behind and still
survive. Hundred-pound loads are cut to forty—thirty for
ski troops. Every squad's gotta carry two radios and extra
batteries because small-unit tactics predominate. And you'd
be surprised how much water and high-energy foods like
fats, breads and sugars you've got to carry. You burn cal-
ories like a runner just keepin' your body warm. And, of
course, you carry automatic weapons. Fighting is at close
range in the Arctic, and therefore you need high cyclic rates
of fire. You'd rather have one machine gun with a thousand
rounds, than a thousand men with one round.''

On the hill below there was a mock attack. The infantry
looked to be stuck in molasses.

The colonel noticed. "You can't mount a classic attack in arctic conditions. You crawl forward, digging in as you go. You can't take advantage of artillery prep because you can't move fast enough. The enemy is heads-up before you even make it to their killing zone. And if your attack bogs down . . . withdraw. Sweat-soaked men will freeze to death in the open in half an hour. As an alternative to direct attack, you could try infiltration. Dress up in captured outer gear. All bundled up you can merge with returning patrols—especially in extended formation—and slip inside the perimeter. We always have somebody with an M-60 doin' a head count at the wire. If you send ten men out, and eleven come back, you start killing."

They talked for half an hour. Of windproof parkas for patrols. Gore-Tex for sweat-prone ski troops. Fur overcoats for sentries and drivers. Saunas that toughen the body, build resistance to illness, and help morale. And dogs to hunt for casualties. "Snow covers irregularities. In arctic whites, lying prone, in flat light, you can't see the wounded. And they don't last long in the cold—ten, fifteen minutes. Plus the Arctic gives pilots a helluva time with navigation. You can't see coastlines if there's ice. Flat vapor layers hanging over the ground are impossible to tell from snow. Landing a chopper can be kinda chancy."

After their long discussion—Clark's cram course in winter warfare—it was a simple statement made offhandedly by the colonel near the end of their talk that Clark remembered best. It crystallized in his mind and in his plans and may have been the most important words of advice that he received. The colonel summed up all the difficulties caused by the harsh elements with a single, sweeping assertion. "Defenders win the battles in winter," he said.

PHILADELPHIA, PENNSYLVANIA
November 2, 0500 GMT (2400 Local)

Pyotr and Olga Andreev were curled up on the sofa under a blanket and bleary-eyed from the election coverage. Behind the anchorman, a map of the United States was evenly divided. The southern and western states were dark Republican red. The northern tier of states were bright Democratic blue.

"I am now being told," the anchorman said as he pressed on his earphone, "that ABC News is ready to make a projection for California, which has a sufficient number of electoral votes to decide the presidential contest." Olga clutched Pyotr in excitement.

There was a loud rap on the door. "With just three percent of the precincts reporting . . ." the anchorman said as Pyotr muted the television and grabbed the shotgun. Olga cowered in the hallway as Pyotr peered through the peephole. "It's just Fred," Pyotr said, and he opened the door.

"Your watch, Pete," Fred said. "All's quiet, but the lady in 304-D asked us to check on her every four hours or so. She's diabetic and needs to take some juice."

Olga handed Pyotr his jacket. "Would you like to step inside for a second?" Pyotr asked. "They were just announcing the winner of the presidential election."

"Oh, who gives a shit," Fred said. "Nothin's gonna change. They forget their promises before the balloons hit the floor, and start linin' up votes for next time. Haven't had a decent president in this country since Abe Lincoln, if you ask me. The place is goin' to hell in a handbasket, and who do we get to choose from? Marshall and Bristol! No-o, I don't even vote anymore. What's the point? We're kaput, I guess they'd say in your country. This time next century, the world'll belong to the slopeheads."

"The who?"

"You kno-ow." The man pulled the corners of his eyes back. "The Japs and Chinks. We used to be a helluva country, but now we're just coastin' down the hill built up by all that hard work. By the time we're old men, Pete"—he laughed—"we'll be talkin' about way back when like them old Britishers after their empire went poof." He shook his head. "But this place used to be somethin', it really did. We had somethin' goin' here. It's damn shame there ain't no Abe Lincoln left in us somewhere. Just a da-a-amn shame."

PART THREE

" 'Does the flap of a butterfly's wings in Brazil set off a tornado in Texas?' In systems like the weather, small perturbations cascade upward, and predictability gives way to randomness. Such is the problem with influencing the course of human events. You can change the direction of history, but you cannot know where that change will lead."

Valentin Kartsev (posthumously)
The Laws of Human History
Moscow, Russia

9

"If you're going to get that driveway clear, Gordon," Elaine said as she cleared the dishes from the breakfast table, "you'd better get started."

"Just a minute," Gordon mumbled. He was right in the middle of a three-part series in *The Washington Post* on life in the UN forces in Siberia. "Did you know," he said, raising his voice, "it gets so cold in Siberia that your breath freezes? When you exhale, it freezes right in front of your face and falls to the ground."

From the center of his newspaper came a loud crumpling noise. Elaine stared at him with one eyebrow raised, her hand atop the paper. "Did you know it gets so cold in Maryland that water freezes and falls right on people's driveways?"

Gordon heaved a sigh and put the paper aside. "You're not supposed to shovel snow first thing in the morning," he mumbled as he climbed into his overshoes. "People get heart attacks."

"Not people with five-thousand-dollar Sharper Image snowblowers," she said as she headed off.

"It was five hundred dollars!" he shouted after her.

"You were the one who wanted that thing," she replied from the kitchen. "It takes up half the garage, Gordon. Do you know how many times," she said, returning for more dishes, "we could have gotten our driveway shoveled if we had paid a neighbor's kid five hundred dollars?"

Gordon was shaking his head. He had her on that one. "That's just the point. Neighbors' kids aren't reliable."

"And *you* are?"

Gordon let out a long, sustained huff. He rose to don his coat. The garage was dark, but the light came on when he hit the opener. The door made its noisy ascent, revealing a driveway covered with four inches of snow.

Gordon smiled. He clapped his gloved hands together and put his goggles over his eyes. The snowblower had a Kawasaki engine in it. He stretched his muscles and touched his toes before he began the effort of yanking the starter cord. Five hard pulls later the cold engine showed no signs of life. Gordon stood and breathed deeply, gathering his strength for another assault. *Man's work*, he thought. Still, he should have gotten the top-of-the-line model. It was another two hundred dollars, but it had a patented "quick-start" ignition.

He began pulling again and again and again. There were some sputtering sounds of life, but the engine didn't catch. "Need some help, sir?" a man asked from just outside the garage. He wore dark sunglasses and a dark suit. An Uzi was slung over his shoulder as casually as a tourist with a camera bag.

"Nope! Almost got it," Gordon said, breathing heavily. He pulled and pulled until finally the motor kicked in. He revved it up and looked at the agent with a smile. "Purrs like a kitten!" he shouted. The agent turned back to the front yard and circled his finger in the air.

Gordon headed out of the garage into the bright sunlight. The engine made so much noise that he almost couldn't hear the shouted commands of the senior agent right by his side. The handle of the snowblower vibrated as he revved it up once again. "Look out!" he shouted to the two men along his property line to the right of the drive. They didn't turn to acknowledge him. Their eyes were peeled and their fingers on the triggers of their own Uzis.

After the warning Gordon began to blow snow. It shot out of the side of the blower in a geyser of white, pelting the backs of the unperturbed agents some distance away. A second agent took up position behind Gordon on his right opposite the senior agent to Gordon's left. They liked symmetry, Gordon had noticed. A third man walked directly in front, his head on a swivel.

The 180-degree turn at the end of the driveway was a little unwieldy. More agents stood around two Broncos parked on the street. Some had long rifles and scopes. Down the street just inside the police barricades, two vans blocked access to Gordon's small stretch of Spring River Drive. One was filled with members of the local SWAT team. The other had satellite antennae raised above it. His entourage had to switch positions around him.

Gordon saw his neighbor two houses down out with his own snowblower. Two agents shadowed the man within easy pistol range. Gordon gave the guy a big wave, which was returned with a broad grin matching Gordon's.

"Sorry!" Gordon shouted to the agent standing guard at the side door. He was removing his sunglasses to wipe the slush from his face. He made sure he powered the baby down before he made his next turn and headed back down the drive. "Beautiful day, isn't it?" he shouted over the noise to the man in the right rear position. The man said nothing. The small earphone with its wire trailed down into the agent's jacket.

When Gordon had finished both the drive and the side-walk, he shut the engine off just outside the garage and took a deep breath of the refreshing air. It was foul with gasoline fumes from the snowblower, but it was cool and dry. Gordon didn't want to go inside right away. He waited while the body heat he'd generated from the exertion dis-sipated. His wrists were sore from the vibrations of the handle. "It's a pretty day," he said to the senior agent. "Maybe I should go knock on doors and try to pocket a few extra bucks clearing driveways." The man's smile reminded Gordon of the *Mona Lisa*.

The man looked over his shoulder at the street just past the barricades. Moments later a car that Gordon recognized as belonging to one of his neighbors appeared. The senior agent seemed distracted by something being said to him over the radio. All the agents now faced the approaching menace—a Volvo station wagon filled with groceries. When it turned into its driveway and a woman got out with her two small children, the men eased.

"Are you going to work the inauguration?" Gordon asked.

"Yes, sir."

The agent turned again and looked around. Gordon could see nothing. *What was it?* he wondered. *"Yellow dog. Range two hundred meters. No tags."*

Elaine stepped out onto the porch. The unexpected appearance of another member of the "secure package" sent several agents scurrying for new positions across the front lawn.

"Gordon!" she yelled. "It's time to come in and get dressed!"

Gordon turned to the agent and frowned. "I've gotta go to this . . . *reception* thing being given by Capitol Hill *spouses*."

The agent nodded, then turned to look down the street. A man in his pajamas and robe was just exiting his house with a white garbage bag. Range: one fifty.

SHENYANG, CHINA
January 17, 0500 GMT (1500 Local)

Chin wanted to leave his seat by the open flap at the rear of the canvas-covered truck and wade into the sea of men away from the bitter cold. But the truck hit a pothole or slid into a rut every few meters, and moving around was treacherous. The next time the truck's brakes squealed, they came to a complete stop.

Chin climbed out over the rear gate onto the frozen dirt road that wound through the mountains. He walked around to the front of the truck and ordered the private out of the passenger seat. His experimental ride with his troops was over. The men hadn't said a word to him, or he to them, and the front cab had a heater. They started moving again, and Chin peered out the frosty windshield. The road ahead curved as it hugged the ridgeline and was filled bumper-to-bumper with trucks under a thick and overcast sky.

He didn't know where they were. He was only a junior lieutenant, and such information was reserved for officers of much higher rank. Officers with maps and binoculars who rode in Jeeps. Chin didn't even know where they were going or what awaited them. There were no questions asked, and none expected. Like the millions of others on the move that day, he just went in the direction in which he was pointed. And that direction was northward.

KHABAROVSK, SIBERIA
January 17, 2200 GMT (0800 Local)

Nate Clark shut his eyes and rubbed his forehead. The phone was jammed hard against his ear. He was sunk deep into his chair. UNRUSFOR now occupied the entire former military headquarters of the Russian Far East Army Command. General Dekker, chief of staff of the army, was on the secure line from the Pentagon.

"Ed," Nate said, "the *entire* Shenyang Army Group is heading north. Five armored divisions, twenty-three infantry divisions—350,000 men. And the Beijing Army Group is clearly staging. That's another four armored and twenty-five infantry divisions—375,000 *more* troops—as a follow-on."

"A *potential* follow-on, Nate," Ed Dekker corrected. But there was no vigor in his voice. He made the point solely as a matter of form.

"It's not just the satellite photos, Ed," Nate said, trying a new tack. "Or the electronic intercepts, or the human intell, or the warnings through diplomatic contacts. There's . . . *something*—all my unit commanders say they can feel it in their gut. It's in the air, in the woods, in the shadows at night. It's been there for days, Ed—for *weeks*."

"What the hell are you talking about?" Dekker replied testily.

"The Chinese—they're coming across. They've been infiltrating in force."

"Where's your *proof* of that, Nate?"

"My *proof* is those fifteen Chinese bodies that German patrol stacked up two days ago!"

"*Fifteen* soldiers, Nate!" Dekker shot back. "That's not coming across 'in force.' "

"For *Go-od's* sake, Ed! Don't tell me *you* are gonna give me the same—"

"Listen!" Dekker snapped, stopping Nate cold. Nate knew he wasn't just crossing the line with a superior. He was trampling it. "I took it up, and they weren't persuaded. Maybe if they'd taken a prisoner who talked."

"The Chinese soldiers were all sappers," Nate said dejectedly. "They killed themselves right after the firefight got started." Dekker said nothing. He knew all the details. "How high did you take it?"

"All the way to Himself," Dekker replied—meaning the president.

Nate pressed down on his sore eyes with his fingertips. "Ed, they could be all over the place. They could be ringing every firebase we got. There's so much goddamn real estate out here—most of it covered in forest . . . I've been patrolling as much as I dare, but I'm terrified, Ed—absolutely *terrified*—at what those patrols might find. That's how that German airborne company found those Chinese sappers—on a long-range patrol. And those Chinese were carrying twenty kilos of C4 *apiece*. That wasn't a recon unit, Ed. They were gonna blow some things up."

"Nate, I'm shooting straight with you. No bullshit. I've

pushed as hard as I can. We're not going to get any reinforcements out of Marshall.''

''How about the 2nd Infantry?'' Nate asked.

''What?'' Dekker shot back. ''Just invite North Korea
into Seoul?''

''We could deploy them to Vladivostok. From there they
could hit North Korea from the Russian border if the North
attacks the South.''

Dekker sighed audibly. ''There's only three days till the
inauguration. Governor Bristol's people tell me he's 'fully
apprised of the situation' and 'is sympathetic to our plight.'
There's nothing he can do right now.''

''That's bullshit. He could get together with Marshall
and Congress and—''

''It's not gonna happen, Nate! We're in a transition period between administrations. From November to January
we're in lame duck limbo. You're not getting any more
troops until after the inauguration. I can't get you more
troops. But I'll do anything within my power to help. What
else can I do for you, Nate?''

Clark filled his lungs and let the air out slowly. ''Just tell
me why I'm here, Ed. What I'm supposed to be doing?
When I can come home?''

There was dead silence on the phone now.

''I'm ordering my troops to take off their blue helmet
covers and put on white camo,'' Nate said. He hung up and
gave the order.

It was a purely symbolic act. But changing from ''blue
hats'' to arctic white at least was something. An act he
could take to prepare for war. Blue hats were for humanitarian peacekeepers. Arctic white meant concealment in
combat. The significance of the change was lost on no one
in his headquarters. The mood changed. The pace of work
quickened. Commanding generals, privates in snow holes—
all braced for the shock that was coming.

FORT BENNING, GEORGIA
January 18, 1900 GMT (1400 Local)

André Faulk read his posting from behind the glass-covered bulletin board. After two months of basic training and two more of advanced individual training at infantry school, the recruits were being sent to the swelling ranks. André's smile drained from his face when he found his name. Others were shouting and slapping backs. André had to look up the strange number he'd found next to his name on the listings of "Military Occupation Specialties."

"André!" Stempel shouted.

Before Stempel could join up with Faulk, a burly, tanned recruit from California grabbed him. He squeezed Stempel's neck and rubbed his knuckles through Stempel's short hair. "Did you hear what billet Fuckup landed in?" the muscular beach bum shouted. He let Stempel raise his head just enough to tell André himself.

"Eleven-B!" Stempel said, beaming. Infantry. "The 25th Light Infantry Division."

"Hawa-ii," the surfer added, using the native pronunciation. "Hey, Stemp, it's possible even *you* might get laid there, troopuh!" He pushed Stempel nearly to the ground. Harold was grinning from ear to ear. He'd been posted to one of the combat arms like all the others. He'd made it.

Men from their training platoon were gathering around.

"What about you, André?" Stempel asked. Everyone waited.

Faulk mumbled, "Second Infantry."

"Aw ri-i-ight!" the surfer said. He punched Faulk on the arm. "They're good to *go,* man. Most combat-ready unit in the army outside the airborne."

"What MOS?" Stempel asked, just as André knew he would.

"Seventy-one-L," André answered. The laughter and noise slowly subsided.

"What's that?"

"Admin specialist," André replied, then walked away. Stempel ran after him and fell into place at his side.

"Hey, André, that admin-specialist thing doesn't matter! Everybody knows you're the best soldier in the platoon! The army's just fucked up. They send you to be a clerk and me an infantryman. Go figure that!" André just stared at his boots. "Look, André, you could use that letter Sergeant Giles got for you."

"Sh-h-i-i. When I joined the army, nobody said nothin' about jumpin' outta airplanes."

"But that must be what *happened*!" Stempel exclaimed. "They had a slot open for you in airborne school, and when you told Sergeant Giles you didn't wannta go, all the combat arms slots were *filled*! So why don't you just go! That letter is supposed to get you straight into airborne school if you change your mind!" Something was wrong. "What?" Harold asked.

André had always been terrified of heights, but he said nothing. He couldn't even look out the windows of his mother's apartment without getting dizzy. He peeled away and headed off toward the obstacle course to think.

"I'd never have made it without you," Stempel called out from behind. André kept walking. He reached up and wiped away the tears of utter humiliation. He'd thought he'd had the makings of a good soldier.

VLADIVOSTOK, SIBERIA
January 19, 2200 GMT (1000 Local)

"Brrrr," Kate Dunn said. She and Woody descended the stairs from the airliner's door to the tarmac. Kate quickly buttoned her parka all the way to the top and then put on her gloves, but she was still cold. "J-e-e-ez," she said through clenched teeth. Her jaw quivered as they walked into the stiff wind that blew across the concrete.

Woody seemed completely comfortable. "Like I said, you need a hat." Kate turned her entire torso to him to avoid exposing any more of her bare skin. One hand clenched the top of her parka closed under her chin. The other was pressed tight against her side. Woody wore the most stupid-looking fur hat Kate had ever seen. "They must've had to k-kill twenty or thirty rats to m-make that thing," she said.

"It's rabbit," Woody said proudly.

"Wood-man!" they heard. The call came from behind a roped-off area where the departing passengers waited. The flight they'd just taken from Anchorage to Vladivostok had been nearly empty. Business was booming, however, on the return trip.

"O-la!" Woody yelled. Kate followed him over to the rope. A waiting man had half a dozen cameras dangling from his body. Woody gave him a soul shake. *"Qué pasa, hombre!"*

"How many times do I have to tell you I'm not Spanish?" the man said with a distinct Irish accent. His white teeth shone through a dark beard flecked with gray. His ruddy face had been turned leathery by the elements.

"But you've got the *soul* of a Spaniard, man. That's what counts! Hey, I'd like to introduce you to Kate Dunn, cub reporter." Kate shook the man's gloved hand with a smirk. She quickly grabbed her collar as the cold air poured in like ice water. But it did little good. The chill seemed to have sunk straight through her Orvis cold-weather gear. "Mick here is black Irish. His people were washed up on the shore of Ireland by the great storm that sunk the Spanish Armada."

"Pleased to meet you," the man said. A gust of wind immersed Kate in the frigid air. She dug her elbows in her sides and pressed her legs close together.

"We'd better let him g-go," Kate managed.

"You need a hat," Woody's friend said.

"I *told* her that, man," Woody said.

Kate rolled her eyes and nodded toward the terminal building. The Russian gate agent—wearing a greatcoat so thick that he looked like a bear—opened the roped-off area. The departing passengers stampeded toward the plane, which hadn't even turned off its engines.

Mick grabbed Woody and whispered into his ear. The

Irishman was looking at Kate. He and Woody laughed loudly. "He-*hey*!" Woody exclaimed. "Always good to *see* ya, compadre!" They parted. Kate practically ran to the terminal and, once inside, went straight over to an old radiator. There she shed the parka and gloves, which had themselves become the source of the cold.

"Ooooh," Kate moaned. She sagged in exhaustion as she held her blue fingers to the hot iron. *"God!"*

"I *told* you it'd be cold," Woody said. "Next time I'd appreciate it if you didn't ask for me by name."

"I fought my ass off for this assignment, Woody," she said. Her teeth remained clenched as she toasted each side of her hands before turning to warm her rear. "You're the very best cameraman there is, and—"

"Yeah, well . . ." he interrupted, then fell silent. "Anyway, *look* at you. I mean, we just like walked from the plane to the terminal, and you're already frozen solid."

"I'll be *fine*! That jerk in San Francisco just didn't know what he was *talking* about. 'Gore-Tex' this and 'polymer' that. My ass!" Woody was distracted. He kept looking around the concourse. "Trying to spot some more old friends like that leering bastard out there?"

"Hey, if he leered any, it's because of his Spanish blood."

"Well, what about that macho male lewd shit he was whispering to you about me."

Woody rocked his head back, feigning shock. "You think that was what it was? Wait here." He headed for the men's room.

Kate began the process of putting her arctic gear on again. The parka was so cold that she held it over the radiator. Then she remembered the salesman's warning that the high-tech fabric might melt. "Gore-Tex my ass," she grumbled as she slipped the parka on. When Woody returned he had a shit-eating grin on his face. "Hee, hee-hee, hee-hee, hee-hee."

"*What is wrong* with you?" she said. "Has that rat hat made you go mental?"

He pulled open his massive overcoat. A large plastic baggy protruded from an inner pocket. In it was a large quantity of pot.

"Jesus, Woody!" Kate whispered. She stepped closer to him and looked all around. The terminal was deserted now. "Where the hell did you get that?"

"Mick-a-roono! He wasn't talking about yer bod, Kate. He was tellin' me where he'd stashed his *sensimillia!*"

"Oh," she said. "Well, what the hell are you gonna *do* with it, Woody?" she whispered. "What about customs?"

He laughed, holding out his arms and looking from one side of the empty building to the other. "This is Russia, Kate. No government. No customs. *Anarchy,* man. You can do anything you want here!"

OVAL OFFICE, THE WHITE HOUSE
January 20, 0230 GMT (2130 Local)

President Marshall already felt like an outsider. All of the Marshalls' belongings in the residential quarters had been packed a week before. Marshall toyed with the pens and pencils on the desk. His staff had already packed up his files. No one expected him to work on a Saturday. The day before the inauguration.

Bristol would be hopping from balls to bashes all across town. They'd be picking up steam and heading into the wee hours of the morning. Looking around the office—stripped bare of anything personal of Marshall's—he saw he was leaving it in good shape for his successor. He wished he could say the same for the world situation. Marshall shook his head and frowned. So much left undone.

The door burst open and the sound of two busy men followed just behind. When they saw him there, they froze. Marshall didn't recognize their faces.

"Oh. I'm sorry, sir," one of the men said. "We didn't know . . ." They held in their hands stacks of files . . . for the new president.

"No, no. Come on in," Marshall said. He swept his arm

across the desk, turning it over to them with a gracious smile.

They looked at each other before tentatively proceeding. Marshall walked along the walls of the office with his hands shoved deep in his pockets. There were portraits of his predecessors. He'd never studied the artwork before. There had always seemed like there'd be time later.

"No, put that one on top. The ones with the red labels go on top."

Marshall looked back around at them and smiled. "You boys aren't out at the parties?"

The one giving the orders and doing the talking shrugged. "We've been spending all our time down in the Situation Room."

"Oh, you're national security?" Marshall asked. The man nodded. "I didn't know—" he began. He stopped himself. He didn't know the national security staffs had already made the transition. He turned away. "I didn't know there was anybody down in the Situation Room tonight." He moved on to the portrait of Washington.

"There was a crisis action team convened, Mr. President," the man said. When Marshall looked up at him, the man stood there awkwardly. He didn't know what to say. "It's a *joint* team. Some of . . . of the *outgoing* staff is down there too."

Marshall nodded, resuming his inventory of the dead presidents. "What's the topic du jour?" he asked.

"Oh . . . China, sir."

"Anything new?"

The man cleared his throat. "Some more troop movements. Closer to the border. And . . . and some patriotic broadcasts have replaced normal programming. Old documentaries about the Long March on TV. Classical music on the radio. That sort of thing. We thought at first that somebody in the leadership had died."

"Wouldn't be surprised," Marshall said. His hands were now clasped behind his back. His eyes roamed the walls. "The youngest one of 'em must be in his nineties." The two men laughed more loudly than was appropriate. They were excited. This was a beginning for them.

"Oh!" the staffer added. "And there was a . . . an order that came down last night from Beijing. Every single soldier from general to private was ordered to shave his head." Marshall turned to look at the man, who was smiling at the humor of it. "Almost three million haircuts. Imagine all that hair." The man wilted under Marshall's worried gaze. "They . . . they have had problems with head lice, NSA said. They think. In the army. The Chinese Army."

Marshall headed for the door. He intended to go directly down to the Situation Room. But he stopped. He looked at the two junior aides standing behind his desk. *Bristol's desk*, Marshall thought. He left the Oval Office for the last time and headed off to a guest bedroom. His late-night snack awaited him . . . as usual.

THE KREMLIN, MOSCOW, RUSSIA
January 20, 0425 GMT (0625 Local)

Kartsev had awoken early to watch the coverage of the inaugural eve gala on C-SPAN. He sat in his office in front of the television. It was the night of his experiment's final catalyst. The last brisk stir of the sociopolitical pot. His few remaining assets had been lying low. Most, in fact, had perished during the extended period of inactivity. Drug overdoses. Violent accidents. Men condemned to Schedule A for risking operational security. Plus suicide was already 10 percent a month.

The television cast the room's only light. On it, a great hall had been turned into a crowded ballroom floor. Kartsev had muted the announcers' running commentary. Only the occasional close-up drew his passing attention. The partygoers were obscure political dignitaries. Kartsev didn't recognize any of the names shown as the camera zoomed in.

When the scene switched to the motorcade pulling into an underground garage, Kartsev turned the volume back up. With it rose his excitement.

". . . have just arrived under heavy police and Secret Service protection. This inauguration will be marked by the tightest security in history after the wave of political terror that flashed across this country last year."

"Excuse me, Tim," another voice interrupted as the president-elect emerged from a limousine. "Governor Bristol is just now arriving." They went on to identify each of the other passengers as they gathered. They all smiled and waved to the cameras campaign-style. When the Bristol and Davis families were assembled, they headed through the cordon of security officers toward the service elevator. Kartsev watched and listened now with rapt attention. His heart pounded in his chest.

THE WILLARD HOTEL, WASHINGTON, D.C.
January 20, 0430 GMT (2330 Local)

The air that rushed through the sheet-metal duct was hot. He was sweating profusely from the exertion of crawling a painstaking pace of a meter or two per minute. Every point of contact with the ducting had to be planned. A hand there—by the jagged rivet he could feel in the darkness. A knee where he estimated the last strap support to be. The noise now poured in through the grating at the end. He inched his way toward it.

The sheet metal had already given three times. Each time it made a loud bang like he'd slammed his fist down. The duct was a meter wide and high. It was suspended above the grand ballroom by black fabric belts looped around it that hung from the ceiling. He could feel the entire thing swaying gently with each movement he made. Each time his weight tested the metal, he cringed in anticipation. Not that he feared death. He would die that night regardless. And he wasn't indifferent to death. He was sickened by the prospect of it. It had been a long run, however. Most of the others from his class were dead already. Siberia, the Bronx, Wembley Stadium, and number 10 Downing Street—he should by all rights be dead. He had faced the void before . . . just never with quite the same certainty.

The metal enclosure resounded again with a bang. It was so loud it sounded like a gunshot, but it was the duct's floor popping back into position after he'd moved on. The noise of the band and the buzz of the room were too loud. Once again they'd missed the sound for which four dozen pairs of ears were intently listening.

He tried to imagine whether he'd left dents that might tip his opponents off. Each time the swinging of the duct became excessive, he froze in place and waited for the motion to dampen. It took an hour and a half to crawl sixty feet.

Finally, he reached the grate. He rubbed his eyes clear of the sweat and peered through. He couldn't see the stage! Enormous nets filled with red, white, and blue balloons hung just in front.

But the balloons will come down, he decided. He took a vise grip and went to work on two neighboring slats. He pried and twisted the thin metal until a hole opened up. That would do for the muzzle. He spread another space several inches above. The bands had stopped and the speeches had begun. He'd barely finished in time.

He replaced the tools in their pouches on his vest. He pulled the rifle off his back where it had been securely strapped. The magazine was already loaded. A bullet was already chambered. The scope was even focused correctly for the range.

The band played "America the Beautiful" as he shouldered the rifle. The muzzle protruded slightly through the hole in the bottom slat. And when he looked into the eyepiece he could see blurry balloons. The upper hole in the slats had been made for the scope. He rested his thumb on the power switch to the laser sight.

Now he waited. The cheers of the throng rose several decibels, and then rose again to a sustained roar. The nets opened up. The balloons began to drop past his scope. His field of view at high magnification was very narrow. All he could see was a falling mass of colorful spheres. All at once the net was empty and the podium came into focus. He flicked on the laser aimpoint.

• • •

Like circus performers Bristol held Gordon's hand aloft. It was clenched in his own as the adoring mass of black ties and sequins cheered. Fifteen, twenty minutes here, tops, before they moved on to the next gathering. Each party was a step up the ladder. At the last stop were the largest contributors.

Gordon waved awkwardly with his left hand as Bristol held his right captive. Every so often he pointed at a face in the crowd. People jumped to punch balloons into the air. The cheering went on and on. Bristol—the consummate campaigner—held Gordon in that pose far longer than Gordon felt comfortable. The grin was frozen on his face and felt unnatural. He looked over to see that Bristol's smile looked the same as always—never quite natural, never obviously staged.

A small red dot wiggled on Bristol's bunched up jacket. It took a moment for Gordon to realize what he saw. In that moment the dot settled squarely on Bristol's chest. Gordon hurled himself into the larger man.

The boom of a rifle shot sounded almost instantaneously. Gordon's momentum carried the two men to the hard floor. They landed in a heap, Gordon on top of Bristol. He rolled off. Screams rose up from the crowd. They were behind the podium. Milliseconds seemed like an eternity. "No," Bristol said just before the podium began to shatter into pieces. Gordon felt the hot daggers in his chest and pelvis. Holes exploded through the podium one at a time. Brilliant footlights shone brightly through each. Bristol's body shook and lurched against Gordon. Searing pain shot from terrible wounds.

Lights hung from the ceiling over the stage. They were hidden from view by short curtains. Like the bottom of his parents' dining-room table. The raw wood underneath the bright polish.

Strings of firecrackers like Chinese New Year in long bursts. *"Cease fire! Cease fire!"* a half-dozen men shouted.

An agent who'd lain on top of Gordon rose. None too

soon, because his weight had crushed the breath out of him. The cool air washed across his soaking chest. Gordon tried but couldn't draw any of it into his lungs. He needed the breath for the words he so desperately wanted to speak. Instead, he just mouthed them over and over and over again. "I've been shot. I've been shot. I've been shot."

10

The snippets of sound and fleeting images whirled around the spinning, sweat-soaked bed. Gordon Davis was so nauseous and drained that he couldn't quite regain consciousness. It was as if he'd tumbled into dark water. He didn't know which way was up. But he saw the anguished face of Elaine. How she gasped for breath as she sobbed like a child. He felt the plastic mask on his face. He heard voices calling out to him from the surface.

"Can you hear me?" a man asked over and over. His voice was deep. He was so close Gordon could feel his breath. There was an awful, steely taste in Gordon's mouth when he swallowed. His eyes were pried open and a painfully bright light appeared.

It was dark again when he lifted his head. Pain split his skull in two. It fell back into the cold, sweaty pillow. Fleeting images of ghostly forms rushed to his bedside in his dreams.

"Can you hear me?" someone asked. Gordon's eyes drifted open. It was a man—a silver-haired man—in a dark suit. Gordon stared at the ceiling tiles in the brightly lit room. He swallowed the fiery bile that threatened to erupt in a gush from his stomach. "I concur," he heard several times amid a confusing jumble of words. They came from different people and different places scattered around Gordon's bed. He tried to lift his head, but pain burst from his abdomen like a tearing of tissues. He collapsed in agony, his eyes jammed closed. But not before he saw the curtain of men in suits that ringed his bed.

Questions. He was being questioned by someone. Prompted. With his eyes closed, he tried his best to croak out the reply the silver-haired man expected. Mere fragments were all he caught. Words that he just repeated. He swallowed over and over to wet his parched mouth. "Swear . . . solemnly swear" . . . something. And "protect and defend." He remembered those words. "Protect and defend."

Gordon opened his eyes. Sunlight streamed in through open curtains. "He's awake!" Gordon heard a man shout. It was followed by the rustling sound of a newspaper and the sudden appearance of several men in suits.

"*Ex-cu-u-use* me," a nurse said, elbowing her way through the crowd.

"Get everybody in here," one of the men whom Gordon didn't recognize ordered. "Now!"

"Good morning!" the nurse said. She fiddled with the drip hanging over his bed and checked her watch. "How do you feel?"

Her voice had the casual sound of a day at work. Gordon realized he was in a hospital.

"Terr'ble," Gordon mumbled. He licked his lips with a dry tongue. The nurse knew exactly what he wanted. She held up a cup with a lid like the one they'd used for the girls when they were toddlers. She let him have only the tiniest sip before pulling it away.

"Ah-ah-*a-a-h*!" she said. "Not too much."

Behind her grew a wall of men, none of whom Gordon recognized. The door opened and closed repeatedly as the bedside continued to fill. He saw Fein. He saw Bristol's campaign manager.

He saw Elaine, for whom the crowd parted. She was crying. But there was a smile on her face as she leaned over and hugged him. Gordon felt the wet tears on his cheeks. It was only when he felt a strange tug that he realized some kind of tube was stuck down his nose. His own eyes filled with moisture.

"Go-o-ordon," Elaine cooed. "Oh, my sweet darling husband. Gordon, I love you so much."

"Elaine," Gordon managed. "I've . . . I've been *shot*."

"I know, honey. I know all about it. And you're gonna be fine. Everything's gonna be all right!" She stared at him through tears and a smile, then lowered her head to his shoulder. "Oh, Gordon," she whispered, "I was so scared. I was so, so scared." The floodgates opened now. He could feel her shaking against him. He cried too, but few tears materialized.

When she rose, she smiled and sniffed. She wiped her cheeks clean with two swipes of her hand. She didn't, however, take the other hand from where she'd lain it flat on Gordon's chest underneath his gown.

"The girls?" Gordon asked.

"They're outside," Elaine said. She turned to the crowd, now four or five deep all around. Gordon looked at them too. "But . . . there's some business these people need to attend to first, Gordon."

She looked back down. She must have sensed something in his face. She bent over to whisper in his ear, her cool hand rising to cup his cheek. "Do you remember what happened, Gordon?"

"I . . . I was on a stage."

"No, I mean after that? Last night." He thought for a moment, then shook his head. She spoke softly. Calmly. Clearly. "Phil Bristol is dead, Gordon. He was shot too, don't you remember? You tried to save him, but it was too late." He shook his head again. "You're the president, Gordon. The president of the United States. You were sworn in last night. You took the oath, can't you remember?" He shook his head. "But there was a competency vote. The speaker of the House is the acting president. These men are here to take another vote. They're here to vote whether you're competent now to assume office. Do you understand?''

Gordon panned the faces around his bed. President Marshall's outgoing cabinet. Would-be nominees for the same posts in Bristol's administration. *My administration*, he thought. His head spun with the unbelievable truth of it.

"Where's President Marshall?" Gordon asked, slurring the words drunkenly.

"He was killed, sir," replied the silver-haired chief justice of the Supreme Court. "He was poisoned by a midnight snack in the White House the night you were shot." Gordon closed his eyes. "Are you ready to proceed, Mr. President?" Gordon looked up and nodded. "Can you state your name, sir?"

"Gordon Davis."

"Your full name, if you please?"

"Gordon Eugene Davis."

"Thank you. Now, sir, can you tell me where and when you were born?"

"Jackson, Tennessee. March seventeenth, 1945."

The silver head bowed in acknowledgment of Gordon's answer. "And can you give me the names and ages of your children?"

"Celeste, she's . . ." he had to think. "She's eighteen. Janet is fourteen."

Again the chief justice nodded. Gordon was doing well. "Now, sir, can you tell me what you know or understand has happened since the night of January twentieth? Since you received your wounds?"

"Well, I was . . . I was shot." The chief justice nodded, coaching now. "And so was Phil Bristol, only Phil . . . he . . . didn't make it. And I remember the ambulance. Elaine," he said, turning to her, "you were there." She nodded, forcing a smile onto her face. "Then not much." Heads turned. "The oath," Gordon quickly added. The chief justice's eyes remained locked on him. The same deep voice had spoken the words—protect and defend. "I took the oath," he said. "You administered it."

That seemed to break the tension. The chief justice had a muted conversation with the speaker of the House, who nodded.

"I'm going to take the poll now," the chief justice said to the gathering. "The question before you is whether Gordon Eugene Davis is competent to assume the office of the president of the United States." He began with Marshall's secretary of defense. "I believe that he is," came the man's reply. "I certify him competent," said the acting secretary of state. The other cabinet secretaries all replied in succession. Gordon, for his part, struggled to keep it all straight in his head. Piercing shots of pain purged his mind of all thoughts. Brief respites were swamped by sickening waves of nausea.

Elaine squeezed his arm. "You did great, darling," she whispered into his ear.

It was quiet now. The room had grown warm. The air stale from so many bodies crammed into it. Arthur Fein stepped through the crowd to stand beside Elaine. He held in his hand a leather portfolio, which he opened.

There was a legal document inside in duplicate. "This is a written declaration, sir," Fein said, "that no inability to discharge the powers and duties of the office of president of the United States exists. If you sign these two copies, sir, and I transmit them to the speaker of the House and the president pro tempore, you will immediately assume those powers and duties."

A sea of faces watched him. Somber men and women. Some of the most powerful people on earth. And by signing those papers, he would become their boss. The leader of the free world. He looked at Elaine. She winked. Gordon saw now that Celeste and Janet had been ushered to the foot of his bed. They smiled and waved, but were inhibited by all the people. Tears filled his eyes. A movie camera and two television Minicams parted the crowd for a better vantage. A boom mike extended high over the bed.

The proffered pen was thick and expensive. Cameras flashed as he scribbled his signature. Elaine kept the pen. Fein squeezed his way to the end of the bed. The speaker and president pro tempore accepted the portfolio. When they'd finished reading, the speaker said, "Congratulations, Mr. President."

The crowd suddenly burst into applause. Cameras recorded it all. Lights flashed. The girls made it to the head of the bed. They hugged Gordon's neck. Their faces were cool, wet with tears. The camera lights fell dark. The applause died out. The room began to clear. Congratulations drifted through his daughter's hair. The sweet smell was what he registered most.

Gordon thought for a moment they were going to leave him alone with his family. But in place of the men in suits came men in uniforms. Rows of ribbons on their chests. Stars on their shoulder boards.

"Come on," Elaine said to the girls. "We've got to let your dad do some work." They each hugged him again. Janet started crying and hugging him. Celeste shook her and said, "Let's *go-o*," in a menacing whisper. Gordon smiled.

Elaine kissed him. She then admonished the gathering generals and admirals not to keep him long. Behind them easels were being set up. Maps were pulled from large, flat cases sealed with combination locks. The soldiers carrying them wore sidearms.

"You need to go potty?" the nurse asked. She was holding a stainless-steel bedpan. Gordon looked at the waiting crowd, their big production ready to roll. He shook his head. She shrugged and showed him the button with which to call her.

Gordon's agony was more or less constant. "What about some pain medication?" he asked.

"Try to cut back. If you really need it, you ask. But we took you off the heavy stuff last night. That's why you're so *chipper* today. But it's going to hurt, Mr. President. For a long time. You're going to have to get used to it."

A trickle of cold sweat ran down his neck. When she left, a Secret Service agent locked the door behind her. Gordon was all alone now with men he barely knew. The joint chiefs of staff. Bristol's proposed nominees for State and Defense. The director of the CIA. A host of others who might be important.

"Mr. President," began Bob Hartwig, Marshall's nominee for secretary of defense, "I'm sorry to have to hit you with this, but we've been paralyzed for the last three days. And the situation is getting worse and more dangerous by the hour."

General Dekker, chairman of the joint chiefs, appeared. He was followed by a large map. It was walked under the brighter lights at bedside. Two men tilted it down toward Gordon. "Eleven hours after the assassinations," Dekker said, "three days ago, the army of the People's Republic of China crossed the border into Mongolia." Dekker held a pointer to the map. Mongolia was almost completely filled with red crosshatched lines. "It was a massive invasion. There was very little resistance. The occupation is nearly complete."

Gordon's eyes roamed the map of Siberia farther to the north. Small islands of blue marked the American and other UN forces.

"Mr. President," Hartwig said. Gordon opened his eyes wide. He had no idea how long he'd slept. He tried to clear the fog. "Mr. President, I'm afraid the news gets worse." Another, more focused map showing the Siberian theater was being held up before him. "About twelve hours ago," Dekker continued, "the Chinese crossed the Amur River into the former Republic of Russia."

"That's when we had the doctors cut your pain medication," Hartwig said. "Mrs. Davis okayed the decision."

Gordon said, "Can't see the map."

The map was held closer. Hartwig and the chief of naval operations raised his head and put another pillow under it. The pain was almost too great. From the sources of the pain, he knew there were multiple wounds. They must have been life-threatening.

Dekker was talking.

Gordon looked up. Red lines slopped over an irregular border. The "former Republic of Russia." The map looked like a child's coloring book in which an unrestrained pre-schooler had drawn. Gordon had no military experience, but he saw red lines of advancing Chinese. On the larger map, they extended from North Korea all the way to Mongolia. On the smaller, they sloped over the Amur and Ussuri rivers dangerously close to UNRUSFOR troops. That left little possibility of mistake. This was no tentative probe meant to take America's measure. This was a war. War. Gordon felt the word for the first time. It mixed naturally with his unrelenting pain.

He focused on Dekker's finger. It lay on the blue unit nearest the invading red. It wouldn't be long until they met.

"We've been in contact in the air but not on the ground," Dekker said.

An air-force general spoke up, "We've been knocking down MiGs and Tupelovs for hours. Most of our intercepts are well inside Russian airspace."

Gordon filled his lungs. The process was painful. "Have we warned the Chinese to get out?" he managed.

"Yes, sir," said Horton Cates, Marshall's acting secretary of state. "They claimed to have warned former Secretary Jensen what would happen if Western troops didn't clear out."

"I'd like to talk to Jensen," Gordon requested.

Cates looked at Hartwig, then down at Gordon. "Hugh Jensen was found dead this morning, Mr. President."

Gordon sighed with a hiss. "Terr'rists?"

Cates shook his head. "Shot himself . . . after news of the border crossings. The FBI is investigating, but they're virtually certain it was suicide."

The extent of the tragedy took shape. Gordon looked back at the map. He struggled to keep his eyes open. He tried but abandoned the effort to draw another deep breath. "All right," he said. His voice was weak. Each syllable sounded like his last utterance. He looked at Dekker. "What do we do?"

Dekker cleared his throat and shifted his weight. "Well, sir, that's not really . . . It's a call that's over my pay grade, sir."

"You're still chairman of the joint chiefs, right?" Gordon asked.

"Well, yes, sir. But whether to pull out or go to war is a purely political question, sir."

"Wait," Gordon croaked. He coughed. Pain racked him. He had to breathe. In. Out. He slowly regained the strength to speak. "I'm not asking you . . ." he continued in a raspy voice, "whether we go to war." He was swimming over great swells of agony. With each dizzying fall he grew nauseous. "I'm asking how do we stop the Chinese? I'm ordering you to expel the Chinese from Siberia by force of arms."

OAHU INTERNATIONAL AIRPORT, HAWAII
January 24, 0100 GMT (1500 Local)

Harold Stempel descended the stairs to the tarmac. He stared at the masses of soldiers dressed in white. There had to be thousands of them in ranks and files. They were loading onto a hodgepodge of dark green military transports and brightly painted civilian airliners.

"Aloha," said a woman in a grass skirt at the bottom of the steps. She hung a lei around Harold's neck and kissed both his cheeks. He smiled at the pretty woman with long straight hair and olive skin. "Aloha" she said to the paunchy man behind Harold. She kissed his cheeks as well.

"Pardon me," Harold said. She seemed surprised he was still there. "But who are they?" he asked, pointing at the troops.

She looked over her bare shoulder. "They're soldiers. Been here all day. Aloha," she said, smiling to the next passenger.

Harold headed toward the uniformed men out of curiosity. It felt good to walk. To unlimber his tight muscles after so many hours of travel. The cruise ship had docked in San Juan. He'd then spent hours in the airport with his parents. They'd said their good-byes and he had flown to Orlando. From there to L.A., then on to Hawaii. He had slept on each of the flights and was only just now waking up.

Two MPs slouched next to their Humvee. They noticed his approach, but were uninterested.

"Pardon me," Harold said.

With a bored look one replied, "Yeah."

"Sorry to bother you, but what unit is this?"

They both turned his way. Both wore sidearms. "Who the hell're you?"

Harold stiffened. "Stempel, Harold, private, U.S. Army, serial number—"

"He *me-eans*," the other man said, "who the fuck do you think you are askin' military secrets, fuckhead?"

"I . . . I'm headed for the 25th. I thought, maybe, you'd know."

"Lemme see yer orders."

Stempel rummaged through his bag. They looked over the orders, then handed them back. They ushered Stempel into the staging area of the 25th Infantry Division (Light).

The hangar was nearly empty, but there were row after row of tables. Everyone looked tired and acted irritable. "You have a will?" the woman asked without looking up from her table. He shook his head. She got his name. The names of his beneficiaries. Stempel signed. "Over there," she said. A man wore a lab coat with camouflaged fatigues underneath. Holding what looked like a staple gun with a long hose, he dabbed cold alcohol on Stempel's arm. "I just got out of basic. I already had shots for—" With a hiss Stempel felt the sting. The man repeated the process with three different injectors. When Stempel picked up his carry-on his arm was sore. "You're done," the man said, pointing at the lone plane on the tarmac. A short line of soldiers ascended the stairs. Leaving his baggage tickets with an NCO, Harold ran across the concrete. The contents of his carry-on jangled noisily. The door of the plane was being closed. The engines started up. A man began to pull the stairs away. "Hey!" Stempel yelled. They waited. He was inside.

The lavatory on the airliner was tiny. Harold barely got the door closed with his "kit," an armload of gear a sergeant had scavenged off other soldiers. He dropped everything, sat on the commode and grabbed his head. The bristles folded first one way, then the other as he ran his palms across his scalp. The day before, he was having a rum swizzle with his parents at a shipboard bar eyeing a girl by the pool in a pink bikini. Now he was on a plane headed for war in Siberia. He'd asked everyone in the hangar and on the plane what was happening. The privates and PFCs had just shrugged. He rocked forward and clamped his hands between his knees, trying to control his breathing. *I'm ready for this*, he told himself over and over. *I made it. I'm a soldier now just like everybody else on this plane.*

Maybe if he got out of his jeans and into a uniform he'd settle down. But that was a chore in the tight quarters. He stripped down to Jockey shorts and a T-shirt on which was printed the torso of a bronzed bodybuilder. Around his neck hung his plastic lei. He began to shiver. The soldiers wore winter battle dress, so the cabin was kept chilly. Harold shoved the lei into a pocket and hurried into the loose, oversized long johns and cushion-sole socks. He bloused mottled green-and-brown camouflage BDUs into white winter combat boots, which were insulated, rubber-lined, and waterproof. A lined woodland camo field jacket completed the standard battle dress.

From there he had to follow the sergeant's instructions. Baggy wool trousers hooked to scissors-type suspenders. A loose, oversized wool shirt covered everything, and an arctic-white nylon shell covered that. He fished in the large cargo pockets until he found tape, which he tied around his thigh to prevent rubbing noise. The shell's drawstrings pulled tight around his boots, which slipped into white arctic overshoes. The solid white parka went over everything. He drew the string at his waist and tied each of the parka's split tails separately around his thighs. On his head went his cold-weather cap, his white, cloth-covered helmet, then the parka's hood. Another pull of a drawstring left only his face exposed. At the edge of the hood he bent a pliable wire inside a fur ruff and covered his face.

Sweat formed at his brow. In the small mirror he looked twice his normal size. He had cotton, anticontact gloves for working on "cold-soaked" equipment. A black "Arctic Mitten System" with thick wool inserts and pile backs for warming your cheeks and nose and a strap for hanging them over your neck. A gauntlet went over his sleeves and an adjustment strap pulled them tight. There was a single little sleeve in the mittens for your trigger finger.

The only spare piece of equipment they didn't have for Harold was a weapon. He was headed off to war unarmed.

Someone banged on the door and Harold jumped. "Quit pullin' yer pud and clear out!" came the muffled voice. Harold began pulling the gear off. He opened the door and apologized to the man outside. He then wandered the aisles with his arms full, looking for a place to sit. The plane was packed. He couldn't find the sergeant. He didn't know anyone. Bags and gear were crammed into every free space. The aisles were cluttered with the overflow. Harold stepped from hole to hole apologizing, smashing his large Arctic Bag into faces. No one talked, but no one slept. A flight attendant finally directed him to a fold-down seat beside the lavatories and behind the galley. He settled in—alone for the duration of the flight—writing his name on his gear. He printed "Stempel, Harold, Pvt." neatly on his parka's label. *Just in case*, he thought. No one on the plane knew his name.

KHABAROVSK, RUSSIA
January 24, 0200 GMT (1200 Local)

"I called this meeting for two reasons," Clark began. He sat at the head of a long table. Aides stood at maps all

around. Before him sat the commanders of each of the coalition's contingents, large and small. Each had his own
agenda. "First, I wanted to inform you of my government's
intentions with respect to the Chinese invasion. Secondly,
I am going to ask you what *your* government's intentions
are."

Heads swiveled. Discomfort was evident.

"First, *my* orders." Most already knew through diplomatic channels what he was going to say. They must also
have known that Clark's worst nightmare was playing out
right before his eyes. "I have been ordered by the president
to repel from Russia—by military force—the People's Liberation Army."

Everywhere Clark looked they stared back at him. It took
willpower to survey each and every face. He was searching
for signs. Who's in? Who's out?

"What are our rules of engagement?" asked General Sir
Arthur Howard. The British commander's businesslike tone
seemed to lift the oppressive weight that had hung over the
meeting. Junior British and American officers began to
chatter in good-natured whispers.

"Conventional weapons only," Clark replied. The room
fell silent.

"Do the Chinese understand that?" Clark's first clear
ally asked. He'd chosen his words carefully.

"They have been informed of the consequences," Clark
said. "I've seen the transcripts of the meeting. The Chinese
ambassador asked for and received clarification in both English and Mandarin. We sent the same message in a telephone call from the secretary of defense to the Chinese
minister of defense." Clark leaned forward. "One *hint* of
chemical, biological, or nuclear weapons and we respond
*dis*proportionately, massively, and without targeting limitation."

Howard's back remained erect, not resting against the
chair. His hands were clasped before him, but he kept his
elbows off the table as if at dinner. "Was there any discussion of . . . of the current hostilities? Any conditions?
Demands?"

"We demanded that the Chinese withdraw immediately. They reiterated their claims to large parts of Siberia."

There came a new voice—the French. "Have you already begun the fight?" the general asked.

"The Space Defense Command has downed all seven Chinese recon satellites. Anything they put up, we'll knock down. They'll be totally blind. And the embargo imposed by the U.S. Navy after Taiwan is now a blockade. Notices have gone out. We'll sink any blockade runners . . . no matter what the flag. The Chinese Navy hasn't put any surface forces to sea. We're sinking them in port. The eleven diesel-electric subs at sea were being tailed. Our attack subs confirmed eleven kills in twenty-seven minutes. The blockade will cut their exports and their access to hard currency. With no way to pay for war materials, their overland imports should be limited. We'll wage unrestricted air war along the coast to a depth of two hundred kilometers . . . and as far south as the Fortieth Parallel."

"But not *south* of the Fortieth?" the French general asked.

"We've got enough targets without including downtown Beijing," Clark replied. "The Fortieth gets us to the suburbs. And it covers all of Manchuria."

Every member of the German contingent had written "40 degrees" on their pads, Clark noted.

"But that doesn't include any action against the Deng Feng missile fields?" the French general asked unexpectedly. The Chinese "East Wind" ICBMs had a nine-thousand-mile range. They were the only Chinese nuclear weapons capable of hitting Europe and the West Coast of America.

"There will be no action taken against Chinese nuclear delivery systems," Clark answered.

"And you will inform us—well in advance—if those rules of engagement change?" It was not a question. It was a condition to French participation.

"Of course," Clark replied, wondering how many other conditions there were. "I *will* tell you, however, that I *have* ordered a full-scale air interdiction campaign. I intend to begin the total destruction of their lines of communication. In addition to air suppression, we'll go after troop marshaling yards, rail lines, supply warehouses. In about one hour, six hundred aircraft from air-force bases in the U.S. and Japan and from carriers in the Yellow Sea and Sea of Japan are going in with raids as deep as Shenyang.''

"Will you hit their army headquarters—northeast?'' General Howard asked.

Clark nodded. "*We're* underground.'' He held his arms out to the bare concrete room. "I want them to be also.''

"Why were we not informed of these raids?'' the commander of French forces asked.

"You are being informed of them now.''

"I do not consider this adequate notice. These strikes have not been authorized by the Security Council.''

"The forces are not part of UNRUSFOR. I called for the strikes in my capacity as commander-in-chief of U.S. Army Pacific.''

"Let's not quibble over the details,'' the British commander broke in. The German commander made a gruff noise and nodded. "Like it or not—and I expect *not*—we have the better part of seventy Chinese divisions bearing down on us. Now, this is General Clark's meeting. We should hear what he has to say.''

Clark nodded to him in thanks. "We of course already have the 10th Mountain, 1st Infantry, and 3rd Marine Divisions in the field. The 82nd Airborne Division is en route to us here. We're projecting brigade strength in the field within twenty-four hours. We'll use them initially to join the 10th and form hasty defenses around Khabarovsk.'' Heads were bowed along both sides of the table. The battles were being fought in their minds. A 300,000-man sledgehammer against thin lines of light infantry and paratroopers. "In addition,'' Clark resumed, "the 25th Light Infantry Division is en route from Hawaii. We plan on placing them in a screen of strong points south and west of Khabarovsk along the Trans-Siberian Railroad.''

"What about more armor?" the German general asked.

"The 2nd Infantry Division will begin immediate trans-shipment from Korea to the port of Vladivostok. Plus, the U.S. Marine Corps has a Marine Amphibious Unit offshore. Within ten days they'll have another half-dozen landing ships giving us a reinforced brigade as a ready reserve. The next forces to arrive will be the 18th Airborne Corps with the 101st Airmobile and 24th Mechanized Infantry Divisions. I also expect an additional four tactical fighter wings inside of thirty days to add to the two that are currently engaged. Plans are for heavy bombers from the Strategic Projection Force based in the continental United States to begin bombing 'round the clock, with aircrews to turn the planes of South Korea and Japan."

"Will your Congress make a formal declaration?" the French commander asked.

"Whatever legal and constitutional requirements," Clark recited carefully, "required to authorize our commitment will be undertaken at the appropriate times." *Jeez*, he thought after parroting the script dictated by the White House lawyer. "Okay," Clark said. "I have now told you the intentions of the United States. I propose that we move on to the second item on our agenda—a declaration of the intentions of your governments with respect to the Chinese invasion." His pulse was racing. He thought it could go either way. He turned first to his most stalwart ally. "Arthur?"

The British general sat forward as if he were ready to answer. "I'm afraid I'm going to have to beg off, for the moment, Nate. Parliament is meeting in closed session. I'm sure it shouldn't be *too* much longer."

Nate was devastated. He tried not to show it. "What about your forces?" he asked the Bundeswehr general.

"I also am awaiting my orders," he said simply. A heavy silence hung over the table. The German seemed most discomfited of all. "My troops do have authority to fire in self-defense, but"—he shrugged—"we are not currently in positions nearing contact."

Clark turned reluctantly to the French officer. The last of the big three. ''General?''

The Frenchman's lower lip protruded from his mouth in a caricature either of a pout or a scowl—Clark couldn't decide which. ''I received instructions from Paris while en route here this morning.'' Clark braced himself. ''If the United States is committed to the fight, so is France. I am personally highly opposed to that decision, but I await your command, General Clark.'' He bowed his head like a courtier.

Clark's forces on hand were now doubled. Just as he tried not to show the defeat, he tried now not to grin like a schoolboy. He moved on to the Belgians, who fell in line with the French. The other exceptions were the Finns, who answered simply that they would fight. And the Danish, whose sole contribution was a medical contingent that would be bolstered to treat war casualties. All of the others deferred until orders were received from home.

Despite that, however, Clark was buoyed. After all, no one had actually backed out. And the French were in and—when Clark asked—seemed ready to send more troops. It was at that point the meeting was interrupted. The commander of a Belgian firebase was on the radio. The call was patched into the meeting. Clark lamented the fact that he didn't speak French as the commander delivered his report. The faces of the officers who did, however, grew increasingly long. The occasional background burst didn't sound like an artillery barrage. He realized suddenly what it was. The Chinese were busting bunkers one at a time . . . with demolitions. They were mopping up the Belgians.

The slow and calm report of the officer on the radio took on in Clark's mind a funereal quality. The sudden burst of noise over the radio ended in static.

No trace of Clark's smile now remained.

NORTH OF AMUR RIVER, SIBERIA
January 24, 2130 GMT (0730 Local)

The rolling landscape slid beneath the helicopter gunship.
Warrant Officer Hector Jiminez sat atop the Apache's chin
gun. His head was level with the knees of the pilot. The
higher elevation gave the pilot a clear view of the snowy
forests ahead. Sitting low gave Jiminez the feel of the gun.

Airspeed, altitude, and heading lit Jiminez's visor. As
copilot/gunner, he wore the Integrated Helmet and Display
Sighting System. He listened constantly for the sound of
warning tones.

"There's the river," Hector heard over the helmet's
headphones. It was the familiar voice of the pilot, fellow
Warrant Officer Steve Tipton.

Up ahead snaked a flat, white highway. Through the armored seat of the AH-64 Hector felt the aircraft decelerate.
Their flight of buglike gunships all pitched nose up in unison. They maintained their stagger—strung out to the right
of the flight leader's stubby winglet. The airspeed shown
in Hector's visor fell from 160 to near zero. The frozen
Amur River—the border between Russia and China—disappeared from view. The helicopters all settled below a
ridge into a hover a few feet above the treetops. Snow was
lashed off the branches of the twisting evergreens in the
narrow valley below.

They waited. Hector looked at the Apaches to his left
and to his right. The crosshairs on his visor traversed the
snow-covered hill just in front. The other gunners did the
same, he could tell. He watched the thirty-millimeter chain
guns under their feet slew from side to side. They were
slaved to the sighting systems, which traversed and slewed
in sync with the copilots' helmets. The long, single-barreled
cannon turned this way and that, their gunners nervous and
ready for action.

Underneath the helicopters' short wings were four pylons. They would normally be filled with Hellfire missiles—
sixteen in all—which could knock out even the most heavily armored main battle tanks. This mission, however, was

against soft targets—trucks and dismounted infantry. They instead carried four fat, round rockets launchers. Each held nineteen 2.75-inch rockets—seventy-six rockets in total. Each Apache packed the equivalent of a two-minute barrage by an eight-gun artillery battery. There were eight Apaches in all.

"Victor Sierra five three, this is Victor Sierra one one," came clearly through the earphones. "Objective in sight. Mounted and dismounted infantry. RWR is negative. Repeat, RWR is negative. Out."

RWR is negative, Hector thought. He took a deep breath and relaxed a bit. No Chinese guns or missiles had lit up the Kiowa Scout's Radar Warning Receiver.

"All units, this is Victor Sierra five three," came a new and familiar voice—their flight leader. "Weapons hot. On my lead. Tallyho."

The chin-mounted guns all swiveled left as the gunners looked at the lead Apache. It banked left and dipped its nose. The other seven gunships did the same. From a line abreast they turned into a single file. They followed in a long line through the valley, twisting and turning around icy outcroppings.

Jiminez could feel the acceleration in his back. The noise and vibration rose until they shook the cockpit controls. At full military power they roared out of the valley. Speed 110. Altitude thirty feet and falling.

They heeled over hard, turning sharply over the Amur. The frozen river snaked through white hills. Tipton rolled the Apache from side to side to follow it. To the right was Russia. To the left—China.

Hector's hand firmly gripped the joystick. His finger was ready to pull the chain gun's stiff trigger. The pilots of the gunships now increased their spacing. The Apache they followed was over two hundred meters ahead. Hector could no longer see their flight leader's aircraft.

"Engaging!" came the lead's shout. The loud rattle of his chain gun was clearly audible in the background. The river turned sharply to the left just ahead.

"Here we go!" Tipton yelled.

They banked hard around the river bend, then flew straight into the drifting smoke. The gunship ahead of theirs opened fire. It belched orange flame toward the ground from its rocket pods. Hector saw the first Chinese.

The river was brown from one side to the other. The Chinese had poured dirt to improve the vehicles' traction. Half a dozen narrow lanes traversed the white ice of the Amur. Each was choked with trucks and scattering infantrymen.

"Goin' *rockets*!" Tipton shouted at a range of two miles. A half-dozen rockets whooshed from their tubes. Tipton wove wildly through the wide river valley as the rockets raced off in straight, smoking trails. Red fireballs burst all along the Amur. Trucks filled with fuel and ammunition added towering secondary explosions.

Hector shut the sights and sounds from his mind. He lined up a group of scurrying infantrymen and squeezed off a short burst. The gun thrummed through the floorboard into his feet. Small orange flames lit the frozen surface, felling men. A truck pulled out around a burning hulk. Hector laid the crosshairs directly atop the fleeing vehicle. He steadied the aim as Tipton rolled the gunship again. A squeeze of the pistol grip let loose a dozen rounds in a single second. Troops tumbled out of the back of the smoking truck. Fire began licking at the green canvas top.

They were fifteen feet over the battlefield flying at 150 miles per hour. Hector aimed and squeezed as fast as he could. The gun gyrated wildly. Shells exploded in orange strings along the white ice.

A crashing blow knocked the aircraft sideways. Hector's breath froze solid in his lungs. His eyes shot to the instrument console. There were no red warning lights. When Tipton fired more rockets, Hector assumed the aircraft hadn't been critically damaged. Red-glowing tracers stretched across the flat, open river. He saw flashes in the trees on the riverbank. He trained the crosshairs on the flaming muzzles and held the trigger down. His 1,100 rounds remaining dropped quickly to under a thousand. The woods were on fire. The Chinese antiaircraft gun fell silent.

The helicopter burst out of the smoke and flame of the battlefield. There were no more targets in the windshield. Hector saw the flight leader's rotor over a hill to the north of the river.

"Five three's at two o'clock!" he called out. "Circling back." Tipton followed the river then banked. Two Apaches hovered on the far side of the hill. They rose in unison above the crest and fired. Their wings belched flame as they expended rockets from the safety of a mile's distance.

Tipton flew up to the ridge beside them. Once in a hover, they began to rise. They peeked out over the rocky spine of the hill. The frozen river lay before them, smoking. The last of the Apaches was weaving its way across the valley. Brilliant flares spat from their tails.

"Better pull on up clear of the ridge . . ." Hector began to say to Tipton, but it was too late. The whoosh of 2.75-inch rockets and blinding flashes of explosions on the hill thirty feet ahead splattered the gunship with rebounding shrapnel. They had made a terrible mistake.

"Auto-*rotating*!" Tipton shrieked. Hector hung on. The Kevlar main rotor hit the rocks. The canopy shattered. Hector was riddled with shards. By the time the helicopter came to rest in the snowdrifts on the valley floor, Hector didn't have long to live. Leaking fuel cut the process short. The fireball lit the surrounding hills.

11

The C-130 revved its engines. Stempel looked back over his shoulder at the noise. Snow flew off the one-lane road behind the engines. The aircraft had just dropped him and 2nd Battalion, 263rd Infantry in Siberia. They had flown them in from Japan via Vladivostok, and now they were leaving. Stempel shivered when the backblast washed over the ranks. The stubby, dark green aircraft lifted easily into the air. It was empty.

"Second *Platoon*," the lieutenant called out, "lock 'n *load*!" Men busied themselves with weapons all around Stempel, reinforcing the nakedness he felt at not having one. It was like one of those dreams where you showed up at school with no pants, only it was happening for real. His field pack weighed heavily on his back. High above it rose his bulging white Arctic Bag. It contained an air mattress and a Mountain Bag with a quick-release zipper.

The platoon sergeant hung four ammo belts for the platoon's two M-60s around Harold's neck. "Stick close to the LT," he said. Stempel was an unknown quantity. They didn't trust him.

"Don't you got a pocketknife or anything, man?" someone asked. Everyone laughed—jittery and nervous. From inside his hood Harold watched their laughter jet smoky white from their mouths. He looked at the clear sky. The sun was still high in early afternoon, but it seemed to emit no heat. The transports were gone. All was quiet except for the crunching noise of units moving off the road.

Cold had soaked straight through Harold's gear and now scraped at his cheeks with each breeze.

Squads filed off in succession as the platoon spread out in a skirmish line—three squads abreast and facing south. The platoon sergeant kept increasing their spacing, and the gaps between the men grew wider and wider. At almost fifteen meters separation, the thirty men covered a four-hundred-meter front. Stempel remained in the center with the platoon leader and a machine gun. He could barely see the platoon's flanks.

Each ten-man squad sent a scout forward a couple hundred meters, and they moved out. Stempel and the small platoon headquarters section were about thirty meters behind the main line. Everyone seemed to know what they were doing. The crackle of conversations from the radio carried on the back of the lieutenant's RTO was reassuring. They reached the tree line and headed into the woods. The going grew more difficult in the scrubby ground. Deep drifts had gathered around every clump of brush. Their progress slowed, and it grew noticeably darker and quieter. The deep woods were still and frozen.

When Stempel sank up to his knees, they had to pull him out. His thighs began to burn. He felt the first trickle of sweat underneath his gear and unzipped his parka, then took his hood off. The tiny hairs on his face were crusted with ice, but he was sweating.

The LT's hand went up signaling a halt. After a quick radio call, the LT put the map in his teeth and jabbed at the ground with his finger. The men dropped their packs and began to dig in the quiet of the snowy cathedral. Stempel delivered the extra belts of ammunition to the machine gunner, then received his orders. "Dig a snow hole, butt-fuck!" He dropped his pack, unfolded his metal shovel, and dug. In no time he was through the white, powdery snow and struck the hard black soil. While the other men set up their weapons and worked out angles of fire with their squad leaders, Stempel dug. The earth was frozen solid, so he expanded outward. When the hole seemed suitably wide, he evened out the breastwork of snow in front until it was a uniform height of about two feet, and about two feet thick at the base.

When he was done, he looked up from the little fort he'd built. The machine gunner lay behind a hundred-round belt of shiny brass. His ammo bearer lay to the side ready to keep the hungry gun fed. The M-60 pointed through gaps in the line into the trackless woods ahead. Stempel heard the pounding of his heart. He felt the artery in his neck pulse against his clothing. Men wearing white parkas and helmets—barely visible in the cottony snow—lay prone.

The cool and collected platoon sergeant strode along the platoon's thin line just ahead of Stempel. He barked out curt commands through teeth holding a stubby, unlit cigar. He left steady, organized soldiers in his wake. Stempel was again in the world of the familiar. He drew a deep breath and relaxed. These were good soldiers—real soldiers—and they were ready.

"Heads down!" the LT shouted. "Splash over!" He held his radio-telephone handset under his helmet and pressed gloved fingers hard against his exposed ear. There was a faint crackling in the sky overhead. Everyone pressed flat onto the snow. A stunning boom rattled Stempel's insides. The shock wave that pounded his ears had a solid feel to it. Snow drifted from the heavily laden limbs of a thousand trees.

Are we shelling them, he wondered, or are they shelling us?

He closed his dry mouth and swallowed. Another crackle sent him to the bottom of his hole. He felt the thump through the ground before he heard the boom. It wasn't that close, so he raised his head. There was no blackened crater, or fallen trees, or smoke drifting on the wind. He took a deep breath to soothe his ragged nerves. Sergeant Giles's warnings about the ferocity of artillery must've been exaggerated.

"Where's that fire, over?" the LT shouted. The platoon leader sat on the edge of his hole. "*Bull*shit, sir!" he yelled. Another boom drowned out more shouts. ". . . expect us to hold this position? We need fire support, goddammit! What about air? Over!"

From the forests up ahead Stempel saw small groups of men hustling back toward their lines. They were shouting both parts of the sign-countersign combination in panicked voices—not waiting for a challenge and reply. "Hold your fire!" rang out up and down the line. One returning group headed straight for the platoon headquarters. The LT hurled his handset into the snow. His radio-telephone operator looked petrified. Stempel began to shiver from the cold. The platoon leader's wide and unblinking eyes looked haunted. Stempel's next breath caught in his throat.

The two men from the observation post slid to the ground beside the lieutenant. "God Aw-mighty, LT!" The large black sergeant gasped for breath. "There's gotta be a whole goddamn *regiment* comin' this way! Fo' hun'erd meters out! *Christ*, sir!" He pulled his helmet and cap off his head. Steam rose from his bare scalp. "Them spotter rounds was bang on! Tell 'em to fire for *effect*!" The lieutenant muttered something. "*What?*" the sergeant shot back. "Five goddamn *rounds*? For the love of *God*, LT, they're gonna . . . We gotta pull back! They jus' ain't no fuckin' way, LT! *No* way!"

Again Stempel couldn't hear what the lieutenant said. But the two men cursed all the way to Stempel's hole. A private first class slid in beside Stempel, who was forced to the far end of his fortress. The sergeant piled in after him. They paid no attention to Stempel at all.

"We 'bout ready to git fucked *up*!" the sergeant growled as he pulled every magazine and grenade he had out. The

PFC looked terrified and speechless. "This is it! Those rear-area mother-*fuckers* jus' sent us here to *die,* man! Jus' sent us here to *die*!"

"Pardon me," Stempel said—his voice trembled. "Could I maybe have a grenade or something?"

"Say *what*?"

"He ain't got no weapon," the PFC said. His breath stank with fear. He laughed as if at a hilarious joke. "Stupid-son-of-a-bitch-is-straight-outta-boot-camp!" he blurted with a laugh as his eyes moistened.

"You a cherry, Snow White?" the sergeant asked.

"Yes, Sergeant."

He laughed, shook his head, and picked up one of his half-dozen grenades. "You gonna use this?"

"Yes. Yes, I will." He tossed it to Stempel, who was then armed.

"Look at that!" someone shouted from the line ahead. From out of the woods—darting and weaving and leaping into the air—was first one, then ten, then nearly thirty deer. They ran and hopped like gazelles, changing course at each clump of snowy brush. In utter amazement, Stempel and the others watched the deer race past the American fighting positions and keep going. They were fleeing in fright. Something massive was approaching.

There were two sharp blasts from a Chinese whistle. The shrill commands were repeated from a dozen other whistles to the left, right, and front. Stempel felt like vomiting. His mouth was as dry as dust. All was quiet save a great scraping noise . . . rising. It sounded like an avalanche of snow.

"It's them," the sergeant said. "They're coming."

The sound of ten thousand scraping feet grew louder and drew nearer. A bitter pit of bile formed in Stempel's stomach and rose toward his esophagus. To the sound of crunching snow was suddenly added a chant. A single voice raised high in words Stempel couldn't make out. It was rhythmic Chinese called out in time, he felt sure, with their pace.

A thousand voices roared as one. The solid wall of voices came from directly to their front, but other choruses rose on separate cues from either side. The white helmets of terrified U.S. troops twisted in their line of holes ahead, catching each other's gaze and measuring the size of gaps between the positions.

A loud *"Hu-u-h!"* erupted from deep in the attackers' diaphragms. The sound was jarring in contrast to the high-pitched voice that led them. Stempel wondered whether they chanted to build their own courage, or to sap the nerves of the defenders. He was freezing and shaking like a leaf. He jammed his gloved hands into his armpits but it did no good. The white shell he wore vibrated and Stempel could do nothing to stop it. His teeth were chattering. His abdomen was clenched so tight that his bowels churned. He suddenly felt an overpowering need to urinate.

The crunching and chanting were suddenly drowned out by a fusillade of gunfire to their right. Units quickly engaged on both sides. But everyone was still in his platoon. The LT had his M-16 raised to his shoulder. He was just a simple rifleman now. In the next few seconds a layer of ice coated Stempel. A lens descended over his eyes. He could never have been prepared for what happened next, but he was numb from shock before the first shot. The few Claymore mines they'd strung blew almost simultaneously. That set off a cacophonous bleating of whistles, bugles, and shepherd's horns. The Chinese all began to shout at once.

The line of American riflemen in front of Stempel opened fire. Their rifles were deafening in the enclosure of the forest. Stempel couldn't even see the Chinese until they too opened fire. Then bright orange flashes lit the woods. The machine gun and the two men in the hole with Stempel began to fire. The first sprays of snow flew into the air around their hole. Stempel ducked . . . and vomited. The world spun dizzily in between spasms. The two soldiers beside him rose up into the storm to fire hurriedly aimed bursts despite the tremendous risk. Another bout of vomiting overcame Stempel. He clenched his grenade tightly to his burning belly. The snow beneath him filled with foul-smelling bile.

When nothing more would come up, Stempel tried to lift his head into the sheets of bullets—cringing with each inch his helmet rose. He heard the *zzzziip* of bullets passing just inches away. Each caused him to pause, but with his eyes almost jammed shut and his jaw clenched, he forced his head up. Smoke filled the woods. Hundreds upon hundreds of men ran in a crouch. Their knees sent heavy coats flapping. Their weapons blazed. They had gleaming bayonets fixed to the ends of their rifles. Just behind the first line was a second. Behind it . . . a third. Buzzing sounds sent Stempel back to the depths of the hole, shivering in fright. The air forced past his vocal cords sounded like moans. The PFC flew backward and sprawled against the rear wall before tumbling onto Stempel.

His deadweight crushed Stempel. Grenades went off all around like firecrackers. They continued to rain down in showers, hitting the upper branches of the trees. Some burst in the air. Others dropped to the ground, which shook with the pounding they delivered. One grenade bounced off the rear lip of the hole right beside Stempel and kept going. Stempel cringed, but it didn't explode—a dud!

Boom! The blow stunned him. The sergeant dropped his rifle and grabbed Stempel's entrenching shovel, swinging baseball-style at the falling grenades. Fire filled the air. The snow walls collapsed into the hole. Everywhere men screamed, "I'm hit! I'm hit!" or, "I'm hit again!" Branches shorn from trees crashed to earth. Explosions amid high branches created a drizzle of twigs.

"Grab his rifle!" the sergeant shouted at Harold, whose stomach began dry-heaving over and over. "Sweet Je-e-ezus!" Stempel heard. Bullets split the snow walls all around. Grenades burst everywhere. Hot fire preceded an avalanche of snow as the walls collapsed. Stempel's eyes were filled with the icy slush. To the heavy weight of the PFC's body was added that of the sergeant's.

TONGDUCHON, SOUTH KOREA
January 26, 0330 GMT (1330 Local)

André Faulk hauled the mailbag into the barracks of 3rd Platoon, Charlie Company, 2nd Battalion. Like everyone on base, they were packing, cleaning weapons, filling packs and pouches with combat loads.

"Mail call!" André announced, which usually began a stampede. "Shhh!" was all he heard from the opposite end of a long corridor. Men in camouflaged fatigues were clustered around an open door. All were intent and quiet. Faulk dropped the bag and approached, passing rooms with new arctic gear piled on bunks. The wavering whine of the radio grew louder. Through the crowded door he saw a soldier on his bunk leaning over a field radio. His hand was constantly adjusting the frequency knob. A distant voice pierced the random white noise, but it was so distorted he could make nothing out. The signal unexpectedly grew stronger, and the voice louder and sharper. The words were being shouted.

". . . zero niner niner Echo! Fire for effect! I say again, fire . . ." The signal drifted away.

A new and clearer voice cut through. "Negative, negative, November Echo seven two. This is Bravo India three niner. Designated grid coordinate is friendly—I say again *friendly*—unit position. I countermand that fire order. Over."

The shouted reply came as a vehement string of unrecognizable electromagnetic squeals. The signal strength grew into a desperate voice, which was warped into a shifting howl. ". . . left! They're a-a-all gone—all gone! The Chinese are pouring through their position right at u-u-us! Fi-ire for effect! Fi-i-ire for e-e-effect!"

"Charlie Foxtrot seven seven?" came the louder voice of the fire controller. "Can you confirm that grid coordinate has been overrun, over?"

The signal was dying, swallowed by the enormous distance. "Fire for effect! Fire for effect! For the love of God *fi-ire fo-o-or effe-e-ct!*"

"Charlie Foxtrot seven seven, do you read, over? Charlie Foxtrot, *do you read,* over?" Nothing. "Charlie Foxtrot seven seven, fire for effect at designated coordinates." They couldn't understand the garbled response. "Fire for *effect,* goddammit! On *my* authority! Out!"

The radio fell silent with a click. It was an ordinary field radio carried on a backpack like the man screamed into while begging for fire. People began to clear out. "Weird atmospherics," someone muttered.

André grabbed the man by the arm. "Who was that?"

He shrugged. "Somebody in the shit," was all he said, but from the look on his face and his lowered gaze André could tell that he was deeply upset. Another man said, "It's the 25th," to André.

André wondered . . . but no, it wasn't possible. Stempel was still on some cruise with his parents.

"Are you gonna hand out the fuckin' mail or what?" one of the soldiers asked. Down the hall he saw them fucking with his bag.

"Hey-hey-*hey*!" André warned. He went and jerked the bag out of their hands, then smiled. "Now this *is* 3rd Platoon, Charlie Company, 2nd Battalion, right?"

"Come on, fuckhead!"

"You gotta *wait,* now. The postal detachment follows pro-*cedure*!" He reached into the bag and pulled out the stack of battered and crushed envelopes and small packages. Two thick rubber bands held everything together. André cleared his throat theatrically and drew more obscenities. "Is there an 'Aguire'?"

"Yo!"

André tossed him his letter. "Okay," he said, fending off an impatient grab at the mail. It had been the same every day. "How about an 'Alvarez'?" The man snatched his package from André's hands. André held the next letter up as if he were farsighted. "Next we got us a 'Be-', 'Bej-' . . . Jesus Christ!"

"Bejgrowicz!" several impatient men shouted all at once. One grabbed the letter and tossed it high into the air, sending Bejgrowicz to the floor on a search. Thus it went until "Wolfson" walked away with the padded envelope clearly holding a videotape. Nearly half of 3rd Platoon, Charlie Company, 2nd Battalion still waited to see if something had been sorted out of alphabetical order.

AMUR RIVER, RUSSO-CHINESE BORDER
January 26, 1400 GMT (0400 Local)

Every day since they were first told that NATO had attacked China, Lieutenant Chin had heard the distant rumble. At first he'd looked for storm clouds. He didn't remember exactly when he'd realized what the deep drumbeats were. He remembered only the sinking sensation. A feeling like when he feared he'd caught leprosy during an outbreak in his province. It had turned out to be a rash, but until a doctor had given him the reprieve it had eaten away at him like psychological rot—less fear, really, than melancholy. The thunder of fate drawing nearer to him and he to it.

At the top of the last ridge he saw the River of the Black Dragon. It looked like a white snake through the hills. He'd known it was their destination even though they'd been told nothing. Chin and his platoon climbed out of the trucks and headed down. The road that descended to the riverbank was clogged with burned-out hulks of trucks. At the bottom, the bank was rocky, and the river was frozen solid. Men traversed it in long lines of tiny specks. Chin stepped out onto the flat surface. His platoon trailed single file. There were at least half a dozen such columns visible before the twists of the river bent the ivory highway out of sight. Chin was nearly halfway across when he passed the two wounded men limping to the south. Their faces were drawn and pallid. One leaned on a crooked branch, his leg a mass of bloody bandages. The other rested his hand on his comrade's shoulder, his head swaddled in gauze. Their progress was slow, but it had purpose. It was homeward bound for the lucky pair.

KHABAROVSK, SIBERIA
January 26, 0730 GMT (1730 Local)

Nate Clark stood before a bank of radios, but it was clear that they couldn't raise the 2/263rd. He stumbled through the busy room. He passed men and women from various nations without seeing them. He sank into his chair. His head, his limbs—they seemed heavy. Like he was pressed flat on the surface of a huge planet by immense gravity.

Clark picked up the telephone. "Get me General Dekker." He waited through a series of clicks and hisses—ever-more-distant connections. The telecommunications net patched him into the Pentagon some seconds later.

"Nate?" Dekker said. No words came out. "General Clark? Are you there?"

"I'm here, Ed. I got some bad news." He took a deep breath. "Second Battalion, 263rd Infantry Regiment's been overrun by the Chinese."

"How bad are the casualties?"

Clark closed his eyes. "I said they were overrun, Ed. They met and engaged advancing Chinese infantry from hastily prepared positions. They were overrun, as were their rear areas. Brigadier General Merrill—commander of the 2nd Brigade—needed a screening force to buy him time to organize defenses around the airbase at Birobidzhan. The 2nd of the 263rd was that screen. Now they're gone."

"Oh, God, Nate," Dekker said. "We lose *squads*, Nate! Sometimes *platoons*! But never an entire *battalion*, for Christ's sake! And you're tellin' me Merrill just sacrificed five hundred goddamn *GIs*?"

"I don't know, sir. But are you ready for the rest?" Dekker said nothing. "We're not going to be able to withdraw Merrill's brigade from Birobidzhan to Khabarovsk. The road was cut by Chinese who'd infiltrated undetected to set up blocking positions."

"Can't they push on through?" Dekker asked. "What's the Chinese strength?"

"We don't know. We got only sporadic radio reports from some of the transportation units that were ambushed.

Aerial recon shows over a hundred vehicles, mostly trucks, destroyed and burning on the road with no sign of their crews.''

"Jesus Christ," Dekker muttered. "This is a disaster of the first magnitude."

"General Merrill had three battalions at Birobidzhan," Nate continued. "On my orders he was packed up to leave. All their supplies were sitting in crates and pallets on the side of the runway. One mortar round would've set 'em off. They would've been reduced to what they were humping in their *field* packs. Merrill had a fourth battalion—the 2/263rd—that was inbound. It was diverted to a road about twelve clicks to the south. I don't know what expectations he had about that battalion, Ed. But Birobidzhan has already fended off three major attacks. They lost a C-130 *with* crew on the ground to a goddamn *RPG*. That battalion bought them a few hours. If they make it, those few hours could be the difference. There's no way they'd have gotten their defenses organized if the Chinese hadn't been slowed. But I'll know more when I get over there tonight."

"When you do *what*? Oh, no you're not, Nate. You can't get yourself tied up in a brigade-level action like that. The damn airbase is *surrounded*! Do you know what the propaganda value of your capture or death would be to the Chinese? That's one of the most selfish acts I've ever heard proposed. What's gotten into you, Nate?"

Clark's head was spinning from lack of sleep. "Goddammit, Ed. What the hell use am I here? I don't have the horses to fight this war. I might as well grab a fuckin' M-16 and lend a hand."

"Nate, you get your shit together, that's an order. I'll bust your ass right outta the army if you crap out on me like this. As it stands now, there are gonna be some long goddamned knives out when word of this massacre gets around." Clark rubbed his sore eyes. Through blurred vision he saw Major Reed holding a message slip. Clark wiggled his fingers and held out his hand. It was a short message. "I might be able to limit the damage to Merrill.

But any more debacles like this and they may stick *my* head on the White House gate.''

"Merrill's dead.''

Dekker's reply was abnormally delayed. "Say again.''

Clark read, " 'General Merrill killed in action by sniper fire . . . ' '' His voice trailed off. He had nothing more to say.

After they signed off, Clark tossed the crumpled message in the trash. He looked at the papers on his desk. He'd read them all hours before. The maps were unchanged. He rocked his chair forward and back and forward. He fished all of the pens and pencils from his desk and lined them up for quick access, then sat there with a deep sigh, staring off into space.

Reed appeared. "Did you tell General Dekker?'' he asked.

Clark nodded. "Get me a helicopter,'' he said.

"Birobidzhan?'' Reed asked. Another nod. "Can I come?''

SOUTH OF BIROBIDZHAN, SIBERIA
January 26, 0800 GMT (1800 Local)

Stempel was lying in a shallow, snowy grave. He'd carefully rummaged through his pockets, still holding his grenade. He'd been looking for the candy bar they'd handed out. He'd found instead the plastic lei hung around his neck in Hawaii. He dug deeper. The credit card his father had given him before boot camp. *If you ever get into any trouble,* he'd said, *any trouble at all—this card will get you out.*

He lay under two dead bodies. He was covered in their blood and gore. He didn't know where he was. He was all alone. He was waiting to die. How long it would take he had no idea. Water, you need water. You'd die in four days, he'd once read, without water. He then spent a while trying to decide whether the cold would kill him first.

He'd heard nothing for a long time. Before that . . . He

jammed his eyes shut. He held in the scream of mental pain. He ground his teeth. He forced the images from his mind by mere negation. *No, no, no, no, no!* was his mantra. It had a remarkably soothing effect. It calmed him. He could again coolly contemplate his demise.

The shallow hiss of his breathing was the only sound. The trees overhead were growing dark. With surprising urgency the need to act—to move—came over him. He had to force himself to remain still. Will himself not to sit bolt upright and peer at the landscape around him.

Slowly, he raised his arm and looked at the black sports watch he wore outside his sleeve. *"This is Siberia!"* the platoon sergeant had shouted on exiting the transport plane. "Local time is fourteen fifty hours—one four five zero!" That was all Stempel knew of the world into which he'd been deposited. His rough position on a continent, and the correct local time.

Which was now eighteen hundred hours. He shook his head and lay back. Three hours since . . . A lifetime. The bodies under which he lay were now frozen. They had given him the last of their heat. A huge cloud billowed out of his mouth. He exhaled again to test the phenomenon. It seemed as if the entire contents of his lungs turned white. He didn't remember that from before. There had been the typical fogging of his breath, but not a thick cloud. He tried one more time, with a similar result.

It was growing dark, and the temperature was dropping. He swallowed, but his mouth was bone-dry. "The canteens'll freeze if you don't keep 'em close to yer bodies!" the platoon sergeant had shouted. Harold was thirsty. Their platoon's only drinking water was kept warm by body heat. All their canteens would be freezing soon. The cold, calculating part of his brain returned to work. He had a canteen. But it wouldn't last long. He could rummage through the gear of the others . . .

The conscious, feeling part of his brain came alive unexpectedly. Stempel had grown accustomed to the weight pressing down on his body. But they were corpses—the sergeant and the PFC. He began to wriggle out from under them reflexively. With his first movement—the first shifting of their weight—the sense of revulsion rose to unmanageable proportions. The workmanlike rise became panicked flight.

Grunts and gasps escaped Stempel's mouth with whining cries. He climbed out of the hole and lay on his back . . . fully exposed.

All around him lay the detritus of war. Still. Lifeless. Chinese dead were strewn about the forest floor in great numbers. But it was the American dead that sent Stempel into shock. He had known, of course, that they were all dead. He had heard them die. The pleas of surrendering men. The merciless executions. Rifle shots in hole after hole . . . coming closer. The flaming muzzle. The gore that oozed from the corpses' new wounds. But seeing them there— half-naked in the snow—just about sent him back into his hole. The Chinese had stripped most of them right down to their underwear. The sight of men lying bare-skinned in the snow was appalling. "Oh, God," he said. He looked up at the sky. An arm—severed at the shoulder—hung from a branch.

If I leave here, he realized, *they'll never find my body*. The army would send people after the war. If he walked even a short distance away from the battlefield he'd forever be "Missing in Action." He'd never have a funeral. Or a grave where his mother could come and be with him.

"Hey!" he heard. He jerked his head around. A man in snowy-white arctic gear crouched beside a tree. There were others, also in uniform, vaguely visible in the snow. All had rifles raised.

I'm alive, Harold thought as he climbed to his feet. He began a slow run toward the men through deep drifts. When he noticed the man's strenuous gestures he stopped in confusion. The man was motioning for him to get down. Harold plopped onto the snow. He didn't take his eyes off the others. He'd never let them out of his sight.

Slowly, cautiously, the man made his way toward Stempel. He advanced a few steps at a time, then dropped. His head was on a swivel. He looked in every direction before continuing on. With a great crunching through the crust that had formed, he dropped next to Stempel, out of breath.

He looked at the blood covering Stempel. "You hit?" he asked. Stempel shook his head. The man's eyes roamed the woods. "You heard anything?" he whispered. Great puffs of smoke emanated from his mouth.

"Not in a while," Stempel replied. The man was a sergeant, Stempel saw from the three chevrons on the front of his helmet.

"Anybody else in your area make it?" Stempel shook his head. He girded himself for the next question: *why aren't you dead?* "Okay, you fall in with us. *No noise!*" the sergeant whispered through clenched teeth. They rose. Stempel's white parka was drenched in a blood. The deep brownish red was almost black. His dirty secret was clear for all to see. "Where's your weapon?" the sergeant asked. Stempel felt tears well up in his eyes. "Never mind," the sergeant said. "There's gear lyin' around. We'll scrounge one up."

Stempel followed the man. Sure enough they found the battlefield rich in equipment. The unit had been fresh from barracks, and each man had carried a full load. The Chinese must have been in a hurry. Some of the bodies were picked clean. But others still wore full existence loads in blood-splattered packs and pouches.

They scavenged everything they needed, and finally found the most prized possession of all. Beside a fighting hole, one of Stempel's new comrades reached down into the snow. He pulled up the black barrel of an M-16 and carefully brushed away the snow and ice. Stempel watched as the man looked the weapon over. Satisfied, he handed the rifle to Stempel.

Stempel made no sound. He gave no outward sign. But inwardly, silently, where it counts, he vowed he would never put the weapon down. He would die with it pressed firmly into his shoulder. He would raise his head up into the storm. *Just like the PFC and the sergeant*, he told himself. *Just like the PFC and the sergeant.*

VLADIVOSTOK, SIBERIA
January 26, 0930 GMT (1930 Local)

"This is the most stupid idea you've ever had," Kate whispered to Woody. They sat huddled together at a table in the center of the dark barroom. Gold-toothed Russians and a smattering of rough-looking foreign oil workers occupied all the other tables. They sat there staring at Kate—the only woman not working the place—getting more and more drunk.

Woody downed a shot of vodka with a backward toss of his head. The fifty-dollar bottle had been their price of admission to the bar. He exhaled, winced, and wiped his lips with his hand. "Nope," he replied. "The *stupidest* idea was to try to *sneak* our way up to the front in the first place."

"But the army hasn't taken the press pool anywhere *near* the fighting, Woody," she whispered.

"Yeah, well, did you ever think there might be a *reason* for that?"

Kate rocked back against the huge, thick Russian fur that she'd draped over the back of the chair. It made her look more like a bear than a fashion model, but it was warm. It also stank. "I can't believe *you,* of all people, would kowtow to the military like that." Woody poured another shot and threw it back. "Don't you think you've had enough to drink?" Kate asked. Woody was the veteran at these things, her navigator through a dangerous world. They had bought a dilapidated Russian car for a hundred bucks from a former officer in the Russian Army. Woody had smoked a joint as thick as her thumb on their drive through town in search of the seediest bar in Russia. Now he drank vodka like it was water.

"Actually," he said, pouring another shot in the dirty glass, "I have not yet begun to drink."

He raised the glass to his lips, but Kate's hand pressed

his wrist firmly down. "Woody, please," she whispered. He sniffed loudly, but left the glass on the table.

Rising up the staircase behind Woody was a hairy, pot-bellied Russian. He grinned lasciviously at two women. His hand firmly grasped their pudgy rears. He kissed one with a disgusting, sloppily open mouth. Kate winced and looked away as the other woman reached to crudely rub at his fly.

"So," Woody said in an argumentative tone, "you want to get to the *front,* as you call it. I happen to call it the onrushing Chinese Army. But let's just use the word 'front' for the sake of convenience. Now, the suits at NBC News say they can't get permission through the Pentagon. And, you might have noticed, they pointedly did not exactly *send* us there. Why do you think there were so many lawyers on the speakerphone? Why'd they use such hypercareful language when you told them about getting up to the action? They were doing some fast legal maneuvering—that's why—so they don't get sued by our heirs when we get our butts killed."

"Come on, Woody. Watergate was a long time ago. Give the paranoid conspiracy crap a rest, okay?"

Woody giggled. "Okay. Paranoia. Fine." He sniffed again. "The army says it's too dangerous."

"Well that's just bullshit!" she replied. She looked around. Everywhere men tried to catch her eye. Brutish men, unshaven and unclean, with bad teeth. "They're just saying that," she continued in a whisper, "because they must have something to *hide*. They screwed something up. Now they're trying to cover it up."

"Who's spinning conspiracy theories now?" He had slumped down into his chair. He looked tired.

"What is it with you?" she asked.

"Nothing," he replied, but she pressed him. "Look!" he finally snapped. "I think it's a fucking *stupid* idea. This isn't the bush leagues, Katie, it's the big show. People die. All the time. The camera and the official UN-accredited press badges don't *stop* bullets!"

"I *know* that, Woody! I know it's a dangerous job. But it's a job that *I'm* still trying to *do*!"

Her last gibe deflated him. He was slumped even lower than before. A door beside the bar opened. The noise of a tiny, smoke-filled casino poured in. There was no law anymore. No police. The British patrolled the streets. They occasionally responded to impassioned pleas for help from foreigners or from Russians who spoke English. Most of the British soldiers, however, trod warily down both sides of darkened streets. Armored cars rolled down the middle at foot pace. The last man in each file of troops spun around to walk backward a step or two—the "Ulster twist."

"If we can't get there officially," Kate said, repeating her earlier logic, "then places like this are the best for making alternate arrangements."

The door to the street opened. Everyone in the bar fell quiet and looked attentively at the new arrival. It was yet another natural resource of Siberia that seemed in virtually inexhaustible supply—scary-looking men. The bar's patrons resumed their silent drinking. They accepted the presumably suitable newcomer into their fold. When the bartender pointed at Kate and Woody, however, Kate grew frightened. "This is who we were *waiting* for?" she whispered, incredulous.

"The bartender said he could help us," Woody replied.

The man turned a chair around and straddled it, seated backward. His hands rested on the chair back, his chin on his hands. He let out a noisy gush of air through his nostrils like a beast of burden and ran his bloodshot eyes over Kate from toe to head—especially at points in between. The large but indeterminable contours of the man's body were hidden from view by a fur coat. Its rough quality made Kate's look like it was straight off a hanger at Saks. He even smelled like a mastodon—completing the image in Kate's mind.

He turned to Woody. "Speak English?" he asked in a thick Russian accent. Woody nodded. "American?" Woody nodded again. "You want to go places?"

"We want to go to the front," Kate said.

The man turned to her. His beard thinned raggedly at the

tops of his cheeks, revealing pockmarked skin every bit as red as his eyes. He didn't grow the beard, Kate thought. He simply never shaved. "Hah!" he belched. It took Kate a moment to realize he'd laughed. The man rose at the same lethargic speed with which he had sat and leaned over the table, eclipsing the long bar with its row of stools. He picked up Woody's shot glass, threw the vodka back, and shook the glass to drain every drop into his open and waiting mouth. His thick tongue darted inside the glass like a frog. Kate cringed. Woody stared up at him in awe, as if seeing some wonder of the animal kingdom. The woolly beast ambled away.

Woody raised the bottle of vodka and took a swig. His face contorted in pain. A shudder rippled down from his head to his shoulders. "I don't think he wants to go to the front, Katie." He wiped his mouth with the back of his hand. "Too damn bad!" He was beginning to slur. "*Pro*-bably a *pos*-thumous *Puh*-ulitzer *Puh*-rize too!" His stupid grin threatened to crack open his chapped face.

MOSCOW, RUSSIA
January 27, 0600 GMT (0800 Local)

"Schedule A," Valentin Kartsev said. "Next?"

"Victor Afanasyev," the young aide read as their limousine raced down the center lane of the broad boulevard. "He laughed when Program 412B was mentioned at a dinner party."

"What program is that?"

"The aborted plan to retrain steelworkers for the lumber industry."

"Oh." Kartsev chuckled. Through the curtains he could see lines of people waiting for something, patient as always. *Food,* he guessed. "That was a real fiasco," Kartsev said. *Who would've guessed that steelworkers didn't want to be lumberjacks?* The aide waited, staring at him. It made Kartsev highly uncomfortable. He loathed the dreary administrative work—especially this. "Schedule A. Next?"

There was a second's pause before the young aide returned to his list. *Surely there's a better way to do this,* Kartsev thought. "Lyudmila Vavarov," the man read.

"Who is she?"

"Substitute secretary in the typing pool working on a sensitive typing job where each secretary got a different page. She took hers up to hand it in, but stopped and talked to another secretary. When she left the other secretary's desk, she picked up the sheet her friend had just finished typing—she said by mistake."

"Did she have a chance to read it?" The aide shrugged. "What were they typing?" Another shrug.

The young man studied Kartsev, and Kartsev stared back until the aide turned away. "You know," Kartsev said, "power—the *accumulation* of power—has always been the ultimate achievement of man. Everything else—fame, fortune, political office—is all just a means of attaining the real goal, which is power over others. And the ultimate power is the power to make each and every human being do *what* you want, *when* you want it done. That requires a close attention to every detail and the willpower to act when you know in your heart what is necessary."

His aide's eyes betrayed no hint of comprehension. No hint of anything, for that matter. Such was the extent of his fear of Kartsev. But it didn't make for stimulating conversation. For that he needed someone fearless. He wondered just where Miss Dunn was, then sighed. "One more for Schedule A," he said, fatigued. *One more bullet to the back of the head.*

12

Clark watched their approach through the windshield of the Blackhawk helicopter. Night was falling slowly. But even in the waning light he saw the ring of smoke that rose around the airbase. Guns on both sides contributed to the haze that defined the perimeter defenses. But most of the fires were from the massive, round-the-clock air raids. They churned the earth just beyond the last string of wire.

Clark stood braced in a wide stance. Trees slid under the helicopter's belly at astonishing speed. He gripped the crew's seats as they weaved to avoid small-arms fire. The corridor down which they flew was particularly smoky. The area had been marked for intense "preparation" like a single spoke from the wheel of the airbase. All the traffic to and from the besieged base would fly down that corridor. In a couple of hours, they'd prepare another spoke.

Choppers headed in with special forces. The Green Berets were Clark's only ready reserve. The same choppers headed outbound filled with wounded. Clark had seen casualties unloaded before he, Reed, two riflemen, two female medics, and a dozen Green Berets climbed aboard.

Out of the upper left-hand corner of the windshield roared an inbound C-130. Painted white, the transport plane blotted out the sky momentarily. It passed close overhead. The turbulence buffeted the smaller helicopter. Clark watched a massive parachute blossom behind the transport. It pulled a pallet down the open rear ramp. Securely strapped crates fell twenty feet to the ground. They burst open and scattered their contents over the near end of the runway.

Clark was distracted by a single clang. A bullet struck somewhere in the rear. When he looked back through the windshield, the C-130 was practically scraping the runway's pavement. Parachute after parachute popped open. The pallets now had less than ten feet to fall. They skidded to a halt—braked by the parachute and the friction. It was a race—prodigious fires versus mammoth payloads. Three thousand men and women firing their weapons continuously. It was the greatest test the U.S. Air Mobility Command had ever faced.

The helicopter neared the base perimeter. It was a scarred zone of felled trees and thick black smoke. A barrage of orange flame boiled from the trees. Streaking tracers lit the growing darkness. It was remarkable, ferocious fighting. There must have been an attack under way that very moment. Several more bullets clanged off the helicopter. Clark turned to look into the crowded but still cabin. He remembered from decades before the flailing arms of a man swatting at the burning tracer in his body like at a bee, and the coughing splutter from the old Huey's single engine.

They burst out over the airbase and dropped still lower. The Blackhawk banked steeply. Clark feared their rotors would strike the earth. His knees buckled. The nose rose. The G-forces ended with a jarring thud. The landing threw Clark forward. Pain shot through his ribs. When he tried to breathe he could draw no air. Pain spread hot fingers across his chest. He couldn't straighten up.

The side door slid open behind Clark. The roar of the rotors' downblast poured in. The engines still whined at high pitch. Reed helped him stumble to the door. The cabin was empty. The first litter was being loaded aboard. On it was a man covered in bloody bandages. Clark leaped to the ground. A searing jolt of pain nearly felled him. Two of the Green Berets with whom he'd arrived pulled him roughly down to the frozen soil.

Tiny holes appeared out of nowhere in the helicopter's fuselage. Sprays of glass exploded from its windshield. It was slow, methodical sniper fire. It was unreal. The noise from churning rotors masked the sounds of the bullets' impacts. The pilots sat motionless at their controls. They were fully exposed inside their Plexiglas canopy. They watched the loading of their increasingly bullet-riddled aircraft. Clark imagined their tremendous anxiety. Their desire to get airborne. To pitch and weave their vehicle as taught. But they sat there . . . waiting.

The helicopter lurched into the air. A man standing just inside was almost thrown to the ground. The aircraft headed back into the wall of smoke whence they'd come.

Clark now heard the full roar of the massive firefight. The popping, bursting, crackling noise came from every direction. He heard also the telltale splitting sounds of bullets through air. The twelve-man special-forces team was spread out in a rough semicircle. Their weapons were raised to their shoulders. Two female medics lay inside the tiny perimeter. So did Clark's group of two officers and two riflemen. All had volunteered to go to the surrounded airbase, whose fate was very much in doubt.

The first Green Berets rose to rush toward the piles of sandbags around nearby artillery emplacements. Bullets cut through the air overhead. The two soldiers dropped, but appeared unharmed.

"That sniper's got us zeroed in!" Major Reed shouted. But there was nothing they could do to fight back. That was the frustrating thing about snipers. Clark remembered the afternoon he'd spent hugging the embankment of a rice paddy. He'd been soaked waist-high in muddy water. His entire forty-man platoon had been pinned down by a lone man with a bolt-action rifle.

But this war was different. It wasn't going to be a decade-long war of attrition between a conventional military superpower and a peasant force of guerrillas and terrorists. It was a massive clash between two huge armies. In such a war you couldn't bide your time and minimize your risks. You had no choice but to take your chances. No choice but to accept casualties. "All right, listen up!" Clark shouted. "We'll all make a run for it at the same time!" The effort sent sharp stabs of pain through his torso.

The captain who commanded the special forces A-team counted down.

Everyone rose at once and began their labored run toward the sandbags. The Green Berets wove this way and that. But Clark knew it was wasted effort. At extreme distance, snipers aimed only at the area. It was luck—the law of averages—on which they counted. Since snipers had a slow rate of fire, going all at once would lessen the number of shots he'd get off. They rose and began their sprint.

Each time Clark's boots hit the hard earth, pain shot through his side. He'd busted a rib, he knew it. His anger at himself made him momentarily forget the sniper. The singing *zzzip* by his left ear, however, refocused his attention. He ran straight toward the booming artillery pieces as fast as he could. The others ran faster. It wasn't just that Nate couldn't draw a deep breath. He felt like an old man.

They all made it safely to the cover of the sandbagged walls. Every few seconds the self-propelled 155-millimeter gun fired, its barrel at maximum elevation. The high-angle fire meant the Chinese were close. The guns were firing at their shortest possible range.

An artilleryman led them to the brigade command post. The Green Berets were all sent to the most critical sector of the defenses. Stairs made of railroad ties led down into an enormous mound of sandbags. The snow covering it was blackened and pitted from mortars. The last vestiges of what must have been camouflage netting hung in tatters from poles and spreaders.

Inside he found a wounded colonel—Brigadier General

Merrill's successor in command. He was sitting at an awkward angle, leaning against a large map table over which
hung the best light in the bunker. He was in too much pain
to answer Clark's questions coherently. Clark understood,
however, that Merrill had led two battalions out to try to
reinforce the 2/263rd. But they'd been hit hard on the way.
They'd barely fought their way back to the base. Merrill
was dead.

It was a quiet story given by a man in great agony. Clark
had seen it all a long time before. Pain had turned him
pasty. Nauseous. Sweaty. He ordered the man to the aid
station. The colonel didn't have the energy to argue.

Clark looked up to see that everyone at brigade headquarters stared at him. Bare bulbs hung intermittently from
the low ceiling by strings of wire. Clark removed his outer
garments and gear. Reed at his side did the same. At least
twenty people were crammed together amid banks of radios
and tables with laptops. They lived in the perpetual darkness of the bunker.

"Call 'em to attention," Clark said to Reed.

"Ten-*shun*!" Reed barked.

The weary men and women stood and straightened.
Everyone but a radio operator. She stooped at her small
table because the wire to her headphones was too short.

"Listen up!" Clark bellowed. "My name is Lieutenant
General Nate Clark! I am the commander of UNRUSFOR,
USARPAC, and now—temporarily—2nd Brigade, 25th In-
fantry Division!"

Clark was astounded at the sudden burst of applause and
cheers. Paper flew into the air like confetti. When he saw
the genuine excitement on their faces, he realized instantly
what it was. It was a lesson he'd learned long before—first
in books, then in the field. It was a lesson he now learned
anew as he watched the suddenly energized soldiers await
their first orders.

"You can't lead from the rear," Clark remembered, then
went to work.

• • •

258 ERIC L. HARRY

As Clark and Reed waited for the commanders of the French and Belgian units to arrive for the first full brigade meeting, there was a stir at the bunker's entrance. A small crowd in arctic whites led a captain up to Clark's small desk. The captain was carrying a white towel on a stick.

"Sir," the haggard, unshaven man said, "I've been sent as an intermediary from the Chinese. Captain Lawrence, sir. Bravo Company, 2/263rd." Clark offered the man his seat and ordered hot food brought in on the double. "I was captured when they overran us," he said, his voice breaking. He licked his chapped lips and coughed. "They're promising good treatment of prisoners and to turn the wounded over to friendly lines, but they're demanding the immediate surrender of Birobidzhan. And, if I don't return," Lawrence added, looking Nate in the eye, "they've promised to kill all their prisoners."

Nate was relieved to hear that at least the Chinese were taking prisoners. Everyone stood around Captain Lawrence in obvious discomfort. Nate realized that all eyes were fixed on him. They were waiting for him to decide whether Lawrence would be allowed to stay, or ordered to return to his captors. Nate briefly considered giving the man the choice, but decided that would be nothing more than a cowardly attempt to relieve himself of responsibility. He turned to the disheveled captain. "You go on back," he said. The man looked down and nodded. "You can write a letter home, if you want, before you leave. And we'll give you a list of units along the road to Khabarovsk that will surrender so you can have something to take back." Clark turned to his operations officer. "Tell those units to begin destroying their weapons once they've made contact with local Chinese commanders." He turned back to the captain. "But as for this base, you tell the Chinese that the only way they're gonna get it is to come in here and take it." The captain raised his head. "Use whatever words you want."

Hot food was brought in on a metal mess tray. The captain gobbled it up in huge bites.

"I want him debriefed," Clark said quietly to his S-2, the brigade intelligence officer. "Troop strengths and deployments. Names or descriptions of all prisoners of war he can remember."

Captain Lawrence wrote a letter to his wife and children at Clark's desk, and then he returned to Chinese lines—to Chinese custody—with Clark's answer. As Clark watched the man shake hands on his way out, Reed informed him that the brigade staff and subordinate unit commanders were all gathered. Clark greeted each of the new arrivals with brisk shakes of their hand, but he couldn't escape the emotions he'd felt on sending the man back to the Chinese. He looked around the bustling headquarters. Would the same fate befall everyone else there?

Nate felt goose bumps ripple up his arms and across his chest. It wasn't fear at the thought, but anger. Reed quietly asked if Nate would grant an interview to a *Newsweek* reporter. Nate shook his head. "All right," he said overly loudly as he turned to the map, "our objective is to defend as wide a piece of real estate as possible with inadequate resources against an unimaginably large enemy force. That means we're going to have to consolidate our position. Tighten our perimeter. Give *up* ground we want and are fighting to hold right now. Ground we'll have to take back in a week at heavy cost to be able to operate this airfield."

He picked up a blue pencil and drew an irregular circle around the airfield. Its radius was about two kilometers, and it was well inside the sagging lines of their current, heavily dented perimeter.

"Even after the consolidation, we still won't have enough people to man a continuous defensive perimeter. So I want an intelligence assessment by twenty-four hundred hours telling me what the most likely Chinese objectives are. We'll defend those, and cover the undefended areas with artillery fire only. That means our lines are going to be porous. Chinese sappers, stragglers, even whole units are going to get through. So I want all the service and support units in the rear to put pickets out at night. They'll also need to form provisional infantry platoons to sweep designated sectors clear of infiltrators after every attack. If the Chinese get through the lines in force, they'll have to defend their own positions against direct assault. And since we've given up these dominating heights around the airfield," he said, drawing red *X*s on three hills, "we'll be under direct fire from those hills round the clock." They all stared down at the *X*s. "So I want those hills under air and artillery attack round the clock, too. I want every Chinese soldier up there either heads down or killed in action."

The enthusiasm they'd shown upon his arrival was gone.

"We'll *also* have to draft men from the service and support units for infantry fillers," Nate continued. "We'll form them into provisional infantry companies. We need at least one infantry battalion as the brigade reserve. We can add line crossers from units out in the field who make it back inside the perimeter.

"The provisionals in the brigade reserve will counterattack to plug breaches. They'll go three ways as three separate companies, or all together against one point of attack—whichever I say."

No one seemed particularly happy with Clark's plan. A lieutenant colonel—the operations officer—was the first of his staff to speak up. "Sir . . . those provisionals are clerks and cooks and mechanics, not infantrymen. They can clear out a few holes. But to maneuver against an enemy under fire they need time to organize."

"They're soldiers, Colonel. They wear the same uniform as you and I."

"Just keep their tactics simple," Reed jumped in. "Nothing complicated. Just single-line, massed frontal assaults for sweeping operations." He turned to Clark. "I could put the battalion together," he said.

And command it, he knew Reed to be proposing. It would be an awful job. Clark worried that losing so many men might ruin Reed. You'd never convince him it wasn't his fault . . . if he lived.

But Reed was good. Those men deserved him. Clark nodded. "Take off," he said.

Reed flew out the door still climbing into his parka.

The group waited for Clark, who still stared at the exit. When he turned back, he said, "Okay. What's our current fire support plan?"

The operations officer pointed at the artillery symbols, hand-drawn rectangular boxes with a single cannonball in the center. "We've got a collection of about three battalion-strength artillery units. They're all firing 155s, which helps with supply. One unit is American, one Belgian, and one French. They're each covering the areas defended by their nation's contingents."

"Who directs them?"

"They're under the control of the three different commands."

Clark stood upright. "You mean to tell me their fire control isn't integrated?"

"We didn't want forward observers controlling fire-direction centers they hadn't worked with. Plus, there's the language barrier. And the different national commanders all wanted their own people available to *them* in case—"

"And *un*available to everybody *else*!" Clark exploded. He tried to rein his temper in. But it was a critical mistake. He was sure men were dying—right at that moment—because of it. "I want centralized fire direction. I want a single, integrated fire plan for every mortar, rocket, and artillery tube on this base. I want to be able to lay preregistered fire—from every gun on this base—wherever the Chinese mass for an attack. But only *I* will have authority to release all three battalions' guns to a single forward observer." He leaned out into the light. His hands pressed heavily on the table. "We *own* the terrain inside those guns' ranges! They will stop the Chinese—dead in their tracks—if used properly. If used intensely. If concentrated. Search and traverse—box patterns—poured out as fast as those crews can cycle their guns. Forget what happened with the 2/263rd. Those guns will cut exposed infantry down. They'll butcher them. It can be made to work. It has to be made to work . . . if we're gonna hold this base."

He waited for someone to tell him it couldn't be done. No one took that opportunity. If they had, Nate would have quietly taken him aside and reassigned him to different duties.

"Do we have any Firefinder radars?" Clark asked.

"They're packed up and ready to move out," replied his chastened operations officer.

"Unpack them. I want counterbattery fire laid against any guns before they get off a second shot." Clark looked down at the map. "Now, why is this artillery unit here," he said, pointing, "deployed out so close to the perimeter?"

"They're still providing fire support for units strung out along the road to Khabarovsk. Those units are at the extremity of the guns' ranges, sir. If we pull them back, they won't be able to support—"

"Pull them back, Colonel," Clark said. He got looks that verged on contempt. Clark resented it. They didn't have to make the hard decisions. "I'll authorize all the unrecoverable units to surrender. We can't risk those tubes that far forward. Pull them back safely inside the perimeter." He ran his finger back and forth across the map. "And make some sense of these deployments. If it takes moving gun emplacements, then move them. If it takes blasting and bulldozing new positions for every last gun, then do that. I want those guns protected, and rationally dispersed. I want them interlocked and capable of responding to calls from every fire-direction center on this base no matter what nationality. And I want it by twenty-four hundred hours."

Their faces were set in grim masks.

"Now, do we have an inventory of exactly who is on this base?" Clark asked.

"Not exactly, no, sir," the operations officer replied. "We've spent the last forty-eight hours collecting units from smaller firebases all around. We were also a transit point for units moving down the road to Khabarovsk before it was cut. Some units we thought were here had already headed on toward Khabarovsk. Others we thought were gone fought their way back down the road to us. There are plenty of others I'm sure we don't know about—bits and pieces, some of them smashed, from a half-dozen different nationalities.''

''I want an inventory by twenty-four hundred,'' Clark ordered.

The man nodded.

''And I want everyone else digging,'' Clark said.

At first it was as if they hadn't heard him.

''Digging,'' he repeated. ''Get engineers to blow the top-soil with shaped charges. You'll be amazed how good an entrencher man with long-handled shovels can be. Men properly organized. Well led . . . by *you*.'' He had their attention now. ''You structure their lives for them. They'll be getting no sleep, so their minds will be mush. We will do their thinking for them. We tell them what to do. When to do it. How to do it. We'll motivate them to keep going. Give them a direction to head in—an objective. And if that objective is directly related to holding this base . . . you've done your job just as they will do theirs. That's all they want out of you right now. And that's all you can ask of them.''

''Should we . . .'' the operations officer began, then shrugged. ''Pass any words of encouragement down to the troops?''

''You tell them we're going to hold for the night. Then tomorrow you tell them again. And the next day—again. If they haven't taken us in three days, they never will.'' Clark looked each of them in the eye, then straightened. ''Twenty-five percent strength in fighting positions till dusk. All patrols in before dark. Starting at dusk, I want automatic weapons moved to alternate weapons pits and test-fired every hour to prevent freezing. We go to fifty percent strength on the line from dusk till twenty-two hundred hours. Seventy-five percent till oh four hundred. Then one hundred percent through the dawn attacks. Afterward we'll send out patrols—*combat* patrols. We'll take the fight to the enemy. It'll police the battlefield. It'll keep the Chinese from digging in within small arms' range of our lines. And it'll build morale. Everyone not on patrol or in their fighting posts . . . digs. Every day. Every night. Till I say stop.''

SOUTH OF BIROBIDZHAN, SIBERIA
January 27, 1245 GMT (2245 Local)

Stempel's small band followed the roar of fighting all night. It sounded as if a giant fireworks factory had caught fire and was slowly cooking off its wares. The sounds fell in intensity sometimes for several minutes, then grew again to a fever pitch in just seconds. The flashing light flickered through the treetops.

Every time they'd stopped, numbness spread up his limbs from his extremities. Every time they'd resumed their march, he'd regained some feeling . . . but not all. At the only road they crossed, they saw Chinese. The sergeant, a pair of binoculars to his eyes, had said there were trucks being unloaded on the road's shoulder. It was dark, and they had crossed the road at a dead run—all together. The Chinese obviously had no night-vision goggles because the crossing had been uneventful. After that, however, their rate of progress toward the ever-increasing noise of battle slowed, and their caution grew. There had to be Chinese in the woods.

Stempel felt an odd kinship with the men even though he didn't know their names. He had spoken only once, his first brief exchange with the sergeant. But he felt a bond with them that was hard to describe. He knew their ranks from the black plastic insignia mounted on the fronts of their helmets. They were mostly privates, like himself. But there were The Two PFCs, The Spec Three, and The Sergeant, who gathered everyone around as the night sky crackled. Stempel got the sense that something momentous loomed. The Sergeant whispered, ''That's the airbase,'' and nodded toward the sound of the fighting. Stempel knew nothing about any airbase. The noise rose several decibels as a flight of jets roared in. A string of thudding explosions sounded in their wake. "The fighting is too hot. We're gonna have to wait. It'll be light soon. We gotta spread out. Dig in. Don't mess the snow up. We want concealment, not cover."

"What about our bootprints?" The Spec Three asked. "If we stop here, they may lead the Chinks straight to us."

"Shit," The Sergeant replied. "Okay, listen up. You know that little stream that we passed? It's iced over. There's not much snow on the ice. We'll double back, keep to our old tracks, then head down the streambed a ways and dig in on the bank. Everybody okay with that?" No answer. "Let's go."

They all rose and began to follow the bootprints back toward the streambed. They took high, awkward steps. Their boots squeaked as they descended through the holes in the snow. Someone grabbed Stempel's arm in the darkness. It was one of the privates. Stempel could see in the starlight that the man's brow was deeply furrowed. "I cain't feel my toes!" he whispered. There was an angry shush from up front.

Stempel could only shrug. He tried to wear a sympathetic expression. He watched the man head on. His steps were even more awkward than the others'. The guy's feet dropped down through the snow in an ungainly plop. Stempel wondered whether the problem wasn't worse than just numb toes. Thereafter, Stempel had a name for the man with the dark eyes and deep furrow. He became The Private Who Couldn't Feel His Feet.

BETHESDA NAVAL HOSPITAL, MARYLAND
January 27, 1430 GMT (0930 Local)

"How are you feeling this morning?" a smiling Elaine asked.

"I hurt all over," Gordon said.

She kissed him, careful not to lean on the mattress. "Do you need anything?"

"A new kidney. Maybe a new hip."

"I mean painkillers. Do you want me to get you some?"

"Can't." He took a deep breath and winced. Gordon didn't waste words anymore. He had only about an hour per day of alertness. The rest of the time he was either asleep or adrift in a sea of nausea and pain through which he wished he could sleep. Any more painkillers and he wouldn't be alert enough to listen to the five-minute updates on the war. The reports were almost universally bad. But they were so couched in bureaucratese that Gordon could only guess how bad the situation really was. And he was too weak to ask pointed questions, or to press for a more complete briefing. "Got an NSC meeting," he said. "Then congressional leadership."

"I know I saw them all gathered out in the hall—arguing."

"About what?"

Her gaze dropped. "This war, Gordon. It's awful."

"*All* wars are awful!"

She immediately placed her hand on his chest. "I know, Gordon. I know. It's just . . . why *this* war? Why are we there? Don't you think maybe we bit off a little more than we can chew?"

" 'We' who?" he croaked.

Elaine reached for the cup and gave him a drink. "I mean America," she said softly. "Honey, those early reports sound terrible. Three thousand dead—most of those Americans. And the numbers of *Chinese* killed . . . ! Can that be right? Forty-five thousand in just four days?"

Gordon lay back. There was so much he wanted to say. Impassioned arguments he wanted to make. The Europeans were committing their troops. They would provide half the manpower. But America was the glue that held the coalition together. Gordon's resolve was its most visible manifestation. America had been leader of the free world since World War II. Was it ready to slough off that mantle because the burden had grown too great? To allow the balance of world power to shift to China? Totalitarian rule to dominate the

Asian landmass? The future was being decided today.

But the most compelling reason for war was completely unrelated to geopolitics. It was simple, to Gordon. To capitulate in the face of naked aggression would be humiliation. Not just for Gordon. He could beg for a cease-fire, get everyone out, then tender his resignation for reasons of health. His footnote in the history books would be kind. But he'd leave his countrymen utterly defeated. That would deal a blow to their self-image. Their self-respect. It would mar the psyche of a generation. The so-called Vietnam syndrome would be nothing compared with what would follow. It would mean isolationism instead of leadership. It would mean the end of the ''American Century,'' and the beginning of the Chinese one.

Character, he thought. The nation would lose some element of its character. And it was character that had made America great. It was the engine of the most powerful country in history. It had been forged in the crucible of war. It could be shattered by a cowardly retreat. War carried a terrible price. But Gordon was not willing to allow *his* weakness to put at risk his country's greatest asset.

Gordon had all those thoughts. But all he had the strength to say to Elaine was, ''We'll win.'' His head felt light. She came into and out of focus . . . talking. Soothing.

''The tree of liberty . . .'' he remembered.

''What?'' Elaine asked.

He'd read it once. The tree of liberty must be refreshed from time to time with the blood of patriots and tyrants. *Thomas Jefferson* . . .

''Mr. President,'' said the minority leader of the Senate. Gordon opened his eyes. How long had he been asleep? He was in the middle of a meeting. ''There's going to be a resolution on the floor of the House to cut off funding for the war after ninety days. If it passes, the cutoff will be automatic. Only another vote by a majority will authorize more funds.'' He paused to let Gordon digest the terrible news.

ERIC L. HARRY

"Will it carry the Senate?" Gordon asked.

His former colleague shrugged. It was a gesture of defeat. "Gordon, I'm gonna just lay it out for you, okay?" Gordon nodded. "Nobody wants this war. Nobody. Not in Europe. Not on the Hill. Not even in your own administration. Ninety percent of the American people oppose it. This is shaping up to be *the* most unpopular war in our country's history—the Civil War *included*. Everybody on the Hill is getting bombarded with faxes and letters and calls and E-mails."

"That's not the people."

The senator smiled. "No. You're right. But I guess you haven't been reading the papers, either."

"Can't hold 'em up," Gordon croaked.

"Well, according to the front page of *The New York Times*, there are over two thousand AWOLs reported. And the number may be going way, way up. And there have already been the first demonstrations."

"So you're pulling the rug out from under me?" Gordon asked. He turned to the leadership. They were clearly uncomfortable.

"I'm sorry, Gordon," the speaker of the House said finally. "The measure will pass. You've got three months to bring our people home."

They waited, but Gordon said nothing. He couldn't. He was too angry. Too busy planning. When the room was cleared of all but a sheepish Fein, Gordon knew what he was going to do. He gave Fein his orders.

"Get me Daryl Shavers."

BIROBIDZHAN AIRBASE, SIBERIA
January 27, 2000 GMT (0600 Local)

The winter sun had yet to rise into the misty sky. But flames lit the breach in the lines they'd just closed. Reed and Clark stood staring as the already frozen Chinese bodies were being stacked like cordwood. "They completely shattered the single platoon manning the perimeter," the dazed Reed said. "They broke clean through. They had open field running ahead of 'em." He shook his head. "But they stopped here."

Men were pulling bodies out of the tattered rags of the mess tent. Huge, gleaming pots still steamed where the starving Chinese had stopped to fill their stomachs after overrunning a battalion field kitchen. Major Reed's provisionals had counterattacked, pouring fire and grenades onto the absurdly exposed Chinese. Over a hundred Chinese soldiers, crammed inside the mess tent, died amid the pots and pans.

Clark's radio crackled. His radioman announced that another Chinese attack was coming. "Where?" Clark asked tensely. "Southern perimeter," the man repeated as he listened to the radio. "In the gap between the U.S. and Belgian positions." A wave of relief washed over Clark. It was exactly where and when he'd expected. He ordered the prearranged call to go out to the air commander. Pilots sitting in their jets on the runways of Khabarovsk a hundred and ten miles away would be there in ten minutes on afterburners. Plenty of time to form up for the attack.

Before departing, Clark shook hands with Reed. "Good job," he said tersely.

Reed held Clark's gloved hand. The major looked back at Clark through puffy, bloodshot eyes. They were surrounded with growing mounds of the dead. Men Reed had ordered slaughtered as they desperately tried to fill their starving bellies.

"You did what you were supposed to do, Major." Reed opened his mouth to speak. Clark squeezed his hand tight. *Not now*, he thought. Don't start asking the questions. "You did what you were *supposed* to do, Major," Clark repeated. "Now get your provisionals ready for another counterattack."

Clark headed for the perimeter.

The Chinese were going for the lone rise on the base to the south of the airfield. Clark had dug in a half-dozen .50-calibers near the crest. The heavy machine guns were awesomely destructive. They had devastated the light probes the Chinese had sent in the night for the sole purpose of mapping the positions of the guns. Now they'd come back to root the weapons out. The fire support plan was ready. All forty-eight tubes—too close to be brought to bear on the battlefield—would begin firing at extreme elevations onto the immediate rear of the attacking Chinese. But the support on which Clark pinned his hopes would be orbiting above the clouds—unbeknownst to the Chinese—with wing pylons heavily laden with high explosives. Clark stopped to look at his watch. All forty fighter-bombers should be on station in fifteen minutes.

Clark edged his way through the narrow slit in the earth. He was bent in a stoop just below the snowy surface. The slit trench connected the defensive perimeter with the command and aid posts to the rear. It would soon be jam-packed with traffic. Ammo and fast reaction teams would move outward. The dead and wounded would be evacuated to the rear. Bugles and whistles began to blow just as Clark got to the deeper and wider main fighting trench. His radioman and two-man security team followed close behind.

The soldiers in the main trench all sat or stood with their backs pressed to the outer wall. Their heads hung down. They eyed Clark with bleary eyes sunk deep into their sockets as he moved down their ranks. "How's it goin'?" Clark asked. He slapped men's shoulders and shook hands. They were so weary that it took time for his presence to register. But in his wake the men stirred and came to life. An officer stood on a step carved out of the wall. He peered at no-man's-land through periscope binoculars. By the time Clark got to the young platoon leader, his men were doing a double take. They thought they'd seen it all in the last seventy-two hours, but this was something new.

"What'cha see, Lieutenant?" Clark asked in a loud voice.

"More fuckin' Chinese," he said. He then took his face uncertainly from the binoculars. His feet slipped off his precarious step. "S-s-sir?" he said. He saluted awkwardly.

"No saluting, Lieutenant. No sense giving those snipers a target."

"Yes, sir!" he replied.

"Where's the nearest gap in the lines?" Clark asked.

"About a hundred fifty meters that way," the young man replied, pointing toward their right. "We've turned back the last platoon on the line along that flank. It's about a two-hundred-meter gap to a Belgian company on the opposite side that's turned back its left flank. We're planning on plugging the hole with four-point-two inch mortars and some heavy machine guns on the hill behind us."

"Sounds like a plan," Clark remarked. "You mind?" he asked, nodding at the binoculars but not waiting for a reply. He stepped up onto the perch. The binoculars had mirrors inside that allowed the viewer to remain safely below the lip of the trench. Its massive lenses were pointed at the wire. When Clark adjusted the focus slightly he saw the Chinese sappers stealthily creeping forward. The cleared killing field had been tortured and blackened by the awful violence of modern war. "What's the range to the tree line from here?" he asked. "Tree line" was hardly descriptive. They were shattered and blackened trunks pointing skyward.

"Two hundred meters, sir," he answered.

Clark whistled. "Pretty tight quarters. You got any claymores out?"

"We blew the last ones about zero three hundred. We haven't been able to get back out there 'cause of the snipers." The Chinese soldiers moved slowly. They never rose much above a squat. Their moves were unhurried. They held their new CQ 5.56-millimeter automatic rifles, a Chinese derivative of the ubiquitous American M-16, high and in front like they expected imminent hand-to-hand combat. *They're all about to die*, Clark thought.

"Can I ask you a question, sir?"

"Sure," Clark replied. He panned the binoculars to the left. The picture was the same all up and down the wire.

"Who are you?"

Clark looked around at the man and held out his hand. "Lieutenant General Nate Clark."

A small crowd had gathered. Clark shook everyone's hands.

"You're the commander of . . . of the whole thing, right?" the lieutenant asked. "Of the whole UNRUS-FOR?"

Clark nodded. "Yep. That and fifty cents'll buy me a cup o' coffee," he said. The tired old line drew laughter from the exhausted men.

"Well, um," the lieutenant began, "wh-what're you doin' *here*?"

Clark laughed, and they all joined in. He considered making a joke—*I was beginning to wonder the same thing.* Or maybe bravado—*Brushin' up on my target practice.* But men had died there, he realized. In a dirty trench that smelled of urine. There was blood on the icy floor. A crimson bandage on one man's neck. An arm in a sling. An NCO who'd lost part of a foot. It was a hallowed place. Consecrated by these men and their dead friends.

"I'm here to fight," Clark replied simply.

The smiles remained on some of the grimy faces. On others, there were different emotions displayed. All, however, were alert and alive. Clark and his small entourage moved on. They followed the winding trench to the right. Toward the gap. He pressed the flesh on the way like a politician. After he passed what had to be over two hundred defenders in the already reinforced sector, the sky lit up with trip flares.

Nate decided he'd fight from right there. "How far out are the flares, Lieutenant?" he asked the platoon leader. He then checked his M-16. He had a full magazine—twenty rounds.

"Three hundred meters, sir," the nervous twenty-something replied.

"You lay any mines?"

"No, sir. But we strung some booby traps between the trees on a wire. Grenades with the pins pulled in tin cans."

The grenades started to go off. The Chinese ran into the wire in the darkness, spilling the grenades to the ground. Freed of the confines of the can, the grenades' handles flew off. They popped by the dozens.

"How far out are the booby traps?" Nate asked.

"Two fifty, sir."

Then came the first shouts of "Rifle grena-ades!" from the trench's observation posts.

Everyone pressed themselves low to the front wall. The rifle grenades came arcing down from the mist on long smoking tails. They were slow enough for Clark to watch before ducking his head. The explosions rippled up and down the line. The closest shook ice loose from the sandbags. Poor man's artillery.

The American guns opened up. "Commence firing!" the platoon leader yelled. The men all climbed up to their firing posts. Brass rained down onto the trench floor from all manner of infantry weapons. The M-60 crews had sandbagged roofs built over their nests. But the soldiers with SAWs and M-16s had to duck with each bursting grenade.

Clark climbed up onto the earthen step of an empty firing post. Peering over the sandbags, he saw two things. Hundreds upon hundreds of running, weaving Chinese, each of whom would have to be killed. And caked black blood that ran down the sandbag just in front. The post was empty for a reason.

He glanced at his watch. The fighter-bombers were just a couple of minutes out, he guessed.

Clark raised his M-16 and lined up the nearest Chinese infantryman. He flicked the selector switch to "semi" and gripped the trigger firmly with his index finger. When it came time for him to fire, he found it remarkably difficult. At first he thought maybe he'd left the safety on and the trigger wouldn't pull. But it wasn't the rifle's mechanism that prevented him from killing. It had been a long time since he'd killed a man.

Clark jerked the trigger, releasing a round just to get it over with. The rifle bucked. The boom of the round's release rang in his ear. All was as he expected. Even the thin swirl of smoke from the muzzle was as it should be. Clark centered the next shot on a man's chest and squeezed. The rifle bucked and boomed and smoked. This time his target fell. Prostrate. Unmoving. Dead.

He had forgotten how hard it was to kill a man. How much it took out of you emotionally. The men firing weapons all around him weren't exhausted from lack of sleep. They had been deprived for too long of something else. Mercy, kindness, forgiveness—all those things man calls "humanity." Clark fired again, and missed. He fired again. This time a hit. The man he'd shot writhed on the ground. He thrashed about in pain from a high-velocity round that had just shattered bones and jellied tissue.

Clark pulled his eye back from his sights. The Chinese were dying in numbers he had never before witnessed first-hand. Some of the grizzled old vets in 'Nam had told stories of the human waves in Korea. But words could never do the scene justice. When men fell and died by the thousands, individual targets quickly lost their significance. There were so many they just became a part of a whole. Clark was killing a platoon, a company, a regiment. Whether one at a time by the pull of a trigger, or en masse by issuing orders from his CP. The targets weren't individual human beings. They had no face. No family. No past. That would've been too much for him to bear. The scale of the slaughter forced him to wall his mind up. To shut out reality.

His two riflemen and even his radiomen were on the wall now. They all fired across the two-hundred-meter shooting gallery. The smell of the gun smoke made Clark vaguely nauseous. Still the Chinese came. A fresh wave appeared in the broken trees even before the last of the ranks before them had fallen. *What were the Chinese commanders doing?* Clark wondered in sudden confusion. *Entire regiments hurled against well-prepared positions? How could they possibly be expending men's lives in such a coldly calculated fashion?* Then he remembered Brigadier General Merrill. You did what you had to do.

The depleted front ranks of the onrushing infantrymen were now at one hundred meters. Clark began to fire three-round bursts. He quickly ran through two magazines. He then grabbed three more from a man who carried a rucksack up and down the trench line. A new wave of attackers leaped over the flattened razor wire in the killing zone.

He turned to his radioman and shouted, *"Find out what's keeping that air!"* He then returned to his rapidly fired bursts. The sandbag on which he steadied his aim jerked and split open. It leaked its contents just like a human body would.

Another shot whizzed by his head. Clark caught himself feeling momentarily amazed. He then raised his rifle almost in reflex. He had been a green second lieutenant three decades ago. Somehow the greenness had grown back.

The air was now filled with the enemy's return fire. Out of the corner of his eye Clark saw the first man fall. The ragged but still charging line was now seventy-five meters away. He glanced back at the fallen, writhing man. Most wounds in the trench would be like his, he realized. Head wounds. A medic was trying to pry the man's hands away from his face without success. He was screaming. It was just like before. It was every bit as awful as he remembered.

"Tango Lima one niner, this is X-Ray Yankee five eight, do you read me, *over!*" the radioman shouted. He got no response. He was sitting at the bottom of the trench, repeating, *"Tango Lima one niner . . . !"*

Every shot counted now. The men nearest the trench were hurling hand grenades in volleys. Just before Clark and all the others dropped, he saw a fresh line of Chinese emerge from the smoky forest.

The spinning grenades rained down all around. The earth shook with several dozen explosions. Fire and smoke shot down the trench from around the bend. A grenade had dropped home on the unlucky squad. Grenades fell end over smoking end from the sky. But an NCO shouted, "Everybody *u-u-up!*"

"Tango Lima one niner . . . !"

When Clark stepped back onto his fighting post he felt fear shoot up his spine. He didn't have time to wonder what had gone wrong. He didn't have time to rage at the forward air controller. He had time only to fire his rifle. The first Chinese were fifty meters away. This time he jerked at the trigger. His targets fell at nearly every pull. They were right at the end of his front sight, impossible to miss. The searing heat of grenades licked at his skin. Their thunderous booms frayed his nerves to a jangled mess. Violence raged around him. Grenades burst in and all around the trench. Bullets ripped through the air at supersonic speed. Clark killed without thinking.

"Tango Lima one niner, do-you-read-me-ove-e-e-r?"

Clark dropped down and ejected an empty magazine. He could hear the full-throated shouts of the massed Chinese. Suddenly the world erupted in fire. The air at the bottom of the trench shook. Choking dust rose. Snow cascaded from walls onto his helmet and shoulders. Everybody had fallen from their posts and lay now on the icy floor. Men leaped down into the trench or onto the far wall just as another earth-shattering roar shook the darkening sky. Flame shot out of rifles, lighting the trench with flashes as men killed other men. All was noise and confusion and death. Soldiers of both armies clawed at the walls to escape. Another thunderous vibration filled the air with falling and burning debris.

The fighting inside the trench was over. The survivors hugged the walls for their lives. The staggering, earth-shattering, end-of-the-world violence was near constant. Clark rolled himself into a fetal ball. He didn't know if they had won or lost. The bombers had arrived out of nowhere to begin the apocalypse. They had become everyone's enemy. Bombs kill indiscriminately.

His heart was still pounding when he realized the worst had passed. The intense bombing had moved farther away. "Come on!" someone shouted before choking on the smoke and coughing. "Sweep the trench!" Clark rose back up to the wall. The misty morning sky was now obscured by a pall of black smoke. A shroud over the countless dead. Crackling fires burned near and far. No one moved. Nothing lived. The battle was won.

"I know where the hell you are!" General Dekker shouted over the satellite phone. "God*dam*mit, Nate. We've soldiered together for years, but you disobeyed an express order! I don't need to tell you where I'm headed with this. You put the commander-in-chief of *all* forces in theater into a *surrounded* airbase under *imminent* threat of overrun! You're risking getting yourself killed in a *sideshow*, Nate! A fuckin' *sideshow*! *Jesus* Christ!" Dekker's sigh sounded like a gale wind blowing into the mouthpiece. "Why'd you do it? Why'd you disobey my order and go in there?"

"I'm sending men off to die, Ed." Clark's voice quavered. "You should see them. You'd be proud of 'em. All these years and I still don't know what makes 'em lace up their boots and head out into that shit. I swear to God it amazes me more today than it did back when we were their age. They don't have a clue why the hell they're here. They just . . ." He choked. "They just . . ." He shook his head. Goose bumps rose on his arms as he spoke, "By *God* they're fine soldiers, Ed. Every last one of 'em. I don't care what they did before or what they'll do if they make it home. Nothing can take away the fact that right here, right now, they're the best goddamn army that's ever taken to the field."

Dekker was silent. When he finally spoke, he sounded drained of his earlier anger. "You know I should yank your goddamned command. I should bust you down two grades and retire your ass on half pension. But if that base holds, they'll pro'bly pin a fuckin' DSM on your chest."

"I won't take it. As far as I'm concerned, my visit here didn't happen. It's off-the-record. This base is gonna hold, I can feel it. We're gonna start sending out combat patrols to clear the snipers. These guys've got the starch to hold the place, and it doesn't have *anything* to do with me."

"Tell that to *Newsweek* magazine," Dekker said.

"They've already called. Your picture's gonna be on the goddamn *cover*—'Come and take it!' printed in big letters. I can't fire you now, Nate. You're a *hero*. But if you *ever* disobey another order that I give you—I don't care *how* trivial—I'll stand you up against a wall and make your goddamn death wish come true! *You* read me?"

"Yes, sir," Clark replied.

Dekker slammed the phone down.

A man was waiting with a radio message. It was from one of the surrounded units on the road to Khabarovsk that Nate had personally decided was unrecoverable. "Ammo is gone. All weapons destroyed. No sign of relief. Will surrender my unit as ordered. Am destroying radio. Please pray for us. Out."

13

Things had grown worse and worse as the night wore on. Columns of Chinese had come close to Stempel's small band. There had to be tens of thousands of them, all moving toward the airbase. Finally, one long file of men walked straight through the middle of their dispersed hiding places. Lying under his blanket of snow, Stempel didn't even breathe for fear of exhaling a white vapor that would begin the killing. But no one saw them. The frightened Chinese soldiers were too concerned with what lay ahead to pay any attention to their immediate surroundings.

By dawn, the last waves of Chinese had passed, and the battle had begun. So many Chinese had passed that Stempel couldn't imagine how the airbase could've held. The sounds of fighting were intense, but they were nothing compared with what was to come next.

The woods exploded. That was what it seemed like to Stempel. Wave after wave of concussions. A flight of four jets screamed overhead. In their wake, a storm of fire rolled through the forest. The last bomb in the string was barely a hundred meters away. The ground vibrated under Stem-

pel's back. Then came the Chinese stampeding the other
way. They ran like wild animals. Leaping fallen logs. Darting this way and that. Crashing through limbs that hung
low with their weight of snow, falling and being half-
covered by the avalanche. Stempel feared the retreating infantry. But he feared death from the sky the most. The thick
drifts of snow beside the streambed had been a natural place
to hide. But the streambed also offered pilots a break in the
thick forest's canopy.

Gunships flew straight down the narrow stream. Their
chopping rotors and whining engines changed pitch as they
twisted and turned in air. Fleeing Chinese who crossed the
stream were mowed down. The Apache's chin gun stripped
branches and even felled whole trees. Thick ice was thrown
up in great sheets. The earth shuddered with hundreds of
blows. Chinese caught in the open simply disintegrated.
Desperate mobs, heedless of the sounds of the airborne
predators, crossed the ten-meter cut through the woods.
Turbines whined. Rotors hacked at air above the agile birds
of prey. Snow and ice exploded.

It was impossible to count the dead. The constituent parts
of their bodies littered the landscape. Gunships cut great
swaths through masses of men. Others ran on unharmed.
Life and death were reduced to a senseless, random lottery.
And in the background—far, far away—there was thunder.
The deep, hellish sound of heavy bombing. *B-52s,* Harold
thought. It had to be. Every thirty-second rumble reminded
him that if death sought him out, there was no place on
earth to hide.

When the last of the surviving Chinese were gone, the
whines of the engines diminished until all was quiet. Even
the wails and moans of the wounded quickly fell silent.

The Sergeant rose up. Snow cascaded from his arctic
gear. With vigorous arm signals he waved everyone to their
feet. Six of the men got up. Three didn't.

The Private Who Couldn't Feel His Feet and two others
remained stuck in their banks of snow. During the stillness
of their hours in hiding, they had lost all feeling in their

lower extremities. The Sergeant took a look at them in the dim light, peeling back their clothes and prodding and probing.

He moved away to exchange urgent whispers with the Spec Three. Stempel heard everything.

"They got frostbite bad," The Sergeant said.

"Should we try rubbin' snow on their skin?" the Spec Three asked.

"Naw. They're frozen too deep. Don't rub or massage 'em. Don't even try to bend 'em. They're gonna lose them toes and fingers. They'll be lucky not to lose their hands and feet."

"Can they walk at all?"

"No way."

That started Stempel on his own calculations. There were six of them who could walk. But one was the man Stempel called "The Private With The Leg Wound." There weren't enough healthy guys to go around.

"Everybody down!" The Sergeant suddenly hissed. All those who had risen returned to their spots and covered themselves back up. Stempel barely finished the last flicks of his gloved hands when he caught sight of movement. A point man profiled against the light. Not stooped over, but with his rifle at the ready. Stempel let the man pass before burying his arms and hands, finding the hard grips of his rifle under the snow.

Stempel kept his eyes right on the rounded shape of the helmet. The man wearing it was clearly watching him also.

"All right," The Sergeant said in a normal tone of voice. "Nobody move. You got that flag?" The Spec Three showed him the white towel. The Sergeant nodded. "Okay. Lift it up slowly—*slo-o-owly*—and wave it over your head."

The Spec Three spun the white towel in slow figure eights. Time passed. Stempel shivered in the quiet of the frozen woods. He waited to die. He gripped his rifle so firmly with numb hands that his forearms cramped. His gaze remained fixed on the round, white helmet.

"Freeze!" someone shouted from a distance. The Spec Three's towel hung limply. "American soldier! Identify yourself!"

Stempel couldn't believe it. The Sergeant had a grin on his face. The Spec Three was laughing. The Private Who Couldn't Feel His Feet cried. It was true. Stempel's eyes drooped shut.

"Second of the 263rd!" the joyous sergeant replied.

Stempel opened his eyes. Then they sank closed again. He heard the crunching of snow. His eyes opened just long enough to see GIs with M-16s. They closed again.

"You guys really from 2nd Battalion?" he heard. Stempel forced his eyelids open. Several heads nodded. "Is there anybody else?" he asked. Puffs of smoke shot from his mouth and nose.

No one said a word. Stempel's eyes again closed.

PORT OF VLADIVOSTOK, SIBERIA
January 29, 0200 GMT (1200 Local)

André Faulk headed down the gangplank, exhausted from two days at sea. The combat units had flown over on luxury airliners, but André's postal detachment had been pitched and tossed in the winter seas aboard a smelly, rusty freighter. The cold air cut right through his loosely hanging parka, but he breathed deeply. Ahead was land, fresh air, and open space. He fell into formation on the dock with the others from his unit, a motley crowd of the overweight and the slight of build. He felt himself sway slightly from one foot to the other.

"Listen up!" the lieutenant yelled as he approached the formation. In the heavy winter gear he looked almost athletic. But André had seen him in the gym back in Korea. He was almost six feet tall, but weighed maybe one forty. "You are now in Vladivostok, Russia! There *is* no Russian government left! This whole area is under military government by United Nations Russian Forces! You should consider yourselves in hostile territory anytime you're outside a secure military compound! The Chinese are on the way, but the Anarchists are already here! Plus the civilian population is hungry, so they'll slit your throat to get at your food or your wallets! That means standing orders are no *fraternization*!'' A groan went up. ''Now, I *mean* it, guys!'' the lieutenant squealed, cracking down. André rolled his eyes. ''Okay! We start processing tomorrow! Let's *do* it!'' His fist pumped the air for emphasis. He got no response.

André watched the ship berthed next to the rust bucket on which they'd arrived disgorge Bradley armored fighting vehicles. They'd all been freshly painted white in the division's barns back at Tongduchon. He wondered where Stempel was.

BIROBIDZHAN FIREBASE, SIBERIA
January 29, 1000 GMT (2000 Local)

Only after Harold Stempel woke did he hear the thumping explosions and feel them through the floor of the warm bunker. He'd grown used to the violent background noise, but he couldn't sleep through the shouts of the staff sergeant, who rousted everyone from their sleeping bags. *More digging*, Harold surmised. He sat upright, but his head wobbled and his eyes closed. Since he'd made it inside the perimeter, he'd been on ''excused duty.'' That meant he'd dug, and he'd slept, but he hadn't fought. His ears were numb from the charges engineers had blown to loosen the soil. Their labor detachments would take cover against trench walls, and the smoke and choking dust would roar past them. Before crawling into his gear, Harold took two of the codeine they'd given him at the aid station to dull his many aches and pains.

When he donned his blood-coated arctic shell, the sergeant asked if he was wounded. Stempel shook his head, but that was a lie. He *was* wounded. You just couldn't see the wounds. But he could feel them, especially in his sleep. When he closed his eyes, paranoia slowly gripped him and rose quietly to uncontrollable panic. Light sleep meant nightmares, sweats, sometimes shouting. From the bliss of deep sleep he would awaken to an adrenaline rush—eyes wide open, pulse racing, a sudden wakefulness, and overwhelming fear of imminent danger as he lay in his sleeping bag.

The sergeant led Stempel and a dozen others out into the cold night air. The fighting sounded light and sporadic—occasional rips of automatic fire that died down quickly. A distant grenade. A single shot. Despite the apparent calm, the staff sergeant crept through the slit trench bent over at the waist, holding his rifle out in front of him at port arms. Stempel took his cue from the man. He flicked the selector switch of his M-16 to "burst" and slipped his trigger finger into its sleeve. When they arrived at a bunker off the slit trench, the staff sergeant poked his head into the darkness and asked, "How many you need?" One more, came the reply. The staff sergeant turned to Stempel and said, "You."

Stempel crawled into the bunker, which stank from the fumes of a gas stove. In the light of a lone kerosene lantern, he could make out the large, heavily clad shapes of eight men who faced a ninth. "Take a seat," the ninth said to Stempel. Harold sank between parkas that rubbed together noisily. Everyone looked at the caked brown blood coating Stempel's parka. "You're now in 1st Squad, 3rd Platoon, 1st Provisional Infantry Company." The man's eyes darted from Harold's face to the dried blood. "My name is Harper—specialist five. I'm your squad leader."

"Stempel, private," Harold reported. The squad leader wrote Harold's particulars on a piece of paper then resumed what Stempel's arrival had obviously interrupted. He wrote down the name, rank, and serial number from one of the others, then asked, "MOS?"

"Eighty-two-C," the man replied. "Field artillery surveyor."

The spec five moved on to the next soldier.

"Thirty-one-M—multichannel communications systems operator."

It suddenly dawned on the groggy Stempel that they were forming an infantry squad.

"Sixty-three-B," came a woman's voice. Stempel's gaze shot to the dim profile in the corner. "Light wheeled vehicle maintenance," she supplied. Her chin rested on an M-16's front sight.

"Eighty-eight-M—motor transportation operator," came the quivering response of the man next to Stempel. He wore thick, shatterproof glasses.

"Four-fifty-seven-XB," the next person said in answer to the spec five's query.

"What the hell's *that*?" their squad leader asked.

"Airlift aircraft maintenance/C-5," the guy replied. "I'm air force, not army."

"Gre-e-eat," somebody mumbled. The spec five was himself incredulous. "Is there anybody *else* here who's air force?" he asked. The rubbing sounds of fabric drew the bunker's attention to two others who raised their hands. "Ah, sh-*sh-shit*!" the spec five cursed. 551XO—pavements maintenance, and 703XO—administrative/reprographic were their specialties. The spec five huffed loudly and asked, "We got any navy? Coast guard? Boy Scouts?" There were chuckles. "Okay, who have I missed?" Again a rubbing sound from the darkness. "Speak up!" the spec five barked.

"Well, m-m-my *official* specialty is zero two B, sir . . . Sarge . . . But, well, I was called up as ninety-two B—medical laboratory specialist—which is my civilian job."

"You're army *reserves*?" the spec five asked.

"National guard," the guy replied.

There were groans. "Shut the fuck up!" the spec five snapped as he wrote. "What's an oh two B?"

"Um." The guy chuckled nervously. "It's actually—you're gonna get a kick outta this—cornet. I'm a cornet player. Zero two B is for cornet and trumpet players."

"Oh-oh-oh," somebody groaned in the darkness. "We're dead meat, man."

"Shut the fuck up!" the spec five shouted again. "Nobody says another goddamn word unless I tell him to . . . or her!'' He turned to Stempel. Again he glanced at the blood of the sergeant and PFC on his shell. ''What about you?'' he asked in an almost deferential tone.

''Eleven-B—infantryman,'' Harold replied. The man next to him sighed in relief. Another shook Stempel's hand in a sixties-style soul shake.

As the spec five wrote, a question was directed to him from the darkness. ''What's *your* specialty?''

The spec five busied himself with a recount of the ten names and replied, ''Zero zero J.'' The man asked what that was. ''Club activities manager, *okay*?'' was their squad leader's answer.

No one said a word. The only sound was the crack of high-powered assault rifles outside.

An officer arrived carrying a heavy sack. ''My name is Lieutenant Dawes.'' He seemed confident, and Stempel clung to that. ''We've got to clean out some Chinese that smashed through the perimeter. They're pinned down in some old mortar pits, but we've got to attack to reestablish the line.'' There was dead silence. ''I know you're all nervous, but you gotta do this. It's gonna be real straightforward. I'll take you guys, and Sergeant Brunner'll take Second Squad. We'll form a single, tight line and do a simple leapfrog. One squad advances twenty meters, drops, and lays down covering fire for the other squad's advance. No fallin' behind! When we get to the pits, we kill the Chinese. But listen,'' he said, clearing his throat, ''you're gonna have to maneuver under fire, understand?'' Apparently only Stempel did. No one else seemed to register the fear he felt crawling up his spine. ''Our approach is across an open field. I'm sorry, but that's just the way it is.''

Now they all got it. Their expressions ranged from anger to disbelief. Dawes dragged his sack in front. ''Everybody take five grenades.'' The motor transportation operator next to Stempel unexpectedly gulped air and coughed. He put his hand on Harold's shoulder as if to rise, but he never got off his knees. Harold thought he was going to vomit, but Dawes gave him some water and he didn't.

"Fire at their muzzle flashes," Dawes said as the heavy bag was dragged around. "That'll keep their heads down. When we get in grenade range, start tossin'."

They filed out into the slit trench one by one. Nobody said a word.

Dawes put everyone in their places along the wall of a slit trench. It was a tight, five-meter spread. When all was set, he waved his arm and they crawled up onto the snow. The staccato pops of Chinese guns began immediately. Bullets whooshed through the air overhead. They'd been spotted and were being fired on by prepared troops. Stempel pressed low to the crusty, windblown snow. To his left and right the rest of the terrified provisionals joined him.

"First Squad," Lieutenant Dawes shouted, "pick a target and prepare to fire!"

Stempel raised his rifle to his shoulder. The snow-covered ground was uneven. It rose in places just enough to obscure all but one blazing Chinese gun. He aimed at the bright muzzle flashes and flicked the selector to "semi." From his left he heard, "Second Squad, prepare to advance in line! On my command"—there was a moment's pause—"go!"

"First Squad open *fi-i-ire*!" Dawes shouted.

Stempel squeezed the trigger, and his M-16 rocked hard against his shoulder. It was the same rifle he'd fished out of the snow. He'd cleaned it once in the bunker, and it functioned perfectly. All of a sudden the field ahead came alive with Chinese guns. Each was marked by its flashing muzzle just like Stempel's position would be fixed with his every shot. He fired rapidly at the new targets—moving from gun to gun and squeezing his trigger as fast as he could take aim. The snow around him began to spray into the air. Out of the corner of his eye he saw the ghostly, white-clad forms of 2nd Squad all drop to the ground at once.

"*First Squad,*" Dawes shouted over the roar, "*advance twenty meters!*"

Stempel and his squadmates rose into the swarm of angry bees that buzzed by them at supersonic speed. For him to stay on his feet required the complete abandonment of reason and sanity. Every rational thought screamed at him to dive to the ground, but he shut them from his head. He detached his mind from a body that might at any second be ripped to shreds or cored by hot steel. His mind remained above the fray, focusing on such minutiae as staying in line with the others as if on parade ground.

"First Squad, *down!*" Stempel hit the ground hard, first knees then face plowing into the snow. "Fire at the *gu-u-uns!*" Dawes yelled. Stempel spit the cold grit from his mouth and wiped the back of his glove across his face. Second Squad was leapfrogging ahead. He switched the selector to "burst" and fired a three-round burst at the now closer muzzles. The blazing Chinese gun was extinguished, and Stempel smiled in surprise. He fired at the next hole and knocked out that gun too, but his bolt remained open. His magazine was empty. He ejected it.

"First Squad, *adva-ance!*" Dawes shouted.

Stempel rose slowly as he fumbled with the snap on his ammo pouch. He ran forward as the guns from 2nd Squad roared from his left. He was falling behind, but he couldn't get the goddamn plastic *snap* open on the goddamn *pouch*! He stumbled through the drifts. The air around him was filled with zips and zings of random death. He got the pouch open and reached inside.

He snagged his parka on a tree limb, jerking his sleeve around. "First Squad, *down!*" Dawes shouted. Stempel dropped and slapped the new magazine into his rifle. That's when he saw the hole in his parka and realized two things—there were no trees on that field, and he'd been hit in the right arm. The scratch rapidly became a sting, then a throbbing ache, then a searing fire. A bullet had passed between his right biceps and his chest. When he probed inside, he saw blood on his glove.

A grenade burst up ahead in a jarring crash. Then another. They illuminated the sixty or so meters that now separated the two sides. It was tabletop flat and covered in a blanket of sparkling snow. Stempel raised his rifle and fired burst after burst.

"First Squad, *u-u-up*!" Dawes screeched.

It took all the will Stempel could muster to rise. To abandon the soft snow for the hail of bullets and sprays of grenade shrapnel. Gone was the pain from his arm. Gone was the shockingly cold snow that had found its way inside his collar. With clenched jaw he rose into near-certain death. The random zips of passing bullets became a constant roar. *You're a dead man if you run straight!* he remembered Sergeant Giles had shouted, and he began to zigzag. To his right and his left he saw men fall. Their screams now joined the buzz of bullets, pops of rifles, and crash of grenades. A stunning blast of hot fire from nearby dazed Stempel. He grew dizzy but labored forward despite feeling like someone had kicked his helmet and slapped open palms on his ears all at once. Somebody was shouting *"Grena-a-ades!"* at the top of his lungs. They were bursting everywhere. Snow and flame shot skyward.

Stempel suddenly realized it was Sergeant Giles yelling for First Squad to throw grenades. *No,* he thought as he dropped, *it was Lieutenant Dawes, not Sergeant Giles*. He patted his cargo pockets and fished out a steel pineapple. Another explosion almost knocked the wind from him. The ground underneath him bucked and he registered the heat on his exposed face. Snow fell all around him, first in huge gobs, then in a fine, frozen mist. Harold looked down and saw his left index finger in the metal ring. He twisted and pulled and twisted and . . . The ring came out. He squeezed the grenade and handle in his right hand. Another blast peppered his neck and face with ice, stinging terribly and causing his eyes to water.

When yet another grenade burst nearby, Harold looked around and realized that he was all alone. That meant only one thing—those grenades were being hurled at him and him alone. The Chinese were out to kill him. His clenched teeth popped so loud he thought he'd broken a tooth. He rose to one knee. Drew the grenade back to his right ear. Pointed with his left hand at a group of flashing muzzles. And hurled the grenade with a grunt. He dropped down to his stomach. The effort had wrenched his shoulder painfully. The air above him filled with lead. By the time his first grenade went off, he was pulling the pin of a second. He reared up—heedless of the terrible danger—and threw at a different cluster of flashes. He pressed himself flat, and the buzzing bees above him had never been angrier. His parka was jerked by a passing bullet. Another bullet stung his boot, and pain shot through his ankle. He contorted his body and looked down to see that a piece of rubber had been peeled off the sole of one boot.

The thwack of a jarring blow to Stempel's helmet simultaneously stung his ears, wrenched his neck, and gave him an intense headache. A bullet had glanced off the Kevlar, and more skittered through the snow on both sides. The pain meant nothing now. He had to save his life. He frantically pulled the pin of a third grenade and again tempted fate to rise. He hurled it with all his might, shouting "A-a-ah!"

As he again dropped, he caught sight of a black object disappearing into the snow in front of him. It felt like he was inside the explosion. He stared up at the starry sky and could make no sense of the battlefield. He groped for and found his rifle, but as if in a dream couldn't clear his head enough to use it. He was still patiently brushing ice from the M-16 when he felt a hand grab his parka and shake.

"Charge those holes!" Lieutenant Dawes shouted, pointing.

"You're bleeding, sir," Stempel said on seeing a huge gash along his jawline.

"Come on, soldier!" Dawes shouted. Blood that hung from his chin fell in large, black drops.

Stempel rose, rifle in hand, and charged in the direction Dawes had pointed. He ran straight at the Chinese guns. When he zigged, he saw no friendly troops. When he zagged, he confirmed he was all alone. He ran like a maniac straight toward the nearest mortar pit. Chinese guns fired on either side, but in the center—where he'd thrown his grenades—it was dark. He was so, so exposed that the last few steps before the sandbags seemed to take forever. The dark round pit looked still, but moments earlier it had been filled with flaming muzzles. He leaped over the sandbags and fell through the air into the mortar pit. He landed feet-first, but it did little good. He slipped on the ice and crashed hard onto the ground.

Onto the bodies of Chinese soldiers. The dark pit was full of them. Corpses were lit with every burst of American grenades from the pit in front of 2nd Squad. They were still, but they weren't all dead. He didn't know why he felt sure, but someone was hiding under the bodies, he could feel it. He raised his rifle to his shoulder and threw himself back against the wall. His finger was on the trigger. He traversed the pit with his muzzle, the sight to his eye. *Where are you?* Stempel raged in silence.

A man scampered over the wall in a shower of snow. Stempel almost shot Lieutenant Dawes. Instead he shot at a lunging Chinese soldier. He saw the man die at point-blank range in the blaze of the muzzle. The bullet struck the man's ear just below his helmet. Brains sprayed onto frozen sandbags. Dawes began firing single shots into each of the Chinese. A dozen bullets for a dozen bodies. No others made a move. None showed any signs of life before they were shot. All were certainly dead after. The pit was filled with their viscera and gore. The lieutenant made his way over to Harold. The large gash along his jaw still dripped blood. He patted Harold down, finding the wound on his inner biceps and the matching scratch on his chest. Harold's eyes sank closed.

"Just a scrape," Dawes said after probing the wound and sending hot stings of pain through Stempel.

Scraping and sliding sounds drew Harold's rifle. Dawes slapped the barrel down before Stempel killed his squad-mates. They piled into the mortar pit one at a time. The "fighting" in the near distance was now execution-style.

Single shots, single grenades, death by ones. Dawes pinched Harold's face as if examining pimples. Harold hissed in pain. "You got some metal splinters from a grenade," Dawes reported. "You'll have to get 'em out at an aid station."

"Hey, man," the artillery surveyor said to Stempel. "You got *way* outta line. We couldn't throw any grenades 'cause you—"

"He fuckin' saved your *ass*!" Lieutenant Dawes snapped. The man fell silent. "You can't go to *ground* out in the *open*! When you attack, you gotta *take* the goddamn position! This private here is an *infantryman*, and you should all spend the rest of your miserable fuckin' lives thanking God that he knows what the fuck he's doin'!" The angry Dawes told the squad to wait there and went off. The men spent the time trying to figure out where the others were. Only five members of the squad had made it to the pit.

"The spec five's dead," the multichannel communications guy finally offered. He was seated comfortably atop a Chinese soldier in the black, still night. "Checked him myself. Bullet must've gone right in his mouth 'cause I didn't see no hole. But when I took his hood and helmet off, the back of his head sorta . . . came *with* it."

"Oooh, *gross*!" the cornet player said.

"Where the hell're those air-force fucks?" the artillery surveyor asked. The implication was clear.

"I saw two of 'em get hit," the motor transportation operator reported.

"Well, what about the third guy?" No one knew. He was, therefore, either a coward or dead.

"Where's that woman?" Stempel asked.

"Dead," the motor transport man said. "Grenade blew up right in front of her."

"*Je*-sus," the cornet player said. "That's *half* of us . . . dead."

Lieutenant Dawes returned with a sergeant. Stempel thought it was their new squad leader. But he saw too many rockers and chevrons on the man's black plastic insignia. "Listen up," Dawes said. "We're gonna combine you with Second Squad. This lodgment has been reduced, but there're still infiltrators running around loose. We're gonna form a skirmish line and sweep the runway. When we find 'em, just drop, return fire, and wait for orders. Let's go." Stempel started to rise. "Not you," Dawes said. "You go with the first sergeant here. The line companies need infantry fillers."

"Well, *shit!*" the motor transportation guy said. "We need him *too,* sir!"

"He's infantry," Dawes replied. "This is a provisional company."

"Yeah, but I don't see *them* out here attackin' Chinese '*lodgments.*'"

"*You* wanna go out to the perimeter?" Dawes snapped angrily. He turned to the first sergeant. "I *know* it must be a little *slow* up there, Top! But you think you can use one more man?"

The man's slow laugh sounded like a smoker's cough. "*Well*-sir, we *do* have this patrol goin' out come sunup." The soldier didn't say another word. Harold parted company with his second unit since the war began. They shook hands and wished each other luck. Dawes led the small group off. That left Stempel alone with the first sergeant. "You were with the 2/263rd?" the senior noncom asked. Stempel nodded. The man looked around at the dead Chinese. Stempel had grown so accustomed to their presence he'd forgotten about them. He was safe there. "We tried to come help," Top said. "Ran right into the main force coming in to attack this base. Made it back with the whole People's Liberation Army on our asses."

Stempel didn't know what to say. "Thank you," he managed.

The dark profile of the helmet slowly turned Stempel's way. He reached out to Stempel's shoulder and squeezed. "You got that the wrong way around, Private," the raspy-voiced first sergeant said softly.

• • •

It was a bad time for introductions. Stempel's new comrades had just survived a major attack. "Private Stempel, here, is joining First Squad," Top announced. The hollow-eyed men sagged low against the main trench wall. No one rose, or nodded, or extended a hand, or said a word. The first sergeant took Stempel's new squad leader aside for a few private words. The men sat facing Stempel, their backs to the fighting steps and covered machine-gun revetments into which were frozen heaping mounds of spent cartridges. Some looked down at his blood-caked parka. Not in horror, or even curiosity, it seemed to Stempel, but in a daze. The first sergeant left and the squad leader stepped back up to Stempel. "We better get those wounds seen to," he said as he peered at Stempel's face. Harold remembered the wound on his arm and chest and showed the sergeant the bloody hole in his sleeve.

"Let's get you some new gear," the squad leader said. He went and got a new parka. Stempel quickly changed. The new jacket was freezing cold, but clean. "Just toss your old one over there," the sergeant directed him, pointing. Stempel went over to the heap. When he got there, he realized it was a pile of gear. Webbing. Packs. Wool underclothes. Arctic whites. All of it was ripped open and covered in blood and gore. He added to the pile, tossing the caked brown parka with his name neatly printed inside on top.

BETHESDA NAVAL HOSPITAL, MARYLAND
January 31, 1300 GMT (0800 Local)

The knock at the door woke Gordon Davis. When he opened his eyes, he saw Daryl Shavers. Gordon smiled. He could hear a faint chant of, "Hell no, we won't go!" in the distance. "You made it through that all right?" he asked.

Daryl smirked. "They're passivists, not anarchists. They got doctors in green scrub suits standing in front of the cameras protesting your drafting them. Haven't seen 'em this mad since that managed-care legislation.'' Daryl sat. ''So, what's it like to be president? Is it everything you dreamed it'd be?''

''No jokes, please,'' Gordon said. ''It hurts to laugh.''

There was an awkward pause. ''Helluva mess you got yourself into, Gordon. I think you've single-handedly set the civil rights movement back thirty years.''

''Is my 'honeymoon period' over?'' Gordon asked. ''Are they bringing up race?''

Daryl shook his head. ''The only things you've got *going* for you is that you're black and all shot up.'' He attempted a smile. ''Seriously, Gordon, how do you feel?''

''What did that drunk cowboy say down in Dallas? 'Rode hard and put up wet.' ''

''I don't know,'' Daryl replied. ''I wasn't in Dallas.''

There was another strained interlude. ''Listen, Daryl. I'd like to talk about what happened.''

''Yeah, well . . . I've moved on. Got a job at a company that makes biodegradable bags for potato chips. Hires inner-city workers. Donates one percent of its payroll to liberal causes. That kinda shit.''

''Are you . . . wed to this potato chip thing?''

''What kind of question is that?'' Daryl snapped angrily.

The door opened. Two Secret Service agents stood in the narrow space looking in. ''Could we have some privacy?'' Gordon said. The men disappeared. ''Daryl, I'd like you to be my chief of staff.''

Daryl snorted in derision but couldn't quite keep a smile from parting his lips. ''You're serious.'' He shook his head. ''Man, I thought you had better political sense than that. What's in that IV bag? Demerol?''

''I need you, Daryl. I'm all alone. Stuck in this bed. I don't know the people who work for me. They don't tell me things I need to hear. I find out more from listening to *that*,'' he said, jabbing his thumb at the window, ''than from talking to my advisors. I need somebody I can trust.''

Daryl laughed. ''Running for cover, are they?''

"Like scalded dogs." They laughed. "Daryl, I'm going down in flames, here. I need you."

"To do what, Gordon?" Daryl asked. He hovered close by Gordon's bed. The hook was in deep.

"Pull up a chair."

"I wish you'd worn a tie," Gordon mumbled to Daryl, who stood at the head of his bed. Entering the map-filled room were some of the most powerful people in Washington. Each new political animal to arrive sized up Daryl, the new beast at the watering hole. Each smiled and greeted Gordon and then Daryl—the latter with an abundance of grace and enthusiasm. "I remember you from the . . . the *Houston* convention, wasn't it?" the secretary of defense said. "You were a *floor* manager, tha-at's right!" He shook Daryl's hand a second time as if Daryl had not yet been properly greeted.

"Daryl's going to be my chief of staff," Gordon lobbed into the gathering.

Good-natured smiles never left the faces of the well-mannered men and women. They descended on Daryl anew. Shaking his hand again. Congratulating him. Even grabbing and squeezing his shoulders with their free hands. But by lunchtime, Gordon knew, the long knives would be out. Dirt dug up and leaked to the press. Snide remarks made off the record. Political sabotage of the upstart challenger. Gordon decided to make a preemptive strike. "Daryl has agreed to take a look at the staff—top to bottom." The grins now grew more strained. "He'll have carte blanche to trim things up for the rough sailing we've got ahead of us." *Always good to use sailing metaphors,* Gordon thought.

Their ears were all twitching at that. No longer did they lap at the still pool. They now scoured the terrain for the sound of breaking twigs that announced the approach of a predator. It was probably enough of a charge, Gordon decided, to break up the cliques and make it every man for himself. If not, he could up the voltage. Like Daryl had said after agreeing to take the job—"Hey, Gordon, *fuck* them! You're the president of the United States!" The pain from his laughter was still fresh.

OUTSIDE KHABAROVSK, SIBERIA
February 2, 0400 GMT (1800 Local)

Chin stopped long enough to look at his new watch. The impressive radium dial glowed in the dark. They had two hours to be in position for a dawn attack. But the going was slow through the thick woods and heavy snow. It was then that the worst happened.

A stunning display of noise and fire tore the forest apart. Snow fell from the limbs above and bounced from the ground in a fine mist of ice crystals. Chin was so shocked by the violence of the explosions that he didn't dive to the ground as he'd been taught. He sank onto his haunches and sat—his head swimming. In the moment before the second wave of explosions, Chin heard the crackling of dry ever-greens and the wails of the wounded. He willed himself lower into the powdery snow. The ground slammed against him and a tidal wave of suffocating fire passed over him.

When Chin awoke, he was all alone. The cloak of darkness and silence had again descended on the woods. His head hurt so much the first thing he did was probe his bristly scalp for a wound. There was none. But his limbs were numb from the cold. His fingers and toes ached menacingly when he flexed them repeatedly. He half rose, and his skin tingled like at the onset of a fever. He retched and then collapsed back into the snow. There he lay sweating and cold. Time seemed to slip.

The sky was noticeably lighter. A dusting of snow lay like a blanket over him—saving his life from the frostbite that was near certain to grip him in the open. Again, how-ever, he had to work his deadened extremities until they burned with pain—a good sign. He then struggled to his knees. The world was spinning, and he almost blacked out completely when he rose to his feet. Chin had to support himself with his hands on his thighs and stood bent half over his burning stomach. The forest was shattered. Healthy evergreens were cracked in two. Green bristles littered the snowy ground. Huge splinters of shredded white wood protruded from broken trunks like exposed bones. Gaping black craters—yawning holes blasted out of the earth by huge explosions—lay less than fifty meters from where he stood.

Bombs, he realized. They'd been bombed.

He suddenly panicked. Could it be that . . . he was dead? That his spirit had just risen . . . uncertain what to do next? He looked down and saw no corpse. *Where is everybody?* He looked around and at first saw no one. Then—slowly— the crumpled shapes that had moments before been logs metamorphosed into human form. Half-covered in snow. An elbow. A helmet-covered head. A severed leg. Chin stood there . . . alone among the dead, but alive. If they were dead, he must be alive. He groped in the snow with numb hands and pulled his rifle from the powder, then he listened. Nothing. The attack must have been called off. They'd been discovered and bombed before they had even made it to the American guns.

He took one last look at the brightening sky to the east and headed back in the direction from which they'd come— away from the American base. When he got back to his platoon, his senior sergeant gave him the head count. Twelve missing. Two wounded. Fifteen present and ready for duty.

His platoon was down to half strength and they had yet to fire their weapons in combat.

UNRUSFOR HEADQUARTERS, KHABAROVSK
February, 3, 1730 GMT (0330 Local)

The French colonel took the radio microphone himself. The interpreter whispered the translation into Clark's ear. "Do you read me, Firebase Toulon, over?" But Clark had been listening to the repetitive calls for so long that he needed no translation. Two hundred French paratroopers and engineers had been helicoptered into Firebase Toulon. Their mission was to prepare the base for a brigade that had gotten bogged down by a series of minor ambushes dozens of kilometers away. The colonel repeated his call. Clark walked over and put his hand on the man's shoulder.

The officer lowered his chin and continued to call out over the radio. Clark left him alone. But the spell his vigil had cast over the group around the radio was broken. By returning to his desk, Clark had pronounced the unit dead.

Papers lay spread over his working area at one end of the operations center. He had a spacious office with Oriental rugs and dark hardwood furniture. But he preferred this spot—in the company of others—to the quiet of the tomb-like room.

The calls in French drowned out the other noise and chatter of the spacious op center. It wasn't that they were any louder. It was the regularity of the man's efforts. First a call, then a pause to listen for a response, then the exact same call again. Clark sat there staring at the paper. Waiting for the next try. It was like water dripping from a leaky faucet. As the man's wait for a reply grew longer, the silence grew more oppressive. Clark listened intently. All that was missing in the din of activity were the few words called out in French. The silence went on and on.

It was over. Even the colonel had finally given up. There was no one single event that marked the death of a unit, Clark thought. Like the death of a single human, the line was a wavering one. Was it when the heart stopped functioning? Or respiration? Or the brain?

A unit was a living organism too. Its death was also purely a matter of definition. When the last man had been chased down and shot like a dog, the unit was clearly dead. But its death really occurred sometime before that. *Was it when the main line of defenses was breached?* he thought. No. The unit still lived. It still fought hand to hand in trenches and holes—the commander desperately sending his last feeble reserves into the gap. Was it when the command post was overrun? The commander killed? No. The military made its units tough. Resilient. Even after the command post was overrun, the subordinate commanders held their panicked men together for the final phase of every decisive battle—the slaughter.

Clark was tired, but he forced his mind to focus on the question he'd posed. He knew he couldn't sleep now anyway, even if he wanted to. When is it that a unit dies? When is it that he knew to take the marker off the map? To declare its men "Missing in Action, Presumed Dead or Captured"?

The radio traffic that poured into Clark's nerve center was growing by the minute. The operators' replies formed an ever-louder buzz in the background of the windowless shelter. He looked at his watch—the only way to learn the hour in his perpetually darkened world. Dawn was approaching. Each cell of the UNRUSFOR organism was preparing for the inevitable "contact." Clark realized just then he had his answer. A unit dies when it quits calling him on the radio. It no longer exists when he can't talk to it. No matter that the last soldier hasn't yet been tracked down. When a unit's radio goes off the air, it's dead.

Clark pulled out a pad and a pen and began to write.

Dear Lydia:

By now you must have read the accounts of my visit to Birobidzhan, and I know you must be worried sick about me. And added to those worries, I know, is the already heavy burden of caring for the children alone. But I have to write this letter, because I have no one to whom I can speak these words that now crush me so completely that I can hardly breathe. Please forgive me, but I must put them down on paper and ask you to help shoulder their weight because I absolutely cannot bear them alone any longer.

War is the saddest thing I have ever known. Individual human tragedies abound in this world, but in war the horror and grief is widespread. Huge armies of the young rip the life from one another. Healthy, strong, and brave, they are the brightest hopes of a million mothers and a million fathers. And those young soldiers know where they're going and what lies ahead. God Almighty, Lydia, how do they do it? What cause could be so great as to bind them to their duty? To hold them to a course which leads only to deafening noise, and sudden and random death.

At times my strength fails me. I cannot remember the cause for which I send those young men and women to their deaths. I know the words, but they're like mental tricks which work sometimes and fail me at others. They are failing me now, Lydia. At times like these, I feel I owe a duty greater than to my country. A duty to God or to nature or to those hundreds of thousands of men and women whose lives are being wasted. Wasted. I feel an overpowering urge to step out into the middle of no-man's-land and shout "Stop!" at the top of my lungs. "Nothing matters more than life! None of this will change anything!"

But I could no more stop what is happening here than I could alter the drift of the continents. We were always going to fight here, in this awful place. Some immutable law of nature bound us to this battlefield as surely as gravity holds our feet to the earth. I have been through war before, Lydia, as have you, and I know that my present weakness will pass. I will banish it, because it is defeatist, which goes against who I was taught to be. But what if I'm wrong? What if the deeds I believe to be so heroic prove to be nothing more than base sins against the innocent? Lydia, if I'm dragged down into the fires of hell to pay for the evil that I am committing, I will go without complaint. I will wish nothing more than that I spend eternity paying the price for my corrupted ideals. I

will bear all, suffer all, pay whatever toll with a light-
ness of heart, Lydia, if only you will forgive me those
sins. If you will know and believe my one excuse
that I give only to you, Lydia, only to you. I didn't
know what I was doing was wrong. I didn't know. I
didn't know.

Clark sensed Major Reed standing patiently beside his
desk. He had no idea how long he'd been there. Clark
looked up and drew a deep breath with difficulty. "Yes?"
he said.

"J-STARS has positive contact with a five-hundred-plus
vehicle convoy. It's crossing the Amur near Madagachi.
The joint controllers have asked to divert the morning's B-
52 raids to hit the convoy. Their targets are a hydroelectric
plant and some munitions factories at Harbin that we can
hit anytime. The convoy is hemmed into a pass between
steep hills waiting to cross. Estimates are that it could be
an entire infantry division. The joint controllers need your
authority to divert and hit those passes."

Reed stood there, waiting. After a moment he said, "We
could knock out a whole division with one *air* raid, sir."
Clark forced his eyes to focus on the man. "We've got
three cells—nine B-52s—chock-full of five-hundred-pound
bombs. They could overlay a single-plane bomb box one
after the other." He fell silent, waiting. He seemed not to
understand what he was asking Clark to do. That he was
asking him to sign the death warrant of thousands of human
beings with no more reflection than one would give an
everyday chore.

Clark closed his dry mouth, swallowed, and nodded.
Reed ran off. The letter awaited his signature. Lieutenant
General Nate Clark slowly crumpled the thick stationery
into a ball and tossed it into the trash.

14

There they are, Chin thought to himself as he peered over the shredded trunk of a tree. He scanned the small dale that separated his ridge from the southern edge of the small Russian town. In the early-morning light he could clearly see the American soldiers scurrying around and digging in. He wished that he had binoculars to survey the approaches to their objective. The amazing view given by the pair his training class had passed around had amazed the officer candidates. But in the five months Chin had been in the army he'd only seen two other pair. Both were dangling from the necks of colonels like all their other badges of rank.

Chin spotted his platoon's objective, the lower of two stone walls that traversed the gently rising hill opposite him. "You see the wall, Senior Sergeant?" Chin asked the man lying next to him.

The sergeant was a veteran of several years. He was the only man over the age of twenty in the platoon. "Yes-sir," he slurred.

Chin eyed him for signs of disrespect, but could detect

none. "Do you have any questions?" Chin asked.

The senior sergeant stared out across the dale at the busy Americans. "Did they tell you how many of them are over there?"

"No."

The sergeant didn't respond for a few moments. "Did they say anything about getting a third magazine of ammunition for the men?"

"They said regimental stretcher bearers will bring ammunition up and take wounded back," Chin replied. He was growing more and more wary of the man's tone.

"Did the company commander give us a second objective?" the senior sergeant asked.

"*No*," Chin answered testily. He looked over at the man. The senior sergeant stared out at the three-hundred-odd meters of open space that ran down their hill and back up to the edge of the city. He nodded his head slowly, almost imperceptibly, and fell silent.

Chin rubbed his eyes, which were bleary from lack of sleep. They had been spared the last few days of furious assaults on the American base while their platoon awaited replacements. Then their commanders changed their plans. They had marched cross-country right past the surrounded Americans. It was a great victory, he'd told his men. The airbase's defenders would wither on the vine. Even as he'd repeated the words passed down to him by the company commander, the air overhead was filled with the sound of huge transport planes. They landed at the base every couple of minutes.

Chin forced his mind back to the present. The enemy lines across the valley didn't look so formidable. The open fields below had only traces of snow and ice. They wouldn't have to slog through knee-deep drifts while exposed to fire.

But the sun was well up now. *We're over three hours late*, Chin saw, looking at his wristwatch. They had intended to take advantage of the darkness for the dash across the open dale. *But now?*

He looked up and down the line of helmets. The men of his battalion lay in the brush, their packs on the ground around them to be left behind, per the battalion commander's orders. Twisting around, he caught glimpses of 1st Battalion's line thirty meters behind. They were poised to rush forward and fire at the Americans as Chin's 2nd Battalion advanced. He looked down at the floor of the valley. The distance suddenly seemed far greater than before. He felt his normally calm heart beating strongly in his chest.

The lower of the two stone walls—his company's objective—sat about a third of the way up the opposite hill. The route he would take to it seemed smooth and unbroken. There was good footing except for the small clumps of manure that dotted the valley. The animals that had been penned between the two walls were nowhere in sight. *Sheep and goats*, he reasoned. *Oxen would have wandered right through the loose stones.*

He smiled and felt calmed by the thought. He'd been an ox boy as a youth on his family's farm. He'd seen the animals use their tremendous strength to simply walk through most man-made obstacles. Sheer, brute force—almost nothing could stop the massive beasts.

Chin closed his eyes, feeling bathed by the crisp morning air. He took a deep, refreshing breath. When he opened his eyes, he saw the platoon leader to his left—Lieutenant Hung—staring blankly into the dirt beneath him. *College boy*, Chin thought with disgust. *City puke.*

The sound of shells overhead ripped the fabric of Chin's fragile calm. He cringed and hunched his shoulders in anticipation. But the first explosion burst not over their heads but on the opposite ridge just short of the American positions. The men of his platoon began to cheer. He turned and snapped "Quiet!" at their stupidity. His hand fell to his rifle—as taught—to reinforce his particularly important order.

Chin heard a whistle from his far left and his heart skipped a beat. A flare shot into the air and burst as whistles

sounded on both sides. His skin crawled. A slight shiver
shook his body. The last of the Americans leaped into their
holes at the town's edge, and then their positions were still.
The time for the attack had seemed so far away just minutes
ago. A full company of men to his left rose from the low
brush and moved forward. The shells now fell randomly
amid the Americans.

Another whistle sounded. Two shorts, one long—his
company commander's order. Chin reached into his parka,
placed the warm whistle to his lips, and blew it with all his
might. His men rose to their feet and advanced past him
through the light brush. He and the senior sergeant followed
at the prescribed distance. Everyone began to shout as they
burst out into the open and the slope fell away under their
feet. The full-throated roar of the attacking battalion filled
the valley and inspired Chin with its volume and mass. He
was not alone. He felt a part of a great process many
thousands of years old. Always the outsiders came. Always
this was the way they left.

A phenomenal burping and cracking roar erupted from
the American lines. Chin's whole body flinched as if struck
by a blow. The battalion's shouts—which were almost
drowned out—trailed off to silence as men began to fall in
the line ahead of Chin. Some stumbled, others stood
straight up then slid to the ground awkwardly, still others
cartwheeled or spun to the ground with a dramatic flourish.
Some emitted bloodcurdling screams, others not so much
as a grunt. Buzzes and zings rushed by Chin's ears, setting
off an almost electric sense of alertness that vibrated every
nerve ending. His legs propelled him forward, but the rest
of his body froze in anticipation of the impact that would
end his life.

Fully half his men fell before they reached the valley
floor. Small geysers of earth erupted with sharp booms as
American mortars dropped in their path. Machine-gun fire
came in sheets. Their advance slowed as if running against
a stiff wind and the line began to grow ragged. Chin
clenched his teeth and ran harder to catch up with his flag-

ging platoon. "Keep moving!" he yelled, but the sound of his voice was lost against the stunning noise from the guns toward which they raced. Looking to the rear to make sure no one lagged, he saw the slope littered with wounded and dead. Behind them appeared 1st Battalion, which charged out of the tree line and began to fall. Chin almost stumbled on the flat valley floor and turned back to face the enemy. A series of explosions suddenly burst up and down the battlefield to each side of him, and his platoon came to a complete stop. They pressed themselves to the ground and curled themselves into fetal positions, holding their helmets or hugging their bodies, but it did nothing to ward off the bullets that hailed death from a range of 150 meters.

Chin dropped to the ground. He opened his mouth to yell at the man lying barely five meters away, but great splashes of frothy orange blood erupted from the smooth white parka stretched over his back. The sod splattered into Chin's face. The *whiz-z-z-z* of bullets passing and the thud as they pounded the earth around him grew nearly continuous. With death mere seconds away, he willed himself as high as his rebellious body would go and zigzagged up the hill toward the low wall.

In his path lay a small round object. Its green plastic was meant to blend into grass, but it stood in stark contrast to the gray patch of ice beneath it. Wires like a spider's legs radiated outward in all directions. They were everywhere. *A minefield!* But Chin couldn't slow down. High-stepping as if through puddles, he wove his way through the sinister tentacles by staying as far as possible from their explosive center. He completely lost track of his platoon and its fate as his toes dug into the uphill slope. He dodged and wove, each second a game of chance with bullets that sliced through the air all around. Giant explosions burst on both sides of him, but he thought nothing, saw nothing, felt nothing but fear. He was frozen in motion. Eyes peeled to the ground. Legs pumping. Neither alive nor dead, but instead walking a tightrope in between—awaiting the outcome.

Suddenly Chin was confused. He was running as if in a

dream. He wasn't exactly sure what he was doing. A choking smoke made him begin coughing, and a great wave of nausea swept over him. Nothing seemed right as he sought out reality. The first thing he found was terrible pain emanating from his ears and the center of his head. The pain deluged him, and his body hummed with the agony of it. He opened his eyes, lifted his wobbly head, and saw a smoking hole not ten meters away. Behind it was the ridge from which his battalion had attacked. A ragged collection of men crawled across the forward slope or flopped from side to side. In their midst, geysers of dirt erupted in great sprays. In the woods behind them he saw muzzle flashes. *3rd Battalion*, he remembered. *That's 3rd Battalion.*

A pair of jets flew wingtip to wingtip. They banked steeply to align themselves with the hill's tree line. Chin fought to focus his blurred vision. Four canisters—two from each plane—tumbled end over end. They fell into the trees on top of 3rd Battalion. Billowing flames mushroomed skyward. The heat was searing even at two hundred meters. Chin's eyes teared and he jammed them tightly shut. The heat and noise grew more and more painful as the air rumbled and the ground shook. Oily fumes filled Chin's nostrils and mouth.

Just as suddenly as it had erupted, the noise was replaced by the crackle of a roaring fire. The valley was quiet. Then the cracks of individual American rifles resumed their methodical killing. Chin forced his watering eyes to look back across the dale. A huge black cloud rose into the air above the ridge. The entire crest was charred black and flattened. It was broken only by small licks of flame that still found nourishment from unburned wood. A forest of trunks pointed skyward like broken spears. It and everyone in it had been incinerated in seconds.

The pall of thick black smoke drifted in the gentle breeze. The taste of petroleum fouled Chin's mouth. He lowered his head to the ground in great fatigue. Several of his men cowered behind the stone wall, which was being chipped into fragments around their hunched shoulders.

We took it, Chin thought as he lay down to die. *We took it.*

When Chin came to, it was night. Thick snow fell. The noise and the smells of battle were gone. He was alive! The Americans hadn't policed the battlefield to kill the wounded. For all Chin could tell from listening, they might even have withdrawn. He ran his hands over his body, patting and squeezing in search of pain. He found none. In the darkness he groped for and retrieved his rifle then rose hesitantly to his knees. Despite the cold he felt the prickly feel of coming sweat ripple across his torso. They could see him in the dark. They had special binoculars that lit up the night, but only for them.

Just in case, Chin raised his hands in surrender. He knelt on the ground in that pose for almost a minute. There was no sound. Without lowering his arms, he labored to his feet. There he stood, surrendering to the invisible army with their batlike view from above. His throat was thick with fear. If they were there, rifles would be aimed at him now. Strangers with the power to kill him with one squeeze of the trigger. With no more care for him than for a stray dog.

His arms were growing tired, so he lowered them. He picked up his rifle, turned, and headed down the hill. *The mines!* he remembered, and stopped. The tiny green bombs with their web of deadly legs that Chin would never see in the darkness. He willed himself onward, grimacing with each crunching footfall. The scene ran over and over in his mind. A blinding flash of light. A wall of fire. Excruciating pain. Then darkness. But his boots found only the squeaking snow. The land underneath flattened, and his inner sense told him he'd made it. He began to walk at a more natural pace. By the time he reached the far ridge, the terrors of the night had receded.

Until, that is, he came to the charred remains of the tree line. The air was heavy with the stale smells of a long-dead fire. The ground was littered with heaps of ash-coated debris. He stumbled every other step, finally strapping his rifle

over his shoulder and groping through the obstacles with
his hands held in front. It was nearly impossible to tell what
he felt through his thick boots and gloves. He tried his best
to shut the thoughts from his mind. But in the blackness of
the burned forest Chin's senses were alert and alive, and
touch was the most intimate of all the senses. The discov-
eries made in that fashion were not easily ignored. Among
the fallen trees and cratered earth in that terrible place, he
came to realize, were charred remains of 3rd Battalion.

VLADIVOSTOK-USSURIYSK ROAD, SIBERIA
February 6, 0030 GMT (1030 Local)

Kate and Woody had finally talked their way to the front.
Their cramped Humvee cruised along the snow-covered
road. Ice framed the windshield outside the wipers' reach.
Kate searched the endless forests for some sign that a war
was on, but saw nothing other than a perpetual succession
of trees.

"You want to do the interview now?" the scrawny lieutenant asked from the front seat. Kate sat in back between
Woody and a sullen private who held a large bag in his lap
that Kate guessed normally occupied her seat.

"Here?" Kate asked. Woody cleared his throat. "Sure!"
she blurted out. "Great idea." Woody unzipped his camera
bag. Kate reached into her backpack for a stick mike.

"Batteries won't last long in the cold," Woody reminded
her for the hundredth time.

"Then use the special battery *saver*," she said. Woody
didn't get it. "The *battery* saver, Woody!" She reached up
and turned the camera off. The red taping light went out.
The soldier beside her smiled. "Testing, one, two, three,"
she said into the dead stick mike. The lieutenant combed
his hair with his fingers. She had him state his name, rank,
and serial number, and identify the unit that he commanded—2nd Infantry Division's postal detachment. She
dipped the microphone back and forth for each question
and response.

"Are you getting this?" the officer asked.

Kate realized she'd left the mike beneath her mouth as she searched for burning hulks or shell craters. "Oh, it's a special, multidirectional microphone. Latest stuff. You getting all this, Woody?"

"Yep," he said, squinting into the dark viewfinder and grinning. He reeked of pot smoke. Kate caught the young soldier beside her watching them. He was onto them. She realized the officer had finished. "And you go right up to the battle lines to deliver the mail?"

"If we have to, ma'am. 'Course the unit we're delivering to today hasn't seen any combat yet."

"*What?* What do you mean?"

"Well"—he shrugged—"the Chinese haven't gotten here yet. They're still a ways off."

"*Shit!*" Kate said, dropping the mike into her lap.

"I couldn't take you up to the front if there was *fighting,* ma'am. It wouldn't be safe."

A smirking Woody lowered the camera, replaced the lens caps, and closed the control panels. The soldier beside her was grinning. "*Shit!*" Kate cursed.

The reporter and cameraman followed André Faulk on his mail runs interviewing soldiers about their feelings on the eve of battle. The lieutenant had gone on to the next battalion to deliver the mail, doing the job of a private to get his face on TV. The quiet woods were filling with snow, which drifted through the dense trees and piled onto the thick blanket already there. The only sounds were the crunching of their feet and the occasionally profane outburst of the woman reporter. "I can't fucking believe it!" she went on and on. André walked in front lugging the bag, which grew lighter with each stop. The woman was short but very pretty. The cameraman older and with a ponytail. Both acted like André wasn't there.

"Ma-ail call!" André heard shouted—as always well before he got there. By the time he put the bag on the ground, there were a dozen men gathered around. "What platoon is this?" he asked.

"Third Platoon, Charlie Company, Second Battalion," someone called out. André remembered them from the barracks in Korea where they'd listened to the sounds of fighting over the radio. He began to call out the familiar names. "Aguire!" He ran the envelope under his nose. "Mm—mm! Smell go-o-od, Aguire!" The soldier snapped the pink envelope out of André's hands and brushed it with his mittens. "Alvarez!" André pulled the package out of the bag like Santa Claus. He raised and lowered it to judge its heft. "I delivered one o' these yest'day. It's one o' them inflatable rubber dolls, ain't it?" Everyone laughed. "Bej-gro-wicz!" André called out. "You still ain't changed that to English?" More laughter.

The woman was already interviewing a soldier at the edge of the semicircle around André. "But don't you normally ride around in Bradley armored fighting vehicles?"

"Yeah, well, usually. But they dropped us off up here and we ain't seen 'em since then."

"So you're just up here by yourself with no support?" the woman asked. "Chinese combat troops outnumber UN-RUSFOR's four to one. I thought the arrival of 'heavy' units like the 2nd Infantry Division was supposed to cut down on the high rate of infantry casualties?" The guy's face, which moments before had shone with happiness at André's arrival, now showed deep concern. "Are you supposed to fight right here—from these holes—without your armor and other vehicles?" she asked.

The microphone was stuck in the guy's face. He arched his eyebrows and shrugged. "I dunno. We'll fight when we see any Chinese, I guess."

"But you do know that the Chinese have eleven divisions headed down this way to try to take the port at Vladivostok. That's over a hundred thousand men. They're going to hit these lines, right here, anytime now. How does that make you feel?" She held the microphone to his mouth, but he didn't reply. He didn't need to. His face said it all.

"Wolfson!" André called, a scowl on his face. "That's

it!'' He hoisted his lighter load onto his shoulder and
headed off, leaving the sullen group. They'd been robbed
of the cheer that André felt was his job to dispense, and
that pissed him off. The news crew trailed him and jab-
bered.

"Those poor guys are being sent out here to get slaughtered!'' she bitched. "It's *criminal*! They take kids and
brainwash them so they don't think! Don't question! They
just trundle off to their deaths without a care in the world!''
André spun around, and the woman jumped in surprise.
White vapor jetted out of his nostrils, and they shut the
fuck up. He headed on to the next unit.

THE KREMLIN, RUSSIA
February 9, 0200 GMT (1600 Local)

The heavy lunch and hot tea cast a blanket of drowsiness
over Valentin Kartsev. His eyes drooped as he reclined in
the chair behind his desk. Although his mind was mush, he
tried one last time to grasp the elusive words that described
the concept with which he was grappling. It was a process
analogous to the complexity of the balls' motion on a billiard table. You excite them all and they begin to strike
cushions and each other. Newtonian physics described perfectly the forces at work, and a supercomputer could predict
the balls' travels for the next thousand years. But there were
so many variables that affected the outcome that to the
naked eye their motions quickly seemed so impossibly
complex as to seem random. But they were not random,
and Kartsev sought to explain their mechanics.

He had excited all the balls on the world table. He had
stirred the political pots of dozens of major powers. He had
known that there would be motion, but he still had no idea
what the outcome would be. He yawned. The sofa beck-
oned, but there were three new messages on his computer.
He clicked on the mailbox icon. The first two messages
both contained long lists of names. The previous day he'd
sentenced two men to Schedule A but had them watched

for twenty-four hours. These were lists of people with
whom the two had made contact during their last day on
earth.

Kartsev checked boxes with clicks of the mouse. A check
by a name meant death. Short descriptions of the contacts
were all Kartsev had to go on. "Lunch in Kremlin cafeteria." *Too public,* he thought. They'd never conspire together there. *Ah, but dinner in a private restaurant.* He
checked the next box beside the name "Chapaev, Stepan."
He'd never heard of the man. Rare was it that he knew any
name on these lists. Such was the price of power. Computers helped him wall himself off even from his closest
aides. These E-mails allowed him to do his work at a distance that he imagined his staff greatly appreciated.

He checked or skipped the boxes absentmindedly. The
process was arbitrary, but he did try to be fair. He even
went back and checked the box by the woman who'd had
lunch in the cafeteria. After all, lunch, dinner, what's the
difference? Besides, what better place to plot his demise
than the middle of the Kremlin cafeteria?

The third E-mail was a refreshing change. It was a short
message and a video attachment. He clicked "play" and a
window appeared with a clip. "Is there anything you'd like
to say to your folks back home?" Kate Dunn asked a soldier in snowy woods. In the dim, flickering light, Kartsev
smiled. Even tired old questions seemed fresh when asked
by Miss Dunn. The soldier struggled with his reply. "Well
. . . 'Hey,' I guess. I'll be all right. Don't worry." The pathetic reassurances dimmed Kartsev's smile. The camera
switched to Miss Dunn—the young interviewing the young.
"How about you?" she asked, and the camera swung onto
a young black soldier with a rifle and heavy bag. "Where
are you from?"

"The Bronx," he replied.

"Do you know what you're fighting for?" she asked.
"What you're doing here?" The question was posed so
forthrightly that Kartsev loosed a chuckle. The soldier
looked at the others gathered around, then shook his head

and shrugged. "I'm s'posed to deliver the mail." Everyone laughed to the kid's embarrassment. The satellite feed was replaced with color test bars. Kartsev sighed.

All was still and quiet. Kartsev yanked the chain that dangled beneath the stained-glass lampshade, and the room fell dark with a click. Unencumbered by sights or sounds, his mind roamed the vast expanses of the east. The chill had put color in Miss Dunn's smooth cheeks. He'd loved the purity of the cold during the years he'd spent in Siberia. Most people—prisoner and guard alike—had relished the short summers during which life had bloomed with stunning intensity. Nature had so little time to flourish that it burst into a verdant display as if to scream out, "I'm alive! Look at me!" The same was true of the people. Prisoners who from a distance had appeared little more than trudging greatcoats bared their skin to the summer sun. Guards who in winter only left their warm huts after bracing for the cold with vodka drank less, exchanged crude jokes with the prisoners through the wire, let parcels from home slip through. To Kartsev, summers in the camps had meant smells and mosquitoes and mud . . . and the discipline that only killing could bring. For when nature lifted her firm grip from men's souls, Moscow had sent Kartsev in to replace it.

The words returned now in a gush. He turned the lamp on and wrote feverishly in longhand. "It is the most oppressed among men that possess the greatest potential energy. In them, life lies coiled to its greatest tension. When the repression of their spirit is eased, there is a brief and spontaneous flowering. Nature's force is released onto the streets. The populace is invigorated. And if uncontrolled, that release is always violent." Kartsev wrote for six hours straight, recording the torrent of new ideas. Then, exhausted, he went to his sofa, pulled the covers up to his chin, and closed his eyes. He smiled as, in his mind, billiard balls bounded off felt cushions in a deliciously complex way.

PHILADELPHIA, PENNSYLVANIA
February 11, 0300 GMT (0800 Local)

From the way the passersby were bundled up, Pyotr Andreev would've thought it was cold. He jogged down the sidewalk wearing gloves and a towel wrapped around his neck and tucked into his Adidas warm-ups. The walk was icy, but the already bright sun would soon melt it away into a warm winter day.

He rounded the block, startling a woman in a heavy wool coat walking her small dog. When Andreev turned to apologize, a car pulled up to the intersection. Two men in the front seat were looking his way. The driver extinguished his left turn signal and proceeded straight through the intersection.

The nondescript government car sped away. Pyotr scanned the streets ahead for the team that would pick him up next. It was too cold for them to leave their heated cars. Plus, their sunglasses and dark suits always gave them away.

UNRUSFOR HEADQUARTERS, KHABAROVSK
February 13, 2200 GMT (0800 Local)

Clark could barely bring himself to watch the disgusting spectacle. A closed special inquiry in an underground briefing room. "Please state your name," the congressman said into the microphone.

"Henry Adams," the shaken officer replied. He faced the committee, the microphones, the cameras that were there for "historical purposes." "Lieutenant colonel, United States Army."

"And you were commander of the artillery supporting 2nd Battalion, 263rd Light Infantry?" the committee's chairman asked. His suit jacket was bunched up around his fat neck as he leaned forward.

"Yes, sir. I was."

"And on the day of that battalion's engagement with the Chinese, how many guns did you field?"

The lieutenant colonel cleared his throat. "I laid thirty-two 155-millimeters on the battlefield."

"And how many rounds did those thirty-two guns fire?"

The ashen man hung his head. "One hundred and three."

The congressman nodded. He already knew the answers to the questions. They were all in the colonel's after-action report. He asked them only to ruin an officer who already looked shattered by the experience. "That's a little over three rounds per gun. Is that the amount of fire support your battalion was expected to deliver?"

The colonel shook his head. "No, sir. The support plan called for concentrated fire once the enemy was massed in the open for their attack. We should've gotten off at least two dozen rounds per tube—seven to eight hundred total." He couldn't even look his accusers in the eye.

"In your opinion, Colonel Adams, would it have made a difference if those guns had fired eight hundred rounds instead of one hundred?" The officer nodded. "Please answer for the record."

"Yes . . ." he blurted out. His head dropped. Clark wondered whether he'd thought of anything else since that day. "The measure of artillery performance is placing as many rounds as possible on target in the shortest amount of time. It would've made a difference . . . yes."

Clark closed his eyes and shook his head. The man had decided to accept full responsibility. When he opened his eyes, the chairman was nodding. "Why didn't those guns fire the expected number of rounds, Colonel?"

The answer was delivered in a monotone. He knew it by heart. "The guns' lubricants thickened because of the cold. Some recoil mechanisms didn't bring the guns back into battery for three or four minutes. The guns that *could* fire tried to cover but ran out of ammo. The cold also affected a lot of the rounds that we did get off. Their propellants and fuses were frozen, which resulted in a high percentage of shorts, overs, and duds."

"And why is it, Colonel, that you experienced so many problems from the cold weather?"

The man finally raised his head. He looked his inquisitor straight in the eye and said, "We didn't have time to winterize. To acclimatize. To train in a Siberian winter so we could fix the problems before they . . ." He lost his train of thought. His haunted eyes drifted off.

"Please state your name," the chairman said into the microphone.

"Clark, Nate, lieutenant general, United States Army."

"And you are commander-in-chief of U.S. Army Pacific and of United Nations Russian Forces, is that correct?"

"Yes, sir. That's correct."

"Now general, on January twenty-sixth—three days after the Chinese invaded Siberia—they cut the road leading from Birobidzhan to Khabarovsk, is that correct?" Clark confirmed the facts. "And that resulted in Birobidzhan Airbase—which was being evacuated at the time *to* Khabarovsk—being surrounded, is that correct?" Again Clark agreed. "Can you tell this committee how the Chinese managed to cut that road before the evacuation was complete?"

"The Chinese had been infiltrating Siberia for weeks in force. According to prisoners we've interviewed, they were under strict orders to avoid any contact with UNRUSFOR troops. The enormous size of our theater of operations and the thick forest canopy prevented our discovering where and in what strength they were concentrating."

"And for some hours *after* the Chinese had cut the road with probably a division-strength unit, the commander at Birobidzhan—the late Brigadier General Merrill—still sent lightly armed convoys down the road toward Khabarovsk, is that correct?"

"The first word anyone had that the road was blocked came from aerial reconnaissance, which reported abandoned vehicles on the road. General Merrill correctly concluded they'd been ambushed and sent a battalion-strength task force up the road on a clearing operation. He continued to send truck convoys behind the mixed armor-infantry force because of the severe time constraints imposed on the evacuation by the advancing main Chinese force and on the presumption that the road would be cleared.''

''And was the road cleared?'' the chairman asked—the answer patently obvious.

''No . . . sir. The clearing operation was turned back with heavy losses. The trucks were ambushed and had to be bulldozed off the road. Very few of the unarmored vehicles made it back to Birobidzhan. And there were approximately five hundred men killed or missing and presumed killed or captured.''

The chairman was nodding. ''How do you personally rate General Merrill's performance at Birobidzhan, General Clark?''

''I firmly believe that Brigadier General Merrill, Lieutenant Colonel Adams, and every other soldier in my command has fought bravely and well under the most difficult circumstances imaginable. None were as prepared as they should have been for what hit them. I also, however, firmly believe it is not the government which sent them here who should be asking *them* why . . . but the other way around.''

BIROBIDZHAN FIREBASE, SIBERIA
February 14, 1200 GMT (2200 Local)

''You sure you're ready for this?'' Stempel's new squad leader asked. His voice was already lowered in anticipation of danger. Stempel nodded, trying to slow his breathing. The sergeant moved on to check the others. He tugged on equipment to see if it made noise and asked if they knew their radio call sign and that of the company commander and battalion fire support officer . . . just in case. They each practiced giving the password that would get them back in through the wire. When the sergeant talked to his men, he grasped them firmly by their shoulders and squeezed, sometimes using a gentle shake to reinforce his comments. He was only twenty-three, but he was a good NCO.

The waiting left Stempel's stomach churning. His mouth was dry. Tremors shook his limbs. While the others in his unit had been outside the wire several times, Harold had been excused duty because of his minor wounds. But no more. This would be Harold's first combat patrol.

It was pitch-dark and seemed to grow colder the closer they came to going over the top.

"All right, Second Squad," the sergeant whispered. "Let's go. Unsafe your weapons when we get up." The men began to scale the trench wall using crude ladders made from wood packing crates. Stempel got in line. There were twelve in all—their squad's ten men, plus one of the platoon's two-man machine-gun crews. The climb required tremendous effort. He was carrying eight magazines in pouches on his belt and another eight stashed in thigh pockets. But that burden was physical. Far heavier was his psychological load.

Ice and snow covered the sandbags at the top. An alien landscape lay ahead. He'd been out numerous times to police the battlefield after ritualistic dawn attacks, but never beyond the wire. He rose to his feet. Everything looked different. When the terrain was viewed from just above ground level at a fighting post, every undulation was mountainous, as if to an ant who saw peaks and valleys measured in inches. But now—in the dim starlight—he saw that the killing ground was tabletop flat.

They headed toward the wire at a trot. Harold leaped over the first strands of concertina wire, which were half-buried in snow. They were less an obstacle than a boundary. A border. The limits of relative safety and the beginning of extreme danger. They slowed. Stempel was breathing hard. He searched for the Chinese through the billowing fog of starlit breath. He stayed in exactly the same path as the man in front, placing his feet in the man's tracks. Maybe those places wouldn't explode.

At the trees, they all dropped. Harold raised his rifle and aimed into the dark woods ahead. He'd followed Patterson, who lay three meters away. At night, the spacing was tighter. You risked bunching up to maintain contact. If you got separated from your unit—which happened all the time in firefights—you couldn't exactly call out. You were on your own, and both sides' guns would shoot you on sight.

He glanced over at the short and wiry grenadier on his right, who carried an M-279 grenade launcher mounted underneath his M-16. He'd arrived the day before to replace a guy who'd been blinded when a light mortar round landed in front of his fighting post. Stempel knew nothing about the replacement other than what he'd noticed that morning. When they awoke in the trench under a light dusting of snow, he looked as if he'd grown a white beard that stood out starkly against his dark skin. It had taken him several minutes to scrape the ice crystals off his two-day-old beard.

The squad rose and followed Chavez, their semipermanent point man, who wore their only pair of night-vision goggles. Everyone else stumbled forward blindly in a roughly wedge-shaped formation. It was an inverted *V*, with the point man truly at the "point." Four men formed each flank of the wedge with Stempel next to last on the left. The squad leader and the machine gun took their place in the center. Their firepower would be able to refuse contact to either flank. The only sounds were crunching snow and fabric-covered thighs rubbing together. Stempel saw target after target. The thin trunks of trees constantly appeared from behind other trees. Brush and stumps and fallen branches protruded, black and menacing. The night was moonless, but the stars still cast shadows, and when the wind blew, the shadows moved.

The snow was tramped down in places into a slick shine. Masses of Chinese had been canalized by artillery fire into the killing fields at the wire. But the platoon leader had told them there should be only snipers and observers and men with shoulder-fired SA-7 antiaircraft missiles. Like a snake they would strike only if the patrol walked right over them. But that was the whole point of the patrol—to sweep those Chinese from the woods. The lieutenant's talk had seemed more comforting half an hour before. Why they called it a "combat patrol" Stempel didn't know. They couldn't do much fighting. They had a radio and were supposed to call in the base's mortars or—once they were a couple of kilometers out—their 155-millimeter howitzers. But combat patrols as opposed to recon patrols were supposed to engage the enemy. He couldn't imagine twelve men doing much against the Chinese Army other than simply trying to survive, especially six kilometers out—the planned depth of their patrol.

The man ahead of Stempel went to ground with a crunch. Stempel plopped down into the thick snow. His heart thudded. He waited for the night to explode. He pressed his cheek to the cold, hard stock and found he couldn't breathe. The lump in his throat choked him, but he couldn't swallow the obstruction. He panicked that he'd have to call out for some sort of Heimlich maneuver to clear the fear that blocked his windpipe, but finally he managed to draw air. All across his assigned free-fire zone the woods were still. He spotted the white helmet of the last man on his flank and saw the Siamese twins lying side by side behind the machine gun on the other side. It was that awesome gun that might save them if they ran headlong into an inbound attack. The squad's wedge would collapse into a ring around the gun—their only strongpoint. But he remembered the waves that had crashed against the wire in the major attacks. If their patrol ran into a company, a battalion, a regiment . . .

Stempel shook his head to rid himself of the dreamlike images. Of the faces of the men from that first engagement. Their features were quickly growing indistinct, but not so their identities. The LT's shouts into the radio that had given way to stunned resignation. The angry bitching of the PFC and sergeant in their last moments of life. The cries of nameless men trying to surrender.

Stempel jammed his eyes shut and dropped his face till he felt the cold sting of snow. He flooded his head with wildly dissociated thoughts till he scattered the visions like rings of smoke with a wave of his hand. ''Pssst!'' he heard, and raised his head. Patterson was on his feet. Stempel quickly rose and labored forward. It wasn't bravery that kept him moving. It was fear. Demon-filled nightmares.

Evil figments who eyed him from the dark periphery of his sleep. Ghosts of men he'd never known.

Harold had decided that the first time didn't count. He'd pledged, however, that the next time he would die fighting.

ALONG URMI RIVER, SIBERIA
February 16, 0630 GMT (1630 Local)

At four-thirty every afternoon, Chin's war against the Europeans ended and his battle against the cold began. Not that UNRUSFOR was ever the greater threat. The cold dominated the battlefield completely. Every morning they awoke to an inspection from Chin. More often than not one or more of his men would require medical attention for frostbite. Several times men never awoke at all—frozen, dead, on sentry duty. It usually took them till ten in the morning to break camp. They would then march a kilometer, eat their last rations, and march another kilometer. At two they began searching for a bivouac. By four it was a race to survive. He had to strike camp before the temperatures plummeted at sunset or no one would make it to morning.

Chin had learned to read the company commander's mind. In the briefings he said nothing, but in his choice of campsite he told all. If he'd been worried about contact with the enemy, they would've camped on high ground or under a canopy of trees. But the CO always camped in the open, where it was warmer, and in ravines or on flat terraces at the bases of hills, where snow wouldn't collapse the tent while they slept. But never a valley, where the killing cold would settle.

"I'd rather eat reindeer than horses," Chin overheard as his men erected their platoon's single tent.

"Me too. But there are plenty of dead packhorses along the supply routes, and their meat is frozen."

"Quiet!" Chin snapped. He didn't think it right that his men discuss their hunger so openly. All they'd had in four days was field rations—frozen sugared blocks of crushed sesame seeds, peanuts, and rice.

There was a commotion. The two newest replacements were returning from their trip to the battalion supply depot. Everyone dropped what they were doing—even Chin. The men pulled a sled heavy with supplies and collapsed in the snow sweating. "Back off!" Chin shouted as men tore at the covering tarp.

"There's no food, sir," one of the new men reported, out of breath.

"*What?*" Chin yelled. "What the hell is *this*?"

"Ammunition, blankets, soap . . ."

Everyone was incensed. Several kicked the new guys, and Chin didn't stop them. When one of his wounded limped up, he ordered the two men to unload the sled and pull the man back to the aid station. "And this time don't come back without food! At least some cabbage! I don't care how you get it, understand?" They understood. "Back to work on that tent!" Chin ordered. He shoved them back toward the campsite. They would anchor one side of the tent to a small humpback ridge that would form a natural windbreak. One detail had cleared the snow to the relatively warmer ground, and Chin ordered them to begin laying a bed of spruce twigs for flooring. Larger branches first, then successively smaller twigs for comfort. In the center, men set up the lone wood-burning heater. Another detail built one-meter-high snow walls along the three unprotected sides to block the wind from those directions. The tent's entrance would be placed at forty-five degrees to the prevailing winds, which Chin was still trying to judge.

Chin would arrange the men in the tent according to the duty roster. The first men on sentry duty or tasked to clear drifts from the lee side of the walls would sleep nearest the entrance. Their relief would sleep in the next row so they could be located without waking everyone else. Shift by shift they slept in rows for four hours at a stretch. If they all fell asleep they'd all die. Chin cast a nervous eye to the low and anemic sun. "Let's start driving those tent pins! Where the ground's frozen, look for natural anchors! Hurry up!"

In the near distance, more new replacements were completely stripping a tree of its branches. Chin stormed over to them. "Don't take *all* the branches! The enemy can see bare trees from the air! Take a few lower branches and move on to the next tree! There are *millions* of trees all *around*!" They dropped their load and moved to comply. "Well take *those* branches!" They picked them up. "Which are upper branches, and which are lower branches?" Chin asked. They clearly had no idea. "I told you we burn *upper* branches before dark because their smoke is white! *Lower* branches have tar and resin! They burn better and are warmer, but give off dark smoke! We switch to them after sunset!"

The men hurried past like frightened rabbits. Chin rolled his eyes and shook his head. *No wonder they don't live long,* he thought. The wind whistled by. But the frigid gust could do nothing to increase his misery. He was already frozen to the bone. Hungry. Dying slowly, along with all his men.

BETHESDA NAVAL HOSPITAL, MARYLAND
February 17, 1300 GMT (0800 Local)

The Senate and House leadership gathered in a semicircle of seats pulled up to Gordon's bedside. Their faces were grim. The chants of the demonstrators outside the hospital, now nearly ten thousand strong, were clearly audible in the silence. Gordon knew the meeting would be contentious. His visitors had all just run the gauntlet of protesters at the gate. But it was the quieter protests that worried Gordon most. The flood of antiwar sentiment conveyed by phone calls, letters, and faxes. It was the collective roar of the politicians' constituents against which Gordon would fight his battle.

"The question has been raised," he began, "why are we fighting in Siberia?" Almost all of the politicians facing him had voiced vocal opposition to the war. "I called you here to answer that question." Daryl handed Gordon a glass of water. The painkillers gave him cotton mouth, and the words sounded as if they were stuck together. Gordon cleared his throat. "Siberia has a landmass equal to that of the U.S.,

Western Europe, and India combined. It had a pre–Civil War population, however, of only nine million, and that has now dropped by half. Yet Siberia contains the greatest deposits of natural resources on the planet. Its cobalt, chromium, iron ore, molybdenum, nickel, vanadium, tungsten are still virtually unexploited. Gold, copper, mercury, lead, platinum, tin, and zinc are all buried there in abundance, as are diamonds, emeralds, graphite, mica. And, of course, the fuels that run the world—oil, natural gas, coal, and uranium. There is not a region on earth richer in resources, and those resources are now 'in play.' They're up for grabs.''

He paused to take another sip. ''The fight over Siberia is between China, and the U.S. and Western Europe. In the era of imperialism it would be quite correct to say that we were the imperialist exploiters. We were in the wrong, then, but that era is gone and we are now in the right. We have just completed a half century of ideological competition in which our principal foreign policy was to contain the spread of totalitarianism, whether fascist or communist. We expended vast sums from our treasury and paid dearly for that policy in blood. This current war between East and West is a continuation of that competition. It is not racial or even particularly ideological. If the world's most populous country, which is a totalitarian dictatorship, were to acquire control over the world's richest supply of natural resources, we will one day again have to pay a great price. We are fighting today to avoid an even greater fight in the future, and that, in and of itself, is just.''

His voice had grown weak, and he again paused to take a drink. This time several of the congressmen glanced at each other. ''Finally,'' Gordon resumed, having to clear his throat repeatedly, ''we are fighting for something more important than natural resources or totalitarian containment. We are fighting for our soul—our identity. Many are tempted to cast that identity in terms of how the rest of the world sees America. Whether we will show resolve when committed to a cause, or cut and run in the face of adversity. But the more important question is what lies inside us? What is the true character of the people of this country? Do Americans see America as a powerful force on the side of right and justice? A nation that, once committed, will not back down even from war if that war is just? Or will we ignore the call to duty whenever the price we have to pay is high? How many times can we back out, fail to commit, look the other way, and still retain our national identity? And what could be more important than our self-image? Americans are not defined by any race or religion. We don't have a single, distinct culture. It is Americans' image of themselves that defines what this country is. We become, over time, who we believe we are. And if we are not today the triumphant United States of 1945, then just how different *have* we become? Who are we? That's the question that this war poses."

Even before he'd finished, Gordon knew his effort to win support had been a failure. What he hadn't done was express his deepest fear. What if America's grand social experiment with democracy was losing steam? What if the Anarchists were correct and liberal democracies were in incipient decay? What if they'd lost their vigor and were on the long, slow slide into decline? Did some immutable physical law make anarchy the eventual result? Gordon was more frightened of shrinking from a just war than of prosecuting an unpopular one.

The Democratic majority leader of the House cleared his throat. "Mr. President, I think I can speak for everyone here on at least one matter. We all appreciate the considerations you so eloquently expressed just now. They are surely weighty matters, and I feel certain that all of my colleagues on the Hill have paused to reflect upon them in a thoughtful manner. But I also can tell you that the issue of continuing this war has been so clearly resolved by Congress as to be a thing decided. The funding, as you know, will be cut off automatically on April nineteenth. We have agreed to schedule another vote before the funding cut off. But I'm sure your people will tell you the same thing that mine do: that vote won't even be close. I'm sorry, Mr.

President, but the American people don't want this war, and Congress is heeding their cry. I must respectfully counsel you, sir—as a friend—to listen to that voice as well."

As if on cue, a faint roar rose up from the protesters on the street.

"Gordon," the minority leader of the Senate and a good friend said, "you inherited this thing from Tom Marshall. We all opposed his deployment." The "we" was the Republican Party. "There were ample warnings that the Chinese were spoiling for this fight. It's never too late to start talking to Beijing. We don't have to cede them anything, just get their agreement to a halt so we can get the hell out of this awful mess. There are great forces at play in the world, I totally agree. But those forces are natural ones. Siberia is part of Asia, not Europe, and we're standing in the way of a natural realignment of geopolitical boundaries. That opposition may or may not be beyond our capabilities, *but*, Gordon, it is clearly beyond the mandate that the American people have vested in this government. I'm afraid that I have to agree with my Democratic colleagues on this one."

That left Gordon all alone. His own party—the leadership of the Senate in which he had been a member—was closing ranks with the Democrats. And their stand came on the crest of a popular backlash that had left Gordon—who had not even been elected to the office which he now held—at an historic low in public opinion polls. Gordon knew they would not be persuaded. They could be cowed into submission by critical letters, faxes, phone calls, polls, press, but when all that feedback was on *their* side of an issue, they were emboldened and would fight to their political deaths. They had to have some principle to live by, and it was those "voices from the heartland" in which they believed.

"It's one, two, three, what're we fightin' for?" the singer blasted over the loudspeakers outside. No one turned to look at the window, but all heard the lyrics.

"April nineteenth is the date for the second vote, Mr. President," the House majority leader said quietly. "The Senate will vote in the morning. The House in the afternoon.

The cutoff would take effect immediately afterward.''

It was a clash of titanic proportions. The White House contended that congressional authorization of the UN deployment gave Davis the authority to fight the war, but on April 20 there would be no funds with which to prosecute it. Any attempt to purchase war materials, to ship them to the Far East, to do any of the million and one things that the executive branch was charged with doing to keep the effort going would be rendered illegal. And it wouldn't be Gordon who would be confronted with violating the law. He had presidential immunity. It would be tens of thousands of bureaucrats who manned tens of thousands of offices who would each—personally—be faced with criminal prosecution. No matter how bravely Gordon stood, those men and women would falter. All it took to gum up the machine of government and bring the war to a grinding halt was one minor functionary refusing to follow Gordon's unlawful orders. And there would be not one, but hundreds—thousands—who would hesitate, defer, seek clarification, consult counsel. The congressmen knew that. They knew they held the winning hand. It would cost America the war, but that loss would be blamed on Gordon. And the end they achieved of bringing the troops home would be welcomed by a hair over 88.2 percent of the population.

Gordon took a deep breath. ''Very well,'' he said. ''On another topic, my health will not permit me to deliver my state-of-the-union address for some time.'' The congressmen all nodded in complete agreement. Gordon cut off their words of understanding. ''I should be well enough in a couple of months, so I will appear on the Hill for the address on April eighteenth.'' Mouths hung open and eyes caught each other's glances, but no one objected to Gordon's proposal.

15

Clark saw the thick torso of Admiral Ferguson emerge under the still-spinning helicopter rotors. The four-star, who as commander-in-chief of the Pacific Command was Clark's immediate superior, looked out of place in his navy-blue greatcoat and green Kevlar helmet. Major Reed led the admiral and his large coterie of aides to Clark, who saluted then shook Ferguson's hand. "Welcome to Khabarovsk, sir," he said loudly over the dying whine of the rotors. They headed toward the sandbagged headquarters entrance.

"Not as cold as I thought," Ferguson said in between the heated helicopter and the heated bunker.

Clark was already pissed at the surprise visit, but he let the comment pass. "How was your trip?" he asked as he fell naturally into step with the admiral along with the entire phalanx of aides and bodyguards.

"Flight was smooth as glass. No thermals, which must mean it's cold." They descended the frigid staircase to the operations center. Ferguson stopped abruptly at the bottom and Clark almost ran into the mountain of navy-blue wool.

One of his aides entered the operations center first and shouted, "Attention on deck!" Ferguson then briskly entered, boomed "Carry on!", and began to wander among the staff. "Where ya from, soldier?" he asked.

"Lyons," replied a French officer, who wore cold-weather gear from American stocks.

Ferguson didn't miss a beat. "Ah, *comment allez-vous*?" he asked, beginning a conversation in French that brought smiles from the French contingent. Ferguson slapped the officer on the back, interrupting the man's intended response and moving on. *Like a politician,* Clark thought as he followed. *Is that what it takes?* Ferguson left a broad wake through the center of the room, completely disrupting the harried officers' routines. At the opposite end of the main area, he suddenly turned to Clark and said, "Let's go to your office." Clark led his boss not to the desk in the corner of the big room, but to the office that he used only for sleep. Luckily, someone had gathered the pillow and blankets from the sofa.

"An uncluttered desk means an uncluttered mind!" Ferguson bellowed. He and Clark peeled off their cold-weather gear, then Ferguson turned to his aide and brushed the air with his fingers. As the navy captain cleared the room, Ferguson fiddled with the tape dispenser, the letter opener, the Dictaphone. He even opened a stapler to confirm it was loaded. When the door was closed, they sat and Clark opened his mouth to inquire as to the reason for the visit, but Ferguson beat him to the punch. "I *suppose* that you're wondering just what the hell I'm doing here?" He looked directly at Clark. "I'll get right to the point. I've had some misgivings about the strategy you've employed in this war, and I want to discuss some changes."

Clark arched his brow as if to say that of course he would be receptive to any advice about the conduct of his ground war by the former carrier pilot who by historical accident happened to be his superior. "You're fighting not to lose," Ferguson said. "This strategy of pulling everybody back into tight groups of mutually supporting firebases cedes the initiative to the Chinese. We let them do what they will in the field while we hoard assets here and in Vladivostok. By doing that, we fail to make use of our superior mobility. We could be out there running circles around their infantry. Hitting them *hard*"—he slammed one meaty paw into his palm—"then outrunning them to set up another ambush."

Ferguson sat back, and Clark gathered that it was his turn to speak. He cleared his throat. "It is true, Admiral Ferguson—"

"Franklin," Ferguson insisted.

"—Franklin," Clark continued, "that UNRUSFOR's nominal tables of organization and equipment provide us with superior mobility. But that advantage has been substantially degraded by a variety of factors, not the least of which was the failure to deploy the service and support units necessary to maintain that equipment in a harsh environment. Most of the allied units were deployed without their heavy equipment. What they did have has deteriorated through lack of maintenance."

Ferguson was not the most patient of men. Before Clark had finished, he was already shaking his head. "You're talking maintenance. I'm talking about the operational *art,* General! Campaigning. Our fundamental strategic approach to halting the Chinese advance." Clark tried to speak, but "Franklin" wasn't through. "I'm gonna shoot straight with you. There's been talk by the desk jockeys back at the Pentagon about you being gun-shy—our 'General McClellan.' " Clark set his jaw firmly to mask his sudden anger. West Pointers like Clark knew their history. The Civil War general had been accused by many in the North of cowardice for his tentative use of superior forces against the South. "They say you were traumatized by that Birobidzhan thing," Ferguson went on, "and that you're now afraid to commit."

Ferguson shrugged and shook his head as if to explain that he was, of course, Clark's great and tireless defender. "Now, I know what you're going to say. You warned everybody who would listen about the risks of this war.

You clamored for more men and heavier equipment that you still haven't gotten, et cetera, et cetera. But the fact is most of the allied units that are in the field right now haven't even fired a shot. There's a perception by many—and that includes the media—that we're just letting them waltz in and take the place. Plus, there are the parallels to the firebase strategy in Vietnam. Sure, sure, defense is stronger *tactically* than offense, but assuming the defensive *strategically* can *lose* this war, General.''

An incredulous Clark had no idea where to begin. He tried to compose a response while vigorously reining in his temper. Where should he start? With the politics of the shaky UN coalition, which might bust apart if he ordered a risky counterattack? Or with the utter nonsense that large units could regularly hit the Chinese hard, disengage, and set up again without getting so entangled that they'd be fixed in place and lost to the man? Better to use airpower to punish the Chinese, who were exposed on their road marches and—

''Washington wants you to change your strategy, Nate,'' Ferguson said simply. ''That's why I'm here.''

So that was it. Nate didn't flinch, or nod, or even blink. ''Admiral Ferguson,'' he began in as even a voice as he could muster, ''Franklin, I have the better part of 800,000 Chinese troops coming my way and less than 200,000 men in the field to oppose them. Four-to-one numerical inferiority. In a couple of months we'll have narrowed that gap to three or even two to one by attriting the Chinese and building up our forces in theater. At three to one, I can show the world something. At four to one, I'm hanging on by sacrificing ground *and* men's lives to buy time!''

''That's one strategy,'' Ferguson said coolly, ''but it's not the one endorsed by the joint chiefs.''

''It's the one endorsed by the joint command of UN-RUSFOR.''

The two men stared silently at one another until Ferguson finally burst out, ''God*damn* but you're a thickheaded son of a bitch!'' He rocked back, his hands gripping his thighs as he sat there rigidly. "Listen, Nate, you're not leaving me much wiggle room here. You've been fighting this war out here all by your lonesome for three weeks without hearing word *one* out of me but 'What can I do to help?' Am I right?" Nate had to nod. "Now why, all of a sudden, do you think I come here and tell you you've got to change your fundamental strategy for fighting this war?" Nate didn't reply. "The decision has already been made . . . back in Washington."

"By the joint chiefs?" Ferguson nodded. "Dekker?" The admiral nodded again. Clark was furious. He rose and began to pace the office. "I could lose *more* than the war! I could lose the war *and* every last man in my command! What the hell do they think they're doing? I'm hangin' on by my fuckin' *fingernails*!"

"Don't shoot me," Ferguson said. "I'm just the messenger. Hate to say this to you, Nate, but this is over my pay grade."

"Over *your* pay grade?" Clark said. Ferguson nodded again in reply. Clark thought for a moment, then said in low tones, "I'm not ordering those men out of their firebases. It's suicide—murder—and I won't be a party to it."

"Sounds like you've got some talking to do back in D.C." Nate was again confused. Ferguson was again frustrated. "Nate, if you don't get your ass back there chop chop, you won't have to issue those orders because you won't have a *command*! Timmy Stanton'll get it, and he'll order the counterattack on the flight over from Seoul."

Clark was shaking his head. "I don't believe it. Tim's a good man. He wouldn't do it either, not after he saw what he's got, and what he's up against."

"Maybe you're right, but it wouldn't change the fact that you'd be out of a job, General. It's check. You've got one move left to you, Nate, and that's to hop on a plane and get back to Washington pronto. You know how fast things move in that city. It may already be too late, I don't know."

"What the hell am I going to say to Dekker that could possibly—"

"Nobody said anything about you talking to Dekker," Ferguson interrupted.

Nate slowly turned, increasingly astonished. "Are you suggesting what I think you're suggesting?"

Ferguson rose and began to put the gear back on. "I didn't say anything. I'm just a dumb country boy from Tennessee. Don't know why I even joined the navy seein' as there's no ocean anywhere near Clark County. I'm just going to take a nice, long tour of the battlefront all the way over to Chita in the west and back to Pearl. I'll have to report that you refuse to change strategies when I get back, but I'll probably be out of direct communications for a day or so. Sat phone's on the fritz, you know?" Nate understood and nodded in appreciation. "He's at Bethesda," Ferguson said. "Good luck."

"Thank you . . . Franklin," Clark said.

"One more word of advice, Nate. By the time you land in D.C., you'd damn well better have a plan to win this war tucked under your arm. Capisch?"

VLADIVOSTOK-USSURIYSK ROAD, SIBERIA
February 19, 2100 GMT (0700 Local)

André Faulk trudged through the snow with the heavy mailbag slung over his left shoulder. He held his M-16 by the pistol grip with his right hand. Ugly black holes scarred the virgin snow. Exposed, fresh wood dotted the pockmarked trunks. He finally saw a fighting hole with a white helmet protruding above snow level, and headed toward the position. When he was a few feet away, the head jerked around and the rifle followed. "Hey!" André shouted. "Be cool, man!"

"Jesus, get down!" On hearing the tone of the man's voice, André dropped immediately. He crawled forward into the man's hole. "God*damn,* man!" the soldier whispered. "Are you fuckin' *crazy*? *Jee*-zus!" All across the snow-covered field ahead trees had been felled by great violence. "Are you our relief?" the guy asked André. He was nervously gripping and regripping the forward plastic guard of his rifle. He took his eyes off the woods in front only briefly.

"Naw, man. I'm lookin' for Third Platoon, C Company, Second Battalion. You know where they are?" The guy just lowered his helmet to the front edge of the hole and mumbled something André didn't understand.

"Say what?"

"This *is* Charlie Company!" he snapped as his head shot up to his rifle sights. The woods were still.

"Take it easy, man. Could you just point me to Third Platoon?"

The man looked like he was going to be sick. His head wobbled. His chin was covered in black stubble. Tiny beads of ice dangled from each follicle. His eyes were red and sunken into swollen sockets above black bags. His jaw drooped, leaving his mouth open. André looked around the desolate defensive line in search of someone else, but the guy seemed to be the lone defender.

The soldier turned slowly to André. "You got a truck or somethin', man?" He spoke in a whisper. "Take me back with you."

André snorted and half grinned. Then what he was asking sank in. "Man, you gotta be kiddin'. *Shit*." It was then that he noticed the change in the man. He grew nervous and looked back through the woods toward the supply road where the Humvee was parked. He clenched his rifle tight in both hands.

"Say," André reasoned, "listen, I rode in here with a spec four, and . . . you know." The man didn't seem to be listening. "He'd fuckin' . . . I dunno! He's carryin' a goddamn grenade launcher. And he's got about eight mags on his skinny-assed chest. He'd pro'bly, you know, shoot you or something if—"

"Not if I greased his ass first." The soldier's face changed completely. "*Please*, ma-a-an! Jesus *Christ*! Do you know what this shit is *like* up here? It's motherfuckin' goddamn *hell*!" he shouted. The guy sort of rolled over onto his back and stared at the overcast sky. André watched his rifle, which he hugged against his chest. "You want 3rd Platoon, C Company?" he asked, sounding exhausted. "They're out there." It wasn't much, but André understood that there was "in," and there was "out." He looked toward no-man's-land, but he saw nothing but trees, snow, and here and there . . . an arm. Frozen at a right angle. A helmet half-covered in a drift. The boot of a soldier fallen face forward that was draped over a log. It was a cemetery, with all the bodies sloppily buried. But André could tell from the shape of the helmets that they were Chinese soldiers, not American. Third Platoon, he concluded, lay somewhere beyond, similarly half-buried in snow.

"What do you mean you couldn't find them?" the lieutenant asked. André explained that the entire 3rd Platoon was missing in action and that he couldn't find their company headquarters section. "But who was in charge, then?" André shrugged. The lieutenant sent André off to process his undelivered mail. He sat in a windowless room no bigger than a closet and pulled out a thick stack of letters. The first was pink. It was addressed to "Aguire, Todd C., Pvt. USA" in a woman's hand. André's eyes flooded with moisture, and it angered him. He took the red felt-tip pen and held it poised over Aguire's name. The tip left a splotch where it rested against the absorbent paper.

"Return to Sender," André scrawled across the neat hand of some woman named "Laney Aguire." He dropped it in the outgoing bag. The return address on Alvarez's letter had a stick-on label with Christmas holly swirling around the corners. Letter by letter the job grew more difficult. André angrily smeared the words he was writing over the cards, envelopes, and packages. By the time he had finished, it had come to him. Somewhere between "Aguire" and "Wolfson," he realized he knew each of those men.

He went to his quarters, got the letter from his AIT school commander that was supposed to get him into air-

borne school, and marched into the LT's office. He spent
fifteen minutes arguing, holding his ground, waving the letter in the air. "All right, already!" the lieutenant said finally. "It's your funeral!" He sent André out and got on
the telephone. A half an hour later he emerged from his
office. "Classes are full at airborne school, but a buddy at
Fort Campbell said they got a spot open in air assault
school. It lasts ten days, and it's supposed to be absolute
hell." André said nothing. "Look, André, the 101st Airborne is pouring into Vladivostok right now. If you think
this is a ticket home or something, I mean . . ." He was
shaking his head. "You're gonna be right back over here,
and the shit's gonna be thick. Those guys are the fire brigade. They're bein' choppered in when the Chinese punch
through, dropped smack-dab in their line of advance, and
told to hold." André said nothing. "Okay!" the frustrated
lieutenant said, and he called his secretary into his office.
"André, here, wants to part company with our happy band.
Type up some travel orders for air assault school at Fort
Campbell. Is that right, Private Faulk?"

André nodded.

ABOARD C-141, OVER CENTRAL PACIFIC
February 20, 1000 GMT (2000 Local)

Clark had left his British deputy commander in charge of
UNRUSFOR. With him he'd brought his J-1, J-2, J-3, and
J-4—all generals—and Major Reed. Once again it was
Reed's study that had yielded the basis for Nate Clark's
plan. "In 1939, the Japanese Army in China attacked
Georgi Zhukov's Russian forces in Mongolia. Zhukov ordered his frontline troops to hold while he marshaled arriving reinforcements for a counterattack. He mustered
overwhelming force under strict operational security and
obtained air superiority. He concentrated his armor and lav-
ishly employed swift-striking forces. When he counterattacked, he drove the Japanese back deep into China."

The German staff officer nodded. "He did the same at

Moscow, Stalingrad, Kursk-Orel, and Berlin.''

"But how do we stop the Chinese?" Clark asked the man.

"We must use the *Stützpunkt*—the strong point," Reed replied. "A network of loosely connected defensive positions backed by local reserves. When the Chinese attack, we kill them in huge numbers. When the pressure grows we pull back to the next line. A properly organized time-phased delay path is our only hope of stabilizing the front when we don't have the troops for a continuous line."

"Hitler tried that last," the Russian advisor said. The former general spoke in a slow and thickly accented voice. "The fascists' 'hedgehog' defense on the Eastern Front was a tactic of weakness. Hitler said no retreat, so German units tried to make their stands in open fields. When we attacked in morning, we found men frozen in bottom of holes. And so Nazis pulled back into villages and built these strong points. They gave open fields to us and we infiltrated between their positions easily. When we attacked in strength, we were able to shoulder our way through."

"Strong points saved the Wehrmacht," the German general replied. "A continuous line across three thousand kilometers would be like paper. We needed elasticity—defense in depth—to stop offensives. Two rows of firebases. The ones in back manned by support troops. Artillery and air bombardment will fill the gaps."

"But there is no shelter in Siberia," the French member of Clark's staff pointed out. He spoke directly to his close comrade the German. "There are no villages like there were in western Russia. How will we protect our troops from the weather?"

"We have engineers. We will make our own shelter." He turned to Clark. "And when the pressure isn't great, we can push the perimeters out beyond the firebases to interlock."

One of the American officers was shaking his head. "Your firebase system sounds too much like Vietnam. It's

reactive, defensive, tailored for long security duty. The operational art has come a long way since Vietnam . . . and World War Two. We need to be proactive, aggressive, decisive.''

''This *will* be aggressive,'' countered the German. ''We'll use air, indirect fire, and special operations to interdict supplies and reinforcements. If we isolate the battlefield, the tactical commanders can attain local superiority over the Chinese and win their engagements. These defenses are not static. They can be made very active. The terrain will canalize the Chinese through mountains and valleys. We will be waiting for them with prepared defenses and concentrated fires.''

''But where will we ultimately stop them?'' Clark asked.

The German officer's pen traced the northern branch of the Trans-Siberian Railroad—hundreds of miles north of the border—which stretched across the map from east to west. ''That is the line where we must stiffen and hold.''

''But all they need to do is break that rail line in one place and they win,'' the British officer commented. ''They sever the east from the west. How can we be certain we will stop them?''

Without a moment's hesitation, the most junior officer at the table answered. ''Supply,'' Reed said. ''That is the one major weakness of the Chinese Army.'' Clark followed Reed's eyes down to the map of the vast Siberian wilderness. ''Somewhere, they'll reach the 'culminating point'— the point beyond which they can't maintain continuous supply of their frontline troops. They have no road/rail grid. Rugged terrain. Brutally cold weather. *We* have total air supremacy. We have to degrade their supply capabilities through air attack. Make sure that they reach their culminating point somewhere south of the rail line.''

''And then what?'' the French general asked.

Clark stared back, unflinching. ''We hit them as quick as we can, as hard as we can, where it hurts the most, when they aren't looking.''

McLean, Virginia
February 20, 1900 GMT (1400 Local)

The moment Nate Clark arrived home, he knew something was wrong. He had called ahead, and Lydia had picked up the boys from school. They had hugged him, but they were subdued. Lydia, too, seemed different. Tired.

They sat at the dinner table. Nate drank the coffee he'd made while waiting for them to arrive. "I don't have long. I've got to go see the president." The boys nodded. Everyone seemed ill at ease. The boys' eyes darted up at Nate's, but didn't linger. "What the hell's going on?" Nate asked.

They all looked at him. "I'm sorry, Nate," Lydia said, forcing a smile. "It's just . . . you don't realize what it's been like. For the boys, I mean."

"What *what* has been like?"

"The war. The protests."

The boys were looking down. Dejected. "Are you being bothered by someone?" he asked.

"They've picketed our house," Lydia said softly. "The police ran them off. But I've been thinking about moving. The owner of the house . . . he's agreed to let us out of the lease." There was pain in her eyes. Embarrassment at having raised the subject on Nate's brief return home.

Nate was seething. Lack of sleep. Too much coffee. Frustration and setback and criticism from all sides. And the immense strain of all that was happening. He knew he was on the edge. He ground his teeth and kept quiet. "I thought I was a national hero after that *Newsweek* cover story."

"I'm sorry, Nate," Lydia said. "I wasn't going to tell you. There are just as many idiots on TV, saying what we should do or should've done."

Nate turned to his sons. "Would one of you please just say something to me?"

They looked up at him finally. "When are we gonna start fighting?" Jeffrey asked.

"*Jeffrey!*" Lydia chastised.

Again the boy's head hung low. But in that instant of candor Nate caught a glimpse of what was being drummed into everyone's heads. The commanding general was too cowardly or inept to put up a fight. But it was worse than just that. "People say," Jeffrey ventured slowly, "it's because Mom is Chinese." He couldn't look either parent in the eye. "Because we're . . . half-Chinese."

All Nate felt was blinding anger. Lydia took him into his study and closed the door. He couldn't bring himself to speak at first. "What is it, Nate?" she asked.

He felt overwhelmed. "I'm considering requesting relief," he replied in a monotone.

"From your *command*?" she asked. She tried not to sound surprised . . . but failed. "Nate . . . that's not *like* you."

"I'm not running *away*! Is *that* what you think?" She eyed the door. The boys were still there. "I'm sorry," he said, and they embraced each other. "I'm going to propose a plan to the president. A plan to win the war. If he rejects it, I'm thinking about submitting my request for relief. It's a one-shot weapon, but I believe in the plan I'm taking to him."

She remained pressed against him. "What if he doesn't grant your request?"

"Then I'm still legally obligated to carry on in command. But he wouldn't reject my request. I'd be out. Out of my command. Out of the army. Out."

"Would that be so bad?" she asked. He tried, but couldn't reply. The lump in his throat prevented him from speaking. Lydia squeezed him tight. She understood it would mean defeat, no matter what the outcome of the war. And, inevitably, cowardice. Desertion of his troops during a desperate war. In his own eyes. In the eyes of his sons.

BETHESDA NAVAL HOSPITAL, MARYLAND
February 20, 2100 GMT (1600 Local)

"Mr. President?"

Gordon Davis opened his eyes. A man towered over his bedside. Gordon blinked several times before his blurry vision cleared. He didn't recognize the man who stood before him wearing slacks and an open-collar shirt.

"Yes?" Gordon croaked. He struggled to push himself a few inches up his pillow. The man helped.

"My name is General Clark." Gordon's eyes shot up to him. "What . . . ?" he began, but then coughed. Clark poured some of what used to be ice water into a paper cup. Gordon drank and cleared his throat. "What are you doing here?"

"I came to talk to you about the war, sir. Nobody knows I'm here." He held up his arms as if to display his camouflage—civilian clothes.

The room was empty. Gordon looked Clark up and down. He was shaven and appeared clean, but he looked exhausted. "I'm listening," Gordon said.

The general pulled his chair over to the bed and sat. "I'm sorry to bother you, Mr. President. But what I'm about to say may mean the difference between winning and losing this war."

"Is this about the change in strategy?"

Clark nodded. "It's a mistake."

Gordon took as deep a breath as he could risk—just short of the point of pain. "This is outside my area of expertise, General. The joint chiefs have recommended that we take a more aggressive approach."

"I know, sir. But it's wrong. The coalition will fall apart. The Germans, maybe even the French, will withdraw. The casualties will skyrocket on both sides, but *we* can't sustain the losses . . . politically. The American people won't tolerate them. We'll be forced to negotiate a cease-fire and pull out."

"You're asking me to reject the unanimous advice of the joint chiefs of staff and accept your opinion? General Clark, no offense . . . but I don't even know you. They had charts and maps and quotes from Sun Tzu and von Clausewitz. It was a helluva show. Made it sound like . . . well, maybe you were too hesitant."

Gordon studied the soldier. He seemed unfazed by the

words. He spoke slowly, and with conviction. "We have the best army in the world. The soldiers and equipment are unequaled anywhere. But there's only so much they can do in the face of four-to-one numerical inferiority. We have to rely for the time being on the inherent tactical advantage of defense over offense. We have to entrench, dig in, and then pummel the attackers with our firepower. We've got air superiority, so we know where they are and can hit them virtually at will. But if we come out of those holes, Mr. President, our casualty rates skyrocket. And for what? The territorial gains would be minimal."

"But what about morale? I thought it was lagging because of the defensive strategy."

"It's *lagging*, sir, because it's winter in Siberia. A land war on the Asian continent against the Chinese Army. They're barely holding on, Mr. President. To ask those men to crawl out of their holes and attack now would be disastrous."

Gordon had a sinking feeling. The man was, it seemed, just as he'd been described—timid. Generals were supposed to say things like, "All seems lost, so I'm attacking." But this man wasn't like that.

"I'm sorry, General Clark. I'm not going to bullshit you. I'm not convinced."

"Would you give me one chance, sir? Would you let me tell you what I propose?" Gordon nodded, waiting. "The Chinese have given up trying to take Vladivostok in the east, Khabarovsk in the center, and Svobodny in the west. They're pushing instead for our only remaining east-west rail connection in the north. I propose using existing ground forces in-theater to stop the Chinese south of that line. We'll pound their main supply routes from the air round the clock. All the while we're building up war stocks and massing reinforcements along the rail line. We'll mass two more corps—one American arriving from the east by sea and rail; one European arriving by rail from the west—to add to the there we've already got in the field."

Gordon interrupted with a question. "How will the Chinese not know what we're doing?"

"Sun Tzu said it first, sir. 'All war is based on deception.' If the Chinese haven't pulled back into defensible
positions before we launch our massive, setpiece attack, the
war's over. *We* have mobility. *They* don't. And they have
no way of seeing the attack coming. With no space-based
or aerial reconnaissance assets left, their battlefield intelligence is purely tactical—thirty kilometers beyond their
lines, at most."

"They have CNN," Gordon noted.

"CNN and all the other media are a major part of our
strategic deception plan, Mr. President. That plan is to make
everyone think we're losing the war. Since the Chinese will
know we're staging somewhere, we'll make them think it's
for the limited purpose of relieving Khabarovsk and Birobidzhan. While we're staging for the *main* attack farther
west, we'll set up decoy bases in Komsomolsk—north of
Khabarovsk. Mock fuel dumps, trucks, armored vehicles,
multispectoral close combat decoys. Fake headquarters will
broadcast huge volumes of encrypted radio traffic. The
Western media is an asset we can use to create the impression that the *most* we could be planning is to liberate Birobidzhan."

"And how would we win this war, General?" Gordon
asked.

"We invade China," Clark replied simply. "Strike
straight into Manchuria from the northern rail line and from
Vladivostok." Clark stared back at him with an unwavering
gaze. "Mr. President, when the Chinese invaded, our mission changed. War is simple. War is about extreme commitment. On the individual level, it's about killing or being
killed. On the national level, it's about total victory or total
defeat. And nothing short of taking the war to the enemy
will win it. We've got to go into northern China. Cut the
roads. Take the cities. Rock the Chinese back on their heels
so hard that the war is ended on our terms. Decisiveness,
Mr. President. It's a quality all great leaders possess. Before
you take risk, you must stand to gain something of com-
mensurate importance. To go from defense to offense is to

risk everything. Therefore, total victory must be what we stand to gain.''

Gordon looked the man over one last time. He was the first military man to propose a plan for total victory. But there was still one more piece that had to fit. ''Just when would this counterattack come?'' Gordon asked.

''The timing is tricky, Mr. President. For the plan to work the Chinese supply network has to be exhausted, and all of our stocks and reinforcements have to be in place at precisely the same time. Plus, there's the terrain and weather. For ten days when the ice melts the rivers are unbridgeable. And if we wait too long, the rivers flood and the ground turns to mud.''

''When, General Clark?'' Gordon tried again.

''Mid to late April, sir.''

Gordon smiled. The answer struck the mark. ''Then I approve the plan.'' Clark looked up in surprise. ''You will launch the counterattack on April fourteenth.'' Clark appeared confused. ''April fourteenth, General Clark. A major operation of the sort you propose must take months of preparation. I'm giving that time to you. You will attack on April fourteenth—four days before my state-of-the-union address; five days before the War Powers Act vote. But let's not tell anyone we've agreed on that date, understand? That's just between the two of us.''

Clark understood. He nodded slowly. As commander-in-chief of UNRUSFOR, he always looked at the big picture. He was beginning to get a feel for an even larger perspective still.

NEW YORK, NEW YORK
February 25, 1300 GMT (0800 Local)

Roger Stempel fumbled with the antacids his doctor had prescribed. The metal foil wouldn't tear, and he quickly grew angry. He was a wreck, and the list of medical complications from the stress was growing. His wife was having lunch with her sister. If he had a heart attack now, he'd die alone. *Like Harold,* a voice whispered. Roger winced and covered his face. He dragged his hands down his cheeks. His eyes shone back at him from the mirror bloodred.

The last weeks had been the worst of his life. "Missing in Action—Presumed Killed," the army had said. First shock, then agony and despair. Their only child. Their little boy. The sadness had evolved into depression. His son's death had become handling the details. The army could produce no remains. No remains, no funeral—Gay had said. Graves Registration had only a blood-soaked parka with Harold's name printed inside. *Not "bloodstained,"* Roger thought. The man had clearly said "blood-soaked."

The mail clapped onto the floor of the foyer. A flood of catalogs, junk mail, and the occasional bill. Roger trudged into the study to be near the trash can, the repository of at least half their mail. Catalog. Catalog. Encyclopedia offer. Magazine subscription offer made to look like a check. Preapproved credit card. Charitable donation solicitation. A letter slipped out of a magazine. It had the rare look of personal correspondence. He turned the envelope over.

It was in Harold's handwriting! Roger sank into the chair behind his desk in shock. With trembling hands he tore the envelope open. The letter was dated less than one week earlier! The first paragraphs were about Harold's unit being overrun. The trouble they had getting back onto base. His slight wounds while fighting with the provisionals.

"He's *alive*!" Roger shouted, reveling in the relief the letter brought from his unrelenting grief. His joy subsided with Harold's every word.

I know now what "biting" cold means. Your teeth chatter. Your body clenches so hard it's exhausting. Your breath freezes into large sheets of ice outside the towel or strip of wool blanket you wrap around your neck. When you don't shave, tiny droplets of ice cling to the tips of the hairs. It's painful to pull them off, especially with windburned cheeks. Frozen tears weld your eyelashes together in big clumps and form long, white mustaches of ice. When we come in from trench duty, our weapons steam when you put them near the fires. Every square inch of skin is chapped, especially your hands, face, and lips. If you leave your nose or cheek exposed even for a few minutes, you get frostbite. Red skin is okay, but pale yellow is trouble. The only way to get the color back from yellow is to rub snow on it. But sometimes that doesn't work. Two guys in our platoon on sentry duty crawled behind a log to get some sleep and froze to death.

But it's when the wind blows that it's the worst. It's like a bath of cold water being poured onto you no matter how warmly you're dressed. At least when it blows hard, you know the Chinese won't attack. Then everybody's just trying to survive. The wind feels like it cuts your skin when it hits your face. And when there's snow, it's like little darts, a handful of pebbles that someone throws at your face. Even inside the shelter, the wind whistles and howls through the cracks in the roofing timbers so loudly you can't sleep.

At night, when it's the coldest, we go out patrolling. You can see that the Chinese have been there, and if you turn your ear to the wind you can hear all kinds of things. The woods are alive and filled with tracks. Every step anyone has taken is recorded in the snow. Your tracks, theirs—they're all mixed. The guys in the next battalion down the line swear they patrol their front aggressively, but we always draw fire from their sector. Once, we swept their sector and found bunkers the Chinese had lived in for days! But I understand. Patrols are spooky. We fire white phosphorus marker rounds for artillery spotters all around the base, and the shadows are always moving. The sound of the snow squeaking under your boots carries a long way in the cold, especially downwind, and gives your position away. And under the snow, the ice is as slippery as a skating rink. The sunshine at midday melts the top layer, and it freezes again at night. You're constantly at risk of falling, especially on the roads. They were muddy from the summer rains when they froze, and the deep ruts are now sharp ridges. When the wind blows the snow off, they look like six-inch-high black marble knives. If you fall on them, you break bones because they're as hard as iron.

I don't want you to get too scared. Most of our time is spent in the trenches, where we're relatively safe. Our stretch of the perimeter is fairly solid. The Chinese haven't once made it within grenade range of the main trench, and they're in terrible shape. They loot the dead and crawl through piles of our trash for food and clothing. They're hungry and ragged and more frightened than we are. A lot of the corpses we police up are wearing scavenged U.S. uniforms. We even found some Christmas packages we think came from the convoys that got overrun on the road to Khabarovsk. I feel a little sorry for them. One patrol came back after a blizzard and reported they'd found an entire regiment frozen to death. I don't know how the Chinese do it, especially the second and third waves, which have to pass mounds of the dead and dying.

Please don't think everything here is horrible. We sometimes get fresh food from the French. It's usually frozen by the time they bring it to the perimeter, but we reheat it and it tastes great. Everything freezes. Even in the warming huts or the bunkers where we sleep, you have to chop the food with a hatchet or an ax to cook it. We usually don't cook in the bunkers, though, because of the smell. They're also our bathrooms. But trench duty is fine when the weather is clear. The skies can be pure as crystal and a pale blue color I've never seen before. And the ground is like a winter wonderland, entirely covered in white. If you don't police up the dead, they're just covered up by the snow, at least until spring. And even the night, which almost always brings an attack if the weather permits, has a beauty of its own. The air is so dry that you can see every star. And when the fighting starts, the tracer rounds look like fireworks. Long, continuous bursts from each side intermingle and look almost like bouquets of flowers. Green ribbons of light from the Chinese. Yellow beads on long strings from the good guys.

So don't worry, Mom and Dad. I'll be fine. They say if you make it past two weeks, your odds go way up, and I'm past two weeks. I hope you don't get all stressed out over this. I'll make it. Lots of people live through war without anything terrible happening. It's just a job. I'll write again soon. Love, Harold.

OUTSIDE USSURIYSK, SIBERIA
February 27, 2330 GMT (0930 Local)

Kate Dunn positioned everyone. "All right, Woody! You get the shot from on top of the trench. Okay, Jurgen. You go about your business." Woody scampered up to ground level with his Minicam. But the German and American paratroopers hesitated.

"Is there a problem?" Kate asked. The sky was perfect. The sun was nicely covered by thin clouds. But soon it would clear. Direct sunlight would change everything. Shades. Shadows. They'd lose this shot.

"What do you want me to do?" the German asked.

"Just do what you were doing," Kate said. "I don't *stage* shots." They didn't understand. They looked at each other. Kate explained by grabbing the man's parka. She moved him to the trench wall just below Woody. "Now go. Teach the Americans how to fight the Chinese."

The GIs stirred and snorted. The German shook his head. "No, no. Not how to fight. How to prepare positions. Winter positions."

"Right. That's what I meant. Just go back over what you were telling them before you stopped. Only for the camera." She smiled and pointed up at Woody. He waved from behind his eyepiece.

Kate placed the American paratroopers in a semicircle around the German. She held a boom mike over the group just off-camera. She had the German give his name and rank. He spoke English very well. No on-screen transcripts were needed. Woody gave her a thumbs-up. The taping began.

"Okay," the German advisor said, "the best cover in the trenches are ice parapets. They are bulletproof. You make them by taking a poncho . . . like this." He held the thin fabric up with a rustling noise. "You roll small sticks inside it like this, *ja*?" The crinkling of the poncho was far too loud. Plus Kate saw Woody have to shift position. Kate motioned for the Americans to kneel. They did. The advisor held a thick bundle of small sticks. They were rolled into the poncho. He climbed a raised step on the trench wall. Kate's mike followed. He placed the bundle in front of the firing post. "Now, please, would you hand me the water."

Snow was being melted in fires up and down the trench line. An American carefully handed him a heavy can. The men all stood back from the liquid. They handled it slowly as if it were a vat of acid. The German used a stick to break the thin ice that had formed at the top. He raised the can. He poured the water onto the poncho.

The Americans—all in their teens, from their looks— marveled as the water froze. The poncho was slowly covered in translucent layers of ice. They thickened right before their eyes. *Too long,* Kate thought. But the advisor took his time emptying the bucket.

Kate was reminded of high-school science projects. The "gee whiz" experiments meant more to intrigue than inform. Maybe they'd see that angle back in New York. Or maybe she should mention it.

"Pour slowly, *ja*? So the ice will freeze." When he was done, the bundle of sticks was frozen solidly onto the front lip of the trench. "An ice parapet," he said, showmanlike. "Let the ice set. Then cover it with snow for camouflage. You can bank the snow. Pour water over it. Two of this-size buckets. That will make a 'snow-und-ice glacis.'"

The Americans laughed. "Snow-und-ice" was repeated.

"Okay, *cut*!" Kate shouted. She lowered the mike. "Great! Did you get that, Woody?" He gave her another thumbs-up. He wasn't talking because of a sore throat he was protecting with scarves and mufflers. "Okay, I need to do the story's lead-in. I'm going to stand right up there where he is. Everybody down here just go about your business." She showed with her hands the camera's field of view. They stood there. "Good. Say, you all have your rifles, don't you?" They showed her. They weren't even loaded.

She climbed up the wall rolling her eyes. Woody held the camera to her face. She took a quick glance in her compact, cleared her throat . . . and looked around.

Soldiers cleared the gentle slope in front. Engineers cut tree trunks with noisy chain saws. When she was trying to decide which story to do, the unit commander had told her it was a dangerous job. You could hit an ice core, break the chain, maybe send the saw flying back at you. *Boring,* she thought. Backhoes carried brush to the rear. Soldiers sawed logs for ceiling timbers. Kate had chosen to stick with the paratroopers. She had Woody try to get it all. Engineers preparing the killing fields in the background. Troops in the trench below. A close-up of Kate.

Woody counted down with his fingers, then pointed.

"The 82nd Airborne Division was the first major unit to arrive in Siberia after the war began. But this fabled unit has yet to see action. Traditionally reserved for the ultimate in national emergencies, the 'All-American division' is now about to get into the fight. They're bracing for the shock of the main Chinese assault. At night, the wind carries the sounds of approaching combat. The German Army will soon 'pass the line' to their American comrades, and these paratroopers will learn firsthand the brutality of winter infantry war.

"But lessons are already being passed from ally to ally. German soldiers have been pulled back from the lines, and the experience of battle they have had visited upon them is helping fellow UN troops to better prepare their icebound positions." She lowered the mike. "We'll cut here and insert the scene we just taped."

Woody shook his head and spoke in a raspy voice. "That form you signed with the public affairs guy is gonna haunt you. It's a pact with the devil, Kate. The censor's gonna hold the tape. They won't let you mention the 82nd till they start fighting."

Loud gunfire erupted from the hills. It wasn't close, but it was near enough to cause everyone to turn. Even in daylight you could clearly see the flashes. They lit the clouds.

Kate smiled. She had Woody start taping. Scenes of officers shouting. The men on the slopes dropping their logs and saws and coming back up the hill. A sergeant marching down the trench and magazines being loaded into weapons. Kate couldn't believe their luck.

"Hey!" an officer shouted. "Get down from there!"

"We're from the press," Kate said.

"*I* know who you are!" The man was a captain. Kate and Woody climbed down. Woody filmed the paratroopers' grim preparations close-up. "Show's over. Out of my trenches," the captain said.

"But we want to get this," Kate pleaded. She was outraged. Artillery shells cut through the air overhead. They exploded on a ridge a mile away. Kate flinched at the loud booms. *"Besides!"* she yelled, stopping the man. "It's probably too dangerous out there already."

"What's too dangerous is what's comin' this way! Now, lady, there's *no* way—*no* how—you're stayin' here!" He left.

"What an asshole!" she said. Men laughed. They all stood on or near their fighting steps. Woody's camera whirred. More shells rumbled through the sky. She ran out in front of Woody, having to rely on the camera's built-in mike. "Have you been told what is happening?" she asked a soldier. "We were told the Chinese were thirty miles from here."

"One of our patrols ran into one of their patrols," he said. He kept turning to look at the camera. "It's just sorta . . . escalatin'."

"But how could they get so close without us knowing? With satellites and spy planes and—"

"There's only one way to know where the enemy is, ma'am. That's to bump into him. That's what patrols do. That's how we know they're comin'."

Kate glanced to make sure Woody got the sound bite. He wasn't there! "Shit!" she snapped. She found him around a turn in the zigzagging trench. He was hovering above the German advisor and two kneeling Americans. Their heads bowed. Their eyes closed. One was muttering Hail Marys. One clenched a tiny, homemade cross—short strips of leather bound by string.

Kate couldn't help herself. She balled up her fist and pumped her arm in the air. *Yes!* she thought. Before they got to the Humvee, she'd composed the words for her voice-over.

16

Normally Clark wasn't much for theatrics, but he was play-ing this for all it was worth. He'd left most of his senior officers out of the planning. He'd been ordered to wait until the last ally had committed. That had occurred the night before. "Are they all there?" he asked Major Reed, who nodded. Clark took a deep breath, tugged down on his BDU blouse, and straightened his back. He turned to ensure that his aides all stood ready behind him. "Okay, let's do it."

He opened the door and entered. Conversations in a half-dozen languages fell quiet as the national commanders of the various UNRUSFOR contingents turned their attention to the procession of American officers. Clark was at its head. As he sat, his aides arrayed easels in a semicircle behind him. The maps remained covered with an opaque plastic sheet.

"Good morning, and thank you all for coming," Clark began. "I am fully aware of the internal debates each of you has been having with your capitals ever since I returned from Washington. And I apologize for not consulting with you earlier. But I am also informed that your political lead-

Operation Winter Harvest
Anticipated troop dispositions on Z-Day

Sea of
Okhotsk

R u s s i a

Svobodnyy
XXX
I BaroCorps

II BaroCorps
XXX
XXX
III Corps
Urgal

Shenyang
Army
Group
(North)

Komsomolsk

XXX
I Corps

Beijing
Army
Group

Birobidzhan
Airbase

Khabarovsk

Amur River

Vanin

Jinan
Army
Group

Jiamusi

Amur River

Shenyang
Army
Group
(South)

©China

Harbin

Tatar Straits

Zeda
Khanka

XXX
Tibetan
Amphibious
Corps

Suifenhe

Ussurisk
XXX
Wild Airborne
Corps

Vladivostok

Yalu River

North
Korea

Sea
of
Japan

Hokkaido

J a p a n

Honshu

| Miles | 0 | 50 | 100 |
| Kilometers | 0 | 81 | 161 |

ership and mine have agreed to broad strategic plans for prosecution of this war to its conclusion. Therefore, I am here this morning to issue the operation order. The plan's code name is Winter Harvest.''

Clark could hear the theater map being uncovered behind him. Reed had hit his cue perfectly. Everyone's eyes turned to the map. To the two sweeping blue arrows stabbing deep into the heart of Manchuria.

''To put it simply,'' Nate said, ''we will marshal and hold in reserve every soldier and weapon that arrives in-theater from this point forward. We will hold our current lines with units currently in the field. And in a little under two months we'll strike the Chinese with everything we've got.''

He didn't tell them the deadline for the counterattack was April 14. After all, he reasoned, Davis could be convinced of a better time, if necessary. But he knew he'd made a pact. Davis was issuing statements vigorously defending Nate. Neither Ferguson nor Dekker had interfered much in his planning.

Reed stood at the map wielding a pointer. He'd gotten little sleep the past week. ''The first column,'' Nate began, ''will move west from Vladivostok toward Kirin, China. The second will move south from the Trans-Siberian Railroad west of the city of Urgal. Its objective is also Kirin. The objective of Winter Harvest is to pocket the entire offensive threat of the People's Liberation Army between the twin pincers . . . and destroy that threat.''

Heads turned. ''Any questions?'' Clark asked.

''How will we maintain operational security?'' the British deputy commander asked. ''The world press is running rampant throughout the theater.''

''Our strategic deception plan,'' Clark answered, ''is this—we are defeated. We are barely clinging to our positions. We are reeling under the weight of unstoppable Chinese assaults. Our troops are dispirited and demoralized. In short, they pose *no*,'' Clark said slowly, ''offensive threat whatsoever. That shouldn't be too much of a leap for our news media to make.''

There was laughter—a release of pent-up, nervous tension.

"The Chinese will know," the Dutch commander commented. "They won't be swayed by news reports."

"We intend," Nate replied, "to begin vigorously demonstrating against China from the sea. We'll sail U.S. Marine amphibious forces up and down the Chinese coast. Put SEAL teams on their beaches. They'll gather intell on beach gradients, sand firmness, minefields, troop dispositions. Only one of those landing ships, however, will be loaded with marines. It will also carry the press."

Amid the laughter, a British officer noted, "The empty ships will ride high in the water."

"We'll offload the marines and equipment at Vladivostok. They'll fight with the southern prong of the advance into China. We'll load Russian trucks filled with rocks as ballast."

"Where will you hold landing exercises for the press?" the grinning German officer asked.

"Korea. It'll be the best-trained amphibious assault battalion in Marine history." More laughter. "In addition to achieving strategic surprise, we hope to tie down at least thirty Chinese divisions along the coast."

"What will the dummy target be?" the French general asked.

"Hong Kong," Clark replied.

"What about the flanks of the main attack?" the French general asked. It was a far more serious challenge. He waggled his finger at the twin arrows, which extended far into northern China. "You don't seem to broaden the neck of those advances at all. Once UNRUSFOR crosses the Amur and Ussuri into China—*if* we can cross it—the PLA is going to pull everything back. Those troops will be positioned to attack straight into the flanks of our advances."

"*We* will make it across the rivers," Clark replied. "The Chinese won't. We will put at least one armored corps across in each prong before the ice breaks. Once the ice breaks, my engineers tell me that no bridging equipment made can stand the flow. The People's Liberation Army will be stranded on the Russian side for ten days. In those ten days we will win the war.''

THE KREMLIN, RUSSIA
February 29, 0900 GMT (1100 Local)

When Kartsev returned from the bathroom, he froze in the door to his office. Someone had been there. A letter sat in the middle of his desk chair. All was still.

He chided himself for being so anxious and walked around to his desk. He returned to his running, subvocal conversation with himself—half mumbled aloud—but then looked up startled. For a moment he thought he'd seen the door open a few inches.

He tried to steady himself. Why worry about such things? No force on earth could change the outcome if his complex system of reward and terror failed. *Besides*, whispered a voice, *that end is inevitable*.

Kartsev smiled. It was a voice with which he was well acquainted. It had been his counsel on many a long, cold Siberian night. Most people, he knew, shut out those awful whispers that arose from the dark recesses of their minds. Kartsev, however, listened attentively. They had served him well, for they spoke terrible truths. Truths about the nature of man. About himself.

The envelope lay in the seat of his chair. It was thick and unopened. He never opened his own mail. He never received anything personal. At the very least he hoped they'd X-rayed the letter. People could make bombs out of the most innocuous and compact packages.

There was no return address, just Kartsev's typed name. He opened the letter. It was from the president of the United States.

Kartsev settled into his chair with a smile.

After reading and then rereading the letter, he slipped out of his shoes and lifted his stockinged feet onto his desk. *Well argued*, he thought as he reclined with his computer keyboard in his lap. The man has a well-ordered mind. He proceeds logically from point A to point Z, connecting all his arguments in between.

"But, alas . . ." he said to no one. He typed the short reply himself.

> Dear Mr. President. Pardon so informal a reply to your letter, but I find E-mail suits my needs best for the moment. With respect to your reasoning as to why I should relinquish my role as ideologean for the "Anarchist Movement," I must say that I find your logic to be impeccable. I am certain the world would be a better place if I were to do as you requested . . . from where you sit. However, we do seem to find ourselves with slightly divergent interests, don't we? As for your appeal to my patriotism in reference to the war in Siberia against China, might I remind you what anarchy stands for?
>
> The border over which you fight is an arbitrary line demarcating the limits of power presently exerted by two competing systems of human tyranny. The concept of a "nation" is itself what anarchy is meant to abolish. You are the leader of the strongest nation on earth. You may draw whatever conclusions you wish from that about my desire to cooperate with your government.
>
>   Sincerely, Valentin K. Kartsev.

Without so much as a second read, Kartsev hit "send." After a momentary delay his message was at the White House.

So easy, Kartsev thought. He then resumed his writing with newfound vigor.

BETHESDA NAVAL HOSPITAL, MARYLAND
February 29, 2130 GMT (1630 Local)

"So this is it?" Gordon Davis asked as he took the sheaf of papers from the young White House counsel. There was

a select and oddly diverse gathering there to witness the
event. In addition to Gordon's personal lawyer, he had in-
vited the chief justice of the Supreme Court, the chairmen
of the two houses' intelligence oversight committees, and
the director of the CIA . . . of course.

Gordon leafed through the pages until he found the section entitled "Findings." "Based upon the best evidence
available," Gordon read, "Subject is responsible for planning, training, and directing over 147 acts of international
terrorism leading to 429 dead and 238 wounded." The second paragraph levied new charges. "National intelligence
sources estimate that Subject has personally ordered the
murder of over 1,200 of his own citizens. In addition, his
repressive state security apparatus has summarily executed
between 10,000 and 60,000 civilians." On and on the allegations went. "Subject's crimes against humanity also include instigation of a civil war which left over 100,000
dead and another 160,000 wounded."

The sheer weight of the numbers was numbing. Was 429
dead from terrorism somehow more heinous a crime than
100,000 Russian dead from war? Why else was it that such
a small number warranted anything more than a footnote?
But it would've been a footnote that included heads of state.
Members of Marshall's cabinet. Phil Bristol. And twice,
almost, Gordon himself. Everyone in the room watched
him. Gordon didn't need to read on, but he did for appearances' sake. The grounds for the Executive Order grew
more shaky. "Subject personally ordered policies leading
to starvation and disease that have claimed upward of
300,000 lives." Gordon would have left out that count. It
sounded like bad economic policy even though he knew it
was ethically equivalent to the most loathsome of criminal
acts. And then he came to the last paragraph on the single
summary page. "Subject is the motive force behind the
spread of an ideology that debases human institutions and
values and seeks to undermine the moral and ethical pre-
cepts from which democratic governments derive their legitimacy."

Gordon looked up at his counsel. "I want this last paragraph out," he said. Heads dropped to read.

"All right, sir," the lawyer replied. "We were just giving you the full menu."

"And you might as well take out the paragraph before it about starving his people."

"Well, sir, that one isn't legally distinguishable from the paragraph preceding *it*. Instigation of civil war is as accepted a crime against humanity as a war of aggression."

"All of which," the chief justice intoned, "are based on *dubious* jurisprudential reasoning."

Gordon's lawyer didn't reply.

"Why not just stick with the first couple of paragraphs?" Daryl Shavers proposed. "We got him dead to rights on international terrorism and mass murder of his own people."

"I agree with Daryl," Gordon said, taking a pen and striking everything but the first two paragraphs.

"We do have some evidentiary problems with even that intelligence," Gordon's personal lawyer pointed out.

"Look," the director of the CIA said impatiently, "I *know* this has to be done legally, but do the words really matter so much? Can anyone dispute the fact that the son of a bitch is a mass murderer?"

"Done," Gordon said to cut the debate short. He flipped to the signature page. "By order of Gordon Eugene Davis," he read out loud, "president of the United States of America, be it hereby resolved and directed that Valentin Konstantinovich Kartsev be apprehended and brought to trial or, failing apprehension, executed by appropriate means and in a manner designed to cause minimal collateral damage."

"*My* counsel," the CIA director interrupted, "has *real* problems with that phrasing, Mr. President."

Gordon looked up at White House counsel. "We have to try to apprehend Kartsev *first*?"

The young man shrugged. "If the opportunity presents itself . . ."

"There'll *be* no opportunity," the CIA director snapped. "The bastard never leaves his *office* anymore! Even his *aides* don't see him." He turned to Gordon. "Hell, sir. I don't even know how we're gonna do it, much less 'by *appropriate* means and in a manner designed to cause minimal *collateral* damage.' Now, what the hell does *that* mean?"

White House counsel bristled. " 'Appropriate' means you can't pour hot *lead* down his throat!"

The rotund CIA director squinted. "What in God's name are you *talking* about?"

"I'm explaining that first *clause*."

"Are bullets 'appropriate means'?" the director asked. The lawyer pursed his lips and nodded. "Explosive devices?" Again Gordon's counsel nodded, a little more slowly this time. "Incendiary devices?" The question drew hesitation and the beginnings of a shrug. "Poison? Garrote? Gas? Ice pick in the ear? Electric charge in a door handle? Prolonged exposure to microwaves? Accumulated doses of iridium? Biological contamination of the Kremlin water supply?"

"You see," the lawyer responded, "this is why we went with the generic language 'appropriate means.' It's impossible for me to say which of the ways Subject could be executed would or wouldn't be acceptable."

"You *wrote* the goddamn language!" the CIA director burst out. "If *you* can't tell me what it means, how the *fuck* can *I* figure it out!" He turned to Gordon. "He's trying to hang CIA out to dry."

"That's enough!" Gordon snapped. "Here's what we're gonna do." He raised his pen and drew a line straight through the middle of the words. "What if we say, 'By order of me, et cetera, et cetera, be it hereby resolved and directed that Valentin Konstantinovich Kartsev be executed'—period."

White House counsel reluctantly assented. The director said, "I love it."

Gordon pointed his finger straight at the smiling CIA

man. "Now I want to tell *you* that I *personally* want to approve every aspect of that operation. I don't want to be surprised, do you read me?" The director nodded. Gordon signed the Executive Order. "You make the changes and I'll sign a new one for the files." He handed it to the lawyer. "And good job. I appreciate somebody trying to cover my ass." There was polite laughter. "Now what's the plan?" he asked the director.

With apologies the man politely cleared the room. When he and Gordon were alone, he said, "We have an asset— somebody who can get close to Kartsev."

"Who?" Gordon asked.

"A Russian ex-pat—former head of presidential security—living illegally in Philadelphia."

PHILADELPHIA, PENNSYLVANIA
February 29, 0245 GMT (2145 Local)

Olga and Pyotr walked arm in arm from the movie theater. It was one of the few times they'd gotten out for an evening on the town. The girls, they finally decided, could be trusted not to tell a baby-sitter everything. But just in case they hired their neighbor's thirteen-year-old daughter.

The downside to choosing the oblivious teenager was that she spent the entire evening on the phone.

"I should try calling again," Olga said as they stood under the bright marquee lights.

"Darling, if she's on the telephone it means she's there. Everything's okay. *Ladno?*"

She wasn't satisfied. But he'd bought enough time to make it to the restaurant for coffee and dessert. There would be a pay phone there. The busy signal sure to come from it would provide a topic for the next thirty minutes of conversation.

The crowds thinned. The streets darkened. Olga was too busy silently fretting to notice the subtle change. But Pyotr grew more and more alert. He hadn't seen the government car that usually shadowed him.

"Pyotr Andreev?" they heard from behind.

Olga gasped. She lowered her head and jammed her eyes shut.

But the accent was distinctly American.

Pyotr turned. Two men in dark overcoats stood behind him. A parked car turned on its headlights. It pulled up beside them. It was unmarked. But to Pyotr it may as well have had "U.S. government" printed on the door.

"It's all right," he said quietly to Olga.

"And what is this 'business' you're talking about?" Pyotr asked.

The man across the small table in the suburban house flicked his cigarette repeatedly.

"It's an operation," he said as if he were breaking significant new ground.

But to Pyotr it was stating the obvious. He drew a deep breath and looked around the room. It was dimly lit except for the bright light over the table. The other agents all loitered at a distance.

"What kind of operation?" Pyotr asked.

There was again a long delay. The talker took a drag of the cigarette. He slowly exhaled. "A foreign operation," he said, each syllable accompanied by puffs that were lit by the warm overhead bulb.

It was almost midnight. Olga would be home worried sick. "Can you be more specific?"

The man had seen too many old movies. He took his time replying. "No," he finally said.

It's in Russia, Pyotr surmised. *And it's so dirty they won't talk about it till I sign on.* "I'd like to help, bu—" he began.

"Good," the man interrupted. "We thought you'd appreciate your position."

Pyotr heard the thudding threat. He sat forward. His weight rested heavily on his elbows. He raised his voice for the microphone—wherever it was. Maybe someone out there was listening. "I have a wife and kids. My first duty is to them. If you're proposing that I take some personal risk, then I cannot help. My wife and children need me . . . *alive*."

Again there was smoke. Only this time the wait was sheer agony for Pyotr.

"All right," the man then said. He reached into his pocket. The agent shoved a card across the table. Pyotr began to breathe again. "If you change your mind, call that number anytime." Pyotr eyed the card without reaching for it. "We can help . . . with things," the man said. "Certain legalities . . . like citizenship." Pyotr couldn't tell whether the man was dangling a carrot or wielding a stick. Probably both. "And I wouldn't take too much time thinking it over."

Pyotr took the card from the table. The agents drove him home. He was shocked that they had simply made a request and then let him go home.

Olga wasn't. "It's *America*!" She clutched him joyfully to her chest. "Everything is different here!"

Pyotr decided not to tell her about the veiled threat. She was too in love with her new home.

FORT CAMPBELL, KENTUCKY
March 1, 1600 GMT (1000 Local)

"This morning we'll teach you tactical rappelling!" the sergeant shouted to André's class. "Heliborne insertion into an inaccessible landing zone!" He turned to the helicopter around which the class sat, and picked up a rope. "Pay attention, 'cause in about one hour you *will* be descending from *this* helicopter to the ground one hundred feet below!" The young trainees fidgeted nervously, but André almost choked in fear imagining himself hanging beneath the helicopter with people shooting at him. "This afternoon we'll go over 'Stabilized Tactical Airborne Body Operations'! In STABO insertions, four of you are suspended side by side underneath the helicopter from hundred-foot ropes and flown to the drop zone!"

There was a snicker.

"You got a problem with that, soldier?" shouted another NCO. "You had better realize that if you get that Air Assault Badge, you're headed for the 101st Airborne Division (Airmobile). You ever heard of the Screaming Eagles? D day! Operation Market Garden! The Siege of Bastogne! The Tet Offensive! Hill 937! You ever heard of *Hamburger* Hill? Well, this is the home of the men who fought there!"

The rappelling instructor raised an all-important "D" ring and ran again through the procedures for attaching a personal harness to it. They had been taught how to rappel on a tall wooden tower, but André was relieved when they went back over everything, especially how to clamp down on the twin ropes to control their rate of descent. The forty-five minutes of instruction seemed like forty-five seconds. "All right, then!" the sergeant shouted abruptly. "Everybody *up!*"

The trainees all looked at each other. *Just like that?* André thought. The helicopter's flight crew, which had been quietly checking out the aircraft, were now strapped into the cockpit. André's class rose. Instructors made their way through, tugging on the harnesses the men wore. The engines began to whine and the rotors turn. "Mount up!" the instructor shouted. The twelve scared trainees climbed through the open side door. By the time they were all aboard, the wash from the rotors was at gale force. André sat on the hard metal floor. With a lurch, the helicopter began to move forward. The grassy field rushed by not five feet beneath them. André felt the rise in his gut. The helicopter banked quickly, turned, and pitched nose-up. The muscles from André's stomach to his shoulders were clenched tight. He had trouble drawing a breath. The helicopter settled into a hover. Below, dozens of aircraft and their trainees filled the open field. The noise of the rotors and the wind that roared through the open doors was deafening.

"When you get to the ground," the instructor shouted, "clear the LZ and set up a perimeter!" André wasn't ready.

He was terrified. "Okay!" The instructor clapped a guy hard on the shoulder and jerked his thumb toward the door. André felt a tap on his shoulder. Another instructor waved him to his feet. There were two instructors. Two ropes. Two open doors. "Let's go!" the instructor shouted.

André struggled to rise, but gravity tugged at him. When he finally stood beside the instructor, the man pressed the spring-closed bar on the "D" ring and wove the two ropes into André's harness. He briefly went back through the principles that would keep André from plummeting to his death. "You ready?" André nodded. "You'll love it! It's better'n sex!" He ushered André to the edge. The void loomed at the tips of his combat boots. It was a hundred feet down to the green field.

"Turn around!" the instructor ordered. "Back up to the door!" André turned carefully. The instructor held the ropes out to him and he gripped them with all his might. "Lookin' good! Now back up!" There was a cliff behind him. André could feel it. The wide-eyed soldier opposite him took baby steps, inching his heels closer to the edge with an instructor shouting in his ear. André slid his boots back without lifting them, and there it was—the edge. He could feel it through the thick soles. A distinct boundary beyond which lay nothing but air. His heels hung out, but his toes still solidly gripped the deck.

"Okay, son! Just lie back!" No matter how hard he tried, André couldn't bring himself to lean backward out the door. Inside the helicopter were the pallid faces of his sickly class. Outside were spinning rotors, a roaring engine whose hot exhaust lapped at his face, and a constant downwash of freezing winter air. "We don't have all day, Private!" the instructor shouted. André saw his counterpart across the cabin sort of sitting out in space. His knees were bent and he kept almost losing his footing, but he managed to struggle back inside and start the process over again with the now livid instructor hounding him loudly.

André let the rope slide through his gloved hands and leaned back. It was only a few inches, but he had crossed the imaginary line between inside and out. The dark green fuselage framed the world of his classmates a million miles away. The guy who'd been opposite him was unhooking and another trainee—a woman—was taking his place. "You're almost there!" the instructor yelled, motioning for André to keep going. He let more rope through his cramping hands until he looked up at the whirring rotor and at the pilot, who had twisted around and looked back from under a large green helmet and black visor. A few more inches of rope and he was reclined almost level with the floor—past the point of no return. A few more . . . and his feet lost their grip and he fell. He grabbed the ropes, stiffened his legs, and hung suspended in air beside the wheels. He tentatively loosed his grip and fell at a dizzying pace before clamping down again. When he looked up he saw the instructor's thumbs-up and the woman's butt protruding from the door.

Down he went in five- and ten-foot drops, every gut-wrenching free fall too fast. But by the time he was halfway to the ground it was the easiest thing in the world. He hung for a moment in the relative peace. The woman was clinging to the rope, even with the wheels. André zipped all the way down with a flourish and landed with a springy thud on his feet. He grinned broadly at the waiting instructor.

"You're under fire, asshole!" the man shouted, peppering André's chest with backhanded blows.

André acted out his part in the pretend battle. He released the ropes from the "D" ring, ran to the edge of the landing zone, dropped and raised his empty M-16. He even lined up an imaginary target—a fire hydrant by the parking lot. "You're under fire, sweetheart!" André heard the instructor shout. The female soldier dove to the ground next to him and shouldered her rifle with a broad grin. "That was easy as *shit*!" she said. "Air assault, buddy!" she said, raising her hand high to André. He slapped it with a flourish, half expecting the instructors to explode in shouts. But the NCOs turned their attention to the next trainee.

ABOARD F-117A, OVER HARBIN, CHINA
March 7, 1600 GMT (0200 Local)

Major Lauren Russell flew the F-117A Nighthawk straight and level ten thousand feet over the sprawling industrial city of Harbin. It was a clear night, but the city lights had been extinguished and all was dark. There was no doubt, however, that she'd arrived over her target. Global positioning signals beamed by satellite gave her her location within five meters of accuracy. The amber triangle representing her aircraft on her navigation/attack screen straddled her course line. Up ahead, the line bent—her final turn to target.

Suddenly tracers rose into the air ahead, followed almost immediately by "Triple A"—antiaircraft artillery—being fired randomly into the sky from every quarter of the city. The night was no longer dark. It flamed with brilliant displays of fireworks, which would have been beautiful had they not been deadly. They must have heard her twin, non-afterburning turbofans as she passed over Harbin's outskirts and given an order to fire blindly skyward. Unfortunately for Russell, her route took her straight through a thicket of crisscrossing white tracers and clusters of fireworks left by large, prefused cannon rounds. All around the burning embers of the heavier shells were lethal spheres of expanding shrapnel.

It took all Russell's willpower to stay the course as balls of fire bloomed in her path. She had to make a choice, and one thing the F-117A gave you was time to think. The indicator on her heads-up display read 460 knots. If she'd been flying an F-15E Strike Eagle from her old squadron, she'd have been doing Mach 1.5 at treetop altitude listening to the blaring tones from threat warning receivers. Russell could still hear the radar paints, but their volume had been turned way down. They were only a remote threat to the stealthy F-117A. Maybe if she passed directly over a Chinese radar, it might paint its multifaceted fuselage. But with a radar cross section the size of a seagull, they couldn't track her for a kill.

Still, the pointed nose led straight into a solid ball of flame. She knew it was just an illusion. There was nothing solid about the sky in front. It was filled with empty spaces, but she experienced an almost overwhelming desire not to risk it. She was a "stick-and-rudder" woman, and it went against her every instinct not to bank clear of the danger and then reacquire the target visually. But years of training for just such a mission bound her to the course. Her grip on the stick grew tight. The cockpit lit with strobes of soundless lightning. Tracers streaked past the flat-paned canopy. Long glowing strings formed a "golden BB." Russell flew straight into the thick of it. Her heart skipped with each and every burst. She cringed as gunners slewed their weapons every which way and looping chains of tracers swung by her. A spotter had presumably heard her engines, and they now fired with wild abandon.

She heard nothing but a steady whine and the soft tones of her nav/attack system. They reminded her to begin her descent to point-blank bombing altitude. Russell cut the throttle, lowered the nose, and made a cruising descent while under furious fire from below. The radio was eerily quiet. Stealth aircraft needed no entourage. No aircraft packages for air defense suppression. No fighter escort. No AWACS controllers with their steady patter of warnings and contacts. Just one plane, one pilot, and two bombs . . . and a thousand Chinese guns all firing blindly in air. Flame shot from the ground as a missile rose with astonishing speed. In less than three seconds it flashed by on a ballistic trajectory. The heat seeker could find no heat. The Nighthawk's inboard engines, platypus exhausts, and twin butterfly tails reduced its infrared emissions to near zero. The missile detonated harmlessly thousands of feet overhead.

But a loud knock and a slight roll got Russell's full attention. It sounded like a rock striking the undercarriage of a speeding car. The warning lights, however, remained dark. The digital fuel gauge ticked off consumption pound by pound. Russell took a deep breath of pure oxygen and exhaled slowly. *Must've been a spent round falling back to earth*, she thought. *Or a bird startled to flight by the guns.* The sky grew dark again. She was through the wall of fire. Another tone announced her arrival at five thousand feet. Another sounded shortly thereafter at the last heading change—a thirty-degree turn to the left.

In the dim starlight, the tall smokestacks rolled into view. Russell could've flown by sight and released her bombs visually from there if she'd had to. But the planners had chosen the two release points very carefully. The first bomb was destined for the tailgate of a production line for 155-millimeter artillery shells. The shells were loaded there onto trucks and carted away. Russell's two-thousand-pounder would fly straight into the loading dock. The explosion should rip into the plant from its one unhardened Achilles' heel. The second bomb would fall straight through an air shaft into an underground explosives bunker.

Russell had little to do now. The computer would open the bomb-bay doors just before release. The carefully designed lines of the stealth aircraft would be disturbed, and it was then that enemy radars would have their best chance. Russell shut the thought from her head as she eyed the looming smokestacks. The computer automatically handed off targeting from the forward-looking imager to the downward-looking imager. Russell—the computer's backup system—kept her thumb on the bomb-release ''pickle'' and her eyes on the nav/attack screen. When the range to the first release point hit zero, the bomb-bay doors flew open and the computer released a bomb. The aircraft floated upward but remained straight on line. Russell corrected the altitude. The bomb rode a laser beam fired from under the nose down toward the aim point. The range numbers to the second target all reset instantly. Almost as soon as Russell digested the new readout, it came time to drop the second bomb.

A brilliant flash lit the instrument panel and dash. Russell hit the pickle a split second after the computer release just in case, and again the F-117A soared. She rolled the ship on her side and jammed the throttle to the stop. The bomb-bay doors thudded shut. A second and brighter flash lit the night. As the plane banked, she saw the blazing display. The entire factory was rapidly being engulfed in flame. When she returned the F-117A to straight and level exactly on her egress heading, the sky was lit repeatedly by explosions from her first bomb. The target area of her second, however, remained dark and still. In the light from the flames, however, Russell noted black smoke jetting from the air vents with such force that it looked like the exhaust from a revving engine.

Russell blipped the prerecorded "Mission Accomplished" message back to the 49th Fighter Wing. She then settled peacefully onto the course that led back to the sea. There were more guns firing now than before, but her windshield was dark and clear.

AMUR RIVER, SIBERIA
March 10, 1600 GMT (0200 Local)

The moon was full. The cloudless night was brutally cold. They had lain still and quiet for three hours, buried in thick banks of snow at the Amur River's edge. There had been no sound, no movement, no sign of the Chinese.

Captain John Hadley rose first. One after the other his "A" detachment of eleven U.S. Army special forces crawled from the snow in rapid succession. The nine NCOs and two officers didn't need to be told what to do. They deployed in a semicircle to give as much defense in depth as a twelve-man unit could. His two lieutenants approached Hadley in the darkness. The only sound was the squeaking snow.

Hadley and his two officers knelt. "I want this over with fast," Hadley said. He spoke in just over a whisper. "The clock starts when the first man's on the ice. Got that?"

There were two quiet "Sirs." Army shorthand omitted the implicit "yes." They were off. The snow was so dry that it reminded Hadley of the beach near his home town in Florida. The saccharine sand there squeaked loudly as you trudged across it.

There was some time spent assembling the equipment. But it was all done under the cloak of strict noise and light discipline—no sounds, no flashlights. Hadley searched the bends of the river in both directions. They had seen nothing of the armored cars that patrolled the flat ice pack. His two Dragon teams would have little trouble knocking them out. But one word by the vehicle's crew over the radio and he and his men were as good as dead. To get in, spend a day and night deep behind enemy lines, and get out depended not on his "A" team's ample firepower. Their survival relied one hundred percent on stealth.

Four men rose and headed onto the ice. One measured distance by rolling a large wheel at the end of a pole. The two behind him lugged the heavy drill between them. The fourth, a lieutenant, rode shotgun. His M-16 was raised high and at the ready. They all wore night-vision goggles, but Hadley chose not to don his. There was no need. The four figures threw shadows onto the ice from the bright moonlight.

Hadley took another nervous check in both directions. A single man sat hunched over earphones. He'd cleared snow from a patch of ice. He listened to the ice through a flat microphone for the sound of an approaching vehicle.

The man measuring the distance stopped. The distinct whine of an electric motor easily carried the distance. The tone sank nearly instantly as the bit hit ice. The operator kept its motor humming. He was wasting no time standing exposed in the center of the river.

The whine finally fell silent. The two men extracted the bit and took off running. Their bulky gear and heavy load slowed them to a lumbering pace.

They were breathing hard when they reached the bank. "Lemme see it," Hadley said. Two men hoisted the drill into the air. The stainless-steel teeth were covered in white shavings. Hadley brushed the slush clear and saw the four-inch-thick tube of solid ice. That core sample was the sole purpose of their mission.

"All right," Hadley announced, "let's get the hell outta Dodge."

Hadley felt relief at leaving the river behind. But egress was the most dangerous phase of all. They followed their tracks back toward the landing zone. A scar across the virgin snow. If it were snowing hard or blowing briskly, the tracks would be covered in a matter of minutes. But on relatively still nights—like that night—the deep indentations were a dead giveaway. For the only two-legged creatures in the woods were soldiers. If a Chinese patrol found the tracks, they'd either hunt them down or lie in ambush. The twelve-man detachment was strung out in a line over a hundred meters long. They pulled two-hundred-pound ahkio sleds filled with gear, weapons, and ammo.

The soldier in front of Hadley raised his right hand and knelt. Hadley and the men behind him did the same in rapid succession. Hadley turned to ensure that everyone was still and ready.

Ready for what? he wondered. It wasn't an ambush because they'd never see it coming. The woods would simply erupt in flame and screams of pain. A good number of his men would die in the first frenzied volleys. It would depend from there on reaction times, correct guesses, and luck. At ten meters separation Hadley had no chance of issuing orders. It would be every man for himself. Relying on training and instinct.

The man in front of Hadley rose and shoved the heel of his hand toward the sky. Everyone rose, made the same hand signal, and moved on. *He must've seen shadows*, Hadley thought. *Or mounds in the snow. Fallen trees. A ghost in his peripheral vision.* Walking point did a number on your head.

BUREYA MOUNTAINS, SIBERIA
March 12, 0000 GMT (1000 Local)

Lieutenant Chin led his eighteen remaining men down a winding path. Snow drifted to the earth amid tall hills. Were it not for the tire ruts, the road would have been indistinguishable from the surrounding landscape. It was a flat gouge out of the flanks of the undulating earth.

At least the wind is down, Chin thought as he pressed his aching legs on. All morning they had lurched forward under heavy direct fire. A hundred meters forward, and three men dead. They lay low for thirty minutes under whizzing machine-gun bullets. One wounded and left for dead as a result. Then another rush toward the shelter of a ledge. It turned out to be no shelter at all, as the enemy opened up from a previously silent position. Two dead. The enemy were like ghosts. They fired their weapons from such long range that Chin had never even learned whom he was fighting, much less been able to bring his platoon's small arms to bear. Rumor was that they were Germans, but they might have been British or French.

The entire time they were under fire, the wind had whistled past Chin's covered face. It had whipped snow and ice off the tops of drifts that stung his eyes and exposed skin. After a while the blasts of cold had seemed every bit as much a threat as the enemy . . . until, that is, the airstrike. Then everything had simply come apart. Chin could no longer hear the whistles from over the hill that were his only contact with company headquarters. His men began to rise and flee in bursts of panic timed between dives from enemy bombers. When Chin had risen to chase them—firing into the air over their heads—he was quickly overtaken by the rest of his platoon. Everyone took the opportunity to save their lives . . . Chin included.

And it did save their lives, he had to admit. Most of them, anyway. He had started the day with thirty-one men. Thirteen lay somewhere behind them, either dead or soon to be dead. The enemy never bothered collecting Chinese wounded. They fired from armored vehicles far away, pulled back under covering airstrikes, and set up again a few kilometers to the north.

"Did you see that guy in the tree?" one of his men asked from behind.

Chin didn't turn, but he kept his ears peeled. He'd had to fire over the heads of his fleeing men. The unpleasantness hung in the air between them.

"He must've been a sniper," another soldier ventured. "Got killed, but his gear kept him from falling."

"No. He wasn't strapped to the tree. He was hanging *over* the limb. He got *blown* up there! Did you see him? It blew his skin right off his *bones*!"

"Maybe he wasn't even Chinese," a third guy joined in. "Maybe he was American."

Everyone laughed. "*Yeah,* you dumb shit! How many dead Americans have you seen? One? Three? And how many dead Chinese?"

"A thousand," someone guessed.

"Oh, more than *that*. What about that grave?" Chin remembered the long cut in the earth. Men with white cotton masks had been pouring white powder over mounds of bodies. An army of men with shovels waited by the side of the hole.

"The Americans do it right," came from one of the men who'd spoken before. "They don't just piss their men away like last night's beer."

"Enough!" Chin finally shouted. He wheeled on the loose gaggle of men. They stopped in their tracks and eyed their platoon leader. Chin stood facing eighteen armed and brooding men. Men he'd fired shots toward not three hours earlier. He swallowed the lump of fear before continuing. "Keep quiet!" he shouted. He then tried to think up some reason why they should follow his order. "The Foreign Enemies might have microphones planted in the woods!"

There was a smattering of chuckles that almost brought the muzzle of Chin's Type 68 assault rifle around. "Keep quiet!" he shouted. He turned and proceeded down the path.

They walked for almost an hour before they saw another soul. Chin was looking for an alternate route, having decided the road led too far to the east, when shots rang out from the hill to their right.

"Drop your weapons!" a man ordered. Chin and his men all turned to see an officer waving a pistol from which hung a lanyard. "Drop them or we'll fire!" he yelled. Chin saw the other guns in the rocks pointed at the trail.

"We're Chinese!" Chin replied.

"You're under arrest by order of the supreme commander of the People's Liberation Army!" the pistol-toting officer shouted officiously. "Now drop your weapons or we'll open fire!"

"But why are we under *arrest*?" Chin challenged. He was suddenly outraged. "What the hell did we *do*?"

The arresting officer, who looked to be around Chin's age of twenty, seemed hesitant. "You . . . you are *deserters*! I have orders to arrest all deserters, and to shoot them on the spot if they resist!"

"We're not deserters!" one of Chin's men yelled. The officer turned his pistol and almost fired.

"Shut up!" Chin shouted at his man. Saving his life. Maybe all of their lives, judging from the number of weapons pointed their way. Chin saw too that his men's weapons were generally pointing toward the rocks. A single shot could be the spark that sent flames raging out of control. He turned back to the officer with the pistol. "We're not deserters. We're loyal soldiers. These are my men. I am their platoon leader. How can you have deserters when I— as their commanding officer—led them down this trail?"

He felt rather than saw his men's heads turn. They were watching Chin now. He felt a sense of pride in that fact.

"The enemy is *that* way!" the officer shouted, pointing back up the path down which they'd come.

"We *know* that," Chin replied. He was beginning to prevail, he felt, and he pressed home his advantage. "We've been fighting for the last three days straight. I lost thirteen of my men this morning." He raised his voice to address his real audience, the dozen or so men holding rifles pointed their way. "I lose thirteen men to the Americans," he said, choosing Americans to create the proper impression. "And now I'm going to lose *more* to my comrades-in-arms?"

No orders were issued, but the rifles in the rocks above pointed away.

The little man with the pistol, however, wouldn't let it

drop. "You are deserting your *unit*!" he screeched. "The enemy is *that* way!" he repeated. Again he pointed.

"But didn't you hear?" Chin asked. "The Americans got around *behind* us." He looked down the trail in the direction they were headed. He hoped that his irreverent men could keep from sniggering. "They swung around us and cut off the roads to our rear." The heads of the men in the rocks began to swivel. "Don't you have a radio?" Chin asked. The now sheepish officer replied that he did not. Chin knew then that he had won.

"And they have microphones in the woods," one of his men blurted out. Chin cringed in anticipation of laughter. But none came.

The man with the pistol suddenly seemed to grow anxious. He no longer was certain of his position. He looked around warily. And when he spoke, he did so in lowered tones. "How did they get behind us?"

Now, Chin thought, *for the capper*. "Tanks," he whispered, just loudly enough for all to hear.

The talking was now among his would-be captor's men. "Quiet!" the lieutenant shouted. He quickly checked all around for the enemy.

"Can we go now?" Chin asked.

The distracted man peered in both directions down the road. He craned his neck to look up the hill above his head. His stern warning to Chin was whispered. "Don't come back down this road again without signed orders! Do you understand?"

There were chuckles from Chin's men. Chin himself had to smile. He hadn't seen a written order since the war began.

They marched on. The talking and whispering resumed. When a single shot rolled over the hills from the distance, the grumbling grew more open. "Fuck them," someone said in a tone he obviously didn't mind being overheard.

At first Chin was incensed. But he reconsidered when he realized what it meant. They trusted him. They felt that he was one of them. People didn't openly criticize the government unless they were certain about everyone within earshot. And they certainly didn't say "Fuck them" about the army after hearing the execution of a deserter.

Chin stopped and turned to his men. They'd grown quiet after the comment. They all watched Chin intently and waited. "Be careful," he said in a reasonable tone. Chin turned to lead his platoon on. A grin lit his face that they couldn't see. For the first time he walked with his back to his men without fear. Without that keen sense of alertness to the danger they posed.

17

André straightened his tie before knocking. He could hardly keep the grin off his face. The peephole grew dark. There was a squeal and a metallic jangling of locks and chains. The door flew open.

"*Ba*-by!" Evelyn shouted as she leaped on her son. Her joy was so unrestrained that André started to cry even as he laughed. "My *baby*! My baby! My baby!" She twisted his neck and shook him from side to side. André's sisters came running. The family hug was all noise and celebration. His mom pulled back, smiling through tears, and said, "Look at you! All dressed up in that uniform!" She pulled André into the apartment. "Why didn't you call? What are you doin' home? I thought you was in Ko-rea."

"I was. I came home for more trainin'. I had a two-day leave, so I caught a flight home."

"Listen to you! 'Caught a flight'! Aren't you a world traveler! My little boy." She pinched André's cheek. He pulled free. "But you only got two days? Where you gotta be in two days?"

André hesitated. He turned away. "I gotta go back."

"Go back where?"

"To join up with my new unit." He glanced up at her. She was squinting.

"What kinda trainin' you been up to?" André shrugged. She grabbed his chin and forced his face up. "You answer me."

He pulled his chin free. "Air assault school. I'm now an air cavalryman. Instead of horses, we use helicopters."

Evelyn Faulk pushed through the girls, headed into the kitchen, and started cooking.

André followed. "Mama." She wouldn't turn around. "I got into First Brigade, 101st Airborne Division." His sisters trailed behind. "I wasn't in a good spot before. I was deliverin' the *mail*, Mama!"

"Ain't nothin' wrong with deliverin' the mail!" she said. She turned to him in anger. "Mr. High-and-Mighty! Who are you that deliverin' the mail ain't good enough for you?"

André shrugged. "I'm a soldier, Mama."

Her hands went to her hips. "A soldier? A soldier? You're *seventeen years old*! You ain't a *soldier*! You're a little boy playin' army." She threw her dishrag onto the counter. It slid all the way to the corner.

"But I'm good at it, Mama. I'm a good soldier."

She nodded, her mouth open. "You kilt anybody yet?" André shrugged. "You been shot at?" André rolled his eyes. "Answer me, boy! Have you shot your gun at another human bein' even once? Answer me!"

"No."

"So what makes you think you're a soldier?"

Her last words hurt André. His mother's hand rose to his cheek, and her head tilted. "It's the only thing I ever been, Mama," he said. She froze. When André felt the tears welling up, he got his hat and headed for the door. She grabbed his arm and pulled him back. The family hugged again, but not in joyous celebration.

NEAR ALDAN, SIBERIA
March 17, 2000 GMT (0600 Local)

"We've gotta drop off this load, Miss Dunn," the driver
said. He turned the wheel of the large truck and pulled to
a stop. "We'll meet you back here in one hour."

Kate and Woody climbed down to the deserted street of
the ramshackle village. The U.S. Army truck rumbled off.
When it was gone, all was quiet. There was no sign of life
anywhere. The entire town appeared to have been abandoned.

"Well," Kate said. She slapped her hands on her thighs.
"*This* is exciting."

"Hey, you wanted to go somewhere off the beaten path.
It doesn't get much farther off than this."

"Yeah, but . . . The point was to dig up a story." She
looked up and down the empty road. Nothing moved, not
even a stray dog.

"So let's go dig," Woody said. He took off walking past
buildings whose windows were blackened. By the time
Kate caught up with him, he was lighting a joint.

"Wo-o-ody," she chastised.

"*What?*" he snapped. Kate frowned as he pointedly took
a long toke, his cheeks sucked into his face. "What are
you?" he managed to say without leaking too much of his
precious smoke. "My mother?"

"I just don't like being the designated driver in the middle of a goddamn *war.*"

"Here, then," Woody said, holding the joint out to Kate.

She sighed and rolled her eyes. She walked up to the
small garden in front of a house that was deeply pitted and
burned. "Where are we going?" she asked.

"*I* dunno," Woody replied. He took a deep breath of the
frigid morning air. He wore a huge grin on his face.

"There's no story here," she said, looking all around.

"Sure there is, Kate. There's a story everywhere." He
stepped up on a low stone wall, balancing himself with his
hands out to the side. The joint was pinched between his
gloved thumb and index finger. "The White Army troops

came into town with their guns blazing.'' He held his imaginary machine gun up and trilled out a few rounds with his tongue. "Aaah!" he screeched in mock agony. "Lots of people died. There was blood everywhere. Two minutes of prime time—guaranteed! But with their black flags flying, the Anarchists beat the White Army back, slaughtering them by the *thousands*." Again he acted out the massacre. "Both sides were exhausted, and both tried to surrender to the other. In the end they decided to simply lay down their arms and go home. Right here, Kate, in this little village. Right here is where the collapse of Russia occurred.''

Kate looked at Woody, then at the meager collection of shacks along the side of the road. They were all burned and shelled out. "How do you know all that happened here?" she asked.

Woody shrugged and stepped down off the wall. "How do you know it *didn't*?" He relit the joint.

"*Jesus*, Woody!" She huffed, expelling her breath in a puff of white fog. "What do you propose we do? Give me the camera while you do a one-man dramatization of the Russian civil war?"

Just then they heard the heavy rumbling of a train. They both stared in the direction from which it emanated. Kate wandered through the yard of the abandoned house and to the edge of the snowy woods behind it. Woody followed. The supply truck with which they'd hitched a ride generally followed the rail line to the west from the port of Vanin. They'd seen several long trains hurtle past them on the five-hour ride. But the sounds to which they now listened were different. This train was stopping.

"Come on," Kate said. She trudged out into the deep snow of the woods.

"Hey, Kate," Woody called out from behind. She turned. "I'm not so sure this is a good idea."

"What? I just wanna go see why that train stopped."

"Yeah, but . . ." He faltered.

"But what?"

"What if they don't want us to see? I mean, UNRUSFOR put this whole area off-limits."

"So? You mean to tell me you're perfectly happy smoking *pot*," she said sarcastically, "but *tre-espassing! Well . . . !*"

"I'm not worried about getting busted, Kate. I'm worried about getting shot."

She laughed dismissively and turned. "We'll just be quiet and take a look over this hill." She labored through the snow with loud squeaks from her boots. Woody followed. She heard the flicking of his lighter and his renewed sucking on the ever-shortening joint.

It was slower going than she'd expected, especially during their ascent of the hill. The snow was up to her knees. Woody had to help her in some spots where she sank particularly deep. Finally, they reached the crest of the hill.

The rail line ran to the east and west for as far as she could see. About a quarter of a mile away, the train they'd heard sat parked in the middle of nowhere. At least seventy cars long, the train was brimming with military vehicles of every size and description. The only uniformity to its cargo appeared to be the two dozen flatbed cars in a row. They each had the same vehicle on top. M-1 main battle tanks, painted white. Car after car was loaded with the monsters. Their thick barrels were all pointed toward the rear.

Several people walked along the train's length. At first Kate surmised that it had broken down. It was parked in the middle of nowhere. The snow was particularly deep on the open fields to the sides of the tracks. All of a sudden the snowy ground started to open. The mound of snow parted, changing instantly Kate's perception of the world before her. The deep fields of snow became acres of tarpaulin as two men peeled back white fabric to reveal the artificial light inside.

"Holy *shit*!" Woody whispered. He raised the Minicam to his shoulder on reflex. It began to whir quietly. A large truck emerged from the opening towing a wedge-shaped green ramp. The men and vehicle gave everything a scale. The snowy field was in fact the polyurethane roof to a massive depot of some sort. The thick metal braces that

held the fabric aloft attested to the enormity of the subter-
ranean labyrinth.

Soldiers crawled over the tanks. One fired up an engine
with a puff of smoke. The engine's growl was audible despite the distance. Still more smoke belched from its tailpipes as the tank pivoted toward the ramp. The driver
nudged the tank forward. Its nose dipped and it descended
to the ground.

The tank disappeared inside the white cavern. Behind it
came other tanks.

The camera fell silent. Woody lowered it from his shoulder.

"Wait," Kate said, transfixed by sight of the earth consuming the massive stores of equipment. "I wanna do a
stand-up."

"Kate . . ." Woody began woodenly.

"I know, I know!" she interrupted. "But if I look like
a camera hog we'll edit it out. I just don't want the network
taking the raw footage and doing their own—"

"Kate," Woody interrupted, whispering.

She turned. A team of men moved silently through the
trees toward where they stood. Their weapons were raised.

BIROBIDZHAN FIREBASE, SIBERIA
March 17, 2000 GMT (0600 Local)

"Everybody *up*!" the platoon sergeant barked. For a moment Stempel thought he couldn't possibly move. He lay
at the bottom of a deep well of sleep. Fatigue pressed down
on him. Gravity tugged at every molecule in his body. Harold couldn't leave the warm womb of his bag. He coughed.
Pain shot through his head. His sinuses were parched from
the frigid air and bled constantly. His throat was raw and
eyes as dry as paper. The "army cough" was epidemic in
the bunkers and trenches.

The platoon sergeant shouted again. Stempel grabbed but
couldn't will himself to pull the bag's zipper. The bladders
of the air mattress were warmed by his body and softened

to a luxurious cushion. Half the men stayed at fighting posts
every night with weapons in hand. The other half were
roused only when an attack was under way. The previous
night, Stempel's squad was in the latter group and there
had been only one perfunctory assault. Beginning at first
dark, they would man the walls all night long.

The nights on trench duty were the worst. Bundled up in
an extra layer of clothing with your head covered with a
knit liner, helmet, and hood, he felt like he was in a cocoon.
He withdrew into his sluggish mind. Three nights earlier,
he'd been slouched in a fighting post cut out of the trench
wall along the outer perimeter. He'd peered out into the
open killing ground with his rifle on the sandbags beside
him. Although he was wide-awake and his eyes were open,
he saw nothing. He thought nothing. He felt nothing. When
the flares went up they illuminated a misty field full of
Chinese infantry. In the back of his mind he'd seen them
all along. But like all the machinery they'd brought to Siberia, his mind slowed in the cold.

He unzipped the bag. A freezing gush of cold air followed. He quickly donned his cold-weather gear. The body
heat accumulated from four precious hours of sleep was
totally lost. At the door men lined up with their injuries
requesting excused duty. First was a man with a terrible
"cold burn" where he'd grabbed a rifle barrel with bare
hands. He'd mistakenly thought it was his, but the cold-
soaked weapon had just been brought in after a night in the
open trenches. He was the only man the sergeant excused
from duty. The platoon sergeant handed Stempel a Snickers
bar for energy, and he exited the bunker through two layers
of tarpaulin frozen as solid as plywood. They blocked the
wind and masked the light, but they didn't hold in the paltry
heat from the chemical burners. Eight guys in a maintenance platoon had sealed their bunker off and were found
dead from the fumes the next morning.

It actually felt good to be in the fresh air. Stempel paused
to devour the candy before it froze. *Snickers for breakfast.*
Mom would be appalled. He joined his squad in the roomy

main trench fifty meters from the sleeping bunker. They all
slung their rifles over their shoulders and heads. They were
going out—probably to raise the wire above the latest
depths of snowfall.

Harold saw the trash bags. Every third man got one. He
counted as the squad leader neared. One, two . . . *Shit!* The
sergeant handed one to Stempel. *Shit!* He climbed over the
front wall into the flat light of the morning sun. Thick mists
limited visibility. The first men from the neighboring platoon were returning in pairs. The man in front carried the
head and shoulders, the man in back the feet. Stretched out
in between and hard as a board was a dead Chinese soldier.

"We oughta burn 'em for firewood," the tall Arkansan
next to Stempel said.

"It'd smell like shit," a wiry kid from Detroit replied.
Both men—one white, one black—looked the same inside
their mound of thick clothing.

"Why don't we just leave 'em out there?" asked Jumpy.
Stempel had never seen anyone so nervous. His mere presence had a calming effect on Stempel. Jumpy proved to
him again and again there was always someone more frightened than he was.

"When the thaw came, they'd rot," someone suggested.

"Naw, it's on account of wolves," came another view.
"They'd come lookin' for food." He loosed a laugh.
"That's just what we need on trench duty. To have to fight
fuckin' wolves every fuckin' night!"

"Snowdrifts!" they all heard from behind. They slowed
up to admit their squad leader. "The bodies would gather
snow. The drifts would fuck up our firing lanes and give
'em concealment. Plus, there'd be a health problem come
spring."

They passed men probing with long poles, searching for
Chinese snow tunnels. Harold's squad found the first bodies
lying in ranks where they'd been mowed down when machine guns suddenly opened fire. Ribbons of viscera. Contorted bodies in pools of crimson ice. Frozen forever in the
most grotesque and ridiculous of poses. It reminded Stem-

pel of an exhibit about Pompeii to which his parents had taken him as a child. He imagined these Chinese being buried in the permafrost and unearthed thousands of years later. Scientists would study their remains to discern how they lived and why they died.

"This one got hit so hard his *eyeballs* popped out," a squadmate commented. "Musta been a .50." He had a dozen automatic rifles slung over his shoulder. Some were American M-16s, which were surely from Stempel's lost battalion. "He's all yours, Stemp," the man said as he left with his load of weapons.

Stempel began to search for his bounty. Men grunted under the strain of their frozen cargo. "Here ya go, Stemp!" another of his squadmates shouted. He pointed at a brown crater before picking up a severed torso, which was light enough to carry unaided. Stempel went to the edge of the hole, which was rapidly filling with fluffy white snow. He tossed an index finger wrapped around an imaginary trigger into the bag.

In his mind, he was a scientist—a paleontologist—a long, long time in the future.

BETHESDA NAVAL HOSPITAL, MARYLAND
March 17, 2200 GMT (1700 Local)

"Thank you, Mr. President, for agreeing to meet with us," the anchorman said.

CBS, ABC, NBC, CNN—the anchors were almost invisible in the glare of the television lights. A film of perspiration had formed on Gordon's forehead and neck. He didn't want to mop his brow. The dreadful image of a wounded and weak chief executive would be beamed into every set.

Gordon lay in bed wearing a royal-blue robe. A gold presidential seal adorned his left breast pocket. The tubes, wires, and other medical paraphernalia had been moved away from the cameras' cruel, unblinking stare. All of the details of the interview had been thoroughly negotiated.

The number of cameras. Their positioning. Which could zoom in for close-ups. The format of the questioning. They had even obtained the network's agreement not to edit the interview or to lead into it with any editorializing about the war.

In fact, the restrictions imposed by the White House had themselves become a story. They had led to yet another onslaught of negative press.

The CBS moderator began. "By prior agreement, the first question will be from ABC." He turned to his counterpart from the rival network.

"Mr. President, the casualty figures from the war with China just announced by the Department of Defense are horrible. Three thousand two hundred and twelve U.S. servicemen dead, another seven thousand wounded or missing. The latest CNN/*Wall Street Journal* poll from *before* that announcement revealed that a striking seventy-two percent of Americans polled oppose the war. And reports out of our allies' capitals indicate that the governments there are making contingency plans for a hasty withdrawal from Siberia should the war take a turn for the worse."

"Is there a question in there somewhere?" Gordon interrupted as Fein had coached when the question turned into a speech.

"Is it your intention to announce the complete and total withdrawal of American forces from Siberia as has been rumored in Washington for days?"

"No," Gordon replied.

"Then you intend to continue the fighting?"

"That is my intention, yes."

"To what end?" the ABC anchorman asked.

"To win the war."

The man shifted in his seat then leaned forward. "But . . . why? What is the purpose of the war?"

"The Communist Chinese invaded Siberia, leaving us with two options: flee in the face of aggression and cede to China control over whatever territory it can grab by force, or not. It was not a war of our choosing, but once the die was cast those were our options. We chose the latter. We chose not to flee.''

"You say 'we,' Mr. President," the NBC News anchor joined in, "but it was really 'you.' Word out of your administration is that—almost to a man—no one outside your inner circle agrees with this war. To put it bluntly, sir, your people have been running for the hills. Putting as much distance between themselves and perhaps the most unpopular war in this country's history as they can. Given that, why are you, sir, so personally committed to a war that you could very easily have passed off as your predecessor's doing? You were, after all, a vocal opponent of President Marshall's deployment to Siberia in the first place.''

"We're fighting not because we want to, but because we *have* to. We're fighting because we cannot allow rogue nations to gain from aggression. We are the most powerful nation this earth has ever known. Our system of government is the wonder of the world. We do *not* shrink from punishing injustice. We will *not* back down from our duties as world leader. And first and foremost among those duties is to protect the weak from the strong. To punish aggressors who, despite all the lessons of history, still choose the path of blood, and death, and destruction to further their goals of domination over their fellow man.''

For a moment the four journalists were quiet. It was enough to prove to Gordon that he was right.

Even as the questioning continued, Gordon's optimism rose. The men before him were undeterred. They jabbed over and over, emboldened by the polls. But Gordon rested secure that a principle had been proven to his satisfaction. If you speak the truth boldly, people will listen. They will be forced to think, however briefly, about what it was you said.

UNRUSFOR HEADQUARTERS, KHABAROVSK
March 18, 0100 GMT (1500 Local)

Major Reed handed Clark the large-format videocassette. It was high-quality three-quarter-inch tape.

"They're in there, sir," Reed said. He opened the door and stood back. Clark entered the small room.

There was a woman at a table complaining nonstop.

"You should put *signs* up or something," she said to a military policeman. The ponytailed cameraman kept his eyes fixed on Clark.

"Is this the only tape?" Clark asked the man, who nodded.

"You're General Clark, aren't you?" the woman said. She rose and extended her right hand. "Katherine Dunn, NBC News." She waited. He stared back at her. She lowered her hand.

"Let's get one thing straight," Nate said. "We're not dealing with some petty violation of military security ground rules, here. We're not talking about suspending your press credentials and expelling you from the combat zone. You're both under arrest, if you haven't noticed."

The ponytailed man understood. But the female reporter challenged him. "On what charges?"

"Suspicion of espionage."

"*What?*" Kate exploded. "We're *journalists,* for God's sake!"

"Kate," Woody said, putting his hand on her shoulder.

"What?" she snapped at him, then twisted free of his grip.

Woody spoke in a calm voice. "Just listen to the man, okay?"

In the center of the table was their gear. In one of the pockets, Clark knew, the MPs had found marijuana. He looked first at the cameraman. "We have a problem, don't we?" Clark asked. He turned to Kate. "You two now know something. And, as journalists, to conceal is contrary to your every instinct. But to me, to conceal is to gain advantage. To deceive is an art." He stared straight at Kate now. "What you know could, if revealed, cost the lives of thousands of my men. I would do anything within my power to save their lives."

Kate felt Woody looking her way. She returned his look

with a shrug. "Just what is it we know that's so important? That you've got a secret base out in the middle of nowhere?" She shook her head, at a loss. Woody cleared his throat, which annoyed Kate. He was being overly defensive. "Just what do you want, General Clark?"

The man looked tired. He had a large frame, but it was slouched in the chair opposite her. There were lines in his face around bloodshot eyes.

"I want this tape, first of all," he said. He handed it to the officer standing next to him. "Secondly, I want your cooperation. I want your silence."

Kate listened until it was clear he had nothing more to say. "So . . . what? Do you mean, like, our *total* silence?" He nodded, and she chuckled. "Listen, General Clark, I *understand* the need for discretion. And I'd even understand if you just told us flat out what needed to be edited out of our report. But to just tell us to not *do* a report . . ." Kate felt she wouldn't need to complete the thought. But looking at the expression on Clark's face, she realized she would. "General Clark! I have no intention of jeopardizing the lives of your troops. But First Amendment rights still apply even during time of war. You can't just throw us into the *stockade* because we were going to air something you didn't want aired."

He stared back for a few moments in silence. "Are you telling me that imprisonment is the only way I can keep you from broadcasting a report on what you saw today?" he asked . . . carefully.

"Kate," Woody whined in a whisper.

"No, General Clark, it is not," she said, ignoring Woody. "There's another way." Both Clark and Woody waited. From their body language, it was clear that Woody waited with the greater interest. "I'd be *perfectly* willing," she continued pleasantly, "to work *with* you and your staff on this story."

Kate wasn't sure he had a clue what she was suggesting. "What *'story'*?" he asked.

She shrugged. "Whatever it is that's such a big secret,"

she replied nonchalantly. "I presume there's a day coming when it'll all become totally public. I'll agree that I won't air a word about any of this until that day comes. You can have guys with guns follow me everywhere. In return, you give me the whole story. Background, interviews, the opportunity to record everything—like your army historians do—so I can do a truly insightful piece . . . when the time comes."

Clark sat there, unblinking, for a moment. "All right," he replied quietly.

Woody let loose a loud sigh and relaxed.

"All right . . . what?" Kate asked warily.

"All right you can do that story. I'll give you the access you need to do it right. And you'll not breathe a word of anything till I give the go-ahead."

Judging from Woody's obvious relief, he was taking the offer at face value. But Kate was determined not to compromise her journalistic integrity. "I won't do a white-wash," she said firmly. "I won't propagandize or sugarcoat." Clark nodded, but she continued. "When I make a legitimate request for access, or ask a question to which you or anyone else knows the answer—"

"*About,*" Clark interrupted, "*this* operation—no others."

Kate considered the modification, then replied simply, "I want my questions answered."

Clark nodded again.

Kate sat up straight and shrugged. "Okay, then. Can we have our equipment and tape back now?"

Clark nodded at Major Reed. Their camera and cassette were returned. The cameraman at first protested when the reporter had him hoist the camera to his shoulder. But then the ponytailed man maneuvered around the table for a shot. "Go," he said finally.

"We're here in UNRUSFOR headquarters with Nate Clark, commanding general of UN troops. General Clark, what was it we saw under that camouflage covering today along the rail siding?"

She stuck the mike in Nate's face. "Equipment, ammunition, fuel," he answered.

"So . . . you're saying that those are ordinary supplies?" She felt the first twinge of disappointment at the deal she'd struck.

"Yes."

"Why, then, the extraordinary security precautions that you've taken around such an ordinary supply depot?"

Again the mike was dipped to Clark's chin. "Because of where those supplies are. They're much farther to the west than the Chinese expect them to be. And there are much larger stores building there than the Chinese believe there to be."

Kate didn't even know how to proceed. She considered briefly even abandoning that line of inquiry and just blurting out an unrelated question. But she tried once again. "Can you explain, General Clark, what those facts would tell a Chinese general that makes them so vitally secret."

"It would suggest that UNRUSFOR is planning a massive counterattack. It could be evidence that we are marshaling our supplies far to the west for a major offensive that would threaten to encircle the entire Chinese expeditionary force. It might cause the Chinese to moderate their advance and assume a more defensive posture instead of pressing on into what might be a trap."

"Are you . . . are you saying that UNRUSFOR is planning a major counteroffensive against the Chinese?" Kate asked, feeling a stir of excitement at the prospect. The stick mike hovered just in front of Clark's face.

"No," Clark replied. "I'm saying that intelligence would *suggest* those things to the Chinese."

"But . . . is it true? *Are* you planning a major counteroffensive?"

"Yes."

Kate regripped the mike, and then regripped it again. "Cut!" she finally snapped. She looked at Woody. He leaned out around the eyepiece. "General Clark," she said, "are you sure you want to *say* that?"

He shrugged. "You wanted the whole story."

"Yeah, but . . . All right." She nodded at Woody and raised the mike. "What is your plan?"

"To push south from our supply nodes along the Trans-Siberian Railroad, outrace the retreating Chinese, and cut them off at the Amur River, encircling them north of the river and winning the war before the spring thaw and flooding."

Kate's mind reeled with questions, but one was first and foremost. "Do you intend to enter the People's Republic of China?" she asked.

"No," Clark replied.

"Cut," Kate said, lowering the microphone. The faint whir of the camera fell silent. "Jesus," she murmured.

"Now you know," Nate said. He turned to Major Reed. "No calls, no contact with anyone outside our people, nothing. They can film anything they'd like, talk to anyone they want, but they're to be sealed off tight. Twenty-four-hour armed escorts everywhere they go." He turned back to Kate and Woody. "If they attempt to make any unauthorized contacts, the MPs orders are to stop them. They have my authority to use deadly force."

Kate looked back at him without flinching, not intimidated by his little show. "Anything else?" she asked.

"No pot."

"What?" Kate asked, laughing.

"Nobody smokes pot in my headquarters," Clark said.

"You think this place is bugged?" Kate asked as she walked through their underground quarters.

Woody was working intently on the camera. "No-o-o," he said, disparaging the notion. "These're military types, not spooks. They'll just shoot us if they don't like what we're doing."

Kate laughed at Woody's naïveté. "You don't really think they'd shoot us!"

"The hell they wouldn't!" he said, tightening some loose screw with a tiny tool. "That's what they're in the business of doing. It's bugging rooms that's not their thing.''

Clark had been generous in every way. They'd been given free run of the former Russian military base. Their ''quarters'' consisted of a large conference room off which their choice of four small bedrooms opened. On entering the underground room, Woody had locked the only door into and out of the room and tested the security of the bolts until satisfied. He'd then opened the door briefly and waved at their escorts just outside. They made no move to intrude upon their privacy even after Woody noisily relocked the door.

''We've been had, Woody. Clark suckered us in and then sprung the trap. Now this is basically over for us. Everything we learn from here on out is classified.''

''Uh-huh.'' Woody squinted and tilted his head this way and that, scrutinizing the inner workings of the Minicam.

''What are you *doing*?'' she asked as he pried open a circuit board with his screwdriver. His mouth remained open as he concentrated, his tongue sticking out between parted teeth.

''Got it!'' he said finally, removing a small baggy.

''Got what?'' Kate headed for the table but ended up following Woody toward the bathroom. ''What *is* that?'' Inside the small room, Woody motioned for her to close the door. She finally saw what he was unwrapping. ''Woody!'' she shouted.

''Shhh!'' he hissed back.

''But that's *pot*!'' He opened the plastic to reveal a round bundle of joints held tightly together by a rubber band.

''Like I said, they're soldiers. They're not spies, and they're *sure* not cops!'' He was grinning ear to ear over his little coup.

''Clark said no getting stoned!'' Kate reminded him.

Woody sat on the commode and flicked his lighter.

''Wo-o-od-y!'' Kate whispered through teeth clenched in anger. The tip of the joint glowed. ''You could get us in real trouble, *Woody*! This is the most totally stupid thing you could ever do!''

"Don't worry," he said with a grimace, smoke drifting from his pinched lips. He stood up on top of the toilet seat and exhaled slowly into a large vent. "These are air filters," he said. "This is a bomb shelter. They'll never smell a thing."

"Is this really worth it to you?" Kate asked in a plaintive tone. "Is getting high so goddamned important?"

"Well . . . *yeah*! Why do you think I go to so much trouble?" He toked hard on his joint.

"Why?" Kate asked.

Woody turned to her with a serious look on his face. He took his time again to exhale, eking out the maximum buzz for his buck despite having what appeared to be ample supplies. " 'Cause . . . I got a bad feeling."

"What could you possibly complain about *now*?" she asked. "We're at UNRUSFOR headquarters. Sleeping in a bomb shelter. How much safer does covering a war get?"

"And you'll stay here?" he asked, suddenly animated. "For the duration of the war? You'll agree to . . . to sit back and let the *biggest* military operation since I-don't-*know*-when go off while you twiddle your thumbs in this bunker?"

Kate shrugged. They'd only just gotten there. It was hard to say. "Clark didn't agree to us covering the actual offensive," she said. But already her mind was filling with the arguments she could make to him. She'd have an unprecedented understanding of the operation once it rolled around. She'd know exactly when and where the true drama of the story would play out. If she did a straight-up job on her reporting—maybe documentary-style—she might just earn Clark's trust. *A documentary*, she thought. The goose bumps rippled up her arms. *The* definitive *documentary on the Chinese War!*

What she lost was the immediacy of a scoop. A fleeting few seconds of nightly airtime. What she gained, however, was possibly a special. An hour—maybe even *two*—of exclusive, behind-the-scenes coverage of the biggest operation since whenever! It was perfect. Win or lose the battle, there was no need to manufacture the drama.

And the topper, she now realized, would have to be action footage. Not just any fighting, but the most crucial battle of the whole war. The most desperate, the most evenly matched, the most important. She'd remain on the lookout for that battle. Even though she knew nothing about military science, she was confident that one battle would stand out from all the others. She would talk her way into covering it. She just *had* to!

Woody drew another toke from his joint.

THE KREMLIN, MOSCOW, RUSSIA
March 21, 0830 GMT (1030 Local)

"Vasiliev," Kartsev read on the screen, "Lyudmila. Teacher in Kalina. Anonymous denunciation."

Anonymous denunciation? he thought. That wasn't enough. She was denounced for *what*, this Lyudmila Vasiliev? "No," he half uttered, and clicked "down." Kartsev's eyes and shoulders were both growing sore. He sat hunched just in front of the bright screen.

Another name scrolled into view . . . another box. *To check, or not to check,* he thought in English. "*To suffer the slings and arrows . . . slings and arrows*" bounced through his mind. He'd always wondered what "slings" were. He had to remind himself to refocus on the screen.

"Ivanov," he said out loud, "Grigory." As nondescript a name as he'd ever seen. "Mechanic, central Moscow. Possible conspiracy involving unknown persons." That was it? What persons? Conspiracy to do what? "It's unbelievable, these people," Kartsev slurred. *I really* have *to get at least two lines*, he thought. He skipped another potentially guilty suspect because of insufficient information. *But they'll come back with more*, he knew. There was really only one way to get off the surveillance list.

The charge levied against the next man was much more useful. "Andreev, Pyotr. Former commander, Presidential Security Force. Met with CIA in America." Well, it wasn't actually a charge. Just a status, really. He was potentially dangerous.

And in America, Kartsev thought as he arched his stiff back. He'd totally lost interest in America after the presidential assassinations. Three of five missions had been foiled. The two that were successful didn't seem to have any further effects. He'd written an entire chapter on the observation, entitled "Diminishing Marginal Effects of Terror: an Econometric Analysis." But maybe those effects would return with the passage of time.

Kartsev clicked, checking the box next to "Andreev, Pyotr." His hand was beginning to cramp.

PHILADELPHIA, PENNSYLVANIA
March 24, 2000 GMT (0600 Local)

"Should we get Oscar Meyer?" Pyotr Andreev asked.

"Are zey turkey baloney?" Olga asked. A woman glanced her way on hearing the accent.

"That's what's on the label." He dropped the package in the basket. "I don't think shopping is supposed to take hours," Pyotr grumbled. He brushed the cookie crumbs off Mashenka's sweater.

"It doesn't take hours," Olga retorted. She stopped at a display filled with cheeses. There were dozens of wax-wrapped brands. Pyotr knew she would study them all.

"I'm going on ahead for the Cheerios," he informed her. He rounded the end cap into an empty aisle.

"Honey *Nut*!" she called out from behind.

"Honey-*Nut*-Honey-*Nut*," the kids began chanting from the basket. Pyotr could detect no trace of an accent.

There were a million brands of cereal. Special K, Kellogg's Corn Flakes, Cap'n Crunch, Pyotr read.

Pyotr noticed something at the end of the aisle. He looked up. A man with an overcoat raised a machine pistol. Pyotr dove to the floor behind a stand of iced orange juice. The angry roar of the gun splattered sprays of cold liquid onto Pyotr. Boxes of cereal burst and flew to the floor.

There were shouts, and then screams . . . and then footsteps.

Four, three, two . . . Shot after shot rang out. The machine pistol clattered to the floor just beside him. He peered around the edge of the display to see two men in dark suits. They were making their way down the aisle toward the gunman. He lay prostrate in a widening pool of crimson blood.

The screams, the screams . . .

Pyotr turned. They were from Olga. She was bloody and clinging to the side of the basket . . . to the limp shapes of his children. *Oh-God-oh-God-oh-God,* he thought as he ran to them. With every step his fears were confirmed. They lay in the basket covered in blood. He quickly found the open artery in Masha's thigh. He pressed it closed with his thumb and index finger. Poor Oksana sat at the back in total shock. She didn't scream like little Mashenka. She didn't move much, or even look around. Her skin was pale with fright. She stared straight at her screaming mother.

The two government agents rushed to their side. The other shoppers were horrified and kept their distance, but the two agents swung into action. One checked under Oksana's coat. The other pinned his thrashing wife to the slippery floor.

"Shit!" the man checking Oksana hissed.

Oksana began to cry. She had been shot like her mother and little sister.

The stranger now fought for the life of Pyotr's oldest daughter. The life of his youngest seeped through Pyotr's cramping fingers ounce by ounce. It seemed like hours before the ambulances arrived. By then the two girls had both fallen unconscious.

Olga screamed till she too gave out.

The rest of the night was all plastic tubes and hospital smells. Sweat-soaked doctors coming to see Pyotr with somber words. He lost track of what was being done. Mostly he just sat. He broke out crying only when he saw the two agents. They were covered head to toe in his family's blood. The men stayed with him the whole time like old friends.

Early in the morning the doctors told him they'd all live.

WEST OF URGAL, SIBERIA
March 27, 0730 GMT (1730 Local)

Chin and his three fellow platoon leaders sat hunched in the small tent.

"Here he comes," one of the university snots said. He closed the tent flap.

The company commander crawled in and instantly began to bitch. "What are you doing?" he snapped at the four lieutenants. Chin and the others stared back in stunned silence. "I could see the light from a hundred meters!" His voice was hushed. But from the strain showing in his body and face he might as well have been shouting. "You men are my officers! I've got to count on you to use your heads!"

Chin didn't dare look at the others. He'd never seen the captain this mad. Plus his fellow platoon leaders were all pricks anyway.

The captain removed his gloves and pulled a beat-up plastic tube from inside his white poncho. He unscrewed it and extracted a rolled-up paper map with care. His fingers were already trembling from the cold. He noisily flattened the map, the paper crackling under his hands and heightening Chin's sense of anticipation. It wasn't often they got a chance to look at a map.

The colorful paper coiled back up as the captain tucked his hands under his armpits. "Okay," the captain said, his words quaking from a chattering jaw. "I called this company meeting to pass down word from army group command. These orders are to go no lower than your rank." He looked each of his four subordinates in the eye.

Chin felt a stirring of his blood at so solemn a charge. It was a privilege to learn so important a secret—whatever it was. He looked around and immediately grew annoyed.

The other platoon leaders' faces all showed disrespect. One man—Lieutenant Hung, whom Chin had caught reading the subversive text back in barracks—even wore a sneer.

"The Peoples' Republic is engaged in a glorious victory," the captain recited woodenly. The tone dampened the excitement Chin had felt. "You are each to be commended for your efforts." Lieutenant Hung drew an unusually deep breath, almost a sigh of impatience. He drew a squinting, menacing look from the captain. The company commander then turned his attention to the map. There were a variety of colors and symbols marked in pencil. "We have to be ready to repel attacks on our flanks from here, here, and here." He pointed. Everyone now hunched over the map, eclipsing most of the light from the single lantern. "Get back!" the captain shouted. Everyone sank back onto their haunches but still studied the unit positions and terrain.

"You're pointing at our left, our center, and our right," Lieutenant Hung said. His tone was just this side of insolence.

"*Good,*" the captain said sarcastically. "You can read a map!" Chin kept his mouth firmly shut.

"If we're in the middle of a glorious victory," Hung continued, "why are we worried about our flanks?"

"Those are our orders!"

"And why do we alternate between ridiculously loose dispersion of our units during the day," Hung pressed, "and tight defensive groupings at night?"

Chin had never realized it before, but every day and night it was the same. When they broke camp in the morning, the four platoons scattered widely before moving out. But they bivouacked just meters apart.

"Yeah," came a seconding voice. "We used to maneuver at night. The *Europeans* curled up into a ball when the sun went down, and *we* hit *them.*"

"Do you like patrolling at night?" the captain finally barked. He shot challenging looks at each face in succession. "Do you want to go up against those bases—night after night—again? To run into their patrols and wait for the artillery to come raining in?"

Chin remembered those scary nights with a shudder. The only way to survive the artillery was to hug the Westerners so tight the big guns couldn't fire on them.

"Our *orders,*" the captain shouted, "are to pull into a defensive mode every night and to be prepared to repel advances against three of our four fronts!" He was staring the smart-assed platoon leader back against the tent wall.

But Lieutenant Hung didn't flinch. He didn't recoil—as Chin would have—expecting blows. He sat there unmoving, and that in itself was almost insubordination.

"Is that clear enough for you?" the captain asked in low tones.

It seemed to be, for Hung nodded.

Chin tried to comprehend what it was that both Hung and the captain understood. He gave up, however, and drew only the most basic facts from the captain's briefing. China was losing the war—not winning, as he had thought—and they should prepare to be attacked from all sides. And he could also tell from the interactions of his comrades that the glue of army discipline was weakening.

But it was also quite possibly being replaced by an even stronger bond. For there was a palpable sense of fear in that tent. From then on, the bickering came to an end.

18

The snoring kept André Faulk awake on his first night in his new job with his new unit—infantryman, 1st Squad, 3rd Platoon, Alpha Company, 3rd Battalion, 1st Brigade, 101st Airborne Division (Airmobile). He lay in his bunk in barracks kept frigid so everyone could sleep in full battle dress. Like firemen, they had to respond to desperate calls. A firebase on the verge of being overrun. A hole in a line to be plugged. A last-ditch effort to stop a breakthrough. Human filler plugged into a dam that was leaking in a hundred places.

André's stomach gurgled loudly. He rolled over onto his back in a series of twists that left his clothes askew. The metal bunk creaked and squealed. The snores of the bulge in the bunk above sputtered. He saw in the dim light from the duty room that several metal links were missing from the Russian bed. The mattress poked through like bald spots on an old tire. He sighed, and his breath fogged.

There were nine new guys who'd joined the air cavalry platoon with André. Ten replacements for a unit of only thirty-three men at full strength. Ten divided by thirty-three was one out of three or four. Those had been the odds of being wounded or killed in about six weeks of fighting, André reasoned, although maybe they weren't the first replacements. His stomach lining burned.

What the hell am I doing here?

A telephone rang in the duty room. The muffled sound of the old-fashioned bell penetrated the walls. André focused on that sound. The phone was picked up just as the second ring began. The distant voice of the duty NCO ended abruptly as the phone was slammed down. In the terrible few moments of silence that followed, André heard every snore, sniff, and cough from the two dozen sleeping men.

He also heard the whining windup of a helicopter's turbine.

The door burst open, and André just about jumped out of his skin. The flickering of the fluorescent lights overhead announced the coming of a man-made dawn. "Mission call!" Everyone groaned and rolled out of bed. No one moved faster than André—the petrified seventeen-year-old.

Just outside the barracks the brutally cold night air at the helipads was astir in the wash of forty helicopters' rotors. Amid the noise and under the bright lights of the base André and his squad scrambled single file toward the helicopter with 110-pound packs on their backs. All around them brilliantly lit Blackhawks began to rise into the night sky filled with troops.

"Air assault!" someone shouted over the roar. A smattering of "*A-a-a-air*-borne!" came in reply, but the enthusiasm was not particularly contagious. In fact, no one in André's squad said a word as they climbed through the open door of their white helicopter. The sky was alive with red and green running lights and flashing white tail beacons. It was a full battalion-sized deployment complete with nets full of ammo boxes slung underneath giant utility helicopters.

André stood last in line. He involuntarily stooped under the idling rotors' wash. The swirling Siberian air felt like a cold shower, and he could hardly see through his watering eyes. His squad leader—Sergeant Moncreif—stood at the open sliding door and grabbed André's M-16 to ensure it was safed. He returned the rifle and slapped André on the helmet. Two squadmates helped pull André aboard, and a crewman closed the door shutting out the howling gale.

André dropped his field pack and dragged it across crowded floor to the rear wall. He hugged the pack to his chest. The muscles along his stomach cramped from their tight clench, so he arched his back and took a deep breath. His jaw vibrated and teeth chattered from the lingering cold. The engines vibrated through the armored pads on the deck and straight into his itching testicles. With a lurching, crushing jolt the aircraft leaped into the sky, hovered momentarily in the turbulence of the downdraft, then pitched forward suddenly. The acceleration in the odd, nose-down attitude was sickening. Almost instantly all was black through the frosty windows of the Blackhawk as they tore through the heavy, cold air. The cabin lights were a dim red to preserve their night vision.

The walls of the troop compartment were lined with the ten men of his squad plus two medics. The center was piled high with gear. No one talked, they just stared straight ahead. André closed his eyes. *Two medics*, he thought. Time passed. The helicopter hurtled toward the LZ with its engines at full military power. Five minutes? Ten? Thirty? The cabin was warm, and the tension was exhausting physically. He tried to sleep, but the fear impaled him—stifling his breathing. He was far more terrified than he thought he'd be. He'd have to deal with it, he knew, to survive on the battlefield.

There were two loud knocks in rapid succession, and the helicopter pitched over onto its side. For a split second André thought it was the end, but the dive seemed to be controlled. There was another sharp thwack like the sound of a hammer pounded against the helicopter's thin skin. They were taking fire. The ballistic mats on the deck jumped with more blows. Another jarring string of fire thudded beneath their butts. Men raised their feet into the air, shying away from the ground fire. André could smell smoke. The helicopter wove from side to side as sparks flew up the wall. A window shattered. Air whistled into the cabin. A heavy thud pressed André's head toward his chest with a grunt.

The door flew open. "Everybody *out*!" A constant rain of bullets struck home. Holes were punched through the walls as men leaped into the maelstrom outside. André dragged his pack toward the door and ducked as each new hole puckered the bulkheads. Death—ruthlessly random—stabbed into the cabin. In the red glow of the cabin lights the swirling snow looked like fireflies being blown up—not down—by rotors turning at full power. Snow peppered his face and forced his eyes closed. He judged his odds now from the frequency of loud smacking sounds to which he was helplessly exposed. A drumroll of thumps hit the aircraft like buckshot from a shotgun. A man at the door fell backward onto André.

"Aaa*aaa*HH!" came a bloodcurdling shriek, then screams in rapid howls made at the limits of a human's vocal cords.

"Jesus *Christ*! Give me a hand!" one of the crewmen shouted at André. Bullets smashed into the metal fuselage like rocks thrown against tin siding. André helped the crewman pull the wounded man back into the helicopter. Blood poured through his fingers where his hands covered his face.

"Get *out*!" the crewman shouted at André. He groped blindly for his pack, jumped to the ground, and dragged the pack out with one hand. His other hand firmly grasped his rifle. A man appeared out of nowhere. "I got hit," he said, holding his rib cage just below his left breast. He was pale, and his eyes were glassy. Another *zzzip* of bullets sent André to the ground. He pulled his pack around in front as the helicopter lifted off. The force of the downdraft redoubled, filling the air with snow and ice. When the artificial blizzard subsided, André raised his head to see that the helicopter and the wounded man were gone.

Its noise was replaced by booming explosions and rips of gunfire. Tracers streaked all through the woods ahead. Ricochets off trees shattered into sparks of shooting stars. Grenades lit small patches of the forest floor in fiery geysers of snow. One illuminated for the briefest of moments a standing human form. The LZ was on a frozen lake, André realized, and forested hills rose on all sides. The white bowl formed by the ridges was a carnival of noise, but there were no soldiers anywhere to be seen. It was almost peaceful.

André struggled to his feet and headed for the violence. He ran, bent at the waist, as fast as he could toward the awesome roar. At the edge of the frozen lake he knelt behind a tree and flicked his M-16's selector to "burst." He then began the ascent of the snowy ridge, which was difficult with the heavy pack on his back. His thighs began to burn. He gave up weaving through the trees and focused solely on making it to the crest. Stray bullets hissed through the branches high above. Halfway up André heard voices . . . in English! He headed for the sound and smashed through a low branch laden with snow.

Flame erupted from just ahead of him. He collapsed facedown as a muzzle blazed straight at him. Bullets pounded into the pack on his back, yanking his shoulder straps repeatedly with their impact. The fire was clearly from an American M-16.

When the magazine was empty, there was the clacking of a reloading soldier. André raised his head and screamed, *"American so-o-oldier!"* He dropped exhausted. His heart pounding. Waiting to die.

"Come out so I can see you!" came a shout from close by.

André gathered his strength and stood slowly. The man whispered to guide André to him. Two men lay at the base of a thick tree. One clutched his hands to his bloody stomach. The other held a smoking rifle. "Jesus!" he said to André. "I almost *shot* yer ass!"

"Goddamn mother-*fucker*!" André snapped. *"Sh-shit!"*

"You don't come runnin' *up* on somebody like that! What are you, a fuckin' *cherry*? *Christ!"*

Booming explosions from an air raid in the distance lit the scene with their brilliant fire. The two men stared at each other with teeth bared in anger. André broke the stand-off by asking, "Where's Second Squad?"

"*Which* Second Squad?"

"First Platoon."

"*Which* First Platoon?" the guy asked André. "What fuckin' comp'ny are you in? Fuck it. The fightin's up there." He pointed toward the glowing crest. The treetops shone with flashes from ordnance large and small. The continuous roar of small arms was punctuated by huge blasts from artillery shells.

"What're *you* doin'?" André asked the man.

"I'm fuckin' *wounded*!" His calf was wrapped in a small bandage. "Plus, I can't leave the LT."

The other guy was lieutenant, André realized. "Is he gonna be okay?" he asked.

"How the hell should I know?" shot out of the man. "I *tried* to find a medic, *okay*? I ain't seen one!"

"He needs help," André said.

"I *know* he needs help! Didn't I *tell* you I looked for a fuckin' medic? Didn't I already *say* that?"

André wanted nothing to do with the shithead and headed uphill. "Here!" the guy said, tossing him a heavy canvas sack. "They sent me back for these grenades." André slung the bag over his shoulder. His legs felt like jelly when he rose. He barely made it to the top of the ridge carrying the enormous load. It was much louder there, and he dropped to crawl and peer over the snowy knob. There he saw everything, and nothing. Muzzles spit flame in a saddle between two hills. Artillery burst every few seconds, lighting the contours for André to see. There were gaps in the trees that could be ponds or streams. The crack of rifles and booms of machine guns blared across the valley like car horns inside a tunnel. Under the canopy of evergreens was a world filled with noise and danger and death.

He girded himself and headed down into the battle. Each step was a controlled slide through the deep drifts, which served to brake his too rapid descent. At the bottom he was physically spent. He sank to one knee and sucked gulps of dry air. His lungs ached. His legs were on fire. He rose and pressed on—ever closer to the thunderous violence. An unnatural cnill crawled up his chest like the onset of the flu, but it was fear, he quickly realized. Palpable, tangible fear was seizing control of him, its progress measured in quivering body parts.

André almost made the same mistake twice. He heard the raspy static of a nearby radio and headed for the sound, but caught himself and dropped to the ground. He drew a deep breath and shouted, *"American soldier! American soldier!"*

"Over here!" he heard. "Keep it slow!" André rose and walked forward at a deliberate pace. He practically stepped on the man and immediately dropped into the snow. He felt drained to the point of a nervous breakdown. "Private Faulk," he managed, "reporting for duty."

"Dundrey, PFC! Glad to see ya."

"Where's Second Squad, First Platoon, Charlie Company?" André asked.

The guy laughed. "How the fuck should *I* know? I'm just an RTO! This is Alpha Company, Third Platoon. You'd best check in with the LT up there." He pointed into the furnace of muzzle blasts and hand grenades. The radiotelephone operator then answered a call over the radio. André began to crawl forward. The RTO grabbed his leg. "Roger that, India Tango. Out." He put the handset down. "Tell the LT there's a flight of tac air comin' in. The forward controller says heads down, pass it along."

André crawled on with a greater sense of purpose now that he had a mission. A rational reason to explain his otherwise suicidal advance toward the front. His ears began to ring from the deafening noise. Air-splitting sounds pressed him facedown in the snow. The flashbulbs of muzzle blasts popped from the darkness ahead. It occurred to him for the first time that he could shoot back. He even paused and took aim at where he'd last seen a muzzle flash, but something held him back. Maybe it wasn't a Chinese soldier, but an American. He crawled on.

"Hey!" somebody yelled from behind him. "Where the hell you *goin'*? Get back to the line, you crazy mother-fucker!"

André had crawled right past the forward most American positions. He scampered back as fast as he could. The man who'd called out to him blazed away with a machine gun. André rolled over the log behind which the two-man gun crew had set up. The weapon was so loud he couldn't make himself heard. He slapped the gunner on the boot but the man scarcely paid any attention. The yellow fire from the gun's heavy barrel lit the icy brush ahead.

The M-60 fell quiet as the gunner's assistant reloaded. "I'm lookin' for the LT!" André shouted. The gunner jabbed his gloved index finger to their right. André nodded. "Keep your heads down!" he shouted. "There's an air strike comin' in!" The machine gun opened fire again, and a phosphorus grenade illuminated the woods ahead. A solid wall of tightly packed attackers—maybe a company of Chinese—were firing as they trudged forward through the snow.

He released his pack and it slipped to the ground.

André's body clenched up from his shoulders to his crotch like a string had been drawn. Dozens of Chinese grenades went off almost simultaneously up and down the American lines, stunning him with the violence of their blasts. Flames mixed with powdery snow covered him. The earsplitting noise dizzied him and made him nauseous. Despite pain like an ice pick in both eardrums, he raised his head. Blazing muzzles were barely forty meters away. He lifted his rifle to his shoulder. A Chinese soldier hurled a grenade that got caught in the branches of a tree. The guy shouted something. His comrades dove. It burst right in front of them. When they rose again André switched the selector to "semi" and pulled the trigger. The butt jammed hard into his shoulder. His target fell.

He looked over at the machine-gun crew, but saw no

one. He looked everywhere. They were gone. There was
nobody but André and the Chinese. He began to squeeze
off rounds one after the other. The underbrush around him
began to snap into pieces. André split in two and felt his
mind leave his body. Part of him winced at every passing
bullet, and another part was a functioning rifleman. Target
pops up. Swing the barrel. Bull's-eye! The two halves were
totally distinct. One grimaced from the panic so complete
that he was afraid even to flee toward safety. The other
squeezed off aimed fire—focused on the job of saving his
life by taking the lives of others.

Jets screamed by. André's sinuses squealed and ears
popped from the pressure change. A staggering roar shook
heaven and earth. It was like nothing he'd ever experienced
before. Trees were split in two and fell to the ground. Great
geysers of flame rose high into the air. Yet another string
of bombs exploded not three hundred yards away. His ears
itched and stung from the wave of compressed air.

André saw a kneeling man waving at his cowering comrades. He had the man dead to rights in his sights. His rifle
recoiled. The man disappeared. Three more waves of jets
passed with tailpipes glowing brightly through the trees.
Shrapnel sheared large branches from the surrounding trees.
They obscured André's field of fire, so he moved. All fell
still save the crackling fires.

The Chinese were still out there, he knew. *What they
gonna do?* He fished a full thirty-round magazine from his
pouch and seated it with a faint clacking sound. The noise
attracted an undisciplined spray of fire from a single rifle.
André laid his sights on the muzzle flash but held his fire.
He had the shot, but they would see him if he fired. He
carefully reached into the canvas bag and began to pile
hand grenades in front of him. Several single shots were
fired in his direction. Brief bursts of intense gunfire broke
out all up and down the line. Artillery still rained down on
the opposite Chinese-held ridge, but that was another theater of war. André's world measured thirty meters by thirty.

There was hushed talking. They were discussing—planning. When they fell silent, André pressed himself as low as he could. Another Chinese gun lit the night. It sprayed the trees all around. *They know I'm still here*, he thought. *But they haven't fixed me.* He was totally calm now. He pulled the pin on his first grenade. *Let's see if this shakes 'em up.* The tricky part was rising to his knees. He put the grenade to his chin and let it fly like a football to the sound of rustling fabric. The handle sprang off. He heard a shout. A rifle blazed. André grabbed another grenade and pulled the pin, still kneeling.

The first grenade exploded dead center in a cluster of Chinese. A host of new guns opened up. André was invisible to the flash blinded riflemen, but he tossed grenade after grenade at their muzzles. Bullets passed so close he could feel their wake, but one by one the enemy rifles fell dark. His arm was sore after throwing a dozen grenades. The last burst lit several running men in profile, felling two. They were running away. André dropped and wrapped his finger around his trigger. He surveyed the woods for a target but found none. The artillery now lit up a distant valley. The woods all around were still and smoky.

They were gone.

BIROBIDZHAN FIREBASE, SIBERIA
April 2, 1600 GMT (0200 Local)

Harold Stempel cowered on the trench floor against the icy wall. The trench line was inundated with Chinese artillery and mortars. The night blazed with indescribable orange fire. Each of the crushing blasts was a body blow. Each was the end of the world.

"What's goin' on?" screamed the unshaven man next to him.

Stempel didn't budge from his fetal position. He held his helmet to his head with one hand, his knees to his chest with the other. Stempel's hood was drawn tight around his face. The newly issued body armor covered his torso. He watched the bursts of lightning from behind layers of wool and Kevlar. Each eruption of earthshaking violence opened a wound in him, but it was a wound you couldn't see.

His vision tunneled. His eyes filled so fully with tears that the fiery flashes starred. He was frightened by his rapid breathing and pounding heart. He couldn't draw enough air. A near miss bounced him off the ground and covered him in snow. He was stunned—his insides rattled. Now even the earth lashed out at him.

"*Dear God in hea . . .*" Stempel began. But the trench itself exploded. His voice was swallowed by thunder. "*Please sto-o-o-p!*" he yelled.

A medic picked him up. The man was profiled against a low blanket of white clouds that had grounded their air support. He dropped Stempel and ran off toward the sound of the screams. Everyone was standing at their posts and firing. Everyone but Stempel. No one looked at him. Their weapons blazed. Stempel knew he had to get up. He frantically groped for his rifle and slid halfway up the wall.

A massive burst shook the earth. A boiling mushroom cloud rose over the rear wall of the trench. The Chinese had blown an ammo bunker a few hundred meters to their rear. Smaller explosions popped all around. But Stempel saw something even more frightening. Their squad leader came down the trench. "Let's go! Every other man! Come on!" He pulled people from the wall and sent them toward the rear through a communications trench.

A blast from a heavy shell knocked Stempel to his knees. Sergeant Moncreif stopped in front of him. "Come on, Stemp!" Harold didn't understand at first. "They're inside the wire!"

Stempel rose and followed the others—men he now knew better than anybody else in the world. He'd seen them put through every extreme in life. They'd been tested. Some could be counted on. Others you had to watch. But Harold was confident that as a unit they'd do the job.

"*They're inside the wire!*" Moncreif shouted behind Harold to motivate others to their feet. Stempel followed his squadmates down the slit trench that opened off the main trench. It was so narrow he had to turn sideways to squeeze through. When the men in the lead slowed, the men following collided. They were slip-sliding on the slick icy floor, but time was everything now. Every second that Chinese soldiers remained alive inside the main perimeter meant the chances of holding the base fell. If they circled back to hit a section of the trenches from behind, they'd peel open a hole so wide the base's defenses would burst like a balloon. Harold understood that much, as did all the other grim-faced young men.

Someone began a shout of warning that was cut short by an explosion.

Once again, the only thing that saved Stempel were bodies. Layers of people in front of him absorbed the shrapnel from a grenade that burst in the narrow furrow. Searing fire burned into Stempel's right arm. He found himself lying underneath a man's body. Bullets flew over his spinning head. The dying man on his legs clutched his chest, unable to draw a breath.

Stempel ducked his chin and looked down his own body. His flak jacket was ripped open and ragged. The pain from his upper arm was intense. The air all around him was filled with buzzing projectiles. The ice along the walls above him was being sheared away in ledges. He was helpless and exposed.

Two grenades exploded among the Chinese who had blocked passage ahead. French soldiers dropped into the trench with their stubby rifles spraying fire wildly. One of the legionnaires was shot in the back by his own man. Another's helmet flew off and he collapsed backward as a Chinese round struck him. But they killed more than they got killed.

Boots trampled Stempel. Every third or fourth man stomped right on his head or chest. He yelled to them for help. Some responded in incomprehensible French. They all kept moving. Finally, American medics arrived. They cut frantically at the clothing around Stempel's upper arm. Peeling the fabric back caused intense pain. So did the fiery alcohol and the pressure bandages. Stempel cried out and kicked into the dead men who lay at his boots. The medic gave him a pill, which he swallowed dry. "You'll be fine," he said. He sat Stempel up against the trench wall and ran off toward the firefight, which was intense but receding into the distance.

Stempel could hardly remember what had happened. The artillery barrage had stopped. A deep rumble rocked the ground for some time, sending a fine mist into the trench. The sonorous noise was steady and deep like the thudding subwoofer in his father's media room. Like five-hundred-pound firecrackers going off hundreds at a time.

He almost felt good. He remembered weathering the barrage in the main trench. Then squeezing his way through the slit trench. He couldn't remember the attack. He didn't even think he'd fired his rifle, which he was surprised to find still at his side. Another herd of men stampeded past. They stepped on him, but he didn't mind. "Off to war?" he mumbled, slurring.

They stopped to toss the bodies of the fallen out of the trench. "Hey!" Stempel yelled, but not loudly enough to get their attention. "Those are my buddies!" His shout drew glances from the nearest two men.

They lifted the last body out of the trench and carefully laid it in the snow to the side. They moved on. Stempel was alone again with the dead.

UNRUSFOR HEADQUARTERS, KHABAROVSK
April 3, 0800 GMT (1800 Local)

Clark's J-2 reported to the meeting of joint force commanders. "The ice has thinned from over sixty centimeters to under ten." The chief of joint staff intelligence had become an expert on the Amur River ice pack. "We're already seeing the Chinese have trouble with their heavy vehicles. They're laying pontoons to distribute the weight. Plus they halve the loads on their trucks. And it appears to us they're preparing for the ice flow themselves. They're using all their available transport just to get supplies across the river. Pack animals move it from there to the front.''

Clark held his J-2's gaze. ''What's the latest guess as to how long we've got before it breaks?''

''I'd say . . . between two and four weeks from now.''

His answer brought a stir from around the table. The French commander said, ''That means we must attack sometime between right now, and two *weeks*.'' He held his hands up in mock confusion. ''But *which*? How can we know?''

''I've got a team goin' in tonight,'' the commander of Clark's special operations group offered.

''We launch the offensive at zero four hundred local time on April fourteenth,'' Clark announced. There was stunned silence. Everyone knew of the funding showdown. No one directly raised the subject of any connection. The German commander came closest.

''We'll need to get a significant force across the Amur,'' the German general said. ''For your plan to work, the ice must break between seven and ten days after the attack is launched, depending upon the speed of our advance. What if it breaks too soon—before we cross in strength? Or what if it holds too long and the Chinese withdraw their forces from Russia? Since timing the break in the ice is so important, can't we have some flexibility in the launch date depending upon intelligence on ice depth from the Amur?'' Clark replied that they could not. Although the question ''Why?'' hung over the room, no one gave voice to it.

The senior French general asked, ''Has President Davis approved penetration into China to the Jilin-Harbin-Qiqihar line?''

''Yes,'' Clark replied. ''He has assured me that no calls for a cease-fire will be entertained until we've reached those objectives. That line is approximately 560 kilometers, or 350 miles south of the Amur. It should ensure that the bulk of the Chinese invasion forces and mobile reserves are fully enveloped.''

''We can't get tied down in civilian population control,''

the British general pointed out. "Once we drive Chinese authorities from the north, there could be chaos, Mass rioting. Disorder."

"We won't," Clark replied. "If the diplomats start negotiating the shape of the conference table, we'll reduce the pockets of bypassed Chinese by force and withdraw. Our mission is to destroy the offensive capabilities of the People's Liberation Army. We're getting back across the Amur quickly. We have no time for anything more than operational security. No humanitarian relief. No civil administration. Just war, gentlemen. War that will be prosecuted with the utmost violence and skill that we are collectively able to muster. From the moment we launch this counteroffensive, to the moment the last track rolls back across the Amur, I have only one goal. To destroy the ability of my enemy to fight so completely that he will pose no immediate threat to the security of Siberia."

There was no dissension. Clark was sure, however, that there were doubts and fears. And most of those would center on the ice.

BETHESDA NAVAL HOSPITAL, MARYLAND
April 6, 2200 GMT (1700 Local)

"We've been diverting ninety percent of our resources to the staging areas," General Dekker briefed Gordon Davis. "That's put a real strain on the troops in contact with the Chinese. Quite frankly, they're all pretty close to the breaking point. And there's no relief in store for them when the counteroffensive kicks off. We plan on using them for flank and rear area security."

"What are our current casualties?" Gordon asked.

"We have, to date, lost over eight thousand killed and twenty thousand wounded. Those numbers could double before the end of the counteroffensive."

"Will Clark's counteroffensive win this war if all goes according to plan?" Gordon asked.

He was putting the man on the spot. Clark had not consulted Dekker before approaching Gordon, and for all Gordon knew the two men were now sworn enemies. Regardless, because Dekker hadn't signed off on Clark's plan, he was free to criticize—to second-guess—which was good. It gave Gordon a professional check against over-reliance on Clark—a man he barely knew.

Dekker's discomfort was clear. "It has risks and is aggressive, but it's sound. We're satisfied we've built up the manpower and matériel to execute the plan. The biggest wild cards are the ice and the counterattack they're sure to launch out of the Beijing area with their strategic reserve. We've got to stop them, but if the ice starts to flow before we get at least a corps across the Amur . . ." He looked up at Gordon but didn't say anything more.

"You didn't answer my question. What I want to know is this—will Clark's counteroffensive so totally demolish the Chinese Army that I won't have to cut deals with Beijing . . . *if* it goes according to plan?"

The chairman of the joint chiefs took a deep breath. "If everything goes according to plan, sir, we'll hack the PLA to pieces in a Sherman's March from Mongolia all the way to Korea Bay. But, Mr. President, nothing ever goes according to plan."

Gordon nodded. He understood that Clark's plan had little margin for error and practically nothing held in reserve. "What do you think about General Clark's objectives and timetables?" he asked.

Dekker arched his eyebrows. "They're aggressive. *Very* aggressive. If the Chinese south of the Amur resist ridge by ridge, stream by stream, then we'll get bloodied like we haven't been since the Ardennes Forest in 1944. And they *will* be fighting for their homeland."

"They'll be fighting for Communist octogenarians in Beijing," the chief of naval operations countered. "And those soldiers are all third-rate conscripts. We've already seen the best the Chinese have to offer." The navy was, Gordon knew, a tireless supporter of "their" man General Clark, who reported up through the navy billet—CINC-PAC.

The room now fell silent. Everyone had said his piece. None of it had done anything to change Gordon's mind. "All right, I'm ready to authorize the launch of the offensive as planned—on April fourteenth." No one raised a voice of objection. No one commented on the rigid timetable.

Dekker cleared his throat. "What about the congressional deadline, sir? We'll just be breaching the Chinese lines when the clock runs out on our funding. If Congress doesn't—"

"You let me take care of Congress," Gordon interrupted. "All you've got to do is win the war."

The door opened. Gordon's daughter Celeste entered the hospital room alone. Gordon was thrilled to see her, but when she saw him looking at her, her gaze dropped to the floor. She crossed the large room with her hands clasped in front of her. "Hi, Daddy," she said, and kissed him.

"Did your mom pick you up at the airport?" Gordon asked. She nodded. "Where is she?"

"Oh, she had to, you know, run some errands and stuff," Celeste replied. She still wouldn't look at him directly.

"You mean," Gordon translated, "she wanted you to come here by yourself."

"No," she whispered. "I wanted to come by myself."

"Honey," Gordon said, smiling, "is this about that demonstration at school?"

She immediately leaned down and hugged him. "Daddy! I never meant to do anything to hurt you!"

Gordon winced in pain as she squeezed him. "It's nothing, darling. Forget about it."

"But it was supposed to be just, like, a student memorial. And the newspapers and television just blow my picture up like I was . . . Daddy, I left as soon as they started saying all those awful things about you! The press made it sound like I was *part* of that, but I *wasn't*!"

Gordon tried his best to soothe her feelings as she cried.

Elaine had told him how upset Celeste was. When his daughter's tears finally dried up, he said, "Have I ever told you why we're fighting this war?"

Celeste raised her head from Gordon's chest, perplexed and surprised. "You don't have to explain yourself to *me*."

"Yes, I do. You're almost an adult now. You have the right to ask for and deserve an answer." She was shaking her head, but he said, "Celeste, I've got to explain myself to everybody in this country . . . and I will. It's all right to be against the war, Celeste. *I'm* against the war—*any* war. But life presents you with only a limited selection of options, and sometimes they're all bad, but you still have to pick one. You can wish you had more or different choices, but life doesn't work that way. You just make the best decision you can under the circumstances."

"Is this about my trip to Cape Cod last weekend?" Celeste asked sheepishly.

Gordon screwed up his face. "*No*. This is about the *war*. What trip to Cape Cod?"

She loosed a high-pitched giggle. "Oh . . . never mind. I thought maybe—you know—this was, like, some sort of father-daughter advice thing. Like . . . in *code*?"

Gordon was confused. "You went to Cape Cod for the weekend?"

She waved both hands in the air as if to erase her earlier comment and spoke rapidly, leaving no pauses into which Gordon could squeeze. "We don't need to go into that now. I told Mom all about it . . . um, when I got back. She's okay with it. Everything's cool. So, how're ya *feelin'*?"

Gordon didn't raise the subject again. They chatted about school. About whether she could have friends hang in the White House that summer. About the limited number of available roles for her in the drama department's productions of Chekhov, Ibsen, and Wilde. They talked about anything but the war . . . and whether there were boys on this road trip to Cape Cod.

ST. MATTHEW'S HOSPITAL, PHILADELPHIA
April 7, 1300 GMT (0800 Local)

"Mommy," Mashenka said in her girlish pitch, in English, "could you read this bo-o-ok?"

"I can't reach it, *kissa*," Olga Andreev replied. Masha held the book up over the railing, but in the hip-to-toe cast she couldn't put it within reach. Olga was confined to her own bed. She'd been warned not to strain the stitches. She thought about pushing the call button. But she'd already overtaxed the nurses' patience. She resisted making such a petty request.

Oksana lay in the portable bed opposite Masha. As usual, she was disturbingly quiet.

"Where's *Daddy*?" Masha asked in frustration.

"I don't know, *kissa*," Olga said for the hundredth time. In Pyotr's brief absences, the girls had been unmanageable. Or—more correctly—three-year-old Masha had been unmanageable. Oksana hadn't said ten words since the shooting. "Are you all right, sweetheart?" Olga asked the six-year-old for the hundredth time.

"Gdye Papa?" she mumbled, never looking her mother's way.

"I don't know where he is, sweetheart," Olga answered.

The door opened. It wasn't Pyotr, or a nurse, but one of the policemen. Pyotr regularly talked to the men protecting them, but they rarely came in the room.

"This was left for you, ma'am," the officer said. It was a letter with no words of address. The officer left. Olga opened the envelope.

"Dear Olya," Pyotr wrote by hand—in Russian. Olga almost instantly choked and clutched at her chest. "I have had to go away. I hope you understand, but this is something that I must do. I missed my first opportunity. Now I must take my second." Olga drew a deep breath and closed her eyes. *No!* she raged silently. She knew without question what Pyotr was saying.

Repeated demands from Masha forced Olga to open her eyes. She explained again that she couldn't read the book.

Olga glanced back over at Oksana. The girl was staring attentively at her mother with dark eyes. "It's okay," Olga whispered in English. She moved quickly to dry her face. She pressed her hand on Oksana's mattress, the closest she could come to touching her. "*Vsyo* okay. *Ladno*?"

The girl returned to her sad pose. Masha began an incessant repetition of a cereal commercial jingle. Olga returned to Pyotr's letter. This time she reined in her emotions. She bottled them up. She ground her teeth together and read, maintaining a neutral expression.

"This is not something that I want to do. No, that's not true. I do want to do this. But I would not be so selfish if not for the fact that our life can never be normal until this is done. We can never live the life you dream of living unless we are free from fear. We've tried to ignore the evil, to pretend it didn't exist, but it does exist. It lives and it breathes and I must put a stop to it. Fate has punished you and the girls for a single mistake that I made. I will try to correct that mistake, but I will also try to return home to you. For, you see, I want that more than anything else, Olya. And I swear by God Almighty that I will try. I swear to you that I will, Olya. With all my love to you, Oksana, Mashenka—Pyotr."

Olga began to sob. She couldn't help it. Even the searing pain from her incisions couldn't stop it.

The door burst open. It wasn't a nurse but two policemen with guns drawn.

Olga looked around. Oksana lay in her bed staring at her mother with wide-open, frightened eyes—both thumbs repeatedly pressing the call button.

OUTSIDE SOFLYSK, SIBERIA
April 8, 0845 GMT (1845 Local)

Chin's ears were still ringing and his head pounded. He staggered back for a company meeting. Officers only. The other platoon leaders were gathered in the open under shelter of a tree. He stumbled and almost fell right in front of them. He expected ridicule. But instead Lieutenant Hung asked, "How many'd you lose?" All three of the others wore visible bandages from light wounds.

"Four," Chin replied. "I'm down to sixteen men."

Hung snorted. "You know how many I have from my original platoon? *Five!* Five out of thirty-two!" He was shushed by the others.

Chin sat in the silence for a minute. "You had some bad luck on that frozen lake," he sympathized.

The supply platoon leader looked around and whispered, "Where's our air support?" He drew cautionary looks and gestures, but he kept going. "They keep pushing us on and on and on! We're doing *our* job. Where's the air force?"

Everyone looked around nervously. The rumors were that security forces had taken several junior officers in their regiment away in the past few days. They march in, read a charge, take a man—usually an officer—and you never see or hear from him again.

"Where's the captain?" Chin asked. A couple of bitter laughs greeted his mention of their commanding officer. "Is the company meeting still on?" Chin tried. He got shrugs and frowns. "Because I really need some more ammo," he mentioned to the supply platoon leader.

The man could barely contain his disgust. "Get in line. The last supplies we got, we stole out of the 104th's regimental depot."

Chin's fellow officers all wore concerned looks on their faces. "Are you saying our supplies are being cut off?" Chin asked.

His question instantly angered the supply platoon leader. "Why do they *send* us these sodbusters?" he asked the others.

"Our supply lines are stretched too long," Hung explained.

"Because we're advancing," Chin protested. "We're *winning*. We haven't hit anything solid in *weeks*!"

"Until this morning," another officer commented. "That artillery wasn't a hit-and-run attack. It was a sustained barrage—maybe fifteen minutes. And when we pushed on, we ran right into prepared positions. By the time we crawled back, I'd lost *six* men.''

Heads nodded in agreement. "There's something up there," Hung ventured. "When we got the orders to move to our night positions, they were four kilometers back from where we made contact. Four kilometers!" He looked from face to face even briefly catching Chin's eye.

"And those troops you ran into up there," the supply officer said. "They're Americans." The words had an ominous ring. "Everybody was talking about it at the battalion depot."

"What the hell are they doing out *here*?" Chin asked. "We're in the middle of nowhere."

"This is as far as we go," Hung said. He had a distant look. "It's the end of our 'glorious victory'!"

Chin looked around to ensure they weren't overheard. "You think we're gonna *lose*?" he asked to make sure he understood.

"Chin," Hung replied, shaking his head. "I can't decide whether I pity you or envy you. You're the perfect citizen. The 'everyman.' You believe we're winning the war because they tell you so. And when the hammer comes down on the anvil, you'll believe whatever lies they use to explain that too." He was being totally unfair, Chin felt, but there was a strange tone of compassion in his voice. "I'm only gonna say this once." He twisted to make certain they were alone and then caught the return gaze of each man, ending finally with Chin. "The real enemy isn't four kilometers to the north," he said quietly, slowly. "It's two thousand kilometers to the south."

A silence descended on the group. It was a chance Chin welcomed, for he had a lot to consider. Hung had suffered the same hardships as Chin. He and his platoon had more than once laid down the fire that had allowed Chin's platoon to withdraw. Chin had done the same for him. They were joined by a bond of common experience despite their dislike of each other. Chin could conclude only one thing from Hung's comment. He'd just stated that the enemy was not NATO, but the Communist Party. For Beijing was two thousand kilometers to the south.

Lieutenant Hung was a traitor. He'd guessed as much ever since he'd found him reading English in the barracks bathroom. His views were treasonous. He should be shot for them. But he'd shared that most intimate confidence with only three other men in the world. Chin was one of them. A new bond had been established.

UNRUSFOR HEADQUARTERS, KHABAROVSK
April 10, 0300 GMT (1300 Local)

"Cut!" Kate Dunn said to Woody. He lowered the camera from his shoulder. She turned back to the German colonel. "We've got enough footage of people talking about supplies and logistics. What I need now is someone who'll talk about strategy. How you're gonna beat the Chinese Army."

The colonel shrugged. "But this *is* how we are going to beat them," he replied. "We are going to keep our vehicles rolling. Our ammunition loads full. Our mobile troops will fight three, four, five engagements in one day. The Chinese may fight only once or twice per week."

"Can you show me when and where on the map?"

"If you want maps and pins, Ms. Dunn, you should be down with the divisions. Better yet the brigades. We provide heavy weapons and air support, but our job is mainly to build up and move stores." He shrugged.

Woody flashed a goofy smile. They headed back to their cavernous quarters. Kate looked at her notes. Their coverage was dry as dust—headquarters shots, over and over. Woody lit another joint in the bathroom. He sat on the toilet with the door open. "They don't air interviews about building log roads. They get *pictures* of it! And what do we have tomorrow?" She tapped her pad. "Tagging boxes with bar codes!"

From the bathroom came a loud sucking sound. "We could use that stuff from the officers' club."

"What?"

"Yeah. It kinda reminded me of that scene in *Star Wars*. You know. From that bar with all the aliens. Everybody speaking different languages."

"That's a *great* idea, Woody! Just great! I think blazing battlefields and rows of attackers coming straight at you are a bit *derivative* by this point! We could do a two-hour documentary on how people relaxed from all the *stresses*. Maybe viewers are ready for the *entertainment* side of war!"

Woody didn't respond. Kate threw her pen to the pad. The most dramatic footage they'd shot was of the quiet perimeter thirty miles out. The defenses were so well manned that the Chinese hadn't challenged them since the early days of the war. There were combat flights lifting off at the airbase. But how many night afterburner shots can you use?

Woody emerged from the bathroom. He sat at the desk beside Kate. "Go see Clark. Tell him you need to get up to the front. Work your magic on the guy. He's already gotten out of you what he wanted."

"And what was that?"

"How many stories have we done about outnumbered defenders? A dozen? And how many have we done about the counterattack we know is coming? Any other questions?"

Kate was incensed. She tried to force out a laugh, without much success, then rose and headed for the door.

"Come in!" Clark said from his desk.

"It's a Ms. Dunn," the NCO announced from the doorway to his office. "She's with NBC News."

"I know who she is." Clark covered some of the paper on his desk. "Bring her in." He rose.

"General Clark," Kate said the moment she entered. "I have a proposition to put to you."

"Won't you have a seat?"

She hesitated, then said, "No, thank you. I'd like to

stand." Clark sank into his chair. She began to pace. "Here's my problem. I've gotten some great background stories. I can truly say that I now appreciate just how dedicated all the people you've got working for you are. And the perspective I've gotten from Khabarovsk . . . ! Well! It gives me an excellent understanding of all the behind-the-scenes work that goes into running an army. However—"

"I'm glad you came by," Clark interrupted. "You've kept your side of the bargain, so I was going to ask if you'd be interested in getting some shots of the action? Being there when the balloon goes up? Maybe follow some of the lead elements in the counterattack? Meeting the men and women at the sharp end of the stick? What do you think?"

"Well . . ." She grinned. "That's a *great* idea! Yes! Thanks! I think I'll take you up on it."

Clark nodded. "Get your things packed. It's time."

PART FOUR

*"The microsocial laws control the individual.
They define human interaction on the small
scale. They tend to restrain, to inhibit, to control.
The macrosocial laws control the masses. They
define human interaction on the large scale.
They tend to liberate, to unchain, to unleash. The
same person who would cry at the pathetic sight
of a wounded animal might chant loudly for war,
for death, for the indiscriminate destruction of
men, women, and children by bomb and by bullet. Civilization has tamed the individual. But in
the collective heart of the mob there courses the
blood of primitive man. Both the micro- and
macrosocial laws must be understood for the effective manipulation of human beings."*

Valentin Kartsev (posthumously)
The Laws of Human History
Moscow, Russia

19

The steps of the portico were filled with friends and supporters as Gordon's wheelchair was lowered to the drive. They all applauded politely, which did little to drown out the jeers and bullhorns of protesters in Lafayette Park. Cameras rolled as the orderly wheeled Gordon up the green ramp. Elaine followed and smiled, followed and smiled.

Staffers lined the halls of the White House. Although his family was now comfortably ensconced in the mansion, it was Gordon's first visit to his new home.

"Welcome back, sir," aides called out—aides whom Gordon had never met.

"Give 'em hell!" someone shouted—a line that drew nervous laughter from the other onlookers.

Slowly, the crowds thinned until the only people lining the corridor were mute, pinch-lipped Secret Service agents. Gordon had grown somewhat accustomed to making the executive decisions called for by the presidency. But he was totally unprepared to enter the Oval Office. His now familiar national security staff mouthed words of welcome as he was rolled up to the beautiful desk. Gordon was nearly overwhelmed with emotion.

He felt anew the truly awesome power he had assumed. He laid his hands on the surface of the desk. All was neat and carefully arranged. Pens, writing paper, a single file folder. He opened the drawer and was surprised to find paper clips, clamps, and other office supplies. Gordon looked upon the desk as a museum piece, but it was obviously intended for real work. *For* my *work*, he thought.

When the group was herded out of the office, the door was closed, leaving Gordon alone with Elaine. They smiled at each other, then broke out laughing. "I'm going to get in the chair," he said, and Elaine helped. He sighed on contact with the soft leather and his eyes began to roam the gallery of American political power. They landed on the lone folder lying atop the desk. He opened it and found a speech printed out in oversized draft type. The first words were "My fellow Americans . . ."

Gordon looked up.

"Daryl had some speechwriters give it a try," Elaine explained, "just to get a first draft on paper for when you got out. He didn't want you to exhaust yourself having to start from scratch."

Gordon slowly turned the pages to read line after line of bullshit. Nothing in a hundred separate sound bites. He tossed it into the trash and searched the drawers for a leather folder enclosing a legal pad. He found a pen and began to write his state-of-the-union address. After a couple of sentences he looked up to see Elaine still standing there.

Elaine rounded the desk and kissed him on the cheek. "I'll just work over there," she said, nodding at a small table. "I'm writing an important article for *Good House-keeping* on what being first lady means to me. They sent my first try back because it didn't make enough references to the debts I owe to my 'predecessors' in the civil rights movement," she said with obvious humor. "I'm thinking about changing the title to 'How Malcolm X Led Me to the Republican Party.' "

Gordon kept writing, but a smile crept onto his face. He wrote for a while longer, then flipped back to the first page.

Without looking up, he said, "Okay, I'm done."

Elaine had barely settled in. "Done with what?"

"With the speech."

She bolted right for the desk and took the pad. The first thing she did was count the pages. "Gordon! That's less than ten minutes *long*!"

"I'll speak slowly."

"But . . . this is the state of the *union*!"

"Lincoln delivered the Gettysburg Address in three minutes."

"But we've pinned *every*thing on this speech!"

"Read it," Gordon replied. Elaine hesitated. "Go on."

She raised the pad and read without saying a word. When she was done, she looked up. "This is what you want to do?" Gordon nodded. "You don't even want to mention the counterattack? How we're winning the war even as you speak? There's a pretty dramatic moment."

"I'll let the war speak for itself. No policy ideas, no programs, no legislative initiatives. Nothing on the budget or taxes or welfare reform. No social issues or doctrines of foreign policy. This speech is about something bigger. I very intentionally didn't write anything down until I was sure in my mind what I wanted to say, and that's it. That's it, Elaine. If the American people rally around me, and the war, and their country after listening to what I really believe, then I should be president of the United States. And if not, we'll go home to Bethesda in four years and live out our lives knowing we tried to do it the right way."

AMUR RIVER, SIBERIA
April 12, 1720 GMT (0220 Local)

The overcast sky blanketed Captain Hadley with a sense of security. He'd never felt it on prior trips to the Amur. The clouds held the warmth of the day beneath them. Hadley found himself unzipping his gear during the arduous trek through the deep forest drifts.

But clouds also meant darkness. No moon or starlight

penetrated the overcast sky. That was both a blessing and a curse. A blessing in that his men carried night-vision goggles and the Chinese didn't. The point and rear men and machine gunner wore theirs constantly. But the dim light was also a hazard. Nothing triggered a firefight more certainly than stepping right on an ambusher.

Hadley heard curses from the line up ahead. It was the second time he'd heard noise from his men. It was probably nothing more than a low branch. They were growing too comfortable with these missions. Not once in their five trips had they seen any Chinese. That bred a sense of solitude. Of being all alone in an impossibly big space. *That,* in turn, led to sloppiness. All it took was one chance encounter for them to get swallowed up by endless forests.

Four men lashed together with rope headed out onto the ice with the drill. The man in front rolled the wheel that measured the distance. The three who followed—

A resounding crunch broke the silence like a gunshot. Hadley scanned the white ice for the source. Three men— he counted only three. Two more men rushed out onto the frozen river. Hadley followed them down the bank onto the ice. It was his first time out in the open. He hadn't realized just how exposed it felt.

Brief shouts and gasps for air could be heard. Everyone was lying on their bellies and inching forward. "Help!" came a watery splutter. It was followed by the splashing sounds of a drowning man. Hadley and the two men with him dropped to their stomachs and began to crawl. He could see two forearms being held above the water. Men were counting in unison. When they said *"Three!"* they pulled with loud grunts. For an instant they hoisted the soldier from the black river.

He gasped for air and coughed before being dragged back under. It was as if a great shark held his feet and fought his rescuers. The soldier slowly sank into the ever-expanding hole. On the next pull the two men got a rope under his armpits. Hadley and the reinforcements went upstream of the hole to begin a tug-of-war against the powerful current. They sat on the ice and pulled against the raging force of the water.

Hadley got to his feet and dug in his heels. Without saying a word the other men did the same. Hadley could feel the ice almost break underneath him. Several times he repositioned his feet at the last second. Two more men arrived just then from the bank. On whispered count, the five of them pulled and dragged the fallen man out of the water. For good measure they pulled him away from the hole. The medical officer slipped an oxygen mask over his face. The others quickly stripped their comrade of his clothing in silence. Off came his parka, his liner, his long underwear. Off came his boots and his shell and his insulated leggings. The dark-skinned African-American sergeant lay naked against the white ice.

They hustled to put dry clothes on him quickly. Everyone carried extra clothing. They dried and dressed the man from head to foot. It was done rapidly, but even so he suffered extreme hypothermia.

"Everybody back to the tree line!" Hadley ordered.

"What about the core sample?" asked the lieutenant who led the team with the drill.

"*Fuck* the core sample!" Hadley replied. "We're outta here! Call for a medevac. Ditch Jeter's wet clothes and the drill through the hole in the ice. We'll double-time it to the emergency pickup zone."

"But our orders are to—" the lieutenant began to object.

"*Listen*, West Point!" Hadley shot back. "They wanna know how thick that ice is? Well, we got their answer! Mission aborted!"

UNRUSFOR HEADQUARTERS, KHABAROVSK
April 12, 2000 GMT (0600 Local)

Clark pinned the new silver oak-leaf cluster on Reed's epaulets. He then shook his aide's hand. "Congratulations, Lieutenant Colonel Reed," Clark said. There was applause from the gathering of staff, who shook hands with an unsmiling Reed.

Clark had a call to make. He went into his office and shut the door. He picked up the dedicated line, spoke to a series of operators, and waited. "General Clark?" finally came the voice of the man for whom he was waiting.

"Mr. President, I've given the action order. Operation Winter Harvest will be launched on April fourteenth—in two days."

"Wonderful!" Davis said. "The timing couldn't be any better from where I sit. You give me five days of battlefield successes, and we'll win that vote on the nineteenth. Then we win the war."

When they hung up, there was a knock on the door. It was Reed. He again looked sheepish. "I have a favor to ask, sir," he said without looking Clark's way. "I'd like to get out into the field. Help out where I can. Even if it's a staff position somewhere. I'd just like to—"

"I understand," Clark said. "But I need you too." Reed wasn't going to object. "I'll keep my eyes open. Maybe something will come along." Reed nodded. "Now let's start issuing unit orders."

BIROBIDZHAN FIREBASE, SIBERIA
April 13, 2200 GMT (0800 Local)

"Light duty's over, fuckface." Stempel looked up from his computer. "Hey!" he shouted at his squadmates, who crowded into the door of the bunker. He greeted the seven men like long-lost friends. He'd been out to the perimeter to visit his squad several times, but this was their first trip to the rear to see him. They exchanged high fives. Harold's wounds had largely healed, but he winced from habit as they slapped his hand. "You guys gettin' some R and R or something?" he asked.

"Knock it off!" an unseen NCO boomed through the open entrance to his office.

McAndrews grabbed his crotch and pulled in a silent insult of the man. He then looked around at the bare sand-bagged walls. "So you got heat in here too, huh?"

"Yeah," Stempel replied, proudly showing off their electric space heater. "And they let us sleep here."

"This is too *fine*!" Patterson said.

The master sergeant emerged. "What the hell're you doin' in here?" he shouted.

"We come to get Stemp," Patterson replied.

"And who the hell sent you?"

"The CO hisself. Said he was takin' Stemp off light duty and that we was to come 'n get him."

"He can't just up and yank one of my people outta here!" the man snarled. "Shit! Who's gonna log supplies in?"

· Stempel's squadmates looked at each other. "I will!" several said at the same time.

The grumbling master sergeant went out in search of an officer. Stempel scrambled to gather his things before he returned. The visitors eyed his laptop computer. On it glowed an inventory management program. They helped themselves to a six-pack of diet Coke they found in a rucksack.

"Shit, man!" Stempel objected. "Sarge is gonna tear you a new asshole if you take those!"

"*Fuck* him!" Patterson replied as he slipped two cans in his parka. "Let him hump his butt outta Club Med here and come find me."

Music began to play from the sergeant's office.

"Jeez!" Stempel shouted. He ran toward the cramped room. Two of the guys were dancing to the country music on the master sergeant's boom box. "What the . . . !" Stempel said, then leaped for the "stop" button. The bunker fell quiet save for the laughter. "If he heard you usin' up his batteries like that he'd *kill* you!"

Chavez's M-16 rose instantly to his shoulder. Stempel stared down the rifle muzzle and the forty-millimeter grenade launcher under its barrel from a distance of two feet. There was a grenade in the launcher's chamber, and thirty rounds in the banana clip. BORN TO KILL was scrawled on the man's white cloth helmet cover. Chavez relaxed and pointed the weapon away. But the grin on the man's face wasn't reassuring. Everyone in the squad kept their distance from Chavez.

They hurried out of the bunker before the NCO returned. Stempel joined his squadmates in the fresh, cool air. The whine of jet engines was nearly constant. Giant C-17s had been landing for days. Their noise had become a part of the background.

Patterson looked at Stempel and screwed his face up. "Ain't that just like a rear area motherfucker." He grabbed Stempel's bulging field pack and rocked him from side to side. "Got so much shit in here he can't even hump it all." The men descended on the overflowing pack.

"Hey, come on!" Stempel shouted as they began to toss his things into the slush. When his load was lighter, they headed down the communications trench toward the perimeter. Stempel collected a few of the essentials they'd discarded, but left most of the stuff where it lay. He hurried to catch up with the others, who walked single file down the narrow slit in the earth.

They passed into the wider security trench that ran alongside the runway. Transports off-loaded huge crates of supplies. Stempel's squadmates yelled taunts at the newly arrived airmen. "Welcome to hell!" one shouted. The air-force shits wore ear protectors, but they took the oversized headphones off and walked over toward them. "You got any booze or pot?" Patterson asked.

"Yeah," one of the airmen replied, laughing. "Sure! What you got to trade?"

"How 'bout a Chinese SKS? Got blood on it and everything! You can tell the folks back home you killed him yourself!"

The air-force troops all stood around their low-slung tractors and forklifts laughing. They'd obviously just flown in to help unload. In the day or so since Stempel had last been by, the airfield had become jam-packed with crates, fuel bladders, trucks, and Humvees.

"If you got a string of Chinese ears or noses or somethin', " came the reply from an airman, "I'll get you a fifth of Scotch!"

Patterson wheeled to walk backward and shouted, "I'll get you a necklace of *dicks* for a fifth of Scotch, motherfucker!" Everyone laughed. The airmen donned their ear protectors. A giant C-17 lumbered to the edge of the tarmac. "Who's policin' the wire this morning?" Patterson asked.

"They don't got no fifth of fuckin' *Scotch*!" McAndrews replied derisively.

"You heard the guy!" Patterson shot back. There were snorts from his squadmates. "No, really! They're just lyin' around out there. It ain't like they're gonna use 'em again!"

"Patterson, you are one *sick* motherfucker!"

When Patterson finally gave up on his impossible dream, Stempel asked, "Is there any news about reinforcements?"

"Ain't you heard?" McAndrews said. "Man, Stemp's gonna drop a load in his trousers when he hears this." There were chuckles.

"What?" Harold asked. The line of men halted, bunched up in the trench by their momentum. Men rested against the walls and looked Stempel in the eye. "What the hell's goin' on?" Stempel asked again.

"Some asshole general back in the Pentagon thinks we've been fuckin' off around here," Patterson said. "Thinks maybe Uncle Sam ain't gettin' a fair day's work outta us."

Stempel shook his head. "I don't understand."

"We got 'The Word.' We're climbin' into full battle rattle and goin' over the top."

"What?" Stempel said. "Like a patrol?"

Heads shook. "We're goin' on the offensive," McAndrews said. Although his squadmates' looks ranged from excitement to exhaustion, most were grim. "Tomorrow morning before first light we're packin' up and pushin' south."

"Toward the *border*?" Stempel asked, incredulous. "Toward *China*?"

No one answered his question, but they didn't need to. The looks on their faces told all.

"Hey!" Patterson said. "Look at that!" He pointed back toward the newly arrived transport plane.

A loadmaster was walking backward down the angled rear ramp of the C-17. He waved his two flashlights like traffic batons. In the dim light of the cavernous cargo bay you could see the metal tracks of an armored fighting vehicle. A white-painted Bradley with its twenty-five-millimeter chain gun and four TOW antitank launchers rolled into the sunlight.

"Son of a *bitch*!" McAndrews slowly intoned.

A ripple of excitement registered by smiles quickly spread through the infantrymen. "Guess we're ridin' in *style*!" Patterson chirped. There were high fives of celebration. They hurried toward the perimeter, stopping along the way to pass news of this latest development.

OUTSIDE SOFLYSK, SIBERIA
April 14, 1600 GMT (0200 Local)

Chin almost didn't see the others in the darkness. They were squatting and totally silent. "Where the hell have you been?" the company commander hissed.

"I brought a man back with me to look for an ambulance," Chin explained.

"And so you go roaming around the countryside while we sit here waiting for you?"

"Where's your man?" Hung asked Chin.

"He died."

His fellow lieutenants all fell silent. The company commander let it drop. "All right," he said, "we're pulling back." That was it? Three months of driving ever northward—three months during which suggestion of retreat could get you shot for treason—and now the orders to withdraw were so casually delivered?

"What's going on?" Hung asked.

"None of your business!" the captain shot back. "You

don't get paid to ask questions! You get paid to follow orders!''

"I haven't been *paid* in two months," Hung mumbled.

"*What did you say*?" the CO replied. He was so angry his voice rose. Chin could hear the rustle of fabric as he twisted around and checked the trees.

"I said I haven't been paid in two months . . . *sir*. And I haven't eaten in almost two days. And none of us has had a day off from combat in almost three weeks."

There was silence. Everyone waited. "Are you looking to get arrested?" the company commander asked in a low and menacing tone. " 'Cause if you are, you can *forget* it! And while we're on the subject, orders have come down that if there are any more self-inflicted wounds in this regiment, the colonel will personally finish the job!"

"My man didn't shoot himself!" Hung objected. "He was wounded in a firefight!"

"In the foot? It just so *happened* that he only lost a toe— his little toe at that?"

"It happens! People get shot all over! I had a man get his balls shot clean off! You think he did that on purpose? Two of my men lost their lower jaws . . . from the *same bullet*! One man got a flesh wound in his shoulder! Only he died, 'cause the bullet didn't ricochet out from his bone, like we thought! It tumbled *into* his chest! I lost my senior sergeant when he started complaining about a headache after an artillery barrage! When he passed out, we looked all over his body for the wound! We stripped him naked right in the snow 'cause he was turning white as a sheet! Somebody finally noticed he had a ti-iny speck of blood on his temple, and another under his hairline on the opposite side of his head! A metal splinter from one of the shell casings had gone straight through his brain! He didn't even know he'd been hurt till he keeled over. He died four hours later.''

Hung had clearly forgotten whatever point he was making. But in his agitated state no one made any attempt to shut him up. When he ran out of steam, the company commander said simply, "Get your men packed up and ready to pull back in an hour."

"In the middle of the night?" Hung questioned. "We're heading back toward our own guns in the middle of the night?"

"Everybody's pulling back!" the captain explained. "Don't you understand? Can't you get what I'm saying through your thick skulls? One hour! Listen for the whistle!"

Chin had pulled his platoon in tight around him so as not to get separated in the darkness. In the distance he heard several tentative toots from whistles. They weren't the vigorous, repeated blows signaling an attack, but brief and hesitant sounds emanating from men who clearly cherished anonymity. Invisibility. Chin couldn't tell the one meant for his company from any of the others, but he decided it didn't really matter. "Everybody up!" he ordered.

His men rose. They followed him back over ground they'd fought for the day before, and then over ground from the day before that. The woods around them were filled with movement. They completely lost contact with their brother platoons. After the first few tense encounters with strangers, Chin and his men let down their guard. They even took comfort from the shadowy figures streaming south alongside them. The thought occurred to Chin that some might be American infiltrators. But he silently just wished the concern away. He was determined to avoid contact no matter what.

The first sign of danger he saw was lightning. At least that's what it looked like. But it lasted too long, and the rumble that arrived seconds later went on and on and on. The unearthly noise of the distant air strike set his men talking.

"Quiet!" Chin snapped.

The next strike was much, much closer. The booms could now be made out individually, though they still sounded out of time with the flashes. They were loud enough, however, to be jarring. Chin flinched with almost every string. They were brief strobes of a man-made thunderstorm that rattled the air and lit the dark woods. In the flickering light he could see fear quickly taking hold of his men's faces. Their eyes darted this way and that. Even their pace began to pick up.

Chin found himself being passed by jogging troops. His initial reaction was to command them to slow down. They were supposed to be following him. But on second thought he instead quickened *his* step, as did the other units against whom they brushed in the night.

The dark forests suddenly erupted with fire. Everyone threw themselves to the earth as the screeching jets tore through the sky overhead. They bombed the now distant positions Chin and his men had just abandoned. From a distance of several kilometers the explosions did little more than shake loose snow from the trees.

At least that was what Chin thought at first. When everyone rose to their feet, they didn't jog away from the sound of the bombs . . . they ran. "Hold on!" Chin shouted, but they didn't listen. The few men who remained by his side nervously searched the woods. When the bombing began again—much closer—someone shouted, "*America-a-ans!*" at the top of his lungs.

That began the panic. All Chin could see in the fiery flashes were the moving forms of fleeing Chinese troops. Like a herd made anxious by an unfamiliar scent, they fled now from demons only imagined. He rose to run after his men. To collect them as a shepherd might round up his flock. But the *pum-pum-pum* of a loud cannon to the rear drew his complete attention. It's rapid fire was like nothing he'd ever heard.

He knelt behind a tree and saw a large armored vehicle approaching through the woods to his right. As it raced past the thin trees and crashed through the thick snowdrifts, its gun again opened fire. Glowing tracers shot far into the distance at incredible speed. It was already firing well past where Chin lay. Firing at some target that Chin couldn't even see. But the batlike gunner on the speeding vehicle could see. The night was bright with targets for him.

An identical vehicle raced by on the opposite side of Chin. And there was another even farther away. They were barreling at thirty kilometers per hour into the Chinese, who were panicked and offered no resistance. And how could anyone stop such a thing? All Chin had was his rifle and a single hand grenade.

Just before a second line of armored vehicles pulled even with Chin, he lay behind a tree and pressed himself flat. The sound of machine guns and rifles fired from parts filled the woods. He lay there until the sound of the engines receded into the distance behind him. Then he lay there until he could no longer hear the guns and the bombing runs. Then he waited for the sun to come up.

He didn't rise from that spot, in fact, until ordered at gunpoint. Then he rose carefully, slowly, his hands high in the air as the nervous Americans shouted orders he didn't understand.

SOUTH OF URGAL, SIBERIA
April 14, 2300 GMT (1800 Local)

The crowded Bradley armored fighting vehicle rocked and bumped along at high speed. Kate and Woody were thrown every which way, banging shoulders and knees with the mechanized infantry squad. Woody had tried at first to shoot the scene, but he'd given up with mumbled complaints about bad light.

The men sat with their backs to the walls. They were quiet and wore looks of deep concern. They were new to the war Kate had learned as she did eve-of-battle interviews with several. They'd only just flown into Siberia, having remained in Japan as part of the "strategic deception plan." They looked little older than high-school boys, and they had attempted unsuccessfully to hide their fears. All of which, Kate knew, made for the first good footage in weeks.

The squad leader began talking on the radio. His words were almost shouted, but Kate could barely hear them over the whining engine. He traced coordinates on the map with his finger. He repeated, "Roger that! Roger that!"

When the sergeant got off the radio, he squatted in the narrow center aisle. "Listen up! We're gonna provide flank security to the main breakthrough! When we dismount, I want everybody to follow me toward a line of low ridges! We'll set up there and refuse to the east! One of the recon units up ahead sighted dismounted Chicom infantry moving toward that ridge! We're gonna drop our packs and double-time it so's we get up that ridge first!"

Even before he'd finished, the Bradley began to slow to a stop. The engine noise dropped off noticeably. Men scrambled to get a hold of their gear. The sergeant pulled his bulging pack toward the rear and knelt awkwardly amid the press of knees. The double doors opened. Men raced into the darkness outside. Kate and Woody were the last two out.

The doors closed and the Bradley took off. The soldiers all dropped their loads and raced for the dark outline of a hill. She and Woody followed, but very quickly they lost contact with the men. Woody grabbed Kate's arm and pulled her down into the snow.

"Woody!" Kate objected, but he hushed her angrily. "Woody," she whispered, "we can't just loiter around here in the dark. That's more dangerous than—"

He tackled her flat to the ground. She didn't know what possessed him to crush her like that, but she lay there scanning the woods for danger. It took her a few moments to see the dark silhouettes of moving men.

Nearly a dozen men emerged from the tree line. They walked slowly like a wary patrol. At first she felt sure they were Americans. But their differently shaped helmets were a dead giveaway.

Chinese!

Kate and Woody lay absolutely still, but it was no use. The Chinese headed straight for them. Each step of their approach was announced by the crunch and squeak of their boots . . . ever nearer.

Kate raised her head. The Chinese soldiers stood all around. They had thrown down their weapons. Their hands were raised to the tops of their helmets. Woody got to his feet.

"You guys are all under arrest," Woody said. "Get down on your knees." He motioned, and then demonstrated what he wanted.

"Woody!" Kate cautioned. But the Chinese slowly sank to the ground, their hands still atop their heads. Some whimpered pathetic pleas in Chinese. Some cried. Their faces were frostbitten. One man who was missing several teeth held up family photos and begged. By the time the first American soldiers arrived, the number of prisoners had grown to almost a hundred.

"THE FARM," WEST VIRGINIA
April 15, 2300 GMT (1800 Local)

Pyotr Andreev followed the instructor to the range. It was a sunny day. The place looked like a public park. They stopped at a picnic table with bench seats covered by a small shingled roof. On the table lay a half-dozen weapons.

"All right, two fifty-three," the instructor began, calling Pyotr by his anonymous case number. He had a gray, "flat-top" haircut and the protruding stomach of a middle-aged man. "What we have here is your primary weapon—a semiauto .50-caliber sniper rifle, military issue—and your choice of secondary weapons." The selection included an Uzi, a Heckler & Koch MP-5, and an Ingram MAC-10. The man started to go over the strengths and weaknesses of the lot, but Pyotr picked up the Ingram. It was the .45-caliber version, not the lighter nine-millimeter. He slapped a magazine into the pistol grip.

"Okay," the instructor said, following him the short distance to the target range. "The MAC-10 is a helluva weapon for close-in combat." The man stopped beside

Pyotr. Three plastic jugs filled with water sat atop a pitted
wall of concrete blocks. A thick earthen embankment lay
behind. Single shots cracked rapidly—at killing pace—in
the distance. Pyotr held the weapon at his hip. He grasped
the pistol grip firmly with his right hand and wrapped his
left in the leather strap that hung from the muzzle. "It fires
standard .45-caliber pistol ammo. The rounds' tremendous
stopping power is also the weapon's main drawback. It
tends to ride straight up into the air when you—"

Pyotr squeezed the trigger. The weapon thundered. It
bucked and shook and shot flame a foot out of the end of
its short barrel. Pyotr fought a losing battle to control the
machine pistol for a second and a half, then the weapon
fell silent. "God*dam*mit!" the instructor yelled. "I give the
goddamn order to fire on this range! You do that one more
time and . . . !"

He fell silent. His mouth was still open. He stared down
the range toward the targets. There were no jugs on the
wall. "Cease fire," he said as an afterthought. He took off
down the range. Pyotr followed. Shredded and twisted
pieces of plastic lay on the ground behind the wall. The
gray concrete blocks beneath the targets were dry. The water had been sprayed all over the soggy embankment behind
the wall.

The instructor never looked his way. "*Don't* fire any
weapon on *my* range again without my *go*-ahead! You *got*
that?"

Pyotr nodded. They had asked him to say as little as
possible. His accent betrayed too many things.

The instructor picked up a new jug of water and put it
on the wall. When he turned, Pyotr poured water from the
container down the wall on the right-hand side. "Hey!
Leave it full. We use these gallon milk containers 'cause
they're the same density as a human torso when filled with
water." When the light gray blocks on the right were dark,
Pyotr placed the jug atop the wall on the left-hand side and
headed back to the picnic table. "So," his trainer said,
"you'll take the MAC. Let's move on to this mother." He

raised the huge black rifle. "This is a Barrett 82A1 ten-shot, .50-caliber. It fires these," he said, tilting the open top of an enormous black magazine so that Pyotr could see the stack of rounds inside. They were over five inches long. The thick, metal-jacketed bullets were propelled by an enormous charge. The cartridges were the width of a man's thumb. "Standard .50-cal. BMG cartridge made for the Browning M-2—'Ma Deuce'—machine gun. Been around since 1917. Longest confirmed kill was February 1967 in Vietnam. Lance Corporal Carlos Norman Hathcock the second—2,500 yards." He looked at Pyotr. "One-point-four-two miles."

"I would prefer a manual bolt," Pyotr said, "instead of a semiauto."

"I know where you're headed," the instructor replied, shaking his head. "But this bolt is rock solid. It gives an excellent, stable base to the chamber. It's every damn bit as accurate as any Springfield ever fired and it's got six times the killing power."

Pyotr just frowned. The other rounds in the magazine were just excess weight. Like the old adage about striking at the king, you had to kill with your first blow.

"Get a feel for the weapon's weight," the instructor said. It had a trimmed-down, tubular construction. Not much stock to speak of. Built-in scope, bipod, and carrying handle. The only things disproportionately massive about the weapon were the thick barrel and enormous magazine. Pyotr took the long rifle from his hands. "Weighs thirty pounds with the scope and bipod." Pyotr took the magazine from him as well. "Thirty-four fully loaded." Pyotr slammed the magazine home and yanked the bolt back against the stiff spring. "No firing till I say, remember?" Pyotr safed the weapon and nodded. "Let's head back a ways. You don't get any fifty-foot shots with this thing."

As they walked, the instructor lectured on the principles of sniping. Elementary things like surveillance, conceal-ment, light, wind. The effects on the round's trajectory of humidity. An introduction to long-range killing. They reached their destination—250 meters from the target, according to the sign. The instructor climbed up to the firing position. Pyotr didn't follow. ''My range will be 425 meters,'' Pyotr replied.

''Well, I know, but this is the first day.''

Pyotr and the man eyed each other. ''Four hundred and twenty-five meters,'' Pyotr repeated.

The instructor picked up a small sandbag and they continued their walk. He also resumed the lecture. When the man informed Pyotr that the rifle wouldn't break down, Pyotr stopped in surprise. ''It'll be zeroed in right here—on the range. The elevation set for 425 meters. The round's trajectory will send it about nine feet above your line of sight. You just need to make sure you don't bang it around too damn much.''

''How the hell am I supposed to—'' Pyotr shut himself up. Infiltration was an operational detail. This man wouldn't know anything about it. The remainder of the way, Pyotr fumed over such a ridiculous choice for a weapon. Standing on the ground, it came up almost to his chest. And he was supposed to walk straight into Red Square carrying it.

There were range markers every twenty-five meters like on the driving range of a golf course. At 425, the instructor dropped the sandbag to the ground. Pyotr laid the rifle on its side with the barrel resting atop the bag. He began to stretch his muscles.

''Good, good,'' the instructor said. ''A lot of people overlook the importance of good muscular relaxation. Do you have any natural tics or muscle contractions?'' Pyotr shook his head. He leaned over to pull up a few sprigs of grass. ''Marksmanship is also a lot about breathing.'' Pyotr let the grass fall from eye level. It drifted slightly to his left. ''Deep, regular breaths.'' Pyotr lay on his stomach behind the weapon. The instructor lay down beside him, taking the lens covers off his oversized binoculars. ''When you get ready for the pull, switch to shallow, rhythmic breathing.'' Pyotr pressed the huge butt plate of the rifle firmly against the hollow of his shoulder. He reached up and turned the windage knob one click to the plus side. "Then, when you're settling in on the target, fill your lungs halfway and hold it."

Pyotr peered through the sights with his eye nearly four inches behind the padded rear lens. At that distance, the scope's field of view tunneled to near extreme. But that was preferable to the telltale bloody ring around the eyes of rookie shooters. Besides, the water-soaked concrete blocks filled the sight nicely. By feel alone Pyotr switched the selector from "safe" to "fire."

"*Hey*, douche bag!" the instructor snapped immediately. The man handed Pyotr large ear protectors. The two men put the oversized headphones on. "The Barrett uses muzzle brakes to diffuse recoil. The old guns kicked like mules. These are more like a twelve-gauge. But the brakes make 'em loud as hell. You'd be deaf as a post if you fired this mother unprotected."

"May I fire?" Pyotr asked.

"Not till I say!"

Pyotr waited. "May I fire now?" he asked after a few seconds.

"All right, Mr. Professional. Mr. I-Know-What-The-Fuck-I'm—"

The shot sounded like an explosion even with the ear protectors. Pyotr would've fired a second round almost instantly had his hand not risen out of habit to work the bolt. As it was, he got another round off in a heartbeat. Then another, and another, and another. Pyotr looked over at the instructor.

The man lowered the powerful binoculars from his eyes. "You ready to do some listening for a change?" he asked testily.

"I always listen," Pyotr replied.

"Yeah, well, I know you're on a fast track here, but there are some fundamentals that will help you hit your target next time. 'One shot, one kill'—that's our motto."

"But I hit the target," Pyotr objected politely.

The CIA man raised his binoculars. "That jug's still sittin' there. If one of those rounds had even nicked the thing it'd be . . .'' He froze. He presumably saw now the opposite end of the wall. The right-hand side that Pyotr had darkened with water until it was approximately the width and height of a man's torso. He lowered the binoculars and got to his feet without looking at Pyotr. ''Safe that weapon,'' he said as he headed for the target area. Pyotr followed.

There was a man-sized gap in the wall. The water-soaked concrete blocks were gone. Obliterated. Pieces no larger than a fist littered the ground all the way back to the embankment. All the instructor said was, ''You fucked up our wall.'' Pyotr apologized.

20

The table was abuzz with excitement when Clark entered the room, but the din quickly died down. The commanders of the various national forces were obviously far too pleased with the results only three days into the campaign. Clark resolved to set them straight.

"The ice is already breaking at Luobei," he announced. The intensity of the men's expressions rose a notch. "Recon overflights report black water visible across fifteen percent of the surface." He tossed photos of the Amur River onto the table. The generals all reached for them at once. In moments they were scrutinizing the black-and-white high-altitude shots. The previously solid white highway of ice was spotted with black like a dalmatian. "That ice could go any minute now, gentlemen," Clark warned ominously.

"Thank God we're ahead of schedule," the British commander said. He held his reading glasses at an angle to study a photo.

"We're not ahead of schedule, we're behind," Clark retorted, drawing quizzical looks from the joint staff. "I've accelerated the timetable. I want first units across that river in three days."

A commotion now filled the room. "That is impossible!" the French commander objected. He drew vigorous nods of support. "That is demanding too great a price from the troops. And," he said in a lowered voice and a sweep of his gaze around the table, "it will leave us exposed to local attacks all along our flanks. Is the ice breaking more quickly than we thought?"

"No," Clark replied. "The Chinese are." He nodded to Lieutenant Colonel, who began handing out the new timetable. "The objectives are all the same," Clark continued. "On the basis, however, of our initial success in breaching the Chinese lines—and after review of the state of the ice on the Amur—the time to take those objectives has been reduced by half."

Again there was a stir. But this one was decidedly less vocal. What Clark was proposing was a risk-laden change of plan. "What about the danger to our flanks?" the senior German general inquired.

Clark finally sat. His delay in responding was not simply theater. He too was concerned about advancing so rapidly. Not only were they leaving their flanks largely unguarded, there were forgone opportunities and unforeseeable risks. Field commanders would be ordered to disregard their better judgment. To let pass chances to consolidate their positions by seizing terrain. To plunge ahead with inadequate reconnaissance. To bypass immobilized Chinese formations who might spring to life and hit them from behind.

"We either win this war," Clark began slowly, "with *this* operation, or we lose it. Not to win the war here and now *is* to lose. That isn't a military fact, it's a political one. Each of us now knows after seeing Chinese units fold one after another that we can defeat their armies *north* of the Amur. We can kill or capture 600,000 men, destroy all their heavy weapons, seize their stores of supplies, retake *all* of the territory they seized from Russia . . . and still lose the war in the process. Because no matter how successful this operation is *militarily,* our troops are going home soon. And when we leave Siberia, we cede it to the half-million Chinese troops *south* of the Amur . . . *unless* they too are defeated.''

Clark knew he was stating the obvious. *Re*stating it for the hundredth time. But by their silence the joint staff allowed him to continue. To focus them on the war's bigger picture. For Clark's primary function as commanding general was to translate the broader perspective on the war into orders. To ensure that their missions and plans remained consistent with overall geopolitical objectives.

''In order to achieve total victory we have to risk total defeat. We have to put people across the Amur into China even though powerful forces remain operational to their rear. Even though we know that the day will come quite soon when they'll be cut off by the flowing ice. We're going for broke, gentlemen. *All* out. Starting right now, with those timetables you have in your hands.''

''Since you broached the subject,'' the British commander interrupted, his brow knit as he studied the thick sheaf of papers, ''it appears you've made an error on page four.''

Everyone began flipping pages in their copies . . . except Clark. ''It's not an error,'' he said.

''Pardon me, Nate,'' his good friend from the British Army said, departing from his usual crisp, professional tone, ''but this is *suicide*. You are consigning a *brigade* of your troops and your entire 75th Ranger Regiment to a mission that . . . that even if we're *successful* in crossing the Amur in accordance with the new timetable could result in their total annihilation! You're sending troops into that valley far, far too soon. I'm sorry, Nate, but I must object.''

Clark took a deep breath. ''The Jinan Army Group is already moving up—we just got the intell.'' There was a stir. ''But at this *very* instant there's a gap, and I'm inserting that brigade into it. If we take that valley now, we'll block the road-rail line. We'll isolate the north from the rest of China. And we'll pocket fifty divisions—over three quarter of a million troops—south of the Amur.''

The French commander checked the table of organization

and equipment in his briefing book. "But they have to hold off an entire army group by themselves. Two armored divisions. Ten infantry divisions. Three airborne divisions. Over 175,000 *men,* General Clark."

Nate replied. "We have air supremacy, and I've ordered the air commander to pound every kilometer of those columns with everything we've got round the clock. Fewer than half should arrive in that valley. Those who do make it will be disorganized, exhausted, terrified, and green. The men I'm committing against them are hardened professionals, and they're fighting in terrain that's *perfect* for defense. On-the-ground recon reports the hills are broken by deep furrows, pointed outcroppings, and shallow cuts. The defenders will have good cover, the attackers will be canalized into firing lanes, and we will own the air." Clark felt a heavy weight descend around him. "They're my troops, they can be put in with lighter loads than the 82nd Airborne, and Brigadier General Lawson asked for the job. I take full responsibility for the 75th Ranger Regiment, and for First Brigade, 101st Airborne." Clark rose. "Meeting adjourned."

VLADIVOSTOK, SIBERIA
April 18, 0600 GMT (1600 Local)

"Things must be goin' to shit," one of André Faulk's squadmates said.

"Naw, *man!*" another retorted. "I hear from this jerk-off over in signal corps that the Chinese are runnin' like scalded dogs! This war is *over,* man!"

The door burst open. In walked two clerks from battalion headquarters.

"Close the goddamn door!" came a shout as the cold air quickly chilled the room. The clerks extracted a thick bundle from a sack. It reminded André of a mail call from long, long ago. Of Aguire and the others, ending with Wolfson . . .

The clerks pulled rubber bands off the bundles with loud snaps.

"What the hell's that?" asked one of the guys.

"What the fuck does it *look* like?" a clerk replied.

"It *looks* like a goddamn map! But you ain't answerin' my *question*!" He had to be restrained by his squadmates. The clerk threatened to bring an end to their hopes.

The headquarters guy smirked. He handed out the new maps. "There's a battalion meeting at eighteen hundred hours. Hangar B." They left. The mood in the room turned foul.

"What the fuck is this?" Men opened the fan-folded maps. "Su-i-bin? Tang-yu-an? That don't sound Russian to me."

André focused not on the towns and streams and mountains. He traced the single salient feature on the map. A river snaked along the top—to the north. Its name was the Amur.

There was abundant noise in the large hangar. It was like a bitch session on a battalion scale.

"Ten-*shun*!" the booming voice called.

Chairs scraped across the gym floor. André Faulk and his entire battalion rose. Nervous chatter died to absolute quiet during the battalion commander's ascent to the stage. André's eyes fixed on the man's face. "At ease!" the colonel called out from the podium. His voice was loud. "Take your seats."

The noise from all the movement ended quickly as the six hundred men settled in.

The battalion commander stared down at a single sheet of paper. He shoved it into his breast pocket when the noise subsided. "I guess you've all been hearing rumors. Some of those rumors are true. We are currently kicking the butts of the Chinese." There was an eruption of laughter and good cheer. A release of pent-up tension. "But this war isn't over yet!" The hanger fell silent quickly. "At least not for us."

The man next to André mumbled, "Oh, shit." A chill ran down André's spine.

The battalion commander's head was bowed. "And I know we've taken more than our fair share of casualties."

Again André's neighbor said, "Oooh, shit."

"But we've got one more mission to execute. One more before we go home."

"This ain't good at all," the talkative guy commented. That drew a "Shut-the-fuck-up!" from the guy behind, and a "Knock-it-off!" from an NCO.

"Four days ago we launched Operation Winter Harvest. That offensive is about to enter a new phase. We are about to cross the border into the People's Republic of China. And this battalion—you men—are going to be sent into China once the first troops cross the Amur River." A minor disturbance was quelled by barking NCOs. A sudden and deep fatigue overcame André, who found himself shutting his eyes as the colonel continued. "We're going on a strike *deep* behind enemy lines." There wasn't a cough, a whisper, an audible breath. "A battalion of rangers will jump to secure the LZ. Our entire brigade will go in heliborne. Wheels up at nineteen hundred . . . tomorrow."

There were a few mumbled curses. André's stomach gurgled.

The colonel continued. "Altogether, we'll number only seven thousand men. Our mission will be to sever the main supply route between Manchuria and Beijing." He strolled out from behind the podium. His head was bowed deep in thought. André's eyes sank closed again. "Our mission is to seize a mountain valley with steep, rocky walls. The Chinese will try to push their way through. It will be mountain fighting. Infantry warfare. A battle for the heights. The fighting will be close-in. If we hold key terrain, we win. If we're pushed off, we lose. It's that simple. I'm not going to shit any of you men. They're gonna throw everything they've got at us. They'll envelop us. Fight us for every crevice, every boulder, every log."

André found himself falling asleep. He caught his falling head once and got nudged by his neighbor the second time. He half listened to the remainder of the meeting. Extra loads. Inspections. Last mail call. Details not bravado. And not a word of complaint from the troops. That André understood. Sickening dread had a deadening effect. In André it caused almost narcotic sleepiness.

SOUTH OF BIROBIDZHAN AIRBASE, SIBERIA
April 18, 0800 GMT (1800 Local)

The two-and-a-half-ton truck bumped along the rough track that passed as a road. Harold Stempel was cold and cramped in the canvas-covered bed. The driver ground his way through the gears, and everyone stared at each other glumly.

It was a far cry from the Bradleys in which they all assumed they'd be riding. The Bradleys were just as uncomfortable. But the ignominy of riding into battle aboard ordinary diesel trucks was a little too much for the light infantrymen to bear.

"You know this whole thing sucks!" Patterson said, bitching yet again about their mistreatment by the army. "Those bastards fly in here from the States or Japan or wherever, climb right outta them warm planes and into them warm Bradleys, and then *ri-i-ide* on off to win the war."

McAndrews replied, "Hey! You wanna be mixin' it up with the fuckin' Chinese? I'm sure a lot of those fuckers'd change places with you about now."

"But that ain't the point, is it? The point is respect, and how we don't get none. Ever since that first day when . . ." His eyes shot over to Stempel. He didn't go on, but everybody knew where he was headed. He was alluding to the "lost battalion," the overrun unit with which Stempel had deployed. They'd all heard the talk. Light infantry wasn't as good as the airborne or airmobile troops, and it wasn't as well equipped as mech or armor. Stempel had heard other talk as well. If the lost battalion had put up a stiffer fight, maybe this or that would've been different.

"Hey, man," Chavez said with a sneer. "We're trench

troops. They'll pro'bly have us pullin' sentry duty at some
supply depot.''

"The *hell* you say!" came one of the several profane
responses.

All of a sudden the truck slowed. The men at the rear
untied the canvas flap of the clunky "deuce-and-a-half."
With a final grinding of the gears, the brakes were set and
the engine shut off.

"Everybody *o-o-o*ut!" came the command from outside.

Stempel and the others piled out through the open flap.
They were in the middle of nowhere, but the crisp air was
invigorating after the carnivallike ride in the back of the
truck. They shouldered their heavy packs at the tailgate.

"Let's go, girls!" Stempel's platoon sergeant commanded. Bent under the weight of their loads, the men
trudged up a low hill. When they reached the crest, they
all stood and stared. Thousands and thousands of Chinese
sat or squatted in the valley below. A lieutenant with an
MP armband ascended the hill to meet them. "Man, am I
glad *you're* here!"

"You had any trouble, sir?" the platoon sergeant asked
the much younger officer.

"No. But we got another few thousand on their way, so
I hear. And night's falling in a few hours."

The platoon sergeant turned to his men and ordered,
"Packs off! Lock and load."

No one said a word as they were led to the prison camp's
perimeter. But they all exchanged looks of rage or disgust.
They'd been assigned, they all understood, the only duty
for which the army deemed them fit.

THE WHITE HOUSE, WASHINGTON, D.C.
April 18, 2300 GMT (1800 Local)

Gordon Davis straightened his tie in the mirror.

Elaine said, "You should sit down!"

"I'm all right," Gordon replied.

She ushered Gordon to the vanity's bench seat. "If

you're going to deliver this speech standing up, you've got to conserve your energy.''

''I'm *fine*,'' Gordon insisted, taking his seat on the upholstered bench. ''Now, tell me how great I am.''

Elaine laughed. ''Gordon . . .'' she began. She bent over and put her hands on his thighs. ''*Gordon*, honey. You're going to be spec*tacular*!'' She hugged him, careful not to get her makeup on his jacket.

He was grinning from ear to ear. ''And?''

''I'm so, so proud of you. Have I ever told you that?''

''Go on.''

''I can't. Any more praise and your head's gonna swell up and apply for statehood.''

They laughed.

''Mo-*o-om*!'' Celeste whined from the sitting room outside. ''This dress makes me look ten years *old*! Can I at *least* take this stupid *bow* off it?''

Her parents' laughter ended with two comfortable smiles. Elaine touched her forehead to his and kissed him softly.

''Mo-o-om! Everybody I *know* is going to be watching this stupid thing! I'll never live this down as long as I *live*!''

''This isn't *about* you, Celeste!'' Elaine finally replied.

''Oh, yeah, well . . . I'm not *going*, then!'' The door to the sitting room slammed shut.

''You want me to handle this?'' Gordon asked.

''Oh, yeah, right! She'd end up wearing a black T-shirt and *hiking* boots!'' Elaine left.

Gordon picked up the three-page speech. He felt a rush of anxiety. You could never know how a speech would be received. His dramatic finish could fall flat on its face. He might walk out of the joint session not to thunderous applause and a standing ovation, but to murmurs of shock and surprise. Nobody had any idea, after all, what to expect. The closest anyone had come to predicting the address's contents had been a *New York Times* story that had hinted the speech would be short—''an attempt at a statesmanlike approach,'' their exact words. But that speculation had been lost in a sea of misinformation. Some analysts suggested that he was going to make a public peace offer. Others that he'd make veiled threats of nuclear attack. Or perhaps even a national referendum on continuation of the war as a face-saving way of exiting the coalition.

Gordon took a deep breath and looked at himself in the mirror. He'd lost fifteen pounds, but the cameras would put it all back on for him. He put his speech on the vanity and headed downstairs to wait. He knew the words by heart. That's where they had come from in the first place.

"I come before you tonight not to talk of politics, or of policy, or of war," Gordon began before the joint session of Congress. "I come to talk to you about the state of our union. I come to talk to you about the character of our people. About something we have lost. Something we must find again. Rudyard Kipling penned words many years ago that still call out to those who will hear them. 'There's no sense in going further—it's the edge of cultivation, so they said, and I believed it'—"

The House chamber was silent.

"But what sense is there in struggling, in striving, in forging ahead? 'It's the edge of cultivation. The trails run out and stop! There's no sense in going further!' Have not we, as Americans, already built a nation as great as any on earth? As great as any nation that ever rose? Why should *we,* the prosperous, the advanced, the comfortable, the *leaders* of the *world,* risk all and press ahead toward a future whose only certainty is of unending troubles?"

Gordon felt a sudden rushing sensation—as if a lens had descended before his eyes. Until that moment he'd been someone else. His mind separate from his body. Banished from it had been the sense of actually being there—of finally delivering the speech that would decide the fate of his presidency. He'd been free of the burden of appreciating just how important the moment was in his life. In the life of his country. He'd strolled like a sleepwalker down the ornate carpet and awoken in front of two TelePrompTers. Behind them lay the largest audience in American television history.

"Something lost, go and find it! The timid, the cautious, the perplexed . . . they have always halted at the edge of cultivation. But the ambitious, the curious, the daring—the men and women who *built* this thing we call America— they have sallied forth to carve out the roads down which we now effortlessly travel! They have listened to the whisper, ladies and gentlemen, of this Congress. They have heeded its call. 'Over yonder—go you there!' "

There was a burst of applause so spontaneous—so filled with unexpected energy—that Gordon felt a tingle ripple up his body and spur him on.

" 'But are not the days of discovery now gone?' you ask!" His shouts jarred the room into stony silence. The commotion had ended with no chatter. They had no copies of his address to distract them. Everyone looked up and waited for Gordon to continue. " 'But does not that whisper merely lead us down a path of fruitless adventurism? There are *fields* to sow. *Fences* to mend. More *barns* to raise right *here*, where we are *now*!' "

Gordon looked up into the gallery. Elaine smiled. The shot was shown, he was sure, worldwide.

"Beyond us lies a vast and untraveled land. The great unknown of tomorrow. You can't see the future, but it's waiting. And like our forebears we have a choice. A choice. Do we venture forth? Do we *explore* those uncharted regions with an aggressive *spirit* and an imaginative *mind*? By *routes* that will at *some* times be true . . . and *others* lead astray? Or do we *abandon* our courage—*neglect* that urge, that force, those smoldering ambitions that have *fueled* the engines of our progress and unleashed the all-consuming *fires* of human achievement?"

There was an outpouring of cheers from the partisan crowd of veteran Republican speechmakers.

"The call beckons," Gordon continued, "yet some will never hear it. They will be enslaved forever to the present. Timid, fearful, they will not understand the glories that rise up all around. The commonplace wonders that they take for granted. Those mere ornaments of convenience that were once *triumphs* of ingenuity and drive! They will memorize formulas, paraphrase words, digest books *filled* with the most powerful and brilliant thoughts of humankind! But they will not reach up to grasp the torch! They will not blaze a new trail! They will not *dare* to see what glories there might have been!

"If we are to survive as a nation of free men and women—if we are to stoke the fires that must burn within us to give us the strength and the will to explore the future in search of its hidden truths—we must first look within ourselves. We must find those beliefs that lie suppressed beneath the weight of convention, and of comfort, and of ease, and we must give them voice! And so to those of you who hear the call I say . . . speak out! Shout at the top of your lungs that we are not a people whose time has come and gone! Stand, and be counted, or *forever* hold your peace!"

There was a cacophonous ovation as floor and gallery alike leaped to their feet. Gordon breathed—deeply—as self-assured as he'd ever felt. He unfurrowed his brow and relaxed. He smiled for the first time. The energy surged through him and left him free of the aches and pains of his days. He waited until there was total quiet.

"Ladies and gentlemen of this Congress, I report to you that the state of our union rests in your hands. To one side lies comfort and security. To the other, a churning sea of foam and fire through which our storm-tossed ship of state must sail. It is our choice whether to transcend our time! To slough off our current prejudices and ignorance! To break the limits that bind us with heavy chains to the dead-weight of our certain present! We, my fellow Americans, must survey the rivers of life! We must not let fear of the difficult inhibit us! For if we do, we may never know the virgin forests that lie at the river's source or the rich low-lands into which the fertile water flows. The state of the union, ladies and gentlemen, rests in your hands. Something lost. Go and find it."

UNRUSFOR HEADQUARTERS, KHABAROVSK
April 19, 0105 GMT (1105 Local)

For a moment the television's small speaker was silent. President Davis's stirring words had left everyone gathered around transfixed.

When the rapturous applause erupted from the joint session of Congress, however, a similar uproar burst forth from the crowded conference room. Officers and soldiers alike seemed ecstatic and exuberant. Nate turned to look at the scene. Even the Europeans were caught up in the emotion, most particularly the British, on whose lips Nate caught repeated references to Kipling in an animated discussion.

Nate turned back to the small television. President Davis slowly made his way down the center aisle. Republicans and Democrats alike stood clapping and smiling. They held hands out as if to some passing celebrity. The camera switched to take in Mrs. Davis and her lovely daughters, who were about the same age as Nate's two sons.

Memories of home made Nate anxious and impatient. In just a few hours it would be his face that filled the screens. It would be his show under the bright lights of international television. He longed for that show to be a success. For his boys to see their father standing tall. Describing their country's amazing victory. He felt guilty for so petty a thought. His men were fighting for their lives. But he closed his eyes and reveled in a victory that was still somewhat in doubt. He relished the triumph over all who doubted—even those who lived in his own house.

"Sir?" Lieutenant Colonel Reed said. Nate opened his eyes. "Seventh Corps commander is on the line. He's got the latest unit positions."

Nate felt a tightening of his chest. The previously boisterous gathering grew quiet. Nate made his way across the large room to the radio. He could already hear the sound of the general's voice. The man was asking the communications officer what he thought of the president's state-of-the-union address. His buoyant tone was a good omen.

"Clark here," Nate said loudly over the speakerphone.

"General Clark!" came the voice of his corps commander. "Are you ready for current positions?"

Pads and paper rustled all around Nate.

"Ready on this end," Nate replied. His heart pounded. His throat constricted. "Give me your forward-most unit first."

"Second Battalion, 173rd Armored Cavalry Regiment," came the tinny voice over the radio, "north bank of Amur River."

The room burst into cheers. "Pipe down!" Nate shouted, silencing the room.

". . . token resistance only. The frontline Chinese units are totally spent. Their stocks of ammo must be extremely low. A lot of their units are flat running out. But intell is speculating that some units in the interior of the main pockets may be sitting on substantial stocks that they never succeeded in moving forward. I'd like to request a delay in bridging operations so we can secure our flanks north of the Amur. We're so far ahead of schedule that a twenty-four-hour pause shouldn't—"

"Negative," Clark interrupted. "You're 'go' to cross the Amur in strength just as soon as the engineers certify the bridge." There was a long pause. "Do you acknowledge?"

There was another brief delay. "I read you five by five, General Clark," the reluctant corps commander replied. "Orders are to begin crossing the Amur."

When they'd signed off, Reed waited on Clark. "What about the 25th LID?" he asked. "They've encountered light resistance and are at the Amur south of Birobidzhan."

"Send them across," Clark said.

"What's their objective?"

Clark turned to Reed. "To cross the Amur River into China," he said simply.

"It's too early to get a read on how President Davis did tonight," one of the American network commentators said. Kartsev shook his head in disgust. "He needed to be bold, given his abysmal approval ratings and the bleak head count on the impending funding vote on the war. But a speech of this sort is truly unprecedented and, I might add, totally unexpected. We knew the address would be short due to the president's still-fragile health. But we'll really have to wait for the first flash polls."

The American media was hedging, but it was an undeniably brilliant speech. Davis had managed both to rise above the fractious political infighting of which Americans had grown so tired, and to defend a highly unpopular war without mentioning it once.

Kartsev turned the television off. He'd seen no reports from Miss Dunn. The other reports on the war meant nothing to him because they affected him so little. As a scientist, he had applied the catalyst to propel the system into action. But thereafter, if he intervened, he might alter the very dynamic he was attempting to analyze. He took a pen and pad and listed the results of his experiment to date. First, the collapse of the Russian government—no mean feat. Then the destruction of Russia's remaining institutions of power in the civil war. Ditto. UNRUSFOR and China had then simply been sucked into the vacuum—pure cause and effect—with war the inevitable result. UNRUSFOR would win that war, due in no small part to Kartsev. It had been his assassin who had killed Governor Bristol, a man more conventional by far than Davis. Had Bristol been president, the outcome of the war would have been very different, he was certain.

Kartsev's pen rested on the blank space at the end of his list. The dividing point between past and future. He wrote, "What will happen in China?" The strained tendons and failing tissues of Russian society had created a once-in-a-lifetime opportunity. Anarchy in Russia had been both an end unto itself and a catalyst of events yet to come. But recording the large-scale social forces his experiment had unleashed involved an element of serendipity. And the scale on which those forces played out could get no larger than China—one quarter of the human population. The unanswerable question loomed before him. *What next for China?*

Kartsev found himself standing in the center of the bright red Oriental rug. He suddenly got the sense of how he would appear to some omniscient eye and moved quickly to the bookshelves beside the fireplace to idly peruse his eclectic collection of treatises. But there was nothing new to be gleaned from them. They were as detached from modern-day life as he was. He should have lived in the nineteenth century. It was a time that better suited him. People had then tackled the broader questions, as was his wont.

"I've got to . . . !" he began, but he didn't know how to finish. With grinding teeth he grew determined to climb out of the malaise into which he had fallen. He marched over to his desk and hit his intercom button. "Hello?" he said, and then waited. Nothing. "Hel-*lo-o-o*!" he repeated impatiently.

The door opened. Kartsev's heart leaped into his throat, but it was only a disheveled aide. *Not yet,* he thought, relieved at his reprieve. He was so near to completing his work. The aide stood there watching him like the omniscient eye. Kartsev looked up so abruptly that the man recoiled noticeably. The reaction was interesting. It was human and involuntary. Kartsev smiled.

I need more contact like this, he thought as the words began to fill his head. Words about the power and purpose of terror. *"Let them hate, so long as they fear,"* he recalled. "Who said that?"

"Sir?" the ashen aide said out of the blue.

Kartsev realized he'd spoken his thought aloud. He ignored the man, thinking, *If I can get this kind of material from just one human interaction* . . . He looked up. "I want to hold a rally."

The man screwed up his face and cocked his head. *"Sir?"*

"A *rally*. You do speak Russian, don't you?"

"Y-yes, sir, but . . . What sort of rally?"

"A large one. I want Red Square filled from end to end."

"With people?"

"No, you idiot! With goats and chickens!" The man looked even more frightened than before. "*Yes* with people! I want to address a gathering in Red Square about the historic times in which we live!" The aide's face was an open book. Kartsev could almost hear him recite a list of practical problems in getting crowds to turn out. "Offer them bread," Kartsev said dejectedly. "And vodka." He walked around his desk to his computer, on the screen of which glowed a waiting, half-written page. *Future historians will write* volumes *about these times*, Kartsev thought in annoyance, *and all those louts are interested in is bread and vodka!*

The aide cleared his throat. "You want me to organize a rally in Red Square and offer bread and vodka to draw people there?" Kartsev waited, then nodded at the dimwit. "And . . . and *you* will address the rally?"

It wasn't really a question. It was an opportunity for Kartsev to change his mind. Kartsev glowered at the man . . . but he hesitated. He ruled, as he had written in Chapter Twelve, through a complex system whose main underpinning was based upon the "principle of codependent interests." *This* man—whoever he was—owed all he had to Kartsev. His comfortable apartment, his food and drink, the girls or boys that amused him nightly. Everything. Therefore any risk to Kartsev was a threat to him as well. That was *why* the system worked as it did with very little maintenance required.

The man clearly sensed danger, but Kartsev wanted something to mark the anticipated completion of his manuscript, and this had a certain symmetry to it. After all, Chapter One had begun with a rally in Red Square. "*May* Day!" Kartsev blurted out, instantly grinning. "We'll have a good, old-fashioned May Day parade, only with no parade—just a rally. All right? Now go! Make all the preparations.''

The aide hesitated, then left. Kartsev imagined that the man's preparations for the event included some of a purely personal nature. Fake passport, cash, airline tickets. Such an escape might be possible for a junior aide. But no escape was available to Kartsev. His remaining days—however many—would be spent in his windowless office. He could never hope to evade the ''justice'' of a vengeful and self-righteous world.

He looked around the empty room. ''But then what is it that I have to lose?'' he mumbled out loud, then began to type, the keys clacking rapidly as if in a race against time.

THE WHITE HOUSE, WASHINGTON, D.C.
April 19, 1100 GMT (0600 Local)

''Who's this?'' Gordon Davis asked.

''Ralph Stevenson,'' Daryl replied. He held the receiver out to Gordon.

''Ralph!'' Gordon's fingers massaged his throbbing temples. ''Have you heard the great news?''

The congressman was uncertain. ''About the *war*?''

''You *bet* about the war! We're kickin' their butts all the way back to Beijing! What do the people in Kentucky have to say about that?'' As the man answered guardedly, Gordon fumbled with his painkillers' childproof cap. Elaine appeared with a mug of hot tea and rested her cool hand on his clammy forehead. ''Well, I *know* you've made commitments to your leadership, Ralph,'' Gordon said. ''But you've got other commitments to honor too, don't you? To the people of Kentucky? To your country?''

''Mr. President, we've given you ample time to bring this war to an end, and—''

''What about bringing this war to a *victory,* Ralph? That's where we are, you know. Right there on the verge of winning this thing! Now, what're you gonna tell the people back in Louisville come election time if you help pull the plug on the single most successful American military operation since D day?''

The man laughed nervously at the mere suggestion that he would do such a thing. Elaine dabbed at Gordon's forehead with a handkerchief. "Listen, Ralph, time's short. Men and women are dying over there trying to win this war, and all you've got to do is vote. Can I count on you?''

He heard a faint sigh, then a tired, "All right, Mr. President.''

"Thank you *very* much, Congressman Stevenson!''

"Jim Berne," Daryl said as he hit line two. "Jim!" Gordon said in a vibrant voice.

"No," came the reply of a small child. "My daddy had to go to the *potty*! His tummy has germs.''

"Well, listen, sweetie. I'm the president of the United States. Do you know who that is?''

"Uh-*huu*uh! I saw you on TV. You're 'The Fool.' ''

"Yep. That's me. But do you know the soldiers who are fighting in the war?''

"Ye-ah. They wear white clothes, 'cause it's *cold*.''

"That's right! Now you tell your daddy the fool says he shouldn't be mean to the cold soldiers. Tell him he shouldn't take away their food and warm blankets and . . .'' Elaine slapped Gordon on the shoulder. "You just go stand outside the potty door and explain that to your dad.''

With an enthusiastic, "*Okay*!" the girl accepted her mission.

"Bill Craft on line four," Daryl said the instant she hung up.

"Bill! This is Gordon.''

"You can't possibly be calling for the reason I think,'' Senator Craft said. "Gordy, I'm one of the goddamn *sponsors* of the War Powers Resolution.''

"Just give me my shot, Bill, that's all I ask. Just let me make my case.''

Craft huffed, but then replied, "Of course, Mr. President. Go ahead.''

•   •   •

When it was all over, Gordon leaned back in the padded
chair behind the historic desk. It was quiet. The Oval Office
was nearly empty. "Get General Clark on the line," he
slurred, and didn't look at anyone in particular. An aide
handed him the phone. "Nate?" he said in a raspy voice.
"We won the vote. You've got thirty more days of funding.
Go win the war."

AMUR RIVER, SIBERIA
April 19, 2300 GMT (0900 Local)

Harold Stempel and the others waited on the riverbank. The
newly plowed road that ran to the edge of the Amur River
was already deeply rutted. His legs and back ached from
the weight of the heavy pack he carried, but he couldn't sit
down or he'd never get back up.

Engineers were stringing additional cables to secure the
pontoons. The floating bridge looked all right. But every
so often the thin ice would shift. The groaning sound of
friction would draw anxious looks from the engineers.

A man on the center of the bridge shouted, twirled his
arm, and pumped his fist in air.

"All right let's *go*!" shouted Stempel's platoon leader.

They headed across the bridge in two files, one down
each solid metal track meant for vehicles. The lieutenant
led Stempel's file. His RTO followed with his radio aerial
whipping the air. Then came Stempel's squad leader, then
Stempel—fourth in line. The men on the other side of the
bridge followed the platoon sergeant. A quick check of the
upstream ice left Harold distinctly unsettled.

From the riverbank the ice looked fairly solid. But from
the bridge it was clearly thin and dangerous. Here and there,
the ice cover had grown thinner and darker on the sunny
day. It was broken straight through around the gently bobbing pontoons. The water there was black and foreboding.

They passed a group of the engineers who were struggling to fasten cables to the bridge, straining to keep the

bridge intact. Harold wanted to quicken his pace, but had to maintain his place in line.

There was another loud groan from the river. Everyone's head turned in search of the ominous sound, but nothing had visibly changed. The long highway of gray ice remained unbroken. Harold felt a trickle of sweat run down his back under the warm rays of the sun.

Several times he felt the bridge sway beneath him. Not a jarring shift, just a gentle drift with the current. He peered out around the bulging pack of the radioman. The bridge was bowed to the left. Long guy wires from the banks held the pontoons in place, but the bridge still bent to the relentless flow. He ached to speed up his pace, but he had to stay in line.

When Harold finally stepped off the metal pad onto dry land, he breathed a sigh of relief.

"I never thought I'd get to China," McAndrews said.

Harold looked down at his boots—at the ruts made by a hundred vehicles' passing. *China*, he thought, utterly amazed.

"What's this?" Patterson asked. He took the large green can proffered to him. It looked like oversized hairspray.

"Tear gas," the squad leader replied. He handed one to each man. Harold took the cold, heavy can. Chavez followed with gas masks in canvas sacks.

"What's *this* for?" an incredulous Patterson persisted. The sergeant's patience was wearing thin, but Patterson kept at him.

The sergeant finally wheeled on him. "You know how many people there are in China, shitface? A billion and a half! They're handin' out tear gas! Figure it out for yourself!"

NORTH OF TANGYUAN, CHINA
April 20, 1100 GMT (2100 Local)

The Blackhawk bucked wildly through the heavy turbulence. André Faulk felt sick to his stomach. It had been hours since they'd refueled and headed in. This was the longest flight he'd ever taken in a helicopter. The weight of the external fuel tanks had forced removal of the armored flooring. After reaching the border, everyone had sat on their packs or helmets. André's back and ass ached.

But it wasn't the threat of antiaircraft fire or the lack of comfort that caused him the greatest distress. The entire battalion had flown straight into a raging cold front. They were being tossed about like a small boat on rough seas. The buffeting was so violent in the mountains it almost knocked his breath out. Several in his squad had already vomited into airsick bags. André had been on the verge of doing the same numerous times. He'd stopped just short, however—his mouth and nose breathing the stale air of a bag.

"Thirty miles!" the squad leader shouted after getting off the intercom. "We're thirty miles out!" He then spilled the contents of his stomach all over the center of the cabin. André felt his capillaries contract, his skin tingle, his hands begin to grow cold. The unchecked fear seized total control over his body.

They all listened for the smacking sound of bullets on the metal fuselage, but they heard none. No one said a word as the engines revved to military power. The deceleration crushed everyone to the deck.

There was a jerking thud. The door cracked open. In rushed the rotors' downblast. The door slid wide. The cabin filled with swirling, frigid wind. The sergeant leaped out. One by one the blackness swallowed men and their gear. André slid on his butt toward the opening. The weight of his pack prevented him from rising. By the time his legs dangled in air under the whirring blades, the first men were returning to off-load crates of supplies.

"*Move it!*" came a shout, almost totally washed away by the engines' roar. André hopped to the ground—misjudging the distance and collapsing to his knees. Two of the returning men hoisted him to his feet. He lumbered into the night across uneven footing. The LZ was filled with dozens of choppers. The sarge shoved André in the right direction. He found the other men's gear piled high. With a quick motion he released his heavy pack. It fell to the ground with a jangling thud.

He felt light when free of the weight. He and another man returned to the chopper and dragged out a heavy crate. André and his partner dropped the load amid stacks of others at the puny battalion supply depot. The choppers were all lifting into the air. They had illuminated their blinking red, green, and white lights to avoid collisions. André monitored the sky. A good number of airmobile troopers had been killed by their own helicopters.

The downdraft from a low chopper hurtling by overhead forced the men to their knees. When it was gone, the night was markedly quieter. It grew quieter still with each helicopter's departure. By the time they reached their packs, the Blackhawks were all gone.

"Head up to the 60," the squad leader said, his voice a whisper. "Everybody clear the zone! Clear the zone!" André and the others marched into the darkness. There were six hundred men and tons of supplies on the drop zone, but after the departure of the helicopters, the night had become still and peaceful. André had experienced the disorienting phenomenon on other insertions. Hours of steady noise, a rush into the rotors' downdraft, then total silence. It was a change for which you were unprepared.

But as soon as your ears adjusted, you had to guard against something else. You couldn't let the roar of a firefight stun you into inaction. You strained to hear even the tiniest sound, but at the same time you prepared for a cacophony of explosions. You steeled yourself against the fire and death that could spring from the quiet at any moment. For if you froze in the first awful seconds, you would almost certainly die. He'd ambushed Chinese like deer in the headlights before. The real killing was in those first terrible moments.

André hooked up with the rest of his squad. By random

luck he lay next to the attached machine-gun crew. On the sergeant's command, they unsafed their weapons and headed into Indian country. He hugged tight to the side of the M-60. The big gun would attract enemy fire, but it was still the safest place for him to be. Because working machine guns almost never got overrun. They were backbreakers—the rocks against which waves of attackers would crash. They were the decisive weapons of modern infantry combat.

The platoon headed for the tall ridges and jagged rocks that rose all around the LZ. André felt tense at facing the great unknown. At stumbling blindly forward with no sense of what to expect. When they left the flats, word was passed from man to man. There were no friendlies anywhere around them. They were in a 360-degree free-fire zone. They would kill anyone they met.

21

There was a knock on Nate Clark's door. It was his secretary. "Sorry to bother you, sir, but that woman reporter is back."

Nate looked up, confused. "Who?"

"Me!" Kate Dunn said angrily. She edged her way into his office. "You said you were sending me to the fighting, but there was hardly a shot fired! And you *used* me! You fed me bullshit stories about how *weak* you were and I repeated them like some stooge!"

Clark nodded at his secretary, who departed. "Have you ever heard of a Strategic Deception Plan?"

"I've heard of *deception*! 'Strategic' just makes it sound okay because it's a *military* thing! But my job is to report the truth, and you've been *fucking* me over ever since we first met!" Kate feared she might be laying it on too thick.

"I didn't arrest your friend for possession of marijuana," Clark replied.

"Possession of *pot* in the middle of *Siberia*? It's *anarchy*! There aren't any laws here!"

"There's military law, and you broke it by sneaking around that supply depot."

"I wasn't sneaking, I was reporting! That's my job!"

"And you doing your job would prevent *me* from doing *mine*! *And* it would've gotten a whole bunch of people killed! *Your* countrymen! *Your* army! You in the press think you're *supra*-national. You follow some ill-conceived '*neutrality* principle'! You think you have to report from midway between the opposing sides even if one side is *right* and the other is *wrong*!" Nate had to stop himself. Months of being ridiculed in the press had built an enormous reservoir of resentment.

Kate switched tone, but not direction. "All I'm doing is busting my ass to do a decent story on what this war is *really* like, and you send me to that Mickey Mouse attack out west. I thought we had a deal. That you were a man of your word." Her last words seemed to have the desired effect.

"Sergeant Scott!" Clark bellowed. They stared at each other across Clark's desk. "Sergeant *Scott*!" he shouted again, then muttered something and went off in search of the man, leaving Kate alone. His office was spartan, nearly devoid of interesting sights other than the colorful map on his desk. It was upside down from her perspective, but she could make out the familiar track of the Amur River. It was a commanding general's map showing the whole war in one oversized picture. The blue marks were UNRUSFOR units. The red for Chinese. Two blue spikes struck deep into the mass of red. A modest advance from Vladivostok pressed from the east, and a huge bulge plunged from the north through starving Chinese troops in search of food, water, and shelter. Kids wanting nothing more than an end to the horror. The offensive looked great on the map, but there was no glory to be found in the field. No human drama. No desperate struggle on whose outcome the tide of the war would turn.

One tiny pocket of blue caught her attention. It was buried deep in northern China far separated from the rest of the allied forces. She half turned her head to read "75th/101st" written beside the blue island. She heard voices

from the outer office. Kate quickly noted three other things from the map. A massive red hammer of a Chinese army was moving north toward the blue dot. The two prongs seemed destined to converge on that same spot in China. And the name on the map closest to the unit was "Tangyuan." *Tangyuan,* she thought over and over.

Clark returned with his secretary and began dictating. "To: All UNRUSFOR Personnel. From: Lieutenant General Nate Clark, Commanding. Today's date. Re: Ms. Kate Dunn." Kate stared back, waiting. "Ms. Dunn is a correspondent for the National Broadcasting Company. On my authority, she is to be given complete access to all areas under UNRUSFOR control, including, without limitation, all theaters of combat and all units engaged with the enemy. You are hereby instructed to cooperate by all means necessary to afford Ms. Dunn and her camera crew the access herein specified."

"Including transportation," Kate added in almost a whisper.

". . . including transport," Clark appended to his memo. "Okay?"

Kate held out her hand. "I truly appreciate your assistance, General Clark." He shook her hand as the phone rang.

"It's the president," Clark's secretary said. He ushered Kate Dunn out.

"Are you ready for your big show?" President Davis asked.

"Yes, sir!" Clark replied. "But you're a hard act to follow, sir. That was a helluva speech you gave."

Davis laughed. "I kind of liked it myself. And I want you to go to that press conference and give 'em hell too, General Clark. Don't hold anything back. I want the people to believe we can win. I want *you* to walk out there and convince everyone that it's possible."

"But, Mr. President, there's still a lot that can go wrong. We only have one division across the Amur and bits and pieces of a half-dozen units from as many countries. If that ice breaks now—"

"I know all that, Nate. But you have a job to do. You've got to help rally the country around this war so you can be freed to win it. I need to convince everyone that this counterattack is *already* a success. Nothing generates support like victory. I want you to get behind the wheel and jam your foot on the gas of that bandwagon. It may be half-empty now, but people will be chasing to hop on. Just put your worries aside for thirty minutes, Nate. Enjoy for a moment what you and your men have accomplished! And be *sure* to let the press see that enjoyment."

"Good morning," Clark's deep voice boomed. The briefing room was still. "I come to report to you a great victory." Two aides lifted the gray plastic sheet off a wall-sized map. There were gasps and a general disturbance when the map was revealed.

Kate and Woody watched from the back row. There were the two blue prongs she had seen in Clark's office, but on this map something was different. One more of Clark's deceptions. There was no tiny island of blue near the Chinese city of Tangyuan. Kate pulled Woody out the door.

"UNRUSFOR forces," Nate continued loudly, "have pushed south of the Amur River into China from the west, and west into China from the Vladivostok region." Again there was a burst of noise. "The results of Operation Winter Harvest thus far have been . . . spectacular." The silver tip of Reed's pointer tapped the main, plunge southward. "In sixty hours UNRUSFOR has advanced over two hundred miles. In the process, they have enveloped over 200,000 Chinese troops."

The room was filled with excited chatter.

"In the east," Clark said as Reed swung his pointer to Vladivostok, "something equally significant is occurring. Chinese lines that had stabilized in the first days of the war have crumbled, and all four main belts of defenses have been breached. Elsewhere," Clark continued as Reed's pointer moved to the center, "units based here in Khabarovsk and at the long-surrounded airbase at Birobidzhan have broken out in individual drives for the Amur River. Casualties everywhere have been lighter than expected . . . on both sides. Field commanders report forty thousand Chinese troops taken prisoner.''

That completed the story of widespread success.

''As you must all understand, I cannot say much more about Winter Harvest due to concerns about operational security. But let me take this opportunity to give you one personal observation. No war is ever popular. It is a terrible, ugly waste. But when all efforts at peacemaking have failed—when the diplomats have given it their best but come up short—you have only two choices. Cut and run— ceding the field to the enemy—or fight. Now I know people have voiced noisy opposition to this war, and that's good. It is *precisely* at times such as these that the right to express your opinions is paramount. But perhaps now that everyone can see our plans to win this war, the debate can reflect the true military reality. *This*,'' Clark said, wheeling on the map with a sweep of his arm, ''is what we've planned to do all along, and it's been successful beyond our *wildest* dreams!'' Every face was raised to his. Pens were frozen on pads. Cameras rolled. ''There's still more fighting to come, but one fact should be evident from this map. The People's Liberation Army is being defeated in the field. We *will* win this war.''

The major on whom Kate and Woody waited was on the phone. He was another insufferable ''public affairs officer.'' PAOs pretended to be on the press's side. They agreed that things were unfair, but what could they do? They were just a ''spoke in the wheel,'' they always said, and the information flowed from the ''hub''—the commanding officer.

There were two signs above the PAO's desk. One read, FOUR HOSTILE NEWSPAPERS ARE MORE TO BE FEARED THAN A THOUSAND BAYONETS. NAPOLEON. The other was of more recent vintage. WHEREVER COMMANDERS GO, THEY SHOULD PLAN FOR CNN. LIKE THE WEATHER, WE'LL ALWAYS BE

THERE—JUST ANOTHER FEATURE ON THE BATTLEFIELD TERRAIN. JAMIE MCINTYRE, CNN CORRESPON-DENT.''

The major hung the telephone up and reread the already crumpled memorandum from General Clark, then left. Kate realized Woody was looking at her. All their traveling gear, his camera included, lay by their sides. ''What?'' she asked.

''Where are we *going*, Kate?''

The major returned with a colonel—the head of army air transport—who held Clark's memo in both hands. ''What can I do for you?'' he asked.

''I want to go to Tangyuan,'' Kate said. Woody's eyes darted her way.

The colonel laughed. ''I don't know what the hell you're talking about,'' he lied inexpertly.

Kate leaned forward and whispered. ''I'm talking about the 75th and 101st.'' Nothing registered on the colonel's face. ''General Clark told me to come see *you*.'' Kate glanced down at the name stenciled above his breast pocket. ''Colonel *Wheatley* at the *airbase*.''

''Whah-tley,'' the major corrected, pronouncing it like ''what,'' not ''wheat.''

''General Clark mentioned me by *name*?'' the colonel asked. Kate nodded significantly.

''Well, all we've got going in there are airdrops, and I don't imagine either of you are airborne-qualified.'' He wore a broad, amiable grin.

''What about medevacs?'' Woody asked, sounding almost reluctant. His voice was wooden and tired.

The colonel looked at the PAO. The public affairs officer shrugged and said, ''Under conditions of open coverage, field commanders are required to permit journalists to ride on military vehicles and aircraft whenever feasible.'' Kate looked at the colonel and arched her brow.

Kate and Woody were taken to a MASF—a mobile army surgical facility. They were escorted by a nurse in a flight suit to a large helicopter fitted with bulging external fuel tanks. Its engines were whining and the rotor was beginning to turn. They hoisted their gear up and climbed aboard. A female medic pulled the sliding door closed with a bang. Kate and Woody found a place among the litters.

The flight was long, but the two nurses remained busy the entire time. There were drip bags to hang on hooks. Oxygen masks to lay on pillows. Trays filled with small bottles whose caps had to be removed. These women were obviously veterans of previous flights. Their combat boots squeaked on the bare metal floor as they bunched towel after towel underneath the litters. As the helicopter began to rock in the increasingly rough weather, Kate's eyes were drawn to the towels. *They had to have good footing*, she thought. *The towels would keep the deck dry.*

She glanced at Woody. His sad, tired eyes were fixed on Kate.

The final few moments of the descent were the worst. The helicopter had flown through a cold front that barreled out of Siberia like an avalanche. Now it bucked and rolled as the pilot fought his way down. Each time the deck pitched, Kate imagined the rotors smacking the ground and disintegrating.

A hard thud sent pain shooting up her back. The door slid open. The blizzard flew into the cabin with full force and fury. Kate and Woody grabbed their gear and headed out. At the door they saw the first bloody body being hoisted aboard through the hellish wind. Kate watched a parade of the horrible. Men were crying. One screamed for his mother. She leaped to the ground, and Woody followed.

The door slid closed, and the blast of the rotors forced Kate and Woody to their knees. The air filled with snow and dirt. When the helicopter was gone, the gusts of the storm seemed tame by comparison.

"What the hell're *you* doin' here?" came a loud voice.

Kate saw Woody staring at her—the same question clearly on his mind.

• • •

Brigadier General Lawson, the brigade commander, took one look at General Clark's memo, crumpled it into a ball, and threw it against the bucking wall of the tent. "You've got *some* fuckin' balls comin' in here! Do you realize what you've gotten yourselves into?"

"We're war correspondents covering a military operation," Kate replied. "We're just doing our job."

"Oh, is *that* right? Fine! O-okay! You want a war, you've come to the right place!" He led them to a map of the mountainous terrain laid out under a battery-powered lamp. "Here *we* are. And everywhere else"—his palm circled the ridges dotted with blue—"is the Jinan Army Group—a quarter-million men."

Kate shook her head in confusion. "I don't understand. How are you supposed to stop a quarter of a million Chinese soldiers with—what—a few thousand men?"

"I believe the plan, as expressed to me, was fight like hell. Live high on rocky ridges. Move fast and at night. Hit 'em hard and then get the hell outta Dodge. That means goin' days without a hot meal. Sleepin' no more'n two or three hours at a stretch. And, if you get wounded, that's not good. Now, *that's* what you've gotten your sorry asses into, *and* you've made yourselves a royal *pain* in *my* ass to *boot*!"

Kate wasn't rattled by the man's shouts, but she was scared to death by what he was saying. "Surely they wouldn't send you here to get . . . wiped *out*."

"They sent us here to isolate the battlefield. To stop Chinese reinforcements from preventing the encirclement of the invasion forces." The general's eyes sank to the map. "The interior and exterior walls of this valley are steep. The floor channels the Chinese and narrows our front. If we dig our toenails in and fight for every rock, we can hold the high ground and win. They'll keep throwing live bodies at our fighting holes, and we'll keep making 'em dead. It's a simple and brutal calculus. Nothin' pretty about it."

NORTH OF TANGYUAN, CHINA
April 22, 2200 GMT (0800 Local)

The lean-to angled away from the gale. It blocked the wind, but snow wrapped around inside. It licked at André's body with chilling gusts. It was mid-morning, but the sky was gray and dark.

A machine gun opened fire.

"Come-on!-Come-on!" was shouted by almost all the men together. It was as if they were cheering for the embattled home team. Twice already they had done this. Both times with no casualties in their squad.

André and the others crawled out into the storm. When he stood upright, the wind rocked him back a step. He had to put his shoulder down to get moving forward, toward his fighting hole. The line of ten men weaved their way through the thick trees of the valley floor. At first, it was just a grueling jog into the impossibly cold tide of air. Then the Chinese began to yell. The howls from their lungs rose up. With the wind at their backs their massed voices carried and were amplified by the narrow mountain gorge.

From a distance of a few hundred meters, the two armies rushed toward each other at a dead run. The Americans raced for their fighting positions. Chinese infantry flooded the southern end of the valley like water from a bursting dam. All at once the heavy crew-served American weapons opened up. Machine guns growled out .50-caliber bullets from high ridges. Launchers thumped grenades out twelve a second. The crackling fire took a toll measured in voices. The Chinese quieted. They were either too scared to shout . . . or dead.

André labored into the stiff breeze. He tried to check his weapon, to eject a round just to make sure the bolt hadn't frozen. But the driving snow stung his eyes so much they watered. He couldn't see, so he abandoned the plan. Above all the noise a heavy rumble filled the valley. Another distant B-52 raid drowned out the sound of the puny infantry weapons. High wind and low visibility foiled most air support. But at fifty thousand feet, the huge bombers merely opened their bellies and gravity did the rest.

They reached their preplanned defensive line, but André panicked when he couldn't find his hole. He'd hurriedly dug it on the eve of the first battle. Up ahead was the cleared field of fire. They'd chopped or torched the low brush and limbs. He was definitely in the right place.

The others were bailing new-fallen powder out of their positions. André stumbled around until his boot sank into his hole. He leaned his rifle against a tree and began to dig. He scraped the snow out with his gloved hands. When his fingers scraped bottom he crawled in. He grabbed his rifle by the stock and looked it over. The bolt looked clear, but still he blew into the mechanism. He brushed it with his glove, but that only put more ice and snow on the black metal.

The platoon sergeant made his way down the line, checking the men. André saw splinters fly off a thin tree beside him. A bullet left a deep gash in the otherwise pristine bark. The Chinese were firing at extreme range. André laid as low in his hole as he could.

"Hold your fire till the guys from the OP pull back!" the platoon sergeant shouted as he knelt beside André's hole. "There are *three* lines! *Three* lines! One battalion in each line! It's a full regimental attack!"

He moved on.

That was it? André wondered. No plans for maneuver? No prearranged signal to fall back? *Three lines. Three battalions. Three waves.* A full regiment was a lot of men. Maybe fifteen hundred Chinese against two hundred Americans, two companies from André's battalion in line abreast.

André popped open the large pockets on his parka and checked. They were heavy with newly filled magazines. He had six in his bulging pockets, plus four tucked away inside the jacket. Together with the full magazine in the rifle that made eleven—a hundred and sixty-five rounds.

He couldn't imagine going through that many magazines, but he also had two grenades. He felt for and found one in each breast pocket. *And then there's the ammo from the dead*, he thought guiltily as he looked around. To his left

the man had a log for protection. To his right the guy—
like André—was in the open. If he had to scoot over for
more ammo—to loot the corpse of one of the fallen—he
hoped it would be the PFC on his left. The log looked at
least eight inches thick.

The wind died down a bit. The heavy bombers had finished working over the Chinese. He could again hear the
machine guns and grenade launchers from the high ridges.
The breeze calmed even further. Suddenly it was still in
the valley. The cracking and deep popping of the .50 cal-
ibers and forty-millimeter grenade launchers still echoed off
the mountain walls. But like in the eye of a hurricane the
storm seemed to pause. The last mist of snow drifted from
tree branches overhead.

"Say, André" the guy to his left called out. "You got
any extra grenades?"

André replied with an exaggerated shake of his head.
"Just *two*."

"I got movement!" someone yelled.

"Hold yer fire!" came an NCO's reply.

GIs raced toward the rear. The men from the observation
posts were sprinting through the woods with wild abandon.
They crashed through low limbs and sent showers of snow
to the ground. They didn't even slow down at the defensive
line. One, two, three men passed on the dead run.

"How many were there at your OP?" one of André's
squadmates asked the fleeing men. They didn't even glance
in his direction. "I count five guys who've passed!" someone shouted. Up ahead, André could see more men.

"Hold your fire!" the squad leader barked.

"Hey!" someone replied. "Those are *Chinese*!"

At twenty meters, the thinly scattered line of Chinese
attackers opened fire.

M-60s cut them down. They rattled the air with rapid
strings of fire. In a matter of seconds André could see no
more targets. But the 60s kept up their industrial killing—
meted out six rounds at a time. The machine gunners
squeezed, traversed, and squeezed again. Their full-sized

NATO rounds flew through the woods for over a mile. Unless, that is, they hit something. Most likely a tree, or an outcropping, or one of the small ridges that ran like ribs up the hills to each side. But every so often they struck something soft. They ripped through flesh, and organs, and bone.

Six rounds, then a pause, then six more. Their squad had one of the guns. André wished he were closer to it. It was twenty meters to his left. And the gun to his right was thirty or more meters away. He was in the weak gap between the platoon's two big guns. Right where the Chinese would have their greatest chance at a breakthrough.

The wind picked up again. In a few seconds the lull was over. Powdery ice crystals again peppered his eyes. The frigid air seeped through his clothing like cold rain. Each touch sent ripples through his body. The sudden chill threatened to overcome him. His muscles quivered and his breath grew ragged.

André tried hard to shut out his many distractions. To concentrate on the hazy woods ahead. The visibility was shit—at times maybe sixty meters, at others no more than twenty. And twenty was way too close. Twenty was hand-grenade range. At twenty, they were mere moments away from being overrun.

He was almost surprised to see the main body of Chinese. Their large parkas were flapping over pumping knees. The snow slowed them down, made them easy shots. But there were hundreds and hundreds of them. The American rifles began to crack. It sounded like the rifle range at boot camp. With his thumb André checked the selector. Single shots, not three-round bursts. The cold plastic stock touched his skin beneath his eye. An oversized white form filled the sight.

The rifle kicked. Its flame lit the gray snow. Down went the large parka. A strong gust sent snow into André's eyes. It was like the frozen spray of whitecaps blown off the tips of ocean swells. He had to wipe his face with the back of his hand to resume firing. But even in the haze of drifting snow, targets made themselves visible. Flickering muzzles lit the woods with orange flame. The Chinese were firing their rifles on full auto. They didn't have orders to conserve ammo like their foes. André forced his watering eyes to line up a muzzle flash. When the faint outline of a human being became visible, he squeezed once and dropped the man at forty meters.

The buzz of a bullet through air made André flinch. The angry sound was unmistakably lethal. You needn't have seen the effects of a high-powered round to be terrified by it. You didn't even need to know what the hell it was. Anyone hearing air split at the speed of sound would know to fear the object's passage. Any sane man would curl up in the bottom of his hole.

André lined up another target and fired. Three-for-fucking-three.

His first miss came on the sudden arrival of a running soldier. The man rushed out of the swirling snow straight at the guy on André's left. André spun his rifle on the man but hurried the shot. The attacker's rifle was blazing from his hip. André and his squadmate both laid the man flat with their next rounds. He collapsed into the snow three steps short of their line.

Directly in front of André's hole he saw three men. They ran straight at him. He flicked the selector and squeezed the trigger in one motion. *Cra-a-ack*, came the roar of three rounds. *Cra-a-ack,* came another three. He had to fire again to waste the last guy, but only two rounds came out this time.

André cursed and ejected the magazine. He sank down into his hole. He'd dropped the three Chinese soldiers. But the woods were filled with hundreds of others. A constant yell again rose up. It had to be the second wave! The snow all around his hole was sprayed into the air. His shaking glove couldn't guide the magazine home. He cradled his rifle against his body and used both hands. It slid in until metal touched metal.

He was terrified by the steady singing sound of passing

enemy bullets. Terrified that he'd see all was lost when he looked up. But he was fighting for his life, so he raised his head into the shooting gallery of high-velocity rounds.

There must've been a hundred shouting men charging forward. André fired and fired and fired. He missed far more than he hit. But it wasn't about marksmanship right then. It was about pouring out as many rounds as he could. It was about turning the ten rifles in his squad into a machine gun. About spraying the woods with as much lead as they could unleash.

He bent over and reloaded again. As he rose something smashed down into his helmet. André was stunned by the blow, but he raised the brim. The nearest attacker was twenty meters away. He jogged forward and fired his rifle straight at André. Orange fire blazed right in André's face. André raised his M-16 and fired. The iron sight of the M-16 was laid smack on the man's midsection. The assault rifle's flaming muzzle swept across André as its owner fell. He hadn't felt any bullets pound his chest. Still, however, he waited. Perhaps he was hit, but in a state of shock. He watched the battlefield slowly empty of Chinese.

When he finally snapped out of his daze, he realized that they had won!

"Faulk!" he heard shouted through numb ears.

He turned to see everyone pulling back from the line. The squad leader was waving for André to come over. The man on his left lay draped across his log. He'd been hit despite the fortification. André climbed out of his hole, his tight muscles aching terribly. His joints unlimbered slowly as if he'd been curled up in a cramped space for hours.

"Come *on!*" the sergeant shouted.

André joined him, taking the sergeant and the wounded man's rifles. The soldier was moaning. His eyes were unfocused. He'd been hit bad. The squad leader hoisted him onto his shoulder. He was hunched over in a fireman's carry. He began to stagger to the rear with André following. Everyone else had already disappeared.

"What's the deal?" André asked.

"We're pullin' back," the huffing man said.

"But why . . . ?"

His question was cut short by the roar of a gun. André flinched on hearing the sound at his back. A half-dozen bullets sliced through the air and slammed into trees. André dropped to fire as the sergeant stumbled onward. Masses of attackers approached unopposed. André fired burst after burst, but it did little good. The few men he felled were just drops in the surging sea. He grabbed the three rifles and quickly rejoined the lumbering sergeant.

The squad leader was sweating profusely. His teeth were set in a painful grimace. André had no trouble keeping up with his slow pace. His only trouble, in fact, was to keep from racing ahead. He glanced over his shoulder. The wind was whipping through the woods. He couldn't see the enemy soldiers, but they would be gaining.

The wounded man was flopping limply like a rag doll. When the sergeant stopped to adjust the load, André checked the man's face. His eyes were glassy and lifeless.

"Hey, *Sarge.* I think he's dead!"

The squad leader didn't respond. He just resumed his trudging flight toward their alternate positions. André glanced over his shoulder and saw hazy forms.

"He's *dead,* Sarge! Jesus *Christ,* man, he's—"

"*Shut the fuck up!*" came the reply through gasps for breath.

A stupendous roar filled the woods. This time the gunfire came from in front. From the Americans who were firing at the three men's pursuers. André cringed and ducked behind a tree. He hid not from the Chinese, but from the blazing line of American fighting holes ahead. When the first volleys didn't kill him, he figured they'd been recognized as friendly troops. He bolted around the tree and rejoined the laboring sergeant.

But now the Chinese were firing also. The volume of guns from the two sides was shocking. It was like racing across a live firing range. The simple act of remaining upright seemed impossibly perilous. André's mind blanked out all thoughts but one. He began to sprint and fled out ahead of the struggling squad leader. When he reached the alternate defensive line he dove to the ground. He crawled behind a tree and watched the sergeant struggle on. He'd almost made it when his legs just seemed to fold. He fell to his knees and the dead man's weight crashed down on top of him. The Chinese poured out of the woods fifty meters away. The sergeant squirmed out from under the weight and began to pull the dead man to the rear.

"Leave him *be-e-e,* Sarge!" André shouted. But his voice was lost in the maelstrom of noise. He raised his rifle and fired repeatedly. But still the Chinese came. *"Come on, Sarge!"* André shouted. He never took his eye from his rifle's sights. He emptied his magazine in seconds.

"Shit!" André cursed. He laid his empty rifle beside the tree and began to crawl forward. Chinese hand grenades began to fall all around. They were hurled on the dead run and burst everywhere.

He crawled as low and fast as he could. By the time he reached the sergeant he could see the bobbing heads of racing Chinese. The squad leader dragged the corpse by the hood. A trail of blood through the white snow marked his path.

"They're too close!" André shouted. The sarge only gritted his teeth and pulled. Stray rounds skimmed through the snow all around. It was only a matter of moments before he was hit. The gusting blizzard rose to a howl. He grabbed the wounded man's arm and began to pull with all his might. He kicked at the ground and propelled himself inch by inch through the thick drifts. Suddenly, through the swirling snow, he saw the Chinese. He lay back in stark terror, awaiting the inevitable. His rifle was ten meters away. *My grenades!* he thought. André ripped open his pocket, extracted a frag, pulled the pin, and slung it side-arm. It didn't go far, but it was just the right distance.

The explosion rattled André's insides. It lifted two men into the air with their feet still running and flattened an entire rank of others. He took his last grenade, pulled the pin, and rose to his knees. He hurled it football-style into the thickest clump of approaching soldiers. The air around him buzzed with bullets thick as buckshot. One caught the dead man's leg and splattered André with blood.

The second grenade lit the snowy woods in a brief orange day. It riddled the attackers with metal knots from the pineapple-shaped frag. André scampered back to the sergeant, grabbed the dead man, and pulled and pulled and pulled. His scream was lost in the turmoil. His curses turned into grunts of exertion as he dragged the dead man back. When his elbows landed hard on his half-buried M-16, he realized they'd made it. The sergeant began lifesaving CPR. André fired up his half-empty magazine. He then fired the sergeant's and his dead squadmate's M-16s. He fired till he heard, "Cease fire!"

Flurries of shots rang out on the still-dangerous battlefield. Between the bursts of gunfire, André heard the puffing breaths of the hardworking sergeant. The man lowered his mouth onto the dead private's lips and blew. André crawled over to him.

"He's dead, Sarge," he whispered. Still the man worked frantically.

A medic slid to the ground and pried open the man's sagging eyelids. He opened his bag, pulled out a pair of scissors, and cut away the man's clothing. The two men applied bandages as others joined the lifesaving effort. André slunk away and rested his back against a tree.

The guy was alive, but André had given up on him to save his own skin. The exhausted sergeant caught his eye and crawled over to where André lay. André braced himself.

"Thanks, 'Dré," the sergeant said.

The man's words should've eased André's wretched guilt. His squadmates came by and added their words of praise. They backhanded André's leg. Said, "Way to go," or things like that. André ignored them all.

The man died before they got him off the battlefield. But even that didn't absolve André of his deep sense of guilt.

NORTH OF TANGYUAN, CHINA
April 22, 0100 GMT (1100 Local)

Woody framed the shot. Kate in the foreground. Rising smoke from the firefights in the background. Kate held the stick mike to her mouth. Woody rolled the tape. "The skies have cleared over this narrow mountain valley. What the sunlight has revealed is death, death, and more death."

She stopped and shook her head. "That's too much, don't you think?"

"Just keep going. We'll edit it out."

Kate fixed the appropriate expression on her face. "To reach this valley, Chinese troops must advance along winding mountain roads through a gauntlet of fire from the air. Sources estimate that as many as forty percent are killed or wounded before reaching the battle. What awaits those who make it can only be called murderous fire. Behind every rock and tree it seems is an American machine gun, grenade launcher, or rifle. The fire pours down on the valley floor from steep mountain walls. An estimated forty thousand Chinese soldiers have tried to force their way into this valley since the fighting began two days ago. Their deepest penetration is less than a mile into a valley that is twelve miles long."

The thrum of engines from another flight of C-130s caused Kate to change the order of her script.

"Now that the weather has lifted, U.S. Air Force C-130s have become a familiar sight in the skies overhead." Woody shifted positions to take in the stubby transport. Kate could see out of the corner of her eyes the very scene she was describing. "Rolling down their rear ramps are the tons of supplies that the intense fighting consumes round the clock. The trees are draped in the nylon of hundreds of parachutes. High above are the crisscrossing contrails of air superiority fighters. This may be Chinese real estate, but the airspace is under UN control."

Woody swung the camera to follow the low and slow transports. They belched supplies into the valley. Parachutes from previous drops were draped over treetops to form an arrow easily seen from the air. More parachutes bloomed out of the backs of the fat planes, pulling heavy pallets filled with boxes or crates down the aircrafts' ramps. The supplies fell in and around the clearing at the tip of the giant nylon arrow.

Woody lowered the camera from his shoulder. Kate sat on a rock. "Aren't you glad I talked you into hiking up here?" she asked.

"I'm tickled pink," Woody said. He read the tape counter and made notes on what he'd shot.

"Are they gonna let you recharge the batteries at the hospital?"

"Yep," Woody replied, not looking up at her. The breeze was cold but not gusting. Woody had a scowl on his face.

"Aren't you going to get high?" Kate asked. Woody shrugged. "Jesus Christ, Woody! What's the *matter* with you? You're not acting like yourself."

He took a deep breath and looked across the rugged landscape. "Has it ever occurred to you that we're sitting on a ridge in the middle of China?"

She waited for more, but that was it. She snickered. "Well . . . ye-*e*-eah! It *has,* as a matter of *fact*." He ignored her barbed reply. "What's your point?"

"My point is that we shouldn't be here. Because sooner or later the Chinese are gonna get real serious about taking this place back."

Kate laughed at the ridiculous suggestion. "And you don't think they're *already* serious? I mean, didn't you just listen to my report? Forty thousand troops sounds fairly serious to me."

"It's a drop in the bucket, Kate. So's 400,000. They've got *millions* of men in their army. They've got a population of a billion and a half, for Christ's sake! Sooner or later, Kate, it's gonna get biblical. They're gonna sweep over these hills and kill everybody and everything in their paths no matter who the hell has air superiority or air supremacy or whatever."

"Well . . . don't you think UNRUSFOR has thought of that? That Clark's got a plan?"

He shrugged. "Maybe that's part of his plan. Maybe these guys are expendable."

"Oh, come on! You don't think he'd piss away seven thousand men!"

"If it meant victory? What's seven thousand men?" Woody frowned and shook his head. "And even if he wouldn't, Kate, shit happens. Things go wrong. He'd take risks. He'd have to take chances to win. And this is bound to be one helluva risk, don't you think? I mean, we're deep, deep inside *China,* Kate. China!"

At first, there was nothing but the whistling sound of the wind. Then came a buzzing sound—like a chain saw high in the air.

"Look, an AC-130 raid," Kate said. She got to her feet and pointed at the orbiting black gunship. You could see the tracer rounds streaking out of the sky toward the ground. Woody just sat there. "Get the *shot,* will you?" Kate said impatiently.

"I've got plenty of AC-130 shots," he muttered lethargically.

"Not in broad daylight and clear weather," she argued. The sky was filled now with a second and then a third set of smudgy streaks. The circling Specter gunships pummeled their targets. Nearly always on call, they responded to fire direction from an AWACS, which monitored ground movement detected by an aircraft called a J-STARS. All of it unleashed punishing blows on the Chinese long before they even came near the valley. The buzzing was from twenty-millimeter cannon and 5.56-millimeter miniguns. Booms resounded from 105-millimeter artillery pieces firing directly at targets below. All of it was mounted on the left sides of the lazily orbiting gunships.

Woody raised the camera to his shoulder and began to tape. Kate kept glancing back and forth between the raid and her cameraman. She was terrified by what he'd said but tried not to show it.

Soflysk POW Camp, Siberia
April 22, 2400 GMT (1000 Local)

"Take your clothes off!" came the female U.S. Army soldier's high-pitched Cantonese. Chin and the others all looked at each other uncertainly. She repeated the command. The dozen or so prisoners just stared at the woman. She looked ethnic Chinese, but her accent was distinctly foreign. And she was a woman.

A large black soldier with a rifle barked something threatening in English. Everyone began to disrobe. The tent was heated, and they were marched into a warm shower. Under the loud urgings in English they washed with soap and then dried with rough cotton towels. When they emerged, a team of doctors and nurses awaited.

Chin covered his genitals and walked sheepishly to the brightly lit station. The doctor prodded and probed, wearing thin, rubbery gloves. He even made Chin bend over and spread the cheeks of his butt. Once the humiliation was over, Chin was issued socks, canvas slippers, and a new uniform. It was a bright orange one-piece with a long number across his breast pocket. Next came an electric razor that clipped off all of his wet hair. They gathered at the far side of the tent.

"We're gonna freeze to death," someone whispered. The tent was nice and warm. But Chin's teeth were already chattering, his eyes fixed on the closed flap in the tent. Two guards stood there wearing armbands and holding rifles. Beyond lay subzero temperatures. Their fears subsided when heavy blankets were handed out. Everyone wrapped the blankets over their heads and around their shoulders. They were herded onto a green bus just outside. It too was warmed by heaters. They sat in padded seats. Smiles broke out on some of the men. Two armed men stood at the front. The driver sat behind a mesh, wire wall. He ground through the gears and they took off down the road.

"Where you think we're going?" the guy next to Chin asked.

Chin shrugged. He just stared out the frost-covered windows. The fresh clothing and warm blanket swaddled him.

He was immersed in a rare sense of comfort. Months of aches and pains eased. He didn't care where they were taking him. He didn't imagine it would be bad. It wouldn't make sense to bathe a man before killing him. And they weren't dressed for labor out in the elements.

The bus pulled through a barbed-wire enclosure. Inside were row after row of barracks. The bus stopped in front of one. The doors opened to admit a chilly blast. Everyone rose and followed a guard to the street. They stumbled inside and were each ushered to a bunk. Half the long, open barracks were already filled. The human cargo from Chin's bus filled the other half. An American with a clipboard pointed Chin to the lower bunk. He wrote the number from Chin's jumper on his pad. On the bunk lay a metal cup. Inside it was a toothbrush and toothpaste. He eyed his new possessions in wonder.

The man in the lower bunk next to his was grinning ear to ear. He sat cross-legged and ate rice from a bowl. "You want some?" he asked. He didn't have much left in the bowl, but Chin was famished. He nodded. "There's all you can eat down there," he said. He pointed with his chopsticks toward the end of the barracks.

Chin immediately got up and headed that way. By the time he got to the stove, he was already third in line. A Chinese cook wore an orange prison uniform. He stirred a vat of hot soup and dished out rice. A tall stack of bowls stood along the wall and Chin took one. There were no chopsticks, so he took a package filled with plastic utensils and a paper napkin.

There was chatter and laughter as Chin returned to his bunk. But no Americans were to be seen in the long barracks. Chin sank down with his steaming bowl of white rice. His bunk had a mattress and wool blanket. Plus he had the blanket he'd brought with him. He tried unsuccessfully to open the clear plastic wrapper. The man next to him laughed at his effort. Chin finally just ate the sticky rice with his fingers.

His yellow-toothed neighbor laughed again. He clicked

his chopsticks together. "Never figure those things out. But everything else?" He looked around the barracks. "Not bad, eh?" Chin was too busy stuffing his mouth to do more than nod. "Been here three days, myself. They come through here twice a day to bring food and coal for the furnace and to take a count. They don't say too much."

"The Americans?" Chin mumbled. He accidentally spilled rice from his mouth.

His bunkmate nodded. "Strange people. But I haven't eaten this well since before the army." He flashed a crooked smile.

"So, is this it?" Chin asked. "No work? Just sitting around here all day?" His neighbor nodded. Chin shoveled more gooey rice into his mouth. "Any word from the war?"

The previously talkative man abruptly lay back on his bunk. He stared up at the mattress above him. He didn't answer Chin's question. He acted as if he hadn't heard it. Conversation over. That was when Chin began to notice the war's effects. He became a student of the sullen and the aching. He flitted around the brooding at a distance but ever watchful. They gave shape and form—and sometimes a name—to the psychological damage done to all. He felt a kinship with his fellow survivors that was unlike any he'd ever felt before.

UNRUSFOR HEADQUARTERS, KHABAROVSK
April 23, 0200 GMT (1200 Local)

"The ice has broken, sir," Lieutenant Colonel Reed reported. Nate Clark and several other officers from various UNRUSFOR armies looked up. Reed lowered his eyes to the printout. "About thirty minutes ago we lost our first bridge. Within about twenty minutes after that we'd lost four others. We've now got reconnaissance both on the ground and in the air indicating that the ice is moving downstream at a rate roughly equivalent to the rate of flow of the water."

"Just like that?" Nate asked in amazement. It was an

event they'd all anticipated for so long, but it had happened so suddenly and without warning. Everyone's eyes were trained on him. He snapped out of his reverie and said, "I want a report of exactly what we've got across. Every unit, every vehicle, what their stores are, where they are, where they're headed, what they're facing. I'm calling a full UN-RUSFOR joint staff meeting for"—he looked at his watch—"sixteen hundred local."

He rose, as did all those gathered around. "We've got work to do, gentlemen. Let's get at it."

JIXIAN, CHINA
April 23, 0230 GMT (1230 Local)

The truck's brakes groaned before the two-and-a-half-ton truck stopped. When the engine was shut off, they all heard the noisy crowd. The truck's canvas flap was thrown open and bright light poured in. They were on a dusty, empty street lined by two-story buildings in what appeared to be a medium-to-large city. "Everybody *out*!" the platoon sergeant barked. "Bring weapons, tear gas, and masks!" Glances were exchanged before they climbed down. Some sort of disturbance raged down the street.

"Form up!" the platoon sergeant bellowed. The incredulous men fell into ranks as if on a parade ground. Stempel's 1st Squad was in the front row. Second and 3rd Squads were behind them. Their entire company formed up platoon by platoon. They now wore mottled green-and-brown woodland camouflage field jackets and BDUs. "Ten-*hut*!" the platoon sergeant commanded. "Dress . . . *right*!" Their drill was less than boot-camp crisp. They held their left arms out to space themselves evenly while their eyes roamed the windows of the surrounding buildings. "What ya lookin' at, Patterson?"

"Private Chavez, Sarge!"

"Cut the shit!" The lieutenant began a formal inspection. The street was filled with shouted commands, but Harold strained to decipher the meaning of the more distant din. The noise was being made by a large mass of people. The platoon leader came up to Patterson. "Where's your bayonet?"

"Shit, I dunno, LT. In my pack, I guess."

"Go get it." Patterson took off for the back of the truck. The lieutenant made a cursory check of Harold and moved on. When the inspection was over, their company moved off down the street. Close-order drill commands were barked. "Right . . . face! Forward . . . march!" No one called cadence, so they looked sloppy. They rounded a corner and came face-to-face with a single Bradley armored fighting vehicle. A thin line of MPs wearing gas masks extended to either side. Facing them was a sea of shouting Chinese civilians.

"Jesus Christ!" Patterson said.

"Shut up!" their squad leader snapped from the head of their rank. The platoons were maneuvered until they were lined up three abreast and three squads deep. They stretched from sidewalk to sidewalk, packed in tight. Stempel was in the front rank thirty meters behind the thin line of MPs.

"Get those masks on!" the company commander shouted to the hundred soldiers. The order was echoed by the platoon leaders, who roamed the street just in front.

"I can't believe this shit."

"Patterson!" the platoon leader snapped. "If I hear another goddamn word outta you . . ."

"*I didn't say* nothin', LT!" Patterson whined.

It had been Chavez. Everybody stole looks at the taciturn guy from L.A. He almost never said anything to anybody. Harold took his helmet off and put the mask on. He sucked down on the rubber and sealed the mask tight. He returned the helmet to his head and looked out through the flat plastic lenses. Everything already seemed unreal. The mask only made it more so.

The company commander raised his gas mask. "Mount . . . *bayonets*!" he shouted. The command caught everyone by surprise. The first grumbling arose. Words whispered in questioning tones. Harold fumbled with his scabbard. It took him a long time to seat the bayonet at the end of his rifle. "Port," came the CO's preparatory command, *"arms!"* Harold brought the M-16 up to his chest.

There they stood opposite the crowd. Instead of the ten-meter spread of late twentieth-century infantry, they stood shoulder to shoulder like in the eighteenth. A few feet in front stood the three platoon leaders with the platoon sergeants at their sides. At the center was the company commander and his attendant, the radio-telephone operator. There had been no radio in eighteenth-century engagements. None was needed in the current encounter. "Company-y-y . . . !" the captain shouted.

The lieutenants echoed, "Platoon!"

"For*ward . . . march!*"

Half the men stepped off in unison. The other half advanced just to stay in formation. Stempel was in the latter group. They halted just behind the Bradley. The semiorganized mob of soldiers now faced the totally disorganized civilians. Gaps began to appear in what had been a solid mass of Chinese. Some who remained shook their fists. Others waved official documents of some sort. Still others hoisted banners across which were scrawled unrecognizable characters. An MP repeated something over and over in Chinese through a bullhorn. A major finally called a halt to the effort and had a word with their company commander. The lieutenants were then summoned for an impromptu meeting.

Harold's platoon leader returned. "Front ranks, listen up! Every other man sling your weapon!" Harold's squad leader counted them off. He pointed at Harold, who slung his rifle over his shoulder. "Men in the front rank with weapons in hand assume riot stance!" The LT leveled his own weapon, his bayonet leading the way. "Jab with each step forward! You men with weapons slung, spray gas! Aim at their faces! *Rear ranks,*" he shouted at the top of his lungs, "lock 'n load!" Magazines were audibly seated into weapons in the two squads behind Harold.

"Whatta those people want?" Patterson asked.

The platoon leader spun on him. "How the fuck should *I* know? Our orders are to clear this street, so shut the fuck up!'' The dissent from that point was quiet, but it continued. ''This sucks!'' someone whispered—a sentiment repeated throughout the ranks. Harold found the button on the top of his oversized spray can. The green metal was replete with stern warnings about which way to point the nozzle. It looked like insecticide.

''Forward,'' the company commander yelled, ''*march*!''

They began their advance, taking baby steps as they'd been taught in one brief drill back in boot camp. In the front rank bayonets were jabbed vigorously at the crowd with each footfall. The stylized lunge was meant to clear the front by intimidation. The pace was menacing and deliberate by design, but to Harold—carrying his can—it seemed slow. At a dozen meters from contact, most of the civilians had fled the debris-strewn street. The solid wall of humanity had been reduced to a scattered band. Most were seething with anger over something—what, Harold had absolutely no idea. But they didn't really confront the Americans like enemies, more like an assembly of protesters and petitioners.

''Grunt!'' the officers ordered. From the ranks arose a muffled but still sonorous noise. ''*Huh!*'' they chanted over and over. The synchronized motion and sound fed each other. It organized the entire formation. They repeatedly stepped forward, jabbed, and grunted. They were in step. They were one. They were braced to sink steel into flesh. Everyone, that is, but the can holders—Patterson, Harold, and of all people Chavez. Harold felt like he was being pushed forward by the formation as if by the blade of a bulldozer. He tried to grunt with the others, but it didn't seem natural without the bayonet. He felt like a bystander instead of a participant in the clash.

The officers sprayed their cans first. The tight squirts of gas jetted across the divide into the crowd. The Chinese flinched and recoiled. Harold shook his can and scanned the battlefield for a target. A man with a kerchief over his nose brandished a long stick and boldly stood his ground. Harold decided he'd try to save the man's life. At a range of six meters he aimed the nozzle and pressed the button.

He adjusted his aim till the spray raked across the man's eyes. He screamed, dropped the stick, fell to his knees, and clawed at his eyes. He rolled to the paving stones in hyperactive agony—writhing, bucking, and yelping. He scraped at the skin on his face and kicked his heels against the ground until his friends dragged him away vomiting. Thereafter Harold sprayed mostly men, but some women. Mostly young, but some old. Mostly angry, but some plaintive. He had no idea what they were mad at, or wanted, or needed, he just sprayed.

When it was over, the street was filled only with trash. They made no arrests but roughed up resisters and sent them away bleeding. They didn't kill anyone, but they didn't treat the injured. As they rested on a side street, the entire company hung their heads and looked exhausted. No one talked. The air was thick with the smell of tear gas. Men spat to rid their mouths of the taste. And they listened as their commanding officer ranted and raved. First to the major who commanded on the scene. Then over the radio to battalion staff. Then right in the face of the battalion commander, whose Humvee had pulled up on the main street.

An endless convoy rolled down the now empty thoroughfare, but you didn't have to strain to hear the captain's shouts. And everyone agreed with the sentiments he expressed, even the battalion commander, judging from the man's surprising patience. None of the men in Harold's unit wanted to fight. They were exhausted and ready to go home. But there was a war taking place, and they were soldiers.

WHITE HOUSE OVAL OFFICE
April 23, 0300 GMT (2200 Local)

Daryl was bubbling over with good cheer. Gordon was concerned, but he didn't know why. Elaine's mood was somewhere between the two. Gordon wanted to know exactly where she stood and why.

"We're gonna *win*, Gordon!" Daryl said. "For the life of me I can't see any downside in this." He tossed the one-

page communiqué on Gordon's desk. "The Chinese are
cracking. This is just their opening bid. Japan's ambassador
to Beijing said so himself."

"Are you considering accepting it?" Elaine asked.

Gordon eyed her before shaking his head. "They're basically just offering a cease-fire," he mumbled. "We've
come too far to settle for that."

With a grin on his face, Daryl said, "Hell, when those two
prongs hook up, we can just do our thing and leave." Gordon nodded slowly. Frowning. "*What*, Gordon? What's gotten into you? Things couldn't have worked out any better."

"I know. I know." Gordon looked at Elaine. "I don't
know what it is."

"Maybe you're just a little blue," she suggested. "I
mean, now that it's coming to an end. Maybe everything's
finally catching up with you. You remember what the doctor said. About people who suffer serious traumas sometimes suffering for a long time . . . emotionally."

"Maybe," was all Gordon could manage. He *was* de-
pressed. But he didn't think that was it. It was something.
Some risk. Some danger. He couldn't put his finger on it. He
looked up at Daryl. "I'll tell State not to answer. Let 'em
stew for a few days while we press on to that valley. But you
talk to the people at the Pentagon yourself. I want plans
ready to withdraw those troops from China at a moment's
notice." Gordon felt another wave of concern. It baffled
him.

PART FIVE

"Power over one's fellow man is the root of all human activity. For what better way to control one's destiny than to bend others to your plans and your will? The urge to amass that power is both irresistible and subliminal. Whether that power is gained by wealth, by beauty, by office, by the muzzle of a gun, or by the moral suasion of one's ideas, its accumulation is the end, in and of itself, of every human alive."

Valentin Kartsev (posthumously)
The Laws of Human History
Moscow, Russia

22

"Miller?" the squad leader asked. Three full mags. Eight rounds in Miller's fourth. "Fifty-three rounds," the squad leader mumbled as he wrote. "Faulk?" Two full plus eleven, André answered. "Squeeze 'em off, Faulk," the sergeant replied. "Make 'em count." André nodded in the darkness as he picked at his MRE—chicken teriyaki and asparagus spears. A spasm of gunfire erupted, but no one bothered to look until it was clear from the rising tide of violence that a major attack was under way. Without being told, the eight remaining men of André's squad gathered their gear. The call came a couple of minutes later.

"We're up!" the new platoon sergeant barked. Everyone rose slowly. There were no groans as the men flexed sore muscles. No words of complaint from André's usually vocal squadmates. There was nothing but the clack of magazines. The metallic screech of a charging handle in need of oil. The snapping latch of grenade launchers being closed, locked, and loaded. The resignation of the eight teenagers was oppressive.

They advanced through the increasingly smoky woods

single file, the better to keep together in the darkness. Their silence contrasted sharply with the thunderclap of Chinese shells bursting along the high ridges on both sides and lighting the upper branches of trees like lightning. The thin needles of the evergreens overhead looked colorless in the flickering light, and each blast drew skyward glances from the frightened soldiers. The sporadic fire from the big Chinese guns was new and worrisome. They ascended a low humpback ridge and stooped low near the top with weapons raised. No orders needed to be given. They'd done this countless times. The increasing volume of the fighting warned of the death that lay ahead. André could no longer make out the sounds of individual weapons among the thousands being fired in the narrow valley. He crested the ridge and saw the battlefield, clearly lit by flashing muzzles and bursting flames.

The knot in his stomach grew as he descended into the streaking fireflies below. The roar was so great only a shout would be heard, so André kept his eyes on the men ahead for signs of danger. A flinch, a drop to a knee, a rifle abruptly raised to a shoulder—any one might save André's life. Like a fidgety herd of potential prey, if the men in front turned and fled, the men in the rear would be right on their heels.

His stomach cramped, his bowels churned, and his mouth was dry and tasted of steel. His palms and armpits grew damp. The line filed past the dark silhouette of a man who shoved soldiers to the left and right. "We dig in here!" came the platoon sergeant's foul breath. He propelled André to the right, where a short while later his squad leader grabbed him and pointed down. André dropped his fighting load and began to dig along with the men on either side, not six meters away. If truth be told, André preferred fighting at night when their spacing was reduced by almost half. He spaded the earth with his metal entrenching tool fixed at ninety degrees, then chopped and scraped until his back ached and his lungs burned. Several times he had to rise up and swallow the choking bile of fear.

"Delta Company's gonna pass the line to us!" the platoon sergeant informed the men as he passed behind their fighting positions. "We've got five minutes! Dig 'em deep, boys. There's a whole lotta hurt comin'!" No one said a word, but André heard their grunts as they dug. Sweat poured down his forehead and neck. He debated taking the time to remove his parka, but the shallow hole would be his grave unless he dug deeper. The next few minutes of preparations were precious.

André didn't know why he looked up into the dark woods ahead, but when he did, he saw movement. He dropped his shovel and sank to his knees to grope for his rifle, but it was only two men helping a wounded buddy to the rear. As they hobbled past, André scraped the loose dirt with his gloves and vowed to pay more attention to their front. If all went well, they'd get plenty of warning. There'd be another visit by the platoon sergeant or platoon leader. Then the retreating D Company would pull back in orderly fashion. The last man through—usually an NCO—would call out "Line passed!" Then the order to fire at will would echo from all sides. But things didn't always go well. If D Company folded or was flat overrun, the first sign of approaching danger would be a brief glimpse of sprinting soldiers. Maybe American, maybe Chinese, maybe mixed. The first Chinese wouldn't stop and fight. They'd try to infiltrate to the rear, where confusion would be their ally, then they'd circle back and attack from the rear.

André returned his shovel to his webbing. In a hasty retreat he didn't want to have to collect his gear, and he definitely didn't want to lose his all-important shovel. He laid his two spare magazines on the ground. His eyes were long adjusted to the dim light, but the first thing to go would be his night vision, so he memorized their location by feel. Now began the worst time of all. He peered into the woods ahead through his M-16's sights, licking his dry lips but not finding the moisture to swallow. Brief strobes from large mortars and artillery gave some illumination, and André grew increasingly familiar with sights. Nothing moved. Nothing changed. All was still. The tension grew steadily into a pounding headache just behind his eyes. He pressed his fingers against his closed eyelids then rubbed his temples.

When he looked up, he saw running soldiers through still-blurry vision. André jerked his rifle to his cheek and flicked the selector to semiautomatic. "Hold your fire!" was shouted up and down the line. André's heart pounded as Delta Company fell back as fast as they could run. Men passed so close he could hear the involuntary yelps and moans of fear through their labored breathing. The groans of wounded men being carried too roughly by comrades. One machine-gun crew dropped to their knees between André and the guy on his left and loosed a long burst into the woods. "They're about two hundred meters behind us!" the winded gunner called out. "Must be about a battalion! Good luck!" With a grunt they rose and trotted off, leaving André's unit the new main line of defense. André glanced back at the retreating men in envy. They were probably done for the night . . . unless everything broke.

"Free to fire!" was passed by shouts up and down the line. André yelled it out himself before settling low in the shallow hole. He set his jaw and scanned the trees for the Chinese. "Don't waste ammo!" and other similar warnings were shouted, then everyone fell silent. It gave André a sense of comfort to hear the voices stretch into the distance to either side. *We'll be all right*, he told himself. The line had been passed in good order. They were braced in semiprepared positions. It was the Chinese who would die that night. A shiver rippled up his torso. Not fear, but a sudden waking jolt of adrenaline. He saw every tree ahead with heightened clarity. He breathed hard as if from heavy exertion. His hands ached, and he loosened his grip on the rifle. He caught himself grinding his teeth so hard his jaw hurt. He tilted his neck to both sides and it popped. When his eye returned to his sight he took a deep breath and tried to ease up.

Machine guns began to spit rounds in short bursts to the

far left. Then came a cascading volley of forty-millimeter grenades, then a fusillade of rifles. "Grazing fire!" the platoon leader shouted, and their own machine guns began spraying the woods. André took a last check to clearly locate the gun, which was maybe fifteen meters away. Worst case, he'd peel back and hook up with it, where they might, in an overrun, hold a small but lifesaving pocket. *Any second now*, he thought, counting down the time with each thudding heartbeat. Mortars whistled overhead and dropped into the trees a hundred meters to their front. They burst in the upper branches, raining shrapnel and wood splinters with surely devastating effects. Grenadiers looking down from the surrounding heights plunked forty-millimeter rounds even closer. André knew the men on the ridges wore night-vision goggles that allowed them to see the surging mass of Chinese infantry through gaps in the trees.

Out of the blazing forest emerged the forms of running men—easy shots at thirty meters. Everyone opened fire all at once. *Slow*, André thought. *Aim. Squeeze.* The rifle bucked, and a man dropped like a limp doll. André concentrated on his breathing as he lined up the next guy. The high-powered assault rifle pounded his shoulder—dead man! *Slow 'n steady*, he told himself as the double stack in his magazine dwindled. But despite the devastating fire from three sides, the number of shouting Chinese grew. He fired, and fired, and lost count of his ammo. When the trigger froze, he dropped the empty magazine and slapped a new one home. Spitting sounds like a striking serpent flew by. The attackers dodged and wove as they fired from the hip. André pulled the trigger as fast as he could but the return fire grew thicker still. Once again he was surprised when the trigger wouldn't pull.

"Shit!" he cursed. He was down to his last magazine. *Only eleven rounds left!* sounded the alarm in his head. *Shit! Shit-shit-shit-shit!* He raised his M-16 but was reluctant to fire despite the multitude of easy targets. Only the straight-on approach of three running soldiers, each spewing great volumes of fire, convinced him to part with precious rounds. Each shot felled a man, but when another attacker leaped from the ground unexpectedly, André hurried and missed his fourth shot, killing the charging man with his fifth.

Six rounds left! he thought in near panic. He saved every one for close combat. Not firing his weapon bred a sense of detachment, the view of an observer instead of a participant. The guy on André's left pasted his M-16 to his cheek. Spent cartridges were methodically ejected. The same sight greeted André's check of his right. Only André lay there useless and inactive in the critical moments of a fight for his life. He thought about rushing out and grabbing a Chinese rifle, but he'd never do such a suicidal thing. He craned his neck to see if any squadmates had been hit. He could render aid if someone was wounded, or scavenge ammo if they were dead, but everyone appeared to be engaged except him.

His neighbor to the left reared up and threw a hand grenade. The smoking trail spiraled a few feet through the air and then sparks flew. André caught a glimpse of the grenade rebounding back off a tree.

André was sitting up. His skin was clammy and cold. "You hear me now?" someone was asking. He smelled strong, acrid fumes and felt a sting in his nostrils. He slammed his head back into the tree behind him, and pain shot through his skull. He leaned over and vomited. "*Je*sus Christ!" the man said in disgust. André opened his eyes and saw the man stand and toss the stick of smelling salts to the ground. André half rolled over onto his side—exhausted. He laid his pounding head on the ground. It felt like his face was split open at the nose. He was sweating profusely. He couldn't find the strength to do even the simplest of things, and he took no interest in anything but breathing without heaving again.

A small penlight shone red through his eyelids, which were pried open into the bright beam. "Is he bad?" André heard his platoon leader ask as the light was extinguished.

"No, sir. Mild concussion, maybe." The lieutenant squatted beside him. "You okay, Faulk?"

André mumbled something so slurred he wasn't even sure what he had intended to say, but the platoon leader rose, apparently satisfied. "What's the count?" he asked. "Two dead—both in Third Squad. Five wounded—two bad." After a moment the lieutenant said, *"Fuck!"* in a quiet tone. André listened with his eyes closed. His head hurt so bad he couldn't open them. The radio crackled. The platoon leader answered. A map rattled. After signing off, the LT said, "We're headin' back, Sarge Davis." André thought he meant to the rear, away from the savage fighting. Just a few hundred meters back where you could sleep. But there was something in the lieutenant's tone.

"We need some *time*, sir!" the platoon sergeant whispered. "We got some people that's shook *up*!"

"I *know* that, god*dam*mit! But what the hell'm I s'posed to *do*? Tell the CO *no*? We're movin' out. The whole comp'ny. Get 'em up." The lieutenant took off. With a rustle of fabric the platoon sergeant reached down and grabbed André's arm. "Let's go, Faulk," he said, still seething, and pulled. André found himself sliding up the tree as his arm was almost yanked from his shoulder, and he found himself confused but standing on his feet. "Let's get you back to yer squad."

"But . . ."

"*But* what?" the man snapped.

André licked his dry lips. "I ain't got any ammo."

The platoon sergeant was older. Maybe twenty-six. "We'll get you a Chinese CQ, or a 56-2. We got stacks and stacks of 'em."

CAMP DAVID, MARYLAND
April 23, 1500 GMT (1000 Local)

The joint chiefs all wore their uniforms. Gordon Davis had on slacks and a shirt with an open collar. Maps stood on easels amid two fireplaces and dark wood paneling. "We're having some real problems with civilian unrest in Jixian and Nancha," General Dekker reported. He indicated two Chinese cities on the map just south of the border. "Civil order has broken down completely."

"Has there been bloodshed?" Gordon asked.

"Yes, sir. But not shed by us. People have been ransacking local Communist Party and Security Ministry offices. We haven't disarmed the constabulary forces, and there have been shootings. So far, we've avoided direct engagement. But the situation is deteriorating."

Gordon felt a rush of anxiety. "How about the military situation?"

Dekker glanced at the other chiefs before answering. The disorder must be a serious concern, Gordon thought. He seemed reluctant to leave the point. "The Chinese are making contact with our flanks. No hard jabs. They're just probing till we stiffen. Since they don't have any aerial reconnaissance to speak of, they're probably trying to determine where we are and in what strength. The best way to do that is to press and see if you bump into anything solid."

"What are our casualties?"

"We've lost about two thousand dead in the counteroffensive, and about nine thousand wounded. Half those KIAs are in the Tangyuan Valley. Overall, we're just over ten thousand dead and thirty thousand wounded for the war."

Gordon held Dekker's gaze. "How long till we hook up with those troops in the valley, General?"

Dekker frowned. "It's difficult to say, Mr. President. We're on our time line right now. That would put us there in five days."

Gordon nodded, satisfied, and turned to the head of the Special Operations Command. "So how goes the rearming of Russia's army in the Far East?"

UNRUSFOR HEADQUARTERS, KHABAROVSK
April 23, 2200 GMT (0800 Local)

"She's been ferrying them out by medevacs," Lieutenant Colonel Reed said. Clark sat in front of the monitor watching videos of parachutes bloom behind fat green aircraft. Guns popped and smoke rose from the battlefields beneath the high ridge. It was his first view of the desperate battle.

And the voice was clearly Kate Dunn's. "Flying low through the valley, transports drop massive loads of supplies, which are consumed at a prodigious rate. Soldiers are engaged in near-constant battle against wave after wave of Chinese infantry. Although the numbers of troops landed deep inside China is classified, this is a major operation aimed straight into the heartland. And the People's Liberation Army is pulling out all the stops to throw the foreign invaders from their soil." There were pictures of men running with stretchers toward aid tents. "The twenty-year-olds weathering that storm have no great desire to be here. But they're among the best soldiers in the world. They've been hardened by months of winter war." There were close-ups of sunken, glassy eyes. "They know that the course of the war—and therefore of history—may turn on the outcome of this one battle. But more importantly they know that they're fighting for their lives and for the lives of their best friends." Two soldiers were crammed together into a hole, sound asleep. "The force of the bonds forged on this anvil of war are so great they can only be broken by death."

The final shot was of a vinyl tarpaulin covering all but the upturned boots of a dead soldier.

"This is Kate Dunn, NBC News, northern China."

Clark looked up at Reed and shook his head. "No way. Confiscate every tape she sends out." Reed nodded. "I would like to take a look at them, though," Clark added. Reed nodded again. "Now let's get going."

Nate Clark's Blackhawk hovered far upstream from the heli-bridge. Huge U.S. Marine Corps helicopters ferried heavy loads from one bank to the other. But the more impressive sight was what flowed down the river. Jagged patches of ice, sometimes piled high, meandering toward the sea.

"Beautiful, don't you think?" General Cuvier said. Clark looked over at the area commander. They sat knee to knee beside the large rectangular window. The French general stared down at the scene. "Before I came here it was impossible to conceive of the scale. Of the distances. Of the wilderness. How few roads and villages and people. At least on the Russian side of the border."

Clark turned back to the window and his mind wandered. They were entering a new country. A new and more populous theater of operations. "I won't miss it," he said without realizing. He looked up into the stare of his escort.

Cuvier was alert and leaning forward. The helicopter's engine was loud. It allowed for the fiction that the six aides in the cabin couldn't overhear their private conversation. "You seem to be afraid of losing," the general said. His voice was low and his accent thick. "If I can speak to you about this." Clark nodded. "What I am saying about you is very *good* for a commanding officer. There was talk, you know. Talk from Paris, which we were told came from Washington. That you would resign your command," he explained, as if Clark would immediately understand. "But I never thought that you would, and I told them this. They just said"—he made a face and waved his hand dismissively—"ahh, you just do your job. Fight your battles. *We* will tell *you* about such things."

He rocked back with a scowl on his face and locked himself stiff-armed with his hands on his knees.

Clark's gaze drifted off again. "At least those bastards back at the Pentagon didn't leave a pistol on my desk."

There was laughter from everyone in the helicopter. Nate turned to see a half-dozen smiles. The captains and colonels in their entourage lightened up. An ease settled over the group that had not been there before.

·   ·   ·

The ear protectors they all wore looked like large head-phones. Up and down the riverside heliport giant CH-53Es dropped their loads onto mesh pads. Their huge engines were revved to full power. The noise was quite literally deafening.

Clark strained to listen to his guide. The Marine colonel and his French commander walked him out onto the bull-dozed and matted landing areas. Men on the ground un-hooked the cargo. The loads dangled a hundred feet beneath the U.S. military's most powerful helicopter. "We got a dozen Echos on loan from the navy!" the colonel yelled.

The ferries didn't have very far to travel. From one side of the river to the other, they shuttled vehicles, nets, and fuel tanks. The traffic was exclusively one-way. They picked up on the Russian side, and dropped off in Com-munist China. As he watched the operation, he experienced a sudden and unexplainable rush. Thoughts and feelings flooded his mind. It was as if he'd awakened to find himself sleepwalking. He looked at the bustling helipad. The crowded truck park. The tent city. The mounds of crates and boxes. The road that led off into the distance that hadn't been there two days before. Everything had been built solely for this crossing. In a month it would be a sea of mud. But for the next two weeks it would be an artery through which would flow the lifeblood of his army.

And it was all in the People's Republic of China.

General Cuvier was pointing out the short turnaround time. How the helicopters never touched the ground. But Clark's mind roamed down the road deep into Manchuria. Dust rose high into the air behind two-and-one-half-ton trucks. The same dust also filled the air on the Russian bank. In Clark's mind he visualized the huge pipeline. From factories and ports in America and Japan to the troops on the main line of resistance, the entire supply chain ran across the earth's surface. Until it reached the Amur River, that is, and its gravity-defying heli-bridge.

The parade of ice down the waterway was a testament to nature's power. Clark found himself increasingly drawn to the riverbank. He saw there with his own eyes what had previously been dry engineering theory. Comparisons of the maximum force that a span would withstand with the energy unleashed by millions of tons of moving ice. The thick slabs were broken in places and piled atop one another sometimes several layers thick. They were white monuments to crushing force. The phenomenal energy of the river's movement. And even over the constant roar of the helicopters he could occasionally hear an unearthly groan from the ice.

"We'll have pontoon bridges across in ten days!" the Marine transportation officer said from Clark's side. "Not here, but about ten miles downriver!" He raised a gloved hand to point. "Had to cross up here with the helicopters because there wasn't flat land downstream for two LZs— one on each bank!"

Clark caught himself thinking it seemed too easy. The Chinese defenses built up to counter the Soviets had seemed insurmountable on paper months before. Intellectually, Clark knew all the answers. Those defenses had eroded. They'd been abandoned by the troops who invaded Siberia. But he knew also that there was nothing easy about it. That men had fought and died for every meter of that dirt road. It was a depressing measure of how detached he'd grown from the killing and the dying in the field. How effectively he had shut from his mind all the horror he'd experienced in his youth.

He turned to his French host and said, "I've decided to make a change in my itinerary."

The helicopter landed on the boulevard of a city. Clark and his entourage got out. A British colonel saluted the American and French generals bare-handed. He then quickly replaced his gloves and glanced nervously over his shoulder. The helicopter rotors spun slowly to a stop.

"I apologize, General Clark . . ." the colonel began. But everyone ducked when a loud boom rang out from the next block. Clark's security troops tightened their ring around the commanding general. Grayish-white smoke rose above the low buildings. Everything seemed to be under control.

"As I was saying," the British battalion commander said, "I do apologize that I am not able to put on a better reception for you, sir."

It was Clark who felt like apologizing. A total of three helicopters had landed unannounced. In the lead were two green Blackhawks—his and the one for his security team. Behind was a Cobra gunship riding shotgun. His half-dozen bodyguards, nonuniformed employees of the Department of Defense, were packed at arm's length around the three officers. And at least a platoon of the colonel's infantrymen had taken up positions around the impromptu helipad.

A machine gun opened fire from the same direction as the explosion. Clark listened to the steady drumbeat of high-powered rounds.

"It seems it is *I*," Clark said, "who has interrupted your afternoon's work, Colonel. I won't keep you long. I just wanted to look around."

"Of course, sir," the man said. Clark could tell nothing from his tone or manner. Was he pissed off and Clark was missing it? The British colonel turned and looked over his shoulder. "It's more like unfinished business from the morning, actually. A few holdouts down in the cellars we're trying to clear out. It is a pity to have to blast them out like that. But I don't want to leave them behind our lines. Could get a tad *sticky* once the sun goes down, what with our perimeter set up about five hundred meters in that direction," he said, pointing down the street past the rattling machine gun.

"Is the perimeter quiet?" Clark asked.

"For the most part, yes sir."

"Can I take a look?" Clark asked.

The colonel arched his eyebrow, looking at the dozen-man entourage. "As you wish, General Clark."

Clark understood the field officer this time. He turned and spoke in a loud voice. "Everyone wait here while General Cuvier and I inspect the perimeter." The chief of the security detail turned his dark sunglasses Clark's way. "You wait here," Clark said to the man, then he pushed his way through the ring of bodyguards.

"General Clark," the security officer said.

Nate set his jaw and ground his teeth. He was, after all, a soldier. He could take care of himself on a battlefield. He turned back. The man held his weapon out to Clark. It was an M-16 shortened to carbine length. Its short sling was meant to hang the weapon at your hip.

Nate took it. He was within five hundred meters of the enemy, and he'd brought no weapon with him at all. He strapped the carbine over his shoulder and took a pistol belt with ammo pouches. He had to loosen the belt for his waist-line. Everyone waited patiently by his side. The belt sagged under the weight of six magazines. Clark had forgotten the heavy feel of a fighting load.

"Perhaps I should get something better than *this, hu-uh*?" General Cuvier asked. He grinned as he patted the pistol in his holster. The two generals and the British colonel hooked up with a squad. Riflemen led the way single file down the street.

"There doesn't appear to be much damage from the fighting," Clark said. The carbine kept sliding off his shoulder, so he let the sling dangle and held it by the pistol grip and front guard.

"We didn't have to do too much fighting, actually," the colonel replied. "We came in with armor and mounted infantry, and the city's militia decided not to give it much of a go."

The streets seemed strangely desolate. No smoke came from the chimneys. "Where are all the people?" Nate asked. "This city had a population of a few hundred thousand."

"We don't know where they are, really. We get reports that the roads to the south are jammed. Refugee traffic must be wreaking havoc on the Chinese."

"And they are in our way also," General Cuvier noted. "Slowing us down."

Another loud explosion rocked the street. The infantry-men instinctively dropped to one knee. They quickly re-sumed their progress toward the perimeter.

"Well, there do seem to be at least *some* militiamen who've chosen to stand and fight," Nate commented.

The colonel looked back over his shoulder. "They're not *fighting,* actually. They just won't come out. When we find them hiding—usually in the cellars—we back off and evac-uate the building of any civilians. We waited several hours for an interpreter, but as the day wore on I decided I couldn't wait any longer."

"Do you mean you're just dropping charges down into those cellars when they don't give up?"

"We *try* to coax them out. But without an interpreter I'm afraid it's no use." He paused at an intersection and turned. "As I said, it *is* a pity what one must do."

The silence was filled only by the steady pounding of a machine gun. The colonel's men finishing their morning's work.

"We'll get you an interpreter by nightfall," Clark said.

They crossed the street one at a time at a jog. The lead infantrymen grew increasingly tense at each intersection. Up ahead there were barricades across the broad street. All the talking was now done by hand. By pointed fingers or blunt fists. By parade-field waves and traffic-cop halts. They raced across open spaces, rifles raised to their shoul-ders. They knelt behind cover with eyes to their sights.

Nate was tense. But that was natural. The most promi-nent recollection of the war he'd fought in his youth was the sickening dread of imminent death. If not you, the guy next to you. And it was mixed with interminable stress and inadequate sleep. Numbing fatigue interrupted by shocking danger. Exhaustion from living unprotected in the elements. Aches and pains from a dozen cuts and bruises. Battling extremes of everything all at once.

Nate's turn to cross the intersection came. He was hu-miliated by the indignity of an escort. A British private crossed the street at his side. He was so angered that he felt no present sense of danger. When he knelt, General Cuvier was smiling. He understood from Nate's frown how Nate felt. "At least I didn't fall and break a hip," Nate muttered.

The amiable Frenchman was just beginning to laugh when a single shot rang out. The British soldiers all began an agitated search. A man lay in the middle of the street cursing and shouting. "God! Ah! Christ!" He clutched his bleeding thigh and writhed in pain on the cobblestones.

"I've got movement in the wind*o-o-ow*!" someone shouted. The bull-pup rifles carried by the British opened up. Automatic rifle fire from six men all at once.

"*I need aid!*" the wounded man shouted, his teeth bared. His eyes were shut in a grimace. His red cheeks bulged out and he began to puff. His mouth formed an *O* and his chest heaved as he gulped air.

Several of his comrades put down their weapons. Clark raised his. He leaned out around the corner and took aim. A second-story window was being peppered with fire. Thin curtains danced with each passing round. With his thumb he selected "auto."

"Go!" the lieutenant shouted.

Clark squeezed the trigger. The stubby carbine recoiled with surprising force. He recentered on the window and put five rounds through and two on the wall. Empty shells chinged off the paving stones. He switched to "semi" and squeezed them off one round a second.

He released the empty magazine as soldiers dragged the wounded man to the far side of the street. The rest of their platoon was just arriving, adding great amounts of fire.

Two men set a machine gun down at the intersection and dropped behind it. As soon as they settled on the ground, the weapon roared. Flame shot two feet from the muzzle. It was a shocking assault on the senses. An elemental eruption of noise made more dramatic by the narrow and curving canyon of walls.

The burst ended.

"*By* twos!" shouted a mustachioed sergeant. "Ready-y! Go!"

ER-H-H-H-H-H-R-R, roared the gun.

No riflemen even bothered firing now. Men sprinted down the side street hugging the walls.

"*Cease* fi-i-ire!"

The street was quiet save the sounds of the front door being kicked in. Then there was no noise till the troops got upstairs. They smashed through the sniper's door. Seconds passed. Then the room exploded.

Flame shot through two windows at once. Black smoke poured out after that.

"It's all cl*e-e*-ear!" shouted a man from the dark window. "Sniper's dead!"

"Safe your weapo-o-ons!" shouted the platoon leader. It was a command that Clark instinctively followed. He was kneeling amid brass shell casings. The stench of rifles filled the air. He rose slowly. His knee ached from the cobblestone on which it had rested. Joints popped. He felt no spring in his muscles. Everyone rose, gathering themselves. Straightening their nerves out after the brief fight.

A lieutenant appeared in the sniper's window.

"Was it a *partisan*?" the British colonel shouted.

"No, sir!" the platoon leader replied. "PLA regular, sir!"

"Oh, thank God," the battalion commander muttered from beside Nate.

"Have you gotten any partisan activity?" Nate asked quietly.

"Not yet, sir."

The two men looked at each other. "Do you have a contingency plan?" Clark asked.

The colonel took a deep breath. "Worst case, we leave the cities. Bivouac in the countryside. If . . . if *you* approve, that is, of course." Clark nodded. "In the country we can maintain some distance. Establish clear fields of fire. Even so, there really is no effective defense against. . . . against a billion and a half *people*. Not if they're roused, sir. Not if they're roused."

Clark was silent. "There's a happy thought," Cuvier said to end the conversation.

"Let me know when you hear how bad your man is," Nate told the colonel. "I'll want to visit him at the hospital. But now . . . let's get moving."

The squad re-formed for the final approach to the perimeter. The "front" consisted of two wrecked buses lying end to end. The crude tank trap built by Chinese defenders was blackened by fire. It provided excellent cover for the small party's last few meters of advance. The men jogged in a crouch down the sidewalk. After a short distance they turned into an open doorway. The room they entered had been shot to pieces.

Four men lay against the walls. They hardly moved, but their eyes were fixed on the new arrivals. And their weapons were all within reach. One clutched his rifle to his chest. Another lay cradled across its owner's thighs. The other rifles leaned against the wall beside the soldiers.

The dozen or so new arrivals crowded into the room.

"How were things today, Lance Corporal?" the battalion commander asked.

"Oh, it was tolerable, sir. Tolerable. And everything is quiet now, sir. Sounded like you had some trouble on the way, though, sir. Anyone hurt?"

"Had a chap catch a bullet—right here," the colonel said. He jabbed his thigh at the site of the wound.

"They can be bad—leg wounds. *Bleeders*."

Several heads around the room nodded.

"Yes. Well . . ." The colonel turned to Nate, who all of a sudden felt awkward and insecure. Guilty for indulging himself in this little excursion. "I'd like to introduce you men to Lieutenant General Nathaniel Clark, United States Army, commanding general of UNRUSFOR."

The soldiers started to get to their feet. Clark motioned energetically for them not to rise. "And it's Nate. My given name is Nate, not Nathaniel."

The four men all nodded and acknowledged him politely. "How do you *do,* sir?" and "It's a pleasure, sir."

"Lance Corporal Sheffield, sir. Edgar, sir. From Spilsby."

A couple of the others snickered.

Nate shook the man's hand. "Spilsby? That's . . . ?"

"In the north, sir. Near the sea."

"Ah," Clark said, nodding.

He then duckwalked around the room to meet the others, making the rounds like a politician. As he did, he took note of the deeply pitted walls. The windows and doors that all lay shattered. The pieces of furniture now tossed into one corner of the room.

Upon returning to Sheffield, he asked, "So how bad was it?"

"Oh," replied the lance corporal, "not that bad, sir. Not as bad as this room makes it look. For us, that is, sir. *We* did all the damage in here. Killed *seven* of 'em, we did. Found the blokes after we tossed three grenades."

"Four," another soldier corrected.

"Four. That's right. It was four, I remember now. We found 'em piled up on *top* of each other." His helmet dropped until Clark could barely see his eyes. "One at the bottom was . . . was still saying something, he was. Talked for quite a while. We just had time to make sure he wasn't armed, you understand. We were going at it with some of his *comrades* in the next room. He was dead when we came back through."

"Every room's different," one of the other soldiers said. He was reclined almost flat on the floor. His words were slurred from the posture . . . and from fatigue. "Some of them *we* wreck. Others *they* wreck. It goes back and forth, usually. When you're done, the whole building looks like this."

Sheffield quickly resumed the liaison with Clark. He'd worn a worried look with every word his man had spoken. He clearly thought himself the more polished representative, and he jumped back in as soon as he could. "They cut these *holes*, you see, sir. Through all the *walls*, you see, sir. It's a *rabbit* warren, it is. A *maze*. You have to *we-e-eave* your way through every flat. But we cleared 'em out, sir. Used a *sack* full of grenades!"

"A sack and a half."

"Almost two sacks," the lance corporal amended. "Every time you find a door, you toss 'em in."

"Sometimes they'd come rollin' back out," another man said. He began scraping his heels noisily across the floor, pedaling his boots like on a bicycle. They left trails in the plaster dust that covered everything, even the men. "They'd *kick* at them. Send 'em right back through the door."

"Took one of our men's *arms* off," the lance corporal said, moderating the discussion. He chopped his left hand on his right biceps just under the shoulder.

"Where're the nearest Chinese troops right now?" Clark asked.

Everyone had an opinion.

"I heard some a few *minutes* ago!"

"They've *completely* buggered out! Every last one of 'em."

"I bet they're lying low, maybe five or six houses down. We cleared about four apartments that way before we pulled back."

"We've put up monitoring devices," the lance corporal said more authoritatively. "And flexible camera tubes that can bend around corners. They're all low-light. There are people watching and listening, supposedly. And if they hear or see something, they call us." He patted the radio beside him. "So the theory goes, anyway."

"Sounds like a good system," Clark commented.

"Till you have to change the *batt'ries*," someone griped.

"You've gotta change the batt'ries every six hours," their leader explained.

"Next change is in four hours," another man said from across the room, staring at the lance corporal. "It's gonna be dark as night in three."

"*We'll go in four,*" the lance corporal said sternly. "If you want to switch, I'll take the first run. You can go in the *morning*."

The private looked away. The offer was clearly far less desirable.

"Well," the colonel said, slapping his thighs and rising to a crouch. "The general has a busy schedule. And you do make the point about sunset."

Clark got the hint. But still he wanted to take a look around. He wandered farther into the ravaged apartment. The four resting soldiers all scrambled to their feet. A hand grabbed Nate's shoulder firmly as he approached a dark hole in the wall. Nate looked around behind him to see the lance corporal. The man jabbed his finger toward the hole and shook his head. Clark nodded in understanding. This room was even more bullet-riddled than the first. The hole in the wall ahead was a meter high, and about the same width. A dozen wires disappeared through it. They ran to sensing devices nearer the enemy troops.

Clark allowed General Cuvier a look. They then went back and crouched by the building's exit, beginning the unwieldy process of departure. The squad of heavily armed troops deployed just outside the door. "Good luck," Clark said to the men.

"Sir!" Clark heard. He turned. It was the lance corporal. "You've done a fine job, sir. We'll do the rest. Don't you worry." There were nods of agreement from the other three men.

"Thanks," Nate said. Then he suddenly remembered the purported reason for the visit. "You've done an outstanding job. All of you. You and your officers should hold your heads high when you get home. And I'll do everything in my power to get you there as soon as I can—I promise."

There were more subdued nods from the men this time. But more heartfelt, he could tell, as well.

Everyone jogged the whole way back to the helicopters. It felt good to get the exercise. No one had given the order to run. They'd all just assumed that pace. The more Nate ran, however, the more upset at himself he became. He'd put all these men at risk. Grandstanding by going all the way to the line just to stick a toe over. As if that in any way compared with the horrors those men faced. And most of all, he was disturbed at how weak he'd become. Not physically, but emotionally. So weak that he had to go to the front under the guise of a pep talk, while really the reassurances he sought were to be received, not given.

Perspiration began to dampen his BDUs. It felt good to sweat it out. He'd spent too many days without breaking a sweat from good, honest exercise. But what he really needed was to rid his body of the emotional toxins. The thousand new memories of tragedy and despair. He felt buoyed by the British soldier's remark. For his, after all, was the opinion Nate cared about most. But it still didn't purge his mind of the anguish he felt. And into his system was injected the poison of one more wounded man.

Nate heard the demolition charges and thumping machine guns in the distance.

NORTH OF TANGYUAN, CHINA
April 23, 2300 GMT (0900 Local)

Kate and Woody watched fighter-attack aircraft sweep down the valley. They had followed the forward air observer to a high ridge. The aircraft flew below their vantage to release loads at treetop altitude. The jets then rose and banked out of harm's way, dropping flares to divert heat-seeking missiles. The jet-black canisters left in their wake spun slowly toward earth. Air brakes popped out to slow the falling high explosives. They arced their way downward along an ever-steepening glide path.

The strings of bombs struck home with devastating force. Rings of white vapor spread from the points of impact at astonishing speed. Trees were flattened as if by the heavy step of an invisible giant. The booming sound waves then crashed across their perch. Kate nearly jumped out of her skin. Her eardrums felt like they'd been jabbed with ice picks. The noise left her head aching as if from a physical blow. And the bombs fell over a mile away.

"Okay, Dodger Two, you're next up on deck," the air-force captain said calmly over his radio. The forward air controller and his army security team sat huddled around the radio backpack. Its aerial soared ten feet over their heads.

But there was another radio from which excited voices squawked. This one was manned by an army lieutenant. The shouts it emitted were distorted and indecipherable. In the background, however, was the unmistakable roar of battle.

"Say again!" the lieutenant replied. "I repeat, will you say again?"

Following a hiss there came shouts of "We've been overrun!" The radio crackled loudly and the transmission broke up. ". . . past our . . . and we're . . . ! We need *air*— right now!"

The air-force captain turned to his Army counterpart. "Get 'em to call in their position."

"Foxtrot Zulu one niner, can you say your position?" the lieutenant shouted.

When he got a reply, the two officers quickly found the coordinates.

"Have him throw smoke," the air-force officer instructed. The orders were relayed. A few seconds later purple smoke began to mix with the gray and black haze of the battlefield. "Tell him to hug the ground. I'm bringin' it in close."

As the army officer shouted to the beleaguered ground unit, his air-force counterpart spoke in measured tones to the pilot. "Make one orbit and acquire the purple smoke. Call it once you've got it. Then come in from north to south and drop just past the smoke. I say again, north to south— drop *past* the smoke. No more than a hundred meters. They've been overrun. Do you copy?"

"Copy that," came the cool voice over the radio. "Beginning orbit now."

Woody tapped Kate on the arm and pointed. A banking F-16 flew just over the opposite ridgeline. It disappeared into a thin white cloud, then reappeared on the other side to complete a wide turn. The air-force radio crackled. "I've got the smoke. Inbound—weapons hot."

"Get your heads down now!" the army officer shouted over the radio. There was a reply of some sort, but no words. Only shouts and blazing gunfire.

As the jet sank lower and lower into the valley, Kate realized how detached you could grow at a distance. From the tops of ridges battles were just loud noise and smoke. What she was missing was the whole point of the story. The real experience of battle could not be acquired by remote observation.

After a final waggle of the streaking jet's wings all six bombs were released. The pilot pulled the nose straight up. Brilliant flashes lit the drifting purple smoke. A burst of static hissed over the army radio. There was no shouting or screaming. No rattling machine guns or bursting grenades in the background. Nothing at all to indicate whether the bombs had struck bull's-eye or fallen short . . . straight into the Americans.

A pall of black smoke rose into the air in a long curtain.

"Foxtrot Zulu one niner, do you read me, over?" the army lieutenant called out. There was no reply. "Foxtrot Zulu one niner, do you read me, over?"

The distant gunfire and explosions continued unabated. There was no further word from the desperate unit. The airforce captain went back to his business of air traffic controller over the busy valley. The pattern was full and he had a long day of work ahead of him. But the army lieutenant sat on his haunches holding the mike. He looked deflated to the point of total exhaustion. Everyone, in fact, seemed more subdued. No one spoke, so Kate got no read on their thoughts. But what preoccupied *her* mind was one, simple question. *Were those men killed by the Chinese? Or by the bombs these men had worked so hard to call in?*

The more she thought about it, however, the more she realized it didn't matter. They were killed in the fighting . . . in the war. Why care by whom or how? "Friendly fire" only seemed criminal from afar. Up close, it was all just killing.

"You want me to get some more shots of the air strikes?" Woody asked lethargically.

Kate frowned and then shook her head. "We've got plenty of bombing runs and artillery barrages and air-drops." She knew what they needed to get next. And to tell the truth, the thought frightened her. Out of the corner of her eye she could tell that Woody was watching her. When she looked up, he caught and held her eyes. She turned away, uncomfortable. "You think," she began, "maybe, they've aired some of the tapes we put on med-evacs?"

Woody took his time in responding. "Why don't you just come out and say it, Kate?"

"I just hope they got past the *censors,* that's all." Still, he stared at her. Finally, she said, "*What*?" His eyes were no longer bloodshot. They bored straight into her. "Just one trip down to the fighting in the valley, Woody! Okay? Then we'll get out. Okay?" He said nothing. "Okay, Woody?"

23

Kartsev's writing had grown stale and forced. His treatise was almost complete, but it suffered from his cloistered existence in the Kremlin. One week to go before his May Day address and he was completely out of touch with the world. How could one comment on a society they didn't know? Under the clutter on his desk he found the intercom. "Would someone come in here, please?" he said. There was no reply. A shot of adrenaline tingled his spine. "Hello-o-o?" he said over the intercom.

An ashen young man finally entered. He couldn't bring himself to look Kartsev in the eye. He stood with his head bowed and hands clasped like a royal servant called into the king's private chambers.

"I want to go out," Kartsev announced. The man's head shot up in surprise.

Mounds of trash were piled against the drab buildings, forcing pedestrians off sidewalks and onto streets. Sprays of slush from Kartsev's motorcade showered the suffering lot. Kartsev wanted a better look and ordered, "Slow down!"

over the car's intercom. His limousine and his guards' two
Mercedes slowed. The lead car turned randomly through
the endless maze of streets. Many people, Kartsev noted,
wore kerchiefs or scarves over their faces. "Do those people cover their faces because of the smell, or because of
fear of some respiratory disease?"

His nervous aide glanced at the driver beside him before
answering. "The smell, I would imagine, sir. The temperature is up."

Kartsev nodded, but then sought clarification. "Is it rotting garbage, or human remains?"

His aide and driver discussed the response. "Probably
both, sir," his aide finally replied.

The refuse went uncollected, but it was stacked neatly,
Kartsev observed. "Stop the car!"

The aide turned around to look at Kartsev through the
glass before issuing the order over the radio. The motorcade
slowly pulled to a stop. Men in heavy black overcoats
poured onto the street. Astonished pedestrians carrying
empty shopping bags cowered in fear. Kartsev didn't wait
for someone to open his door.

The air was crisp—not putrid as he'd expected but refreshing. Kartsev strolled over to a narrow passage through
the heaps of garbage to the entrance of an apartment building. He entered the darkened doorway. His surprised security team shot past him. The stench of urine was
unbearable. Kartsev went up the stairs to the first door. Its
number was stenciled on the flaked plaster wall. He
knocked. No one answered. He proceeded to the next.
Again, there was no one. After he got no response at the
third door, his patience wore thin. He looked at his aide
and nodded toward the door.

A brutish man drew his pistol and aimed at the doorknob.
He fired repeatedly from close range. Each loud boom gave
Kartsev a start. A firm kick opened the door right up. Several men entered with weapons drawn. Kartsev followed,
totally unconcerned. The patient sufferers who lived in
these Soviet-era sepulchers were not the sort who would
make trouble.

The wails of a woman greeted Kartsev's entry into the cramped living room. She was being dragged by her hair from behind a sofa. "*Stop* that!" Kartsev snapped. The man released the kneeling woman, who crumpled to the floor, holding her scalp and sobbing. Barely visible behind the sofa was a boy of five or so.

Guards returned from the bedroom. "All clear. Just the woman and the boy."

Kartsev walked up to the petrified woman. "You, what's your name?" She didn't answer, and Kartsev had to restrain a guard whose boot was already raised. "I won't hurt you. My name is Valentin Kartsev." The woman froze. After a moment of silence, her back bucked once and she vomited over and over. "Oh, *good* Lord!" Kartsev exclaimed. He turned away and pressed a scented handkerchief to his nose. The boy stared out with haunted eyes. Kartsev made his way to the sofa. "What's *your* name?" Kartsev asked.

"*No-o-o-o!*" the woman screeched, lurching toward Kartsev's legs.

A guard stomped his boot on her back before the others could open fire. Her bones showed through a thin print dress as she lay pinned under the man's heavy boot. His pistol was pointed at the back of her head. He wore a disinterested expression as he looked at Kartsev questioningly through red and puffy eyelids.

"Let her *go*," Kartsev ordered. The man lifted his boot. She wasn't fat yet, so Kartsev guessed she was young. "Why don't you get up?" he suggested. She got to her feet and stood slouching before him, staring at the floor. "Now, then. What is your name?" he asked.

Her dress was half again too large for her scrawny frame. "Tatiana, sir."

"Ah, Tatiana! But that's a *beautiful* name." She looked up through unwashed hair. She had a pretty face. "Tell me, Tatiana. Has anyone attempted to organize this building for any purpose? I noticed the tidy walkway through the trash on the street. Is there some system for keeping the walk clear?"

She was already shaking her head vigorously. Her unkempt curls flung across her forehead and eyes. "*No,* sir! I swear it on my life—*no*!"

"Calm *down.* I'm not a policeman. I'm a scholar. A scientist. I just have a few questions."

The woman was swaying. Kartsev thought she'd collapse. "Have a seat. Are you all right?"

"Sit down!" barked a menacing guard. She stumbled to the sofa and began to sob again. Her son clambered over the sofa. Guns were drawn in reaction to the sudden movement.

"*Stop* this!" Kartsev ordered the guards. Despite the apartment's chill, it was uncomfortably stuffy. "Why don't you all just clear out," he ordered as he unbuttoned his overcoat. By the time Kartsev's hat and gloves were off, the room was empty save for him, the woman, and the child. Kartsev pulled a chair up to the sofa. "Go to your room," the woman whispered to the boy. He clung to her. "Go!" she said, prying him loose.

The boy ran to the kitchen and disappeared into a room the size of a coat closet. The woman straightened her hair. She wore no makeup. Her skin was pale. But no lines creased her youthful face.

"Do you have a husband?" he asked. Her eyes caught his as she shook her head. It was Kartsev who turned away. "How do you make do? Do you have a job?"

"No! I swear to God!"

"But it is all *right* to have a job. There has been a great deal of confusion on that point. It is all right to have a job. The only form of prohibited social interaction is *forced* behavior." She looked directly at him and swallowed so hard he could see the contractions in her slender neck. Her arms were like sticks protruding from short sleeves. "How long has it been since you've eaten?"

Her lower lip quivered. "Two days."

Kartsev noted her reply on a pad. "And what did you have then?"

She shrugged. "Some . . . cabbage."

"And how did you acquire this cabbage?"

She again dropped her gaze. "In the trash," she practically whispered. "But I *washed* it!"

Kartsev sat back against the hard wood chair. "Would you say your standard of living is average, below average, or above? Which of the three?" The woman wore a look of confusion. He tried again. "You haven't eaten in two days. Do you consider yourself worse off than your neighbors?"

"They're all *pigs*," she spat, her lips curling.

"Why do you say that?"

"They have food, you know? For a moldy end of a loaf of bread those men expect . . ." She fell quiet.

"They expect what?"

She leaned forward. "I'd do *anything* to get out of here," she whispered. It took Kartsev a moment to understand her. "I'm clean. I have no diseases."

"Yes," Kartsev said, rising. "Well . . ." He began to pace the room.

She grew upset. "I can clean up. The men at the institute where I worked were always hitting on me."

Kartsev wandered to the kitchen, keeping his back to the woman. "That's *not* why I'm here."

From the creaking sound he knew she had risen. He turned to see her approaching with fists clenched. "You'll *not* take my *son*!" she screeched with astonishing vigor.

"No!" Kartsev blurted out, appalled. The apartment door opened. Kartsev waved the guards back outside. "You misunderstood me completely!"

She slumped, but then straightened. Her small breasts pointed through her dress. "You don't like me?"

"Well, you're a very attractive woman, I'm sure."

She came up to him. "I'll do anything you want. You've never had anyone like me. I'm almost a virgin. My son . . . it was one time. I was seventeen." She stepped even closer. "You'd like me."

"*Please*," Kartsev said. He was aroused, which made it worse. "I just wanted to ask you a few questions." She began to cry. "What is it *now*? Because I refuse to *defile* you you're *crying*?"

When she tried to flash a smile his way as if to prove her attractiveness, Kartsev had had enough. "I'm sorry for disturbing you." He headed out. The security troops averted their eyes as he passed them for the stairs.

At the building's entrance, the chill hit Kartsev. He remembered he'd left his outer garments in the apartment. Cursing, he returned past the startled looks of the guards. When he entered, he saw the young woman on her knees. A large brute clenched her hair in his hand as he stood before her. Kartsev walked up to the man, whose eyes were closed. He sensed someone's presence, looked around, and registered instant terror. The woman sank back onto her haunches, coughing.

Kartsev left without his things and found his aide on the landing. "Get the woman and the child and put them up in a Kremlin apartment. Give them everything they need." He looked the man straight in the eye. "And I want you to schedule that man in there." The aide nodded. "Oh, and collect my things."

Kartsev waited in the cold stairwell. They hustled the woman and boy past. She smiled at Kartsev as she got the boy's jacket on. A single shot rang out from upstairs. The woman stopped and looked back toward her apartment, but seemed untroubled. "Your coat, sir," Kartsev's aide said.

NORTH OF TANGYUAN, CHINA
April 24, 1300 GMT (2300 Local)

"Sappers *i-i-in*!" came the cries over the furor.

André Faulk was crammed low in a hole next to a replacement. Bullets chipped off rock around their shallow position, which was dug on the side of a steep ridge. Some of the fire was Chinese. But most was from the three machine guns above them that raked their platoon's positions. When the "sappers in" call was given, the guns killed everyone who raised his head.

It was the third time in ten minutes they'd been overrun.

Faulk narrowed his focus to just his hole. To the strong stench of the unwashed man next to him. He was a private from Iowa or Indiana, who was seeing his first action with the 101st. Rock chips peppered them both. The screeching noise and bursts of flames and ever-present shouting of massed attackers chopped André's thoughts to pieces. He jammed his eyes shut. He grimaced as bullets flew by at supersonic speed.

André was at the limits of his ability to function. But the replacement was long gone. He was no use at all. He'd been choppered in that very day. Said he'd seen action with the 3rd Infantry, but the facts didn't sound right.

The storm of fire in the air above subsided. "Heads *u-u-up*!" shouted the NCOs of their heavily depleted platoon. They'd flown in with thirty-eight. But they were down to twenty-nine *including* nine *worthless* fucking replacements! "Let's *go,* fuckhead!" André shouted as he rose.

Through the dim light crept hundreds of men. The slope was steep. They moved as if their legs were stuck in molasses. André aimed and killed. Aimed and killed. Aimed and killed. His muzzle lit the rock on which he lay with flame. The granite was armor. He'd weathered mortars—even artillery—in the rocks.

The only problem was that the Chinese had the same cover. They dove behind the impenetrable stone. Then in celebration of survival they fired. They seemed perfectly content to set up shop behind good cover. Until, that is, they were prodded on. The shrill whistles of Chinese officers sounded like referees in a basketball game. But the sound sent the men to their deaths. It was as if the whistles' exhortations were too powerful to ignore. André listened for them. He aimed at the men who were flushed from behind their cover by the sound.

His rifle slammed into his shoulder with each round fired. Each flash blinded him for a split second. He kicked the replacement hard and then fired. "Hey! Motherfucker! Get yer ass up here *now*!" There were dark moving figures everywhere. They were profiled against fires in the valley below. "I *mean* it, asshole!" André fired three well-aimed shots, felling two. "You're gonna get stuck like a pig if you don't fight!"

André heard a loud whistle. A man was turned and facing downhill. Bent over with the effort of blowing. *Pow!* came the blast from André's rifle. The man disappeared in the muzzle flash.

The bastard from Iowa or Indiana finally joined him. He laid his rifle on the rock and shot up half a magazine in two seconds. It distracted the hell out of André. The guy dropped back down, apparently done for the night. With gritting teeth André braved the deep shit. He'd have to save their fuckin' asses by himself! He killed Chinese to vent anger at his "squadmate." *Useless fuckin' bastard*, he cursed silently as he relentlessly killed the enemy.

Searing pain shot through his ear. His eyes watered instantly. "*Shit!*" André shouted as the warm liquid ran down his neck. The enemy was fifteen meters away. He fired and fired until his magazine was empty. When he dropped to reload, the guy from Iowa or Indiana rose. But he didn't even fire a fuckin' shot! He jumped right on top of André.

"Mother-*fucker*!" André screamed. The full weight of the man pinned him. When he pushed the guy away he saw the problem. A bullet had smacked right into his face. "*Shit!*" André cursed. On instinct he pushed away from the carnage.

"Sappers i-i-*i-in*!" shouted a half-dozen men.

The machine guns fired. The air filled with death. Bullets whipped by inches away. Spits of granite stung his face and eyes. *This is it!* André thought over and over. He switched his selector to "burst." He didn't risk rising. He raised the rifle over the rock, holding it up with his arms at full extension as he lay on his back in the hole. One, two, three quick pulls of the trigger. Nine rounds at what must be point-blank range. The trigger froze on the fourth pull. The mag was empty. He dropped the rifle and grabbed his dead squadmate's M-16. He lay on his back and waited.

André fired at the first dark form to blot out the stars. The three-round burst threw the man down the hill. The next man must've assumed André was dead. He climbed the hill stooped low under the machine guns. André fired a burst through his knees and laid the man out. He didn't want to have to reload. He flicked the selector to "semi." Just then, two men appeared right over his hole. One opened up on full auto from a range of three feet. The rounds pummeled the replacement's lifeless body. André's single shot stood the man straight up. He tumbled backward over the rock. But the second man kicked André's rifle away. He collapsed on top of André as machine guns raked the position repeatedly.

André grabbed the man's searing-hot assault rifle. A flash of white from an elbow stunned him. The man's knee just missed his groin. But the Chinese assault rifle was pressed tightly between them. They wrestled and the rifle went off, spraying rocks on full auto not two feet away. But the wide-eyed Chinese soldier had made a critical mistake. He was smaller than André, so he'd tried to use his rifle.

André summoned all his strength for one spin move. He surprised the man and threw him off. André followed him without losing his grip on the rifle. The guy was now pinned underneath André and the weapon. He was at André's mercy, and André had none. He lunged forward and head-butted the man's exposed face. André's helmet flew off, but the blow stunned his enemy. Blood began to flow profusely from his nose.

André knew he had to use his knife. He pressed his torso down onto the man and let go of the rifle with his right hand. He crushed the smaller man flat with his chest and shoulders and jammed his chin sharply into his opponent's collarbone. There was panicked breathing in his ear, which was followed by searing pain as the man bit his already wounded ear hard. André seized the combat knife by the handle. It slipped out of its leather scabbard with hardly a sound. But the man beneath him sensed something.

The rifle trapped in between them roared on full auto. The bolt tore back and forth against André's chest until it jammed in the loose fabric of his parka. Horrible pain now shot through André's right side in half a dozen places. He rose up—the assault rifle still snagged on his parka—and in one motion jabbed the knife into his victim's chest. But the blade didn't go in far. It hit something hard—a belt, a pouch, a bone. For a moment the two men were motionless. The man whispered something in Chinese. André brought the knife back up with both hands and sank it with all his might through the Chinese soldier's feeble hands. It was more awful than anything he'd ever experienced. The sickening sound and feel of murder.

André hurled himself backward to get away. He lay bareheaded against the frigid rocks. Sweat streamed from every pore. His left ear burned in pain. And from his thigh to his ribs were agonizing wounds. The trickle of blood from several spots changed course with his new position. André stared up at the night sky. The burning tracers looked like shooting stars. The fire of two M-60s and a .50-caliber overlapped. The killing went on, and on, and on. In the end, it was just American guns. They fired and then fired some more.

André awoke while being dragged out of his hole. Someone was pulling him up roughly by his armpits. André grabbed for his rifle and was dropped to the rocks. "Ah!" he shouted. The world started spinning with the pain. It built and built until he feared the agony alone would kill him. He moaned and yelped with sickening dizziness.

"*Jesus!*" came the voice of his squad leader. He scampered to André's side. André opened his eyes. Everything hurt. He'd never felt worse. He saw it was morning. The sun was up. "I thought you said he was *dead!*" the squad leader snapped at one of the replacements.

"Well, *look* at him! He was lyin' there with his mouth wide open! And his freakin' eyes were starin' up at the freakin' *sky!*"

"Never mind," the sergeant said. He knelt beside André. "You hurt bad?"

"I . . ." The words caught in André's bone-dry throat. He coughed. Incredible pain shot from his ribs. "Water," he croaked. They gave him a taste. The more alert he became, the more pain he felt. It wasn't a good sign.

"What's goin' on?" barked an NCO André had never seen before. He raised his pounding head. The man looked all around André's hole. André's gaze followed his. Bodies, brass shell casings, and equipment littered the hillside. But the two most dramatic sights lay at André's feet. His knife stuck straight up from the chest of the Chinese soldier. And the guy from Iowa or Indiana lay faceless and riddled with holes.

Everyone was staring at him. At the Type 56-2—an AK-47 derivative—whose pistoning bolt had caught in the fabric of his parka. It was now stuck to André's chest. André felt wave after wave of nausea. He couldn't answer their questions. They tried to work the bolt, but it was locked tight and wouldn't come free. They finally cut it loose, leaving a two-inch hole in the outer shell of his parka. The unknown NCO's probing hands elicited yelps from André. *Must be another platoon leader*, André figured. Command of their platoon had been passed several times. They rolled him onto his left side and cut more fabric away.

"You want me to clean this thing up for you, Dré?" asked a squadmate holding André's bloody knife.

A pit of burning vomit boiled up. "I'm gonna puke," he groaned, and they stood back. André emptied his stomach on the ground. "That's all right," the new platoon leader said. "Go ahead and get that bad shit outta there." When André was done, they went back to work. "Tell 'em six shrapnel punctures," the platoon leader said, "plus one wound that looks like a bullet hole." André whimpered as the man probed his side. "It looks like a through-and-through, but they oughta look real good." His squadmates applied pressure bandages.

"There's another hole up here," said the replacement.

He held André's right arm in the air. "But it's little, and it ain't bleedin' anymore."

The air was chilly where they had cut away his clothing.

"Tell the clearing station about it anyway. It looks like fragments from a round that must've hit these rocks. Ain't too deep. I can see a piece right here." André raised his head and watched the man dig a metal sliver from his arm. He used André's black combat knife. Its edges were honed and silvery. André threw up again. He heaved even though nothing came out. The NCO gave them directions to the aid station.

"You mean, like, it's on the other side of this *hill*? We're clearin' casualties *outside* the valley?"

"Just *go*. This man needs *aid*."

They hoisted André to his feet. He cursed and hissed and gasped. With his squad leader on one side and a replacement on the other, André managed to remain standing. For the first time he saw the extent of the battle's devastation. The slope was covered with Chinese dead. And nowhere were the bodies thicker than around his position.

"Did he fight?" his squad leader asked.

"Who?" André replied.

"Hansen! The guy from Illinois. Did he fight, or was all that talk about the 3rd Infantry just bullshit?"

André stared as Hansen was lifted out of the hole by the wrist and ankle. "He saved my life," he finally answered. *Hansen,* he committed to memory. *Hansen from Illinois.*

Moscow, Russia
April 24, 2400 GMT (0200 Local)

At first Andreev thought the sound came from a lunatic. A howling, half-human sound emanating from the desolate streets. But then there was laughter and an attempt at imitation. The mimicked howl ended in boisterous glee.

Andreev was crouched low in a notch taken out of the sidewalk. He squatted next to a window that opened below street level. When he'd heard the noise he'd leaped into the convenient hiding place. He risked looking out through a small railing past some dead flowers. There wasn't much light, but what there was streaked across rain-soaked pavement from a single bright lamp on the opposite curb. The beam skirted a triangular median filled with trees, a bench, and a smallish monument.

Three streets merged at the tiny park. A band of swaggering men strolled down one. The lead held an AK-47 one-handed. It was pointed skyward and casually resting on his shoulder. With his other hand he raised a bottle of vodka. The liquid was sloshing, about half-empty by the sound of it. Andreev felt inside his valise. He'd packed only soft things—quiet things—around his weapon. The Ingram came out without making a noise.

"No-*o*-o-o-o!" wailed a man in the center who fell to his knees. The leash around his neck was yanked. He collapsed. His fall onto the concrete was unbroken. His hands were bound tightly at his back. One of the trailing men kicked him. Pyotr counted four around the prisoner. But a fifth suddenly appeared, straggling behind the rest.

"Oh, look!" shouted the slurring leader. He pointed at the park. "Over there!" From the sound of it the man was drunk, bored, tired. The armed men all wore black from head to toe. Their boots scraped across the pavement as they dragged their captive by his neck. The man struggled mightily to get to his feet. He never managed to rise above his knees. Pyotr sank slowly into the tight space, making sure he made no sudden movements. He listened. All too quickly it became clear what was happening.

"Right here, right *here*!" came the impatient voice of the lead Black Shirt. He'd reached the stage of drunkenness marked by a quick temper.

"*You* pull the son of a bitch if you think it's so easy!" *That's the man holding the leash,* Andreev saw in his mind's eye.

"Get up you miserable f-f-f*uck*!" was followed by a hollow thud. And then another thump and grunt. "*Hey!* You *listening* to the man?"

The two kickers, Andreev surmised. All were safely some distance away in the park. But where was the fifth man— the straggler. He'd not said a word. The others bickered as they dragged their victim to the intended place. "Up, up, *up*!" the exasperated leader ordered. But Andreev was preoccupied by the mystery of the fifth man's whereabouts. He brought the Ingram up—ready to kill any dark shapes that loomed over the narrow slit in the sidewalk. But he didn't dare raise his head.

There was laughter. They were taking turns pissing on the man. "Loo's like e's a fuckin' fountain!" the leader crowed. He obviously had a cigarette in his lips. The four men were all rolling with laughter, but not the fifth. That's when the begging began. The pleading. The last attempts from the battered man to appeal for mercy. His lungs grew ragged with the effort. He ceased completing his sentences. Sobs consumed what little energy he had left.

"*Hang* his ass up there," came the command from the now lucid leader. It was as if he'd been sobered by the episode.

"Wait a minute!" There was the fifth man. "Why hang him? I mean, nobody said to *kill* him. We don't even know what the guy *did*!"

"Don't you *know*?" replied the leader. "He's a *conformist*! Or a believer in *orthodoxy*! Or an *objectivist*!" The others all laughed. "Or . . . or—and *this* is my favorite one—maybe he's an establishment*arian*!"

"*O-o-o-u-u*!" came the voices of the chorus in mock disparagement.

"This *thing*," said the drunk, putting on a show, "in other words, is a *very, very* bad man! And *we,* don't you see, are very, very *good* men. Yes, we *are*!" he said to stem the raging cackles. "We are, because we do *this* to bad people."

A shot rang out—a single shot.

With his eyes closed Andreev listened to the echoes off the buildings. They had done the worst, he thought, till he heard the screams. Their prisoner was screeching at the top of his lungs. He was trying to cry and gasping for breath at the same time.

Another shot stopped everything. The street fell quiet.

"Now, *why* the fuck d'you have ta go do *that*?" exclaimed the drunk leader.

"That's what you wanted!" cried the fifth, the straggler. "That's what we were *going* to do!"

"But not *no-o-ow*! We only just *got* here! We can't just drag the son of a bitch one lousy block from his house and *kill* him! What kind of punishment is *that*?"

"Fuck it," came a voice of reason from one of the others. "It's late."

"No! I wanna hear an answer! What's your answer, little boy? Worried what Mama'd say if she caught you out with us? Maybe she'd make you stay home and help carry the *shit* out to the *curb*!"

"Come on, Seryozha. Let's just go home."

The silence was filled with the sloshing of liquid in a bottle. Next came a tortured exhalation and a burp. The group burst into laughter again. They proceeded down the street, as untroubled as before.

Andreev waited for the sound of them to recede. Then he waited longer just in case someone came out of the apartments to check. So far as he could tell, however, no one even opened a window or a door. The night was deathly quiet. The seven million people who remained in Moscow had receded into the safety of the shadows.

Pyotr raised up slowly. He peered over the curb and checked out the scene. The street was empty. In the park, a man hung limply from where his bound hands had been looped over the outstretched arm of the statue. But Andreev's heart skipped a beat when the dark form by the bench took shape. A lone man leaned his back against a tree. It was impossible to tell which one it was or what he was doing. But Andreev had a guess what the answers to both questions were.

The fifth man rose with an audible sigh. He turned and headed back up the street in the direction opposite his comrades. His rifle dangled loosely at his side. He stared at the glistening pavement.

SOFLYSK POW CAMP, SIBERIA
April 25, 2400 GMT (1000 Local)

Lieutenant Hung—one of Chin's fellow platoon leaders—sat on the end of Chin's bunk. He'd been part of the last wave of new arrivals to crowd the now bursting barracks. There were now mattresses on the floor between the bunks, and Hung had moved onto one. From there he'd told Chin everything that had happened in the two days after Chin had been captured. It was a story of total collapse.

"Would you go back if they gave you a choice?" Hung asked.

"Would I go back where if who gave me what choice?" Chin replied. His voice had assumed Hung's quiet tone despite the noise of a hundred conversations.

Hung leaned forward. "Would you go back to *China* if the Americans said you didn't *have* to?"

Chin arched his eyebrows. "Well . . . of *course*. Where *else* would I go?"

Hung shrugged. "If they said you could go anywhere, you mean you'd just say, 'Back to China, please'?"

It seemed a straightforward question. But Hung's surprise at his first answer prompted Chin to ponder it. *Where else in the world could I go?* he thought. *America?* He looked up at Hung and nodded. His friend rolled his eyes. "What?" Chin asked. "My whole *life* is back in China. My family, my friends, our farm. Why would I go anywhere else?"

"Because," Hung whispered testily, "things are better in other places."

"Better how?"

"Not as—" Hung stopped himself and looked around. There were others within earshot, but they seemed not to be listening. Then again, how could you just come out and discuss such a thing, if it was what Chin was thinking. "Not as bad . . . politically," Hung finally said. His eyes again searched the barracks.

Chin just shrugged. "What are politics to me?"

Hung turned on him now. "They are *everything*! Those old men keep us down! They try to control us like it was the 1950s! To them, nothing has changed! But everything *has* changed! Have you ever heard of the Internet?" he asked. Chin shook his head. "It hooks computers from all over the world together. You can talk—exchange ideas— with foreigners. And there's not a damn thing they can do about it."

Chin thought about it then shrugged. "Why is that so important?"

"Don't you *get* it? We can read what people write in the *free* world. All the great ideas are there on the Internet. You just need a computer that's hooked into it."

Chin shrugged again. "I don't see why I have to do all that reading."

Hung snorted. "*You* wouldn't." He eyed Chin now with open disdain. "Have you ever read a book cover to cover?" Chin felt his face redden. "No," Hung said, but without ridicule, "of course not. You're the perfect Communist citizen, Chin. Even if you bitch and moan, they'd love to have another billion just like you. God forbid you use any of those brain cells up there for *thinking*!" He reached out and roughly rubbed Chin's stubble-covered head.

There was something in what he said that Chin found troubling. He hadn't chosen not to read after thinking about it. He simply didn't have any idea what the point was. He couldn't imagine what someone could possibly write that could be so important. Not that he hadn't been educated. But that had been by teachers or army instructors who'd mixed lectures with practical, hands-on demonstrations. Books smacked to him of political classes, and they were the most useless exercise of all.

"You want me to teach you?" Hung asked.

"Teach me *what*?" Chin bristled, his face reddening.

"You know," Hung said, smiling awkwardly. "Some of

the tougher characters . . . just to get you over the hump. They dropped off some old magazines from Hong Kong. It's not nuclear physics, but they're written, you know, for educated people.'' Chin started to object—to explain that *he* was educated—but the words stuck in his mouth. He hung his head. ''Hey, it's okay,'' Hung said, laughing. ''Maybe you can get into the university when you get back!'' He laughed even more, which rubbed Chin the wrong way. But the offer was meant to be kind, and Chin resolved then and there to take him up on it. What better place to give it a shot?

''What about you?'' Chin then asked.

''What *about* me?''

''Will you go back if they let you . . . if they offer you . . . ?''

''Asylum?'' his new teacher supplied. Chin nodded. ''*Asylum*,'' he filed away, his first new word. When there was no answer for several seconds, Chin realized the question was causing Hung great turmoil. He appeared almost sick with worry. He swallowed, his eyes unfocused and his mouth pressed tight in a frown. ''You know what they'd do,'' Hung said, rather than asked. His voice was far away. ''To my family.'' Chin frowned and nodded. The process of branding families disloyal was fairly straightforward. ''But they may do that anyway,'' Hung whispered.

''Do what?''

''Denounce us because we were captured. Strip our families of everything. Even send us to labor farms, or even *camps*!''

''But . . . *why*?'' Chin asked, growing instantly outraged. Instantly terrified that what had happened to him might ruin his family. ''*We* couldn't do anything about getting captured! The only choice we had was to get killed for no *reason*! The only difference between us and everybody who died is *luck*!''

''No. That's where you're wrong. There's another difference.'' Hung was speaking in even lower tones now. ''The dead didn't spend any time around the foreigners.''

UNRUSFOR HEADQUARTERS, KHABAROVSK
April 26, 0700 GMT (1700 Local)

Nate Clark was taking an early dinner when the news came in. He was ravenous after having missed lunch. He'd taken a tour that morning of an UNRUSFOR hospital. He just hadn't felt like eating after that. But now he was ready to dig into the steaming plate of risotto with wild mushrooms.

The different contingents at UN headquarters took their turns cooking. It provided variety, but it also led to the nationalities vying to outdo themselves. The British had the temerity to try kidney pie. The Americans hadn't fared much better with hot dogs. It was really a battle between the French and the nominal contingent of Italians, and the Italians routinely won.

Clark's stomach growled as he mixed the rice and sauce thick with cheese into a gooey consistency. He raised a fork and let it cool in the air. There was a knock on his door. Lieutenant Colonel Reed stuck his head in. Clark waved him over. He put down the fork and read the terse message Reed handed him. Just twenty-two words, Clark saw from the header before rereading it.

He rose and led Reed to the door. "Get everything we've got in the air. Cancel maintenance, pilot rest, everything. Don't hold anything back."

"What about the White House?" Reed asked, and Clark stopped. "He asked that you call if . . ." Reed didn't finish the sentence.

Clark took a deep breath and looked at his watch. "Go ahead and ring the president for me."

WHITE HOUSE RESIDENTIAL QUARTERS
April 26, 0705 GMT (0205 Local)

Gordon Davis was so deep in sleep that it took Elaine shaking his shoulder to rouse him. "Hmm?" he said when he opened his eyes. The first person he saw was the national security staffer.

"There's a call from General Clark, Mr. President."

Gordon nodded and began the slow process of rising. As always it was filled with hisses and groans. The doctor said the pain would linger. That he'd feel worse on cold, wet days. Sure enough, when Gordon padded down the hall to a small office, he saw the steady rain outside. It fell in the new, bright security lights that bathed the White House grounds for the benefit of Secret Service gun crews. The leather chair was cold against his back through his robe. The aide handed him the phone.

"Gordon Davis," he said, then waited on the satellite delay.

"Mr. President, this is General Clark. Sorry to wake you, sir, but we've had a development here."

"No apologies, General. What's up?"

"It appears we've got a serious push under way against our blocking position in the Tangyuan Valley."

"You mean something more than they've been trying already?" Gordon interrupted.

"Yes, sir. Let me read you the communication I received from Brigadier General Lawson, commander on the ground there. 'Major offensive making progress from south. Casualties heavy. Ammunition low. Situation critical. Last reserves have been committed. Cannot guarantee we can hold.' "

Gordon closed his eyes and laid his head back. "What does he mean 'casualties heavy'? I thought casualties were already heavy."

"They were, sir. We don't get many communications like this, although I've gotten more than I care to count in this war. It's not a good sign. Lawson isn't given to over-reaction. He's been wounded pretty bad for days, but he's refused to accept relief. He's a real steady hand."

"What can we do?" Gordon asked.

"I've ordered everything we can put into the air to head down there. For about twelve hours we can give them a curtain of fire so thick no new reinforcements can move up to the action. But close air support has its limitations and . . . and risks. The terrain is so mountainous that it makes bombing very dangerous. Because of the bombs' trajectories you sometimes have only one angle of approach. And if you're off by even a degree or two on the reverse slope of a hill, a miss of a few meters on flat land could turn into a miss by hundreds down the hillside.''

''Is there anything more we can do to help?'' Gordon asked.

Clark sighed audibly. ''We could drop some airborne troops in there. We've got a German parachute regiment standing by just in case. But we've limited ourselves to ferrying in replacements because our logistics are strained enough with the people we've got there now. Once the new troops run through what they're carrying they'd just be more mouths to feed.''

''Just how bad are their supply problems? Your man there said they were low on ammunition.''

''We've been dropping in supplies around the clock. Our stocks of parachutes are running low, but there's a shipment due in from Belgium today that should get us by. We just don't have the lift to get them much more. We *can* change the mix. Less food, water, and medicine and more ammo—that sort of thing. But there's just not much more that we can do. They're fighting for their lives down there, sir. It's up to them now.''

''Do we have any contingency plans?'' Gordon asked. ''If the Chinese break through?''

The delay was longer than usual. ''They go on fighting for as long as they can. Take to the hills and split into smaller and smaller groups.''

''What would their chances be?''

Again, a delay. ''Some of the Rangers might fare pretty well. It's no knock on the men of the 101st to say this, because they're some of the finest soldiers in the world. But they're not trained for the same kind of fighting. For evasion and survival behind enemy lines. Plus they're mainly positioned in the lowlands down in that valley. They're the hard plug the Chinese are trying to push through. Most of them won't even get the chance to climb out of the valley. The Rangers, on the other hand, are dug in on the valley's outer slopes or are patrolling the surrounding countryside—calling in air strikes.''

"General Clark, what effect would loss of control of that valley have on the war?" Gordon felt compelled to ask.

Clark sighed. "Not a good one, Mr. President. The Chinese could move some major part of the Jinan Army Group up the railroad that runs through that valley. Our forces in China would have to assume the strategic defensive all along the front."

"Could we resume the advance sometime later?"

"Not without major reinforcements, Mr. President. At least one heavy corps—another hundred thousand men when you include associated supply and support personnel."

Gordon frowned. Congress and the American people would never go for that. "I know it's a lot to ask, but is there any chance if the Chinese retake the valley that those remaining men could still shut the railroad down? Harass the Chinese sufficiently from the surrounding hills that they couldn't safely move trucks to the north?"

"For a day or two max, Mr. President. After that, it'd be too much to expect from them. We'd have no way to resupply them, and their stocks are already low. They'd be out of ammo very quickly. And it would soon be the *Chinese* who were dug into those hills, not the other way around."

It all came down to that valley, Gordon realized. Just as he'd been briefed that it would. That and the timing of the ice flow were the two great risks of the operation. Nature had cooperated nicely. An entire Chinese army was stranded on the north bank of the Amur.

"How about the relief column heading down from the Amur toward the valley?" Gordon asked.

The audible puff from Clark's lungs sounded like a roar of air over the telephone. "We're pushing them pretty hard as it is, Mr. President."

"Well, push them *harder*."

"There are problems with that, Mr. President. Their main holdup is that the roads are clogged with several million Chinese refugees heading south. The only way to clear the roads, sir . . . Well, I don't think that would be legal . . . or moral."

"All right. Just keep me informed, General Clark, about anything you hear. No matter how small. I want reports every hour—every *half* hour—whenever you've got anything at all."

"Yes, sir. Oh, you might be interested in some videotape that we confiscated. It was shot by that NBC News crew that's down there in the valley. They flew it out on a medevac chopper, and the censors pulled it because it showed too much. I'll have it sent to you via military satellite if you'd like."

"Yes, do that. I'll wait up. I'd like to see what it looks like down there."

The screen in the underground Situation Room was black. Gordon sat in slacks and shirt at a conference table with the head of the White House Military Office.

The picture burst onto the screen first, followed a moment later by the stupendous noise of battle. The camera lay on its side as bullets audibly whizzed by. The scene quickly cut to a different image. It was a wobbly picture of a female reporter. She now wore a helmet and bulletproof vest and sat on the ground beside the banked shoulder of a railroad. *The* railroad, Gordon realized. The air was filled with smoke and the sound of fighting.

"Got it?" she asked the cameraman.

"Go," came his overly loud reply.

The reporter cleared her throat and looked at her notes. When she straightened, she looked directly into the lens and began. "The fighting in the Tangyuan Valley last night took a dramatic turn for the worse. I'm reporting to you now from the rail line and dirt road that are at the center of the two armies' confrontation. Up until midnight last night—" A huge explosion of indeterminate nature interrupted the report. The camera shook and the woman flinched and ducked her head. The camera steadied. Behind the reporter, a towering black ball of smoke rose into the air above the trees. "Up until midnight last night, the Chinese had fought and died in huge numbers but made progress measured only in meters. But as the clock struck twelve on an otherwise calm winter evening, the roar of the guns once again filled this deep canyon. This time, however, the guns were Chinese and they were mounted on tanks. The surprise armored attack broke through line after line despite withering antitank fire. Missile launchers were fired down from the hills at almost point-blank range. At one point during the dark, early-morning hours the hulks of over a hundred vehicles burned furiously in the valley. But still the Chinese tanks came, and hugging tight behind the shields of their armor were masses of dismounted infantry. With each line overrun, the Chinese gulped up significant stretches of this dusty highway. When the sun came up—instead of being driven back by Americans dug in the hillsides above them—the Chinese came back with still more force."

In the background you could see American soldiers approach. They ran single file along the side of the tracks toward the camera, bent over at the waist to take shelter from the railroad's embankment.

The female reporter turned just as a soldier skidded to a stop. With one hand he held the brim of his helmet. With the other, a rifle. "You're gonna have to pick up and move, ma'am," the out-of-breath man said.

"What's the situation on the ground, Lieutenant?" the reporter asked as the camera took in the long line of men behind him. The others all lay in the dirt with their weapons and faces pointed toward the rear.

"You don't understand. I mean move *now*. On the double."

There was an unartful splice of the tape. They had climbed to higher elevation and were taping the battlefield from behind some rocks. Smoke obscured much of the scene. The woman began.

"We've moved now up into the hills where it's safer. Shortly after we left the rail line, British Tornado bombers dropped canisters of napalm onto the onrushing Chinese forces. The heat was so intense we could feel it even through our winter clothes. Despite the certain devastation wrought by the sticky, flaming petroleum, the Chinese now hold that stretch of road and are surging ahead with suicidal fervor."

The camera zoomed in through a break in the smoke. You could clearly see Chinese soldiers with their guns blazing as they rushed forward. Behind them were the sky-rocketing fireworks from a tank whose turret was missing. Flashing through the air above was a missile trailing thin, silvery wires. Gordon watched as first one and then a second infantryman fell. On hearing the roar of a jet, the cameraman zoomed out. It was just in time to catch the fleeting image of a lone fighter-bomber. At an altitude of less than one hundred feet, the jet's shadow bobbed from the treetop, to bare ground, back to treetop. In an instant both shadow and plane were gone. But they left behind a string of bombs—each with its own smaller shadow.

The camera jumped with the concussion of six blasts. When the cameraman recovered, he panned down the length of the road and rail line and took in the rising columns of smoke. Like from miniature atomic bombs there rose six mushroom clouds. They were spaced every hundred meters or so along the road.

"The American casualties have been heavy," the reporter continued before pausing to swallow, her voice thick as if from nausea or fear, "with many whole units now missing in action. But the death toll among the Chinese is staggering. Little opportunity has arisen for the Chinese to collect their dead under the direct fire poured on by the Americans. As a consequence, the woods and foothills of this valley are littered with uncollected and now decaying bodies. And those woods are being filled at an ever-increasing rate as a result of the obviously growing sense of desperation felt by the People's Liberation Army. With a callous disregard of human life, unit after unit has charged headlong into the American killing fields. American commanders on the ground here have no good estimates as to the numbers of Chinese killed. But surely, as their best guesses go, they run into the many tens of thousands.''

There was yet another jumpy change of scene. When the picture finally steadied, Gordon felt a knot of nausea form in his stomach. Filling the screen was a seemingly unending row of upturned boots. The bodies of the Americans had been laid out side by side under a series of green ponchos. All the boots were the same. Their alignment was neat and orderly. As the cameraman walked slowly down the line, Gordon wondered just when he would come to the end.

''But the cost in American lives has been steep as well. And the supply of Americans in this valley will be exhausted far more quickly than the supply of Chinese.'' The camera continued its close-up procession of boots. ''These men all died in the fighting just last night, and they cannot be replaced in time to affect the current battle's outcome.''

''*Jesus*,'' the White House military officer said in disgust. The army colonel, wearing a crisp green uniform with a white cord under the epaulet on his shoulder, was incensed by the reporter's parading of the dead. But to Gordon, it wasn't a question of dishonoring the fallen. It was a scene that at least *he*—as the dead men's commander-in-chief—should see. The consequence of the actions that only *he* had the power to take. The flag-draped coffins arriving at Dover Air Force Base were too sanitary. Dusty boots turned up to blue sky made the point more clearly. And the point, Gordon thought as the reporter concluded her story, was that the war had to end and end quickly.

'' 'The Lord is my shepherd,' '' the kneeling soldiers read from their tiny Bibles, '' 'I shall not want. He maketh me lie down in green pastures, he leadeth me beside the still waters. He restoreth my soul. He leadeth me in the paths of righteousness for his name's sake.' '' The chaplain stood in full battle dress at the front, his vestments hanging from around his neck. '' 'Yea though I walk through the valley of the shadow of death, I will fear no evil, for thou art with me; thy rod and thy staff they comfort me. Thou preparest a table before me in the presence of mine enemies. Thou anointest my head with oil; my cup runneth over. Surely goodness and mercy shall follow me all the days of my life, and I will dwell in the house of the Lord . . . forever.' ''

''Amen,'' the men concluded, and they rose. Gordon's skin tingled. The camera turned to take in the diminutive reporter. ''This is Kate Dunn,'' she said with a quavering voice and moist eyes, ''NBC News, reporting to you from the valley of the shadow of death.''

24

The joint staff's operations and planning team hovered over the map as if they'd find something new if they studied it longer. But Nate Clark understood his options exactly. They'd been evident in the first five seconds. "Okay," he said loudly. The closed rank of uniformed backs parted. They turned from the brightly lit map to face their commander. "What does the PLA have along the Songhua between the 25th Light Infantry Division and the Tangyuan Valley?"

They all looked at the Dutch intelligence officer. "There appear to be two full Chinese divisions and part of a third along that road. They are survivors of the fighting around Birobidzhan that made it across the Amur before the ice broke. When we inserted the 101st into Tangyuan Valley, they were trapped."

"Will they fight?" Clark asked.

The Dutch colonel shrugged. "The southernmost unit has applied some pressure against the north end of the Tangyuan Valley. But our air strikes reduced that to only token attacks mounted once every day or two. The partial division

was damaged so severely that they amount to little more than walking wounded. It's the third unit—which we believe to be the 549th Infantry Division—that poses the most serious concern. We can't yet measure its strength.''

Clark pursed his lips. ''Can anybody threaten the flanks or rear of the 25th if we send them south?''

The British planner replied. ''The hills in that area are very rugged. The roads and rivers run north and south. To go east and west you have to cross mountain ranges. In my opinion, the only forces the Chinese can bring to bear on the 25th are the three units that lie along the length of the Songhua River.''

''If the Chinese dig in,'' the German operations officer chimed in, ''just like the 101st has in the Tangyuan Valley, the 25th will have to dismount and dislodge them.''

''But we have air superiority,'' Lieutenant Colonel Reed countered. ''That makes for a big difference between our defense of the Tangyuan Valley, and any Chinese defenses along the Songhua.''

The arguments were just building steam. But Clark had already made his mind up, so he headed off the debate. ''We drop the German parachute regiment into the valley as soon as possible. And we order the 25th south along that road at maximum possible speed.'' The disbelievers looked back and forth at one another. ''In road miles, they're half the distance from Tangyuan as the main force.''

''General Clark,'' the British planner began gingerly, ''their mission, if I might say so, was purely in support of the main attack. They have only two heavy battalions attached to them, and the terrain does obviously favor the defenders.''

''We can't drop any more troops into that valley,'' Clark reminded him, reviewing their limited options. ''There's no more room to maneuver. They're already pressed into a four-square-mile box. And I will not consign men to a battle in which they're going to run out of ammunition after the second or third firefight. The 25th Light Infantry Division is the closest unit. The fact that they crossed the

Amur at all was due solely to the speed with which they broke out of Birobidzhan. We didn't even know what to do with them, if you'll all remember, so we assigned them the flank support role down that two-lane, piece-of-shit highway. But now they're our only real hope of saving those men in the Tangyuan Valley, and I intend to ask them to do just that. Now, you go off and come back when you've got a plan.''

Several hours later Lieutenant Colonel Reed knocked on Nate's office door. ''We're ready with an operations plan, sir.'' Nate asked Reed to walk him through it before going in to meet with the others. ''The road tracks the Songhua, which runs through a wide valley and will protect their right flank unless the Chinese put gunboats on the river. We'll fix any indirect fire with tactical acquisition radars, then suppress and destroy them with choppers. But the *dominant* terrain all the way down to the 101st are the hill masses to the left side of the road, which is cut through jumbled hills, slopes, and meadows.''

''Sounds like good country to defend,'' Clark commented, worried.

Reed nodded. ''The risk of them enfilading the 25th's soft vehicles is huge. We've got to push the Chinese back from the road at least to the skyline—about seven hundred yards—the whole way down. We'll try to reduce lodgments on commanding ground with intense air attack, but if we want to go fast, we'll have to mount clearing operations. Luckily, the terrain is covered in thick stands of pine, and there are lots of knobs and finger ridges to screen maneuvering. Good tactical commanders'll make short work of any Chinese bunkers, but it'll be exhausting and bloody. Those men'll be fought out in four to six hours. We'll have to rotate—battalion by battalion—constantly. We'll have to use those men up, General Clark.''

Nate nodded solemnly. ''What kind of defenses do you expect the Chinese to have waiting?''

''There are a few huts along the road that'll have to be

cleared, but our best bet is we'll find hastily constructed, bunker-centered strong points on the forward slope protecting mortars on the reverse slope. The men in those trucks will have cover on the left shoulder, where the road's cut into the hills, but they'll be pretty exposed on the river's side, where most of the draws are flooded with runoff. We can muster one battalion of armor and one of mechanized infantry. We'll put a company of tanks in the vanguard to blast their way through roadblocks and distribute the remainder down the length of the column for local direct fire support. They'll have armored bulldozers so they can widen the road, fill in holes, and push hulks over the side. The mech infantry can be used for attack on level ground. We'll use the light infantry to go up the hills."

"What about our artillery?"

"We'll disperse it, but make sure the vanguard and rearguard are within range of all active batteries. They'll leapfrog, with six batteries ready to repulse an attack or prepare an objective at any given time. And we'll sprinkle the division's senior officers around to organize local action if the column gets segmented by a Chinese attack, which is the main risk of the single-road advance. The Chinese can move along parallel valleys and punch at our flanks. If they break through, there's a risk they could destroy the column piecemeal."

A tense Nate took a deep breath. "What's the Chinese population along that road?"

"Sparse," Reed replied. "The terrain is rugged. Maybe thirty, maybe fifty thousand people."

Nate nodded. "I'm going to . . . to lift all restrictions on the fire controllers." Reed looked down, but nodded. Nate could think of nothing to say that wouldn't betray the guilt he felt on issuing the order.

ALONG SONGHUA RIVER, SOUTH OF SUIBIN
April 26, 1000 GMT (2000 Local)

Night had just fallen, and Harold Stempel was quickly drifting off to sleep. It had been a quiet day. They had taken the luxury of building a small fire. With their boots to the heat and wearing cold-weather gear, the spring night was reasonably comfortable.

"All right!" came the loud voice of the platoon sergeant. Stempel and several others groaned when they looked up. The NCO arrived with the rest of the platoon in tow.

"Gather *around*!" came the command of their platoon leader. "Hope you girls don't mind if we crash your camp-fire." A new arrival tried to take Stempel's place by the warm fire. Stempel kicked him, and muscled his way to the fireside. There was jostling among the cranky men as the lieutenant took his place in the middle. He held in his hand a sheet of flimsy paper. "I've called this platoon meeting 'cause we just got The Word." There were groans and some loud curses, which were followed by threats from the NCOs. "As many of you may have heard, there are some good guys holed up in a valley about a hundred clicks south of here. It was the mission of Third Corps' main heavy forces across the Songhua to relieve them. The 25th was providing their flank security."

There was muttering over the subordinate role. This time the NCOs remained silent.

"I say *was* because we just got *this*." He raised the piece of paper in the air, then held it up to the campfire to read. " 'Today's date. From: Nate Clark, commanding general of UNRUSFOR. To: Soldiers of the 25th LID. I was with many of you at Birobidzhan in the most awful first days of this war. The battle there was one of the most brilliant displays of defense in all of military history. Now, however, I must ask you to do the same on offense. I must ask you to go win this war.' "

The young lieutenant looked up. There was no noise from the thirty men. Stempel looked around to see all eyes raised.

" 'A brigade of the 101st and the 75th Rangers was in-serted into a valley one hundred miles south of you. Their mission is critical. Holding that valley means a successful conclusion to this war. But they have endured a week of

ferocious assaults, and the worst began late last night. The
Chinese launched a full-scale attack from the south and
their situation is desperate. They cannot hold much longer.
The 25th is the division closest to that valley. The 25th is
now the main attack force. I am calling upon you to relieve
those troops. UNRUSFOR will support you with everything
it has. I have every confidence you will now prove your
greatness in the eyes of your countrymen, and I will forever
be in your debt. Good luck, and Godspeed.' "

The lieutenant folded the message carefully, and put it
into his pocket. "There are s'posed to be some trucks down
on the road. Gather your gear and prepare to move out."

Stempel rose, packed his gear, and shouldered his load.
There was no discussion. Nobody commented on the un-
fairness of the orders. The desire for respect was a powerful
motivating force. Each of them accepted the mission in his
own way, and in silence.

TANGYUAN VALLEY, NORTHERN CHINA
April 26, 1700 GMT (0300 Local)

There was a disturbance. André Faulk drowsily opened his
eyes. Running in pairs along the ceiling of the inflated,
polyurethane aid station were rows of bare fluorescent
tubes. André looked at the station's entryway. An officer
was arguing heatedly with two doctors and a crowd of
nurses. The outnumbered man vigorously shook his head.
He spun from a doctor, to a nurse, to another doctor. The
medical personnel all had their say, but in the end the officer won.

André figured it was another hasty move. They'd packed
up twice since he'd arrived at the aid station. He'd not been
carried on a litter but had used a crutch. Both times the
fighting had sounded much closer than it should.

The officer walked to the central aisle and removed his
helmet. "I'd like to have your attention," he called out
politely. "I'm sorry to have to bother you men, but things
have taken a turn for the worse. The Chinese are giving it

their all this go-round. And I'm afraid we're going to have to do the same if . . . if we're going to pull this thing out. Now, I know you've done all your country could ask of any man, but right now we need everyone who can still fire a weapon. All the headquarters, supply, and support units have been stripped clean of fillers. The combat units aren't even sending their wounded back anymore unless they're critical. So I'm gonna have to ask for some volunteers to rejoin the fight. You won't have to do any moving around, just use a weapon from a fighting hole. We won't even make you dig it."

It was intended as humor, but nobody laughed. The doctors and nurses all glared at the staff officer.

André lay on his stretcher and watched the captain nervously twirl his helmet. At first no one rose, and the man stood there all alone. Slowly, however, the first men hobbled up and were sent to the exit. Nurses scolded the wounded soldiers and tried sending them back to their beds. The officer interceded, but finally allowed a doctor to check each volunteer out. Only one man was rejected as too seriously hurt.

"Stupid fucks," the man next to André said. But André was already swinging his feet to the floor.

He hesitated, but decided not to listen to the guy. "Hey, man," he said, "if nobody stops the motherfuckers, we're *all* dead. They'll just toss a charge through that door and move on."

His neighbor made a face—unconvinced, disturbed, or both.

André put weight on his feet. Nothing hurt too badly to walk, but he knew it was in part the painkillers. He limped up to the captain and was directed to the doctor. The man stuck a cold stethoscope onto André's chest as a nurse took his blood pressure. "You feel up to this?" the doctor asked while listening to André's heart.

"*No-o-o,*" André answered.

The exhausted man didn't bother with a reply. "Nurse, give this man some ampicillin and some Vicodin." He turned to the next wounded recruit.

The nurse gave André two bottles of pills, the larger one the painkillers. "Take the antibiotic every four hours—the Vicodin as needed," she said while still holding his hand. Standing close, she whispered, "You don't have to do this."

When the next man arrived, she abruptly left André there holding his pills. He reconsidered his decision to leave the clean, warm hospital. But men arrived with rifles and outer gear, which were handed out to the volunteers. Although André's wounds were impressive enough—large bandages over his left ear and all up and down his right side—other volunteers were much worse off. There were bandaged faces leaving only one eye uncovered. Legs were wrapped so thick they looked like tree trunks. Blood soaked through dressings from all manner of hidden wounds.

André donned the gear and took an M-16.

The provisional platoon numbered over twenty wounded men. They had to climb high into the rocks of a steep hill. About a dozen men preceded André. They turned the light dusting of snow into slick ice. His slips were painful, but André didn't complain about the effort. The higher the better, as far as he was concerned. They all helped each other make the slow trek in the darkness. The more seriously wounded were lent shoulders by the few healthy soldiers. The sound of fighting was a now constant and sonorous roar.

The captain who led them there had lied about the fighting holes. He placed the men among the rocks in unprepared positions. André lay on a ledge behind a jagged outcropping. He could see none of his new comrades. They were hidden—as was he—in the hilltop's dark crevices. But they were so tightly packed the captain addressed them all in a conversational tone. "Your job up here is simple. Don't go anywhere, and don't let the Chinese take this peak." The orders seemed ridiculous. They were as far away from the fighting as they could possibly be. "From up here," the officer said as his men handed out extra ammunition, "enemy troops could fire down on our rear areas. We'd no longer be able to move freely to react to Chinese breakthroughs." A soldier handed André eight magazines. When added to the one in his rifle and two others he'd been given outside the hospital, André had over a hundred and fifty rounds. It was the most he'd had at any one time since the first couple of days in the valley.

He couldn't help but wonder why they were being so generous with ammo.

"Good luck," the captain concluded. "We'll relieve you as soon as we can . . . hopefully in the morning."

After he left, the conversations sprang from the dark hiding places like the chirps of crickets from an empty field. André briefly saw the profile of a helmet about ten meters to his right. From the sound of the voices there were men on each side of and above him.

"Anybody got a machine gun?" someone asked.

After a few moments of silence they all heard, "I've got a SAW."

The answer didn't seem to sit well with the questioner. A Squad Automatic Weapon had an impressive six-hundred-round box magazine. But it fired 5.56-millimeter rifle rounds, not the heavier 7.62-millimeter NATO rounds of the M-60. And it would overheat quickly with sustained firing.

"How about grenadiers?" the same voice asked. "Call it out."

"I got one," someone replied. "Two!" another man said. "Three." The count ended at five.

At least that was good, André thought. Five forty-millimeter grenade launchers—M-279s mounted underneath M-16s—could do some good at such a high elevation.

A deep whine rose to a fearsome roar as a jet passed low overhead. "*Jeez!*" someone shouted as the glowing twin exhausts banked steeply. The jet screamed down the valley and exited uneventfully at the far end. It seemed odd that it would risk flying so low.

Then the night erupted in a string of sixteen brilliant

flashes. The clouds of flame cooled from white to orange to red as the explosions rattled André's insides. Moments later another fighter-bomber crested the ridge. They each wrought the same devastation. In all, eight jets dropped 128 five-hundred-pound bombs. They fell along the road and the surrounding foothills. Despite the painful ringing in his ears, André found the display of pyrotechnics entrancing. Soon after each fighter-bomber streaked a hundred feet over their ridgeline, a ripple of explosions lit the forested valley in brilliant fire. The flashes darkened before their concussion pounded his eardrums. The lightning and thunder were a half second out of sequence.

But the more André watched, the more his sense of dread grew. The strings of bombs fell closer and closer to their hilltop position. They finally pounded the base of the hill where they lay. When the terrible violence came to an end, the nature of the men's chatter had changed. It took on an urgency—a sense of purpose—that was new.

"Look alive!" someone called out. Tracers streaked through the woods below. The fighting raged as the Chinese surged forward.

"Let's do this right! My name is Master Sergeant Golden. I'll command for as long as I can. We appear to be in a semicircle! And we got a 16 on the far right at the edge of a cliff. You're number one. Call it out, son!"

"One!" a man said, sounding fit enough.

There was grunting, then a loud, "Shit!" from the master sergeant. He puffed and hissed his way to the next position. "About five meters to the left of number one we got a grenadier and some flat ground. He's coverin' the approach we took to get up here, so we might have to react this way. If we're threatened with an overrun from over here, I want you two guys to call out 'Right! Right!' We'll organize a reaction team to reinforce this sector. When I get around the perimeter, I'll designate which guys are on the team. You're number two," he said at a lower volume. "Call it out."

"Two!" yelled another voice in the night.

The orientation and shouted orders continued. There was about one grenadier to every two or three M-16s. When the count reached number six, the shout came from the guy just to André's right. There followed a conversation in a much quieter voice. "You doin' okay?" asked the senior NCO.

"I'm not feelin' real good," the guy said. "I think I'm still bleedin', and my leg really hurts."

There was a click. André could see the beam of a flashlight dimly reflected off overhanging rocks. "Yeah, you're still bleedin' some," the older man said. "You just don't do any movin' around. Try to maybe prop yer foot up on the rocks and keep it elevated."

"Like . . . *uh,* like this?" The master sergeant approved.

André's mouth was dry and he got his canteen. He took a swig of the cool liquid and felt refreshed. "Take it easy on that water," ordered the master sergeant. His teeth were bared as he eased himself into the rocks. His rifle was slung over his shoulder and he hopped on one leg. "You're lucky seven—call it out."

"Seven!" André barked quickly and with decent volume. He didn't sound wounded, and he was pleased by that fact.

The master sergeant looked him over with his fading flashlight. "You're on the reaction team." André didn't object. He saw in the reflected light that the man was clearly in agony. His face was shiny with sweat. He appeared to be at least in his forties. Must've been from battalion staff. "Listen for the call. 'Right' means head over to where we came up," he said, pointing up the hill through the huge boulders. " 'Left' means that way." He pointed the other direction—also up the hill.

André nodded, and the man was off to continue his tour. The count grew past ten as the fight below raged on. It poured from left to right—south to north—as it moved up the valley. Marked by flashing muzzles, bursting grenades, and streaking tracers, the beleaguered Americans were clearly in full retreat. André pitied the poor bastards far below. But fear took its place as he watched the fiery lines slowly recede. They were leaving André's hilltop far behind.

"Where the hell're they *goin'*?" asked the man next to André—number six.

The question wasn't directed toward anyone. But when no one else answered, André felt obliged to reply. "They're fallin' back."

"But how far? I mean, it looks like they pulled right on back past where *we* are."

The master sergeant's weakening voice came from the distance. "Last one's a grenadier!"

"Twenty-two!" came a much louder shout.

"And that makes me twenty-three!" the master sergeant managed. His booming voice was failing fast, but he was done. *Twenty-three,* Andre thought. He watched the fighting down below. Thousands and thousands of muzzles spat deadly fire.

The figures looked like stealthy mountaineers as they climbed in complete darkness. André kept his rifle trained at the nearest man. He switched from time to time as a more suitable target appeared. The wounded Americans waited in silence as the Chinese approached.

Pebbles trickled down the hill into André's position.

The climbers all froze. Words were spoken in hushed Chinese. Moments passed before a short order was given and they resumed their ascent toward the guns.

Everyone waited on the master sergeant to fire the first round. André drew a bead on a dark form. The man scaled a steep rock. He stood upright momentarily with his rifle slung over his back. He climbed on, now less than fifteen meters away.

A single M-16 fired. An avalanche of noise thundered down the hill. André fired once and knocked a man off the rocks. For the first few moments the fight was totally one-sided. The Chinese were completely exposed. But even so the pace of the killing was measured. The Americans squeezed off shots one at a time, and at first they were the only ones firing.

That all changed after five or six seconds. The entire hillside came alive with muzzle flashes. Bullets sparked off bare granite. The Americans' forty-millimeter grenades burst almost the instant they were fired. The explosions seemed dangerously close.

André lay on a smooth, cold rock. He did his damnedest to aim each shot. But bullets hit the rocks all around. It was unnerving how thick the fire was. Every squeeze of his trigger was followed by an angry swarm of buzzing death. Both sides sprayed the rocks at point-blank range. When one Chinese soldier emptied a magazine on full auto, every American had a clear fix on him for two seconds. Before André could fire, the man was thrown backward from his perch.

The Chinese soldiers died in such great numbers the battle ended quickly. The Americans occupied a steep uphill position, and had surprise to add to their advantage. André's rifle had killed every second or third shot. A company of infantry lay dead after a minute of combat.

"Cease fire!" the master sergeant called out. "Cease fire! Cease fire!"

The American soldiers quickly ended the killing. The only sounds were now made by the wounded. A lone Chinese gun opened up. Single shots by a dozen Americans sounded like a machine gun. They all aimed at where the flame had been and there followed silence.

After a while André slid back onto the dirt. He replaced the half-empty magazine in his rifle with a full one and rose up. He took long looks into the darkness in search of movement. But there were only the moans, bleating calls, and choking gurgles. They would weaken soon and all would be silent.

The wounds along André's side began to ache with renewed vigor. He wasn't cold, but he began to shiver till he was quickly exhausted. He got his canteen and took a Vicodin to settle down.

"Anybody wounded?" the master sergeant asked.

At first there was no answer. Then, "*Everybody's* fuckin'

wounded!'' came a reply. André joined in the laughter.
That was their brief victory celebration. They rejoiced for
a moment at having survived the first encounter.

"Less than eight hours now," said a jubilant number six.

André wondered at the comment, then asked, "Eight
hours till what?"

"Till they're comin' *back* for us. Didn't you *hear*?"

It was the most stupid remark André had ever heard.
Didn't the guy have eyes? Couldn't he see that their "relief" was being beaten farther and farther away? The guy
chattered on about their impending rescue. Each word
grated on André, but he held his peace. He let the man go
through the night with his dreams intact.

WHITE HOUSE OVAL OFFICE
April 26, 0400 GMT (2300 Local)

Gordon sat at his desk all alone and read Kartsev's letter
one last time before bed. "Dear Mr. President. I suppose
by now you are trying to have me killed. I understand your
decision completely. Every choice you have made to date
has been correct. And the results have been extraordinarily
good for you and your nation. But the outcome which
awaits your next decision will be radically different. You
will err at the most fateful turning point in modern man's
history, and that which you hold dearest will be placed in
imminent danger. What I am talking about now is the
worldwide spread of anarchy."

Gordon felt a rush of anxiety each time he read those
words, and he was no longer sleepy.

> Northern China now lies in ruins. Ten million refu-
> gees cling to life's fringes. Another hundred million
> people are unemployed. Into that mixture of physical
> disruption and economic dislocation will soon return
> a defeated, demoralized army. Hundreds of thousands
> horribly brutalized by your war machine. Many of
> those soldiers will be changed psychologically.

They'll cast about for a meaning to it all. For some belief system which will explain the horrors of their youth. Their answer will be found in the simple word "no." They will say no to everybody and everything. No to all authority. No to every norm. No to every order, every request, every plea. Why the word "no"? Because no empowers the powerless. No denies the dominion of the strong over the weak. *"No!"* is the drug which eases the minds of the tortured, the traumatized, the guilt-ridden. No is the hope that what came before will never be again.

From that one, simple word, mankind will finally taste the milk of true freedom. Not the freedom of your democratic rhetoric. The lawyerly parsing of rights and privileges, checks and balances. But total freedom from all constraints. Men and women free to do whatever they wish. And you are part of that great process. A bead in the necklace of history. Soon your moment of truth will arrive. Should you stay in China and do the dirty business of controlling a restive population? Maintain the pressure necessary to prevent man's baser instincts from percolating to the surface? That course will be opposed by your allies, your Congress, your adoring public. "Bring the boys home for a good parade!" You will, of course, withdraw, leaving a momentary vacuum of power which will trigger an inexorable chain reaction. A burst of freedom followed by fiery repression. Escalating uprisings and backlashes in cycles. With each atrocity the pendulum will swing wider until the violence grows uncontrollable. And from that combustible brew there will arise a leader. A spark for the inevitable explosion. Someone to unleash the suppressed natural behavior of a billion and a half people. Imagine the soaring heights of ingenuity, and the depths and variety of evil. The unprecedented social tidal wave will wash over even your tall bastion of order and stability. Even your ship of state will be rocked,

Mr. President. Welcome to the postideological age.

My purpose in writing you, President Davis, is not to wash my hands of any blame. In fact, I am proud of my contributions to society, for I believe mankind will emerge triumphant from its darkest horrors. It will, via the catharsis to come, transcend one order of human development for the next. Imagine a future in which violent coercion by a king or a court is unnecessary. In which man has been freed of the straitjacket of convention. If my optimism about the human spirit proves correct, how then will historians view heretics such as me, who cried out against the injustices of old? And how differently will they view the old regime's protectors such as you? The defenders of the faith who will unleash great death machines in a desperate attempt to preserve, protect, and defend?

Oh, I would love to study the time that is nearing, but I would not trade places with you. I believe you to be a decent man laboring mightily to do an honest job. Your only limitation is that you have not seen what I have seen. You have not been one of the shiny teeth on a cog which slowly ground human flesh in the machine of state. Viewing life from such an extreme opens the eyes and liberates the mind. It strips away the facade of government to reveal the abomination inside. I am sorry, Mr. Davis, that at this crucial juncture in history the reins of power happened to fall to you. But at every innocuous turn in the road leading to atrocity you find decent men possessing the power of rationalization. I know that to be fact, Mr. President, for I have traveled that road my entire adult life.

V. Kartsev.

SONGHUA RIVER, NORTH OF TANGYUAN
April 26, 0500 GMT (1500 Local)

Stempel and his squadmates heard fighting as they piled sandbags in the trucks. They built walls and sat back-to-back in the center. They faced out with their weapons at the ready. The truck's canvas top was lashed down tight with cord. They'd raise the canvas and fire out the sides if they had to. Harold had no idea what the woman driving the truck would do.

But as soon as they began to roll, the soldiers confronted the real enemy. An awful cold numbed their skin and chilled their bones. The men's combat-ready poses gave way. Hands that had once gripped rifles now clenched the mountain bags into which all retreated. Without the truck's lone heater, they could never have made five miles. Its warm air wafted by Harold intermittently. He longed for every lukewarm touch. Every groan of the brakes meant relief. When the column stopped completely, it was heaven on earth. Men rose up, stretched, looked around. They rubbed their extremities and shook like dogs emerging from water. The whole convoy was ordered to dismount. Thousands of men descended moaning and bitching. They did jumping jacks and squat thrusts. When they loaded up and pressed on, Harold felt warm for five or ten delicious minutes.

The road wound through valleys along the river's side. It was a rough land. But curled up on the floor of the truck Stempel could see only the top of the hills through a slender gap in the canvas. He sat there pinching his parka over all but his eyes. The guns of the M-1A1s up ahead sounded like thunder. Echoes turned the sharp cracks into a rumble. They were blasting a narrow pathway through the hills. Smoke rose from the slopes and from blackened craters dotting the road. Tanks with bulldozer blades smashed through barriers and filled in traps. The two heavy battalions that had led the way south from Birobidzhan were almost invulnerable to Chinese infantry. They had been the spearhead easily piercing poorly prepared infantry positions.

The air above the column buzzed with Apache gunships and Kiowa scouts. Trucks carried the helicopters' ground crews, fuel, and ammo forward, allowing them to be refitted and rearmored on the shoulders of the narrow highway. Men swarmed over them like pit crews at the Indy 500, and they were quickly returned to the air. Their chopping blades sounded a near-constant thwack overhead as they scouted the column's undefended flanks. Calls from forward air controllers sent them heeling over and charging into action. Their rockets and guns made short work of the enemy.

Only once did the Chinese mount an effective ambush. But the attackers received a broadside from over a dozen trucks. Almost two companies fired at point-blank range up the hills. Harold's unit had been too far away to get in the fight. But he'd watched the ambush end with a stupendous, deafening air strike. For far above the tree-skimming helicopters flew a dedicated flight of heavily laden fighter-bombers. They and their tankers orbited in holding patterns awaiting the call. When they swooped down, they made clear the enormous difference between forty-pound aerial rockets and artillery shells and two-thousand-pound bombs.

The column rolled on, and Harold had been pleased with the victory because he'd been worried about getting caught in that truck during a firefight. But he quickly saw that those worries remained justified. They steered around the burning carcass of a deuce-and-a-half. The outlines of the truck were clearly visible in the flames. Tires, canopy frame, chassis. The heat was so intense as to be painful. Harold and his squadmates shielded themselves from the searing fire of the fully consumed vehicle.

The wind didn't seem so bad afterward. Cold was slow death, but fire did the job right away. And the breeze helped rid Stempel's clothes of the lingering stench of the burned truck.

TANGYUAN VALLEY, NORTHERN CHINA
April 27, 0700 GMT (1700 Local)

"This is *it*!" Woody shouted over the noise. "As far as we can go!" Kate eyed in disbelief the smoke rising all around. Woody pulled her to the ground between the thick trunk of a fallen tree and a large boulder. They were ringed in by rattling machine guns, bursting grenades, and earth-shattering bombs. Six air-transportable 105-millimeter how-itzers drowned out ordinary conversation as they rapidly expended their remaining rounds. Their crews would then destroy the guns and pick up rifles.

All night and day they'd retreated from the Chinese, but now they were at the end of the road. Half a mile ahead lay the northernmost lines, and a mile behind them charged an entire Chinese army. Kate felt like she was trapped in-side a forest fire drawing tighter around her unburned patch of woods. Through the meat grinder in which they sat cut heavy machine-gun bullets that would travel for miles. They sounded like firecrackers when they smacked into trees and sent sparks flying when they skimmed off granite as they converged from both directions.

That morning she and Woody had awoken to the sight of parachutes in the blue sky. She'd thought they were more supplies, but the soaring spirits of the soldiers around her had lifted her mood before she'd even realized what was happening. Underneath the chutes hung reinforcements, and she and Woody had hurried to meet them. They were a whole regiment of German paratroopers—saviors sent to stop the Chinese. They meant more than just a thousand additional defenders. They stood for UNRUSFOR commit-ment not to lose that valley. A sign from Clark's Olympus that the defenders in the valley would hold.

But they had quickly joined the ranks, and to all ap-pearances had done little to stop the Chinese. There were more parachutes in the sky later that morning, but they'd held long boxes and crates, not men. After what would've been lunchtime had Kate and Woody stopped running long enough to eat, the skies had been filled again, but this time not with transports. The Chinese sent masses of infantry, and the allies responded with bombers. All afternoon the skies had raged, but even their fire was not enough.

"Okay," Kate said, "what do we do?" Her eyes were

transfixed by the smoky boundaries, the frontiers of their ever-shrinking part of China.

"We either lie low down here in the valley, or hightail it up to the hills."

Kate longed to curl up in a ball right there, close her eyes, and not wake till it was over. Every time she thought about getting captured by the Chinese her thoughts froze. She consequently couldn't prepare herself for the horrors that lay in store. Woody's usually smiling eyes were sunk deep into their sockets even though he hadn't gotten high once since they'd arrived in that valley. "I'm sorry," Kate whispered in a trembling voice. "Oh, Woody, I'm *so,* so sorry! This is my fault!" She dissolved into sobs but quickly grew incapacitated by extreme fatigue. Her store of emotions was empty, and she sat there spent, waiting.

Woody finally broke the silence, speaking slowly. "Have you ever seen soldiers crack? At the end, when they break and just run for their lives?" Kate shivered and buried her hands between her knees. She shook her head. "In Burundi, there was a company of French peacekeepers guarding a Tutsi refugee camp. The Hutus came at them by the thousands with machetes, and the French ran out of ammunition."

"Did the Hutus . . . did they kill the French?"

Woody shook his head. "They killed the Tutsis."

Kate tried to imagine the medieval scene, but couldn't. "What will the Chinese do?" she asked, meaning to the defeated UNRUSFOR soldiers. But she was also thinking about herself. Apart from the nurses, she was the only woman among the Americans.

"The most dangerous time, Kate, is right at first. When they're taking you, but before you're 'in the system.' You've just got to stay alive, understand? Don't try for anything more than that. Put everything out of your mind except survival. Don't judge what happens by any standard other than whether you live through it. Time heals wounds, and life is long. You do whatever it takes. Do you understand what I'm telling you?"

Until the question at the end, she'd remained calm. She hugged her legs as tightly as she could to ward off the chill, nodded, buried her face in her knees, and said, "I vote for the hills, not the valley."

"Then let's go. If the Chinese force their way through, UNRUSFOR's gonna drop everything in their arsenal in this valley. Napalm, high explosives, fuel-air munitions, cluster bombs, and whatever other nasty shit they've hidden away for special occasions. All of which also means we gotta pick the right hill, 'cause they'll drop 'em up there too."

Kate hesitated, but then forced the words out. "We could . . . could try to squeeze on a medevac helicopter," she tentatively suggested. Woody said nothing. "No," she quickly concluded, ashamed that she'd even suggested displacing seriously wounded soldiers.

A thin limb was suddenly sheared from the upper reaches of a tree. Kate and Woody both flinched as the healthy, leafy branch crashed to the ground ten feet away. "Come on," Kate said, rising to her feet.

Tangyuan Valley, Northern China
April 27, 0830 GMT (1830 Local)

The Chinese had made three concerted attempts to take the hilltop where André Faulk lay. The first attempt had just missed what was probably intended to be a predawn start. In the dim gray light they had watched men climb the icy rocks. They had lost one step to slippery footing for each two they had taken, and many had been injured by noisy falls on the sharp crags even before the automatic weapons had mowed them down in huge numbers. Before the grenades had rained onto them by the dozens and canisters of shot had lit the rocks with sparks.

The next two attacks had been slaughters on a brilliant blue morning. The three efforts had been repulsed in bloodbaths that did nothing but diminish the defenders' ammunition and leave hundreds of attackers dead. Afterward,

allied bombers had begun pounding the base of the hill.
André had no idea how many attacks the raids had foiled,
but even at five hundred meters stray shrapnel struck the
hilltop with still-lethal force. He was petrified each time the
bombers came in. The handful of wounded men were a
scratch team with no unit number whose lone radio had
been holed and was useless. But someone must have remembered them, for the bombs all dropped at minimally
safe distances. The Marine F/A-18s came closest of all, and
when the last pulled up, it waggled its wings and everything
suddenly fell quiet. The pop and crackle of fighting was
distant. André took a painkiller and lay back to daydream.
All the Chinese in position to attack lay dead amid the
smoking bomb craters. Overhead were puffy clouds and a
bright moon in the daytime sky.

"There's another one!" croaked number six to André's
right. André had lent him some painkillers, but his voice
was failing him quickly. He seized on any hope for a rescue, this time a helicopter he said he'd seen. André's helmet
struck the boulder behind him as he nodded off to sleep.
That rock had kept him alive. Its downhill face was scarred
and pitted. It was like the armor that wrapped a tank crew
in its shell. Deafening grenades erupted only feet away, but
only a heavy downpour of debris fell on the defenders. It
had kept friendly casualties to an absolute minimum—two
new wounds, both slight. The only bad news had been announced by the master sergeant. Two of their brethren, he'd
informed them, had taken a turn for the worse—not from
new wounds, but old ones. It must have been bad because
a man had limped by to redistribute their ammo. "There it
is again!" number six called out raggedly.

This time André saw the helicopter. Not a long-range
Blackhawk like the one they'd rode in on, but a gunship
firing a podful of rockets. That was now the thin tether of
hope on which number six felt his life depended. "What
kind of combat range do Apaches have?" André's neighbor
asked, but no one answered. "It's only a hundred miles or
something, right?"

More like two or three hundred, André thought but didn't say. Number six was like the old sailors that André had read about back in school. They got excited when they saw a bird because it meant land, only in this case they weren't on a ship searching for shore. Their salvation was drifting slowly toward them like an iceberg. Sliding over the earth like a glacier. So slowly you couldn't tell it was moving. Inch, by inch, by inch, by inch . . .

A loud explosion woke André. His eyes shot open and he grabbed his rifle as smoke drifted over his position. Pain shot through his cramping muscles like hot fire when he scrambled onto his rock parapet. The hill was littered with Chinese as before, but none moved. They were beginning to smell in the late-afternoon sun. Another shell burst, stinging André's face with debris. He dropped down with his eyes watering. A smear of crimson darkened his white glove from a cut on his face, and he cursed. Yet another blast ripped through their positions. They weren't the crushing blows of big artillery tubes, and they couldn't compare with the unearthly hell of an air raid, but the new threat brought ragged breathing from André's chest. *Bam!* shook the hilltop a dozen meters away. *Mortars!* André realized in horror. The simple weapons with the small sixty- or eighty-millimeter rounds could pound them all day long. He looked up at the wispy red clouds drifting overhead. They were fired at a high angle and dropped almost straight down.

Another shell exploded. André was so startled by each blast that he feared death from heart attack. A light rain of rock dust drifted down around him, and he curled up and braced himself. From his fetal position—every muscle hard as the rocks against which he lay—he peered up at the sky. There was nowhere to hide. No shelter to protect him from the projectiles randomly lobbed onto them. To his horror, he caught a glimpse of a plummeting mortar round. *Bam!* It landed a safe distance away.

"Aaaaahh!" came the bloodcurdling screech. *"Ah! Ah!*

Ah! Ah!'' At first André thought someone had cracked, as had happened twice during artillery barrages to men in his old company. The terror and helplessness of lying exposed was too much and they just snapped. But that wasn't the case this time. ''Sixteen's hit bad!'' reported one of the men from André's left.

A bursting mortar interrupted his calls for aid. *''How bad?''* the master sergeant asked.

''Real bad!'' the guy shouted over the screams. ''Took both his legs off!''

André moaned and felt sick, jamming his eyes shut. *Please, God*, he begged silently. *Please, please, please, ple-e-ease!* He tried to force everything that was happening from his mind. There was a thud, but no burst—a dud. The screams went on, but André heard them from his increasing distance. The camping trip—the one to New Jersey—with the Boys' Club when he was nine! His sleeping bag. A flashlight. The buses. All the kids from the Bronx had been so excited because they got to sleep under the stars. It was the only time he had ever left the city before boot camp. He always thought back to that trip late at night when he couldn't sleep. He'd lie in his bed imagining he was underneath the stars. But now those stars had lost their magic—their sense of adventure—that had captivated him and the two dozen other youths. They now meant cold, and killing, and screams of pain . . . like those from the legless man.

Crump! came a burst in the dirt. Whole ledges of earth showered down around him. The wails fell to mewls, then silence. But not so the man rendering aid. ''Listen to me! No, no, no! Open your *eyes*! Don't go to sleep! *Hey!* No, man! Jesus, *come on*! Fight it! *Don't close your eyes!*''
André silently advised the man to give it up. He'd seen it before. Screams of horror on first seeing the massive wounds, then pasty stillness and glassy eyes. The sweat that had flooded from every pore gave way to shivering from the bitter cold of death's grip. In basic they'd taught that shock was the body's defense mechanism to help stanch

massive bleeding, but it seemed to kill more men than it saved. Sure enough, there were no more soothing words. Shock was silence. Shock was private. Shock was death.

For no reason apparent to André, the mortars ceased their deadly rain. Out of ammo. Killed by counterbattery fire. Shifted targets. It didn't matter which. The silence that meant death for the wounded man meant life for everyone else. "All right!" shouted the angry-sounding master sergeant. "*Count* off!"

The rightmost man shouted, "One!" The next guy, "Two!" The next, "Three!" André looked out over the rock—his armor. The hillside was empty. They weren't coordinating an attack with the mortars. "Six!" André's neighbor called out, dissolving into hisses of pain from the effort.

"Seven!" André shouted. The count continued until it was time for eleven. There was silence, a broken line in the chain of positions.

"Eleven?" the master sergeant prompted. There was no reply. "Somebody check!" It took a few moments for the obvious truth to be revealed. "Uum!" came the distressed voice of number ten, more of a quivering sigh than a comment. But it made the rest of his report unnecessary. "He's . . . He took a mortar! Right where he was layin'! Right in the back, it looks like! I can't tell, really!"

It had rained the first night. The heavy droplets had thumped against the tent in a steady drumbeat. Through the thin canvas the thunder had sounded like artillery. But André's memory of the trip had now changed. Instead of the squeals of nine-year-olds trying but failing to be brave, each thunderclap brought the shrieks of grown men calling for their mother.

The count moved on, renumbering for the two KIA. "Okay," the master sergeant shouted, "I'm nineteen! Redistribute the ammo!" A short while later a man appeared. Although André's tears had long since dried, he asked if André was all right. André nodded. "So how much ammo you got?"

André's mags were stacked at the base of his big rock. "Four full, plus seven rounds in a fifth."

The guy's face was pitted with small wounds. He looked down at two blood-spattered magazines. Bandages made his helmet sit high atop his head. "You're flush. I'm gonna pass these out further down."

André nodded, and the man turned to leave. "Hey!" André called out. "Who're you?"

"John," the guy replied, breaking into a smile.

"I meant your number," André said, pissed that he now knew the man's name.

"Oh. Ten. I'm right over there where that little tree is growin' out of the crack in the big boulder." He was pointing. André looked out of politeness. "What's *your* name?" number ten asked.

"Seven," André replied. The guy arched his eyebrows and turned to leave, not nearly as upbeat as before. "Name's *André* . . . Faulk. From the Bronx." He shook hands with the smiling man from Minnesota.

25

Maps of various scales shone from the room's multiple screens. Gordon Davis ate a cheese Danish. "The 25th is making decent progress down the Songhua," General Dekker said. "But the Chinese have figured out what they're up to, and the resistance they're putting up is better organized and prepared. In the last four hours the maneuver battalions have had to dismount and clear the surrounding ridges three times. The column's progress has slowed to just a few miles per hour."

"That's the pace of a road march," the commandant of the Marine Corps commented. "Have you given any thought to just dismounting and plowing ahead?"

"The vanguard of that column is still almost forty miles from the valley," Dekker replied. "We don't want to have them reach their objective on their last legs."

"Well, General Dekker," the Marine general responded, not backing down, "it's the fourth quarter and the shot clock is running down. Those men shouldn't save anything for the locker room."

"Those *men*," Dekker snapped, "have been fighting for

over three months without a break! They've only got two heavy battalions, but they've made better progress than *either* of the two main prongs."

"That's because the Chinese they're facing are *done*! You can stick a fork in 'em. They aren't trying to stop that advance. They're just not falling back fast enough. They're on foot being chased by men in vehicles. They're caught in a *trap,* General Dekker."

"So what would you suggest?" the army general asked. "Try to talk them into surrendering?"

Gordon like all the rest waited on the Marine commandant's reply.

"I would *suggest* that they get outta those trucks and *advance*. Get down to basics. Block and tackle, General Dekker. This isn't rocket science."

"And this isn't a game, either," Dekker replied. Knots bulged from his clenched jaw.

"Is it possible," Gordon said, "those men *could* advance more quickly on foot?" Dekker swallowed his pride and nodded once. "Well, speed is everything at this point. So . . . I'd give the order."

SONGHUA RIVER, NORTH OF TANGYUAN
April 27, 1430 GMT (0430 Local)

"Everybody *out*!" came the command from the truck's tailgate, waking Harold. The order was being shouted up and down the road. The trucks had been parked for almost an hour as the fighting ahead raged. Everyone roused himself in the predawn morning with groans from a deep, deep sleep. "Shoulder your *lo-o-oads*!" shouted the platoon sergeant.

"Why the fuck we gotta hump our *loads* around?" Patterson asked from the dark but bustling road.

"You can kiss these trucks good-bye!" the platoon sergeant answered. "Get yer shit and fall in on the shoulders! First and Third Squads in line on the left! Second and Fourth on the right! Ten meters separation! Let's *go*!"

Quiet dissension spread quickly through the ranks. Men knew better than to openly question the platoon sergeant, but lowered voices were leveled on the squad leader. "Why are we leavin' the trucks?" Patterson asked.

"How the fuck should *I* know?" came the reply from the three-striper. He was two grades junior to the platoon sergeant and often knew no more than his men.

" 'Cause you're our *squad* leader!"

"I've been asleep just like *you*! Get your pack on and shut the fuck up!" That did nothing to put an end to the complaints. Harold grimaced when the heavy pack settled onto his raw shoulders at the tailgate. The same pain was felt by everyone, but the others didn't have the 60 to carry. "Don't forget this," Chavez said, snickering sadistically. He handed Harold his brand-new M-60. Along with the fighter-bombers, gunships, and tanks they'd marshaled for their division, someone had scrounged up extra machine guns. Harold's squad had drawn straws to see who'd carry it. Harold had lost under suspicious circumstances.

Harold strapped the long sling of the twenty-three-pound weapon over his neck and shoulder with a grunt that drew laughter from the others. "How much you weigh, Stemp?" Patterson asked. "One forty? You're like an *ant*, man! Ants can carry ten times their weight, ya know."

"Fuck you," Harold replied to more laughter. They fell into a single file on the left side of the road.

"For*ward*!" came the command from the head of the column. Harold stepped off bent over thirty degrees at the waist. His lungs hurt from the weight of the pack on his back. Sweat popped out in beads along his forehead and neck and began to trickle down his body despite the morning chill. Every footstep had to be carefully placed in the dark. An uneven patch of road threatened an instantly twisted ankle. When they headed up the hill, his legs and lungs began to burn.

Harold waited as the maneuver team crawled forward under furious fire. The Chinese knew exactly where the Ameri-

cans were, where they were going, and what they were
trying to do . . . which was kill them. Patterson and the others advancing slowly on the bunker had some cover, but
not much. The earth and underbrush around them was being
peppered with high-powered rounds. They never raised any
part of their bodies even an inch above the ground. Even
so, he'd seen several of the men stop to bandage small flesh
wounds from ricochets or splattered rock chips or wood
splinters. Harold wished he could help, but his orders were
to lay low till the squad leader gave the signal.

That signal came when the four men of the maneuver
team were twenty feet from the bunker. Now it was time
for Harold's team to pour on the fire. Everyone watched
the squad leader's silent countdown. He curled his fingers
from five, four, three, two, down to one. Harold raised his
M-60 and laid it atop a moss-covered rock. The riflemen
around him began squeezing off rounds aimed at the black
slit in the earth. The grenadiers fired forty-millimeter grenades which burst all around the single long firing port.
Now it was Harold's turn. He lined up the big gun on the
earthen bunker's open slit and pulled the trigger. It roared
and pounded Harold's shoulder and belched flame two feet
from its muzzle. Harold calmly marched the fire into the
opening. At seventy meters, he could easily tell when dirt
was kicked up around the opening by misses, and when the
large 7.62-millimeter rounds went into the bunker cleanly.
Long bursts disappeared into the dark hole where half a
dozen men sheltered.

Out of the corner of his eye Harold could see the maneuver team begin their assault. The four men rose and
rushed uphill at the bunker from directly beneath it. The
Chinese defenders were now as good as dead. Anyone who
raised his head to fire would be killed by Harold or the five
riflemen around him. But if no one stopped the assault
team, they would all die in a meat grinder of hand-grenade
shrapnel.

No one stopped the assault team. The four Americans all
rose in unison and hurled grenades. It was risky because

the toss was uphill. In fact, one of the grenades rolled back down. The four men saw it coming and dove to the ground. It burst safely a few meters away just as the other three grenades lit up the interior of the bunker. Bright flame shot out through the slit, and black smoke billowed out after it.

"Cease fire!" their squad leader shouted. The fire team's guns fell silent. The assault team scrambled up the slope. Harold cringed in anticipation, but there were no mines or booby traps. The men crawled right up to the smoking hole and on silent count easily slipped four more grenades into the bunker. They then slid back down the hill with their ears plugged. Again flame jetted through the firing slit. Harold safed his machine gun and relaxed. He closed his eyes and massaged his throbbing temples. He was too tired to give a shit about the Chinese soldiers who'd just died. Nothing mattered to him anymore.

UNRUSFOR HEADQUARTERS, KHABAROVSK
April 27, 2100 GMT (0700 Local)

"Nate?" Clark heard over the secure, long-distance line. He closed his eyes at the sound of his wife's voice. "Nate, are you all right?"

"I love you, Lydia. And I miss you and the boys." His voice was thick.

"What's the matter?" she asked, instantly on guard. He couldn't answer just then. "Everything seems to be going so *well*! We're all so proud of—"

"I screwed up, Lydia" he said. He then cleared his throat. "I sent some brave men too far behind enemy lines, and now they're going to die. I went too far. I rolled the dice and . . ." He couldn't finish.

Lydia sighed. "Tell me what you think you did wrong—exactly."

Nate described their original plans for a counterattack. Then his revisions to accelerate the timetables. All his gambles had paid off . . . except his biggest and last one. "I should've settled for something more modest. We should've done it in stages. Pocket north of the Amur first, then cross the border.''

''Wouldn't the Chinese have built defenses at the river? Tried to stop you from crossing . . . ?''

''If we lose that valley, Lydia, we could lose this war. Everything we've got is heading toward one choke point. The prize would be two whole army groups—600,000 men and all their equipment—pocketed in the Amur River basin. But if the Chinese take that valley, we're stuck. We can't encircle them, and our flanks are totally exposed. We'd have to withdraw and consolidate our positions. They'd get out of the trap and then there's no end in sight for this thing militarily.''

Lydia remained quiet for a moment. Nate felt the agony of being trapped in a box. Like there was no escape and he was running out of air. ''You said *if* the Chinese take that valley,'' Lydia finally said. ''That means it's not certain yet.''

Nate sighed. He felt exhausted from worry. ''I've done all I can do.''

''No, you haven't. There's always something more! Think! You've always been the best soldier in the world. Now you're the best *general* in the world! You can do it. I *know* you can!''

The special-forces team had black greasepaint on their faces despite the bright morning sun. Clark and the twelve men all sat on the bare metal deck of the pitching helicopter. He'd chosen the Green Berets team over the DOD bodyguards because there was no subtlety to the coming threat. There would be no doubt who and where the enemy was.

Clark and Reed watched the wooded hills of northern China flash by beneath the window. They put down along a narrow dirt road near the head of a column of dismounted infantry. They got out and the helicopter took off. It threw dirt and grit into Nate's eyes. It would fly several miles to the rear, refuel, and return to pick him up.

Even before the roar of the chopper receded, Nate heard

the sound of fighting up ahead. Exhausted infantrymen lay on both shoulders of the road. Their rifles were raised onto their huge field packs and at the ready. The dozen Green Berets spread out to avoid crowding their charge and making him a target. Clark and Reed strode down the road toward the boom and crackle of the guns.

"How're ya *doin'*?" Nate called out to heads raised in surprise. Men woke from their slumber and stared at the strange sight. "Good *morning*!" Nate said to men, who scrambled to get to their feet. He never gave an order. He never said a word other than the polite—but loud—greetings. But all down the road in both directions, soldiers who were previously resting began to rise and shoulder their loads.

A delegation of astonished officers soon approached from the direction of the fighting. They all waved perfunctory salutes and gathered around Nate on the road. Clark shook a lieutenant colonel's hand. "What seems to be the problem?" he asked.

The battalion commander was obviously taken aback by Nate's unexpected arrival. He looked back over his shoulder and said, "Well, sir, the road's not clear. There's a platoon of tanks up there working them over. We're waiting on the call to get moving. Meanwhile, we've begun to draw heavy fire from the knob of this hill right on top of us." He pointed for Nate's benefit.

Nate tried to keep his temper under control. In a low voice meant not to be heard by the nearby troops he said, "We've got a war to win, Colonel. If there's some obstacle up ahead, I'd suggest you march your men up there and destroy it."

The man stiffened. "Yes, *sir*!"

"As for the fire from that hill, I'd send a company up there straight at 'em. If they don't *run*, go to ground, grab 'em by the nose, and maneuver against their *flanks*. Fire and maneuver, Colonel. That's what the taxpayers pay you to do."

"Yes, sir," the visibly miserable man said. He turned

and issued the orders. Nate walked on. The volume of noise rose. The men on the sides of the road now didn't leave the shelter of their packs to acknowledge the commanding general's passage. They lay behind their large loads. Their eyes remained near the rear sights of their rifles.

The captain who led the special forces "A" detachment came up to Nate. "General Clark," was all he said.

"All right," Nate replied. He left the center of the road for the left shoulder. He moved forward in a stoop. Men were firing machine guns in short bursts from beside the road. As he got closer still, he advanced only in short sprints from cover to cover. M-1A1 tanks farther down the road fired their 120-millimeter guns at extreme elevations. The flame from their tubes and the explosion on the crest of the ridge seemed simultaneous. Their targets were only a few hundred meters away.

Another battalion commander met Clark near the rear fender of a tank. Neither he nor the captains and majors of his staff saluted in such close proximity to the enemy. "What's the holdup?" Nate shouted over the roar of battle.

The closest main battle tank fired. Everyone flinched. Dust rose from the road all around its treads. Clark's ears rang loudly. The stupendous noise drew his nervous system taut liked after the slamming of a nearby door.

"We got clobbered by about a dozen machine guns dug in on the crest of that ridge straight ahead!" the colonel finally replied. "They held their fire till the tanks rounded that blind curve! Then they opened up at the bend in defilade—firing straight down this stretch of road! I've got a whole company pinned down about four hundred meters that way!" he said, pointing toward the south—toward the Tangyuan Valley.

Nate asked for and then looked through the man's binoculars. There was a line of evenly spaced dots on the hill ahead. Puffs of smoke came from some, but not all. The rocks around the Chinese fighting holes exploded in bursts both large and small. Down on the road ahead, there were men lying prone. It was impossible to tell the living from the dead. They all lay still and helpless. Dirt spat from the ground around them. Machine guns raked back and forth across the road.

Nate lowered the binoculars. "Well, what the hell are you *doing* about it?" he asked with mounting anger. He could understand someone disregarding Clark's order to advance. Someone unwilling to piss his men's lives away to hurry down a road not yet cleared. But those were *his* men that were pinned down. Those were *his* men in need of relief.

"We've called in an air strike, but there's been some kind of screwup. For some reason everything's been diverted."

Clark was boiling mad. He looked around. All of the other officers were majors and captains. Nate turned to see Reed—Lieutenant Colonel Reed—looking on. In the instant before opening his mouth to speak, Nate considered the possible consequences of his order. What his decision might mean for the son of the man to whom he owed his life. But the steady pounding by the Chinese heavy machine guns convinced him that now he had to call on every resource. Now he had to use the young colonel up. "Colonel Reed, you're now in command of this unit!" The battalion staff was stunned. "Call off that air strike, get up that hill, and *clear this goddamn road*!"

Reed stared back at him unblinking for a moment. In Clark's head there was a ticking clock. Despite the sadness he felt, he was still seething. His eyes were locked onto Reed's. If Reed had cast even a sidelong glance at the others, Clark swore to himself he would've found another commander. If he'd hesitated even a moment longer, Clark would've fired him and picked one of the slack-jawed majors. Not to punish Reed. Not to find a better commander from among the other officers. But to make the point to every soldier in the column—advance means advance.

"Yes, *sir*!" the new battalion commander shouted. His words were pure boot-camp zeal. But his eyes were dreary and lifeless.

By the time Clark's helicopter picked him up twenty minutes later, the road was clear and the column was moving. Reed had personally led a company of 110 men up the hill. They'd cleared the machine-gun nests with bullets and hand grenades. Clark's last glimpse of Reed had come from the Blackhawk's window. He stood silently among the dozen Americans whose lives he'd expended.

Clark watched the fighter-attack aircraft make their runs over Tangyuan Valley from the same window. He had a perfect view of the Marine F/A-18s. They dropped from the hazy sky one at a time, leveling out fifty feet above the trees. The jets' twin engines smudged the air over the forests. Their burning exhausts left a shimmering wake.

They disappeared one after another into the valley. They followed the road that wound its way to the south. Above the surrounding ridges drifted the haze of ground combat. To that was added billowing towers of black smoke. The mushroom clouds from thousand-pounders lost their shapes as they cooled above the rocky crests.

Nate grabbed the extra crewman's headset. It was alive with the copilot's tense warnings.

". . . gun radar. Sounds like a ZSU-24. Pro'bly up on a hill to the south."

"Call it in," the pilot instructed. "Get a mission on it."

"This is General Clark," Nate interrupted. "Can we put down somewhere in that valley?"

There was an information-laden moment of silence. "Well . . . uh, it's pretty tight in there, sir. The Chinese are bringin' SAMs and triple A right up to the front lines. Plus the small-arms fire is thick as molasses."

"But flights *are* going in, right?"

"Yessir. Medevacs are, yes, sir."

"Then let's do it." Clark hung up the headphones and turned to the special-forces captain. He and his eleven Green Berets sat on the metal deck, armed to the teeth. They had M-60 machine guns, Squad Automatic Weapons, and Dragon antitank missiles. Their M-16s had all the bells and whistles—M-279 grenade launchers, long sniper scopes, and shortened barrels with side-mounted flashlights.

The helicopter banked steeply and accelerated.

"We're going into the valley!" Clark informed the captain. Without being told, the men all swung into action. They had unloaded their weapons on boarding. They now worked their weapons' bolts. Twelve rifles and machine guns clacked in unison. Once they all were satisfied that the mechanisms were in order, they extracted black magazines and long belts of brass. All were reverently loaded into chambers by men wearing intense looks. They called out "Weapon safed!" and had them checked by their buddy.

Belatedly Clark remembered his own rifle. He hadn't taken the precautions of his security team. It was loaded with a round chambered but on "safe." All he needed was to flick the switch and fire.

They were low now. The Blackhawk's nose was pitched forward and its engine roared at full military power. Only the loudest shouts could be heard at any distance. Most of the talking among the Green Berets was done by hand. Pointing at men. A sentence spoken in gestures. A point, a point, a splitting of fingers. Two hands curled back-to-back in a swimming motion. A curt nod of acknowledgment. A thumbs-up in reply from the machine gunner. It was quick, efficient, and calm. A team in every sense of the word.

Clark felt a growing sense of selfishness at their mission. What could he possibly do to help the men in that valley? They had no slack left in them. They held no reserve upon which he could call. It was the height of arrogance to imagine they'd even give a shit about his visit. He recalled his days in Vietnam as a platoon leader. How much he hated seeing the battalion commander's helicopter. How he'd felt when men in clean uniforms climbed out.

Once he was trying to retake a hill. They were under murderous fire from an old French antiaircraft gun. The same man who'd ordered him off the hill—and then to take it back—stepped out of his Huey. His backslapping tour of frightened draftees pushed Clark right up to the edge. His helpful suggestions almost brought an end to the exhausted young lieutenant's military career. A rifle butt into the man's double chin was Nate's favorite fantasy. The metal baseplate of the M-16 to the bridge of the man's nose a close second. He gritted his teeth at the memory even now.

Nate was on the verge of countermanding his order to land when they eased into an LZ. He could see the rotors' downdraft flatten purple smoke into the rocky clearing. The door slid open twenty feet from the ground and noise and wind rushed in. The helicopter pitched and rolled until a thudding wheels down planted it on the earth. The Green Berets poured through the opening. By the time Clark got to the door, the special-forces captain was shouting at a stretcher bearer who was stooped under the gale of the rotors. The pilot left the engine revved high and remained strapped into his seat. The stretcher bearers were turned away, and the captain led Clark to the shelter of nearby rocks. Small-arms fire crackled a few hundred meters away. Acrid smoke hung low in the valley.

The small clearing on which Nate's helicopter sat was surrounded by wounded men, and more streamed in from both directions to be deposited in the swirling dirt. The less seriously injured helped the outnumbered medics with those clinging to life. They held IV bags in air, oxygen masks on the faces of men thrashing wildly about in pain, large compresses over massive chest wounds that were quickly saturated with crimson stains. Some of the walking wounded even lay on the ground giving blood through tubes that went straight into the arms of their comrades.

Nate had landed not in the front lines to rally the defenders, but in the rear, where the consequences of his decisions were made manifest. His decision to go to the valley, he decided, would do nothing more than distract the frantic efforts of brave men. Clark's chopper even prevented the landing of medevacs. "All right!" he shouted to the special-forces captain. "Nothing I can do here! Let's board that Blackhawk and get back to Khabarovsk!" They jogged back onto the LZ, which looked like a disaster area. Men were laid every which way—side to side, foot to head—in a jumbled and disorganized mass. Many lay propped on elbows watching Clark amid the dust and dirt kicked up by his chopper.

Nate crawled into the deck of the Blackhawk. He'd never felt like a coward in his entire life . . . until then. But he knew that he couldn't stay there. It wasn't his fear of reprimand from Dekker. It wasn't even his fear of capture. He had to leave because he could do only harm, not good. These men weren't in need of aggressive leadership. They were fighting with all their might for their lives. Giving the full measure of their courage just in surviving.

Clark waited alone in the door of the helicopter. He felt old and tired. His memories had faded and dimmed. But they came flooding back to him. Helicopters. The dead and the dying. Fucking senseless goddamn tragedy.

Outside the special-forces team shouted at the captain. The highly disciplined soldiers engaged in a heated debate with their leader, who then reluctantly came up to the door. "General Clark, are you goin' straight back to Khabarovsk?" The twelve men all faced Nate. Clark nodded. "Then, sir, my men wanna stay here!" Clark's thoughts just then were muddled. He opened his mouth to ask why, but he stopped himself. He looked over the captain's shoulder at the makeshift aid station. The growing lump in Clark's throat prevented him from replying. What special words of encouragement or thanks were due the men gathered at the door of the helicopter? Their only benefit would've been to Nate. "We'll take wounded back with us!" he finally replied. He sat back against the far wall as medics and Green Berets loaded the litters. He wallowed in the sudden realization that all his beliefs about command were illusions. What he did—what he said—made little difference. His army fought because its soldiers were the finest of men. Its backbone of field officers and veteran NCOs held it all together. His only contribution was to stick pins on a map in places like Birobidzhan airbase and Tangyuan Valley.

The terribly wounded soldiers were laid on the bare
metal floor because the stretchers were needed in the valley.
Most of the men were dying, that much Clark could quickly
tell. A lucky few who were lightly wounded came along to
give aid to the seriously injured. The helicopter was quickly
crowded with close to twenty moaning, crying men. Clark
kept retreating till he was jammed tight into the rear corner
of the cabin. Some of the men were barely conscious but
were propped in sitting positions along the walls to make
more room.

The door finally closed on the unending stream of
stretchers lined up just outside. The pilot lifted off almost
immediately as Clark watched a young medic take charge.
He wore a red cross on a white armband and a red bandage
on his face covering one eye.

"That guy's got blood in his IV tube!" he snapped at a
man whose head was rocked back in pain. The wounded
man roused himself and lifted the bag of clear fluids higher.
Gravity sent the precious red liquid back into his legless
patient. The medic tore open another pack of white bandages. "That guy's bleedin' bad!" he shouted at another of
his wounded assistants.

Clark rose and stepped gingerly across the bucking deck
in small gaps between the bodies. "Here!" he said, holding
out his hand for the fresh dressing. The medic looked up
in surprise. "Give me that!" Clark demanded. The medic
complied instinctively. "Where's the bleeder?" he asked.
The medic pointed to a prone man with a thigh wound.

That began Clark's modest effort at atonement. He followed the orders of a specialist third with a medic's armband. By the time the long flight was over, three of the
twenty were dead. And Clark was intimately familiar with
the rest. On the tarmac back at Khabarovsk, he raced alongside the gurneys, shouting reports to startled nurses. "He's
lost most of his foot and a lot of blood! We tried cutting
his boot off but it was too intermingled with some open
fractures!" He dashed over to another team with another
gurney. "No, no! Don't worry about the chest wound! It's

stable! He's got what looks like a bullet or some shrapnel at the base of his spine! I could feel it hard up against a vertebra so I left it alone! Turn him over carefully!''

He was so intent on saving his patients that he chased the wounded men to the ambulance doors. ''Stomach wound!'' he shouted to the nodding nurse. The doors to the green truck slammed closed. ''He needs antibiotics!'' Clark shouted, fogging the two small windows. The ambulance pulled away. Clark's BDUs were splattered in blood and stained in orange antiseptic cleanser.

The helicopter's engine had been cut. The exhausted crew slogged toward the hangar. All was quiet. The only people left were the three men who still lay on the tarmac. Nate sat on the hard concrete next to the three wool blankets and waited for Graves Registration.

SONGHUA RIVER, NORTH OF TANGYUAN
April 28, 0100 GMT (1100 Local)

''No fuckin' way!'' Patterson said to the man handing out ammo.

''Yes fuckin' way!'' the man replied as he handed Stempel two hundred-round belts.

They were all lying low on the side of the road. They were sheltered by a cut carved out of the hill. The company up ahead was engaged in a fearsome firefight. The Chinese they met now were all deeply entrenched. ''General fuckin' Clark *himself*?'' Patterson asked.

The ammo bearer duckwalked past Stempel, dragging the large canvas bag behind him. ''The driver of the deuce-and-a-half where I got this ammo saw Clark's chopper with his own eyes. It was sittin' right on the shoulder of the road.''

''Wait-wait-wait!'' McAndrews jumped in. ''So Clark goes up to the head of the column and does *what* did you say?'' From the high pitch of his voice you could hear the extreme disbelief.

''He orders this battalion commander to take a hill, and

the son of a bitch says no right to Clark's face!''

''*No* wa-a-ay!'' came from all corners.

''It's the God's honest truth!'' the man insisted. The doubters wavered.

''So you're sayin' Clark *shot* the guy?'' Patterson challenged. The ammo bearer nodded. ''Bullshit!'' came from several men at once. Chavez kicked at the bastard for lying. But the guy stuck by his story. ''You mean he just up and wasted a *colonel*?'' an incredulous Patterson persisted.

''The guy's a fuckin' *general*!'' the ammo bearer from headquarters company pointed out. ''A colonel's like . . . like *whale* shit to him, man!''

''Where?'' McAndrews probed. ''Where'd he shoot him?''

''Right in the fuckin' forehead.'' The ammo bearer pointed with his finger just below the brim of his helmet.

''*No,* dipshit! I mean, like, did he just haul off and whack the guy right there on the *road*?''

''How the hell should *I* know?''

''So you know all the *rest* of that shit, but you don't know *that*?''

''Look!'' the guy shot back as he strapped his sack over his shoulder. ''You got any better explanation for why we been double-timin' down this road for the last few hours? Why they decided to take the high ground with infantry instead of turnin' those hills into holes with F-16s?''

With that parting remark he was gone, leaving Harold's squad to contemplate the news.

''You know,'' McAndrews said, ''we *have* been haulin' ass down this road. And how many times have we humped up those hills just to wax five or ten Chinks? Six? Seven times?''

Their squad leader returned from a platoon meeting. He skidded to a stop in the dirt as he stayed low. ''All right, let's *go*!'' he said, out of breath. ''Bravo Comp'ny's pinned down. We're gonna clean up that hill right there,'' he said, pointing over the embankment behind which they lay. ''The attack'll step off from the crest next to that burned out hut.

As soon as we breast the ridge, we'll start drawing fire.''

"What the hell is Bravo Company's *problem*?" Patterson bitched. "*Shit!* Cain't they take one miserable fuckin' hill without our *help*?"

"Cut the shit, Patterson!" the squad leader snapped. "Drop your packs on the road. Take your weapons, ammo, and sleeping bag. Everybody'll get an eighty-one-millimeter mortar round to hump up to the line of departure. We'll file past the mortar, hand over the rounds one at a time, and keep on goin'."

Behind him appeared their ill-tempered platoon sergeant. A thick bandage wrapped his hand, which had been holed clean through his palm. "*Move it!*" he boomed in a no-nonsense voice. The entire squad scrambled to their feet. No one really believed that anyone had been executed—especially a colonel by the commanding general. But one thing was clear in the voices of the sergeants and lieutenants. There'd be no breaks. No fucking off. No rest for weary legs or aching backs. No time to treat the small wounds from ricochets or shrapnel, falls or blisters. Harold couldn't count the number of times someone had shouted "move" or "go" in some combination with other orders. And it was always in an irritated tone that expected no reply.

Tangyuan Valley, Northern China
April 28, 0800 GMT (1800 Local)

Kate and Woody first thought their decision was the right one. They'd climbed to the very top of the hills. All the fighting seemed far away. There was fire and roaring noise from below, but at their height they were detached observers. Kate had even shot a report of the battle's final chapter with the smoky valley as a dramatic backdrop.

But then came an artillery barrage from massed Chinese guns. They'd opened fire and blanketed the hills all around and the valley floor beneath. Woody and Kate were forced to make yet another life-or-death decision. To lie low and hope to ride out the storm of high explosives. Or to take their chances and flee the tall hill on which they'd found refuge. And with the barrage still pounding the north slope there was only one way down their hill. It led toward the south and the onrushing Chinese.

Again they made the right call. They climbed down the hill amid the random bursts of artillery without so much as a scratch. But as they caught their breath in a trough between two crests, the bombers began to sweep in. These were not Chinese aircraft, of course, but American F-16s. Strangely enough, however, they pounded the same hill as the Chinese. The same hill on which Kate and Woody had sought refuge.

The nearest bombs fell only a few hundred meters away. Kate and Woody flattened themselves on the ground as the hill above burst into boiling flame. The bombs had struck right where they'd just taped the report. The next pass rained onto the south slope they'd just descended. There was no debate this time. As soon as the bomber passed, they both rose and labored up the next hill farther to the south. They saw the next jet bank and begin its final approach. They took cover before the bombs rained down. The explosions' concussions were more stunning than before. When they looked up, they saw the bombs had fallen in the trough where they'd only recently rested. The air controllers were rolling the fire to the south. Kate and Woody were where they shouldn't be—in an American free-fire zone.

They climbed the hill with furiously pumping knees, throwing themselves to the ground as bombs fell ever closer. Thin trees were toppled from the force of the blasts alone. Their dry needles crackled in flame from the fiery bursts. When Woody pulled Kate up to her feet she almost fainted. Her head was swimming from the thundering blasts so near at hand. Kate cursed as Woody pushed and pulled her to the top of the hill.

Streaking toward them at eye level was an F-16 heavily laden with bombs. They cowered in the rocks as the jet screamed over the ridge. Kate's throat was pinched tight with fear and she covered her ears. The bare stone crevice in which she lay thudded against her back repeatedly. The world rocked on its axis with each stunning blast. Dust rose up. Clouds of smoke filled the air. Dirt rained down. Kate gagged and gasped for breath. Her head swam and temples pounded and ears rang.

Again Woody tugged at her arms. "*No-o-o!*" she screamed. It was no use. They were losing the race with the curtain of fire. Kate lay on her back, waiting for the end. She stared up at the blue sky visible in gaps through the passing black clouds. She saw crisscrossing contrails and tried to decide which one would kill them.

Woody yanked at her arm so hard it almost pulled her shoulder out of joint. She staggered to her feet with tears in her eyes. He led her down the south face in what became almost a sprint. Her head was spinning and she stumbled and slipped on the rocks. Woody's steadying grip kept her upright—her feet flying.

The next bomber came too fast for them to react. The air thumped her chest, rattled her insides, popped her ears painfully, and shook the earth on which she planted each step. Flames shot skyward all around. But miraculously they kept on their feet until they collapsed in exhaustion at the bottom. To the sound of the bombs, Kate slowly realized, was now added the popping gunfire of a nearby firefight. There was no going on, now.

They were ringed in fire with no way out. No hope of survival. Kate buried her face in her knees. Her tears flowed as she sobbed.

"*Now,* Kate! If you wanna live, come with me *now!*"

She had no reserves of energy, physical or emotional. But for Woody's sake she allowed him to drag her up another hill. They passed rocks draped in dead Chinese. Her lungs burned. Her head swam. Sweat poured out of her hair and down her forehead. The sound of fighting had grown louder than the bombs. Finally, they stopped running. Woody climbed up onto a flat rock and said, "Come here and look!'' When he insisted, she crawled up the smooth granite face of the boulder. Twice she had to grab and hold the rock for dear life. Twice her equilibrium took an unexpected spin. Not from new bombs, but from the after-effects of earlier explosions. When she reached Woody's side, she looked out across a relatively flat and rocky ridgeline. The crest rose gently toward the summit of their hill's higher twin. There, interspersed among the rocks of the neighboring hilltop, were the flaming muzzles of a battle. Slowly climbing the hill under withering fire looked to be the entire Chinese Army.

All of a sudden the wooded valley paralleling their own erupted in rolling flame. The shock waves from a hundred bombs formed rings of white mist—expanding outward from each of the hundred bursts at supersonic speed. The storm of fire raced down the valley wall on the side opposite theirs. ''B-52s,'' Woody said with an awestricken voice.

The man-made earthquake began again with the arrival of another bomber. When it was over, Kate's nerves lay in tatters. She stared at the rising flames and flattened woods. She raised her eyes to the sky and saw the white contrails high above. There were three planes following one after another. The tortured valley erupted in another continuous gush of flame a mile long. It was over in a matter of seconds as the final bomber of the three-plane cell completed the total devastation of their bomb box. Kate screamed at the top of her lungs. She grabbed her hair and shook her head and clenched her teeth. Fire and smoke drifted over their hill and blotted out the sun. The day grew dark and her stinging eyes watered and teared.

Woody picked her up in his arms and ran. He jostled and shook her with each laboring step. When he put her down, she realized she'd drifted off. She looked up at a soldier in an American army helmet. His rifle was cradled against his shoulder. His teeth were parted in a toothy smile in the midst of a thick, graying beard. His hair was bound in a long ponytail.

Another soldier appeared over Kate—this one with short hair and a stubble-covered face. She looked back at the first man and realized it was Woody.

Kate sat up too quickly and almost vomited. She had to lie back down.

"Take it easy, ma'am," came the gravel voice of the real soldier.

"Where are we?" she asked.

Woody answered. "We've gone from being lost to being surrounded. I'd say that's an improvement." He raised a Chinese assault rifle and inspected it closely. "Oh, and they're all wounded," he added. "Every last soldier up here."

SONGHUA VALLEY, NORTH OF TANGYUAN
April 28, 1000 GMT (2000 Local)

Harold Stempel stumbled along the steep slope more asleep than awake. Battles raged on the other side of a finger ridge, near the road below, and in the distance in every direction, but they mattered little to him. His world was small. His concerns narrow. His depth of thinking and feeling shallow. His lungs burned from the cold air that he sucked through chapped lips. Just moving his legs without tumbling down the hill took all the effort he could muster. His legs quivered and shook with every step. His aching knees threatened to buckle each time he called upon them for support. The soles of his feet were a mass of blisters.

When they took to ground under fire, the real pain set in. His joints stiffened. His muscles tightened. He had to stretch and massage them constantly to ward off imminent cramps. He was so exhausted that despite facing the flaming muzzles of Chinese weapons his movements slowed to a crawl. He'd drop to his knees and then to his belly like an old man. He'd unfasten his pack and drag it to the front in slow motion. Bullets whizzed by but he didn't even flinch. With lethargic motions he'd line up the 60 on the bright orange flames and lay down a base of fire while riflemen with grenades maneuvered close. Harold's gun kept their heads low, and the grenades snuffed them out like vermin. One by one the Chinese muzzles would fall dark.

Harold would then doze until he heard "All clear!" Then he'd sleep some more until the squad leader kicked him. The hoarse man could barely croak out a word, so he just shoved and kicked and hissed through teeth bared in unrelenting anger. With the help of squadmates Harold would climb to his feet and reshoulder the 60. Then more foot-slogging across the sloping landscape to the next Chinese lines, all the while in the total darkness of heavy forests. The farther they went the stiffer the resistance, the more frequent the ambushes, the more numerous the defenders. They had given up debating how fucked their duty was. Whether they'd rather hump their asses through the hills rolling up flanks, or march down the nice flat road into the teeth of the enemy guns. After nine hours of unrelenting combat, their minds were a total blank. Their glassy eyes were sunk deep into their sockets. They'd given up caring about anything or anyone.

Harold walked straight into a tree. He was stunned as his helmet slammed down into his nose, but it woke him up. He jogged a few steps to catch up with the skirmish line, and that small effort sapped almost all the reserves he had left. He began to shake all over as if palsied. The quaking came not from muscular fatigue, but from complete, full-body exhaustion. "I can't go any further," he mumbled, hoping someone would hear. But the shadowy figures on either side were insensate. Stumbling toward enemy guns like zombies. They'd been blundering forward for hours with no idea what lay ahead. They just walked straight *into* the shit like human fodder! Worst of all, however, was how quickly Harold's anger faded. How resigned he'd become to death. How little he cared so long as the marching ended soon—one way or the other.

There was a challenge from up ahead shouted in Chinese. Harold sank to his knees and flopped onto his belly. Searing pain shot through his hip as Chinese and American guns opened fire. He'd either been shot, or he'd landed on his canteen. Crushed under the weight of his heavy pack, he sighted down the gun and killed. The gun rocked until the last round on the belt flicked through the chamber.

Harold cursed and reached for a new belt. He wasn't angry that he had to reload, or that a 110-pound pack crushed him, or that bullets whizzed past his face, or that grenades went off in bunches all around. Instead, Harold cursed the merciless orders to advance and the bastards who gave them. Once, when their tired legs had unintentionally angled their march downhill toward the road they were supposed to be screening, some son-of-a-bitch first sergeant had marched up to them and shouted, "You're all yellow, unfit cowards!" *Fucker!* Harold thought as he cursed his squad leader for the firm kicks with his boot, his platoon sergeant for all the shouts of "*Up!*", the pussy who'd commanded the platoon for his pathetic apologies before he was killed in an ambush. Harold cursed everyone right up to General Clark, whom he would've shot had he seen the fucker execute anybody.

He slapped the breech cover closed, shoved the bolt forward, and lowered his cheek to the stock. The big gun was so hot he could feel it on his face. He aimed at the sparkling muzzles and fired. It was like blowing out trick candles at a birthday party. You'd puff real hard with your 60, and the flickering lights disappeared. But sometimes, when you moved on to a new target, the muzzle would flash again. It pissed Harold off so much he'd swing the gun back and fire a long burst of ten or fifteen rounds. They almost always fell permanently dark.

The moment the "Cease fire!" came, Harold laid his head down, closed his eyes, and felt a deep sleep coming. The narcotic need seized him, and he drifted off in seconds. "Let's go!" came the command Harold hated most. He set his teeth and clenched his fist, ready to punch if the bastard kicked him again. But the squad leader moved on down the hill and kicked the next guy instead. Grunting and growling to shut out the pain, Harold rose to his feet with the pack

on his back. The one thing he couldn't do by himself, however, was lift the heavy weapon from the ground. He looked
around at the milling men for help.

"What's the matter?" asked a chipper man Harold didn't
recognize.

"I can't lift the *f-f-fuckin'* gun!" Stempel screeched, then
wiped the string of spittle from his chin. The guy picked it
up and helped sling it over his shoulder. Even in the darkness Harold could see the guy's smiling face. "What's *your*
fuckin' problem?" Harold lashed out.

"Me? I don't have any problems, man? Not a *problem*
in the world!" The guy was as happy as he could be. He
slapped Harold's pack and then trotted off toward the Chinese.

"Hey!" Harold called out, thinking the guy had gotten
turned around in the dark. He ignored Harold's call and
rushed into the unknown that lay beyond their skirmish line.
Other men appeared out of the same dark woods. One approached Harold, grinning with eyes bright with tears. He
wrapped his arms around Harold's neck and hugged him.
It was then Harold realized what had happened. Not just
the fact they had finally reached the valley, but what they
had been fighting for all along. The sobbing man squeezed
Harold's neck tight. "I never thought I'd make it," he kept
saying through the tears. "I never thought I'd make it."

More smelly, grimy men crowded Harold. Some jostled
him good-naturedly. Others shook hands or high-fived.
"Let's *go*, Charlie Compan-y-y-y!" came the booming
voice of the company's first sergeant.

For a moment Harold wondered, *Go where?* But they
formed up and marched through slopes filled with dead
Chinese, passing ecstatic defenders immobilized in fighting
holes by their wounds. Every step they took, the sound of
the fighting grew louder. The trees overhead were clipped
repeatedly by streaking bullets. Everywhere lay the signs
of heavy fighting. Bloody bandages, hurriedly opened
crates, smoking craters. They were headed right from the
march into heavy battle. Harold wasn't sleepy now. He

could hardly feel his aching muscles. Like the cavalry they'd made it in time, but at the end of the road lay still more Chinese. They dropped their packs and moved forward with only their weapons. The storm of bullets grew thick. When they reached the forward-most defensive line, they filled the gaps and opened fire. The massed weapons of the defenders and the reinforcements slaughtered the attacking Chinese. Even as the killing continued, Harold's neighbor crawled over from his hole. He shouted something that was drowned out by Harold's machine gun. "*What?*" Harold asked the man.

"Who the hell *are* you?" the guy repeated.

"The 25th!"

"*Who?*"

"*The 25th Light Infantry Division!*" Harold shouted, then fired a long burst at the fleeing figures—chopping them down like dry weeds. The man next to Harold was lying with his face in the crook of his elbow. "Hey!" Harold shouted. "You hit?" He began to pat the man down for a wound, but he raised his head and Harold saw he was crying like a baby.

"Everybody *u-u-up!*" came the command. Harold rose, and they attacked—massacring the fleeing Chinese army.

WHITE HOUSE RESIDENTIAL QUARTERS
April 28, 1100 GMT (0600 Local)

Gordon wasn't really asleep. He was lying still in bed next to Elaine. He'd given up on any hope of drifting off. Pull out? Stay and keep the peace? He had to make a decision. The army had done its job. The nation had rallied around it. *All is well,* he thought. *All is well.*

But what if Kartsev was right? What if China collapsed into anarchy? Would the world build a wall around the country? Would they quarantine the violent ideology like a plague-ridden city in the Middle Ages? Confine the healthy with the sick in a desperate effort to stop the spread of the disease? Consign a quarter of the world's population to funeral pyres and roving bands of cannibals?

Gordon shook his head at the nonsense. Elaine stirred but drifted back off. *What the hell did Kartsev know, anyway?* Gordon thought. But his attempt at easing his mind with the question had exactly the opposite effect. Kartsev clearly knew something others didn't. Something about man's primitive nature.

In the dark room Gordon's thoughts had no anchor. They were carried by the current toward nightmarish visions. *What if anarchy spreads outward from China?* India, Indochina, the Pacific Rim. Half the world's population could be engulfed in madness. Charismatic psychopaths leading followers to violence like warlords with hypnotic power. Human misery on an apocalyptic scale. What would he do? What could he do?

Someone knocked lightly on the door. Gordon realized he must have fallen asleep. The dreams vanished. His mind cleared. He swung his feet to the floor. The motion was a little too rapid. It brought pain from the sites of his old wounds. The doctor had said the aches would always be with him. And that was good, Gordon thought as he wrapped his robe around himself. He'd just spent hours alone with his guilt. The emotional burden of sending thousands of men to their deaths. Of ordering armies to kill hundreds of thousands. He'd spent hours of doubting, questioning, and rationalizing. Praying, chastising himself, crying. In the end all that was left were cleansing pains. The pains of absolution. And in the clarity of waking he made his decision. It was really the only thing he could do. And it *was* the right decision! That was all that really mattered. The only measure of himself that counted.

Gordon opened the bedroom door. "You've got a call from General Clark, sir," an aide said. He led Gordon down the hall to a phone. The White House military officer waited there with a smile, which tipped Gordon off. He could already feel the excitement of victory as he raised the receiver to his ear. "General Clark?" he said.

"Mr. President!" Clark said from a noisy room. "I've got wonderful news!"

Clark went on, his voice ecstatic. Gordon didn't follow all the details. He got what he needed from the man's tone. He took a breath so deep it felt like the first time since the war he'd filled his lungs. *It's the right thing to do,* he told himself. He repeated it over and over.

26

At first André hadn't heard what number six said. Then he hadn't believed it. Hours had passed before he first saw the two civilians. A long-haired freak and a beautiful woman roamed about the killing fields below. They were gathering Chinese rifles and ammunition belts, strapping them over their shoulders.

He stared intently at the petite woman as she returned with half a dozen Type 56-2 7.62-millimeter rifles. The long-haired guy yelled and had her put the rifles down. He flicked the safeties on one by one. The woman had been carrying the rifles just as they'd been dropped when their owners died. He recognized the two TV people.

André decided the strange coincidence made sense. She was a war correspondent. He'd volunteered for airmobile. They'd both been sent into the deepest shit of the war. But what *was* truly remarkable, he thought, was that they'd both lived through the disaster. The great train wreck on a global scale. The collision had ground up bodies by the thousands. It had an appetite for healthy men and women. It took the youthful, chewed them up, and spat them out. Of all the countless bullets, he thought, how had *none* maimed or killed *him*? Some men like Hansen died in the first minutes of a fight. Others like André made it through more or less intact. And he *had* made it, he was near certain. The Chinese hadn't come back in any strength for a while.

A few minutes after the reporters returned, the long-haired guy climbed down onto the ledge beside André. *"There* you are!" he said. "Jeez! They *said* you were over here, but I couldn't find yer ass." He handed André a Type 56-2. "Magazine's full, and here's two others. If you run out, there's plenty more." André waited, but the guy still didn't recognize him. "Well . . . nice talkin' to ya. I gotta go."

When he turned to leave, André said, "Better check number six."

"Who?" the cameraman asked.

André pointed. "The guy right over that rock."

The man hesitated, then said, "Oh. He's dead, man. He was lyin' curled in a ball—really peaceful. I thought he was just sleepin' but . . . There was a lotta blood." André just stared back at him. After an awkward silence, he moved on.

André had never felt so alone. He'd never laid eyes on number six, but the man had kept him company through the most important days of his life. He had been André's only constant contact with another human being. But now he was alone again. Just like always.

Tangyuan Valley, Northern China
April 28, 2100 GMT (0700 Local)

"Stempel!" the platoon sergeant shouted.

It took all the energy Harold could muster just to lift his head from his pack. They were rounding everyone up. The soldiers began to collect their gear in silence. Nobody bitched or moaned in front of the platoon sergeant, who talked for a moment to their squad leader. The buck sergeant turned to his squad and said, "Don't need to bring

your packs. McAndrews, you stay here and guard 'em.''
McAndrews lay back down with a smile on his face.
"*Guard* 'em, *McAndrews*!" the sarge yelled, his abused
vocal cords barely eking out a sound.

"He'll be asleep in three minutes," Patterson said.

"Two!" someone else snapped, sounding angry.

"*Shut* up and listen!" the sergeant screeched. "We're
gonna go up that hill with First Squad," he said, pointing,
"and help some guys at the top get down."

"*What?*" Patterson squawked. "*No!* Now it's *this* kinda
shit that *pisses* me off! It ain't right! We been bustin' our
asses! Marchin' and fightin'! Lost Chavez last night! Now
they want us to go up that tall motherfuckin' hill and help
some lazy fuckin' assholes get *down*?"

"They're *wounded*," the squad leader said. "We're
evacuating 'em, fuckhead!"

Patterson wasn't convinced. "Well. . . . it's *down*hill for
them. We take care of *our* wounded. Let 'em evacuate their
own!"

"They're *all* wounded! They came and got 'em out of
an aid station! Told 'em to hang on to that hill!"

"*That* hill?" Patterson asked. He looked around to get
his bearings. "But we just *took* this stretch last night."

"They got left behind," the sarge said as Harold drifted
off to sleep. "Been cut off for a long time." Instead of
yelling, the squad leader laughed as if at an hilarious joke.
Harold opened his eyes and looked at the man. "Ain't that
the fuckin' army! They fuckin' *ran* off under cover of some
wounded guys!" He gasped for air amid cackles of laughter. He'd cracked. "Ain't that just the *fuckin'* way, man!
God-*damn*! The army *fuckin'* way of doin' every *fuckin'*
thing the most *fucked* up way you can fuckin' *do i-i-it*!"

"Hey, Sarge . . ." Patterson began.

"Now, we're *goin'* up that fuckin' hill! We're gonna *get*
them off it! And I don't wanna hear another *fuckin'* thing
outta *anybody*! Now *move it*!"

Harold jumped to his feet with the others. The two
squads headed up the steep hill in single file. The base and

lower slopes looked like a moonscape. There were blackened holes. Shattered trees. Severed parts of human bodies thankfully charred beyond recognition.

"Jesus *Christ!*" Patterson said from just ahead of Harold. The dozen men skirted the edge of a half-buried boulder. Before them lay an open slope covered with Chinese dead. It looked as if a plow had tilled a cemetery lawn and disinterred the graves of hundreds. They wove their way in silence past bodies in various states of decay. Some lay twisted into awkward shapes. Others died on their backs as if resting in bed. Some lay in rows—sheltered behind rocks where the death appeared organized. Others died in the open with arms and legs akimbo.

Stempel looked up and tried to imagine attacking that high ground. The only approaches were wholly exposed to fire. And the summit above was all bare granite rock. It was filled with crevices, hollows, and notches. All would've blazed with staccato bursts at point-blank range.

No one said a word till they found the first of the wounded. "Got one over here!" came a call. "Another one!" called a man from the other side.

They brought them all up to the flat hilltop. The only guy that Harold found was dead. A white guy lying in a wide pool of dry blood. There must've been three hundred empty cartridges on the ledge. Some were lined up in neat rows of twenty-four. Hours of the day—days of the week—day after day. *Unbelievable*, Harold thought in amazement.

"Need some help here!" Harold shouted. He and another man hauled the dead guy onto the bald, breezy summit. They put him in a line of twelve other corpses. They then waited while the medics treated the wounded. A nurse and a bearded man with a television Minicam helped out. Nobody said much of anything as they waited. The stench from the killing ground below was overpowering.

"Stem*pel*?" Harold heard. He looked around. None of his squadmates had said a word. "*Stemp!*"

Harold turned to see one of the wounded, who was propped up onto his elbow and staring. Harold rose and walked over to the man. The recognition was slow in coming. The guy struggled to his feet and waited.

"André?" Harold tentatively said.

They stood face-to-face not knowing what to do. André laughed. Stempel threw his arms around his neck. Tears instantly flooded Harold's eyes. They hugged each other tight. The only sound was the whirring of the Minicam held by the long-haired cameraman.

UNRUSFOR HEADQUARTERS, KHABAROVSK
April 29, 1200 GMT (2200 Local)

Outside Nate Clark's office, the mood was exultant. The French opened champagne and toasted the victory. The British solemnly raised their glasses to the fallen. After a respectful silence, there was a gush of laughter when the German commander shouted, "To the field artillery!" and everyone drank. But it was a different story entirely in Clark's office. Lieutenant Colonel Reed had been summoned and sat on the opposite side of Nate's desk.

Nate struggled to put into words the things that he'd kept bottled up inside for too long. Even thinking them sent his mood spiraling downward. The sinking sensation he felt in his chest was almost physical. "Chuck," he said to his young aide, "no one should ever be asked to command troops in war. The toll it takes on the soul is just too great. The memories of the things you wish you'd done differently grow more and more awful, not less. You forget how exhausted you were. How confused things get in the fog of battle. How limited your options are when your back is pressed to the wall. In my mind almost every night I still see the faces of men who died in the platoon I commanded thirty years ago in Vietnam. And the burden of those memories is cumulative. Sometimes, it just reaches the point where it's too heavy to bear. If that happens, you can no longer be an effective military officer. You've got to get out. Heal your wounds. Rest your psyche."

Reed stared back blankly. Nate raised and reread the

short letter. "I hereby tender my resignation from active service with the United States Army. I will finish my tour, complete my duties, and provide for an orderly transition, but I wish to remove my name from consideration for any promotion in next year's cycle. My decision is absolutely final." Nate took a deep breath and handed the letter to Lieutenant Colonel Reed. "I'd like to take this opportunity, Chuck, to tell you that you're the best staff officer I've ever had. And you're one of the best tactical commanders I've ever seen."

Reed opened his mouth, but couldn't speak. What at first looked to be a grimace became an oddly misshapen and sickly smile. He looked away, set his jaw, and clenched his teeth. When he finally spoke, his voice cracked and quavered. "It has been the greatest honor and privilege of my entire life to have served under your command, General Clark. I know you'll want to stop me for saying this, but no soldier did more to win this war than you did. It was your strength, your leadership, that held this command together during its darkest hours. I know it's hush-hush, but I've heard you're going to get your fourth star and succeed Dekker as chief of staff. I honestly believe that your promotion to the joint chiefs couldn't be more deserved."

Nate sighed. He was at a loss for words. Nate felt a kinship with Reed that inspired candor. But he couldn't bring himself to describe the cowardly way in which *he* had coped with the psychological load. The burden that Reed couldn't seem to bear. The terrible, invisible scars left on the young officer by repeatedly ordering men to their death. Nate was simply too embarrassed of the bandage that he still applied to ease his own emotional wounds.

He couldn't tell Reed that his memories of the men who'd died were indistinguishable from his memories of the survivors. That in his mind those men were still alive. Healthy twenty-year-olds in the prime of their youth. Simple denial was all it was. At night—when his mind still raced with a million things left to do—he had silent conversations with his old comrades. The imagined talks had

a calming effect. It was a mental trick he used to help
himself fall asleep. To ease the rising tide of guilt he felt
when his mind roamed. Nate exchanged jokes with them.
Small talk. Complaints about army life. Those men, living
and dead, were so familiar to him that they seemed like old
friends. But Nate was too ashamed to tell Reed any of that.
For Clark's closest friend was a young second lieutenant
named Chuck Reed, Sr.

Nate got up and walked around his desk. Reed rose and
the two men shook hands. Nate then grabbed Reed's shoulders and hugged him as he would his own son. Reed shed
tears he'd have to learn to live with for the rest of his
natural life.

VLADIVOSTOK, RUSSIA
April 30, 1300 GMT (2300 Local)

Kate zipped up her ski jacket as she waited at the door of
the smoky coffeehouse. Woody still sat at the table filled
with Dutch journalists. He was taking one last hit off their
brass ''traveling'' bong. Chilled vodka gurgled in the tube.
''Woody-*y-y-y*!'' she called out. ''Come on!''

That began his ridiculous good-byes. There were soul
shakes that led to hugs. They stood holding each other
locked in tight embrace. She could've sworn they would
break out crying after having bonded so completely around
the bong. He parted with his fingers making a peace sign.
The aging Dutch freaks responded in kind.

When Woody joined Kate at the door, she said, ''What
a *truly* moving moment.''

Woody was stoned out of his mind. ''Did you see the
size of that *hash* rock?'' he asked in a tone of awe.

''Is this like a *religion* to you? Like those Indian tribes
who eat those . . . What do they eat?''

She opened the door.

''Peyote!'' Woody grinned and shouted.

Kate was grabbed roughly by two men. They pulled her
out and shoved Woody back inside. One man pinned the

door closed. Kate screamed into the empty street. They pushed her into a van and slammed the door behind her. She sat in complete darkness as the van rocked from side to side through the abandoned city.

NEAR RED SQUARE, MOSCOW, RUSSIA
April 30, 1600 GMT (1800 Local)

Pyotr Andreev carried the rolled carpet through the *perekhod*. He used the dark, underground pedestrian tunnel even though the city boulevard above was barren of traffic. The air reeked of urine and of the unwashed men who lined the walls. It looked like the permanent residence of people driven underground by the terrors of the streets.

Pyotr suddenly saw two men framed in the bright sunlight from the stairs toward which he headed. They strolled slowly, walking side by side, approaching him from the Red Square exit. They both wore jack boots, and one swung a baton. Against the backlighting, he saw only their shapes . . . and the two machine pistols they carried. The guns dangled from straps hung over their shoulders.

Andreev had to make a choice. To lie down in the filth with the dregs of society? Or stroll calmly past the two men? A man coughed, and Pyotr stole a quick glance at him. His weathered face and matted beard resolved his conflict. Pyotr knew he would stand out among such men.

He shifted his grip on the large roll. In the process, his right hand moved nearer his Ingram. He could hand over the heavy load to the Black Shirts. As they reacted in surprise at its weight, he'd extract the MAC-10, flick the safety, and kill them both.

And his mission would be aborted one day short of completion.

A flashlight shone straight into his eyes. Andreev halted and rested the carpet on its end. When the beam ran down the roll, his eyes began to adjust to the darkness. One of the men wore the black garb of the Anarchists. The other wore a garrison cap with a shiny brim—a policeman. The

incredible rise in street violence had forced a police recall.
Pairs like this one were now a common sight in Moscow.
But the Black Shirt was there to keep an eye on the cop.
He could act with impunity while the cop walked a fine
line.

"What's that?" the Black Shirt asked. Pyotr couldn't see
the man's face, but he imagined the sneer that he heard in
his tone.

"A rug," Pyotr answered.

"Where are you headed with it?" the other man, the
policeman, asked.

"To GUM, to trade it for food."

The Black Shirt snorted. "Open it up," he commanded
matter-of-factly.

"But it'll get grimy on the wet floor," Pyotr argued, his
hand inching closer to his Ingram.

The slapping of the Black Shirt's sling against his gun
preceded the sight of a small round muzzle in front of
Pyotr's right eye. The clicking sound of the safety was distinct. Cold metal pressed hard against his cheekbone. Pyotr
stoically kept every motion to a bare minimum. "I won't
tell you twice," the Black Shirt said.

The policeman's flashlight flicked on. "Cover me while
I check it," he said. The Black Shirt stepped back, holding
the machine pistol one-handed and aimed straight at Pyotr's
face.

Pyotr's heart began to race. It couldn't have been a more
impossible situation. The officer raised the flashlight and
peered inside the roll. But Pyotr's entire focus was on the
Black Shirt with the gun. He didn't dare look at the man,
but he saw there was no sway in the large pistol. The man
appeared sober. At three meters, he couldn't possibly miss.

The policeman rooted around inside the roll. Pyotr
worked on a plan. He could grab the officer as a shield and
try to draw the Ingram. But the Black Shirt cared no more
for the cop than for Pyotr. He'd gun them both down without a moment's hesitation. Pyotr had no hope of escape
from that gloomy tunnel. At best his dying act would be to

kill the Black Shirt. It was hardly the great blow for which he was prepared to sacrifice everything. To give up his wonderful new life with Olga and the girls. To never again feel their smooth faces rubbing against his morning beard. To have heard their last squeals of delight at simple things like fresh snow and surprise sweets.

"Turn it over," the cop ordered.

This is it, Pyotr thought in a daze. He tried not to let his eyes water. Maybe if he grabbed the policeman's pistol instead of drawing his own . . . He slowly rotated the rolled carpet in air, raising the open end to the prying man's gaze.

The flashlight clicked on. All Pyotr could see was the top of the hat. Fragments of half-formed plans ricocheted through his mind. His thoughts remained in pieces, however, because of the shattering effect of one thought. He would never see his family again.

The police officer's movements fell still. Pyotr's every sense was focused and intense. From the depth of the cop's probing hand—from the steady beam of his flashlight— Pyotr knew that the man stared right at the black muzzle of the enormous .50-caliber sniper rifle.

"You see anything?" the Black Shirt asked.

The brim of the cop's hat rose slowly. Pyotr knew the time was *now*—the time was *now*! But something made him hesitate. From under the polished black brim there appeared two close-set eyes. They were gray—very Russian— and fixed on Pyotr's.

"Well?" the Black Shirt demanded impatiently.

The flashlight clicked off and the *perekhod* fell dark.

"He's clean," the cop replied. With his eyes still fixed on Pyotr he said, "Better hurry. We're closing GUM early. The big May Day rally is tomorrow morning, you know."

Pyotr nodded, hoisted the heavy rug, and headed toward the gray light of Red Square.

WHITE HOUSE EAST WING, WASHINGTON
April 30, 1300 GMT (0800 Local)

Elaine took Gordon by the elbow. She'd been up and dressed by four. She led him into their private dining room and closed the door. There were heaping mounds of hot food and no people. Gordon smiled, and Elaine smiled back. They sat beside each other, not across the table. She stayed close. They hugged and kissed and laughed. The companionship and closeness was comforting. Elaine knew he was sick with worry.

She didn't bring it up, he did. "You know, Elaine . . ." was all he said. No one else would have understood, but she did. After twenty years of marriage he need only begin a sentence. Sometimes, he only opened his mouth and the words came out of hers.

"What did the State Department say?" she challenged.

He frowned. "Pull our troops out."

"And Defense?" The same, he replied. "And CIA? The UN ambassador? Your national security advisor? Those disgusting, loudmouthed *sycophants* from Congress?" He screwed up his face. "All your *allies* say pull out, Gordon . . . and so do I."

He closed his eyes, sighed, and sank back in his chair. He was relaxed. His guard was down. "This job is too big for one man. Just look at this decision. I mean, what if I do the thing *everybody* recommends, but it turns out wrong? *Sure* nobody wants to keep an army in Siberia. It's not like *I* do! And nobody even *considers* occupying *China* like Kartsev—" Gordon stopped himself short.

"Is *that* what it is? That letter from *Kartsev*?" Gordon felt a twinge of nerves on mention out loud of his innermost fear. "Honey, that man is good at killing defenseless people, that's it! What special insight do you think he has? Do you think he can predict the future? That *anarchy* will spread to China when the Russians *themselves* aren't even Anarchists. His whole system of power is failing completely, Gordon. It's rotting from the top down, and it's about to collapse."

"Isn't that the whole *idea* of anarchy?" Gordon shot back. "Maybe it's part of Kartsev's plan. The state withers away and then . . . nothing. Or something even more awful."

"Gordon, you're doing the right thing. You're taking care of the problem."

"I'm going to kill a man, Elaine. A man I've never seen, or spoken to, or know *anything* about, really . . . except his E-mail and for that letter. Maybe that's why I'm obsessing about the damn thing. It's as if the son of a bitch is taunting me, you know? Because if he turns out to be right, Elaine— if China and Russia both dissolve into true anarchy . . ."

He didn't finish the sentence or complete the thought, but Elaine put her hand on his sleeve. She lowered her head to his shoulder and squeezed his arm. It's a decision you have to make, Gordon, she said without speaking. There really is no other choice.

"My fellow Americans," Gordon said into the TelePrompTer, his hands clasped on the desk in front of him as coached, "I come before you tonight not to talk of victory, but of peace. For this long and horrible war is now over, and the time for a great healing has begun. General Secretary Lin Tso-chang has accepted the Security Council's terms for a cease-fire." He unclasped his hands and leaned forward for dramatic effect. "At eighteen hundred hours Greenwich Mean Time today—approximately six hours from now—all UNRUSFOR offensive operations against the People's Liberation Army will be halted. The Chinese will withdraw all forces in contact with UNRUSFOR to a distance of thirty kilometers. A general and complete prisoner exchange will begin immediately."

Gordon paused as the camera zoomed in. Now, according to the script, the screen framed his head and shoulders. The director's index finger cued him.

"While we have halted offensive operations, let me make this point perfectly clear. All Chinese military equipment and infrastructure within the control of UNRUSFOR will be destroyed. That will include the tanks, armored fighting vehicles, combat aircraft, artillery, trucks, and other equipment used by three-quarters of a million of the PLA's best-armed and best-trained men—over half of their heavy-weapons arsenal. Strict limits will be placed on Chinese military deployments into northern Manchuria. Any violation of the demilitarized zone will be punished swiftly and severely. And any future breach of the peace by Chinese forces or violation of the Russian border will be met with immediate and overwhelming counterforce. We have in this war proven our resolve as a nation and as a people to combat Chinese aggression, and we will continue to do so in whatever form that aggression should take.''

This time the pause was unscheduled. There was no pre-planned gesture. No zooming or camera switches or stage direction. Just one last nagging deluge of doubt. One last echo of Kartsev's warning.

''Although UNRUSFOR,'' Gordon finally resumed, ''will maintain sufficient combat strength in the Far Eastern theater to fulfil its regional obligations, the Security Council has approved a timetable for withdrawal of forces from the Asian continent.''

There, he thought. *It's done.* Somehow, however, he obtained no respite from his worries.

''And so, as of today, this great travail has ended. The sacrifices made by our soldiers, sailors, airmen, and Marines have not been for naught. Siberia is under UN auspices. East Asia is at peace once again. Aggression has been punished severely. China's offensive military capacity has been devastated. And we will remain vigilant against any further crimes against the peace. God bless the United States of America. Thank you. And good night.''

AMUR RIVER CROSSING, JIAYIN, CHINA
April 30, 2200 GMT (0800 Local)

''I'm glad you changed your mind,'' Chin whispered to Lieutenant Hung. His friend said nothing. The bus bumped along the rutted road. "Listen," Chin continued. "You were right about so many *things*. I've learned so much in such a short *time*! The first thing I *do* when I get back is to sign up for college entrance exams. They only take three kids from my hometown, but you can't imagine how dim-witted the others are. I know I'll be one of those three!"

Chin's news didn't seem to make Hung happy. It pained Chin because he owed so much to his friend. He'd known the world was filled with variety. But he'd had no concept of the wealth and diversity of ideas. No understanding of the way things were everywhere else! Hung had translated English magazines day and night, filling in the details and opening Chin's mind. The crash course was cut short by the end of the war. But Chin was a voracious student. And nothing had intrigued him so much as his taste of the forbidden fruit.

"You've taught me so much!" Chin said. Hung, as always, waved for him to lower his voice. "I owe you my life," Chin whispered. Hung rolled his eyes in protest. "No! I *mean* it! I owe you the life you gave me. The life filled with . . . ideas! I mean, who else could've explained the Renaissance in Europe? The fall of communism in—"

"Sh-h!" Hung said, casting Chin a fierce look.

"No one will *ever* take those things away from me! Because I know them now. They're up here," Chin said, tapping his skull with his finger. "I can never unlearn them. And I have you to thank for that!"

"Be careful with what you know," was all Hung would say. His chin was buried to his chest. His voice was low.

"What do you mean?" Chin asked. Hung said nothing more, so Chin moved on to his real point. "There are also things *I* can teach *you*. They're not brilliant things. They're simple." Chin hesitated before broaching the subject. He knew it was off-limits, but he forged ahead nonetheless. "I'm sorry about your brother." Hung's head shot up. "But you can't change what happened to him!"

"What they *did* to him!" Hung corrected, his teeth clenched. This time it was Hung who spoke too loudly.

Chin looked around before continuing in a whisper. "A lot of people have died. Good men. They died in the riots at Beijing University last August. They died before that in Tiananmen Square."

"My brother didn't die in the riots," Hung replied.

"I know, but—" Chin tried to interrupt.

"He died in the basement of some building in Beijing. I don't even know which one. They never let us see the body. Now, why do you think that is?" His eyes rose to challenge Chin.

Chin wilted, his head waggling from side to side. "I *know* that, but the *point* is—"

"*Four* days! They had him for *four* days! We know that much!" There was agony written all over his face. In his mind, Chin knew, he imagined his brother's end. They had been close—just a year apart. They were an oddity, and Hung had been proud of their uniqueness. Two children in one family was rare—*especially* two boys. Almost nobody had a second child after having a boy. Chin couldn't count the number of times the words "my brother" had slipped out of Hung's mouth when recounting some boyhood adventure. Each time it had cast a pall over the conversation.

Chin's mouth was dry, but he tried again. "I guess I mean to say that a lot of people have died. Think about the war. Just think about it." Chin's throat was pinched closed with emotion. "But the war's over. The riots are over. It's time to go home." Hung snorted—like the college puke from before. But Chin wasn't angered this time. "You did the right thing," Chin said. "You'll be glad once you're home and everything's back to normal."

The groaning brakes brought the bus to a stop. Everyone headed out into the cool day. There was a floating bridge across the broad, fast-moving river. "Remember the last time we saw the Amur?" Chin asked excitedly. Hung walked with his hands jammed in his pockets. His chin was tucked to his chest, but his eyes were raised to the bridge. On the opposite side stood a small party of Chinese soldiers. Green army trucks were presumably their ride home.

Four huge tents had been pitched at the small camp. "The river was frozen solid! Remember?"

The dirt road behind them was filled with buses. Hung said nothing as the Americans ushered them toward the bridge. A crowd of almost a thousand Chinese prisoners formed on the Russian bank. All faced south—toward China—with expectant looks. Few said anything at all. After several minutes three men appeared on the far end of the bridge. They walked across the metal span shoulder to shoulder. As they approached, Chin could see they were European. They wore flight suits and one walked with a limp.

When the fliers were almost on shore, several American officers walked out onto the bridge. They wore dark sunglasses, blue caps, and broad smiles. They shook hands and then hugged the returning men. It was a homecoming filled with great emotion and cheer. The returning prisoners were quickly escorted to waiting ambulances.

An ethnic Chinese soldier wearing the uniform of the U.S. Army said, "Go across the bridge!" in stilted and almost monotone Cantonese. There were titters from the mass but they complied. Just before Chin and Hung's turn came to cross, American soldiers blocked their way with rifles. The bridge was filled to capacity, Chin presumed, so they waited. Just ahead, a couple of hundred men slowly shuffled toward the far bank.

Hung kept craning his neck to look back. First at the departing American POWs. Then at the buses, which slowly pulled away. When their time finally came, Chin had to backhand Hung to get him moving.

The bridge swayed and sank with the weight of so many men. Across the river the group ahead had entered a tent. "Must be more medical checkups," Chin said to the taciturn Hung. Chin chuckled. "Gonna stick fingers up our ass again is my bet."

Hung didn't seem amused by Chin's attempt at humor. When they reached the south bank, they saw that their welcoming committee carried rifles. There were no hugs, or handshakes, or even greetings. They were simply herded into a tent filled with cloth partitions, which looked like a field hospital. The process seemed simple enough to Chin. Everyone was crowded into one end of the tent and taken— one by one—into the warren. There arose the clacking of typewriter keys. Hung was called by an armed soldier before Chin.

When Hung was gone, Chin squatted to wait. "Watch your ass," he heard out of nowhere. Chin turned to see a peasant man who had bunked next to him in the barracks.

Chin smiled on recognizing an acquaintance. "What did you say?" he asked the man.

"College shits think they rule the world," came the reply. Chin realized he was talking about Hung. He started to object, but the shout of an armed soldier called him away. Chin was ushered through the maze to a desk. A man sat behind a typewriter smoking a cigarette. He held out his hand to invite Chin to sit.

"Name," the man asked, the cigarette bobbing. Chin answered. Rank. Place and date of birth. Army serial number. All the requisite information. Chin was cooperative and upbeat with his answers. He was eager to board a truck and head home. "Have you observed any antistate behavior?" the man asked in a bored tone. His fingers never left the keyboard. When Chin hesitated, the interviewer squinted and looked up through the rising smoke.

"No!" Chin burst out, then smiled. "All the men in *my* barracks were totally loyal Chinese soldiers."

"Everyone?" the man asked, his fingers still poised. "What about the traitors who stayed with the Americans? Were they loyal Chinese soldiers like you?"

"Well . . . *no*! Not *them,* of course." Chin's eyes darted down to the man's yellow fingertips. They hovered over the keys—still not satisfied.

"Is that your answer?" the man asked. Chin's eyes rose. He could feel beads of sweat forming just beneath his hairline. He nodded.

The clacking keys made their marks on the paper. An

official document filled with Chin's vital records. Chin's mouth was dry and he swallowed. That simple act drew the watchful eye of the interviewer. The man hesitated . . . then continued typing. When he was done, he pulled the sheet from the roller. He laid it in front of Chin and handed him a pen. "Sign that," he curtly directed.

Chin took the pen. "What is it?" The man stared at him through narrow slits. His eyes rose to the trickle of sweat that ran down the side of Chin's face. Chin lowered the pen to the paper. While he was signing, he stole glances at the document. It was a statement of some sort. A claim—sworn by Chin—that the deserters were enemy agents. That they'd been planted years before by the CIA. That they'd worked actively to sabotage the defense of their homeland. That they'd each been given one hundred U.S. dollars by the American government.

Chin laid the pen across the paper and stood. His armed escort took him to the opposite end of the tent. Chin breathed a sigh of relief. He saw Hung squatting off to the side and headed over.

Hung's eyes caught Chin's and he shook his head once. He looked away then as if they were strangers. Chin was instantly alert to danger. He felt a prickly fear spread across his skin. He squatted some distance away from Hung. The short hairs on his neck rose up. The men all now avoided eye contact. No one spoke. They were changed—ill at ease—not like before. Chin acted as anonymous as he possibly could. He knew several of the men right around him, but he dared not look their way.

It took half an hour for the last men to be processed. Out of the maze of partitions emerged a bald officer wearing reading glasses. He held a single sheet of paper. Two guards took up posts beside him. More armed soldiers appeared at the tent's exit. In the center of the guns squatted the former POWs.

The officer began to read off names. One by one the men rose and headed outside. Sunlight streamed into the room with each departure. It was almost blinding after so much time in the darkened tent.

"Hung, Wu shi!" the officer called out.

Hung rose, a fact confirmed out of the corner of Chin's eyes. Hung headed toward the bright sun—toward the trucks waiting outside. Chin gave in to the temptation and looked. Hung hesitated in the door and looked back. A guard pushed him through with a muzzle to his back.

Twenty men departed quietly in that manner. The officer handed the list of names to a senior sergeant and turned to address the remaining men. "You have all spent time around the imperialist war machine! You have seen their *deceits,* their *cruelties,* their *evil* natures! You may have been shown kindness by individual soldiers, who are themselves victims of their oppressive regimes! But their inhumane system brings out the very worst in men! They plunder Asia's resources to feed the factories of greedy capitalists! They drop bombs, massacring innocent Chinese civilians whose sole crime was to demand a return of Asia to Asians! Whose sole desire was to realign boundaries drawn by hundreds of years of aggression by the West! To make *just* borders—founded on *natural* law! To put an end to the looting, the *raping* of Asia's treasure by Europeans! And worse even than block after block of houses flattened by the criminal UN bombing of our cities has been *your* fate! *Yours* has been the worst of the indignities suffered by the People's Republic! You have had to bear the unbearable! But your nightmare has now come to an end! The People's Liberation Army salutes you! The people of China welcome you home!"

With that, the guns were lowered. The guards parted. They were each given a loaf of bread for the journey. They were led out. There was no sign of Hung's group. No sign of Hung's truck. No sign of Hung. Chin never saw or heard from his friend again.

And that began the great awakening in Chin. Not an enlightenment. Not a birth of ideas or a flowering of social consciousness. Beginning on the cold, dusty road heading south from the Amur, there arose instead a hatred that knew no bounds. It was all-consuming. It grew with his visit to

Hung's family. With each furtive stop by Hung's former radical and now cowering university friends. With the one risky trip made to the Defense Ministry, where, Chin found, Hung had never even *been* in the army. He had never even *existed*, a fact the clerk confirmed with confidence after reference to a large book of names. A book that seemed to list the names of nonexistent people.

Chin's anger grew to such proportions that he could express it to no one. No one knew how deep it ran. How his life was consumed by it. How it suffused his every day, his every act, his every thought. How it motivated and inspired him to work hard. To set his goals and excel as never before. For there was no one whom he could trust with such dangerous thoughts but a brother. And his brother no longer existed . . . he never had.

THE KREMLIN, MOSCOW, RUSSIA
May 1, 1200 GMT (1400 Local)

The office door opened, and in walked Miss Dunn. Kartsev confirmed with a tug on his jacket that his pistol remained hidden. He then rose with a truly genuine smile on his face and held out his hand. Miss Dunn hugged her arms across her chest. She wouldn't even raise her windburned and red face.

Kartsev sneezed loudly and unexpectedly. He turned and extracted his handkerchief. "I *apologize*!" he said. "Spring allergies, I'm afraid." She looked up at him defiantly, her lips pursed as she sucked in her cheek on one side, staring. Kartsev had to smile. He hadn't seen such directness since . . . He couldn't remember the last time. "I hope you weren't treated badly. I gave specific instructions that you not be harmed, but . . . but people are getting a little sloppy these days." She frowned, still staring. "I'm sure you'll understand, however, why I brought you here. Why this is such a *momentous* day."

She snorted like a bratty child. "*Yeah! May* Day," she said sarcastically. "Your big speech to an adoring people."

Her smile turned up only one corner of her mouth. She never broke eye contact.

"You've changed," he said out loud. It was a comment made not to her, but to himself.

She arched her eyebrows, her expression a study in boredom. "I've been through too much to put up with your bullshit." Her words were slurred. Her manner nonchalant. She wasn't scared of him at all.

They stared at each other—Kartsev's mood darkening. He walked over to his desk, but she didn't follow. "*Well*," he said, trying to snap out of his funk, "actually I wasn't talking about the rally. Come here. Let me show you."

Miss Dunn hesitated for a moment before wandering over. She shoved her hands in the back pockets of her blue jeans. Slumped and slouching, she stood beside Kartsev.

"You see the document on the computer screen?" he asked. Her head was tilted and her hair half covered her face. But he saw her gaze rise to the monitor. The blue phosphors were reflected brightly in her eyes. "It's my life's greatest work. I call it *The Laws of Human History*. I'm really quite proud of it, if truth be told."

Miss Dunn arched her eyebrows and said, "Hmm." She lifted a paperweight from his desk and turned it from side to side.

Undaunted, Kartsev said, "I wanted to invite you to my 'publishing party.' " He held his hands out to the empty office. She said nothing. The anticlimax was now complete. He didn't know what to say, so he just leaned over to the mouse, rolled the cursor to the "send" button, and clicked. The blue status bar rose slowly till it read one hundred percent. Kartsev stood back. "There!"

After a few moments Miss Dunn asked, "What?" Her interest was finally piqued.

"It's published."

"What do you mean it's published?"

"I sent it via the Internet to a few thousand different servers in about two dozen—" Again he sneezed without warning. "*Excuse* me!" he said, dabbing at his nose. "As

I was saying, I had it translated into a couple of dozen major languages and posted it for all to read. I just wanted you to be here . . . when I published it.''

Miss Dunn was alert now, her old self. Her eyes darted to the monitor. ''What's the book about?''

Kartsev smiled. ''It is nothing more than a . . . a work of nonfiction, if you will.'' He looked down at the floor. ''Maybe you could call it a treatise if you judge by the number of bold statements I make in it.'' He laughed. ''But I did strive to leave a mark.''

''Oh . . . you've left a mark,'' Kate said, feeling her teeth grind. ''You'll be remembered for a long time.''

''But I hope for so much *more* than mere notoriety,'' Kartsev said. ''Social experimentation is a duty we owe mankind. No system is perfect. Pristine ideologies become sullied by implementation. Exemplary organizations lose their way, are corrupted or hijacked, or simply decay over time. Every human institution evolves in a complex but not indecipherable way.''

''And you've deciphered that process?'' Kate asked.

''I have tried to do my part. To describe a piece of the process, perhaps.''

''What piece?''

''Certain . . . *manners of translation* of societal forces. Actually, more like currents that . . .'' He faltered.

After several moments of silence, Kate said, ''You're having trouble answering the question?''

''Well, you're *asking* it in a *rather* rude way!'' He calmed down instantly, ready to apologize.

''You are sick, you know?'' she said with disdain that had never been more evident.

''So I understand,'' he replied with a sigh.

''You think that characterization is *unfair*? After what you've *done*?''

Kartsev ignored the barb and tried again to explain. ''Can you not see the degree of human interconnectivity? The rippling waves of fashion and culture that crisscross our world? They create such deliciously complex patterns of interference. Behavioral trends aren't linear, you know. They are dissonant fields in multidimensional space. Even if they could be plotted mathematically—described by an accurate model—they could not be visualized in the human mind.''

"Then how did you describe the process in your book?''

"Very primitively, I'm sure,'' Kartsev said. He smiled and lowered his head. "I can only hope I've advanced mankind's thinking in some small way.''

"And that justifies what you've *done*?'' she shouted, outraged. "Does that give you license to harm even *one* other human on earth?''

"Who said that I needed license?'' Kartsev asked with an innocent expression. "Why am I not free to do what I please? Because someone wrote a law in a book? I could write *volumes* of rules and regulations. I assume you would find all of them illegitimate.''

"Because you have no mandate from the people to govern.''

"Who said I need a mandate? Empires and monarchies govern quite effectively. Pluralism is simply the dictatorship of the center over the extremes. A distribution of power along the bell curve. Democratic representatives grope for a consensus as if some magical truth lies in that center. What a comical system it is! Who said that conformity to norms is a measure of fitness to govern? Who defines the degree of deviation from the norm that's allowed? Each society draws its own lines. Things acceptable in Amsterdam would get you beheaded in Afghanistan. Where is the sense in that? Who is to judge the right from the wrong? Humans? God? And if God, *which* god? Who's laws and traditions should rule?''

Kate simply shook her head. "You've debased everything good in the name of evil. You've led a counterenlightenment. A Renaissance in reverse. You've led your country into the Dark Ages. You've caused a major war. You've killed millions.''

Kartsev smiled. "Do you believe a man to be responsible

for everything that ensues from his actions?'' She didn't answer. "If the action was well-intentioned, do you still blame the actor for the result?''

"Nothing you've done was well-intentioned.''

"I'm not talking about me,'' Kartsev replied. He grinned broadly, but not menacingly. "I'm a very bad man, yes. To you I must be the epitome of Satan. The incarnation of the Antichrist.''

"You flatter yourself. I actually see you as more banal. A petty tyrant with the aspirations of a Nazi doctor.''

Kartsev shrugged and nodded. His smile was long gone. "I suppose that's an apt description. But perhaps you should read the book.'' He turned and patted his pockets distractedly. He found a pen and stuck it in his jacket. "The Square is full, by now, I would imagine.'' He suddenly had a wonderful idea. "Miss Dunn, have you ever seen Red Square from atop Lenin's Mausoleum? As a reporter I should think you would be very curious. It could be an historic moment, you know. Just imagine looking out on a *sea* of faces. I never have been on the reviewing stand before, actually. But I grew up watching from below. It's really more comfortable down there. Always looking up. Being part of the mass . . . not alone.''

When Kartsev thought to look to Kate for an answer, she almost whispered in a thick voice, "I want to go home.''

There was a knock on the door. An aide stepped in but said nothing. Kartsev nodded, and the aide disappeared. Kartsev tucked his speech into his pocket. "Of course,'' he said. "My people will see to it. Farewell then, Miss Dunn. Farewell.'' He headed for the door, deeply saddened.

"Who were you talking about?'' she blurted out. He stopped and turned. "When you were asking whether someone should be blamed for the results even if his actions were well-intentioned?''

Kartsev beamed. "Oh! Why, your beloved President Davis, of course. This generation's Abraham Lincoln, I believe your colleagues in the press are calling him. Every indication that I get is that he's an honorable, upstanding man. His actions seem to have been taken with the best of intentions, which makes them—of course—highly predictable. And yet who is more despicable? Valentin Kartsev, who caused the deaths of perhaps a few million people at most? Or Gordon Davis, who is directly responsible for the deaths of hundreds upon hundreds of millions of human beings?''

Kate stared back at him. Not understanding. ''You mean the war?'' His only response was a noncommittal arch of his brow. ''Your question doesn't make any *sense*. Hundreds of millions of people didn't *die*.''

Kartsev straightened his tie. He wiped his palms on his thighs as if nervous, then tugged his jacket, stiffened his back, and took a deep, bracing breath. ''But they will.'' He turned and left the chilly, dark room.

The breeze across Red Square gusted slightly. Andreev clicked the windage knob to adjust for the added drift. The sky was a brilliant blue. Heat could be felt in the sun's radiance. The captive mass of pathetic souls below was ringed by black-clad thugs.

Pyotr was calm and focused in the tight space between the ancient chimneys on the roof of GUM. It was the site he'd worried about most as head of presidential security. He'd crawled through the wall space years earlier—just as he had the day before. It was a security nightmare. Ingress was concealed behind the hollow walls of the former government department store. The round, rooftop window was easily opened. Lenin's Mausoleum lay directly in front and beneath the site at a thirty-degree angle of elevation. And there was even rapid egress by climbing down crisscrossing wood bracing to a subbasement. From there you could get into the sewer and out via the subway service tunnels.

He'd written a detailed report and advised how everything should be sealed up tight. But the president himself had interceded. He had rejected the plan without explanation. Pyotr was sufficiently steeped in Kremlin politics not to ask for one. All copies of Pyotr's report were shredded and burned. Thereafter, every gathering in Red Square was preceded by Pyotr's personal check of the site.

A roar rose up, and a waving man ascended to the flat roof of the tomb. Andreev removed the scope's front lens cover from the potentially reflective glass. He twirled his left forearm in the rifle's sling once more, twisting it ever tighter. The sling would limit the circulation in his left forearm, eventually causing shakes from muscles starved of oxygen. But he would be quick. He'd take the first opportunity presented. He wouldn't rush the mechanics of the shot, but there was nothing to be gained by delay.

One shot—one kill, came the words of the American instructor. They were a motto repeated over and over. They were the only words of advice that stuck with Pyotr. He'd never heard them when he went through the Russian Army's special training course twenty years before. The Russians were less concerned with escape, evasion, and survival.

Kartsev mounted the Mausoleum. The rifle was firmly seated in Andreev's shoulder. He lowered his right eye to the scope.

Even though Kartsev knew the cheers were a farce, he got a certain rise out of the sheer volume of crowd noise. When he reached the top of the stairs, however, he was angered to see the waiting collection of toadies. They all stood in front of their seats applauding. They wore black suits like undertakers. But as if that wasn't enough, they wore black armbands and lapel pins in the shape of a black flag. Their fat little hands clapped noiselessly. All turned to fawn over Kartsev.

He'd forgotten that most of them were still alive. Men he'd worked with—organized—in the months leading up to the government's ouster. Their yellowed eyes and pallid complexions reminded him of the living dead. They had feasted on the flesh of their people, and were now reduced to gnawing on the carcass that remained. They held no higher beliefs. Most of the true believers were now rotting in shallow graves dug on the orders of these men. These men were not social scientists. They were bureaucrats of the death machine.

Kartsev greeted no one as he headed for the podium. He weaved his way among the disinterred, the captains and lieutenants of his army of walking dead. Only when Kartsev reached the podium could he truly turn his attention to the crowd. He smiled as he surveyed the pumping fists and bellowing lungs. The streaming black flags. The faces turned expectantly upward—toward him.

What power to summon such numbers. He raised his hand and waved.

The scope wobbled with each beat of Pyotr's heart. At extreme magnification he could see nothing but Kartsev's torso. Always refining—never fighting—Andreev focused all his attention on centering the crosshairs. Nothing existed for him now but the rifle—the scope. His left hand was locked tightly to the stock by the sling. His right hand grasped the pistol grip. His shoulder steadied the rifle stock at the butt. His cheek rested lightly against the cool plastic. The rolled rug lay under the heavy barrel, completing the man-rifle unit.

His index finger held firm pressure on the trigger. A hair more and the weapon would discharge. The crosshairs remained inside Kartsev's torso. It wobbled, but from shoulder to hip to the opposite shoulder. It wasn't Kartsev at which he aimed, but a concept. A defined point in imaginary space. And that point was at the intersection of two lines. The vertical line split Kartsev's necktie down the middle. The horizontal one ran from nipple to nipple. Pyotr waited patiently for the scope's crosshairs to line up. For the momentary unity of imaginary and real lines.

There was an explosion of noise. Pyotr couldn't recall even pulling the trigger. The smoke and haze cleared. The podium was empty. Pyotr slid through the window and was gone.

•   •   •

Kartsev sneezed violently and doubled over at the waist. Even so he heard the booming report of the rifle. There was no doubt in his mind what it was. He remained bent low, shielded behind the thick armored podium. Directly behind him sprawled three dead men. There was gore and shattered bone everywhere. The backs of their chairs each had bloody holes in a descending line. They grew from the size of a melon at the top of the first chair, to a hole the width of a basketball near the seat of the third. The chairs' former occupants had been cored straight through.

Everyone scurried about the rooftop like desperate cockroaches. Some rose, others ducked—all panicked.

But there were no more thunderous blasts from the lone gun. The assassin had missed his target . . . but didn't realize it. The only sound Kartsev heard now was from the crowd. The disturbance and commotion spread quickly through Red Square.

"He's dead!" Kartsev heard someone shout. The words were repeated far and wide. Kartsev realized too late what was happening. By the time he raised up all was lost, and he got a bird's eye view of the end. An end he had guessed might come that very day. It was an interesting footnote to his study of man's behavior. The surging mass confirmed the laws about which he'd written. Staccato bursts of gunfire from the Black Shirts ended quickly. They had little or no apparent effect. Kartsev half turned to see the loyal zombies hurling themselves to the ground. Jumping two stories in a futile attempt to save their skins. But it only hastened their end, he could tell from their inhuman shrieks. From the bloodcurdling screams that rose up from the earth.

Nothing would stop the mob once it was loosed. For it was no longer simply a collection of individuals. It was an entity obeying its own merciless laws of behavior. A detached Kartsev watched the hysteria sweep Red Square. Black Shirts killed, were overwhelmed, then died. Sometimes he glimpsed the living as they were lifted into the air over the masses. After brief torment they descended and were consumed by the crowd.

The most wondrous thing of all was the cacophonous noise. The pent-up potential energy of society turning kinetic.

The fat men atop Lenin's Mausoleum fired feeble shots down the stairs. Their pistols blazed till empty, and then they died. The surging throng devoured their fattened prey like starving beasts. They brutalized some, threw others over the wall, but killed them all.

One by one the gaunt attackers caught sight of Kartsev. He stood all alone to face the wrath of mankind. But they hesitated when confronted by so powerful a man. They were still cowed by their primal fear of Kartsev the Terrible. By the last remaining authority figure in Russia.

Kartsev frowned, drew his pistol, and blew his brains out.

EPILOGUE

"A just system of human government is stable. Unless the catalysts are powerful enough, it will tend to right itself and return to its center. But violence resonates in the unjust system. The vibrations of its excited molecules pass the disturbance along with ever-growing levels of energy. It is in such a system that one man can make a difference. All it takes is one man to send the unjust society careening down the road of history."

Valentin Kartsev (posthumously)
The Laws of Human History
Moscow, Russia

BEIJING UNIVERSITY, CHINA
October 27, 1300 GMT (2300 Local)

Late at night, the university library was empty. Chin still had one hour left before it closed. Janitors mopped the floors. But most of the staff was congregated at the main desk talking.

Chin sat at the computer—one of a few dozen now available to university students. He was logged onto the Internet. He dared not take what might appear to be a suspicious check of his environs. He stared instead at the on-line drawings of a patent application for a water pump. He'd already completed his report on the pump's design. He'd deliver it to his first-year engineering class in the morning. Now he just waited till he was absolutely certain no one could see his computer screen.

When that moment came, he typed in the long and complex URL. He hit "enter" and waited as the server made its connection. Soon enough the familiar title page appeared. He waited as the table of contents and each chapter loaded sequentially. Page after page was beamed electronically into his computer. Until the process was complete he was at the greatest risk. His trigger finger lay poised on the mouse button. The cursor sat atop the "exit" icon. But when the 1.6-megabyte document was inbound, the computer was slow to respond. Its windows closed sometimes in unpredictable ways. A small box filled with the dangerous words might linger on the screen. Chin knew that being caught would mean certain death.

The tiny LEDs flickered as the book poured in. He had a backup plan. You always needed a fallback. He'd flick the power switch on the computer and flush the RAM. Any trace of what he was downloading would then be erased. But at a minimum such an act would cost him his computer privileges. At worst he'd be sent to reeducation camp for years.

Hung had not been so lucky. Chin tried again to imagine who had squealed. Who from POW camp had turned in his friend. It must have been the peasant man Hung had so often and so viciously derided. But he'd never know who it was in the end. It was just one of the mysteries that seemed to abound in the world. Mysteries such as the cause of Russia's now raging second civil war. Everyone knew that the violence had started in Moscow. At a rally in Red Square, he had read. The Anarchist leadership was literally torn limb from limb. And there were rumors of a sniper that had never been confirmed. Confusion always surrounded events on so large a scale. They were a blurred swirl of action and reaction—force and counterforce.

But Chin knew now that the chaotic "dissonance" was caused by "complex, interrelated social variables"—words he'd never even heard before that now explained so much. He was fascinated by his new world of ideas. Especially those that explained things dear to him. Stealing a foreign patent was certainly a challenge for an aspiring engineer. But water pumps held limited appeal in Chin's new order of things. There was so much more to be gained by study and, increasingly, by action.

The red light at the top of the browser finally went black. Chin rolled the mouse and clicked the "back" button. The drawings again flashed onto the screen. *Safe*, he thought, relaxing. He clicked "forward" and the banned book reappeared instantly.

He was over a third of the way into the treatise. It was one long and fascinating lesson in the nature of man. It answered questions Chin had never pondered before the war. What drives man to extremes of behavior? How does violence reshape personality? It described the micro- and macrosocial models with mathematical precision.

The only way he could find his place in the book for each furtive late-night read was to memorize the last words he'd read and search for them the next day. That wasn't difficult. He'd already committed much of what he'd read to memory. Nothing had ever spoken to him like this book did. He'd found it late one night while browsing the Web. The propaganda about the great victory in the north obviously held no answers to any of Chin's questions. Neither Chin's family nor his friends discussed what it felt like to return home from hell. But Chin had found newsgroup postings by soldiers of Western armies that had been translated into Chinese. He dared not reply, of course, but he relished their discussion of the great emptiness both he and they felt. From continent to continent, everyone talked about the great void that had been left inside them. About the end of life's most cathartic experience and the beginning of the great nothingness that followed. "I was in the 1st MEF west of Vladivostok . . ." would begin the heart-wrenching message. The replies would be from Germany, Belgium, Holland, France.

Chin barely held in the surge of emotions when he read what the men had to say. It took the greatest willpower he could muster to keep his facial expression neutral. One was a tortured cry from a traumatized American soldier. He had described how he'd spent his nineteenth birthday behind the flaming barrel of a machine gun. What it was like to go home to his family after killing hundreds of human beings. When Chin had finished reading, he'd run all the way from the library back to his room, where he'd lain in bed and sobbed. Part in joy on realizing he wasn't alone. Part in sadness on reliving the ordeal. For the experience of the cogs was universal no matter what the machine. And he felt a kinship that cut across national boundaries. A closeness that linked brother to brother by spilled blood.

He'd learned many things from those postings. That the panicked, sweaty awakenings were quite normal. ''Posttraumatic anxiety attacks'' were their name. No one ever talked of them in China. But his brothers described it exactly, just as they did the now constant pain in his joints. According to a British vet, one in four in the UN army had been medically discharged due to ''cold-induced rheumatism.'' The doctors at Beijing University clinic had denied there was any such thing. But he trusted only his brethren, and the news from them wasn't good. The pain Chin felt now would worsen steadily for decades to come.

But his greatest discovery had come ten nights ago. It was a posting by a French combat veteran. One of the war-related sites he listed in his message contained the book Chin now accepted as his bible. It was the Rosetta stone of his attempt at understanding why his life had changed. It not only answered all his questions, it posed new ones he hadn't thought to ask.

But the most fascinating thing of all was its breadth and scope of subject. It not only answered whys—and the far simpler when, where, and who—but it spent long sections discussing the ever-practical hows. The cause and effect of human behavior—both mass, and individual. The universal truths about man no matter how dark and base.

What had happened in the north after the UN withdrawal was only a precursor. But it was enough of a shock to Beijing that they'd quarantined all of Manchuria. No news or people flowed into or out of the rebellious provinces. But the fighting there still raged, according to reports he'd read on the Internet.

Chin fantasized late at night in the darkness of his room. In his mind he saw wave after wave of stimuli washing over a seething population. They would unleash violence on a scale never seen before. The destructive potential of a billion and a half people. He imagined the feeble efforts of the decrepit Communist government to stem the tidal forces. He imagined the liberating blows that would topple the weakened state. He went from grinding teeth to smiles to blissful sleep. Then he'd awaken the next morning to aching knees, hips, shoulders, and elbows. He took pain-killers he'd bought off the black market in ever-increasing doses.

It was, in fact, his first forays in search of drugs that had led to his great breakthrough. He'd thought at first of organizing the students at Beijing University. Of forming "study" groups that he could carefully lead into social discussion and eventually criticism. But when he ventured into the back alleys of Beijing to find relief from his incessant pain, he realized what a waste of time dealing with students would have been. Instead of nudging them warily into subversion, he could step into opium dens filled with hatred. And while university groups were closely watched, commoners were too numerous for scrutiny. There were brutalized veterans like Chin. Angry men like Hung who'd lost loved ones in windowless basements and labor camps. Refugees fresh from bloody reprisals in Manchuria. And a vast sea of the disenfranchised, whose bleary eyes lit up when Chin spoke of a world in which they would be free to say the word "no." For what he offered them was priceless. A relief from dreary existence. A break from constant boredom. A justification to swing the fist they'd long held balled up in white-hot anger. A sense of belonging that was more addictive to society's outcasts than the opium that they smoked around the clock.

Already Chin had gotten them to kill. It was no more difficult than issuing orders to his platoon. Part challenge, part coaxing, part plea—the result had been three dead policemen. Three slit throats. Three service pistols added to their budding arsenal. But it was discovery of the treatise on the Internet that had given Chin focus, direction, and drive. For armed with the tools that the book provided him, he could send masses crashing against the bastards who'd killed Hung. The fucking assholes who'd sent hundreds of thousands to their deaths. Who'd consigned many more men—like Chin—to a life filled with physical and emotional agony.

The clicking heels across the library floor elicited the same reaction from Chin as a boot squeaking in snow. He calmly hit the "back" button even as the sweat beaded at his forehead. As his heart raced. As his entire body tensed up and he experienced a clarity of vision and of thought he'd never known before the war. The enemy passed uneventfully. He wore the uniform of an ordinary police officer—white belt, white gloves clasped behind his back, white holster with a white lanyard hanging from his black automatic. Nothing but the finest for China's most elite university. But Chin and everyone else knew that he and the others like him were from the Ministry of State Security. You could tell it from the way the real police officers at the university's gates acted. They wore the drab uniforms and bored looks of the low-paid, and they snapped to attention when such men stopped by. Chin couldn't wait to see the blood drip from the fine, white accoutrements.

The government kept a watchful eye on Beijing University. After years and years of turmoil, admission was now limited to the trusted few. To the sons of peasants, to war heros, to the apolitical. They'd done checks in Chin's village and he'd scored high on all three. "Congratulations!"

the admissions officer had said. "We not only turned up *no* politically insensitive remarks in your past. We apparently turned up no remarks of a political nature whatso*ever*. And *that's* rare."

But that had been before the war. Before *The Laws of Human History*. Before Valentin Kartsev.

The cop was flirting with a girl who worked at the main desk of the library. Chin switched back to the book and hit "find." In the small window he typed the last phrase he'd read before being kicked out the night before. "It is man's most basic nature," Chin typed, "to subvert all attempts at control." When he hit "go," the computer quickly found the passage. As he began his night's reading, he had to force himself to remain alert. He got so absorbed in the book that he was at risk of ignoring the danger signs. For the words sparked wildfires of imagination. Streaming banners. Barricades manned by armed and defiant people. "The creative potential of destruction."

He set his jaw, and ground his teeth, and clenched and reclenched his fists. His body was tensed in preparation for action, but now was not the time or the place.

The day will come, he thought—he pledged. *Soon . . .*